THE HAMMER &
THE EAGLE
– ICONS OF WARHAMMER –

THE HAMMER & THE EAGLE

– ICONS OF WARHAMMER –

CHRIS WRAIGHT, RACHEL HARRISON, JUSTIN D HILL,
SANDY MITCHELL, DAN ABNETT, DANIE WARE,
DAVID ANNANDALE, NICK KYME, GRAHAM MCNEILL,
DAVID ANNANDALE, GUY HALEY,
AARON DEMBSKI-BOWDEN, JOSH REYNOLDS,
GAV THORPE, JOHN FRENCH, DAVID GUYMER,
NICK HORTH, ANDY CLARK, C L WERNER

BLACK LIBRARY

A BLACK LIBRARY PUBLICATION

'Chains of Command' first published in 2001.
'Thorn Wishes Talon' first published in 2004.
'Shadow Knight' first published in 2009.
'Of Their Lives in the Ruin of Their Cities' first published in 2010.
'Extinction' and 'The Smallest Detail' first published in 2012.
'Argent', 'Eclipse of Hope', 'Rite of Pain', 'The Wreckage' and 'Veil of Darkness'
first published in 2013.
'Prodigal' first published in 2016.
'Blood Guilt', 'Endurance', 'Fireheart', 'The Dance of the Skulls' and 'The Old Ways'
first published in 2017.
'Battle for Markgraaf Hive', 'Execution', 'Ghosts of Demesnus', 'Gods' Gift', 'Mercy',
'One, Untended', and 'The Absolution of Swords' first published in 2018.
'Blacktalon: Hunting Shadows', 'Redeemer' and 'Shiprats' first published in 2019.
This edition published in Great Britain in 2020 by
Black Library,
Games Workshop Ltd.,
Willow Road,
Nottingham, NG7 2WS, UK.

10 9 8 7 6 5 4 3 2 1

Produced by Games Workshop in Nottingham.
Cover illustration by Stepan Alekseev.

See Black Library on the internet at

blacklibrary.com

Find out more about Games Workshop
and the worlds of Warhammer at

games-workshop.com

Printed and bound by CPI Group (UK) Ltd, Croydon, CR0 4YY

Editor's Introduction

The mark of a great character, a truly *great* character, is that they stick with you. They endure in the memory, they bring the page alive and give life and verse to the worlds they inhabit. They steal our hearts or they boil our blood (or sometimes both...).

The rich background of the Warhammer worlds is replete with such characters, true icons, a cast of literally thousands, all vying for the light, for our attention. Through their eyes we experience these fantastic worlds, share in the character's triumphs or commiserate their losses. Possibly even celebrate their demise.

Strong characters resonate. They attain form and personality that goes beyond the story. They become *real* and their trials and tribulations matter. We actually care about and become invested in them and, most importantly of all, we want to know *their* story.

The Hammer and the Eagle is a rare publication for Black Library. It's an unprecedented collection of stories about great characters but, and here's the thing, it straddles two worlds. And when I say 'worlds', I mean that in the largest and most expansive sense. Both the far-future setting of Warhammer 40,000 and the gritty fantasy realms of Age of Sigmar are represented within this anthology.

You probably already know them, these icons. Names like Ibram Gaunt and Uriel Ventris; or Ciaphas Cain and Gotrek Gurnisson. Characters like Gregor Eisenhorn, Neferata and Cato Sicarius will have graced battlefields the length and breadth of gaming rooms across the world. Others you will come to know, or may be meeting for the first time: Severina Raine, Adrax Agatone, Gardus Steelsoul, Hamilcar Bear-eater and Minka Lesk.

The list is long and vaunted, each a touchstone to greater and more epic stories. Treat this as your guide, your lodestone to the icons of the Warhammer Worlds, the fantastic characters that through Black Library bring these universes to blistering, eye-watering life...

Nick Kyme
Black Library Managing Editor
Nottingham, August 2019

CONTENTS

Icons of Warhammer 40,000

Icons of Warhammer Age of Sigmar

ICONS OF

For more than a hundred centuries the Emperor has sat immobile on the Golden Throne of Earth. He is the Master of Mankind. By the might of His inexhaustible armies a million worlds stand against the dark.

Yet, He is a rotting carcass, the Carrion Lord of the Imperium held in life by marvels from the Dark Age of Technology and the thousand souls sacrificed each day so that His may continue to burn.

To be a man in such times is to be one amongst untold billions. It is to live in the cruellest and most bloody regime imaginable. It is to suffer an eternity of carnage and slaughter. It is to have cries of anguish and sorrow drowned by the thirsting laughter of dark gods.

This is a dark and terrible era where you will find little comfort or hope. Forget the power of technology and science. Forget the promise of progress and advancement. Forget any notion of common humanity or compassion.

There is no peace amongst the stars, for in the grim darkness of the far future,
there is only war.

ENDURANCE

Chris Wraight

Introducing

DRAGAN

PLAGUE MARINE, DEATH GUARD

They are coming again now, stumbling out of the sulphurous night with their demented grins and their glowing eyes. Lystra is a hive world, populated by billions. Contact has been lost with most of it, indicating that the majority have been turned or are turning, and so the crowds are endless.

Brother Sarrien does not use his bolter. The last ammunition for it ran out three weeks ago, and it has been stowed reverently in the Thunderhawk *Votive IX*, which will lift off, piloted by serfs, when the last wall is broken. He fights on the walls with his power sword and his gauntlets, slaying like a warrior-king of his old home world. His limbs are heavy and flooded with lactic acid, and it feels like powering through deep water.

He is positioned at the jutting salient of a long, south-facing bastion. This is manned by the hastily amalgamated regiments of the surviving Lystran Proximal Guard, who are exhausted down to their marrow. Far off, chem-works are burning, making the horizon smoulder and the freezing air taste like gall. The spires at their backs glow with a million points of fading, flickering light.

He chants as he fights. If he were fighting with his own squad he would have been roaring war cries or calling out tactical movements, creating the auditory hell that daunts the enemy and propels his battle-brothers to greater feats, but his battle-brothers are all far away with their own contests, and so he chants now, in the manner of a Chaplain, to inspire the Guard.

'Stand fast, for Him on the Throne!' he shouts, smashing his fist through the neck of a grasping stumbler.

That is the word they use to describe them: 'stumblers'. The euphemism hides the horror of it. It says nothing of their rictus faces and their awkward splayed limbs, their grey flesh hanging from yellow bones and the hot glow behind their bloodshot eyes. They are climbing up the high walls now, hoisting themselves atop piles of their own dead, limping blindly into the path of lascannon stations. Once they crest the parapet's edge they start killing, grinning the whole time.

'Remember your vows!' Sarrien chants, swinging the bloodied stump of one stumbler-corpse into another, sending both sailing over the edge. 'Endure! Remain steadfast!'

The defenders would have collapsed by now, if he had not been there to keep them fighting. They are staring into the twisted faces of those that were once men and women. Perhaps, every so often, they come up against those they knew, and have to cut them down. Killing one of them is not difficult, for they make no effort to evade the las-fire. Killing hundreds is back-breaking, and every time a mistake is made and one gets through the gap, then the slaughter is prodigious.

'Keep on your feet!' Sarrien shouts, breaking the spine of a stumbler, kicking out to upend another, slicing his blade around to take out two more. His hearts are thudding out of sequence – they are becoming dangerously swollen. He is perspiring too much despite his dehydration. His hands are bleeding freely within his armour – the product of fighting the long retreat for weeks without respite. 'Stay firm! *Endure!*'

The world of Lystra will fall. All but the blindest of the blind see that now, and even the baseline troops are beginning to disbelieve their commissars. Sergeant Cleon of Sarrien's squad knows it too, but he will not order evacuation. The orders remain the same as they were when first given – hold the line, make the enemy pay the maximal price. Distant minds on peaceful worlds have determined that it is worth the sacrifice of a single squad of Imperial Talons to keep Lystra out of the enemy's hands for another month or two, perhaps longer.

Orders, orders. Discipline. Resolve.

For now, the defenders respond to his injunction. The walls are held. The lascannon turrets spit metronomically into the seething dark. Lystra Primaris remains inviolate, an island of purity within the gloom.

But they keep coming, more and more of them. Their deranged smiles become maddening to witness.

He hates them. He hates what they are doing to him. He hates that he will be ended by one of them – a foe without honour or stature – and not some champion worthy of his attention.

Sarrien's voice becomes hoarse.

'Remember your vows!' he cries again.

The attack ship swaggers through the void. It has no need of subterfuge, for it is a predator gliding within a sea of prey. It is not large – by Imperial standards, it might be destroyer class – but there is little in this volume of space that could stand against it and so the designation hardly matters. The great warships are all gone, pulled into the wars that engulf the Carrion Empire and sap its strength. Out here in the wilds, there is only chaff and fodder, only grist to the ever-grinding soul mills.

Dragan takes some pleasure in that. One day, greater battles will call him. One day, the Lords of Silence will convene again for something mighty, but until then he has learned to enjoy the licence. This is leisure for him – a casual slaying, a little light slaughter between so-serious campaigns.

He stares out into the void, at the stars swimming across blurred viewports. His ship, the *Incaligant*, does not have a soul. Not like *Solace*. It is merely a machine, albeit one riddled with cankers and growths. Its weapons fizz with bacteria, and its old phosphex launchers have developed intriguing viruses within the decayed canister-barrels. Its decks run with rust and there are phages fermenting in the infested bilges.

Death Guard, the enemy calls them. That is an irony. The Legion is more alive than anything left in this stagnant galaxy, albeit in ways not entirely in concordance with nature. Its days of glory are within spitting distance now. After a long time nursing grievances spawned at the dawn of the Imperium, the Death Guard are strutting. They are powerful, they are united. Only the Despoiler's mongrel Legion of vagabonds and strays surpasses them in numbers, and those turncoats have their own problems. One day, Dragan is sure, the last doors will be blown open and the Eye's borders will become irrelevant. Until then, there is killing in the emptiness to be had, and that is a fine enough thing to be going on with.

Dragan's eyes narrow. The *Incaligant*'s bridge crew respond. Something has strayed into sensor range.

'Show me,' he orders, his words grinding out from a rust-clogged vox-grille. His fingers, stiff from eroded cartilage, curl around the terminals of a verdigrised command throne.

'Imperial,' confirms his master of sensors, a man in a grease-streaked apron and a pox-red face who cannot leave his seat due to gurgling tubes inserted at regular intervals. 'Running hard, plasma drives only. It can be taken.'

Dragan nods. 'Agreed. Come about.'

The *Incaligant* swings towards the enemy. At this stage the ships are many thousands of kilometres apart, mere specks on the face of the void, but both of them know the score. More data comes in, streaming across cracked and blurry pict-feeds. It is a troop carrier, slow, armed only to the standard level required by the Navy. It should have escorts, but does not. So this will be easy.

Dragan reflects that victories are coming more easily than ever before. Fortune seems to favour them. Every move they make results in triumphs. Perhaps the long-promised turn is coming quicker now. Perhaps they will break the back of the Carrion Empire even before the millennium ends.

'Full burn,' he commands, remaining seated.

It does not take long to catch up. The transport is a typically uninspired thing – a hunk of dirty grey metal as long as it is high, all riveted slabs and heavy blast-plates. It has overloaded its engines trying to get away, and they are sputtering now like half-snuffed candles.

The ship is disabled quickly – a scatter of shots across its bows knocking out its weaponry and blowing the void shields. Then Dragan sends the boarding parties in, composed of his battle-brothers and their slaved adjutants. He lets them slaughter for a while, leaning back in his throne and listening to the cries over the ranged comm. It amuses him to watch the silent, tranquil outline of that ship while knowing the carnage is taking place within it.

Then he moves. He gets up, feeling his disease-thick bones creak. He does not reach for a weapon – his taloned gauntlets are enough for this. He stalks his way down the dank corridors towards the miasmatic hangars staffed by hunch-spined servitors, and takes an encrusted shuttle out across the gulf. He lands it in the corresponding intake hangar and thuds down the ramp and into action.

Dragan never hurries. The decks around him are already filthy with clotted matter – body parts slapped on the metal grids, blood pooling with oils and coolants into a viscous slime. He can hear screaming and shouting from far off. The main lumens have been smashed by bolter fire, but he can see all he needs to.

He kicks through the debris of his brothers' attack, making for the hatchways beyond. He can smell the antiseptic barrenness of the original ship, now overlaid by altogether more vivid aromas. Soon he is nearing the bridge, and ascends a tight set of meshed-metal stairs, ducking under a lintel designed for smaller bodies than his.

He meets his first resistance there – serfs in flak jackets carrying solid-round weapons. He does not break stride, but walks straight through the light dusting of impacts, feeling his armour absorb and spit out the bullets as they come. He reaches out to seize the closest of them, breaking her neck and flinging her to one side. Then he works through the rest, his mind only half-engaged on the task.

They are absolutely terrified of him. In brief snatches of focus, as he breaks their helms open or is struck by a distinctive bodily reaction, he inhales raw, crippling fear. That means very little to him. He does not revel in it, nor does it distract him. It is just the way of things – he is strong, and they are weak. The weak have always been purged, creating room for the strong to flourish. To the extent Dragan has a creed, that is it.

He kills the last of them with an absent-minded backhand, just as his second in command, Glask, emerges at the entrance to the bridge. Glask is a bloated creature, his armour blistered as if thrown into some heat-sink and left to stew. Glask's lone eye glares from a wet helm-face, and his trailing left leg limps.

'All done, brother?' Dragan asks.

'All done,' says Glask.

'What's the tally?'

'A few thousand,' says Glask. 'The brothers will be busy for a while.'

A few thousand troops heading at speed into the void, unescorted. That indicates a degree of desperation. Perhaps a last throw of some dice.

Dragan shuffles over to a command post, wheezing thickly. The cartilage issue seems to be spreading to his other joints, and he moves stiffly. That might mean that a true Gift is emerging, pushing its way through his body as a benison from the god he's supposed to worship. Or it might mean he's getting old.

He punches depressors on a bronze-lined cogitator face and calls up a trajectory skein. It's hard, for a moment, to remember how the Imperium represents void-volumes – that curious mix of archaisms and high technology, never truly understanding what they're playing with – but then he gets what he's after.

'Might have been heading here,' he says, pointing towards a blot of phosphor with his grimy thumb. 'Lystra. Heard of it?'

Glask shakes his head.

The word means nothing to Dragan either. Then again, there are so many worlds and so many battles that very little stands out, his memories a long fog of patient hunting and slow corruption.

'We'll head there next, then,' he says, turning away from the column. 'Should be fun.'

He has been alone for a long time now. Cleon left to spearhead the defence of the main land-gate, far to the north. Talis and Kerenon are roving through the underhives, knee-deep in sewage. The rest of his battle-brothers are dead, their gene-seed lost to this rabble-world.

That angers him more than anything else. For Sarrien, for all of them, that is the sacred part, the thread that binds the Chapter to itself and to its distant progenitor. An individual brother might die, the spark of his life might be ended, and that is accepted. But to have the immortal remnant lost... that is infuriating. They have saved so little of it during this wearying campaign, and there is no guarantee that the last gunship will even make it back to safety.

It feels futile. It feels like a decision has been made by tacticians a long way away, with no understanding of what priceless assets they are allowing to be cast into the wind. Does it really matter that Lystra stands for another month? What was the purpose of that order – to genuinely buy time for other, more strategic conflicts, or to burnish the ledgers of some scholar in a strategium on Terra?

But Sarrien is a creature of command. He will follow an order or die in the attempt. His personal fury, his individual fatigue – these are irrelevant things. He cultivates the qualities taught to him by Chaplain Geracht: defiance, steadfastness, sacrifice to the will of the Throne.

The southern walls of the city are overrun. They are fighting street to street now, making the stumblers suffer for every spire-crown they swarm through. They are beset by eruptions of plague at their backs, as well as the hordes closing in on them from the front. What is left of the Proximal regiment comes with Sarrien on his long retreat, and together they bolster what they can.

He speaks to Lieutenant Voorn, the most senior soldier remaining in his segment of the city.

'You had word of incoming relief forces,' Sarrien says. 'Before the long-range comm-net went down.'

'I did.' Voorn used to treat Sarrien with a kind of awestruck timidity. Now, like all of them, he is too damned tired for anything but grey-faced mumbling. 'Nothing further.'

That is that, then. The brief hope that the sector authorities had managed to scrape together reinforcements proves as illusory as every other half-glimpsed snatch of redemption. Perhaps nothing was ever sent. Perhaps something was, and it never made it.

Sarrien looks around him. The command chamber is an old chapel, barricaded with piles of rubble and smashed woodwork. Clusters of Guardsmen sit on the stone-piles, cradling their guns, some drinking from near-empty canteens, others staring blankly at the floor. They will not be able to assist him this night – they need at least an hour's rest before they will be good for anything.

'I will hunt, then,' said Sarrien, reaching for his blade and activating the power. The weak energy field throws pale, shifting light across the chapel floor. 'Remain in position until I return.'

Voorn salutes, even though he can hardly lift his arm.

Then Sarrien is moving again, slipping out of the chapel and into another seamy night. He glides almost silently, making use of his capacity for stealth as he has done so often over the past months. He looks up and sees artillery positions among the hab-units, still manned. He knows there are a few more stationed further back – clusters of lascannon teams behind barricades. They wait in the stinking gloom, knowing what comes for them.

Soon he is beyond the regions still in nominal Imperial control, and out into the no-man's-land beyond. He ghosts through craters filling with brackish liquid, and skirts the soundless, grave-dark silhouettes of bombed-out buildings. He smells the enemy before he sees them. He detects the faint buzz of flies, and hears the patter of vermin through the heaps of stone. His body twinges involuntarily, a disgust-response that he should be able to better suppress.

He nears the skeleton of a manufactorum-unit, still hot from its bombardment, and scans body-signals within. There are fifty-seven, at least as far as he can detect.

Sarrien takes a breath. Those numbers would not have troubled him at the start of this campaign, but now he is weaker, deprived of adequate food and rest for a very long time, and must go warily.

He leaps up, grips the lip of a window and swings himself through it, smashing the last shards of glass across a rockcrete floor. Figures turn in the gloom, startled. Before they can react he is right in among them, slashing and punching. Two are bifurcated instantly, another three fall before the next heartbeat. Then he is fighting hard, cutting them down as they shriek and swing at him. He smacks away crude machine-tool weapons and veers out of the path of poorly aimed las-blasts. He slices, switches, feeling the effort drag on his raw muscles.

He is quickly panting. He feels old wounds open up. He slips, and nearly lets a whirring saw through his guard. After that he works harder, punishing himself, taking out his exhausted anger on those before him. His retinal lenses become translucent slicks of blood, and still he has to kill, for they do not run. They never run. It is as if they welcome release for what fate has made of them, despite the demented smiles.

Sarrien hurls a snake-armed brute into the far wall and rips the throat out of a green-eyed stumbler. He breaks into a narrow chamber, lined on either wall with dormant, semi-smashed machines. The buzz of flies becomes pervasive, as does the soup-thick stench. The air seems syrupy, as if time itself has become sluggish in there.

He feels dizzy, and pushes back harder against the signs of bodily weakness.

A man lurches into view, huge, his bare skin taut with muscle. His head is bald and studded with iron ingots. He has green eyes, and a tattoo of death's heads suppurating on a leather-hard, lumpy chest. He might be as big as Sarrien, out of his armour, which is astonishing.

Sarrien moves to kill him, but his muscles do not respond readily to his command. He feels like his gauntlets are pinned down by lead bars.

'Enough now, lad,' the man says.

Light-headed, Sarrien drops to one knee to catch his breath, gripping his blade tight lest he lose it. The rest of the stumblers seem to have melted away. Has he killed them all? It's hard to be sure.

'You're killing yourself,' the man says. 'That seems wasteful.'

Sarrien pushes himself up from the floor. Blood splatters against the inner curve of his helm as he exhales. He thrusts his blade against the man's neck and drives the metal into the flesh.

'Silence!' Sarrien hisses.

The man bleeds freely. 'Yes, that's the thing.' He licks his scabby lips, and the sinews of his neck slip over the crackling sword-edge. 'He's very close now. He's coming. The Gallowsman.'

Sarrien wants to push the blade in further, to finish the task, but he can't. He looks into the man's eyes, and suddenly feels tired. So, so tired.

'It's over, lad,' the man says, and a black line of blood bubbles down over a blotchy chin. 'He's almost here now.'

At that, Sarrien feels fire kindle again. He cries out – a wrenched sound of mingled anguish and defiance. Strength returns and he hauls his sword clean across, severing the neck. Flesh parts, bone cleaves, and the huge man subsides into a leaking heap.

Sarrien swings around, breathing heavily, looking for more of them.

He is ankle-deep in corpses, but none of them are moving. His boots slip on the gore, making him stagger. He feels suddenly cold, chilled to his core, and starts shivering. Despite that, he is still sweating too much.

He starts to walk. He needs to get out of this place, to get away from the stench, to draw purer air into his lungs.

All he can see is the man's sympathetic expectancy.

He's coming.

Sarrien keeps walking, not hearing the crack of bone under his boots, struggling to keep the blackness from narrowing his vision into nothingness.

'Endure,' he whispers, little more than a croak from blood-raw lips. Then he says it again. And again.

Dragan looks down at the world he will kill. He and Glask stand on the observation deck and take in the flickering scan-feeds. From far below, he can feel the heavy clunk of lander-pods being lifted into position.

'A hive world, Gallowsman,' Glask says.

Dragan snarls at him – he hates the title, a typical piece of Barbaran whimsy, and he is no Barbaran. He can't even remember where he heard it first, or how it got attached to him, but he's never been able to shake it off.

'There,' he says, gesturing to the greatest area of conurbations, a huge tangle of interlinked hive-spires high up on the northern continent.

'Already under attack,' says Glask doubtfully. 'Invested, cut off. Can we add much to this?'

Dragan finds he has a certainty about this place, more than is generated or explained by his usual excessive confidence. He stares into the scanner.

'Not just filth down there,' he says, blink-summoning his honour guard and issuing follow-up orders to the rest of the Plague Marines in his war band. 'Adversaries worth our blades.'

The two of them head to the pod-bays, where they rendezvous with the rest. The *Incaligant* has a single Dreadclaw lander, salvaged some-how from the ancient wars and still in working order, plus a brace of more cumbersome ways of getting down. Centuries of contiguous service with Death Guard war bands have seen the Dreadclaw's sides break out into pulsing sacs and its metallic spines erupt with bony outgrowths. When they get into it, gripping on to glistening tendrils strung from the spiny roof, the floor flexes under them.

'Are you... all right, Gallowsman?' asks Glask uncharacteristically, and bravely.

'Do not call me that,' Dragan says.

Then the Dreadclaw unlocks, and the dizzying descent begins. They are thrown about, slammed into the pod's yielding innards. For a few moments there is nothing but the internal roar of the engines, but then the greater boom of atmospheric burning surrounds them. The speed builds and builds, reaching a crescendo just before the retros fire and the plummet ends in the familiar bone-jarring crash of planetfall.

Dragan is first out. He lumbers into a cityscape ravaged by the close attentions of his Legion's god – spires hollowed out into rusted lattices, great black vines strung between rotting nutrient processors. The air is humid and rot-sweet, the ground crawling with blowflies. It is raining in a steady torrent, the drops as viscous as mucus. The Dreadclaw has driven a crack into the rockcrete, and it is already filling up with a sticky swell.

'Good place,' Glask says, lurching into shattered streets.

Dragan hesitates. He lets his warriors go ahead of him. He looks up at the distant pinnacles, mobbed by specks that look like crows but are in likelihood something altogether stranger. He breathes in the torpid atmosphere, detecting the familiar strains of sickness and flesh-decay. Rain runs down his armour, streaming in rivulets over his many corruptions.

He starts moving, stirred by the sound of distant munitions. Fighting is taking place here, despite all the signs of deep and ingrained corruption. His war band heads towards the heart of the mouldering city, passing under the thin shadows of skeletal hab-structures, and sees the first poxwalkers lurch out from under cover. Those wretches are, as ever, happy to see Plague Marines, and begin to gibber. One comes close to Dragan, simpering, and has its spine snapped.

'They have been here a long time,' Dragan remarks, casting a troubled gaze across signs of deep-set corrosion. 'What still fights them?'

The Plague Marines stalk through the steady downpour, gathering a train of limping poxwalkers behind them, who paw and gurgle like domesticated cattle. Some carry shocking wounds, barely caked over by the regenerative powers of their many diseases. Glask remains at the forefront, and the others begin to fan out. Their helm-lenses shimmer with pale green light in the murk. Dragan has a sensation that he cannot name and cannot shake, humming behind his eyes, nagging like an insect he cannot swat.

Then he smells it. Even under the fug of festering organics, ceramite armour has a certain odour, carried by lubricants and ritual oils.

'Be wary,' he voxes, extending rust-flecked talons from his gauntlets. 'A serious enemy is here.'

They do not hurry. They never hurry. They stalk their way deeper into the rain-soaked plague-city, cloven boots splashing into the claggy mire, neither hiding their approach nor advertising it. As they have done on a thousand battlefields, they gauge the threat, they measure their strength against it, they close in on it. Soon they are pushing their way under the looming shoulders of streaming spires, burned black and dripping with stringy lines of pus. Their tactical displays, smeared and thick with condensation, pick up heat-markers, and they head towards them. The poxwalkers come with them, more every moment, flocking around the lords they revere and wish – futilely – to one day become.

Glask is first into battle. As he limps down a snaking transitway clogged with the carcasses of charred transports, the first bolt-round cracks out, punching a hole in his right pauldron. He reels, keeping his feet, then returns fire.

Dragan, a few paces back, scans for the source. He sees it – a hundred metres further up, under the cover of a tangled mass of steel wire and crumbled concrete, a lone warrior in unsullied battle-plate clambering into view, firing as he emerges.

Then there are more of them, all in gunmetal-grey armour, emblazoned with yellow-and-black chevrons. A dozen, smelling strongly of engine oil and promethium. Behind them, something boxy, huge and wreathed in smoke is ploughing its way through rafts of detritus.

Dragan smiles. Sons of Perturabo. A serious enemy indeed.

'Engage freely, my brothers,' he commands, slowly lumbering into a ground-cracking charge, his talons crackling with strings of disruptor-charge. 'Let's see what they've got.'

The last lines are broken. Cleon is out of contact. As far as Sarrien knows, the sergeant and all the others are dead now. He gave the order himself for *Votive IX* to evacuate with the last of the sacred weapons and scarce vials of recovered gene-seed, but has no idea if the command made it through in time.

He has been fighting without any kind of pause for longer than he can remember. One leg is broken, and splinters of bone graze up against his armour cabling. He is nearly blind from the blood pouring down his forehead. His powerblade has finally extinguished, its energy unit smashed, and now he wields it like the mute blades of antiquity.

He is backing away from the hordes, slashing in weary, two-handed curves. All he can see is the ocean of corrupted humanity sweeping towards him, every one with that damnable grin on their stretched faces. The air is hot, dry and caustic.

'For the Emperor!' he cries out for the thousandth time that day, in defiance, his voice weak and liquid through a blood-filled throat.

Flies have got in through the rents in his armour, and they burrow into his flesh, snapping and sucking. Foul gases burst up from the ground beneath him, lurid greens and yellows, old toxins now released into an already putrid atmosphere.

He is the last. He has watched all the others die, one by one, selling themselves for a world the Imperium has clearly forgotten. He has no idea if their sacrifice bought time for victories elsewhere, and no longer cares. He cannot remember his own name, nor the chants given him by the Chaplains. He can only remember how to fight, and those three words – *For the Emperor* – that have burst from his lips since before his ascension to the Chapter itself.

A flayed canine horror bounds towards him, its mouth open to expose concentric rings of curved teeth, and he wearily hacks it down. He is aware that stumblers are clambering in the scaffold above him, coiled ready to pounce, and can do nothing about it.

For the first time, despair rises to choke him. There is nothing noble to fight here, nothing to test himself against, just this hateful, *hateful* swell of twisted and destroyed flesh.

'For the Emperor,' he gasps, his body flaring with agony.

He staggers into a cavernous interior of a roofless cathedral, pursued all the way. A great stone aquila hangs from a broken archway, still suspended by corrosion-eaten chains. He fights his way towards it, panting, limping, feeling the insects burrow deeper into his skin. They get into his helm, suffocating him.

'For. The. Emperor.'

Just as he draws closer, a blunt blade chops out his good leg from under him, and he stumbles. He hacks the blade's bearer apart, but has to crawl now. The aquila is swaying, rocked by hot plague-winds gusting along the nave. Even as he watches, the chains break, and the mighty stone sigil crashes to earth. It breaks into three pieces, rocking amid the detritus of the altar beneath.

'For. The...'

No breaths will come now. Every time he tries, more blowflies clog his throat.

'For...'

He looks up. High above him, hidden behind a haze of dust and insects, the heavyset tattooed man is there again. A livid weal runs along his flabby neck.

'That's enough now, lad,' the man says, 'don't you think?'

'For...'

Sarrien is trembling all over. He can feel his body giving up. His organs are full, pulsing as if worms might burst from them. His sword drops from his trembling fingers.

'You want to keep fighting, do you not?' the man asks.

He struggles. All is going black.

'There's a better death for you. If you want it. You won't even remember you were here.'

His head cracks to the ground, and he feels the weight of the stumblers as they land on him. Lice swarm up into his carapace, lodging deep within the interface nodes. His secondary heart bursts, and he feels the hot, wet pain within him.

He manages to look up, one last time. The tattooed man has come closer, and is squatting over him. There's a strange breaking of the light over his green-eyed, bloodshot face.

'So what do you want now, lad?' the man asks.

Just as before, it seems as if it is just the two of them. He can still see the man's features, but the rest is a blur. He can still feel the pain of his body's disintegration, but the shrieks of the stumblers are muffled. The world shrinks around him like gauze over a wound.

'*Resist*,' Sarrien croaks, though his voice is coming from a long way off.

'You could do.' The face looms. It has an unhealthy pallor up close, grey-green like moss on stone. 'You have done for months. You never broke. But then, you can resist anything, can't you? Except, perhaps, pointlessness. This has all been pointless. That is the real torture.'

Sarrien feels the words penetrate like fingernails. Something within him uncurls, a tumour or a blight, flexing into birth. He sees the iron ingots on the man's shaven head, and they look like elongated service studs. He sees the lumps under the man's skin, and they look like the ancient, decayed remnants of a black carapace.

'I killed you,' Sarrien says.

'You may do so again. And that, too, you will never remember.'

He has been fighting for so long. He has forgotten so much. The pain is unbearable. He knows nothing. He has been destroyed. All around him, the city is becoming a shrine. All it lacks is an offering.

'What do you *want*?' the tattooed man asks again.

Sarrien looks up at him.

'To keep going,' he says.

'There's only one way to do that.'

For a long time Sarrien makes no reply. It feels like he's falling, tumbling into a cold well. He can hear someone screaming.

To ask the question is the beginning. He knows this. But that is the easiest way to set off, to soften the hard path ahead.

The green eyes never let him go.

'What do you want?'

The *pain*.

'More,' Sarrien says.

Dragan takes joy in the fighting. The enemy is pushed back. They resist, and do well, for they are as stubborn and strong as the Death Guard, but this world belongs to the god and they are on foreign ground, and so they will lose in the end.

In truth, he does not know why there are poxwalkers in this city. They must have been here for years, corroding and infesting the entire planet in a slow vice of decay. He assumes they were spawned in some ancient war, and have since changed it from its cold Imperial template and transformed it, as they are wont to do, into a little mirror of the Plague Planet.

Dragan launches into the next adversary, plunging his talons into thick ceramite, relishing the Iron Warrior's grinding death. A final death blow rattles his helmet, grating up against the swollen iron studs in his skull. Dragan seizes the dying Iron Warrior and hurls him aside. As he does so, his chest spasms with pain – the old flesh-cut tattoo over his ribcage is suppurating again.

He presses on, flanked by his brothers. They drive the enemy into the rotting shell of what might have been a cathedral, its walls heavily green with glowing vegetation and its floors spongy with saturated spores.

He sees the ruins of an old stone Imperial aquila, half-buried in the mats of rain-spattered fungus. It is in pieces, as if it fell from the open roof a long time ago.

That makes him pause. He freezes, and for a moment feels an old memory tug at him. When he blinks, for a split second he is looking down at a crippled, bedraggled fighter half-buried in the debris, as if they had been speaking, the two of them. A dim memory swims close to the surface, and he reaches out to it and almost gets hold of it.

But then there is a heavy crash, and Glask is forging ahead. The others are going with him. Dragan pulls back. He blinks again, and there is only rubble.

He shakes his head. He barks out a caustic laugh and starts walking again. He finds new targets and selects which ones he will end.

'Gallowsman!' Glask calls out merrily. 'We have them on the run!'

Dragan glowers at him and takes up the slaying afresh.

'Do not call me that,' he mutters and strides across the broken aquila, grinding what remains of its outline into the rotting dust.

YOUR
NEXT READ

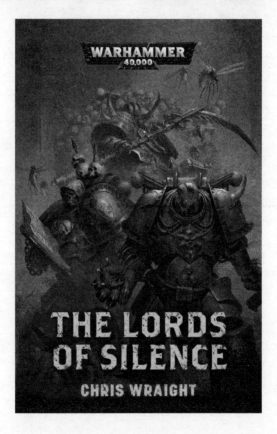

THE LORDS OF SILENCE
by Chris Wraight

The galaxy has changed. Armies of Chaos march across the Dark Imperium,
among them the Death Guard, servants of the Plague God. But shadows
of the past haunt these traitors…

EXECUTION

Rachel Harrison

Introducing

SEVERINA RAINE

COMMISSAR, ELEVENTH ANTARI RIFLES

The sky screams. The ground underfoot screams. In the distance, men and women scream too. The noise is catastrophic, underpinned by the thunder of artillery and the crack of the void shields protecting the rebel-held fortress of Morne. They are the sounds of a siege.

A siege that is failing.

Commissar Severina Raine ignores it all. She's focused on the man in front of her. Captain Tevar Lun of the Eleventh Antari Rifles stands with his lasgun held loose at his side. His grey eyes are locked on hers, unflinching.

It's admirable, considering her bolt pistol is pointed at his face.

'You are refusing your orders,' Raine says coldly.

Lun puts down his rifle, leaning it against the rough wall of the earthworks. The stock of his gun and his flak armour are scored with kill-markings and prayers carved in spiked Antari script. White scratches against the grey-and-green camouflage plates.

'I will not do it,' he says. 'Not my brothers. Not my sisters.'

Lun's eyes flicker to the fortress walls. The wall-mounted guns are firing into the dawn sky, tracking after a flight of Valkyrie gunships that pull up and away, tearing holes in the clouds.

'Those guns are built to kill tanks and aircraft,' he says. 'They turned Keld and his squad to mist.'

Raine saw it too. Not just that, she smelled it on the wind. Rich iron in the cold air. The rebels had disengaged the overrides on the guns and used them that way as a show of force. It was a show of something else as well.

Arrogance.

'Keld was foolish, and slow,' she says. 'Be neither, and the Emperor will see us across. *I* will see us across.'

It's his one chance. A chance she would not give to most of the guardsmen serving with her. She extends it to Tevar Lun because of what he is. A clear head. A faithful heart. A captain respected by all of the squads under his command.

But Tevar Lun doesn't take the chance he's offered. He shakes his head instead.

'What you ask of us,' he says, 'it's suicide.'

There's a break in the noise of the artillery, as if the world is waiting for her reply. Raine lets out a slow breath. Her aim doesn't waver.

'That is your mistake,' Raine says. 'You think that I am asking.'

And without pause, without doubt, she pulls the trigger. The report of the bolt pistol is a loud, flat bang. Blood spatters her face. She doesn't flinch. Doesn't blink. The blood is hers to bear. As Lun's body collapses, Raine hears the slow release of breath from the other Antari standing around her. The flexing of gloved fingers. A snatch of whispered prayer. Then the artillery starts up again. Compared to that quiet moment, it almost seems a relief.

Raine looks at each of them in turn. At Sergeant Daven Wyck and his Wyldfolk, twenty-five strong. At Lydia Zane and the medic, Nuria Lye. At the storm trooper captain, Andren Fel, and his squad of four. None of them look away, even as their captain's blood soaks the ground at their feet. He made them unflinching too. She is thankful for that.

'We have our orders,' she shouts over the noise. 'We know what needs to be done.'

They all nod, still not looking away. That's how Raine catches the open resentment in some of those grey Antari eyes. First Wyck, who is no surprise, and hardly needs more reason. He resents her because she is not of Antar, though he masks it with careful words. She expects it from him, but this time he isn't alone. It's Varn, too. The big man is breathing hard through his teeth, his fire-scarred hands clenched into fists. The third is Lydia Zane. She was standing close to Lun when he was shot. The others keep a superstitious distance from her. From her pale-veined skin and her crown of cables, and her eyes that see even when they are closed. Zane's face doesn't change, but she puts her hand to her throat. To where her captain's blood has dashed across it. Raine knows that the next moments are critical. That she must turn that resentment against the enemy, against the fortress, or they will fail here and now.

She also knows that if it comes down to it, she will bear more Antari blood to get it done.

'The orders that Captain Lun refused are not just my orders,' she says. 'They are the orders of Lord-General Serek. They are the orders of High Command.'

She looks at Wyck, then Varn, then Zane.

'Above all, they are the orders of the Emperor himself.'

There is no change in Wyck or Zane, but Varn blinks. His face drains of colour. Raine hears a muttered prayer from the group.

'So it is that I speak for the Emperor,' Raine says. 'Refuse me, and you refuse Him.'

Zane glances down at her bloody fingertips. Wyck shifts his weight. Around them, the trench network stretches for miles. More than half of the regiment has been deployed outside the fortress of Morne. Over three thousand Antari souls. Infantry, mechanised and artillery. They are not alone, either. The Kavrone 21st took heavy losses recapturing the city of Thadar, but they have brought everything they have left in support of the Antari. Tracks and tank-frames rattle. Petro-chem engines roar. Mortars fire. The sky is lit with explosions. A second sunrise over the world of Drast, and the fortress on the hill. Raine tightens her fingers around the grip of her bolt pistol.

'Will you refuse?' she says.

There is a solid, shouted chorus of 'No, commissar,' from every soldier in the trench. It is loudest from Varn, who has his head bowed now, penitent. Zane and Wyck are less so, but they say the words like everyone else. That sits fine with Severina Raine. She doesn't care about their hatred, as long as they obey. Her finger moves away from her pistol's trigger.

'We will open the way for our forces to take the fortress,' Raine says. 'To *break* it.'

The combat engineer Crys bares her teeth in a smile. It's a white stripe in her bloody face.

'Aye, commissar,' she says.

The Antari shift. Their mood is turning. Their conviction growing.

'The rebels in that fortress think that this noise they make is thunder,' Raine says. 'But they have heard nothing of the Antari Rifles.'

They all salute her, arms snapping up to make the sign of the aquila.

'In His name!' Raine cries.

And it isn't just Crys that answers, it's every soldier in the trench.

'In His name!' they shout over the roar of the guns.

Raine can never sleep the night before a deployment. Instead, she sits out on the ridge, watching the sky light with distant fires. The wind brings her the sounds of war. The taste of smoke and burned earth. She finds it a comfort.

In her hand she holds her timepiece, the same way she always does on those nights. It's brass and bone, marked with her family seal. The only piece of her family that Raine has managed to hang on to.

'Thought I'd find you here.'

The voice comes from behind her. Raine doesn't have to turn to see who it is. She puts the timepiece back into the pocket of her greatcoat.

'Come,' she says. 'Sit.'

Andren Fel sits down beside her on the ridge. He is holding two battered tin cups, and he hands one to her. It's tea. She can see the loose, flat leaves floating in it, even in the dark. Raine had never once had tea. Not until her assignment to the Rifles. Not until she started meeting with Andren Fel. Now it's tradition, and the Antari take their traditions very seriously.

'The burned reaches, then.' Andren follows her gaze. 'At first light.'

'That's what they are called now,' Raine says. 'They were grain fields, once. Crops for miles, like an ocean of gold.'

There is nothing left now of the fields, or anything else, thanks to the rebellion. It had started with small betrayals, as such things often do. A spike in the murder rate. Banned texts found on factory workers. Great, ugly symbols burned into the fields of crops. After eight days, the cities were gripped by riots. Eight days after that, a great pyre was raised in Drast's sprawling capital city of Thadar. Thousands blinded themselves and leapt into the flames one after another in the name of something false and frightening: in the name of the Baleful Eye. Since then, it has not rained, and the sky has become heavy and sick, draped over the world like soaked bandages.

'They're calling it the unbreakable fortress of Morne,' Andren says. 'Saying it's where the rebel leaders are hiding.'

The rebel leaders. Once Lord and Lady Morne, servants of the Imperium, now traitors. Heretics. Their own heirs were among those sacrificed in Thadar. Raine watches as a bolt of light spears into the sky in the distance. The boom comes a moment later.

'A half-truth,' she says. 'But no fortress is unbreakable. We will drag them out of it, or crush them under it, by His grace.'

Andren puts down his cup, then steeples his fingers for a moment. It's a superstitious gesture that Raine has only ever seen from the Antari. Andren does it often.

'By His grace,' he says.

'The guns fire six hundred rounds before they need to cycle.'

Raine watches the walls as she speaks. She watches the streaks of white-hot gunfire against the grey sky. Her eyes flicker to the time-piece. The hand ticks down.

Three.

Two.

'There,' she says.

The guns cease fire. There's a high-pitched whine as they run dry, then a grinding clatter that echoes across the open ground as the rebels reload. It is answered by shelling from the Antari lines. Dirt is thrown into the air in great plumes, each shell landing closer to the void shield until they impact against it with loud cracks. Even this far out, Raine can smell the ozone.

'How long?' says Daven Wyck, from beside her.

'Five minutes,' she says.

The sergeant narrows his eyes and spits on the ground.

'Plus one or two for them to realign to point downwards,' says Yulia Crys. 'If we're lucky.'

She looks up at the guns, shielding her eyes. Crys is taller than Raine by a head. Broad in the shoulders and hips. The left side of her face is a mess of old burn scars that run up into her hairline and around the ragged mess of her ear.

'You're sure?' Raine says.

'That's what it looked like,' Crys says. 'When they took out Keld's Fenwalkers.'

Raine nods. Deaths can be costly, but they are rarely purposeless.

'You're confident you can breach those walls without heavy weapons?' she says.

'I wouldn't say no to heavy weapons, but yes, I can breach it. Anything that's built, sir.'

Raine can believe it. The units in her company specialise in demolition, but Crys is an expert among experts.

'It'll be the getting there,' Crys says. 'Sure as anything there'll be rebels in the field, and longshots on the walls, in the towers.'

'We have the Duskhounds,' Raine says. 'They will get you there.'

Wyck smiles. Unlike the others, he isn't scarred or tattooed. He is tall and lean with handsome, even features and fair hair, like the old illuminations of saints. Despite all of that, his smile is wholly unpleasant.

'More importantly, we have faith,' he says. 'And our blades.'

The words sound right, but Raine knows Wyck. He casts good words about him like a cloak to hide the sharp edges of his soul; the part that truly enjoys killing. That's why he's wound tight, his hands white-knuckled on the stock of his gun. That and the stimms. He thinks that she doesn't know. That he's capable of hiding it from her.

Things don't remain hidden from Severina Raine. She digs them out and drags them into the light. When he ceases to be useful, she'll do exactly the same to Daven Wyck.

'There is one more thing,' Raine says. 'Zane.'

There's a flicker of distaste in Wyck's eyes.

'Where is she?' asks Raine.

Crys looks past Raine, back up the trench.

'She's with Lun, sir,' she says.

Lydia Zane sits cross-legged in the trench beside the body of her former captain. He's been draped with his Antari rain-cloak. Zane has hold of the corner of it between her thumb and forefinger. She doesn't open her eyes, doesn't let go.

'I will do what you ask,' she says, before Raine has the chance to speak. 'Whatever you ask.'

'I know,' Raine says.

'Good,' Zane says. 'Duty comes first in all things, though I do not need to tell you so, commissar.'

Raine nods, though Zane's eyes are still closed. She knows that the psyker doesn't need them to see.

'In the moments before he did it, I knew Lun would refuse you,' Zane says. 'Just as I knew how you would answer his refusal. Strange, how even the deaths you expect still sting.'

Zane opens her eyes. They are bloodshot, like always. She smiles, and her thin skin crinkles like parchment left too long in the sun.

'Which I also do not need to tell you, of course.'

Raine doesn't nod this time. She doesn't acknowledge Zane's words at all. The deaths she carries with her are not for sharing. Zane's smile disappears and she looks down at Lun's body.

'He was not afraid, you know,' she says. 'Well, we are all of us afraid sometimes, but that is not why he stood against you.'

Raine looks down at Lun's body as well.

'It doesn't matter why,' she says. 'It was a moment of weakness, and weakness cannot be tolerated. If you allow cracks to appear in glass, then you should not be surprised when it breaks and bloodies you.'

A long moment passes between them.

'You are correct, of course,' Zane says. 'I know this better than most.'

She lets go of the corner of the drape and gets to her feet, leaning on her staff. It is made of a dark wood, set with gems and wound tight with cables. More cables snake from her hairless head, glimmering silver. A witch's crown. The psyker is tall, like most Antari, but her limbs are corded and thin, the bones showing easily through her skin. It could be mistaken for fragility, but Raine knows better. She has seen Lydia Zane pull apart a tank, piece by piece, peeling the armour back with a curl of her hand. It was chilling to watch, though it was nothing compared to what Zane did to those cowering inside.

'Stick close to the Duskhounds,' Raine says. 'They will watch you. Whatever Fel says, do it without question. As if it were me.'

Zane nods.

'As if it were you, commissar.'

'So, then,' Raine says. 'I believe you owe me a story, captain.'

Andren's posture changes slightly. A shift in his shoulders. It's how he looks at ease, or as close to at ease as a man like Andren Fel can get.

'Sure enough,' he says. 'And what story would you like me to tell?'

The two of them began sharing stories as a way for her to better understand the regiment. At least that's what she told herself it was. Raine couldn't say what it is now, but she knows that she has grown to need it. Another comfort, of a kind.

'Tell me about the Wyldfolk,' Raine says. 'Where does the name come from?'

Andren takes a drink from his cup. The steam catches in the air like gun-smoke.

'The Wyldfolk are Wyck's squad,' Andren says. 'You should ask him.'

'I'm asking you,' she says.

Andren laughs. He does it easily, and often. It's a peculiarity of his.

'That you are. They are a folk story, like all of our squad names.'

Raine nods. She knows this. Andren's own storm troopers are the Duskhounds. It's another Antari story. One about a great hound made of shadow that tears out the throats of those who refuse to die when they are fated to. It's wholly apt for what Andren and his squad do.

'The wyldfolk are forest spirits,' he says. 'Wicked ones.'

Andren puts down his cup and rolls back the sleeve of his black fatigues. His arms are tattooed with lines of scripture. Entwined around the verse, there are figures. Raine sees the duskhound, inked in grey. Andren points to another tattoo just above it of twisted briars that look like clawed hands.

'Wicked is right,' Raine says. 'So, how does the story go?'

'It goes that a woodsman and his family lived on the edge of the great black forest,' he says. 'The woodsman knew that before anything was taken from the forest, something must be given, lest the wyldfolk grow angry.'

He draws his combat blade from his belt and turns it, resting it against the pad of his thumb.

'Every day, before the woodsman felled timber, or took to the hunt, he would cut his thumb and let three drops of blood fall onto the stump of the same tree.'

Andren presses his thumb against the blade, just hard enough to draw blood. He waits for three fat drops to fall onto the ground before he continues.

'Then he would go into the forest and claim his prize. On his return, the blood would be gone without trace.'

Andren turns his hand, watching blood paint a line down to his palm.

'One day, the woodsman's wife came down with a sickness,' he says. 'And so he sent his son to take the hunt alone. He gave him his bow, his arrows and his cutting knife. The woodsman's son went to the stump of the same tree, but he was too cowardly to cut his hand. Too selfish to pay the price. Thinking he could fool the forest, the woodsman's son tipped three drops from his waterskin onto the stump, then slipped between the trees, laughing.'

The first time Raine saw a forest was after the scholam, when she first went to war as a junior commissar. The smell comes back to her as Andren speaks. Such a strange smell. Wet and rich and living.

'The woodsman's son followed his father's path, but soon found it blocked by coiling briars,' Andren continues. 'When he turned back, they stood behind him too. The woodsman's son waited, hoping they would uncoil and let him pass. The forest grew dark. The shadows long. The woodsman's son grew hungry. He could not wait any longer, so he pushed his way through the briars. They snagged at his clothes and raked him with their thorns. The boy cursed the briars. Cursed the forest. Then he set to running, bleeding from the dozens of shallow cuts they had given him.'

Andren wipes the blade of his knife on the leg of his fatigues and sheathes it.

'The woodsman's son tried to run home, but the path seemed to wend in ways it hadn't before. The cuts he had been given kept bleeding until he was weak. Until he stumbled and fell. Still, he did not stop bleeding. Not until every drop was spilt and taken by the forest. For cuts from the wyldfolk never close, and they always kill.'

'That is how it goes?' Raine says.

'That is how it goes.'

For a moment, they both just watch the blood well up on Andren's thumb.

'A whole year, and I haven't heard an Antari story yet that isn't made up of blood and death,' Raine says.

Andren looks at her and laughs.

'Aren't everyone's?' he says.

* * *

Raine watches her timepiece again as the mounted guns roar. The glass is scuffed from use, and there is a tiny fracture in the edge of it, right at the very top of the face. The fracture has been there since the day it came into her possession. It does not seem right to fix it. To undo the damage.

She opens a vox channel to two of the other sergeants that fell under Lun's command. Now her blood to bear. They are far along the line from her position, hunkered in their own stretches of the earthworks.

'Hartkin,' she says. 'Mistvypers. Acknowledge.'

'Aye, commissar,' says Selk in reply. The Mistvyper sergeant's voice is a semi-mechanical rasp, thanks to the augmetics replacing a good deal of her larynx.

'Receiving, commissar.'

By contrast, Rom Odi's voice is soft, with the strong lilt of Antar's southern settlements.

'We move on the next cycling,' Raine says. 'Up to the shield and through it. Once we reach the other side, the guns will no longer have sight on you.'

'Nor will their rebels, when I have finished with them,' Selk says.

Raine would expect nothing less of Selk. The Mistvyper is one of the regiment's best marksmen. Andren often says she should have been a Duskhound.

'Breach at the base of your target bastion, then make haste to the twelfth level,' Raine says. 'We will silence the guns from there.'

Her eyes flick to her timepiece. There are mere moments until the guns cycle. Her limbs burn in anticipation of the charge.

'Ready yourselves,' she says.

'Aye, commissar,' Selk says.

'On your mark,' says Odi.

She looks along the line.

'Ten seconds,' she shouts.

Around her, the Antari brace themselves against the earthworks.

Raine can hear Zane humming to herself in the scant moments between the firing of the guns. It's a song Andren hums sometimes. Something from Antar.

'Five!'

The hand ticks down, approaching that tiny fracture in the glass.

'Four!'

Wyck laughs, all edges.

'Three!'

Andren Fel steeples his fingers, that same Antari gesture.

'Two!'

Crys puts her hand on the top of the earthworks.

'Forwards!'

Raine calls the charge as she leaps up the slope and out of the trench. The mounted guns run dry with a whine. The cycling starts, the clatter echoing across the open ground in front of her.

Raine runs. Her heart hammers in her ears. The air is dust and dirt and smoke that catches in her throat, stings her eyes. Beside her, the Wyldfolk run too. Andren's Duskhounds are a couple of paces behind with Crys and Zane. She can hear the psyker's ragged breathing. The Mistvypers and the Hartkin are moving up from their own positions along the trench network.

As they run, the Antari forces still within the trench line start their own concentrated assault, pummelling the void shield with mortars and rockets and long-range autocannon fire. The void shield flickers, but doesn't fall. It's not expected to. Their assault is a distraction. A means to draw that baleful eye away from Raine and her company. Spears of light punch up into the sky far to Raine's left, and the vox crackles in her ear.

'We have been noticed, commissar. They aren't pleased.'

Devri sounds pleased, though. The captain of the fourth company is the type who wants desperately to prove his worth. To write legends. That fervour makes him endlessly useful.

'Keep it up,' Raine says, between breaths. 'As much noise as you can.'

'More thunder,' Devri says. *'Aye, commissar.'*

A moment later, Raine hears a distant series of booms, as if the surface of Drast is trying to throw them all clear. Devri's thunder. The noise makes her heart sing as she runs.

The land they have to cross to reach the fortress walls was once fortified with forward staging posts and bunkers, and expansive airfields for the Drastian airforce to mobilise from. The berths and refuelling stations are now blasted wrecks, the smooth rockcrete cracked and torn up. Trench lines have been carved into the earth by both sides, wounds cut deep into the face of Drast. Raine and her soldiers run between the slumped remains of fortifications and foxholes; between the burned-out shells of tanks and jagged-edged craters. Everywhere there are coils of razor wire. Those Antari soldiers who pushed forward the previous day are tangled in them, bloodied, torn and dead. They are not the only bodies. Rebels and Antari alike lay all around, whole and in pieces. Looming over all of this is the fortress, a slab-sided edifice that has stood, unbroken on the hill, for a thousand years or more. It is still unbroken. Untouched, even. Protected by a void shield of ancient design, there is not a mark on the stone that the rebels did not put there themselves. The greatest of these is the baleful eye that the rebels have taken for their name, rendered in crimson and gold on a ragged banner that hangs half the height of the fortress wall.

'They do not see us!'

The shout comes from Gryl. He is running ahead and to Raine's left.

'An eye like that, and still they are blind!'

Gryl laughs loud at his own joke, at least until a bolt of high-powered lasfire silences him. He falls forwards, dead. A series of cracks follow, and more lasbolts blaze the air. It's not coming from the fortress. There are rebel soldiers firing from their own trenches and emplacements all around them. Raine sees the glint of rust-red carapace armour, deliberately dulled with mud and dust. She hears the lies the rebels shout, carried on the wind. Blasphemies that make her grit her teeth.

'To those without faith, we bring thunder!' she cries. 'Put them down!'

She aims her bolt pistol at the closest of the rebels as he comes up over the top of his own trench. He is an officer, wearing a curved chestplate trimmed with gold. Across the silver surface he has carved that baleful eye. He's done the same to the skin of his face. Dozens more rebels swarm behind him, clawing their way up and out of the earthworks. The officer raises his own bolt pistol. Opens his mouth to shout. For a moment it is like looking into a dark mirror.

Then Raine fires.

That chestplate can't protect him from a headshot. His body falls backwards into the trench. Onto his own rebel soldiers. The Antari cheer.

'Forwards!' Raine shouts.

She sees Wyck up ahead. He's firing his rifle in twitchy bursts. Twice she sees him shoot out their knees, rather than go for a clean kill.

Yulia Crys ducks into the shadow of a collapsed hangar, then takes a grenade from the bandolier slung across her chest. She pitches it hard and high. It lands well within the rebels' trench network, detonating with a throaty boom.

Lydia Zane flicks her hand upwards and a rebel soldier flies ten or twelve metres into the air. He screams until he hits the earth. Andren Fel and his Duskhounds move around her, making clean kills, never passing in front of one another. Five shadows in matt-black armour with snarling faces painted on their masks.

'How long before we have the big guns to worry about?' Andren says over the vox.

Raine fires her bolt pistol. The soldier charging her falls backwards, his rifle firing wildly into the sky. She has been counting since they left the trench.

'Three minutes,' she says. 'Roughly.'

'We are wading when we should be running.'

'Agreed,' Raine says.

She's about to call out to push through when a bolt of lasfire hits her shoulder and knocks the breath from her lungs. It spins her. Staggers her. Her cap of office falls from her head, landing in the dirt. Raine stops. A second lasbolt scores her thigh, burning like a brand.

Pain blooms in her shoulder, in her leg. It's dizzying, but she does not falter. Raine finds her breath. Grits her teeth. Then she stoops and picks up her peaked cap, letting lasbolts crackle around her. She puts it back on her head, square and straight, then looks to the rebel soldier who shot her. Like the officer, he has cut his face into patterns. Between those angry red lines, his mouth splits, showing blackened stubs of teeth.

'Theatrics,' he says, in accented Gothic.

He drops his rifle and draws a long, curved combat knife from his belt. His intention is to charge her, to force her to duel him. Severina Raine does not enter into honour duels with heretics. She shoots the rebel soldier before he can put one foot forward. The bolt-round makes a crater of his chest, and he falls backwards, bloody foam spilling from his mouth. She keeps moving, firing again to finish him.

When she looks around, Raine sees Andren watching her. He doesn't say a thing, just turns away and goes after the rebels. But Andren Fel isn't the only one. She can feel the eyes of all of the Antari on her, even as they fight and die. Just glimpses and glances, but each one significant. Each one followed by a battle cry.

Not theatrics, Raine thinks, as she draws her sword. *Symbolism.*

'One for one,' Andren says. 'Now you owe me a story.'

It's fully dark now. In the landing fields behind them, the Antari are performing combat drills. Raine wonders if they would be sleeping either, if they could. The fortress keeps drawing her eyes. A distant grey shape, lit by floodlights and fires. The unbreakable fortress of Morne.

'I was raised in one of the scholams on Gloam,' she says. 'Do you know it?'

Andren shakes his head.

'Gloam is a cold world with a dim star,' Raine says. 'No forests. No fauna but vermin. The oceans that remain are made black by industry. It hates life, yet we persist there, as if to spite it.'

'We are at our best when we are pitted against things that hate us,' Andren says. 'Worlds included.'

Raine nods.

'There was a task they had us do,' she says. 'A test, I suppose.'

'I can imagine,' he says.

She knows he can. He lived it as well, in the scholam on Antar. She's heard the stories. Seen the scars.

'Gloam is a hive,' she says. 'Layers stacked up on one another so you can't say for sure where the real ground is anymore. In the deeper layers, the vermin grow big. They are numerous and cunning.'

Andren looks out to the fortress. The shadows catch in the deep scar that runs up his cheek and across the bridge of his nose. His grey eyes narrow.

'As vermin are inclined to be,' he says.

The void shield that protects the fortress is invisible, but Raine knows when they are getting close. It's not because of their position relative to the grey stone, or because of how far they've run.

It's how the fortress looks, slightly out of step with the world around it. How the air is sharp with ozone. How minute reverberations run along her bones and rattle her teeth. Somewhere between pleasant and painful.

'That feeling is hateful,' Wyck says, clearly tending more towards the latter. 'It's like being boiled from the inside.'

The sergeant is breathing hard as he runs. It isn't because he's tired. It's because he's frenzied. His arms are scorched with lasburns, and the bayonet has snapped clean off his rifle. He left it buried in a rebel soldier's chest.

'So we just go right through?' Wyck asks, as he runs up the shattered hull of a tank.

'Right through,' Raine says. 'The shield might be proof against bombardments and energy weapons, but it won't stop us.'

That's what every report and technical specification she has read says, anyway.

In front of them, a full squad of rebel soldiers charge from the shadows of a collapsed pillbox. They are screaming, but the words aren't Drastian. They are something odious that turns Raine's stomach. The Antari clash with the rebels, green-grey striking against crimson. Wyck drops two of them with bursts of lasfire, then slides down the other side of the tank. A third charges Raine. He is clad in thick red armour plating from his knees to his neck. Imperial sigils have been scratched out. Defaced. He bellows at her. She should see the whites of his eyes this close, but there are no whites to see. Just black orbs that shine like ocean stones. For a moment, she thinks of nightfall on Gloam. Of the sound of the sea, hidden by the darkness. How it roars, hungering for the land.

The rebel swings at her with a jagged-edged sword; the kind that will snag when it cuts. Raine knocks the blade aside with her own. The power field of her sword crackles. She ducks under the next swing, dodges the one after. It reminds her of close-quarters training with new recruits back at the scholam. The rebel is bigger than her, so he thinks he's stronger.

He's wrong.

Raine turns away another frenzied blow. The rebel curses in his own tongue, but he's cut short when she drives her sword through his chest. Raine pulls downwards, shoulder to hip, splitting the plated armour just as easily as the flesh beneath it. When she pulls her sword free, blood clings to the blade, despite the power field. It is black too, like his eyes. She kicks the gutted soldier onto his back and sets to running again, her legs burning. That's the last of them. There's not another rebel standing between them and the void shield.

'How long?' says Wyck, keeping pace with her.

Raine is about to answer when the clattering noise from the fortress grinds to a halt. It is swiftly replaced by a building whine.

The rebels have finished reloading the guns.

They are out of time.

'There's a particular kind of vermin on Gloam,' Raine says. 'An especially dangerous kind. The drill abbots called them sin-thieves, because they would come from their holes to gnaw on the wicked and the weak, growing fat on their sin.'

'Sound like rats to me,' says Andren.

'Perhaps they were, once,' she says. 'But they'd become something else. Something worse. As things often do when they are left to their own devices.'

Andren nods.

'One of the scholam boys awoke screaming one night because one of them was sitting on his chest, biting the flesh from his arms. It was the size of a mastiff.'

Andren does a low whistle.

'He killed it, him and one of the others, but his wounds went bad by morning. Everyone said that all the sin they stole had poured back into him.'

'And you call us superstitious,' Andren says.

Raine permits herself a smile.

'The drill abbots could not bear it, nor could we. None of us wanted to go bad. To have stolen sin poured into us by a vermin's teeth.'

'So what did you do?'

Raine's smile fades.

'We went to find the nest.'

'Through the shield!' Raine's vox broadcast goes out to the Wyldfolk and Duskhounds with her. The Mistvypers and Hartkin along the line, too.

'Crys,' Raine calls the combat engineer to her side. 'Gather up the demo charges. We need that breach as fast as you're able.'

Crys grins and tugs at her bandolier.

'I even saved my grenades, sir,' she says. 'Well, most of them.'

She looks back over her shoulder to another of the Wyldfolk. One who is a good way behind.

'Varn,' she voxes back. 'Hey, Varn, move your arse! I need your charges.'

Varn shakes his head. He is a big man. Big enough to make the grenade launcher he carries look small.

'I am not built for this sort of running,' he says, picking up his pace. *'Not with all this kit.'*

'I carry kit just like yours,' Crys says. 'You just like your rations too much.'

Lydia Zane is close by when she turns to look at Varn. Her eyes go wide.

'Run,' she says, in her rough-edged voice.

'What?' Varn says, panicking.

'Move!'

Raine yells her order at Varn, but her voice is lost beneath the roar of the wall-mounted guns as they fire. Raine sees Varn duck his head and throw up his arms, but the rounds never hit him, they stop short and burst instead into dozens of bright white blooms of light. Zane's hands are up, curled like claws. She's shielding him. The psyker starts to bleed from her nose and ears.

'Through the void shield!' Raine shouts to the others over the vox. 'Through the damned shield, now!'

Varn keeps running. High above, the guns track across the line, angling to follow him and the others that Zane is protecting. Her kine-shield starts to crack.

'Run!' Crys shouts. 'Run, you great big fool!'

Zane wavers. More rounds impact against her shield. The cracks spread.

'Varn!' Raine shouts with her. 'The charges!'

The kine-shield fails when Varn is seconds away from the shield's edge. He tries to throw his bag of demo charges the rest of the way, but it never leaves his hands. The rounds from the wall-mounted guns are made to punch through tanks. They punch through Varn with no trouble at all. Even over the racket, Raine hears Yulia Crys cry out. Then the demo charges Varn was carrying go up and Raine is thrown backwards. The world becomes a series of sensations:

Heat.

Light.

Noise.

Then something else, a stinging, like knives running over her bones. Sound drops away. The siege drops away. Raine hits the dirt, landing flat on her back. She watches as the explosion that killed Varn washes upwards and away from her across the surface of the void shield. The explosion hurled her straight through it. The ringing in her ears fades. The fortress guns can track no steeper. They strafe along the line on the other side of the shield, churning the earth, splintering rock and armour and bone. Raine lets out a slow breath. Then she hears something else. A booming voice coming from inside the fortress.

The Imperium of Man is dead, it says. *The Imperium of Man is dead.*

Raine gets to her feet, her mind reeling at the rebels' blasphemies. She's still reeling from the explosion, too, but she doesn't have time for that.

The Imperium of Man is dead.

The Wyldfolk surround her, burned and battered. Depleted. There are eighteen of them still breathing, and only fifteen standing. Nuria Lye is already bandaging wounds and staunching bleeds. Crys is alive, though. And Zane. Andren and his Duskhounds are with them, their armour scorched, peeled back to silver. He looks to her. They all do.

Raine speaks up over the distant voice.

'They say the Imperium of Man is dead,' she says. 'But the Imperium of Man is every one of us. Every soldier. Every tank on the field. Every ship in orbit. Every single faithful heart from here to Holy Terra. Soldier, citizen, priest and pilgrim.'

She looks up at the fortress, and the ragged banner emblazoned with the baleful eye.

'We are many. We are strong. Most of all, we are *right*.'

Severina Raine spits blood and ash onto the ground.

'And that is something you cannot kill.'

Raine drags Crys to her feet and into the shadow of a crumpled Chimera chassis. The hull is caved in, flattening the crew compartment. This close, Raine can smell old blood.

'The wall,' Raine says. 'Can you still breach it?'

Crys looks down. Her left arm is limp and useless, the wrist completely shattered. Nuria Lye sets to strapping it with the supplies from her kit.

'I favour my right hand, so yes.'

'And with the charges you have?'

Crys looks past Raine for a second, out beyond the curve of the shield.

'Without Varn's?' she says.

It seems an effort for her to say his name. Her throat works and her eyes flicker, but when she looks back, she's composed. Everything pushed down inside. Raine knows this, because it's the way you keep going. The way you get your duty done.

'Yes, sir,' Crys says. 'But I'll need Gereth Awd, if he's still walking.'

'To help you set the charges?' Raine says.

Crys smiles, all teeth.

'No, sir,' she says. 'I need his flamer tanks.'

Raine watches from behind the shell of the tank as Crys sets her improvised charge against the fortress wall. They are breaching at the foot of one of three bastions, equidistant around the central keep. One for the Wyldfolk, one for the Mistvypers, and one for the Hartkin. Three cuts in the fortress' flanks. Three wounds that will not close.

Crys stays low and flat against the wall. She picks a join in the stone where it will be weakest and packs it with grenades. First, two melta bombs. Next, her own bag of demo charges, except two, which Raine told her to save. Lastly, she binds the lot together with Awd's flamer pack and sets a detonator line. All the while, that voice echoes from inside the fortress, bellowing heresies at the sky.

'The emplacements and the guards are silenced,' Andren Fel says. 'They won't know we're here until we tell them.'

There are few who can approach Raine without her hearing it, but Andren Fel can. He crouches down beside her, his hellgun slung. The snarling face on his mask is painted anew with spatters of blood. There are deep scores from knife blades on his carapace plate.

Raine looks past him to where Lydia Zane waits. The psyker has her eyes tightly closed. Blood has dried around her mouth and nose. It makes her look like a winter-thin wolf that has been at the kill.

'Remember what I said,' Raine says to Andren.

'Protect Crys,' he says. 'Protect Zane. No matter what.'

Andren looks back at the psyker.

'Though what I've seen Zane do…' he says, in a low voice.

'Makes you wonder who needs protecting,' answers Lydia Zane, as her eyes flicker open.

Andren sighs.

'No offence meant,' he says. 'And I wish you wouldn't do that.'

Zane grins. It makes her look even more wolfish.

'None taken,' she says. 'Though perhaps you should not think so loudly, captain.'

Andren shakes his head. The vox crackles in Raine's ear.

'*Mistvypers, ready to breach.*'

'Hartkin?' Raine says. 'Are you ready?'

More crackling. Raine's chest aches. She realises it's because she's holding her breath.

'*Aye,*' comes the answer, after a moment. '*Just had to quell a little resistance here, commissar.*'

'Good,' Raine says. 'Crys?'

She doesn't have to see the combat engineer to know she's grinning.

'*More than ready,*' Crys says.

'All squads,' Raine says. 'Breach.'

Raine ducks down behind the cover and jams her hands over her ears. The Antari do the same.

A few seconds later, Yulia Crys' improvised charge detonates. The noise is catastrophic, even with the distance and cover between them and the blast. Raine hears fragments of rock clatter against Andren's carapace armour. She clearly hears Crys whoop in the aftermath. When Raine looks over the cover, she sees why.

There's a hole blown clear through the fortress wall. Fire clings to the stonework. Some of it has run like slag from the heat. It's an impressive mess.

'She has got a gift,' says Andren from beside her, and he laughs.

'Good work, Crys,' Raine says over the vox.

She sees Crys salute her from where she kneels behind shattered lumps of masonry.

'*Anything that's built, sir,*' she says.

'*We followed the smell down into the lower levels under the scholam.*'

Raine thinks back to the dank tunnel. The sagging support beams. Water ran everywhere down there, dirty and black.

'*There were three of us. Me, Lem and Bayti.*'

Raine hasn't thought of them in a long time. Lem with her wide eyes, like the porcelain dishes the drill abbots used. How she could turn a knife on you with just a flick of her thin wrists. Bayti with his void-born height and pale skin.

'*We had fuel-lit torches that made the shadows flicker. No pistols, just short training blades.*' *She pauses, remembering.* '*Our shoes were soft and thin. They let in all of the water.*'

Raine takes a sip of her tea.

'*The nest was in one of the old store-chambers. You could see where the sin-thieves had worried away at the stone and metal to make a hole.*'

How it had been made wider over time. Cut by claws and teeth and smoothed by the water and the passing of the vermin.'

The whole tunnel had been dark. Gloom itself was dark. But that hole had seemed the darkest thing she'd ever seen.

'The door to the store chamber had been closed for decades,' Raine says. 'It was frozen stiff and warped in the frame. The handle was rusted and weak. Even if we could have broken it down, the vermin would have fled by the time we'd done so.'

Andren looks at her.

'You had to go through the hole made by the rats,' he says.

The explosion didn't just make a mess of the stone and metal of the fortress. Dozens of rebels lie crumpled and broken just inside the breach, caked in blood and thick stone dust. Some haven't had the grace to die. They gasp and whisper and drag themselves after the Antari, digging their hands into the churned earth like claws. The Duskhounds finish them with single shots from their hellguns.

'Keep moving,' Raine cries. 'Into the bastion!'

Even as she gestures to the nearby structure with her sword, a tide of rebels spills out of the base of it. A klaxon blares. The Antari cannot afford to stop, so they push into the Drastians. The gunfight quickly becomes a melee. A press. Raine draws her sword, cutting her way through turncoats and heretics. Not all are soldiers. Raine sees the remains of courtly dress and serving clothes alike. Every one of them has marked their face with that same symbol. Some are raw and bleeding. They smell as if they've been dead a week, their black eyes glassy and unblinking. Their breath is hot on her face. She is hit with the butt of a gun. A knife slices her arm. None of it goes unanswered as she strikes back with sword and pistol, pushing through into the bastion. In scant moments between each swing and each cut, she catches sight of the muted grey-and-green splinter camouflage of the Wyldfolk, and the black carapace and red eye-lenses of the Duskhounds. The robes of Lydia Zane. Raine can hear the psyker snapping bones and armour alike, even over the racket.

Raine smashes the butt of her pistol into the face of a man who tries to bite her. No, not a man. Not anymore. The impact breaks apart the pattern carved into his face, and he sinks at her feet. She feels the press start to ease. The shouting eases with it. The smell doesn't. If anything, it gets worse.

Raine looks around, catching her breath. She is inside the bastion. The Antari are all still with her.

'Keep moving,' she says.

They all do, save for one. Daven Wyck is crouched over one of the rebels, his knee pressing on the soldier's throat.

'The Wyldfolk have you,' he says, sing-song.

Raine sees the rebel's hands opening and closing, scrabbling at the stone floor.

'Wyck,' she says.

He draws the combat blade from his belt and buries it in the rebel's stomach in one swift movement.

'Cuts from us always kill,' he says, with a smile.

He pulls the blade free and gets to his feet.

'Yes, commissar,' he says.

'Quick kills,' she says. 'We are not animals.'

Every Antari she's met has grey eyes. When Raine was first assigned to the regiment, she thought that they were all the same grey. After a while she began to notice the differences. Wyck's are a cold grey, like chips of flint. Right now, the grey is almost swallowed by the black of his pupils.

Those eyes flicker down to the combat blade in his hand, then Wyck wipes it against the leg of his fatigues. It leaves a black stain. His smile disappears slowly, like clouds moving in front of the sun.

'Understood, commissar,' he says, softly. 'My apologies.'

Commissar Raine follows after him up the stairs, knowing that sooner or later, she's going to have to do something about Daven Wyck.

Raine and the Wyldfolk push their way up the bastion's central stairway, towards the mounted gun. The Mistvypers do the same to the east, the Hartkin to the west. Despite the odds against them, the Antari still treat it like a contest.

'*Third level secured,*' says Odi over the vox.

Wyck laughs.

'Hurry your feet, Rom,' he says. 'We have already taken the fourth.'

The sergeant of the Hartkin's displeasure can be heard in his reply.

'I bet you have,' he says, over the sound of lasfire. 'You have the Duskhounds, and the witch.'

Wyck snorts a laugh.

'Exactly,' he says. 'Even with them slowing us down, we are still one level above you.'

Zane bares her teeth in a scowl. Andren shakes his head. Neither get a chance to answer, because they are interrupted by a throaty bellow from the stairs leading up to the next level. A figure emerges, overmuscled, abhuman, clad in crimson armour. It is so big that the armour plates on its shoulders scrape along the walls. A slab shield protects it, ankle to throat. In its other hand it carries a power maul half as long as Raine is tall. Through the vision slit in the shield, Raine sees deep-set black eyes under a heavy brow.

'Kill,' the bullgryn says in a low, slow voice.

Behind it, two more bullgryns clatter their weapons against their shields.

'Kill!' they echo.

They thunder out of the stairwell and into the room, armour clanking, power mauls humming. The Antari cannot go backwards, and they cannot slip around them. It leaves them only one option.

'Through them!' Raine shouts.

The lead bullgryn swings for her. Raine steps backwards, feeling the rush of air as the maul misses caving in her chest by inches. The head of the maul buries itself in the floor, shattering the stonework with a burst of energy. The bullgryn roars and wrenches it clear. Raine brings her sword down, but the bullgryn's shield comes up. Her sword slides across it, putting a deep furrow in the metal without parting it. The bullgryn twists at the waist and swings again, pushing her further backwards. This time, she barely blocks with her own sword. The force of the blow rattles her arm, sends it numb to the shoulder. The maul comes down again. She blocks a second time, her back against the wall now. That arm isn't numb anymore. It's in agony, probably fractured in a dozen places. Her grip starts to loosen. The bullgryn is laughing, a wet, throaty bark. It twists and raises its maul again. Raine hears the distinct sound of hellgun fire from behind the bullgryn, punching into the few areas of exposed flesh on its back. The bullgryn roars. That's the moment. The break in its guard. Raine spins away and the bullgryn drives its maul into the wall where she once stood. Stone and plascrete explode outwards. She feels a shard cut her face. Blood runs into her eyes.

Raine jumps on the bullgryn's back and grabs hold of its armoured collar. Her injured arm sings with pain. She yells and brings her sword down, cutting its head free from its shoulders. It takes her two strikes to get through the thick, overmuscled neck. More blood spatters into her eyes.

The bullgryn's headless body falls forward, crashing into the wall and sliding down it. Raine tumbles free. Somehow, she's still holding on to her sword. She has to lean on the wall to get to her feet. The other two bullgryns are still standing, laying about them with their crackling mauls and bellowing wordlessly. The Wyldfolk are backing up, lasguns blazing. The bullgryns shrug off wounds that should slow them. Yulia Crys is busy firing at the second bullgryn when the first swings at her. Andren interposes himself and takes the hit. Raine hears his chestplate crack from across the room. His Duskhounds riddle the bullgryn with lasfire. Andren is on his knees, but he keeps his aim and fires too. The lasbolt tears out the bullgryn's throat, and it falls backwards with a crash.

The throat, Raine thinks. *He is a Duskhound to his bones.*

Daven Wyck ducks under the remaining bullgryn's swing and buries his combat blade between its armour plates. It bellows and knocks him clear off his feet with a thrust of its shield. He lands on his back and goes still. Raine only knows he's still alive because she can hear him trying to get air. The bullgryn goes after him, roaring, Wyck's knife still sticking out of its gut.

Raine sheathes her sword and raises her pistol. Her vision swims as she takes a few steps closer. The bullgryn slides in and out of her gunsights. She blinks the blood out of her eyes.

Then the bullgryn is lifted bodily into the air and slammed against the ceiling. It falls to the ground with a boom that rivals Crys' improvised explosives. Raine can hear it panting wetly. Lydia Zane approaches, hand outstretched. She is bloodied, but serene. She flicks her wrist and drives the bullgryn up into the ceiling again and again, as if it weighs nothing. After the fourth impact, Raine can't hear panting anymore.

Well, not from the bullgryn, anyway.

Daven Wyck eases himself onto his elbow. He is winded, his flak armour splintered and dented. His breathing skips and wheezes.

Lydia Zane pulls his combat knife out of the bullgryn's broken body and walks over to him.

'Do not let me slow you down,' she says, throwing the blade onto the ground.

There's a mixture of fury and fear in Wyck's eyes. He snatches up his blade and gets to his feet.

'Funny,' he manages to say, between breaths. 'Very funny.'

Across the room, Andren Fel starts to laugh, though it clearly hurts him to do it.

'Oh, I think so,' he says. 'I really do.'

'Bayti started talking in his starborn tongue,' Raine says. 'I hadn't heard him do it since he first arrived at the scholam. I didn't know it well, but I knew enough.'

Raine remembers Bayti splashing backwards through that glossy water, his eyes glossy too.

'It is an interpretive language. Heavily contextual. What he was saying either meant "can't" or "won't".'

'So, what did you do?' Andren says.

'I told him that there was no room for either can't or won't. That cowardice was a sin. I told him that the vermin would smell it and come for him. That they'd strip the sin from his bones and his flesh with it.'

'Did he refuse?' Andren asks.

She remembers the way her fists had curled, ready to strike Bayti. Clammy palms. She remembers the way her heart hammered in her chest. Then, finally, she remembers the way Bayti had looked at her then, as so many others had since.

'No,' she says. 'In that moment he was more afraid of me than he was of the sin-thieves.'

Raine leads the Antari to level twelve of the bastion. It's not the top level, where the mounted gun itself sits, it's a few floors below, protected by double-thick walls and a unit of well-armoured and well-armed rebel soldiers. Once Raine and her Antari have killed their way through and breached the chamber, they see why.

'Golden *Throne*,' says Crys. 'What have they done?'

The huge, square chamber is the munitions store for the wall-mounted guns, and the armoury for every rebel soldier on this section of the walls. Belts of shells shine with a dull gleam. Demo charges and mines are crated and boxed. There are missiles and promethium canisters. Rockets and grenades. Every single one of them has been marked with that baleful eye, painted on or scratched into the metal. There is another painted on the floor in the centre of the room. From the smell, Raine thinks probably in blood.

'I need you to detonate it,' Raine says. 'All of it.'

Crys nods once, her jaw set.

'With pleasure,' she says, then glances over. 'You mean remotely, right, sir?'

Raine doesn't break eye contact. She has considered both options. She has considered all of the options.

'If you can.'

Crys lets out a long breath.

'I can rig it,' she says.

'How long do you need?' Raine asks.

Crys looks around at the heaped munitions. She rubs absently at the ruin of her left ear.

'Ten minutes,' she says. 'Give or take.'

'You'll have it,' Raine says. 'Just concentrate on rigging the explosives, and get the Hartkin and the Mistvypers on the vox. Make sure they're doing the same. Walk them through it if you need to.'

Crys nods, already pulling what's left of her kit out of her bag.

'Sir?' The call comes from by the door. It's Andren. 'We have company incoming.'

Raine doesn't need telling. She can already hear the thunder of feet, the bellowed blasphemies and all the while underneath that booming voice.

The Imperium of Man is dead.

Not today, thinks Severina Raine.

She draws her pistol in one smooth action, even with her shattered arm bound loosely to her chest.

Not ever.

Raine ducks back behind the door of the arming chamber as solid shot rounds impact the wall beside her head. They are keeping the Drastians out, but it gets more difficult with every passing second.

'Crys!' she shouts.

'Almost there,' the combat engineer yells in reply.

Opposite Raine, Ekar Wain takes a solid round to the face. It shatters the storm trooper's mask, and he slumps sideways. Three more rounds punch into him, torso and legs, before his squad can drag him back into cover. He leaves a dark smear of blood on the stone.

'Mists take them,' Andren snarls.

He leans around the doorframe and fires twice. Two dead rebels. More push their bodies aside and take their place.

'Commissar,' Zane calls out.

Raine moves over to her, keeping low. The psyker has her eyes closed and her hands curled. Blood runs sluggishly from her nose as she projects a kine-shield around Yulia Crys.

'What is it?'

Zane frowns more deeply.

'The three bastions,' she says in a low voice. 'The fire that we make of them. I try to look further, but it is the last thing I see.'

She opens her eyes, just barely.

'I can smell it. Hear it. I see nothing but fire.'

Zane's mouth quirks up in a pained smile as she looks at Raine.

'But I do not need to tell you this,' she says. 'Do I?'

Raine meets Zane's eyes. She lets out a long, slow breath. She has, after all, considered all of the options.

'You know what must be done,' she says. 'Duty comes first.'

There's a flicker in Zane's expression. A momentary tremor. Then she laughs, a hollow sound.

'That it does,' she replies. 'In all things.'

'Done,' shouts Crys. 'It's done!'

'Cover me,' Raine shouts, before running across the room to Crys. She feels the kine-shield envelop her, a distinct winter chill.

'It'll go remotely, as you asked,' Crys says. She's wound her two demolition charges in parchment from her kit. Each strip is marked with prayers in her spiked handwriting. 'The range is enough for us to make it back outside the walls. Odi and Selk had their teams do the same.'

There's a solid boom from the stairwell outside. Raine hears Andren curse.

'All squads,' Raine says, over the open channel. 'Do not detonate until I give the order. They must all go at once, or this will have been for nothing. Is that clear?'

'*Understood,*' says Odi.

'*Yes, sir,*' says Selk.

Crys' gaze slides to the door, to where the fighting is still thick and furious. She closes her grey eyes for a second and mutters a prayer. It's in Antari, but Raine knows it.

May He be with us as we live and die, it goes. *For it is not ours to question why.*

Then she sets the charges.

'We came out of the passage inside the nest. It filled the storeroom, wall to wall. Made of parchment and filth and bones. Human bones. Small ones that broke underfoot.'

Raine pauses and drains the last of her tea. Even after such a long time, thinking of those bones still sends a chill up her spine.

'Bayti cried out,' she says. *'It was the bones that did it. The vermin heard him and came hissing and baring their fangs.'*

She shakes her head.

'Bayti panicked and threw his torch hard and high into the centre of it. Lem followed suit. The vermin started to scatter. I could see that we wouldn't catch them all, that some would pass us and escape.'

She keeps her eyes on the distant fortress as she speaks.

'I threw my torch behind us, setting everything around the entrance alight. It caught so quickly, all that parchment and oil and filth. The vermin were mewling. Bayti was screaming. I grabbed him, and Lem, and pulled them down into the shallow water at our feet.'

Raine remembers the black water, gritty and vile in her mouth. The vermin, scrabbling around and over them, all aflame. Bayti, thrashing and getting to his knees even as Lem tried in vain to keep him under the water.

Screaming. Fire. Smoke.

'There was a huge rush of heat and light. I closed my eyes and I prayed.'
She lets out a slow breath.

'When I opened them again, I had been dragged clear of the storeroom and into the tunnel. The door was open, broken from the hinges. Drill-abbot Ifyn was there. He had been all along, I suppose.'

'What about Lem,' Andren says. *'And Bayti?'*

'He told me that Bayti died trying to run. That Lem died trying to save him. He said that their choices had cost them, as all choices do. I interrupted him then, for the first and last time. I told him that I had made Bayti crawl through the hole. That I had thrown the torch and

cut off our own escape to ensure our success. That surely their deaths were in part due to me.'

She remembers the way Ifyn had looked at her then. Pitiless but patient.

'What did he say?' Andren asks.

'That I was right. That my choices also had a cost.'

She finally looks at Andren.

'And that my purpose was to bear it.'

Fighting out of the bastion is bloody work. They lose the youngest of the Wyldfolk, Ludi, to a tripwire set by the Drastians. It happens so quickly that Raine is dazzled by the burst of flame. No time to blink. Those closest are cut by stone chips and bits of bone. There is no time to stop either. They keep running instead, the sound of their ragged breathing echoing off the walls as they descend the stairs. Raine can feel the adrenaline wearing off. The skin of her injured arm feels tight under her greatcoat and she's lost all the movement in her wrist.

When they reach the foot of the steps, the vox crackles in her ear.

'Hartkin are out and free,' says Odi. *'Who is quickest now, Wyck?'*

Daven Wyck spits blood on the floor. His nose is badly broken from where the bullgryn hit him. It's changed the shape of his face, making it better match the ugliness he carries with him.

'Mists take you, Odi,' he says. 'Trust you to win at running away.'

The words that come back are Antari, and clearly colourful. Raine doesn't even know all of them.

'Cut the chatter,' she says. 'Odi, hole up and wait to trigger on my command.'

They get clear of the bottom of the tower, and make for the breach point in the wall.

'Just how big are we expecting this explosion to be?' Wyck says as he runs.

Crys glances backwards, her eyes wide.

'If I reckon right, it'll do more than just quiet those guns,' she says. 'It'll bring the whole bloody bastion down.'

Andren Fel slows pace, just barely. He looks at the bastions, then at Raine. She sees herself reflected in his eye lenses. Painted in red from the glass and from the blood on her face. Her own and theirs.

'Not just the bastion,' he says. 'It's the whole thing. We're collapsing the nest.'

Raine doesn't get a chance to answer. She is interrupted by a loud crack. A solid shell hits Andren in the shoulder, right between his armour plates. The other two Duskhounds, Tyl and Jeth, return fire as their captain stumbles. Watching Andren Fel bleed, Raine feels something she can't afford. Something she has no time to feel. The first shot is just the edge of the coming storm. More follow as a noise grows that threatens to drown out even the booming voice. It's the sound of boots on stone. The Antari fire back, but it's like spitting into the wind. Together, they fall back into the shadow of the tower as the might of the Drastian forces spills out of the central keep.

'*Commissar,*' the vox crackles. It's Odi. '*They are coming. We cannot stay here.*'

Raine fires her pistol at the oncoming rebels until the clip runs dry. Most of her shots miss. She's struggling to keep the gun steady. To see. The rebels seem to smear like ink.

The Imperium of Man is dead, says the voice.

'All squads,' she says. 'Detonate, now.'

Crys looks at her.

'Now!' Raine cries.

She hears two acknowledgement clicks over the vox from Odi and Selk.

Crys thumbs the detonator.

'Zane!' Raine shouts.

The Imperium of Man is–

The words are stolen as the towers detonate in almost perfect synchronicity. The sky becomes fire as three colossal explosions reach upwards and join, curving on the inside face of the void shield. The pressure wave is repelled by the shield, and every ounce of force is directed back down at the fortress. At the towers. At the Drastian rebels.

At Severina Raine and her Antari soldiers.

The rebels out in the open are silenced. They fall to the ground, dead. Their lungs burst. Their eyes bleed. They are turned to black dust by incredible heat under pressure. Masonry and twisted metal rains to the earth. The great grey shape of the unbreakable fortress of Morne shifts. Cracks.

Then, with a thunderous boom, it breaks.

It's like the Time of Ending, Raine thinks, as she and her Antari soldiers watch the fortress die from their knees, through Lydia Zane's kine-shield. The psyker is screaming, lightning arcing across her limbs and from her eyes. None of them can touch her. Her shield is crazed with cracks. Even as the world stops ending, Zane keeps screaming until the cables that crown her flare with light, and she collapses. Her kine-shield collapses with her. Gentle curls of smoke drift from the ruin of her eyes. Raine puts her fingers to Zane's throat, and the psyker stirs.

'It is the last thing I see,' she says, before falling unconscious.

Around them, the fortress caves inwards, momentous and slow, burying anyone still left inside. Scraps of the tattered banner float to earth, still burning. The baleful eye, consumed by fire.

'Spared,' Andren says, barely audible over the ringing in Raine's ears. 'By Him, and by her.'

Raine nods. It makes her vision swim. The psyker had saved them, just as Raine knew she would, and she had paid for it with her grey Antari eyes. It isn't the only price paid. The vox-link to the Mistvypers returns only static, and when Raine gets through to Odi, he barely acknowledges. Before the link is cut, she hears the sergeant of the Hartkin mumbling the Antari words for the dead. The sound of it will stay with her, always.

With the fortress broken, the clouds choose that moment to break too. Drops begin to fall, cold against Raine's skin. The Antari stir around her, dazed and shell-shocked. Andren unfastens his mask and pulls it off. His dark hair is matted to his head. Blood pinks his teeth.

'The armour was never coming,' he says. 'Was it?'

Raine keeps looking at him, right in those grey eyes.

'No,' she says.

'You kept it from us,' he says. 'The truth of it.'

Raine nods. She had known before she'd led the charge. Before she had executed Tevar Lun. Before sharing stories with Andren on the ridge. She had also known that the fortress could be broken without the armour as long as she kept them strong. As long as they did not falter. So she had made a choice to keep it from them.

That choice, like the cost of it, is hers to bear.

'I did,' she says. 'As is my right, captain.'

Andren looks as if he might say something else, but then he blinks. Straightens his shoulders. It's as though he remembers himself. Where he is. What she is. He bows his head.

'As is your right, of course,' he says. 'Commissar.'

Raine gets to her feet. Her limbs don't feel like her own. Blood gums her eyelashes. Her ears ring and her head aches. Around her, the Antari start to rise. Those that can. They lean on one another, breathing ragged. She turns to them and draws her sword with her one good arm. She can hear the distant sound of the other forces moving up. Engines and armour and boots on the ground. Hymnals, sung loud. A flight of Valkyrie gunships split the sky. Under all of that, the drum of the rain as it washes the world clean.

'The Imperium of Man can never die,' she says, her voice hoarse.

'Not today,' say the Antari.

'Not ever,' says Commissar Severina Raine.

YOUR
NEXT READ

HONOURBOUND
by Rachel Harrison

Commissar Severina Raine and the Eleventh Antari Rifles fight
to subdue the spreading threat of Chaos burning across the Bale Stars.
Little does Raine realise the key to victory lies in her own past,
and in the ghosts that she carries with her.

THE BATTLE FOR MARKGRAAF HIVE

Justin D Hill

Introducing

MINKA LESK

TROOPER, CADIAN 101ST

'What the hell is happening?' Madzen shouted across to Minka as auto-rounds ricocheted off the rocks about them.

Minka threw the straps of the vox-box off her shoulder and threw herself forwards into cover. She had one eye closed. The other lined her sights up with the head of a heretic. 'They're trying to kill us,' she said between gritted teeth as she moved on to the next target and fired again. A double shot, just in case.

'I guessed that,' he snarled, his cheek pressed against the stock of his own lasrifle. 'I meant...'

She didn't bother to hear what he meant. And when Grogar's heavy bolter opened up, it filled the subterranean chamber with muzzle flashes, fist-sized bolts and a thunder that drowned Madzen's explanation.

A few moments earlier they'd stumbled out of an old sewer pipe into this vaulting space, lit throughout by the luminous green mould that covered ceiling and walls. The catacomb had been broken and reshaped by millennia of hive-quakes. The cracked ceiling sagged, the floor slanted steeply to the left, and a filthy pool filled the sunken end, where vast stalactites stabbed down from the ceiling like the fangs of some prehistoric monster. They'd had a brief moment to get their bearings, and then the ambush had been sprung. And now they were fighting desperately for their lives.

Minka fired a quick salvo into the darkness, lasrifle ready at her shoulder.

The heavy bolter roared once more, strobe-lighting dirty bestial faces swarming forwards through the gloom.

The Cadians did not panic. They knelt and fired, and fired once again. They were tight, disciplined, experienced. Like Minka, they'd all learned how to strip and fire a lasrifle before they could read. Fighting was more normal than civilian life.

If their attackers had been half-trained, the Cadians would all have been dead now. But they were not. They were hive scum. And worse than that. They were *heretic* hive scum who'd turned their face from the light of the Emperor and deserved nothing more than a las-round to the face. It was like a wild force of nature coming up against the indomitable brickwork discipline of Cadia. And the Cadians cut the heretics down in droves.

At last the roar of the heavy bolter subsided and, for a moment, it seemed the attack was over. All Minka could see was twitching piles of dead and wounded. She scanned the chamber then lowered her lasrifle.

'Over there!' Sergeant Gaskar shouted from the middle of the line. In the darkness and confusion she couldn't see where he was pointing to, but at that moment more heretics erupted from the pool water only yards behind her. Spray hit her face and hands as she spun about.

Too late.

The blow hit her in the middle of her back and punched the air from her lungs. It slammed her face against the rockcrete slab and cut her lip as well. There was blood in her mouth as she whirled round and fired wildly.

The heretic was on her, and she knew in an instant that he was bigger and stronger than her. He bundled her face first into the dirt, his filthy and emaciated arms and legs enveloping her like a spider on her back. His black nails were in her mouth, grabbing at her throat, scratching for her eyes. But she was Cadian. She broke his fingers, dislocated his arm, and then dragged herself up to one knee and gutted him with her bayonet.

She put a pair of las-bolts into his belly, as well. Frekker.

The second wave came up out of the water and through a crack in the ground that allowed them to sneak right up to the line of rubble the Cadians were holding. It got tense, then. And close quarters.

Minka could never tell how long a battle lasted. It could be seconds or hours. The bark of the heavy bolter, the brief flashes of las-bolts, the scrape of knife on bone and steel, the shouts and screams of orders and of pain. She killed and killed and killed, and the intensity of the moment seemed to fill time. But at last Sergeant Gaskar put up a hand and shouted, 'Hold!' and Minka rested a shoulder against the fallen roof-beam before her and realised how much her ribs hurt.

The vox-unit lay on the floor, and two yards from that Madzen lay on his back. His throat had been cut from ear-to-ear. His head was pillowed in a pool of his own gore. She felt sick in her gut. Markgraaf underhive wasn't worth the loss of Cadian lives, especially not Madzen's. Any dead Cadian was a waste. She cursed the braid-wearing frekker who'd dreamed up this mission.

The heretic who'd jumped her was lying a stone's throw away, face down, his back twisted at an unnatural angle. She couldn't see what he'd hit her with, but Throne it hurt. For a moment she relived his attack, felt his fingers on her face, scrabbling for her eyes, in her nostrils, in her mouth. She wanted to kick him again as she pulled her flak-armour plates forwards to see how bad his blow had been. There was no blood. Her fingers felt along the line of her ribs. Nothing broken, she thought, and then let out a long breath.

Sergeant Gaskar started the roll call. Grogar. Matrey. Rellan.

Leonov. Aleksei. Isran. Artem too, unfortunately. She shouted her own name.

'Anyone else?' Gaskar shouted.

'Madzen's dead,' Minka shouted, and one by one the fallen were named. They'd lost six troopers. Three in the first seconds to auto-rounds and the others in hand-to-hand combat. Minka watched as the medic, Leonov, knelt by the wounded. There'd been ninety-six troopers in Fifth Platoon when they'd entered the under-hive five days earlier.

They had stood on the pollution-grey ashen earthworks and looked up at Markgraaf Hive: a teeming termite mound of humanity that rose precipitously into the sky, burning and trailing a banner of smoke.

'They're under siege up there,' her sergeant said, meaning the patrician hive lords of the Richstar family. The sergeant's name was Fronsak. His regiment, the Cadian 2050th, had been amalgamated with Minka's the year before. He was a solid commander, with the professional manner typical of the Cadian officer class, and made it his duty to obey orders, take objectives and to keep them all alive, as much as possible. 'They're fighting a slow retreat up the hive.'

Minka stretched her head back to take in the mountainous bulk of the hive city. The peak of the massive conglomeration was too high to see with the naked eye. Fronsak handed Minka the mag-noculars. She looked up, past the layers of smoke and burning, five miles above her head, to where the isolated white pinnacles and buttresses of the hive sparkled with ice. The hive lords couldn't have had more than thirty levels left to go before they were driven from the top of their home.

She handed the magnoculars back and looked about. Lines of Chimeras idled as the rest of the Cadian force disembarked, pla-toon by platoon. Further off, Hydra platforms scanned the sky for any counter-attacks, and over the mounds and heaps of slag, she could see lines of local Calinbineer troops filing towards them.

They looked weary and stoic, quite unlike the Cadians, who stood about with a business-like readiness.

And over the slag heaps a procession of skitarii accompanied three huge, tracked transporters that made the files of armour seem as small as beetles upon the plain.

Upon the back of each carriage, tended by servitors and fussing tech-priests, lay a vast tube hastily painted in the colours of the Richstars, the family whose various branches seemed to run this whole sector of Imperial space.

'What are those?'

'Hellbores,' Fronsak said.

Minka said nothing. They looked like armoured tubes set with drill-teeth at one end. Each of the monstrous forgings was large enough to fit a platoon inside. A tunnelling transport that ground its way through earth and bedrock, under fortifications and behind the enemy lines. Which meant they would be sent deep into the heretic territory. A suicide mission if ever she'd seen one.

An hour later her platoon had filed up the ramp into the cramped troop compartments inside the Hellbore. They were rammed in. Face-to-face. Shoulder-to-shoulder. No room to drop a grenade, no way to pull a knife. The doors slammed and locked. A grating whine started as the tunnelling mechanism began to turn, and they were all thrown violently forwards as the Hellbore slid from its mountings and started to drill through the topsoil as easily as ploughing through snow.

The difficulty began when its ceramite teeth came up against bedrock and rockcrete foundations. The grinding mechanism screamed. The tube juddered, and they could hear the rumble of hive-quakes set off by the burrowing. From there on the journey stretched for hours, a gut-wrenching ordeal almost as unpleasant as warp transit. There had been sickening lurches, the constant noise and the habitual terror that their transport might break down or fail, or that a hive-quake might crush them all.

The heat and motion made her feel sick. What if we meet rock too tough to grind through? she thought. A cold sweat covered her hands, her forehead, the small of her back. Her stomach lurched. Her mouth was full of saliva. There was no room to vomit, though others did. She swallowed her bile back. It went up her nose. She could not keep it down. She shut her eyes as the stink began to fill the stifling chamber. She prayed to the Throne, to the Omnissiah, to Saint Hallows, the patron saint of Cadia.

Hellbore indeed, she thought, finally realising how apt the name was.

It was almost a relief when the thing finally jolted to a halt, throwing them all forwards into each other. Lights flashed, a klaxon rang, the assault ramps crashed down and they spilled out into the half-collapsed tunnels of the lowest strata of Markgraaf.

There had been no sign of the enemy, just dripping catacombs that dated from the earliest days of the hive. The broken tunnels and sump-holes forced them to break into small units. It was slow-going into a world that had not seen the light of the sun for thousands of years. At first they used lumens, but everything was covered in a thick, wet mould that gave off a faint green luminescence, and once their eyes grew accustomed to its illumination, they saved their power packs for moments of need such as when consulting their maps.

Each squad had been issued with a rudimentary schematic, a rough impression of the hive, with their objective – the Great Chamber – clearly marked. They picked their way along crazed tunnels that meandered away, some collapsed, others flooded, or cut their way through vast pale slugs of congealed fat and filth from the city above, not knowing if they were drawing closer to the centre of the hive or not.

'What is this Great Chamber?' Ansen asked at one point.

'There's some kind of contraption apparently. Old mine shaft,' Fronsak told them. 'It's the only place where there's access to the upper levels.'

Or that was what they all had thought. The heretics clearly had other ways down into the underhive, because within hours it seemed that the Imperial counter-attack had been discovered and heretics were swarming into the underhive like rats. They were a motley band of tattooed gangers and underhive scum, drawn from the deepest pits of the mountain-city, their emaciated bodies burning with the conviction of heresy.

The Cadian thrust turned into a nightmarish city-fight in the collapsed intestines of the underhive. Sergeant Fronsak died on the second day of fighting, and there'd been three more sergeants since as the sump-war became a living hell of heretics and rock falls. Life by life the strength of the Cadian 101st was being whittled away, like a cathedral full of candle flames extinguished one by one. The longer it went on, the more Minka felt that she was part of a dying breed, a lost way of life, a species on the edge of extinction.

Now she crouched in this unknown chamber, her ribs aching from the blow the heretic had dealt her. She looked to Sergeant Gaskar. 'So,' she said, 'which way now?'

Frekked if I know, Gaskar's expression said. He jumped one of the cracks in the rockcrete floor, skirted the side of the water, pulled out his lumen and used it to pick his way round the edge of the flooded end of the chamber. A fallen metal joist blocked the way between two stalactites. It was embedded in pale drip-lime. He clambered over it, brushed the luminous mould off his hand. It was an unconscious gesture that left a glowing smear across his chest. Perfect target for a sniper to aim at. Gaskar clearly thought the same thing. He cursed and rubbed at the smear with the cuff of his sleeve, scratching his chin as if thinking. 'Looks like the hivers came this way,' he said, pointing to the far end of the chamber.

He turned and looked at them. From where she sat, Minka could see what Gaskar saw. The squad needed to rest. They were exhausted. You could read it in their faces.

Gaskar spat and pushed his helmet back from his head. 'All right. Rellan and Aleksei, stand guard. Everyone else, get some rest.'

Grogar and Matrey set up the heavy bolter in the middle of the chamber while Minka found a hole next to Isran where they could watch the pool. Isran was one of those strange creatures who kept his lean body going on a combination of liquor, stimms and lho. He sat with his lasrifle between his legs, his hands folded over the top end, staring out into the darkness. Minka took a ration pack from her breast pocket. The foil seals were broken. She used her nails to pick the foil from the semi-hydrated slab within and held it out. 'Want some?'

Isran shook his head. 'Nah,' he said, still staring out into the dark.

There was a tremble in the air. She lifted her hand and felt the vibrations come again, stronger this time. Dust drifted down from a crack in the ceiling and freckled the dark water's surface. She thought for a moment of the vast, oppressive weight of the hive above her head and wished she hadn't.

The rumble came again, longer now.

'Think that's a hive-quake?' Minka said.

'Could be,' Isran said. His tone said there was nothing they could do about it.

The trembling faded. Minka ate some more. It came back a few moments later. It didn't sound like hive-quake. But there was another sound. 'What the hell is that?' she said. It sounded like wet mouths feeding, out there in the shadows.

'Rats,' Isran said. Vermin and battlefields went together. It was nothing to be surprised at.

Minka washed the dehydrated food down with a short swig from her battered tin canteen, then dropped the ration pack to the floor. She looked about. Leonov had shut his eyes, but the rest of them were sitting watching, cleaning their weapons, checking their webbing, smoking lhos. Minka shut her eyes and imagined herself anywhere but here. She found her memory taking her back to a Whiteshield camp in the highlands above Kasr Myrak. She had been only fourteen or so, a young Whiteshield with a head full of dreams of fighting for the Imperium of Man. She remembered how her hair had whipped across her face as she watched the dawn breaking over Cadia, how the rising sun had lit the jagged mountain peaks, before cresting the ridge and bathing the world with light. The sun did not give heat at dawn, but it did give hope, and she closed her eyes and remembered that moment now. Cadia. Sunrise. The promise of another day to fight against their foes.

The trembling came again. Isran smiled. 'Maybe that's our rein-forcements coming.'

Minka reached back for the vox. She'd been lugging this useless box around with her ever since the operator, Hama, got himself killed. It was three days ago that they'd last heard anything from HQ, and that had only been some high-ranking idiot giving orders as if there were any order down here to impose. Almost out of boredom she lifted the receiver and flipped it on. There was noth-ing but static. She tapped it against the wall. The note of the static remained unchanged.

'Turn that off, will you!' Artem hissed.

Every squad had a bastard, and Artem was theirs. Minka ignored him.

'I said, switch it off.'

'Frekk you,' Minka told him.

Then Artem was looming up out of the shadows. His eyes were wide and white. They shone in the sickly light of the chamber. He grabbed the vox handset and slammed it against the broken slab of rockcrete. It was Munitorum issue, designed for rough condi-tions – the toughest the galaxy could throw at them – and the blow barely scratched it.

She gave him a look that said, *That's Munitorum equipment, break it at your peril.* But he slammed it against the rock again.

'Sit down!' Gaskar told him.

'Turn the frekking thing off will you!' he shouted and threw it back at her. 'It's useless,' Artem said. 'Useless. Understand?'

Minka despised weakness, and she saw how the underhive had broken him. When he came forward she shoved him back, both hands, the heels of her palms connecting with his sternum. 'Get a hold of yourself!' she said, but he kept coming, and the third time she reached for her knife. The sharp, ground steel gleamed pale green in the luminous light.

Minka wasn't letting a frekk-head like Artem screw about with her. Her hand trembled. Not with fear but with fury. She could feel that surge of strength rising through her. 'Try me,' she said as he came for her again.

Suddenly Sergeant Gaskar was between them. He shoved them both back. 'Stop this now,' he shouted. 'Throne! You're Cadians!'

'Cadia's fallen!' Artem hissed and threw his hand off. 'Didn't you hear?'

'I said sit down, trooper. That is an order.'

Artem hesitated for a moment.

'I said that's an *order*.'

Artem turned and sat down. Gaskar turned to Minka.

'You, too.'

'Yes, sir,' she said and smiled as she slumped back against the cavern wall. Isran gave her a sideways look that was hard to read. Minka realised she still had her knife in her hand. It was non-standard issue, a heavy blade that curved in on itself. Colonel Rath had given her one after Cadia. 'You cannot unsheathe it without giving it blood,' he said.

Minka had been with Rath throughout the siege of her home kasr. Now it was in her hand, unbloodied. In a casual, almost practised gesture, she ran the blade along the inside of her arm. Just enough to raise a bracelet of blood beads along her skin before slamming it back into the sheath.

She flicked the vox off. The sound of munching grew louder. She sat up and looked about. No one else seemed to have noticed it.

'Sergeant Gaskar,' she called. 'Can you hear that?'

'What?'

Something was tugging at her foot. She thought it was Isran at first, then remembered the rats. She looked down and saw what looked like a giant maggot fretting at the leather of her boot. It was as long as her forearm, a blind, translucent creature with a dark head and round, munching jaws.

She leaped up in disgust, stamped on the thing, ground her heel on its head. Even Isran stared down. 'Throne,' he said, and called out to the others. 'You should see this!'

Gaskar and Matrey stared at the maggot. Leonov found another one as big as a dog and lit it up with las-bolts. The smell of burnt flesh hung in the air. The sound of eating mouths grew louder. 'Oh, Throne,' Rellan said, his lumen stabbing out into the darkness. 'There are hundreds of them.'

The floor of the chamber seemed to be moving. 'Time to move out,' Sergeant Gaskar announced abruptly. They stood up, slinging their packs onto their backs. Minka hauled the vox up as Gaskar led them down the centre of the chamber. He jumped the crack and started along the middle of the room, keeping well away from where the maggots were feeding on the dead.

They were halfway along the chamber floor when they came across another crack, deeper and darker than the rest. It was nearly two yards wide and exhaled a cold, rancid smell. Gaskar led them across, and when it was Minka's turn, she put her thumbs through the vox-unit straps, checked her footing and jumped. Isran caught her and hauled her forwards. She turned, about to help Leonov across, when a las-round flared out from across the sump-lake. It hit Matrey in the shoulder, and he grunted with pain. More las-bolts flashed in from the right, and then the left, and in an instant it seemed they were surrounded, half on one side and half on the other.

Isran pulled Minka down to the side of the crack, where a roof-fall provided cover. Gaskar shouted bearings to each pair as they started to return fire, and Grogar set the tripod down, kicked the ammo feed to the side and started to shoot.

In a moment the sump-lake surface was wild water, with the boots of charging warriors, stitched shots of heavy bolters and the hissing steam of las-rounds all churning it up. A small figure climbed up between two stalactites. It stood for a moment, hands on the stalactites to either side, silhouetted by the luminous glow, crucified in silhouette. Minka fired and missed. She cursed herself. She had a moment to aim once more and made sure this time. She felt the hum of her lasrifle as the power pack engaged and spat a bolt of blue-white out of the barrel.

The flare filled her vision, and the bolt lit an eye-searing stripe across the pool surface. It up-lit the target's face for a moment – a shaggy mess of hair, a snarling face that might once have been human – then the las-bolt connected and kinetic energy turned to searing heat.

Minka had seen the puff of steaming flesh many times. The figure fell into the lake with a splash, but where it had stood, three more figures appeared, clambering forwards. And when they were down, there were five behind them.

'They're coming up out of the water!' Isran said.

She nodded and saw the point on the far side of the pool where they were emerging.

They worked together. She was in awe of his ferocious rate of fire. He was calm and methodical, as if he were working his way through the firing range. 'It's easy,' he always said. 'You pick out the highest priority target, kill it, then move on to the next.'

Minka felt a maggot at her boot. She kicked at it and aimed once more. Gaskar was shouting orders. It sounded like Aleksei had been hit as well. Leonov crawled over to him.

'Flesh wound,' Leonov called out. He was scrabbling through his pack for a medikit. Artem was shouting about the worms. Minka was too busy shooting to turn and look at what was behind her.

'They're coming up from the crack!' Gaskar shouted.

Minka risked a look behind her, and at that moment she saw a spinning grenade land near her elbow. Time slowed. She saw that it was Munitorum issue. Plain green drab with stencilled white serial numbers. She knew that it would kill both her and Isran if it went off, and that it would go off within seconds or even milliseconds, so instinctively she screamed a warning as she batted it back into the crack. She had no idea if Isran heard or not. She was ducking when the explosion went off. Shrapnel hit the back of her head and, to her left, a demo charge went off with its sudden distinctive *whoosh!* which brought part of the roof down. The force of the blast threw her down hard enough to knock her face into the rock before her. She couldn't tell if her flak jacket had saved her. Her shoulder ached, her lip was bleeding, there was blood on her chin and on the back of her palm.

A shape loomed over her. Her helmet clanged as metal scraped along it. It connected on her collarbone. She snarled and drove her bayonet into the figure's groin. She fired twice just to make sure, the las-bolts burning deep holes as they buried themselves into her assailant's soft, coiled guts.

She had to twist out of the way to pull the bayonet free. She staggered to her feet and slammed the lasrifle's butt down into the heretic's face, before loading a fresh power pack into the weapon.

To her left she heard Rellan go down. Isran was half-buried in rubble. Throne knew how they'd get out of this fix. Isran was moaning. She wanted to help him, but her focus was forward. So much so that when a hand rested on her shoulder she jolted and spun about, expecting a knife in the kidney or neck. But looking down at her was a Cadian face. An older man. Grey stubble. Lop-sided face. His name-badge read 'Bardski.'

Bardski barely acknowledged her. He didn't stop to talk but knelt beside her and started to pump las-bolts across the chamber. Through the green glow she could see more Cadians picking their way stealthily forwards. A motley collection of about thirty survivors, pausing every so often to aim and fire. Thank the Emperor, she thought, but then she saw the figure at the back. He wore a dark leather cloak and a peaked hat. She caught Bardski's eye, and he gave her an apologetic look.

'Why the Throne did you have to bring him along?' Minka said. A commissar was all they needed.

Minka helped Isran pull himself out from under the girder that had fallen over him. His left arm was clearly broken. His face was pale. He swallowed back his pain as Minka plunged the needle into his shoulder. 'Morphia,' she said. 'Won't take long to kick in.'

Isran nodded. His eyes wandered, and she thought he might faint. 'Heh,' she said, tapping his cheek. 'You were right. It's our reinforcements.'

Commissar Haan wasted no time in introducing himself to those who were left of Minka's platoon. His face was disfigured by an old burn scar that pulled the side of his mouth back into a fierce snarl, and he seemed almost angry that Minka's squad had got to the cavern before them.

Minka could see at least five different units within his warband. Mostly Cadians; a couple of local Calibineers, their velvet jackets smeared with mud and mould; and a lone Valhallan Ice Warrior in a greatcoat and fur cap. The coat looked two sizes too big, like he'd taken it from a dead body, and his face was gaunt.

The commissar looked over his ragtag collection of troopers as a butcher would inspect his knife. 'Any sign of the Great Chamber?'

'None, sir,' Gaskar said. 'The hivers came from the water. And from up this crack here.'

The commissar looked down into the darkness and seemed not to find what he was looking for. He looked across the pool. 'I don't see where.'

'They came up out of the water. There must be a sump-hole there.'

The commissar seemed to like this. 'Right,' he said. 'That must be the way up.'

Gaskar didn't wait for the order. 'Cadians, forward!' he called out, and stepped down into the water, pushing the floating bodies aside, feeling his way as he waded knee-deep towards the other side of the chamber.

One by one the troopers followed, strung out with their lasrifles raised high through the dragon-maw of stalactites. Gaskar shone his lumen down into the water. 'I can't see anything,' he said. The spear of white light panned back and forth, looking for an opening among the sunken rocks.

Commissar Haan pushed forwards. 'It's there somewhere.' He took the lumen himself, but couldn't find anything. At last, he said, 'You, soldier. Give me your lasrifle.'

'Me, sir?' Artem said, blinking as the lumen shone in his face.

'Yes,' the commissar said, turning the light down into the water again. As he did so something flicked through the beam. It was the tail of a maggot, twitching itself through the water.

'What is that?' Commissar Haan said.

'Hive maggots,' Sergeant Gaskar said. 'This room seems to be full of them.'

Commissar Haan pulled out his bolt pistol, used the lumen to locate the maggot's body. It was a yard long and thick as a man's waist, wriggling as it tried to push itself through the water. He fired a single bolt-round into the water. The spray hit them all. No one could tell if he'd killed the maggot or not.

'I can feel one,' someone said behind Minka. 'Throne! It just bit me.'

Minka could feel unseen creatures brush past their legs. Two maggots surfaced next to her. She drew her knife and slashed at them, but even cut in half they continued to writhe. She could feel discomfort start to turn to panic as another man was bitten.

'I said into the water!' the commissar ordered.

Artem's hand started shaking. 'But the maggots…' he started.

Commissar Haan's face showed disgust. 'The God-Emperor of Mankind does not care about hive maggots!'

The leather-coated figure stepped up beside him. Minka knew what was coming. She'd seen it before. Heard the moment recounted many times around campfires and during long warp transits. Seen men lift up their fingers, pistol-style to the side of the head and say the words 'In the name of the God-Emperor!'

She felt that it could have been any of them. Anyone could be standing there now with the cold barrel of a bolt pistol resting against their skin. 'Into the water, trooper,' the commissar ordered.

Artem closed his eyes and the sight transfixed Minka for a moment. She willed him to move. Willed him not to let his life end like this. At least for Cadia, she thought. For the shock troopers.

But then the bolt pistol fired: a bright flash of light and a moment later the report. The shot floored Artem sideways like a hammer to the head. Minka felt cold dread. This was how it would end, she thought, as the commissar turned towards her.

'You!' he snapped.

Minka could not move.

'Yes, sir!' It was the man beside her who spoke. The Valhallan. She turned in astonishment as he pulled off his greatcoat and his cap and let them drop. She felt a moment's shame as the Valhallan plunged into the water and the commissar used the lumen to follow his course. But then the man exploded out of the depths and the commissar caught hold of his webbing and dragged him up. The largest maggot they had seen was hanging off his shoulder. Its body was pulsing as it tightened its grip, dark gobbets of blood moving down into its gut.

Minka slashed with her knife. The first blow ripped the maggot's belly open, the second cut it in half, but still the head clung on, and even as she dragged at it, the mouth-part would not come free. Suddenly the chamber shook. It was the dull roar she'd heard before, but now it was raging, and loud, and closing.

The whole company stopped and stared behind them. They looked back in disbelief as a lone figure entered the chamber and straightened to its full height. It seemed to fill the vaulting space. It was a giant – eight feet of power-armoured horror – with glowing red eyes that turned towards them and focused on them.

The thing was wrapped in chains; skulls hung from its loincloth, and impaled on the brass spikes that rose from its pauldrons were the decapitated heads of Imperial Guardsmen – Cadians, by the look of it – from which fresh gouts of gore still dripped. The monster stalked forwards, exuding pure evil.

Each leg was a column of plated might; each footfall was the crunch of ceramite on shattered rockcrete. It paced to where they had fought the last engagement and crossed the two-yard crack in a single stride. One great boot splashed down into the water. Only then did it engage the weapon that it held, a giant chainaxe that made the whole chamber shake. It was the roar she had heard as she'd eaten. It was the sound of doom. Of murder. Of unrelenting frenzy.

And then the axe fell silent. 'Throne help us,' Gaskar said as the figure took another giant step closer. Minka took an involuntary step backwards. She had a brief awareness of the Valhallan struggling to find his footing as it approached. It had the manner of a jungle cat coming across a wounded gazelle. It savoured the expectation of slaughter.

Commissar Haan rallied them. 'In the name of the Emperor!' And somehow Grogar spun the heavy bolter round, and shots hammered the air about the giant. The beleaguered soldiers of the Astra Militarum fired in a blinding fusillade. Las-bolts flared out and many of them hit, but nothing stopped it. Not bolt-rounds. Not las-bolts. Not hive maggots. The single warrior was like a tank rolling towards them. It did not slow or pause, nor did it accelerate. It triggered the chainaxe again just as it reached their lines.

It cut the next Cadian into two unequal halves, and stoved in the ribcage of another with a massive armoured fist. Commissar Haan held his ground, but it didn't help him. His bolt pistol barked, the rounds pinging off the ruddy armour as he went for a weak spot. He did not find one. The gory blades of the chainaxe whined as their attacker swung, and the pitch of its engine went up a note as the ceramite teeth snagged on skull – but then it was through, and the chainaxe opened the commissar's torso up from neck to sternum, like a zipper on a camo suit. The commissar splashed down to his knees, and he paused for the briefest of moments as if praying in front of the Golden Throne, before slamming ruined face first into the bloody water.

The remaining men panicked. It made no difference. There was nowhere to flee to.

Isran shouted something about Cadia before he died to a blow of the chainaxe, which sprayed shreds of flesh and flak armour, bone and blood, webbing and human hair across those remaining.

Leonov's head tumbled before her as her blade scraped uselessly across the ceramite, and snagged in the piping of a knee joint. The vast creature pistol-whipped Bardski. The casual blow dislocating his skull from the vertebrae of his neck and showering his teeth across the chamber. Matrey went low, hoping to stab through the thing's groin-armour, but he died as its power-armoured knee connected with his face and broke his neck with a sharp snap.

Terror held Minka in its cupped palm as the denizen of hell turned towards her. It seemed to fill the chamber, four-foot broad shoulders and visored mask turning as one to focus on her with the eyes of a predator. She took another step back, and another, and stumbled as the ground beneath her gave way.

The liquid was shockingly cold on her scalp and neck. Something squirmed past her face. She felt the rough surface of a maggot's mouth brush past her ear and kicked furiously down. She kept expecting to hit the bottom but she fell a yard or more. She kicked up for air as the chainaxe roared down at the place where she had just been. Water erupted from its spinning teeth as she sucked in a breath and ducked down once more, pulling herself deeper. Something caught her ankle. She wanted to scream but she couldn't waste the breath. She felt for the edges of the rock. They cut and stung, but she did not care.

A maggot's smooth, bulging body pressed against her face. Her hands scrabbled forwards, searching for an opening. As she went deeper she could not tell what was a passageway and what was a contour of the rock. She found what she thought was an opening but butted up against stone. She backed up, found another and hit a wall of slime that might have been a maggot nest, and had to retreat again.

She had to exhale. The need went from insistent to a compulsion. But if she did she knew she would die. She had to go down. The heretics had done it. They must have come this way, and if they could do this, then by the Golden Throne, she could as well.

At last she found a way forward, but it was too narrow. She let the vox-unit go, but felt her shoulder pads catch on either side. She tore at her webbing. She could feel her lungs bursting within her chest. She fought so violently she cut her hand on the sharp rocks. There was something behind her. She felt her feet being grabbed and let her scream out in bubbles, and sucked in a lungful of filthy water that made her choke and gasp. She couldn't go forwards. Couldn't go back. She kicked free, but her lungs were full of filth.

She wrenched at the clips that held her armour in place. She got one arm free, then the other, and suddenly a hand was on her, dragging her up.

Minka found herself lying on a stone floor. She wheezed and coughed for what seemed like an eternity as vomit and filth came out of her nose and mouth.

At last, she opened her eyes and sucked in the sweetest breath she had ever inhaled. Wiping the water from her face, she blinked, trying to see where she was.

'Are you all right?' a voice said.

She blinked again as she pushed herself up to her knees. She couldn't make out who was talking to her. 'Who is that?' she said.

'Me.'

'Who the frekk is me?'

'Grogar,' the voice said.

She cleared her eyes and looked at the heavy bolter gunner in disbelief. She was full of questions but they could wait. None of that mattered. They were here and they were alive.

'Where are we?' Minka said.

Grogar pulled his lumen from its pouch. He wiped the casing dry, and gave her a look to say, *Let's see if this works.*

It did. The light flickered for a moment, then held true. He turned the beam upwards. In the circle of light, they could see a vaulted ceiling, mouldy plaster shapes crumbling away and, here and there, the glimmer of gold.

In niches in the wall there were statues. Somewhere nearby they could hear running water.

'Is this the Great Chamber?' Minka said, her feet squelching within her sodden boots.

'No,' he said slowly. 'It can't be. It was supposed to be a way up into the hive.'

They emptied water from their footwear, then Minka led Grogar over the fallen masonry to the nearest statue, which was about thirty feet across the tiled floor. It stood in a niche carved with interlocking aquilas. The figure stood on a bronze pedestal, thick now with verdigris, half-buried in dust and dirt and rubble.

It looked like it had once held a spear, but the spear had gone, and the other arm was broken off at the elbow. Despite the mould and the dust, it was unmistakably the figure of a female saint. Minka looked for an inscription. She could not find one, but she felt an immediate closeness with the helmed figure. She reached up and put her hand on the saint's leg and flinched for a moment.

'Do you feel that?' she said to Grogar.

He put out his hand and touched the statue as well. 'It's warm!' he said.

'I don't think any heretics have come here. They would have defaced it.' She closed her eyes and let the warmth in the statue calm her. Conviction that she would not die here filled her. This must have been a chapel once. Whatever it had been, there was a power here still that the heretics avoided.

Grogar looked about. 'This is some hole we've found ourselves in. Just the two of us. No las. No vox.'

Minka had seen tighter scrapes than this. 'You weren't on Cadia,' she said. 'I mean, at the end.'

'No,' he admitted. 'I wasn't.' The big man's cheeks coloured. The 2050th had been recalled to Cadia, but they'd been held up in the warp, and never made it. They felt guilty and resentful that they had not been there, to see Cadia fall.

'I was,' Minka said. She remembered the flight from her home and how, despite the terror and the horror and the loss, there was hardly a trooper who had not seen angels protecting them, or showing them the way.

When you were in a hole as deep and dark as this one, faith was the one thing that kept you alive.

'Do you remember Cadia?' she said urgently. 'I mean, can you picture the place still, in your mind?'

Grogar pulled a face. 'Not really. I mean, I was only fifteen when I left...' He trailed off. 'It's been twenty years. I've seen so many other planets, they all start to blur.'

Minka was intense. 'Try and remember,' she said. She reached out and touched the statue. 'Picture yourself on the Caducades. Or picture the first time you saw Kasr Tyrok.'

Grogar pulled a face but she was insistent.

'Do it!' she ordered.

He shut his eyes, and she put his hand back to the statue and held it in place. Then she shut her own eyes. 'Think of Cadia. Can you see it?'

Minka could. The recollection of her home world was so powerful it almost made her weep. She pressed her eyes together and could smell the distinct salt-air smell of the rocky beaches along the Caducades coastline. She could feel the wind on her face, could feel herself clambering up the rocks to the top of the island, to listen to the moan of wind in the honeycomb of the pylon that stood there. She could see the searchlights of Kasr Tyrok, the flights of Thunderbolts heading into the sunset, and hear the klaxon sounding as the night watch began.

She did not know how long they stood there. The sensation of warmth grew, then receded. When it had gone entirely Minka felt almost deflated. But then she noticed something had changed. 'My clothes are dry,' she said. She took his hand and put it on her sleeve.

Grogar looked at her, and then looked down at his own Cadian drab combat suit. Only his boots were still wet. His jacket, trousers, flak armour were crusted with dry salt. He started to laugh. 'I'll be damned,' he said, but he was a simple-minded warrior and this was beyond his understanding.

But Minka understood. It was a miracle or a sign. Of that she was sure. She slapped his arm. 'Defeat is not an option. We have to get out of here. Don't you understand? This is the hour of utmost darkness. But we're Cadians. We survived. And the Imperium needs us.'

He nodded slowly, only just grasping what she meant. But one thing was easy enough to comprehend: this was the hour of darkness, and the Imperium needed them more than ever.

YOUR
NEXT READ

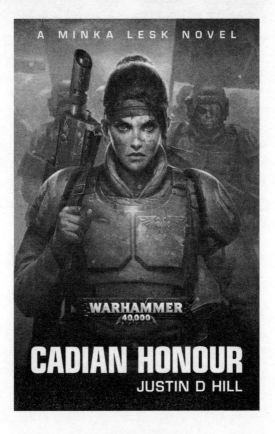

A MINKA LESK NOVEL

WARHAMMER
40,000

CADIAN HONOUR
JUSTIN D HILL

CADIAN HONOUR
by Justin D Hill

Sent to the capital world of Potence, Sergeant Minka Lesk
and the Cadian 101st discover that though Cadia may have fallen,
their duty continues.

THE SMALLEST DETAIL

Sandy Mitchell

Introducing

CIAPHAS CAIN

COMMISSAR

Jurgen had never liked people very much, and their returned indifference was fine by him. That was the main reason he'd joined the Imperial Guard: they told you what to do and you got on and did it, without any of the social niceties of civilian life he found both tedious and baffling. Since becoming a commissar's personal aide, however, he'd been forced to interact with others in ways which went far beyond the simple exchange of orders and acknowledgement, although he remained obstinately wedded to the most straightforward approach in dealing with them.

'What do you want?' the sergeant in the blue and yellow uniform of the local militia asked, looking warily at him from behind the flakboard counter walling off most of the warehouse-sized room. 'The Guard have their own stores.'

Jurgen nodded, unable to argue with that, having already worked his way through the inventories of every Imperial Guard supply depot close to the commissar's quarters. He didn't suppose there would be much here worth his attention, but you never knew, and it was a point of personal pride to know where he could lay his hands on anything Commissar Cain might feel the lack of at a moment's notice.

'Dunno yet,' he said, choosing just to answer the question, and ignore the statement of the obvious which had followed it. 'What have you got? And I'm not here for the Guard.' He readjusted the shoulder strap of his lasgun, so he could rummage in a pocket without the weapon slipping to the floor. After a moment he extricated a grubby sheet of vellum, embellished with a seal, and leaned across the counter to bring it within the sergeant's field of vision. The man stepped back hastily, as people so often did when faced with clear evidence of Jurgen's borrowed authority from close at hand.

'The bearer of this note, Gunner Feric Jurgen, is my personal aide, and is to be accorded all such assistance as he may require in the furtherance of his duties.

Commissar Ciaphas Cain.'

'You're with the Commissariat?' the sergeant asked, a nervous edge entering his voice, and Jurgen nodded. It was a bit more complicated than that, he was technically still on secondment from a Valhallan artillery regiment he never expected to see again, but he'd never bothered to find out precisely where he now fitted into the inconceivably complex structure of the Imperial military. No one else seemed to know either, and he found the ambiguity worked to his advantage more often than not.

'I work for Commissar Cain,' he said, keeping it simple, folding his well-worn credentials and returning them to the depths of his pockets as he spoke.

'So I see.' Sergeant Merser forced an ingratiating smile towards his face. Though he outranked this evil-smelling interloper, he'd long since learned that his status in the planetary militia didn't mean a thing to most Guardsmen; they regarded all locally raised units as little more than a civilian militia barely worth acknowledging, let alone according any sign of respect. Besides, this particular

Guardsman appeared to be running an errand for a commissar, one of those mysterious and terrifying figures seldom encountered by lowly militia troopers, and a good thing too if even half the stories he'd heard about them were true. Not just any commissar either, but Cain, the Hero of Perlia, who even now was giving the rebel forces infesting the city the fight of their lives. However unwelcome his visitor may have been, it was probably best to appear co-operative, at least until it became clear what he wanted.

Jurgen leaned on the counter, and raised his gaze to the racks of neatly shelved foodstuffs in the cavernous space beyond. 'Can't see a lot from out here,' he said.

'No, of course not. Come on through.' Reluctantly, the sergeant lifted a hinged flap in the boardsheet countertop, enabling him to tug open a sagging gate of the same material beneath it. Jurgen ambled through the gap, making a mental note of the man's name at the top of the duty roster tacked to the wall as he passed. Even the most trivial detail could turn out to be important, the commissar always said, and Jurgen had taken the precept to heart, squirreling away whatever nuggets of information he could find as assiduously as pieces of unattended food or kit. You never knew when something you stumbled across might come in handy.

'Got an inventory?' he asked, and Sergeant Merser nodded reluctantly.

'It's around here somewhere,' he said, making a show of rummaging through the shelves under the counter. After a moment or two of Jurgen's patient scrutiny it became obvious there was no point in attempting to stall any further, and he hauled out a venerable-looking book, leather-bound and battered, trying to hide his annoyance. 'I think you'll find everything's in order.'

Jurgen said nothing as he took it, but his scepticism was palpable, hanging around him like the peculiar odour which had accompanied him into the stores. Merser found himself edging away from his unwelcome visitor, unsure of which he found the more unsettling.

'I'll get on, then,' Jurgen said, dismissing the sergeant from his mind as thoroughly as if the militiaman had evaporated.

Merser watched, as the Guardsman worked his way methodically along the storage racks, periodically pausing while he leafed through the pages of the venerable tome. Now and again he glanced in Merser's direction, with an expression of patient inquiry.

'Some local thing?' he asked, as a sliver of dried meat disappeared through the hole in his beard, accompanied by the squelching sounds of mastication.

Merser nodded. 'Sand eel. From the Parch. Only things that can live out in the open down there, so the locals raise them for food.' Aware that he was beginning to babble, he clamped his mouth firmly shut. The less he said, the less could find its way back to the commissar's ears.

'Had worse,' Jurgen conceded, slipping a couple of packs of the leathery shreds into one of the pouches hanging from his torso armour. There had been none of that in the Guard stores, and Commissar Cain generally appreciated the chance to try new flavours. Come to that, they were both seasoned enough campaigners to find the idea of emergency rations which tasted of anything identifiable at all a pleasant novelty.

By the time Jurgen had finished working his way round the shelves, the pouch was considerably fuller than it had been, stuffed with other local viands which the offworld-supplied Guard stores had been without. There was little enough else to like about Helengon, a world which, in his opinion, was aptly named. He'd seen worse, of course, and at least the heretics they were fighting here were human enough instead of gleaming metal killers or scuttling tyranid horrors, but like most of the places he'd been since enlisting, the air was too warm and dry, and the ground too firm underfoot.

'Anything else I can help you with?' Sergeant Merser asked, and, reminded of his presence, Jurgen shook his head.

'Got what I came for,' he said, passing the book back.

'I see.' If the sergeant's voice trembled just a little, or his face seemed a trifle more ashen than it had been, Jurgen didn't notice: but then he seldom noticed things like that anyway.

One kind of subtle cue Jurgen was pretty much guaranteed to pick up on, though, was intimations of danger. By this point in his life he'd been on the receiving end of enough ambushes, berserker charges, and incoming fire to have taken it pretty much for granted that if something wasn't trying to kill him now it was only a matter of time before it did. Accordingly, it didn't take him long to realise he was being followed.

He glanced around, tugging gently on the sling of his lasgun, to bring it within easy reach of his hand without appearing to ready himself for combat. Sure enough, a faint scuffle echoed in the shadows behind him, as someone took a half-step too many before realising their quarry had become stationary, and froze into immobility in their turn.

Jurgen felt his mouth twitch into an involuntary sneer. Typical militia sloppiness, he thought. Not a bad place for a bushwhacking though, he had to give them that. He'd cut down an alleyway between two of the big storage units, which, from the signage stencilled on the ends, he'd deduced contained small-arms and ammunition, neither of which made them worth a visit. Those he could obtain directly from the Guard if he wanted them. Besides, most of the las weapons around here were of local manufacture, adequate, but no match for the products of an Imperial forge world; he had no desire to find a power pack shorting out on him just when he needed it the most.

Which could be any time now. Seeing no point in letting his followers know he was on to them, and needing a plausible reason for his sudden stop, Jurgen unsealed his trousers, and relieved himself against the nearest wall in a leisurely fashion. While he did so, he let his gaze travel around his immediate surroundings, as though simply passing the time until nature had run its course.

There were two men trailing him, trying to make themselves

invisible behind a stack of corroding metal drums. They'd almost succeeded, but not well enough to escape the notice of a combat veteran of Jurgen's calibre. A faint clank of metal against metal meant that at least one of them was probably armed.

In the other direction, a jumble of crates narrowed the gap between buildings; a soldier in blue and yellow was lounging casually against one, puffing on a lho stick, and apparently keeping an eye out for his immediate superior; a performance which would have been a little more convincing if his head had spent more time turned in the direction of the alley mouth than towards Jurgen.

Completing his task with a sigh of satisfaction, Jurgen rearranged his clothing and his dignity, and resumed his unhurried progress towards the smoking trooper. As he'd expected, the soft padding of stealthy footsteps followed him. Only one pair, though, by the sound of it. That meant the other man would be lining up a weapon of some kind. His opinion of the Helengon militia plummeted even further, if that were possible; the gunman would be as much of a danger to his confederates as to Jurgen. More of one, even: Jurgen had a helmet and flak vest for protection, while the troopers stalking him were dressed simply in fatigues.

It never occurred to Jurgen to wonder why these men appeared to be after him; they just were. Reasons were irrelevant.

As he passed the smoker, the man attacked, lunging with the combat knife he hadn't quite managed to conceal behind his body while leaning against the crates. Either he knew what he was doing, aiming a single, precise blow at one of the vulnerable points in Jurgen's body armour, or he was an idiot, striking out blindly in the vague hope of finding an opening. Whichever it was, he was out of luck; Jurgen pulled the lasgun off his shoulder, ramming the barrel into the side of the man's arm, and deflecting his aim with a *snap* of shattering bone. The blade skittered off the tight carbifibre weave of his flak vest, and Jurgen pulled the trigger, putting a couple of rounds through the smoker's chest before he even had time to finish inhaling in preparation for an agonised scream. One down.

Jurgen turned, seeing the man behind him pick up the pace, hoping to close the distance between them before he could bring the lasgun round to bear. He was a slight fellow, whose uniform hung oddly on him, as though it was a little too large for its wearer; which might have struck Jurgen as odd, if he hadn't spent most of his life being issued with kit which didn't quite fit. Imperial Guard uniforms only came in two sizes, too large and too small, a problem most troopers solved by swapping what they'd been given with others in their unit; an option Jurgen had never felt inclined to pursue.

The running man was carrying a weapon in his hand, a crude stubber, which he brought up and fired as he came. Jurgen didn't flinch; the chances of hitting a man-sized target with a handgun while firing on the run were minimal, he knew, and his flak vest would probably hold even if the fellow got lucky.

Which he didn't. A burst of lasgun fire from a stationary shooter, on the other hand, was a lot more accurate, especially if the shooter in question had spent years bringing down moving targets in the middle of a firefight.

Stubber man folded and fell, his torso pitted with the ugly cauterised wounds characteristic of lasgun fire, his pistol skittering away as his flaccid hand smacked against the ground. He was probably dead before he hit the ground, but Jurgen put an extra round through his head anyway. He'd seen enough people keep going on the battlefield by sheer willpower, long after they should have laid down and died, insulated by shock and a final adrenaline surge from the full effect of their mortal wounds.

As Jurgen ran forward, angling for a clear shot at the man behind the barrels, his boot kicked against the fallen gun, and he glanced down at it disdainfully. It was an old-fashioned slug thrower, crudely made, and clearly not standard issue, even to the militia of a backwater world like this one. No wonder its owner had missed him; it was beyond Jurgen why anybody would choose to use a weapon like that, instead of the lasgun he'd been issued with.

The man behind the barrels had no such compunction, it seemed, a hail of las-bolts chewing up the rockcrete footings of the storage blocks, gouging a line of splinters across the crates and the knife-man's corpse behind Jurgen as he returned fire on full auto. That would deplete the power pack uncomfortably fast, he knew, but there was no cover he could take, and throwing himself flat to min-imise his target profile would simply allow the hidden gunman to pick off an immobile target at his leisure. Better to advance behind a blizzard of suppressive fire, hoping that would be enough to keep his quarry's head down, until he was able to get a clean shot at him.

The tactic worked better than Jurgen had dared to hope. The hail of las-bolts threw up sparks from the metal drums, punch-ing dents and ripping holes in them with a clamour which would have struck terror into the heart of an ork. It certainly terrified the hidden gunman, who stopped firing to retreat behind the metal cylinders' meagre protection, huddling in their lee.

Not that it did him much good. Liquid began seeping from the punctured drums almost at once, the thick, acrid smell of prome-thium lacing the air around them. As Jurgen continued to advance, firing as he came, either a spark from an impact or the heat of a las-bolt itself ignited the escaping vapour.

With a muffled *whump*, the whole stack exploded, making Jurgen stagger with the sudden wave of heat. He backed up fast as a lake of burning fuel began sloshing in his direction, scrambling over the crates which were already beginning to blacken in the intense heat, just as the blazing tide began to lap against them. From some-where in the middle of the inferno, he thought he could hear a prolonged, agonised scream, which was mercifully cut short in a sudden secondary explosion.

Choking from the smoke, eyes streaming from the acrid fumes, Jurgen stumbled into the open, gasping for breath. A thick, dense coil of smoke followed him like a questing tentacle, but he ignored it, sweeping his immediate surroundings for any further signs of hostility. Attracted by the noise, a score or more of the local militia were running towards him, some carrying fire suppressors, others with weapons ready, no doubt under the impression that the rebels were attacking.

'You! Guardsman. Drop your weapon!' someone shouted, and Jurgen turned, prepared to fight his way out if he had to; but this time it wasn't an option. Five troopers had their lasguns trained on him, and it was clear that these ones knew what they were doing. They were too widely dispersed to take down; if he tried, he'd only be able to get a couple of them before the others returned the favour. They were dressed differently from the others too, in body armour and full face helmets, unit insignia which meant nothing to him stencilled on their chestplates.

He knew what they were, anyway, he'd seen plenty like them in his time in the Guard. Provosts, or whatever they called themselves in the Helengon militia.

'Can't do that,' he replied evenly. 'It's against regulations.' Imperial Guard troopers were responsible for their lasgun at all times, and although simply putting it down wouldn't be a technical breach of standing orders, the next step would most likely be someone taking it out of his reach altogether. Even an ordinary Guardsman would find the threat of being disarmed well nigh intolerable, but for a commissar's personal aide, it would be a mortal wound to his dignity. On the other hand, being shot five times at close range wouldn't do a lot for it either. 'But I'll take out the power pack and stow it.'

'Good enough,' the squad leader agreed, after a moment's hesitation. She raised her visor to look at him directly, then back to the column of smoke still billowing from between the warehouses. 'Then you and I are going to have a little chat.'

'You've got no idea which unit they were from?' the provost sergeant, whose name had turned out to be Liana, asked, not for the first time.

Jurgen shook his head. 'Never saw any patches,' he repeated, and shrugged. 'Probably wouldn't have recognised 'em if I had.'

'Probably not,' Liana agreed. 'But they should have had something.'

She gestured at the bustle of activity surrounding them. By now, over a hundred militia troopers had arrived to fight the fire, clear up its aftermath, and, in many cases, simply take advantage of the free entertainment. Every single one of them had insignia of some kind visible on their uniforms.

'These ones didn't,' Jurgen insisted, mildly irked at having his word doubted. The commissar would have believed him at once. He glared balefully at the charred cadaver being carried past by a group of troopers who must have seriously annoyed a superior to be landed with that particular duty, and spat vehemently, to relieve his feelings. 'Not that you could tell from that.'

'Special forces, maybe?' Liana speculated, at least willing to entertain the idea that he might not have been mistaken.

'They'd have had better equipment than a backstreet stubber,' Jurgen said, 'and they'd have been better shots.'

'Good point,' the provost conceded, to Jurgen's faint, and pleased, surprise. She turned to Sergeant Merser, who was hovering uneasily nearby, a data-slate in his hand. 'Any luck tracing the lasgun one of them was armed with?'

Merser nodded, looking distinctly unhappy. 'We managed to find a serial number. I would have thought the metal had melted, but the body...' he swallowed, turning another shade paler, 'what was left of it, had fallen on top. Protected it a bit.'

'So who was it issued to?' Liana asked.

'That's just it. It wasn't.' Merser held the data-slate out, as though he expected it to snap at his fingers. 'It's listed as still in stores.'

'So it was pilfered,' Liana said, and Merser nodded unhappily.

'Looks that way,' he replied.

'Then we need to know who by,' Liana persisted.

'If we find out what's missing, we should be able to deduce who's responsible,' Merser said. 'I'll start going through the inventories.'

'We could start with yours,' Liana suggested, fixing the heavyset sergeant with a calculating look.

Merser flushed indignantly. 'My records are fine,' he snapped.

'What's in the files is on the shelves.' He looked at Jurgen for con-firmation. 'He'll tell you.'

Jurgen nodded. 'Everything matched,' he agreed. He jerked a thumb in the direction of the latest corpse to be recovered, being dragged along in a tarpaulin by sweating, swearing troopers, leaving a faint trail of ash and flakes of charred meat in their wake. 'And I'd have a roll call if I were you. Whoever's missing's probably them.'

'Good idea,' Liana concurred. 'Then we can start chasing down their contacts. Wouldn't be the first time a quartermaster started diverting stuff to the black market.'

'I'll leave you to it, then.' Jurgen shouldered his lasgun, and turned away. 'I'm done here.'

'Maybe you should stay,' Merser said hastily.

Jurgen turned back, surprised. 'What for?' he asked.

'Yes, what for?' Liana turned a questioning gaze on the portly ser-geant. 'It's not as though Gunner Jurgen's a suspect.'

'Of course not,' Merser said hastily. 'But he must have assisted the commissar in his investigations. Maybe he can spot something we might overlook.'

'Maybe he can,' Liana agreed, after a moment's consideration. She turned to Jurgen. 'Do you think you might?'

'Dunno.' Jurgen shrugged. 'Worth a try, I suppose, so long as it don't take too long.' In truth, his involvement in investigations gen-erally went no further than processing the paperwork and shooting the occasional traitor who resented his unmasking, but an appeal had been made to his sense of duty, and he felt honour-bound to respond. It was what Commissar Cain would wish, he had no doubt.

'Right then,' Liana said, looking from one man to another, and wondering if she'd just made the decision to consign her career to oblivion, 'might as well get started, I suppose.'

'What do you mean there's no one missing?' Liana asked, hand-ing the data-slate she'd just been shown back to the provost who'd brought it in to her office; a small cubicle on the western side of the militia barracks, which would have seemed crowded with only one occupant. Currently it had three, Jurgen observing from a corner near the window, which Liana seemed to like jammed open as wide as it would go. He had no objection to this, as it gave him a good view of the militia compound, and the city beyond, from which the occasional crackle of small-arms fire could be heard. The rebels were making a concerted attempt to hold on to the southern quarter, with the Imperial Guard equally determined to dislodge them, and show the militia how it ought to be done by breaking the year-long stalemate in a matter of days.

'I mean everyone's accounted for, ma'am,' the provost said, and withdrew, a little hastily it seemed to Jurgen.

'Someone's playing games,' Jurgen said. 'Answering twice to cover for them.' A common enough dodge in the Guard, when troopers had overstayed a pass, or been too hungover to report for duty.

'Unless the men who attacked you weren't soldiers at all,' Liana said thoughtfully.

'They were in uniform,' Jurgen objected.

'I went to a party dressed as an ork once,' Liana retorted. 'That didn't make me a greenskin.'

Jurgen nodded, the way he'd seen the commissar do while considering an unexpected suggestion, and tried to see what she was driving at. 'You mean they were pretending to be militia troopers,' he said at last, reasonably certain he got it.

'That's right,' Liana said, looking at him a little oddly. 'Using stolen uniforms to get onto the base.'

Which sounded reasonable to Jurgen. If they could steal guns, they could steal uniforms just as easily. 'If it was me,' he added, 'I'd have set charges in the armoury as soon as I'd finished helping myself.'

'First thing we checked, believe me,' Liana assured him. 'Nothing there.'

'Hm.' Mindful that he was a guest in her office, Jurgen spat out of the window, rather than letting the gob of saliva land where it would. 'Even the rebels here aren't up to much.'

If Liana realised that was a thinly-veiled criticism of the local forces, she was tactful enough to let it go. Instead, she looked thoughtful. 'You're right,' she said. 'If rebels could sneak in and steal weapons, they'd definitely have sabotaged what was left so we couldn't use them.'

Jurgen's brow furrowed. 'Who does that leave?' he asked.

'Gangers, I suppose,' Liana said. 'Plenty of those around, carving up territories for themselves while the fighting keeps us too busy to rein them in.' She looked up, as Merser entered the office. 'Any luck?'

'I can tell you the records are a mess,' Merser said. 'Overstocks, items missing, half the inventories read like fiction 'zines.'

'No change there, then,' Jurgen said, shrugging. 'Yours are the only ones I ever saw that tallied exactly.'

Merser flushed. 'I like to pay attention to the details.'

'I noticed,' Jurgen said. He glanced at his chronograph, and stood. 'I need to get back. Anything I can help with, contact the commissar's office.'

'Of course.' Liana stood too, began to hold out a hand, then withdrew it hastily. 'We'll keep you informed.'

'Of course we will,' Merser added, standing aside to make room at the door. 'Where's your vehicle?'

'Came on foot,' Jurgen lied, and left them to it.

In fact he'd commandeered a motorcycle, which someone had been careless enough to leave unattended in the regimental motor pool, the better to navigate his way around the warren of streets surrounding the Imperial Guard deployment zones. He'd have preferred a Salamander, but he'd have had to divert around so much rubble if he'd chosen one that it would have all but doubled the distance he would have to travel.

After retrieving his mechanical steed, he coasted into the lee of a battle-damaged Chimera, which a party of enginseers were energetically reconsecrating, and waited a few moments.

As he'd expected, the distinctive figure of Sergeant Merser emerged from the building almost at once, at the closest to a trot he could manage. The heavyset non-com swung himself into the cab of a parked truck, against which a soldier with no visible unit patch had been lounging, and gunned the engine, while his companion scrambled up beside him. No sooner were they both aboard than Merser slammed the lorry into gear, roaring out of the yard as though half the daemons of the warp were after him.

It was almost too easy. After a quick conversation over his vox-bead, Jurgen opened the bike's throttle, and set out in pursuit. He hung well back, keeping the luminator off, despite the rapidly gathering night, well able to judge the presence of any major obstacles in the carriageway by the intermittent flaring of his quarry's brake lights. The risk of being spotted was minimal, he knew. Merser's attention would be entirely on the road ahead, looking for a solitary pedestrian.

Before long, the lorry coasted to a halt at an intersection, where Merser paused, glancing up and down the converging carriageways. Nothing moved in either direction, except a Chimera patrolling the deserted streets. With nightfall came the curfew, and nothing would be moving now except military traffic. Nothing legal, anyway, but there was nothing to worry about. No one would look twice at a militia truck.

'Where is he?' his companion demanded, nursing a laspistol the armourer still hadn't noticed was missing. 'You said he was on foot.'

'He can't have got far,' Merser said, still hovering indecisively. If he picked the wrong direction, the Guardsman would be safely back in the Imperial Guard compound, reporting to the commissar before they could double back and correct their mistake. Before he could make up his mind which road to take, a motorcycle roared up out of the darkness behind them, and parked, its engine revving, next to the cab.

Merser glanced down, and found himself staring along the length of a lasgun barrel, with a well-remembered face at the opposite end.

'I thought you'd leg it,' Jurgen remarked, conversationally. 'But I wanted to be sure. The commissar always likes to be sure, before he accuses anyone.'

'Accuses them of what?' Merser blustered, playing for time.

'Trying to kill me, for starters,' Jurgen said, as though that had been a perfectly reasonable thing to attempt. 'You sent those frakkers after me, didn't you?'

By way of an answer, Merser floored the accelerator. Jurgen debated pursuit for a fraction of a second, then squeezed the trigger of his lasgun instead. There was no way the cumbersome truck would be able to outrun the motorcycle anyway, so he might as well bring things to an end now. The hail of las-bolts shredded the lorry's tyres, and he watched it veer off course and collide with a half-collapsed storefront with detached interest.

As it came to rest, amid a small landslide of displaced brick, the passenger door popped open, and the ersatz soldier bailed out, firing wildly as he came. He was no better a shot than his deceased companions, and Jurgen dropped him easily, without even bothering to dismount. As he swung his leg over the saddle, and began to walk towards the crippled lorry, the Chimera ground to a halt a few metres away.

'Took your time,' he said, as the hatch clanged open.

'What can I say. Traffic,' Liana said, which didn't make much sense to Jurgen. So far as he could see, the streets were still deserted. She flung the truck's tailgate open, and a cascade of ration packs spilled out onto the cracked pavement. 'Looks like you were right.'

'Course I was,' Jurgen said. 'Inventories never match up to what's actually in stores. The only reason Merser's would is if he was covering something.'

Liana nodded. 'The way things are now, food's like currency on the streets. Better. Him and his ganger friends must have been making a fortune.' She paused to glare at the sergeant, who was being prised, none too gently, out of the battered cab by a couple of her provosts. 'He must have realised you'd spotted something was wrong, and sent his accomplices to keep you quiet.'

'That's how I see it,' Jurgen agreed. 'I still don't get why he wanted to keep me around, though.'

'So we could try again, you idiot!' Merser called, as he was half-dragged, half-carried towards the Chimera. 'If you told the commissar, we'd be finished!'

'Told the commissar?' Jurgen repeated, in tones of honest astonishment. 'Why would I bother him with a bit of pilfering? Everyone's at it.'

Merser's response was vocal, prolonged, and unflatteringly inaccurate about Jurgen's genealogy.

Jurgen listened impassively for a moment, before quietening him down with a well-aimed punch to the face. 'Ladies present,' he admonished, although he suspected Liana had already heard a good deal of profanity in her line of work. Besides, he resented people trying to kill him.

'We might need a statement,' Liana said, after a moment, during which the power of speech seemed to have deserted her for some reason.

Jurgen shrugged, his attention already on the crippled truck. 'You know where to find me,' he said.

After all, he still had a bit of space left in his utility pouches, and the motorbike he'd borrowed had commodious panniers. And you never knew when a few extra ration bars might come in handy.

YOUR
NEXT READ

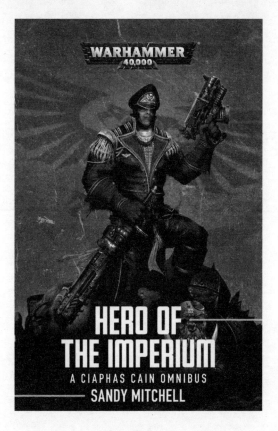

CIAPHAS CAIN: HERO OF THE IMPERIUM
by Sandy Mitchell

In the 41st millennium Commissar Ciaphas Cain, hero of the Imperium,
is an inspiration to his men – at least that's what the propaganda
would have you believe…

OF THEIR LIVES
IN THE RUINS
OF THEIR CITIES

Dan Abnett

Introducing

IBRAM GAUNT

COLONEL-COMMISSAR

It feels like the afterlife, and none of them are entirely convinced that it isn't.

They have pitched up in a cold and rain-lashed stretch of lowland country, on the morning after somebody else's triumph, with a bunch of half-arsed orders, a dislocating sense that the war is elsewhere and carrying on without them, and very little unit cohesion. They have a couple of actions under their belts, just enough to lift their chins, but nothing like enough to bind them together or take the deeper pain away and, besides, other men have collected the medals. They're out in the middle of nowhere, marching further and further away from anything that matters any more, because nothing matters any more.

They are just barely the Tanith First and Only. They are not Gaunt's Ghosts.

They are never going to be Gaunt's Ghosts.

Silent lightning strobes in the distance. His back turned towards it and the rain, the young Tanith infantryman watches Ibram Gaunt at work from the entrance of the war tent. The colonel-commissar is seated at the far end of a long table around which, an hour earlier, two dozen Guard officers and adjutants were gathered for a briefing. Now Gaunt is alone.

The infantryman has been allowed to stand at ease, but he is on call. He has been selected to act as runner for the day. It's his job to attend the commander, to pick up any notes or message satchels at a moment's notice, and deliver them as per orders. Foot couriers are necessary because the vox is down. It's been down a lot, this past week. It'd been patchy and unreliable around Voltis City. Out in the lowlands, it's useless, like audio soup. You can hear voices, now and then. Someone said maybe the distant, soundless lightning is to blame.

Munitorum-issue chem lamps, those tin-plate models that unscrew and then snap out for ignition, have been strung along the roof line, and there is a decent rechargeable glow-globe on the table beside Gaunt's elbow. The lamps along the roof line are swaying and rocking in the wind that's finding its way into the long tent. The lamps add a golden warmth to the tent's shadowy interior, a marked contrast to the raw, wet blow driving up the valley outside. There is rain in the air, sticky clay underfoot, a whitewashed sky overhead, and a line of dirty hills in the middle distance that look like a lip of rock that someone has scraped their boots against. Somewhere beyond the hills, the corpse of a city lies in a shallow grave.

Gaunt is studying reports that have been printed out on paper flimsies. He has weighed them down on the surface of the folding table with cartons of bolter rounds so they won't blow away. The wind is really getting in under the tent's skirt. He's writing careful notes with a stylus. The infantryman can only imagine the importance of those jottings. Tactical formulations, perhaps? Attack orders?

Gaunt is not well liked, but the infantryman finds him interesting. Watching him work at least takes the infantryman's mind off the fact that he's standing in the mouth of a tent with his arse out in the rain.

No indeed, Colonel-Commissar Ibram Gaunt is not well liked. A reputation for genocide will do that to a man's character. He is intriguing, though. For a career soldier, he seems surprisingly reflective, a man of thought not action. There is a promise of wisdom in his narrow features. The infantryman wonders if this was a mistake of ethnicity, a misreading brought about by cultural differences. Gaunt and the infantryman were born on opposite sides of the sector.

The infantryman finds it amusing to imagine Gaunt grown very elderly. Then he might look, the infantryman thinks, like one of those wizened old savants, the kind that know everything about fething everything.

However, the infantryman also has good reason to predict that Gaunt will never live long enough to grow old. Gaunt's profession mitigates against it, as does the cosmos he has been born into, and the specific nature of his situation.

If the Archenemy of Mankind does not kill Ibram Gaunt, the infantryman thinks, then Gaunt's own men will do the job.

A better tent.

Gaunt writes the words at the top of his list. He knows he'll have to look up the correct Munitorum code number, though he thinks it's 1NX1G1xA. Sym will know and–

Sym *would have* known, but Sym is dead. Gaunt exhales. He really has to train himself to stop doing that. Sym had been his adjutant and Gaunt had come to rely on him; it still seems perfectly normal to turn and expect to find Sym there, waiting, ready and resourceful. Sym had known how to procure a dress coat in the middle of the night, or a pot of collar starch, or a bottle of decent amasec, or a copy of the embarkation transcripts before they were published. He'd have known the Munitorum serial code for a *tent/temperate winter*. The structure Gaunt is sitting in is not a *tent/temperate winter*. It's an old tropical shelter left over from another theatre. It's waxed against rain, but there are canvas vents low down along the base hem designed to keep air circulating on balmy, humid days. This particular part of Voltemand seldom sees balmy humid days. The east wind, its cheeks full of rain, is pushing the vents open and invading the tent like a polar gale.

Under *A better tent* he writes: *A portable heater*.

He hardly cares for his own comfort, but he'd noted the officers and their junior aides around the table that morning, backs hunched, moods foul, teeth gritted against the cold, every single one of them in a hurry to get the meeting over so they could head back to their billets and their own camp stoves.

Men who are uncomfortable and in a hurry do not make good decisions. They rush things. They are not thorough. They often make general noises of consent just to get briefings over with, and that morning they'd all done it: the Tanith officers, the Ketzok tankers, the Litus B.R.U., all of them.

Gaunt knows it's all payback, though. The whole situation is payback. He is being punished for making that Blueblood general look like an idiot, even though Gaunt'd had the moral high ground. He had been avenging Tanith blood, because there isn't enough of that left for anyone to go around wasting it.

He thinks about the letter in his pocket, and then lets the thought go again.

When he'd been assigned to the Tanith, Gaunt had relished the prospect as it was presented on paper: a first founding from a small, agrarian world that was impeccable in its upkeep of tithes and devotions. Tanith had no real black marks in the Administratum's eyes, and no longstanding martial traditions to get tangled up in. There had been the opportunity to build something worthwhile, three regiments of light infantry to begin with, though Gaunt's plans had been significantly more ambitious than that: a major infantry force, fast and mobile, well-drilled and disciplined. The Munitorum's recruitment agents reported that the Tanith seemed to have a natural knack for tracking and covert work, and Gaunt had hoped to add that speciality to the regiment's portfolio. From the moment he'd reviewed the Tanith dossier, Gaunt had begun to see the sense of Slaydo's deathbed bequest to him.

The plans and dreams have come apart, though. The Archenemy, still stinging from Balhaut, burned worlds in the name of vengeance, and one of those worlds was Tanith. Gaunt got out with his life, just barely, and with him he'd dragged a few of the mustered Tanith men, enough for one regiment. Not enough men to ever be anything more than a minor infantry support force, to die as trench fodder in some Throne-forgotten ocean of mud, but just enough men to hate his living guts for the rest of forever for not letting them die with their planet.

Ibram Gaunt has been trained as a political officer, and he is a very good one, though the promotion Slaydo gave him was designed to spare him from the slow death of a political career. His political talents, however, can usually find a positive expression for even the worst scenarios.

In the cold lowlands of Voltemand, an upbeat interpretation is stubbornly eluding him.

He has stepped away from a glittering career with the Hyrkans, cut his political ties with all the men of status and influence who could assist him or advance him, and ended up in a low-value theatre on a third-tier warfront, in command of a salvaged, broken regiment of unmotivated men who hate him. There is still the letter in his pocket, of course.

He looks down at his list, and writes:

Spin this shit into gold, or get yourself a transfer to somewhere with a desk and a driver.

He looks at this for a minute, and then scratches it out. He puts the stylus down.

'Trooper,' he calls to the infantryman in the mouth of the tent. He knows the young man's name is Caffran. He is generally good with names, and he makes an effort to learn them quickly, but he is also sparing when it comes to using them. Show a common lasman you know his name too early, and it'll seem like you're trying far too hard to be his new best friend, especially if you just let his home and family burn.

It'll seem like you're weak.

The infantryman snaps to attention sharply.

'Step inside,' Gaunt calls, beckoning with two hooked fingers. 'Is it still raining?'

'Sir,' says Caffran non-committally as he approaches the table.

'I want you to locate Corbec for me. I think he's touring the west picket.'

'Sir.'

'You've got that?'

'Find Colonel Corbec, sir.'

Gaunt nods. He picks up his stylus and folds one of the flimsies in half, ready to write on the back of it. 'Tell him to ready up three squads and meet me by the north post in thirty minutes. You need me to write that down for you?'

'No, sir.'

'Three squads, north post, thirty minutes,' says Gaunt. He writes it down anyway, and then embosses it with his biometric signet ring to transfer his authority code. He hands the note to the trooper. 'Thirty minutes,' he repeats. 'Time for me to get some breakfast. Is the mess tent still cooking?'

'Sir,' Caffran replies, this time flavouring it with a tiny, sullen shrug.

Gaunt looks him in the eye for a moment. Caffran manages to return about a second of insolent resentment, and then looks away into space over Gaunt's shoulder.

'What was her name?' Gaunt asks.

'What?'

'I took something from every single Tanith man,' says Gaunt, pushing back his chair and standing up. 'Apart from the obvious, of course. I was wondering what I'd taken from you in particular. What was her name?'

'How do you–'

'A man as young as you, it's bound to be a girl. And that tattoo indicates a family betrothal.'

'You know about Tanith marks?' Caffran can't hide his surprise.

'I studied up, trooper. I wanted to know what sort of men my reputation was going to depend upon.'

There is a pause. Rain beats against the outer skin of the tent like drumming fingertips.

'Laria,' Caffran says quietly. 'Her name was Laria.'

'I'm sorry for your loss,' says Gaunt.

Caffran looks at him again. He sneers slightly. 'Aren't you going to tell me it will be all right? Aren't you going to assure me that I'll find another girl somewhere?'

'If it makes you feel better,' says Gaunt. He sighs and turns back to look at Caffran. 'It's unlikely, but I'll say it if it makes you feel better.' Gaunt puts on a fake, jaunty smile. 'Somewhere, somehow, in one of the warzones we march into, you'll find the girl you're supposed to be with, and you'll live happily ever after. There. Better?'

Caffran's mouth tightens and he mutters something under his breath.

'If you're going to call me a bastard, do it out loud,' says Gaunt. 'I don't know why you're so pissed off. You were walking out on this Laria anyway.'

'We were betrothed!'

'You'd signed up for the Imperial Guard, trooper. First Founding. You were never going to see Tanith again. I don't know why you had the nerve to get hitched to the poor cow in the first place.'

'Of course I was coming back to her–'

'You sign up, you leave. Warp transfers, long rotations, tours along the rim. You never go back. You never go home, not once the Guard has you. Years go by, decades. You forget where you came from in the end.'

'But the recruiting officer said–'

'He lied to you, trooper. Do you think any bastard would sign up if the recruiters told the truth?'

Caffran sags. 'He lied?'

'Yes. But I won't. That's the one thing you can count on with me. Now go and get Corbec.'

Caffran snaps off a poor salute, turns and heads out of the tent.

Gaunt sits down again. He begins to collect up the flimsies, and packs away the bolter shell cartons holding them down. He thinks about the letter in his pocket again.

On his list, he writes:

Appoint a new adjutant.

Under that, he writes:

Find a new adjutant.

Finally, under that, he writes:

Start telling a few lies?

He pulls his storm coat on as he leaves the tent, partly to fend off the rain, and partly to cover his jacket. It's his number one staff-issue field jacket, but it's become too soiled with clay from the trek out of Voltis City to wear with any dignity. He has a grubby, old number two issue that he keeps in his kit as a spare, but it still has Hyrkan patches on the collar, the shoulders and the cuffs, and that's embarrassing. Sym would have patched the skull-and-crossed-knives of the Tanith onto it by now. He'd have got out his sewing kit and made sure both of Gaunt's field uniforms were code perfect, the way he kept the rest of Gaunt's day-to-day life neat and sewn up tight.

Steamy smoke is rising from the cowled chimneys of the cook-tents, and he can smell the greasy blocks of processed nutrition fibre being fried. His stomach rumbles. He sets off towards the kitchens. Beyond the row of mess tents lies the canvas city of the Tanith position, and to the north-east of that, the batteries of the Ketzok.

Beyond that, the edge of the skyline flicks on and off with the unnervingly quiet lightning, far away, like a malfunctioning lamp filament that refuses to stay lit.

Slab is pretty gruesome stuff. Pressure-treated down from any and all available nutritional sources by the Munitorum, it has no discernible flavour apart from a faint, mucusy aftertaste, and it looks like grey-white putty. In fact, years before at Schola Progenium on Ignatius Cardinal, an acquaintance of Gaunt's had once kneaded some of it into a form that authentically resembled a brick of plastic explosive, complete with fuses, and then carried out a practical joke on the Master of the Scholam Arsenal that was notable for both the magnificent extent of the disruption it caused, and the stunning severity of the subsequent punishment. Slab, as it's known to every common Guard lasman, comes canned and it comes freeze-dried, it comes in packets and it comes in boxes, it comes in individual heated tins and it comes in catering blocks. Company cooks slice, dice and mince it, and use it as the bulk base of any meal when local provision sources are unavailable. They flavour it with whatever they have to hand, usually foil sachets of powder with names like *groxtail* and *vegetable (root)* and *sausage (assorted)*. Ibram Gaunt has lived on it for a great deal of his adult and sub-adult life. He is so used to the stuff, he actually misses it when it isn't around.

Men have gathered around the cook tents, huddled against the weather under their camo-cloaks. Gaunt still hasn't got used to wearing his, even though he'd promised the Tanith colonel he would, as a show of unity. It doesn't hang right around him, and in the Voltemand wind, it tugs and tangles like a devil.

The Tanith don't seem to have the same trouble. They half-watch him approach, shrouded, hooded, some supping from mess cans. They watch him approach. There is a shadow in their eyes. They are a wild lot. Beads of rainwater glint in their tangled dark hair, though occasionally the glints are studs or nose rings, piercings in lips or eyebrows. They like their ink, the Tanith, and they wear the complex, traditional patterns of blue and green on their pale skins with pride. Cheeks, throats, forearms and the backs of hands display spirals and loops, leaves and branches, sigils and whorls. They also like their edges. The Tanith weapon is a long knife with a straight, silver blade that has evolved from a hunting tool. They could hunt with it well enough, silently, like phantoms.

Gaunt's Ghosts. Someone had come up with that within a few days of their first deployment on Blackshard. It had been the sociopath with the long-las, as Gaunt recalled it, a man known to him as 'Mad'. A more withering and scornful nickname, Gaunt can't imagine.

Rawne says, 'Here comes the fether now.'

He takes a sip from his water bottle, which does not contain water, and turns as if to say something to Murt Feygor.

'But I paid you that back!' Feygor exclaims, managing to make his voice sound wounded and plaintive, the wronged party.

Rawne makes a retort and steps back, in time to affect a blind collision with Gaunt as he makes his way into the cook tent. The impact is hard enough to rock Gaunt off his feet.

'Easy there, sir!' cries Varl, hooking a hand under Gaunt's armpit to keep him off the ground. He hoists Gaunt up.

'Thank you,' Gaunt says.

'Varl, sir,' replies the trooper. He grins a big, shit-eating grin. 'Infantryman first class Ceglan Varl, sir. Wouldn't want you taking a tumble now, would I, sir? Wouldn't want you to go falling over and getting yourself all dirty.'

'I'm sure you wouldn't, trooper,' says Gaunt. 'Carry on.'

He looks back at Rawne and Feygor.

'That was all me, sir,' says Feygor, hands up. 'The major and I were having a little dispute, and I distracted him.'

It sounds convincing. Gaunt doesn't know much about the trooper called Feygor, but he's met his type before, a conniving son of a bitch who has been blessed with the silken vocal talent to sell any story to anyone.

Gaunt doesn't even bother looking at him. He stares at Rawne.

Major Rawne stares right back. His handsome face betrays no emotion whatsoever. Gaunt is a tall man, but Rawne is one of the

Tanith he doesn't tower over, and he only has a few pounds on the major.

'I know what you're thinking,' Rawne says.

'Do you, Rawne? Is that an admission of unholy gifts? Should I call for emissaries of the Ordos to examine you?'

'Ha ha,' says Rawne in a laugh-less voice. He just says the sounds. 'Look, that there was a genuine slip, sir. A genuine bump. But we have a little history, sir, you and I, so you're bound to ascribe more motive to it than that.'

A little history. In the Blackshard deadzones, Rawne had used the opportunity of a quiet moment alone with Gaunt to express his dissatisfaction with Gaunt's leadership in the strongest possible terms. Gaunt had disarmed him and carried Rawne's unconscious body clear of the fighting area. It's hard to say what part of that *history* yanks Rawne most: the fact that he had failed to murder Gaunt, or the fact that Gaunt had saved him.

'Wow,' says Gaunt.

'What?'

'You used the word *ascribe*,' says Gaunt, and turns to go into the cook tent. Over his shoulder, he calls out, 'If you say it was a bump, then it was a bump, major. We need to trust each other.'

Gaunt turns and looks back.

'Starting in about twenty minutes. After breakfast, I'm going to take an advance out to get a look at Kosdorf. You'll be in charge.'

They watch him pick up a mess tin from the pile and head towards the slab vat where the cook is waiting with a ladle and an apologetic expression.

He sits down with his tin at one of the mess benches. The slab seems to have been refried and then stewed along with something that was either string or mechanically recovered gristle.

'I don't know how you can eat that.'

Gaunt looks up. It's the boy, the civilian boy. The boy sits down facing him.

'Sit down, if you like,' Gaunt says.

Milo looks pinched with cold, and he has his arms wrapped around his body.

'That stuff,' he says, jutting his chin suspiciously in the direction of Gaunt's tin. 'It's not proper food. I thought Imperial Guardsmen were supposed to get proper food. I thought that was the Compact of Service between the Munitorum and the Guardsmen: three square meals a day.'

'This is proper food.'

The boy shakes his head. He is only about seventeen, but he's going to be big when he fills out. There's a blue fish inked over his right eye.

'It's not proper food,' he insists.

'Well, you're not a proper Guardsman, so you're not entitled to a proper opinion.'

The boy looks hurt. Gaunt doesn't want to be mean. He owes Brin Milo a great deal. Two people had gone beyond the call to help Ibram Gaunt get off Tanith alive. Sym had been one, and the man had died making the effort. Milo had been the other. The boy was just a servant, a piper appointed by the Elector of Tanith Magna to wait on Gaunt during his stay. Gaunt understands why the boy has stuck with the regiment since the Tanith disaster. The regiment is all Milo has left, all he has left of his people, and he feels he has nowhere else to go, but Gaunt wishes Milo would disappear. There are camps and shelters, there are Munitorum refugee programmes. Civilians didn't belong at the frontline. They remind troopers of what they've left behind or, in the Tanith case, lost forever. They erode morale. Gaunt has suggested several times that Milo might be better off at a camp at Voltis City. He even has enough pull left to get Milo sent to a Schola Progenium or an orphanage for the officer class.

Milo refuses to leave. It's as if he's waiting for something to happen, for someone to arrive or something to be revealed. It's as if he's waiting for Gaunt to make good on a promise.

'Did you want something?' Gaunt asks.

'I want to come.'

'Come where?'

'You're going to scout the approach to Kosdorf this morning. I want to come.'

Gaunt feels a little flush of anger. 'Rawne tell you that?'

'No one told me.'

'Caffran, then. Damn, I thought Caffran might be trustworthy.'

'No one told me,' says Milo. 'I mean it. I just had a feeling, a feeling you'd go out this morning. This whole taskforce was sent to clear Kosdorf, wasn't it?'

'This whole taskforce was intended to be an instrument of petty and spiteful vengeance,' Gaunt replies.

'By whom?' asks Milo.

Gaunt finishes the last of his slab. He drops the fork into the empty tin. Not the best he'd ever had. Throne knows, not the worst, either.

'That general,' Gaunt says.

'General Sturm?'

'That's the one,' Gaunt nods. 'General Noches Sturm of the 50th Volpone. He was trying to use the Tanith First, and we made him look like a prize scrotum by taking Voltis when his oh-so-mighty Bluebloods couldn't manage the trick. Throne, he even let us ship back to the transport fleet before deciding we should stay another month or so to help clean up. He's done it all to inconvenience us. Pack, unpack. Ship to orbit, return to surface. March out into the backwaters of a defeated world to check the ruins of a dead city.'

'Make you eat crap instead of fresh rations?' asks Milo, looking at the mess tin.

'That too, probably,' says Gaunt.

'Probably shouldn't have pissed him off, then,' says Milo.

'I really probably shouldn't,' Gaunt agrees. 'Never mind, I heard he's getting retasked. If the Emperor shows me any providence, I'll never have to see Sturm again.'

'He'll get his just desserts,' says Milo.

'What does that mean?' asks Gaunt.

Milo shrugs. 'I dunno. It just feels that way to me. People get what they deserve, sooner or later. The universe always gets payback. One day, somebody will stick it to Sturm just like he's sticking it to you.'

'Well, that thought's cheered me up,' says Gaunt, 'except the part about getting what you deserve. What does the universe have in store for me, do you suppose, after what happened to Tanith?'

'You only need to worry about that if you think you did anything wrong,' says Milo. 'If your conscience is clear, the universe will know.'

'You talk to it much?'

'What?'

'The universe? You're on first name terms?'

Milo pulls a face.

'Things could be worse, anyway,' Milo says.

'How?'

'Well, you're in charge. You're in charge of this whole task force.'

'For my sins.'

Gaunt gets to his feet. A Munitorum skivvy comes by and collects his tin.

'So?' asks Milo. 'Can I come?'

'No,' says Gaunt.

He's walked a few yards from the mess tents when Milo calls out after him. With a resigned weariness, Gaunt turns back to look at the boy.

'What?' he asks. 'I said no.'

'Take your cape,' says Milo.

'What?'

'Take your cape with you.'

'Why?'

Milo looks startled for a moment, as if he doesn't want to give the answer, or it hadn't occurred to him that anyone would need one. He dithers for a second, and seems to be making something up.

'Because Colonel Corbec likes it when you wear it,' he says. 'He thinks it shows respect.'

Gaunt nods. Good enough.

The advance is waiting for him at the north post, the end marker of the camp area. There are two batteries of Ketzok Hydras there, barrels elevated at a murky sky that occasionally blinks with silent light. Gunners sit dripping under oilskin coats on the lee side of their gun-carriages. Tracks are sunk deep in oozing grey clay. Rain hisses.

'Nice day for it,' says Colm Corbec.

'I arranged the weather especially, colonel,' replies Gaunt as he walks up. The clay is wretchedly sticky underfoot. It sucks at their boots. The men in the three squads look entirely underwhelmed at the prospect of the morning's mission. The only ones amongst them who aren't standing slope-shouldered and dejected are the three scout specialists that Corbec has chosen to round out the advance. One is the leader of the scout unit, Mkoll. Gaunt has already begun to admire Mkoll's abilities, but he has no read on the man himself. Mkoll is sort of nondescript, of medium build and modest appearance, and seems a little weatherbeaten and older than the rank and file. He chooses to say very little.

Gaunt hasn't yet learned the names of the two scouts with Mkoll. One, he believes, he has overheard someone refer to as 'lucky'. The other one, the taller, thinner one, has a silent, faraway look about him that's oddly menacing.

'It may just have been me,' says Corbec, 'but didn't we spend an hour or so in the tent this morning agreeing not to do this?'

Gaunt nods.

'I thought,' says Corbec, 'we were to stay put until the Ketzok had been resupplied?'

They were. The purpose of the expedition is to evaluate and secure Kosdorf, Voltemand's second city, which had been effectively taken out in the early stages of the liberation. Orbit watch reports it as ruined, a city grave, but the emergency government and the Administratum want it locked down. The whole thing is a colossal waste of time. Voltis City, which had been the stronghold for the charismatic but now dead Archenemy demagogue Chanthar, was the key to Voltemand. The Kosdorf securement is the sort of mission that could have been handled by PDF or a third-tier Guard strength.

General Sturm is playing games, of course, getting his own back, and doing it in such a way as to make it look like he is being magnanimous. As his last act before passing control of the Voltemand theatre to a successor, Sturm appointed Gaunt to lead the expedition to Kosdorf, a command of twenty thousand men including his own Tanith, a regiment of Litus Battlefield Regimental Units, and a decent support spread of Ketzok armour.

Everyone, including the Litus and the Ketzok, have seen it for what it is, so they've started making heavy going of it, dragging their heels. At this last encampment, supposedly the final staging point before a proper run into Kosdorf, the Ketzok have complained that their ammo trains have fallen behind, and demanded a delay of thirty-six hours until they can be sure of their supplies.

The Ketzok are a decent lot. Despite a bad incident during the Voltis attack, Gaunt has developed a good working relationship with the armoured brigade, but Sturm's edict has taken the warmth out of it. The Ketzok aren't being difficult with him, they're being difficult with the situation.

'The Ketzok can stay put,' says Gaunt. 'There's no harm getting some exercise though, is there?'

'I suppose not,' Corbec agrees.

'In this muck?' someone in the ranks calls out from behind him.

'That's enough, Larks,' Corbec says without turning. Corbec is a big fellow, tall and broad, and heavy. He raises a large hand, scoops the heavy crop of slightly greying hair out of his face, and flops it over his scalp before tying it back. Raindrops twinkle like diamonds in his beard. Despite the bullying wind, Gaunt can smell a faint odour of cigars on him.

Gaunt wonders how he's going to begin to enforce uniform code when the company colonel looks like a matted and tangled old man of the woods.

'This is just going to be a visit to size the place up,' says Gaunt, looking at Mkoll. 'I intend for us to be back before nightfall.'

Mkoll just nods.

'So what you're saying is you were getting a little bored sitting in your tent,' says Corbec.

Gaunt looks at him.

'That's all right,' Corbec smiles. 'I was getting pretty bored sitting in mine. A walk is nice, isn't it, lads?'

No one actually answers.

Gaunt walks the line with Corbec at his side, inspecting munition supplies. They're going to be moving light, but every other man's got an extra musette bag of clips, and two troopers are carrying boxes of RPGs for the launcher. Nobody makes eye contact with Gaunt as he passes.

Gaunt comes to Caffran in the line.

'What are you doing here?' Gaunt asks.

'Step forward, trooper,' says Corbec.

'I thought I was supposed to stay with you all day,' Caffran replies, stepping forward. 'I thought those were my orders.'

'Sir,' says Corbec.

'Sir,' says Caffran.

'I suppose they are,' says Gaunt and nods Caffran back into the file. *A march in the mud and rain is the least you deserve for talking out of turn,* Gaunt thinks, *especially to a civilian.*

There's a muttering somewhere. They're amused by Caffran's insolence. Gaunt gets the feeling that Corbec doesn't like it, though Corbec does little to show it. The colonel's position is difficult. If he reinforces Gaunt's authority, he risks losing all the respect the men have for him. He risks being despised and resented too.

'Let's get moving,' says Gaunt.

'Advance company!' Corbec shouts, holding one hand above his head and rotating it with the index finger upright. 'Sergeant Blane, if you please!'

'Yes, sir!' Blane calls out from the front of the formation. He leads off.

The force begins to move down the track into the rain behind the sergeant. Mkoll and his scouts, moving at a more energetic pace, take point and begin to pull away.

Gaunt waits as the infantrymen file past, their boots glopping in the mire. Not one of them so much as glances at him. They have their heads down.

He jogs to catch up with Corbec. He had hoped that getting out and doing something active might chase away his unhappiness. It isn't working so far.

He still has that letter in his pocket.

'Back again?' asks Dorden, the medicae.

The boy hovers in the doorway of the medical tent like a spectre that needs to be invited in out of the dark. The rain has picked up, and it's pattering a loud tattoo off the overhead sheets.

'I don't feel right,' says Milo.

Dorden tilts his chair back to upright and takes his feet down off the side of a cot. He folds over the corner of a page to mark his place, and sets his book aside.

'Come in, Milo,' he says.

In the back of the long tent behind Dorden, the medicae orderlies are at work checking supplies and cleaning instruments. The morning has brought the usual round of complaints generated by an army on the move: foot problems, gum problems, and gut problems, along with longer term conditions like venereal infections and wounds healing after the Voltis fight. The orderlies are chattering back and forth. Chayker and Foskin are play-fencing with forceps as they gather up instruments for cleaning. Lesp, the other orderly, is bantering with them as he prepares his needles. He's got a sideline as the company inksman. His work is generally held as the best. The ink stains his fingertips permanent blue-black, the dirtiest-looking fingers Dorden's ever seen on a medical orderly.

'How don't you feel right?' Dorden asks as Milo comes in. The boy pulls the tent flap shut behind him and shrugs.

'I just don't,' he says. 'I feel light-headed.'

'Light-headed? Faint, you mean?'

'Things seem familiar. Do you know what I mean?'

Dorden shakes his head gently, frowning.

'Like I'm seeing things again for the first time,' says the boy.

Dorden points to a folding stool, which Milo sits down on obediently, and reaches for his pressure cuff.

'You realise this is the third day you've come in here saying you don't feel right?' asks Dorden.

Milo nods.

'You know what I think it is?' asks Dorden.

'What?'

'I think you're hungry,' says Dorden. 'I know you hate the ration stuff they cook up. I don't blame you. It's swill. But you've got to eat, Brin. That's why you're light-headed and weak.'

'It's not that,' says Milo.

'It might be. You don't like the food.'

'No, I don't like the food. I admit it. But it's not that.'

'What then?'

Milo stares at him.

'I've got this feeling. I think I had a bad dream. I've got this feeling that–'

'What?'

Milo looks at the ground.

'Listen to me,' says Dorden. 'I know you want to stay with us. This man Gaunt is letting you stay. You know he should have sent you away by now. If you get sick on him, if you get sick by refusing to eat properly, he'll have the excuse he needs. He'll be able to tell himself he's sending you away for your own good. And that'll be it.'

Milo nods.

'So let's do you a favour,' says Dorden. 'Let's go to the mess tent and get you something to eat. Humour me. Eat it. If you still feel you're not right, well, then we can have another conversation.'

The lightning leads them. The rain persists. They come up over the wet hills and see the city grave.

Kosdorf is a great expanse of ruins, most of it pale, like sugar icing. As they approach it, coming in from the south-east, the slumped and toppled hab blocks remind Gaunt more than any-thing of great, multi-tiered cakes, fancy and celebratory, that have been shoved over so that all the frosted levels have crashed down and overlapped one another, breaking and cracking, and shedding palls of dust that have become mire in the rain. A shroud of vapour hangs over the city, the foggy aftermath of destruction.

Overhead, black clouds mark the sky like ink on pale skin. Shafts of lightning, painfully bright, shoot down from the clouds into the dripping ruins, straight down, without a sound. The bars underlight the belly of the clouds, and set off brief, white flashes in amongst the ruins where they hit, like flares. Though the lightning strikes crackle with secondary sparks, like capillaries adjoining a main blood vessel, they are remarkably straight.

The regular strobing makes the daylight seem strange and imper-manent. Everything is pinched and blue, caught in a twilight.

'Why can't we hear it?' one of the men grumbles.

Gaunt has called a stop on a deep embankment so he can check his chart. Tilting, teetering building shells overhang them. Water gurgles out of them.

'Because we can't, Larks,' Corbec says.

Gaunt looks up from his chart, and sees Larkin, the marksman assigned to the advance. The famous Mad Larkin. Gaunt is still learning names to go with faces, but Larkin has stood out from early on. The man can shoot. He's also, it seems to Gaunt, one of the least stable individuals ever to pass recruitment screening. Gaunt presumes the former fact had a significant bearing on the latter.

Larkin is a skinny, unhappy-looking soul with a dragon-spiral inked onto his cheek. His long-las rifle is propped over his shoulder in its weather case.

'Altitude,' Gaunt says to him.

'Come again, sir?' Larkin replies.

Gaunt gestures up at the sky behind the bent, blackened girders of the corpse-buildings above them. Larkin looks where he's pointing, up into the rain.

'The electrical discharge is firing from cloud to cloud up there, and it can reach an intensity of four hundred thousand amps. But we can't hear the thunder, because it's so high up.'

'Oh,' says Larkin. Some of the other men murmur.

'You think I'd march anyone into a dead zone without getting a full orbital sweep first?' Gaunt asks.

Larkin looks like he's going to reply. He looks like he's about to say something he shouldn't, something his brain won't allow his mouth to police.

But he shakes his head instead and smiles.

'Is that so?' he says. 'Too high for us to hear. Well, well.'

They move off down the embankment, and then follow the seam of an old river sluice that hugs the route of a highway into the city. There's a fast stream running down the bed of the drain, dirty rainwater that's washed down through the city ruin, blackened with ash, and then is running off. It splashes and froths around their toecaps. Its babbling sounds like voices, muttering.

There's the noise of the falling rain all around, the sound of dripping. Things creak. Tiles and facings and pieces of roof and guttering hang from shredded bulks, and move as the inclination of gravity or the wind takes them. They squeak like crane hoists, like gibbets. Things fall, and flutter softly or land hard, or skitter and bounce like loose rocks in a ravine.

The scouts vanish ahead of the advance, but Mkoll reappears after half an hour, and describes the route ahead to Corbec. Gaunt stands with them, but there is subtle body language, suggesting that the report is meant for Corbec's benefit, and Gaunt is merely being allowed to listen in. If things turn bad, Mkoll is trusting Corbec to look after the best interests of the men.

'Firestorms have swept through this borough,' he says. 'There's not much of anything left. I suggest we swing east.'

Corbec nods.

'There's something here,' Mkoll adds.

'A friendly something?' Corbec asks.

Mkoll shrugs.

'Hard to say. It won't let us get a look at it. Could be civilian survivors. They would have learned to stay well out of sight.'

'I would have expected any citizens to flee the city,' says Gaunt.

Mkoll and Corbec look at him.

'Flight is not always the solution,' says Mkoll.

'Sometimes, you know, people are traumatised,' says Corbec. 'They go back to a place, even when they shouldn't. Even when it's not safe.'

Mkoll shrugs again.

'It's all I'm saying,' says Corbec.

'I haven't seen bodies,' replies Gaunt. 'When you consider the size of this place, the population it must have had. In fact, I haven't seen any bodies.'

Corbec purses his lips thoughtfully.

'True enough. That *is* curious.' Corbec looks at Mkoll for confirmation.

'I haven't seen any,' says Mkoll. 'But hungry vermin can disintegrate remains inside a week.'

They turn to the east, as per Mkoll's suggestion, and leave the comparative cover of the rockcrete drainage ditch. Buildings have sagged into each other, or fallen into the street in great splashes of rubble and ejecta. Some habs lean on their neighbours for support. All glass has been broken, and the joists and beams and roofs, robbed of tiles or slates, have been turned into dark, barred windows through which to watch the lightning.

The fire has been very great. It has scorched the paving stones of the streets and squares, and the rain has turned the ash into a black paste that sticks to everything, except the heat-transmuted metals and glass from windows and doors. These molten ingots, now solid again, have been washed clean by the rain and lie scattered like iridescent fish on the tarry ground.

Gaunt has seen towns and cities without survivors before. Before Khulan, before the Crusade even began, he'd been with the Hyrkans on Sorsarah. A town there, he forgets the name, an agri-berg, had been under attack, and the town elders had ordered the entire population to shelter in the precincts of the basilica. In doing so, they had become one target.

When Gaunt had come in with the Hyrkans, whole swathes of the town were untouched, intact, preserved, as though the inhabitants would be back at any moment.

The precincts of the basilica formed a crater half a kilometre across.

They stop to rest at the edge of a broad concourse where the wind of Voltemand, brisk and unfriendly, is absent. The rain is relentless still, but the vapour hangs here, a mist that pools around the dismal ruins and broken walls.

They are drawing closer to the grounding lightning. It leaves a bloody stink in their nostrils, like hot wire, and whenever it hits the streets and ruins nearby, it makes a soft but jarring click, part overpressure, part discharge.

An explosive device of considerable magnitude has struck the corner of the concourse and detonated, unseating all the heavy paving slabs with the rippling force of a major earthquake. Gravity has relaid the slabs after the shockwave, but they have come back down to earth misaligned and overlapping, like the scales of a lizard, rather than the seamless, edge-to-edge fit the city fathers had once commissioned.

Larkin sits down on a tumbled block, takes off one boot, and begins to massage his foot. He complains to the men around him in a loud voice. The core of his complaint seems to be the stiff and unyielding quality of the newly-issued Tanith kit.

'Foot sore?' Gaunt asks him.

'These boots don't give. We've walked too far. My toes hurt.'

'Get the medicae to treat your foot when we get back. I don't want any infections.'

Larkin grins up at him.

'I wouldn't want to make my foot worse. Maybe you should carry me.'

'You'll manage,' Gaunt tells him.

'But an infection? That sounds nasty. It can get in your blood. You can die of it.'

'You're right,' Gaunt says. 'The only way to be properly sure is to amputate the extremity before infection can spread.'

He puts his hand on the pommel of his chainsword.

'Is that what you want me to do, Larkin?'

'I'll be happy to live out me born days without that ever happening, colonel-commissar,' Larkin chuckles.

'Get your boot back on.'

Gaunt wanders over to Corbec. The colonel has produced a short, black cigar and clamped it in his mouth, though he hasn't lit it. He takes another out of his pocket and offers it to Gaunt, perhaps hoping that if Gaunt accepts it, it'll give him the latitude to break field statutes and light up. Gaunt refuses the offer.

'Is Larkin taunting me?' Gaunt asks him quietly.

Corbec shakes his head.

'He's nervous,' Corbec replies. 'Larks gets spooked very easily, so this is him dealing with that. Trust me. I've known him since we were in the Tanith Magna Militia together.'

Gaunt throws a half shrug, looking around.

'He's spooked? I'm spooked,' he says.

Corbec smiles so broadly he takes the cigar out of his mouth.

'Good to know,' he says.

'Maybe we should head back,' Gaunt says. 'Push back in tomorrow with some proper armour support.'

'Best plan you've had so far,' says Corbec, 'if I may say so.'

The Tanith scout, the tall, thin man with the menacing air, appears suddenly at the top of a ridge of rubble and signals before dropping out of sight.

'What the hell?' Gaunt begins to say. He glances around to have the signal explained by Corbec or one of the men.

He is alone on the concourse. The Tanith have vanished.

What the feth is he doing, Caffran wonders? He's just standing there. He's just standing there out in the open, when Mkvenner clearly signalled...

He hears a sound like a bundle of sticks being broken, slowly, steadily.

Not sticks, las-shots; the sound echoes around the concourse area. He sees a couple of bolts in the air like luminous birds or lost fragments of lightning.

With a sigh, Caffran launches himself from under the cover of his camo-cloak, and tackles Colonel-Commissar Gaunt to the ground. Further shots fly over them.

'What are you playing at?' Caffran snaps. They struggle to find some cover.

'Where did everyone go?' Gaunt demands, ducking lower as a zipping las-round scorches the edge of his cap.

'Into cover, you feth-wipe!' Caffran replies. 'Get your cloak over you! Come on!'

The ingrained, starch-stiff commissar inside Gaunt wants to reprimand the infantryman for his language and his disrespect, but tone of address is hardly the point in the heat of a contact. Perhaps afterwards. Perhaps a few words afterwards.

Gaunt fumbles out his camo-cloak, still folded up and rolled over the top of his belt pouch. He realises the Tanith haven't vanished at all. At the scout's signal, they have all simply dropped and concealed themselves with their cloaks. They are still all around him. They have simply become part of the landscape.

He, on the other hand, nonplussed for a second, had remained standing; the lone figure of an Imperial Guard commissar against a bleak, empty background.

The behaviour of a novice. A fool. A... what was it? *Feth-wipe*? Indeed.

Corbec looks over at him, his face framed between the gunsight of his rifle and the fringe of his cape.

'How many?' Gaunt hisses.

'Ven said seven, maybe eight,' Corbec calls back.

Gaunt pulls out his bolt pistol and racks it.

'Return fire,' he orders.

Corbec relays the order, and the advance company begins to shoot. Volleys of las-shots whip across the concourse.

The gunfire coming their way stops.

'Cease fire!' Gaunt commands.

He gets up, and scurries forwards over the rubble, keeping low. Corbec calls after him in protest, but nobody shoots at Gaunt. You didn't have to be a graduate of a fancy military academy, Corbec reflects, to appreciate that was a good sign. He sighs, gets up, and goes after Gaunt. They move forwards together, heads down.

'Look here,' says Corbec.

Two bodies lie on the rubble. They are wearing the armoured uniform of the local PDF, caked with black mud. Their cheeks are sunken, as if neither of them have eaten a decent plate of anything in a month.

'Damn,' says Gaunt, 'was that a mistaken exchange? Have we hit some friendlies? These are planetary defence force.'

'I think you're right,' says Corbec.

'I am right. Look at the insignia.'

'Poor fething bastards,' says Corbec. 'Maybe they've been holed up here for so long, they thought we were–'

'No,' says Mkoll.

Gaunt hasn't seen the scout standing there. Even Corbec seems to start slightly, though Gaunt wonders if this is for comic effect. Corbec is unfailingly cheerful.

The chief scout has manifested even more mysteriously than the Tanith had vanished a few minutes ago.

'There was a group of them,' he says, 'a patrol. Mkvenner and I had contact. We challenged them, making the same assumption you just did, that they were PDF. There was no mistake.'

'What do you mean?' asks Gaunt.

'I thought maybe they were scared,' says Mkoll, 'scared of everything. Survivors in the rubble, afraid that anything they bumped into might be the Archenemy. But this wasn't scared.'

'How do you know?' asks Gaunt.

'He knows,' says Corbec.

'I'd like him to explain,' says Gaunt.

'You know the difference between scared and crazy, sir?' Mkoll asks him.

'I think so,' says Gaunt.

'These men were crazy. There were speaking in strange tongues. They were ranting. They were using language I've never heard before, a language I never much want to hear again.'

'So you think there are Archenemy strengths here in Kosdorf, and they're using PDF arms and uniforms?'

Mkoll nods. 'I heard the tribal forces often use captured Guard kit.'

'That's true enough,' says Gaunt.

'Where did the others go?' asks Corbec, looking down at the corpses glumly.

'They ran when your first couple of volleys brought these two over,' says Mkoll.

'Let's circle up and head back,' says Corbec.

There's a sudden noise, a voice, gunfire. One of the other scouts has reappeared. He is hurrying back across the fish-scale slabs of the square towards them, firing off bursts from the hip. A rain of las-fire answers him. It cracks paving stones, pings pebbles, and spits up plumes of muck.

'Find cover!' the scout yells as he comes towards them. 'Find cover!'

They have jammed a stick into the ruins of Kosdorf, and wiggled it around until the nest underneath the city has been thoroughly disturbed.

Hostiles in PDF kit, caked in dirt, looking feral and thin, are assaulting the concourse area through the ruins of an old Ecclesiarchy temple and, to the west of that, the bones of a pauper's hospital.

They look like ghosts.

They come surging forwards, out of the dripping shadows, through the mist, into the strobing twilight. In their captured kit, they look to Gaunt like war-shocked survivors trying to defend what's left of their world.

'Fall back!' Corbec yells.

'I don't want to fight them,' Gaunt says to him as they run for better cover. 'Not if they're our own!'

'Mkoll was pretty sure they weren't!'

'He could have been wrong. These could be our people, come through hell. I don't want to fight them unless I have to.'

'I don't think they're going to give us a choice!' Corbec yells back.

The Tanith are returning fire, snapping shots from their corner of the open space. The air fills with a laced crossfire of energy bolts. The mist seems to thicken as the crossfire stirs the air. Gaunt sees a couple of the men in Kosdorfer uniforms crumple and fall.

'In the name of the Emperor, cease your firing,' he hollers out across the square. 'For Throne's sake, we serve the same master!'

The Kosdorf PDFers shout back. The words are unintelligible, hard to make out over their sustained gunfire.

'I said in the name of the Emperor, hold your fire,' Gaunt bellows. 'Hold your fire. I command you! We're here to help you!'

A PDFer comes at him from the left, running out of the shadows of the hospital ruins. The man has a hard-round rifle equipped with a sword bayonet. His eyes are swollen in their sockets, and one pupil has blown.

He tries to ram the bayonet into Gaunt's gut. The blade is rusty, but the thrust is strong and practiced. Gaunt leaps backwards.

'For the Emperor!' Gaunt yells.

The man replies with a jabbering stream of obscenity. The words are broken, and have been purloined from an alien language, and he is only able to pronounce the parts of them that fit a human mouth and voicebox. Blood leaks out of his gums and dribbles over his cracked lips.

He lunges again. The tip of the sword bayonet goes through Gaunt's storm coat and snags the hip pocket of his field jacket underneath.

Gaunt shoots the man in the face with his bolt pistol.

The corpse goes over backwards, hard. Bloody back-spatter over-paints the dirt filming Gaunt's face and clothes.

'Fire, fire! Fire at will!' Gaunt yells. He's seen enough. 'Men of Tanith, pick your targets and fire at will!'

Another PDFer charges in at him through an archway, backlit for a second by a pulse of lightning. He fires a shot from his rifle that hits the wall behind Gaunt and adds to the wet haze fuming the air. Gaunt fires back and knocks the man out of the archway, tumbling into two of his brethren.

The Tanith advance has been rotated out of line by the sudden attack, and Gaunt has been pushed to the eastern end of the formation. He has lost sight of Corbec. It is hard to issue any useful commands, because he has little proper overview on which to base command choices.

Gaunt tries to reposition himself. He hugs the shadows, keeping the crumbling pillars to his back. The firefight has lit up the entire concourse. He listens to the echoes, to the significant sound values coming off the Tanith positions. Gaunt can hear the hard clatter of full auto and, in places along the rubble line, see the jumping petals of muzzle flashes. The Tanith are eager, but inexperienced. The lasrifles they have been issued with at the Founding are good, new weapons, fresh-stamped and shipped in from forge worlds. Many of the Tanith recruits will never have had an automatic setting on a weapon before; most will have been used to single shot or even hard-round weapons. Finding themselves in a troop-fight ambush, they are unleashing maximum firepower, which is great for shock and noise but not necessarily the most effective tactic, under any circumstances.

'Corbec!' Gaunt yells. 'Colonel Corbec! Tell the men to select single f–'

He ducks back as his voice draws enemy fire. Plumes of mire and slime spurt up from the slabs he is using as cover. Impacts spit out stinging particles of stone. He tries shouting again, but the concentration of fire gets worse. The vapour billowing off the shot marks gets in his mouth and makes him retch and spit. Two or three of the PDFers have advanced on his position, and are keeping a heavy fire rate sustained. He can half see them through the veiling mist, calmly standing and taking shots at him. He can't see them well enough to get a decent shot back.

Gaunt scrambles backwards, dropping down about a metre between one rucked level of paving slabs and another, an ugly seismic fracture in the street. Loose shots are whining over his head, smacking into the plaster facade of a reclining guild house and covering it with black pockmarks. He clambers in through a staring window.

A Tanith trooper inside switches aim at him and nearly shoots him.

'Sacred Feth. Sorry, sir!' the trooper exclaims.

Gaunt shakes his head.

'I snuck up on you,' he replies.

There are four Tanith men in the ground floor of the guild house. They are using the buckled window apertures to lay fire across the concourse from the east. They'd been on the eastern end of the advance force when it turned unexpectedly, and thus have been effectively cut off. Gaunt can't chastise them. Oddities of terrain and the dynamic flow of a combat situation do that sometimes. Sometimes you just get stuck in a tight corner.

For similar reasons, he's got stuck there with them.

'What's your name?' he asks the man who'd almost shot him, even though he knows it perfectly well.

'Domor,' the man replies.

'I don't think we want to spend too much more time in here, do we, Domor?' Gaunt says. Enemy fire is pattering off the outside walls with increasing fury. It is causing the building to vibrate, and spills of earth, like sand in a time-glass, are sifting down from the bulging roof. There's a stink of sewage, of broken drains. If enemy fire doesn't finish them, it will finish the building, which will die on their heads.

'I'd certainly like to get out of here if I can, sir,' Domor replies. He has a sharp, intelligent face, with quick eyes that suggest wit and honesty.

'Well, we'll see what we can do,' Gaunt says.

One of the other men groans suddenly.

'What's up, Piet?' Domor calls. 'You hit?'

The trooper is down at one of the windows, pinking rounds off into the concourse outside.

'I'm fine,' he answers, 'but do you hear that?'

Gaunt and Domor clamber up to the sill alongside him. For a moment, Gaunt can't hear anything except the snap and whine of las-fire, and the brittle rattle of masonry debris falling from the roof above.

Then he hears it, a deeper noise, a throaty rasp.

'Someone's got a burner,' says the trooper in a depressed tone. 'Someone out there's got a burner.'

Domor looks at Gaunt.

'Gutes is right, isn't he?' he asks. 'That's a flamer, isn't it? That's the noise a flamer makes?'

Gaunt nods.

'Yes,' he says.

None of the Munitorum skivvies has the nerve to argue when Feygor helps himself to one of the full pots of caffeine on the mess tent stove.

Feygor carries the pot over to where Rawne is sitting at a mess table with the usual repeat offenders. Meryn, young and eager to impress, has brought a tray of tin cups. Brostin is smoking a lho-stick and flicking his brass igniter open and shut. Raess is cleaning his scope. Caober is putting an edge on his blade. Costin has produced his flask, and is pouring a jigger of sacra into each mug 'to keep the rain out'.

Feygor dishes out the brew from the pot.

'Come on, then,' says Rawne.

Varl grins, and slides the letter out of his inside pocket. He holds it gently by the bottom corners and sniffs it, as though it is a perfumed billet-doux. Then he licks the tip of his right index finger to lift the envelope's flap.

He starts to read to himself.

'Oh my!' he says.

'What?' asks Meryn.

'Listen to this... *My darling Ibram, how I long for your strong, manly touch...*' Varl begins, as if reading aloud.

'Don't be a feth-head, Varl,' warns Rawne. 'What does it actually say?'

'It's from somebody called Blenner,' says Varl, scanning the sheet. 'It goes on a bit. Umm, I think they knew each other years back. And from the date on this, he's been carrying it around for a while. This Blenner says he's writing because he can't believe that Gaunt got passed over after "all he did at Balhaut". He's asking Gaunt if he chose to go with "that bunch of no-hope backwoodsmen", which I think would be us.'

'It would,' says Rawne.

Varl sniffs. 'Anyway, this charming fellow Blenner says he can't believe Gaunt would have taken the field promotion willingly. Listen to this, he says, "what was Slaydo thinking? Surely the Old Man had made provision for you to be part of the command structure that succeeded him. Throne's sake, Ibram! You know he was grooming! How did you let this slight happen to you? Slaydo's legacy would have protected you for years if you'd let it".'

Varl looks up at the Tanith men around the table. 'Wasn't Slaydo the name of the Warmaster?' he asks. 'The big honking bastard commander?'

'Yup,' says Feygor.

'Well, this can't mean the same Slaydo, can it?' asks Costin.

'Of course it can't,' says Caober. 'It must be another Slaydo.'

'Well, of course,' says Varl, 'because otherwise it would mean that the feth-wipe commanding us is a more important feth-wipe than we ever imagined.'

'It doesn't mean that,' says Rawne. 'Costin's right. It's a different Slaydo, or this Blenner doesn't know what he's talking about. Go on. What else is there?'

Varl works down the sheet.

'Blenner finishes by saying that he's stationed on Hisk with a regiment called the Greygorians. He says he's got pull with a Lord General called Cybon, and that Cybon's promised him, that is Gaunt, a staff position. Blenner begs Gaunt to reconsider his "ill-advised" move and get reassigned.'

'That's it?' asks Rawne.

Varl nods.

'So he's thinking about ditching us,' murmurs Rawne.

'This letter's old, mind you,' says Varl.

'But he kept it,' says Feygor. 'It matters to him.'

'Murt's right,' says Rawne. 'This means his heart's not in it. We can exert a little pressure, and get rid of this fether without any of us having to face a firing squad.'

'Having fun?'

They all turn. Dorden is standing nearby, watching them. The boy Milo is behind him, looking pale and nervous.

'We're fine, Doc,' says Feygor. 'How are you?'

'Looks for all the world like a meeting of plotters,' says Dorden. He takes a step forwards and comes in amongst them. He's twice as old as any of them, like their grandfather. He's no fighter either. Every one of them is a young man, strong enough to break him and kill him with ease. He pours himself a mug of caffeine from their tray.

Costin makes a hasty but abortive attempt to stop him.

'There's a little–' Costin begins, in alarm.

'Sacra in it?' asks Dorden, sipping. 'I should hope so, cold day like this.'

He looks across at Varl.

'What's that you've got, Varl?'

'A letter, Doc.'

'Does it belong to you?'

'Uh, not completely.'

'Did you borrow it?'

'It fell out of someone's pocket, Doc.'

'Do you think it had better fall back in?' asks Dorden.

'I think that would be a good idea,' says Varl.

'We were just having a conversation, doctor,' says Rawne. 'No plots, no conspiracies.'

'I believe you,' Dorden replies. 'Just like I believe that no lies would ever, ever come out of your mouth, major.'

'With respect, doctor,' says Rawne, 'I'm having a private conversation with some good comrades, and the substance of it is of no consequence to you.'

Dorden nods.

'Of course, major,' he replies. 'Just as I'm here to find a plate of food for this boy and minding my own business.'

He turns to talk to the cooks about finding something other than slab in the ration crates.

Then he looks back at Rawne.

'Consider this, though. They say it's always best to know your enemy. If you succeed in ousting Colonel-Commissar Gaunt, who might you be making room for?'

'Where's the chief?' Corbec asks, ducking in.

'Frankly, I've been too busy to keep tabs on that gigantic fether,' Larkin replies.

'Oh, Larks,' murmurs Corbec over the drumming of infantry

weapons, 'that lip of yours is going to get you dead before too long unless you curb it. Disrespecting a superior, it's called.'

Larkin sneers at his old friend.

'Right,' he says. 'You'd write me up.'

He is adjusting the replacement barrel of his long-las, hunkered down behind the cyclopean plinth of a heap of rubble that had once been a piece of civic statuary.

'Of course I would,' says Corbec. 'I'd have to.'

Corbec has got down on one knee on the other side of a narrow gap between the plinth and a retaining wall that is leaning at a forty-five degree angle. Solid-round fire from the enemy is travelling up the gap between them, channelled by the actual physical shape, like steel pinballs coursing along a chute. The shots scrape and squeal as they whistle past.

Corbec clacks in a fresh clip and leans out gingerly to snap some discouraging las-rounds back up the gap.

'Why?' Larkin asks. 'Why would you have to?'

Larkin laughs, mirthlessly. Corbec can almost smell the rank adrenaline sweat coming out of the wiry marksman's pores. The stress of a combat situation has pushed Larkin towards his own, personal edge, and he is barely in control.

'Because I'm the fething colonel, and I can't have you badmouthing the company commander,' Corbec replies.

'Yeah, but you're not really, are you?' says Larkin. 'I mean, you're not really my superior, are you?'

'What?'

'Gaunt just picked you and Rawne. It was random. It doesn't mean anything. There's no point you carrying on like there's suddenly any difference between us.'

Corbec gazes across at Larkin, watching him screw the barrel in, nattering away, stray rounds tumbling past them like seed cases in a gale.

'I mean, it's not like your shit suddenly smells better than mine, is it?' says Larkin. He looks up at last and sees Corbec's face.

'What?' he asks. 'What's the matter with you?'

Corbec glares at him.

'I am the colonel, Larks,' he snarls. 'That's the point. I'm not your friend any more. This is either real or there's no point to it at all.'

Larkin just looks at him.

'Oh, for feth's sake!' says Corbec. 'Stop looking at me with those stupid hang-dog eyes! Hold this position. That's an order, trooper! Mkoll!'

The chief scout comes scurrying over from the other corner of the plinth, head down. He drops in behind Larkin and looks across the gap at Corbec.

'Sergeant Blane's got the top end of the line firm. I'm going back down that way,' Corbec says, jerking a thumb over his shoulder. 'We seem to have lost Gaunt.'

'It's tragic,' says Larkin.

'Keep this section in place,' Corbec continues.

Mkoll nods. Corbec sets off.

'What's got into him?' Larkin mutters.

'Probably something you said,' says Mkoll.

'I don't say anything we're not all thinking,' Larkin replies.

Outside, the flamer makes its sucking roar again.

All four of the Tanith men with Gaunt express their unhappiness in strong terms. Gutes and Domor are cursing.

'We're done for,' says another of them, a man called Guheen.

'They'll just torch us out like larisel in a burrow,' says the fourth.

'Maybe–' Gaunt begins.

'No maybe about it!' Gutes spits.

'No, I was trying to say, maybe this gives us a chance we didn't have before,' Gaunt tells them.

He ducks down beside Gutes again, and peers out into the mist and rain, craning for a better view. There is still no sign of the flamer, but he can certainly hear it clearly now, retching like some volcanic hog clearing its throat. He can smell promethium smoke too, the soot-black stench of Imperial cleansing.

He looks up at the ominously low ceiling bellying down at them.

'What's upstairs?' he asks.

'Another floor,' says Guheen.

'Presuming it's not all crushed in on itself,' adds Domor.

'Yes, presuming it's not,' Gaunt agrees. 'Which of you is the best shot?'

'He is,' Domor says, pointing to the fourth man. Guheen and Gutes both nod assent.

'Merrt, isn't it?' Gaunt asks. The fourth man nods.

'Merrt, you're with me. You three, sustained fire pattern here, through these windows. Just keep it steady.'

Gaunt clambers over the scree of rubble and broken furniture to the back of the chamber. A great deal of debris has poured down what had once been the staircase, blocking it. Wires and cabling hang from ruptured ceiling panels like intestinal loops. Water drips. Broken glass flickers when the lightning scores the sky outside.

Merrt comes up behind Gaunt and touches his arm. He points to the remains of a heat exchanger vent that is crushed into the rear wall of the guild house like a metal plug. They put their shoulders against it and manage to push it out of its setting.

Light shines in. The hole, now more of a slot thanks to the deformation of the building, looks directly out on to rubble at eye level. They hoist themselves up and out, on to the smashed residue of a neighbouring building that has been annihilated, and has flooded its remains down and around the guild house, packing in around its slumped form like a lava flow sweeping an object up.

Gaunt and Merrt pick their way up the slope, and re-enter the guild house through a first-floor window. The floor is sagging and insecure. A few fibres of waterlogged carpet seem to be all that's holding the joists in place.

'You're a decent shot, then?' Gaunt murmurs.

'Not bad.'

'Pull this off, I'll recommend you for a marksman lanyard.'

Merrt grins and flashes his eyebrows.

'Should've got one anyway,' he says. 'The last one went to Larkin. After his psyche evaluation, marksman status was the only special dispensation Corbec could pull to get his old mate a place in the company.'

'Is that true?' Gaunt asks.

'You ought to know. I thought you were in charge?'

Gaunt stares at him.

'I'm really looking forward to meeting a Tanith who isn't insolent or cocksure,' says Gaunt.

'Good luck with that,' says Merrt.

Gaunt shakes his head.

'I've got a smart mouth, I know,' says Merrt. 'I said a few things about Larkin getting my lanyard, earned some dark looks from the Munitorum chiefs. My mouth'll get me in trouble, one day, I reckon.'

'I think you're already in trouble,' says Gaunt. He gestures out of the window. 'I think this qualifies.'

'Feels like it.'

'So you reckon you're good?'

'Better than Larkin,' says Merrt.

They settle in by the window. The mist shrouding the concourse and the surrounding ruins has grown thicker, as though the discharge of weapons has caused some chemical reaction, and it's disguising the enemy approach.

Below, about fifteen metres shy of them, they can see the blasts of the approaching flamer, like a sun behind cloud.

'Nasty weapon, the flamer,' says Gaunt.

'I can well imagine.'

'Then again, it is essentially a can or two of extremely flammable material.'

'You going to be my shot caller?' Merrt asks.

'We have to let it get a little closer,' says Gaunt. 'You see where it burps like that?'

Another gout of amber radiance backlights the fog in the square below.

Merrt nods, raising the lasrifle to his shoulder.

'Watch which way the glow moves. It's moving out from the flamer broom.'

'Got it.'

'So the point of origin is going to be behind it, and the tank or tanks another, what, half a metre behind that?'

The flamer roars again. A long, curling rush of fire, like the leaf of a giant fern, emerges from the mist and brushes the front of the guild house. Gaunt hears Domor curse loudly.

'He's widened the aperture,' Gaunt tells Merrt. 'He's seen buildings ahead, and he's put a bit of reach on the flame, so he can scour the ruins out.'

Merrt grunts.

'We've got to do this if we're going to,' says Gaunt.

There is another popping cough and then another roar. This time, the curling arc of fire comes up high, like the jet of a pressurised hose.

Gaunt grabs Merrt, and pulls him back as the fire blisters the first-storey windows. It spills in through the window spaces, roasting the frames and sizzling the wet black filth, and plays in across the ceiling like a catch of golden fish, coiling and squirming in a mass, landed on the deck of a boat.

The flames suck out again, leaving the windows scorched around their upper frames and the ceiling blackened above the windows. All the air seems to have gone out of the room. Gaunt and Merrt gasp as if they too have just been landed out of a sea net.

Gaunt recovers the lasrifle and checks it for damage. Merrt picks himself up.

'Come on!' Gaunt hisses.

As Merrt settles into position again, Gaunt peers down into the swirl.

'There! There!' he cries, as the flames jet through the mist and rain again.

Merrt fires.

Nothing happens.

'Feth!' Merrt whispers.

'When the flame lights up, aim closer to the source,' Gaunt says.

The flamer gusts again, ripping fire at the front of the guild house. Merrt fires again.

The tanks go up with a pressurised squeal. A huge doughnut of fire rips through the mist, rolling and coiling, yellow-hot and furious. Several broken metal objects soar into the air on streamers of flame, shrieking like parts of an exploding kettle.

Gaunt raises his head cautiously and looks down. He can see burning figures stumbling around in the fog, PDF troopers caught in the blast. They sizzle loudly in the rain.

'Let's get out of here,' he says to Merrt.

Gaunt calls to the three Tanith men below, and all five leave the guild house together and work their way back along the edge of the concourse to the advance main force, skirting the open spaces.

'I've been looking for you,' says Corbec matter-of-factly when Gaunt appears.

'Not hard enough, I'd say,' Gaunt replies.

Corbec tuts, half entertained.

'You set something off over there?' he asks.

'Just a little parlour trick to keep them occupied while we got out of their way.'

'"A little parlour trick"...' Corbec chuckles. 'You're a very amusing man, you know that?'

'Wait till you get to know me,' says Gaunt.

Corbec looks at him sadly and says nothing.

'What shape are we in, colonel?' Gaunt asks.

'Fair,' Corbec replies.

'No losses so far?'

'Couple of scratches. But look, their numbers are increasing all the time. Another hour or so, we could start losing friends fast.'

'Can we vox in for support?'

'The vox is still dead as dead,' says Corbec.

'Recommendation?'

'We pull back before the situation becomes untenable. Then we rustle up some proper strength, come back in, finish the job.'

Gaunt nods.

'There are problems with that,' he says.

'Do tell.'

'For a start, I'm still not sure who we're fighting.'

'It's tribal Archenemy,' says Corbec, 'like Mkoll says. They've just ransacked the city arsenal.'

Gaunt touches his arm and draws him out of earshot.

'You never left Tanith before, did you, Corbec?'

'No, sir.'

'Never fought on a foreign front?'

'I've been taught about the barbaric nature of the Archenemy, if that's what you're worried about. All their cults and their ritual ways–'

'Corbec, you don't know the half of it.'

Corbec looks at him.

'I think they *are* Kosdorfers,' Gaunt says. 'I think they were, anyway. I think the Ruinous Powers, may they stand accursed, have salvaged more than kit and equipment. I think they've salvaged men too.'

'Feth,' Corbec breathes. Rain drips off his beard.

'I know,' says Gaunt.

'The very thought of it.'

'I need you to keep that to yourself. Don't say anything to the men.'

'Of course.'

'None of them, colonel.'

'Yes. Yes, all right.'

Corbec's taken one of his cigars out again and stuck it in his mouth, unlit.

'Just light the damn thing,' says Gaunt.

Corbec obeys. His hands shake as he strikes the lucifer.

'You want one?'

'No,' says Gaunt.

Corbec puffs.

'All right,' he says. He looks at Gaunt.

'All right,' says Gaunt, 'if we give ground here and try to fall back, we leave ourselves open. If they take us out on the way home, they'll be all over our main force without warning. But if we can manage to keep their attention here while we relay a message back...'

Corbec frowns. 'That's a feth of a lot to ask, by any standards.'

'What, the message run or the action?' asks Gaunt.

'Both,' says Corbec.

'You entirely comfortable with the alternative, Corbec?'

Corbec shrugs. 'You know I'm not.'

'Then strengthen our position here, colonel,' Gaunt says. 'We can afford to drop back a little if necessary. Given the visibility issues, the concourse isn't helping us much.'

'What do you suggest?' asks Corbec.

'I suggest you ask Mkoll and his scouts. I suggest we make the best of that resource.'

'Yes, sir.'

Corbec turns to go.

'Corbec – another thing. Tell the men to select single shot. Mandatory, please. Full auto is wasting munitions.'

'Yes, sir.'

Corbec stubs out his cigar and moves away. Keeping his head down, Gaunt moves along the shooting line of jumbled pavers and column bases in the opposite direction.

'Trooper!'

Caffran looks up from his firing position.

'Yes, sir?'

'It's your lucky day,' says Gaunt.

He gets down beside Caffran and reaches into his jacket pockets for his stylus and a clean message wafer.

His hip pocket is torn open and flapping. It's empty. He checks all the pockets of his jacket and the pockets of his storm coat, but his stylus and the wafer pad have gone.

'Do you have the despatch bag, Caffran?'

Caffran nods, and pulls the loop of the small message satchel off over his head. Gaunt opens it, and sees it is in order: fresh message wafers, a stylus, and a couple of signal flares. Caffran has taken his duty seriously.

Gaunt begins writing on one of the wafers rapidly. He uses a gridded sheet to draw up a simple expression of their route and the layout of the city's south-eastern zone, copying from his water-proof chart. Rain taps on the sheet.

'I need you to take this back to Major Rawne,' he says as he writes. 'Understand that we need to warn him of the enemy presence here and summon his support.'

Gaunt finishes writing and presses the setting of his signet ring against the code seal of the wafer, authorising it.

'Caffran, do you understand?'

Caffran nods. Gaunt puts the wafer back into the message satchel.

'Am I to go on my own?' Caffran asks.

'I can't spare more than one man for this, Caffran,' says Gaunt.

The young man looks at him, considers it. Gaunt is a man who quite bloodlessly orders the death of people to achieve his goals. This is what's happening now. Caffran understands that. Caffran understands he is being used as an instrument, and that if he fails and dies, it'll be no more to Gaunt than a shovel breaking in a ditch or a button coming off a shirt. Gaunt has no actual interest in Caffran's life or the manner of its ending.

Caffran purses his lips and then nods again. He hands his lasrifle and the munition spares he was carrying to Gaunt.

'That'll just weigh me down. Somebody else better have them.'

The young trooper gets up, takes a last look at Gaunt, and then begins to pick his way down through the ruined street behind the advance position, keeping his head down.

Gaunt watches him until he's out of sight.

* * *

Under Mkoll's instruction, the advance gives ground.

Working as spotters out on the flanks, Mkoll's scouts, Bonin and Mkvenner, have pushed the estimate of enemy numbers beyond eight hundred. Gaunt doesn't want to show that he is already regretting his decision not to pull out while the going was good.

Against lengthening, lousy odds, he's committed his small force to the worst kind of combat, the grinding city fight, where mid-range weapons and tactics become compressed into viciously barbaric struggles that depend on reaction time, perception and, worst of all, luck.

The Tanith disengage from the edge of the concourse, which has become entirely clouded in a rising white fog of vapour lifted by the sustained firefight, and drop back into the city block at the south-west corner. Here there are two particularly large habitat structures, which have slumped upon themselves like settling pastry, a long manufactory whose chimneys have toppled like felled trees, and a data library.

The scouts lead them into the warren of ruined halls and broken floors. It is raining inside many of the chambers. Roofs are missing, or water is simply descending through ruptured layers of building fabric. The Tanith melt from view into the shadows. They cover their cloaks with the black dirt from the concourse, and it helps them to merge with the dripping shadows. Gaunt does as they do. He smears the dirt onto his coat and pulls the cloak on over the top, aware that he is looking less and less like a respectable Imperial officer. Damn it, his storm coat is torn and his jacket is ruined anyway.

They work into the habs. Gunfire cracks and echoes along the forlorn walkways and corridors. Broken water pipes, weeping and foul, protrude from walls and floors like tree stumps. The tiled floor, what little of it survives, is covered with broken glass and pot shards from crockery that has been fragmented by the concussion of war.

Gaunt has kept hold of Caffran's rifle. He's holstered his pistol and got the infantry weapon cinched across his torso, ready to fire. It's a long time since he's seen combat with a rifle in his hands.

Mkoll looms out of the filmy mist that fills the air. He is directing the Tanith forward. He looks at Gaunt and then takes Gaunt's cap off his head.

'Excuse me?' says Gaunt.

Mkoll wipes his index finger along a wall, begrimes it, and then rubs the tip over the silver aquila badge on Gaunt's cap.

He hands it back.

'It's catching the light,' says Mkoll.

'I see. And it's not advisable to wear a target on my head.'

'I just don't want you drawing fire down on our unit.'

'Of course you don't,' says Gaunt.

Every few minutes the gunfire dies away. A period of silence follows as the enemy closes in tighter, listening for movement. The only sound is the downpour. The entire environment is a source of noise: debris and rubble can be dislodged, kicked, disturbed, larger items of wreckage can be knocked over or banged into. Damaged floors groan and creak. Windows and doors protest any attempt to move them. When a weapon is discharged, the echoes set up inside the ruined buildings are a great way of locating the point of origin.

The Tanith are supremely good at this. Gaunt witnesses several occasions when a trooper makes a rattle out of a stone in an old tin cup or pot and sets up a noise to tempt a shot from the demented Kosdorfers. As soon as the shot comes, another Tanith trooper gauges the source of the bouncing echo and returns fire with a lethal volley.

The enemy becomes wise to the tricks, and starts acting more circumspectly. Unable to out-stalk the Tanith, the Kosdorfers begin to call out to them from the darkness.

It is unnerving. The voices are distant and pleading. Little sense can be made of them in terms of meaning, but the tone is clear. It is misery. They are the voices of the damned.

'Ignore them,' Gaunt orders.

They have to stick tight. The enemy has a numerical advantage. By getting out of the open, the Tanith has forced its own spatial advantage.

Gaunt wonders if it will be enough.

The ruins still feel like a grave site, a waste of mouldering funereal rot. He wonders if this place will mark the end of his life and soldiering career; a well-thought-of officer who wound up dying in some strategically worthless location because he didn't make the right choices, or shake the right hand, or whisper in the right ear, or dine with the right cliques. He's seen men make high rank that way, through the persuasive power of the officers' club and the staff coterie. They were politicians, politicians who got to execute their decisions in the most literal way. Some were very capable, most were not. Gaunt believes that there is no substitute at all for practical apprenticeship, for field learning to properly supplement the study of military texts and the codices of combat. Slaydo had believed that too, as had Oktar, Gaunt's first mentor.

The vast mechanism of the Imperial Guard, as a rule, did not. Slaydo had once said that he believed he could, through proper reform of the Guard, improve its efficiency by fifty or sixty per cent. Soberly, he had added that mankind was probably too busy fighting wars to ever initiate such reforms.

There is truth in that. Gaunt knows for a fact that Slaydo had a reform bill in mind to take to the Munitorum after the Gorikan Suppression, and again after Khulan. Every time, a new campaign beckoned, a new theatre loomed to occupy the attentions of military planners and commanders. The Sabbat Worlds, now it was the Sabbat Worlds. Slaydo had committed to it mainly, Gaunt knew, for personal reasons. After Khulan, the High Lords had tempted Slaydo with many offers: he'd had the pick of campaigns. He had turned them down, hoping to pursue a more executive office in the latter part of his life and work to the fundamental improvement of the Imperial Guard, which he believed had the capacity to be the finest fighting force in known space.

However, the High Lords had outplayed him. They had discovered his old and passionate fondness for the piety of Saint Sabbat Beati and the territories she had touched, and they had exploited it. The Sabbat Worlds had long since been thought of as unrecoverable, lost to the predations of the Ruinous Powers spreading from the so-called Sanguinary Worlds. No commander wanted to embrace such a career-destroying challenge. The High Lords wanted a leader who would stage the offensive with conviction. They sweetened the offer with the rank of Warmaster, sensing that Slaydo would be unable to resist the opportunity to liberate a significant territory of the Imperium that he felt had been woefully neglected and left to over-run, and at the same to acquire a status that allowed him much greater political firepower to achieve his reforms.

Instead, Balhaut had killed him. All he accomplished was the commencement of a military campaign that was likely to last generations and cost trillions of lives.

Thus are dreams dashed and good intentions lost. Everything returns to the dust, and everything is reduced to blind fighting in the shadowed ruins of cities against men who were brothers until madness claimed their minds.

Everything returns to the dirt, and the dirt becomes your camouflage, and hides your face and your cap badge in the dark, when death comes, growling, to find you out.

Faced alone, out of sight of the other men, the ruination of Kosdorf brings tears into his eyes.

Caffran understands the urgency of his mission, but he's also smart enough not to run. Headlong running, as the chief scout has pointed out so often, just propels a man into the open, into open spaces he hasn't checked first, across hidden objects that might be pressure-sensitive, through invisible wires, into the line of predatory gunsights.

Caffran is fit, as physically fit as any of the younger men who've been salvaged from Tanith. That's one of the reasons he's been selected as a courier.

The advance came into the grave city as a unit, testing its way and proceeding with recon. Now he's exiting alone, a solitary trooper, protected by his wits and training. There's no doubt in his mind that the enemy will have spread strengths out through the dead boroughs surrounding the fighting zone to catch any stragglers.

Kosdorf reminds him of Tanith Magna. Architecturally, it's nothing like it, of course. Tanith Magna was a smaller burg, high-walled, a gathering of predominantly dark stone towers and spires rising from the emerald canopy of Tanith like a monolith. It had nothing of Kosdorf's dank, white, mausoleum quality. It's simply the mortality of Kosdorf that has stabbed him in the heart. Caffran knows that Tanith Magna doesn't even persist as a ruin any more, but Voltemand's second city, in death, inevitably makes him think of it, and the ruins become a substitute for his loss.

More than once, he feels quite sure he knows a street, or a particular corner. Memories superimpose themselves over alien habs and thoroughfares, and nostalgia, fletched with unbearable melancholy, spears him. He thinks he recognises one flattened frontage as the public house where he used to meet his friends, another shell as the mill shop where he had been apprenticed, and a broken walkway as the narrow street that had always taken him to the diocese temple. A patch of burned wasteland and twisted wire is most certainly the street market where he sometimes bought vegetables and meat for his ageing mother.

This terrace, this terrace with its cracked and broken flagstones, is definitely the square beside the Elector's Gardens, where he used to meet Laria. He can smell nalwood–

He can smell wet ash. Lightning jags silently.

He wipes a knuckle across his cheekbone, knowing that humiliating tears are mixing with the rain on his face.

He takes a deep breath. He isn't concentrating. He isn't paying enough attention. He stops to get his bearings, trusting the innate wiring of the Tanith mind to sense direction.

If the God-Emperor, who Caffran dutifully worshipped all his life at the little diocese temple, has seen fit to take everything away from him except this single duty, then Caffran is fething well determined to do it properly. He–

He feels the hairs prick up on the back of his neck.

The las-shot misses his face by about a palm's length. Just the slightest tremor of a trigger finger was the difference between a miss and a solid headshot. The light and noise of it rock him, the heat sears him, flash-drying the dirty tears and rain on his cheek into a crust.

Caffran throws himself down, and rolls into cover. He scrabbles in behind the foundation stones of a levelled building. Two more rounds pass over him, and then a hard round hits the block to his left. Caffran hears the distinctly different sound quality of the impact.

He thanks the God-Emperor with a nod. The enemy has just provided information. A minimum of two shooters, not one.

Caffran gets lower still. With his face almost pressing into the ooze, he repositions himself, and risks a look around the stone blocks.

Another shot whines past him, but it is speculative. The shooter hasn't seen him. A filthy PDFer is hopping across the rubble towards his position, clutching an old autorifle. He looks like a hobbled beggar. The puttee around one of his calves is loose and trailing, and his breeches are torn. His face is concealed by an old gas mask. The air pipe swings like a proboscis, unattached to any air tank. One of the glass eye discs is missing.

Behind him, a distance back, a second PDFer stands on the top of a sloping section of roof that is lying across a street. He has a lascarbine raised to his shoulder and sighted. As the PDFer in the gas mask approaches, the other one clips off in Caffran's general direction.

Caffran draws his only weapon, the long Tanith knife.

He stays low, hearing the crunch of the approaching enemy trooper. He can smell him too, a stench like putrefaction.

Another las-shot sings overhead. Caffran tries to slow his breathing. The footsteps get closer. He can hear the man's breath rasping inside the mask.

Caffran turns the knife around in his hand until he is holding the blade, and then very gently taps the pommel against the stone block, using the knife like a drum stick.

Chink! Chink! Chink!

He hears the enemy trooper's respiration rate change, his breath sounds alter as he turns to face a different direction. His footsteps clatter loose stone chips and crunch slime. He is right there. He is coming around the other side of the stone block.

The moment he appears, Caffran goes for him. He tries to make full body contact so he can bring the man over before he can aim his rifle. Caffran tries to force the muzzle of the rifle in under one of his arms rather than point it against his torso.

Locked together, they tumble down behind the block. The autorifle discharges.

From his vantage on the fallen roof slope, the other trooper hesitates, watching. He lowers his lasrifle, then raises it to sight again.

A shape pops back into view over the stone slab, a filthy shape, with a grimed gas-masked face. The watching trooper hesitates from firing.

The figure with the gas mask brings up an autorifle in a clean, fluid swing and fires a burst that hits the hesitating PDFer in the throat and chest, and tumbles him down the roof slope, scattering tiles.

Caffran drops the autorifle and wrenches off the gas mask as he falls to his knees. He gags and then vomits violently. The stench inside the borrowed mask, the *residue*, has been foul, even worse than he could have imagined. The mask's previous owner lies on his back beside him, beads of bright red blood spattering his mud-caked chest. Caffran slides the warknife out and wipes the blade.

Then he throws up again.

He can hear activity in the ruins behind him. It's time to move. He stares at the autorifle, and tries to weigh up the encumbrance against the usefulness of a ranged weapon. He reaches over and searches the large canvas musette pouches his would-be killer has strapped to the front of his webbing. One is full of odd junk: meaningless pieces of stone and brick, shards of pottery and glass, a pair of broken spectacles and a tin of boot polish. The other holds three spare clips for the rifle, and a battered old short-pattern autopistol, a poor quality, mass-stamped weapon with limited range.

It will have to do. He puts it into his pocket.

It's really time to move.

It's getting dark. Night doesn't drop like a lid on Voltemand like it did on Tanith. It fills the sky up slowly, billowing like ink in water.

The rain's still hammering the Imperial camp, but the dark rim of the sky makes the silent lightning more pronounced. The white spears are firing every twenty or thirty seconds, like an automatic beacon set to alarm.

The boy's asleep, legs and arms loosely arranged like a dog flopped by a grate. Dorden hates to abuse his medicae privileges, but he believes that the God-Emperor of Mankind will forgive him for crushing up a few capsules of tranquiliser and mixing them into the boy's broth. He'll do penance if he has to. They had plenty of temple chapels back in the city, and a popular local saint, a woman. She looked like the forgiving sort.

The boy's on a cot at the end of the ward. Dorden brews a leaf infusion over the small burner and turns the page of his book, open on the instrument rest. It's a work called *The Spheres of Longing*. He's yet to meet another man in the Imperial Guard who's ever heard of it, let alone read it. He doubts he will. The Imperial Guard is not a sophisticated institution.

Nearby, Lesp is cleaning his needles in a pot of water. He's done two or three family marks tonight at the end of his shift, a busy set. His eyes are tired, but he keeps going long enough to make sure the needles are sterile for the next job. Lesp is always eager to work. It's as if he's anxious to get down all the Tanith marks before he forgets them. Dorden sometimes wonders where Lesp will ink his marks when he runs out of Tanith skin to make them on.

The boy kicks as a dream trembles through him. Dorden watches him to make sure he's all right.

The doorway flap of the tent opens and Rawne steps in out of the lengthening light and the rain. Drops of it hang in his hair and on his cloak like diamonds. Dorden gets to his feet. Lesp gathers his things and makes himself scarce.

'Major.'

'Doctor.'

'Can I help you?'

'Just doing the rounds. Is everything as it should be here?'

Dorden nods.

'Nothing untoward.'

'Good,' says Rawne.

'It's getting dark,' Dorden says, as Rawne moves to leave.

'It is.'

'Doesn't that mean the advance unit is overdue?'

Rawne shrugs. 'A little.'

'Doesn't that concern you?' asks Dorden.

Rawne smiles.

'No,' he says.

'At what point will it concern you?' Dorden asks.

'When it's actually dark and they're officially missing.'

'That could be hours yet. And at that point it will be too late to mobilise any kind of force to go looking for them,' says Dorden.

'Well, we'd absolutely have to wait for morning at least,' says Rawne.

Dorden looks at him, and rubs his hand across his face.

'What do you think's happened to them?' he asks.

'I can't imagine,' says Rawne.

'What do you hope's happened to them?' Dorden asks.

'You know what I hope,' says Rawne. He's smiling still, but it's just teeth. There's no warmth. It's like lightning without thunder.

Dorden sips his drink.

'I'd ask you to consider,' he says, 'the effect it would have on the Tanith Regiment if it lost both of its senior commanding officers.'

'Please, Doctor,' says Rawne, 'this isn't an emergency. It's just a thing. They've probably just got held up somewhere.'

'And if not?'

Rawne shrugged.

'It'll be a terrible loss, like you said. But we'd just have to get over it. We've had practice at that, haven't we?'

The emaciated ghosts of Kosdorf come at them through the skeletal ruins. They have become desperate. Their need, their hunger has overwhelmed their caution. They loom through useless doors and peer through empty windows. They clamber out of sour drains and emerge from cover behind spills of rubble. They fire their weapons and call out in pleading, raw voices.

The rain has thickened the dying light. Muzzle flashes flutter dark orange, like old flame.

The Tanith knot tight, and fend them off with precision. They fall back through the manufactory into the data library.

It's there they lose their first life. A Tanith infantryman is caught by autogun fire. He staggers suddenly, as if winded. Then he simply goes limp and falls. His hands don't even come up to break his impact against the tiled floor. Men rush to him, and drag him into cover, but Gaunt knows he's gone by the way his heels are kicking out. Blood soaks the man's tunic, and smears the floor in a great curl like black glass when they drag him. First blood.

Gaunt doesn't know the dead man's name. It's one of the names he hasn't learned yet. He hates himself for realising, just for a second, that it's one less he'll have to bother with.

Gaunt keeps the nalwood stock of Caffran's lasrifle tight against his shoulder and looses single shots. The temptation to switch to auto is almost unbearable.

The lobby of the data library is a big space, which once had a glass roof, now fallen in. Rain pours in, every single moving drop of it catching the light. Kosdorfer ghosts get up on the lobby's gallery, and angle fire down at the Tanith below. The top of the desk once used by the venerable clerk of records stipples and splinters, and the row of ornate brass kiosks where scholars and gnostics once filled out their data requests dent and quiver. Floor tiles crack. The delicate etched metal facings of the wall pit and dimple.

Corbec looks out at Gaunt from behind a chipped marble column.

'This won't do,' he shouts.

Gaunt nods back.

'Support!' Corbec yells.

They've been sparing with their heavy weapon all day. They're only a light advance team, and they weren't packing much to begin with.

The big man comes up level with Corbec, head down. He's carrying the lascarbine he's been fighting with, but he's got a long canvas sleeve across his back. He unclasps it to slide out the rocket tube.

The big man's name is Bragg. He really is big. He's not much taller than Corbec, but he's got breadth across the shoulders. There's a younger Tanith with him, one of the kids, a boy called Beltayn. He's carrying the leather box with the eight anti-tank rockets in it, and he gets one out while Bragg snaps up the tube's mechanical range-finder.

'Any time you like, Try!' Larkin yells out from behind an archway that is becoming riddled with shots.

'Shut your noise,' Bragg replies genially. He glances at Gaunt abruptly.

'Sorry, colonel-commissar, sir!' he says.

'Get on with it, please!' Gaunt shouts. It's not so much the heavy fire they're taking, it's the voices. It's probably his imagination, but the pleading, moaning voices of the Kosdorfers calling out to them are starting to make sense to him.

Beltayn goes to offer up the rocket to Bragg's launcher, and a las-bolt fells him. Gaunt's eyes widen as the rocket tumbles out of the hands of the falling boy and drops towards the tiled floor.

It hits, bounces, a tail-fin dents slightly.

It doesn't detonate.

Gaunt dashes forward. Corbec has reached Bragg too. Bragg has picked up the rocket. He taps it cheerfully against his head.

'No fear,' he says. 'Arming pin's still in.'

Gaunt snatches the rocket, and stoops to the box to swap it for an undamaged one.

'See to the boy!' he says to Corbec.

'Just a flesh wound!' Corbec replies, hunched over Beltayn. 'Just his arm.'

'Get him back to the archway!'

'I can't leave–'

'Get his arse back to the archway, colonel! I'll do this!'

'Yes sir!'

Corbec starts dragging the boy back towards the main archway. Men come out of cover to help him. Gaunt gets a clean rocket out of the box. He rolls it in his hands to check it by eye. It's been a long time since he loaded, a long time since he learned basic skills. A long time since he was the boy, the Hyrkan boy, apprenticed to war, born into it as if it was a family business.

'Set?' he asks the big man.

'Yes, sir!' says Bragg.

Gaunt fits the rocket and removes the arming pin. Bragg hoists the top-heavy tube onto the shelf of his shoulder and takes aim at the lobby gallery. Gaunt slaps him twice on the shoulder.

'Ease!' he yells.

'Ease!' Bragg yells back. The word opens the mouth and stops the eardrums bursting.

Bragg pulls the bare metal trigger. The ignition thumps the air,

and blow-back spits from the back of the tube and throws up dust.
The rocket howls off in the other direction, on a trail of flame. It
hits the gallery just under the rail, and detonates volcanically. The
entire gallery lifts for a second, and then comes down like an avalanche, spilling rubble, stonework, grit, glass and men. It collapses
with a drawn-out roar, a death rattle of noise and disintegration.

Gaunt looks at Bragg. Bragg grins. Their ears are ringing.

Gaunt signals *back to the archway*.

They run in through the archway, through the smoke blowing
from the lobby. They get down. Corbec has signalled a pause while
they wait to hear how the enemy redeploys.

It gets quieter. The building settles. Rubble clatters as it falls now
and then. Glass tinkles.

Gaunt sinks down next to Bragg, his back to a wall.

'First time that time,' says Larkin from a corner nearby.

'I know,' says Bragg. He looks at Gaunt. He's proud of himself.
'Sometimes I miss,' he explains.

'I know,' says Gaunt. The big man's nickname is *Try Again* because
he's always messing up the first shot.

Gaunt sits quiet for a minute or two. He wipes the sweat off his
face. He thinks about trying again, and second chances. Sometimes
there just isn't the opportunity or the willingness to make things
better. Sometimes you can't simply have another go. You make a
choice, and it's a bad one, and you're left with it. No amount of
trying again will fix it. Don't expect anyone to feel sorry for you, to
cut you slack; you made a mistake you'll have to live with.

It was like failing to play the glittering game when he had the
chance as one of Slaydo's brightest; like leaving the Hyrkans; like
trying to salvage anything from the Tanith disaster; like thinking
he could win broken, grieving men over; like coming out with a
small advance force into a city grave, just because he was bored of
sitting in his tent.

He takes his cap off, leans the crown of his head back against
the damp wall and closes his eyes. He opens them again. It's dark

above him, the roofspace of the library. Beads of rainwater and flakes of plaster are dripping and spattering down towards him, catching the intermittent lightning, like snow, like the slow traffic of stars through the aching loneliness of space.

He remembers something, one little thing. He puts his hand in his pocket, just to touch the letter, just to put his fingers on the letter his old friend Blenner sent him: Blenner, his friend from Schola Progenium, manufacturer of fake plastic explosives and practical jokes.

Blenner, manufacturer of empty promises, too, no doubt. The letter's old. The offer may not still stand, if it ever did. Vaynom Blenner was not the most reliable man, and his mouth had a habit of making offers the rest of him couldn't keep.

But it's a small hope, a sustaining thing, the possibility of trying again.

The letter is gone.

Suddenly alert, torn from his reverie, Gaunt begins to search his pockets. It's really gone. The pocket he thought he'd put it in is hanging off, thanks to the thrust of a rusty sword bayonet. All the pockets of his field jacket and storm coat are empty.

The letter's lost. It's outside somewhere in this grave of a city, disintegrating in the rain.

'What's the matter?' asks Bragg, noticing Gaunt's activity.

'Nothing,' says Gaunt.

'You sure?'

Gaunt nods.

'Good,' says Bragg, sitting back again. 'I thought you might have the torments on you.'

'The torments?'

'Everyone gets them,' says Bragg. 'Everyone has their own. Bad dreams. Bad memories. Most of us, it's about where we come from. Tanith, you know.'

'I know,' says Gaunt.

'We miss it,' says Bragg, like this idea might, somehow, not be clear to anyone. 'It's hard to bear. It's hard to think about what happened to it, sometimes. It gets us inside. You know Gutes?'

Bragg points across at Piet Gutes, one of the men who was in the guild house with Domor. Like all the Tanith, Gutes is resting for a moment, sitting against a wall, feet pulled in, gun across his knees, listening.

'Yeah,' says Gaunt.

'Friend of mine,' says Bragg. 'He had a daughter called Finra, and she had a daughter called Foona. Feth, but he misses them. Not being away from them, you understand. Just them not being there to return to. And Mkendrick?'

Bragg points to another infantryman. His voice is low.

'He left a brother in Tanith Steeple. I think he had family in Attica too, an uncle–'

'Why are you telling me this, trooper?' Gaunt asks. 'I know what happened. I know what I did. Do you want me to suffer? I can't make amends. I can't do that.'

Bragg frowns.

'I thought,' he starts to say.

'What?' asks Gaunt.

'I thought that's what you were trying to do,' says Bragg. 'With us. I thought you were trying to make something good out of what was left of Tanith.'

'With respect, trooper, you're the only man in the regiment who thinks that. Also, with respect to the fighting merits of the Tanith, I'm an Imperial Guard commander, not a miracle worker. I've got a few men, a handful in the great scheme of things. We're never going to accomplish much. We're going to be a line of code in the middle of a Munitorum levy report, if that.'

'Oh, you never know,' says Bragg. 'Anyway, it doesn't matter if we don't. All that matters is you do right by the men.'

'I do right by them?'

'That's all we want,' says Bragg with a smile. 'We're Tanith. We're used to knowing where we're going. We're used to finding our way.

We're lost now. All we want from you is for you to find a path for us and set us on it.'

Someone nearby says something. Corbec holds up a hand, makes a gesture. Pattering rain. Otherwise, silence. Everyone's listening.

Gaunt pats the big man on the arm and goes over to join Corbec.

'What is it?' he asks.

'Beltayn says he heard something,' Corbec replies. The boy is settled in beside Corbec, the wounded arm packed and taped. He looks at Gaunt.

He says, 'Something's awry.'

'What's that supposed to mean?' asks Gaunt.

Corbec indicates he should listen. Gaunt cranes his neck.

The Kosdorfers are moving. They're talking again. Their whispers are breathing out of the ruins to reach the Tanith position.

Gaunt looks sharply at Corbec.

'I think I can understand the words,' he says.

'Me too,' Corbec nods.

Gaunt swallows hard. He's got a sick feeling, and he's not sure where it's coming from. The feeling is telling him that he's not suddenly comprehending the Kosdorfers because they are speaking Low Gothic.

He's understanding them because he's learned their language.

The boy wakes up with a start.

'Go back to sleep,' Dorden tells him. 'You need your sleep.'

Dorden's standing in the doorway of the tent, watching the evening coming in.

Milo gets up.

'Are they back yet?' he asks.

Dorden shakes his head.

'Someone needs to go and look for them,' the boy says flatly. 'I had another dream. A really unpleasant one. Someone needs to go and look for them.'

'Just go back to sleep,' Dorden insists. The boy slumps a little, and turns back to his cot.

'You dreamed they were in trouble, did you?' Dorden asks, trying to humour the boy.

'No', replies the boy, sitting down on the cot and looking back at the medicae. 'That's not why I have the feeling they're in trouble. I didn't dream it, that's just common sense. They're overdue. My bad dream, it was just a dream about numbers. Like last night and the night before.'

'Numbers?' asks Dorden.

Milo nods. 'Just some numbers. In my dream, I'm trying to write these numbers down, over and over, but my stylus won't work, and for some reason that's not a pleasant dream to have.'

Dorden looks at the boy. He asks, 'So what are the numbers, Brin?', still humouring him.

The boy reels the numbers off.

'When did he tell you that?' Dorden asks.

'Who?'

'Gaunt.'

'He didn't tell me anything,' says the boy. 'He certainly didn't tell me those numbers. I just told you, they were in my dream. I dreamed about them.'

'Are you lying to me, Brin?'

'No, sir.'

Dorden keeps staring at the boy a minute more, as if a lie will suddenly give itself away, like the moon coming out from behind a cloud.

'Why do those numbers matter?' the boy asks.

'They're Gaunt's command code,' says Dorden.

'Explain yourself,' the voice demands. It comes out like an echo, from the ruins, the ghost of a voice. 'Explain yourself. We don't understand why.'

The voice tunes in and out, like a vox that's getting interference.

'We're hungry,' it adds.

Corbec looks at Gaunt. He wants to reply, Gaunt can see it on his face. Gaunt shakes his head.

'You left us here,' the voice says. It's two or three voices now, all speaking at once, like two or three vox sets tuned to the same signal, their speakers slightly out of sync. 'Why did you leave us here? We don't understand why you left us behind.'

'Feth's sake is that?' Corbec mutters to Gaunt. All good humour has gone from him. He's looking pinched and scared.

'You left us behind, and we're hungry,' the voices plead.

'I don't know,' says Gaunt. 'A trick.'

He says it, but he doesn't believe it. It's an uglier thing than that. The voices don't really sound like voices when you listen hard, or vox transmits either. They sound like... like other noises that have been carefully mixed up and glued together to make voice sounds. All the noises of the dead city have been harvested: the scatter of pebbles, the slump of masonry, the splinter and smash of glass, the creak of rebar, the crack of tiles, the spatter of rain. All those things and millions more besides, blended into a sound mosaic that almost perfectly imitates the sound of human speech.

Almost, but not quite.

Almost human, but not human enough.

'You left us behind, and we're hungry. Explain yourself. We don't understand why you left us. We don't understand why you didn't come.'

The Tanith are all up, all disturbed. Knuckles are white where hands grip weapons. Everyone's soaking wet. Everyone's watching the dripping shadows. Gaunt needs them to keep it together. He knows they can all hear it. The inhuman *imperfection* in the voices.

'I know what that is,' says Larkin.

'Steady, Larks,' growls Corbec.

'I know what that is. I know, I know what that is,' the marksman says. 'I know it. It's Tanith.'

'Shut up, Larks.'

'It's Tanith. It's dead Tanith calling to us! It's Tanith calling to us, calling us back!'

'Shut up please, Larks!'

'Larkin, shut your mouth!' Gaunt barks.

Larkin makes a sound, a mewling sob. Fear's inside him, deep as a bayonet.

The voices are out there in the dark and the rain. The words seem to move from one speaker to the next. Dead speakers. Broken throats.

'We don't understand why you didn't come. We don't understand. We don't know who we are any more. We don't know where we belong.'

Gaunt looks at Corbec.

'We getting out?' he asks.

'Through the back way?'

'Whatever way we can find.'

'What happened to holding this place until reinforcements arrive?' asks Corbec.

'No one's coming this way that we want to meet,' says Gaunt.

Corbec turns to the advance force.

'Get ready to move,' he orders.

The voice pleads, 'Where do we belong? We don't know where we belong.'

'It's Tanith!' Larkin cries out. 'It's the old place calling out to us!'

Gaunt grabs him, and pushes him against a wall.

'Listen to me,' he says. 'Larkin? Larkin? Listen to me! Get yourself under control! Something worse than death happened here, something much worse!'

'What?' Larkin whines, wanting to know and not wanting to know.

'Something Tanith was spared, do you understand me?'

Larkin makes the sobbing sound again. Gaunt lets him go, lets him sag against the wall. He turns, and the men are all around him. Mkoll's right there, Mkvenner too, looking as if they're going to step in and pull Gaunt and Larkin apart. The Tanith men are all staring at him. No one's looking away.

'Do you understand?' Gaunt asks them. 'All of you? Any of you?'

'We understand what you did,' one of them says.

'Oh, this isn't helping anything, lads!' Corbec rumbles.

Gaunt ignores Corbec and laughs a brutal laugh. 'I'm a destroyer of worlds, am I? You credit me with too much power. Indecent amounts of it. And anyway, I don't much care what you think of me.'

'Let's go! Let's go now,' says Corbec.

'There's only one thing I want you to understand,' Gaunt says.

'What's that?' asks Larkin, his mouth trembling.

'The worst thing you can imagine,' says Gaunt, 'is not the worst thing. Not by a long way.'

In the open, the rain is heavy, like a curtain. Caffran knows he's never going to make it. The straggly figures hunting him are closing in, and they've been calling to him for the last ten minutes, using the voices of people he used to know, twisted by bad vox reception.

'We don't know why you left us,' the voices plead. 'Where do we belong? We don't know where we belong.'

Caffran's feet are sore. He's got the pistol in his hand. Its clip is empty. He's killed three more men on his way out of the ruins.

The voices call out, 'We've forgotten what we're supposed to be.'

He's reached the ramparts of the hills, with the city grave at his back. He kneels down. The Imperial camp is somewhere ahead, below and far away. He can't see it, because rain and night shadows are filling the valley, but he knows it must be there. Too far, too far.

There are signal flares in his message satchel. He's pulling them out as the heavy raindrops bounce off his shoulders and his scalp. Does he need to find higher ground? There'll be obs positions looking this way, won't there? Spotters and look-outs?

The voices call to him.

He stands and fires a flare. It makes a hollow bang and soars up into the wet air, a white phosphor star with a gauzy tail, like a drawing of a comet in an old manuscript. It maxes altitude, and then starts to descend, slow, trembling, drifting.

Caffran's watching it, the other flare in his hand ready to fire. He knows there's no point.

The flare looks too much like the silent lightning.

There are figures on the hillside around him. They come towards him.

They call out to him.

Bonin locates the remains of a depository entrance in the south-western corner of the data library, and they exit, via the basement stacks. They make their break out from there.

The basement is flooded, up to their hips. They have to cannibal-ise an RPG shell to make a charge to blow the hatch open. Then they're out into the street, into the rain, and they're drawing heavy fire right from the start.

Gaunt orders bounding cover, and they push along a street from position to position. They stay in good formation, despite the level of fire coming at them. No one switches back to full auto, despite the temptation.

Even so, the advance is pushing the limits of the ammo sup-plies it's packing.

They begin to string out into a longer and longer line. They make it to the circus where two dead boulevards cross, and pick their way through the underwalks of the crippled tramway shelters to achieve the far side. Volleys of shots rain off the crumpled metal roofs of the shelters. The objective is the arterial route that joins the eastern boulevard. Gaunt and Corbec tell Blane to push ahead and edge back to bring the rear of the line up.

The advance is halfway across the circus when it's rushed by enemy ambushers. The ambushers come out of one of the under-walks that looked like it was choked with rubble. They're armed like trench raiders with clubs and mauls and butcher hooks. They hit the Tanith advance in the midsection of its bounding spread. They rush Gaunt as he's trying to direct the force forwards.

Gaunt goes down and his head strikes something. He's too

stunned to know what's happened. A raider swings a hook to split his head and finish him.

Mkoll intercepts the raider, and guts him with his silver warknife. He meets the next one head-on, somehow evades a wide swing from a spiked mace, and rams the knife up through the throat so the point exits the apex of the skull.

Corbec's also been caught in the initial rush. He takes his attacker over with him, and breaks his neck using body weight and a wrestling hold he'd learned watching his old dad compete at the County Pryze fair.

He looks up in time to see Mkoll pull the knife out. Blood ribbons up in a semicircle, like a red streamer in the rain, and the raider curves backwards in the opposite direction. Through the sheeting rain, Corbec can see more raiders coming out of the underwalk at Mkoll. Corbec's lasrifle is wedged under the corpse of the man he just killed. He yells Mkoll's name. He yells *idiot* and *feth* too, for good measure. Mkoll's las is strapped over his shoulder. He's facing three men with just his knife.

There's the whine of a small but powerful fusion motor, the unmistakable whir of a chainsword firing up. Gaunt comes in beside the scout. Gaunt's got blood down the side of his face and his cap's gone missing. The three raiders are too close to Mkoll for Gaunt to risk a shot with his rifle or his bolter.

He takes a head clean off with his chainsword. The neck parts in a bloodmist venting from the blade's moving edge. Corbec can see from Gaunt's stance and the way he presents that he's been trained in sword work to the highest degree. Covered in dust and blood, on a slope of rubble, fighting feral ghouls, he still looks like a duelling master.

Gaunt lunges and puts the chainsword through the torso of a second raider, freeing Mkoll enough to tackle the last of the group in quick order. More are running in from the underwalk. Gaunt rotates, extending, and slices the chainsword around in a wide, straight-armed arc that neatly removes the top of a skull like a lid.

Corbec's on his feet. He pulls his lasrifle in against his gut and flips the toggle over. Then he rakes the mouth of the underwalk. Full auto flash lights up the rubble. Figures twist and jerk. He exhausts a power clip, and then lobs his last grenade down the underwalk to take care of any stragglers.

Gaunt looks around for his cap.

'Why didn't you do that?' he asks Mkoll.

'You wanted to conserve ammo,' says Mkoll.

'In all fairness, he probably could have taken them all with his knife,' says Corbec.

From up ahead, towards the east boulevard, they hear lasrifles starting to cut loose on full auto. The chatter is unmistakable.

'Ah. I've set a bad example,' says Corbec.

Gaunt moves forward, shouting orders. He heads towards the front of the advance force, trying to restore firing discipline. Right away, he realises how badly broken their formation is. The ambush to the midsection of the spread has almost cut the advance in two. It's the beginning of the end. The enemy is exploiting their flaws, breaking them down, cutting them into manageable parts, reducing them. He knows the signs. It's exactly what he'd do.

It'll be over in minutes.

The back of the party is lagging too far behind. Gaunt tries to get the forward section to drop back and rejoin it, or at least hold position and not extend the break. It's still pushing ahead to try to reach the arterial route. Corbec's hollering at men, calling them by their first names, names Gaunt's never heard, let alone learned. Full auto fire is clattering away up ahead. Some PDFers loom over the rubble line, and Gaunt drops them with support fire from Domor and Guheen.

'Single shots! Single shot fire!' he's yelling.

He sees the Tanith fanning towards him, firing on full auto. At least one of his orders has got through, he thinks. At least they've swung back to keep the unit whole.

Then he's eyes-on, properly. These Tanith aren't members of the advance.

Rawne rakes a couple of bursts into the rubble line, and then approaches Gaunt as reinforcements pour in behind him.

'Major?'

'Sir.'

'Surprised to see you.'

'We ran into Caffran,' Rawne says.

'You ran into him?'

'We saw his flare. He was heading home, but we were already on our way out.'

'Why is that, major?' Gaunt asks.

'Concern was expressed to me by the medical chief that the advance was overdue. A support mission seemed prudent, before it got dark and out of the question.'

'It's appreciated, Rawne. As you can see, things are a little lively.'

Rawne keeps looking at his timepiece.

'Let's keep falling back apace,' he says. 'Let's not outstay our welcome.'

Gaunt nods. 'Lead the way.'

Rawne turns and yells out to the men running his flanking units. Varl and Feygor get their fireteams to interlock firing patterns. They lay down a kill zone of las-fire that moves with the Tanith like a shadow. It burns through ammo, but it covers the retreat off the east boulevard and onto the main arterial route. They leave spent munition clips behind them, and the pathetic corpses of the enemy.

Adare and Meryn distribute ammo to Blane and the forward portion of the advance. Gaunt sees Caffran with Varl's squad. He tosses his rifle and his musette bag back to him. Caffran catches them and nods.

Rawne's still glancing at his timepiece.

'Let's go! Let's go!' he shouts. It's really getting dark. The fluttering, stammering barrage of the gun battle is lighting up the whole city block.

'We're going as fast as we can,' Gaunt says to Rawne.

Rawne looks at him, and sucks in a breath between clenched teeth that suggests that there's no such thing as too fast.

Gaunt hears a noise, a swift, loud, rushing hiss, the sound of a descent, of a plunge, of an angelic fall from grace. It ends in a noise shock that quakes the ground and nearly knocks him down. It feels like the lightning has found its voice at last.

Then it happens again and again.

Light blinds them. Bright detonations rip through the eastern boroughs of Kosdorf, some as close as a block or two away from their position. Blast overlaps blast, detonation touches detonation. It's precision wrath. It's bespoke annihilation.

'The Ketzok,' yells Rawne to Gaunt. 'A little early,' he admits.

Gaunt watches the heavy shelling for a moment, hand half-shielding his eyes from the flash. Then he turns the Tanith out of the zone with a simple hand signal.

It's too loud for voices any more.

Dorden cleans his head wound.

'It's going to mend nicely,' he says, dropping the small forceps into an instrument bath. Threads of blood billow through the cleaning solution like ink in water.

Gaunt picks up a steel bowl and uses it as a mirror to examine the sutures.

'That's neat work,' he says. Dorden shrugs.

Outside, in the morning light, the Ketzok artillery is still pounding relentlessly, like the slow, steady movement of a giant clock. Munitions resupply is an hour away, the bombardiers report. A huge pall of smoke is moving north across the sky over the hills.

'Rawne says you were instrumental in urging him to mount a reinforcement,' Gaunt says.

Dorden smiles.

'I'm sure Major Rawne was simply following standard operational practices,' he says.

Gaunt leaves the medicae tent. There's still rain in the air, though now it's spiced with the stink of fyceline from the sustained bombardment. The camp is active. They'll be striking soon. Directives have come through, order bags from command. The Tanith are being routed to another front line.

He's got things to think about. A week spent getting the regiment embarked and on the lift ships will give him time.

'Sir.'

He turns, and sees Corbec.

'Caligula, I hear,' says Corbec.

'That's the next stop,' Gaunt agrees. They fall into step.

'I don't know much about Caligula,' says Corbec.

'Then request a briefing summary from the Munitorum, Corbec,' says Gaunt. 'We have libraries of data about the Sabbat Worlds. It would pay the regiment dividends if the officers knew a little bit about the local conditions before they arrived in a fighting area.'

'I can do that, can I?' asks Corbec.

'You're a regimental colonel,' says Gaunt. 'Of course you can.'

Corbec nods.

'I'll get on it,' he says.

He grins, flops back his camo-cape, and produces one of his cigars and a couple of lucifers from his breast pocket.

'Thought you might enjoy this now we're outside field discipline conditions,' he says.

Gaunt takes the gift with a nod. Corbec knocks him a little salute and walks away.

Gaunt goes into his quarters tent to spend an hour packing his kit. The rain is tapping on the roof skin.

His spare field jacket is hanging on the back of the folding chair. Someone's sponged it clean and brushed up the nap. They've taken off the Hyrkan badges and sewn Tanith ones on in their place.

There is no clue at all as to who has done this.

Gaunt takes off the muddy coat and jacket he's been wearing all night and slips the spare on, not even sure it's his. He strokes it down, adjusts the cuffs and puts his hands in the pockets.

The letter's in the right-hand hip pocket.

He slides it out and unfolds it. He'd been so certain it was in his number one field jacket. So certain.

He reads it, and re-reads it, and smiles, hearing the words in Blenner's voice.

Then he strikes one of the lucifers Corbec gave him, and holds the letter by the lower left-hand corner as he lights the lower right. It burns quickly, with a yellow flame. He holds on to it until the flames approach his fingertips, and then shakes it into the ash box beside his desk.

Then he goes out to find some breakfast.

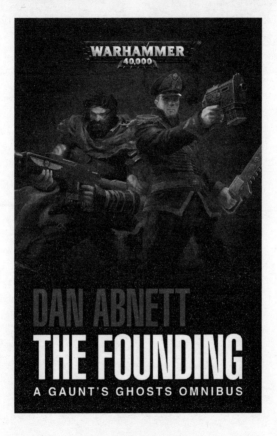

MERCY

Danie Ware

Introducing

AUGUSTA

SISTER SUPERIOR,
ORDER OF THE BLOODY ROSE

The cathedral's corpse was vast.

Standing in its hollow heart, its darkness vaulted huge above her, Sister Superior Augusta rested one scarlet-gauntleted hand on the bolter at her hip. She said nothing, only scanned this icon of the Emperor's might, searching for motion, for threat, for any remaining gleam of His Light.

But there was nothing.

This was Ultima Segmentum's darkest corner, and little reached out here.

Beside her, the missionary Lysimachus Tanichus was speaking in hushed tones. 'From the last years of the Age of Apostasy, sister. Or so they say.' His sibilance coiled in the dark, like echoes of millennia.

Augusta gave a brief acknowledgement and walked carefully through the debris. The air was hot here, clammy with the overgrown jungle-marsh outside; twisted creepers had penetrated the cathedral's crumbling walls and they writhed across the stonework like the tendrils of Chaos itself. Sweat itched at the fleur-de-lys tattoo on her cheek.

'Sisters.' She spoke softly into the vox at her throat. 'Roll call.'

Five voices came back through the darkness. Augusta's retinal lenses tracked their locations: blips deployed in a standard sweep-reconnaissance pattern. Her squad were experienced – all except one – and she had complete trust in their worthiness, and in their love for the Emperor. Together, they had carried fist and faith across every segmentum of the galaxy.

Tanichus, fiddling with his rosarius, spoke again. 'The Emperor's light had not touched this world in millennia, sister, not until I came here, carrying His name. The local townspeople told me of the cathedral. It's a part of their mythology–'

'I trust you've brought them Truth,' Augusta said. Her authority was unthreatened by the missionary, but she needed to listen – the brief from the canoness on Ophelia VII had listed this world as a potential staging point for Chaos, invading from the Eye of Terror, for witchkin or renegades, for marauding xenos of every kind. Augusta was a twenty-year veteran, her bobbed hair and stern gaze both steel-grey, and her experience made her both sharp and wary.

'*Me serve vivere*, sister,' Tanichus said. 'I live to serve.'

'Sister Jatoya,' Augusta said into the vox. 'Anything?'

Her second-in-command responded, 'No, sister. If there's anything here, it's well hidden.'

'Check everywhere.'

'Yes, sister.'

'Very well.' Her touch still on the bolter, eyeing the decaying statues and pillars above her, Augusta gestured for Tanichus to keep speaking.

But he told her only what she already knew: his history with the townspeople, and their rumours of the cathedral. The town held the place taboo, but they'd told Tanichus their local myth – that the ruin had a guardian, an armoured stone icon with a bloodied flower upon its chest. And Tanichus had carried word of this back to the Ecclesiarchy, and to the Sisters.

A member of the Order of the Bloody Rose, Augusta had volunteered for the mission immediately – with the cathedral's age, it was possible that the icon could be Saint Mina herself. 'The Emperor has called me,' she'd said to the canoness. 'And I must go.' Perhaps for more political reasons than visionary ones, the canoness had agreed.

Her boots crunching over ancient, fallen masonry, Augusta climbed the steps towards the high altar. Ruin or not, she paused before the top and dropped to one armoured knee, her black cloak billowing and her hand tracing the fleur-de-lys on her armour.

'Quantus tremor est futurus, quando attingit locum Lucis.'

How great the fear will be, when the Light touches this place!

She felt the missionary shiver as he, too, knelt. Tanichus was a talker, a good man to carry the Emperor's word, but she was His daughter, and her task was clear.

She would find this icon.

'Did the townspeople tell you anything further?' she asked, coming back to her feet. 'You lived with them for several months.'

'Only superstitions,' he told her. 'If this is your patron saint, sister, then we must find her without their help.'

Augusta nodded. She gave her squad orders to structure their search, to move in a standard skirmish pattern throughout the cathedral's cloisters and side-rooms. Sister Viola, the youngest, she ordered to stand guard at the fallen doors. Viola was new from the schola; she was high-hearted and eager to prove herself and that was all very well… but Augusta wanted her close.

'Yes, sister.' Viola, bolter in hand, returned to the doors and took her position, watching the huge and muggy writhe of the outside jungle.

Over the vox, the Sister Superior recited the Litany of Mettle. Whatever was here, they would find it.

In the cathedral's transept stood a colossal thirty-foot statue, its broken hands raised in the sign of the aquila. It had been carved in full armour and, like all such things, it faced Holy Terra as if it still sought the Light.

But if this was Saint Mina, then she had no face, and her insignia had long since fallen to dust.

Augusta was scanning, carefully looking for age and identity, when the cry came from Viola at the doorway.

'Sisters!' The word was soft across the vox, but it carried the faintest of quivers. 'I see movement!'

Augusta felt the touch of adrenaline and inhaled, enjoying the lift, the first flush of faith – as her briefing had warned her, this was a dangerous place.

'Be specific,' she said, turning to crunch back out to the nave, the cathedral's main aisle. 'What do you see?'

'Large force incoming. Seventy, eighty yards. Moving slowly, but heading this way.' Her voice was taut with fear. 'It's hard to see them through the jungle.'

Tanichus followed at Augusta's shoulder. The missionary had unhooked his lasrifle and looked slightly queasy; she hoped he could shoot straight. 'Sisters, to me. Kimura, to the doorway. Jatoya, watch the rear.' Kimura carried the squad's heavy bolter, and its faster suppression would be critical. 'Viola, description.'

'I can't see well, sister, but they're all shoulders. They're huge!'

'Space Marines?' Jatoya's tone was surprised. 'Out here?'

But Kimura was at the doorway now, weapon at the ready. Her voice came back over the vox, her tones shuddering with a rising, burning eagerness. 'They're not Heretic Astartes, sisters.' The words were alight.

'They're orks.'

Orks.

If there was one damned xenos that Augusta loathed, it was the ork. Filthy, stinking things, slavering and disorderly; they were as much the enemies of the Throne as any witch or heretic. She could feel her faith unfurling in her heart like a banner – she had a chance to reclaim this holy place, at the edge of the segmentum...

But Augusta's ruthless discipline was what had kept her alive through twenty years of warfare. She could embrace the love of her Emperor and keep her thoughts clear.

She reached Kimura at the doorway, and used her auspex to look outside.

Immediately, she saw why Viola had made the mistake.

Many of the incoming beasts were enormous, bigger than the Sisters, armour and all. But this was not the disciplined advance of highly-trained soldiers, this was ramshackle, and noisy, and slow. The orks moved more like marauders; they laughed amongst themselves, pushing and shoving and snarling. Their tones were harsh and their voices guttural.

They were hard to see through the steam, through the festooned and looping creepers.

But they were heading straight for the cathedral.

'Sister!' Kimura had reached the same conclusion – her voice was tense. Augusta saw her take a sight on the lead ork, anger radiating from her stance as if her armour burned with it.

'Hold your fire.'

For a moment, she thought Kimura would disobey, but Augusta's command of her squad was too strong. Instead, Kimura paused, quivering, her finger on the trigger, tracking the orks as they approached.

Behind them now, Viola's breathing was swift in her vox. She was afraid – and Augusta understood.

But still, the youngest of the squad had to control herself, and quickly.

Swiftly, the Sister Superior gave orders for deployment. Kimura and Caia at the door, Viola and Melia at the front left archway, Jatoya, with her flamer, watching the rear. Augusta herself, Tanichus still with her, took position at the front arch to the right, its window long since put out by the creeper and shattered to forgotten dust.

Outside, the orks advanced, oblivious. A fight had broken out amongst their number, cheered and jeered by those surrounding.

Beneath her helmet, Augusta curled her lip – she had no fear of these beasts, whatever their numbers. Over the vox, she recited the Battle Hymnal and heard her sisters join her, avidly soft.

'That Thou wouldst bring them only death,
That Thou shouldst spare none,
That Thou shouldst pardon none
We beseech Thee, destroy them.'

She felt Viola stiffen, felt her courage coalesce. She felt Kimura steady, ready to unleash His wrath on the incoming creatures and their blasphemous intentions...

'Wait,' she said, again.

The orks moved closer.

Within heavy bolter range.

Within bolter range.

Any moment now, they would see the crouching Sisters, their blood-scarlet armour and their black-and-white cloaks...

'Sisters, stay down. Kimura, on my command, full covering suppression. For the Emperor... *Fire!*'

The orks had no idea what had hit them.

Raiders and warriors alike, everything vanished in a hail of gore and shredding flesh. The heavy bolter howled in Kimura's hands, and the jungle was ripped to pieces, leaves shining like shrapnel, trees and vines cut clean in half.

One ancient trunk toppled over with a groan, but was stopped by a tangle of creeper. It hung there, creaking, like some huge executioner's axe.

Kimura's voice came over the vox, louder now, '*A morte perpetua, Domine, libra nos!*' The Hymn of Battle raged in tune with the furious barking of the weapon. The Sisters' voices joined her, rising to crystal-pure harmonics as Kimura visited bloody destruction upon the orks.

Augusta was grinning now, tight and violent beneath her helm. She knew this with every word in her ear, every flash in her blood – this was her worship, her purpose and her life. The Emperor Himself was with her, His fire in her heart, His touch in the creak and weight of her armour, in the bolter in her hand. She was here to unleash His wrath against the despoilers of this forgotten and holy place.

And it felt *good*.

At her other hip, her heavy chainsword clanked as if begging for release, but not yet... not yet.

She heard Kimura's singing ring with vehemence as the sister cut the orks to pieces.

'*From the blasphemy of the Fallen, our Emperor, deliver us!*'

But orks, despite many flaws, had no concept of intimidation. They had no interest in the Emperor's wrath, no tactics, and no sense. Another force might have gone to ground, given covering fire, but not these beasts.

Roaring with outrage, waving what clumsy weapons they had, they simply charged.

Over the singing, Augusta shouted, 'Kimura, fall back and reload! The rest of you, *fire!*'

She raised her own bolter, aiming for the largest ork she could see. Greenskins had a very simple rule of leadership – the bigger the beast, the more control it wielded. And if she could take out the leaders, the rest would be easier to kill.

The battle hymn still sounded and she added her voice once again, feeling the music thrill along her nerves like wildfire. A second wave of orks raged forwards, leering and eager.

There seemed to be no end to them.

The beasts were closing fast now, and she could see them clearly: their jutting teeth and green skin, their rusted weapons, their armour all scrappy pieces of ceramite and steel, scrounged from who knew what battlefields.

One had a set of white pauldrons bearing the distinctive fleur-de-lys. Snarling, she blew it away.

But their losses didn't touch them; they picked up the weapons of their dying and their trampled, and they just kept coming.

Bolters barked and howled in red-gauntleted hands. Tanichus took single shots with his lasrifle, picking his targets carefully. The jungle became a mess of blood and smoke and noise, but still the orks came on, slobbering and shouting, ripping through creepers and fallen trees. To one side, there was a lashing and a gurgle and half a dozen greenskins vanished, shrieking and struggling, below the surface of the marsh. Jeers and calls came from the rest, but they didn't slow down.

'There's too many of them!' The youngest sister's cry broke the hymn's purity and Augusta felt her squad waver.

She raised her voice to a paean, a clarion call like a holy trumpet, allowing them no pause.

'*Domine, libra nos!*'

Shrieking with fury, Viola resumed firing.

But the orks didn't care. They tore themselves free from the jungle's tangle and threw themselves at the steps.

The lead ork went backwards in a spray of crimson mist.

The others were already boiling past it. Tanichus kept firing, streaks of light past Augusta's shoulder. Augusta switched to full suppression and heard the bolters of the others, all growling in righteous fury.

Yet the orks still came. They were like a rotting green tide, large creatures and small, no structure, no fear. They bayed and snarled like animals.

The Sisters couldn't stop them all.

Fury rose in Augusta and was annealed to a magnesium-white flare of righteous wrath. *You shall not enter here!*

Viola, afraid, screamed the words of the hymnal, the same verse, over and over...

The advance stopped.

Shredded leaves fluttered slowly to the rotting jungle floor.

The orks had paused. Changing magazine with an action so reflexive she barely noticed, Augusta scanned them through her retinal lenses, wondering what in Dominica's name they were doing.

Had they just been overcome by the holiness of the cathedral itself?

Somehow, she doubted it.

She watched as the creatures at the front moved, taking cover behind toppled statues. She gave the order to keep firing and heard the bolters start again.

The beasts knew the Sisters were here – and they'd responded.

Smart orks? The idea was horrifying.

Yet something down there – the warboss or whatever it was – had intelligence.

It made her wonder if their presence was pure coincidence... and an odd chill went down her back.

The lead orks had taken cover now, and the jungle was ominously quiet. Behind them, through the rising steam, she could see bigger figures, moving forwards. Several had stubby sidearms, luridly decorated; the weapons gave a steady bark of fire. Rounds chewed chunks out of the stone and made the Sisters keep their heads down.

And one of them–

'Get back from the windows! Take cover!'

Her squad were already on the move, throwing themselves back. They didn't wait for the ork with the rocket launcher to loose his leering-skull-painted missile... straight into the cathedral nave.

Augusta hit the floor, taking Tanichus down with her.

The world erupted in fire.

She heard the whistling of shrapnel, felt the whoosh of heat that seared her armour and shrivelled her cloak to tatters. The orks would use the cover of the missile to gain entrance to the building, and she was back on her feet, even as the flame was dying.

'Sisters! Roll call!'

Tanichus was scrambling up, charred but unhurt – Augusta had covered as much of his unarmoured body as was possible. He was coughing, fumbling for his lasrifle amongst the settling dust.

Five voices came back to her, making her thank the Emperor Himself for the courage and experience of her squad.

The orks were on them now, piling through the doors, scrambling over the window ledges – if all else failed, Augusta would bring the building down in a final hail of rounds, and kill everything within.

For the glory of the Emperor!

But they were not done yet. They would fight with the Emperor Himself at their backs, and they would fight to their last breath.

'Kimura–!'

She started to give orders to fall back, for Kimura's heavy bolter to cover them, but her voice was lost under the detonation of a grenade, impacting right at Kimura's feet.

The sister disappeared in a blast of smoke and fragments.

Viola screamed. Chunks of roof tumbled to the floor. Tanichus scrabbled away on his backside, his rifle lost.

Now, the orks were all over the nave. Augusta could see the smaller, darker gretchins, scuttling in among their boots, picking things up and shaking them and biting them, then scurrying glee-fully away.

Slinging the bolter, she drew the chainsword and started the mechanism.

It snarled into life like pure impatience, eager for the blasphem-ers' blood.

Called by the rasp of the weapon, the Sisters were upon the orks with fists and feet and fury, punching one, kicking it to the floor, then ripping the axe out of its grip and using it on the one behind. Their armour, already red, slicked brighter with colours of death.

But somewhere under the combat-high, Augusta was beginning to understand something: this was not just a random raid, it was too big, too clever, too strong. These orks had come here knowingly.

And they'd come expecting resistance.

A hand grabbed her cloak and pulled her backwards.

She spun the chainsword, slashed through the neck of one ork and into the chest of another. Both went over, one still howling, and her thoughts were forgotten – she had other priorities. Stamp-ing at the impertinent gretchins, she slashed at a third ork, and a fourth. She was wrath incarnate, the rage of the Emperor, carving flesh and bone and armour, and spraying gore like red wine.

Tanichus had vanished, somewhere in the mess.

Sister Jatoya shouted over the vox – the orks had got round behind them.

Clever indeed.

The flamer roared as Jatoya retreated, searing the enemy and sending them screaming, burning, stumbling. The wet and seething creepers started to smoke.

And then, Augusta saw something else.

Warboss.

Throne, the beast was big! Seven and a half feet of pure, green muscle. It had metal in its ears, one lower tooth that jutted over its face, and an almost full set of armour that offered more than one well-known symbol – Blood Angels, Imperial Fists, the eight-pointed emblem of Chaos. It was a champion, and the biggest damned ork she'd ever seen.

And if *that* thing was out here scavenging, then she was straight out of the schola.

It had a sharp, sly glimmer in its red eyes – and its gaze stopped on Augusta.

She snarled at it, *'Mori blasphemus fui.'*

Die, blasphemer.

Around them, the melee slowed to a fluid dance of blood and blades. From the corner of her eye, Augusta saw Viola punch her scarlet gauntlet clean into an ork's face, saw the ork rock backwards, then shake itself and grin.

But her attention was still on the leader.

Just as its was on her.

They were the eye of the storm. The ork carried twin axes, each as long as its muscled forearm, and there was a second grenade at its belt.

It said, 'Sis-tah.'

But the snarl of the chainsword was its only reply.

Not only big, but *fast*.

Augusta was used to orks being slow, bearing down an enemy by brute force, rather than by speed or skill.

Not this thing.

In her mind, she recited the Litany of Blood – a reflex, a chant of pure focus. It was part of her combat training, something she'd learned at the schola, and it made her sharp, the tool of the might that flowed through her.

But her first side-slash was blocked, then the second, the rasp of the chainsword rising to a scream as the axes caught in its teeth.

The ork didn't falter. It was controlled and powerful. She went backwards, parrying one blow after another, her boots scattering dust and mess and fallen ork bodies. And it came after her, its breath as foul as its coated yellow teeth. It was still talking; threats and mockery, but she had no interest in bandying words with it. It was defiler and despoiler, and it would die.

Another blow, and another. She tried to press forwards, but it gave her no gap in which to strike. Around her, the rest of the squad fought with knives and fists, hammering the orks to a bloody green pulp.

She saw one sister falter, and fall to her knees.

'Sis-tah.' Grinning, the monster dropped both axes. It grabbed the chainsword, blades and all, in one massive hand, and tore it out of her grasp.

It threw it aside.

She saw Jatoya's flamer in the corner of her vision, saw Caia and Melia together pick an ork up bodily and hurl it into a gathering of its fellows, sending all of them scattering to the floor.

They *would* win this!

It almost made her laugh, the sound like pure, righteous joy. With only her gauntlets, she threw herself at the monster.

But it was too fast – it grabbed her, its chainsword-carved hand around her gorget, and it lifted her clean off the floor.

Furious now, she kicked it.

Again.

Again.

She split the beast's lip, but its grin only widened, its teeth now streaked with its own blood. Furious, she took its wrist in her gasp and tried to twist and crush its arm, force it to drop her.

It shook her like an errant underling.

'Sister!' Across the vox, she heard Jatoya's cry. Her second in command couldn't use her flamer but Jatoya barked a clear order at the rest of the squad.

'Take it down!'

The warboss didn't care. It shook her again, her armour clattering.

'Sis-tah,' it said. *'Know* you. Came to *find.'*

What?

'Wait!' The word was a gurgle over the vox.

The beast was laughing at her. 'We take all. Kill sis-tahs. Take *weapons.'*

Understanding grew up her spine like ice. She stared at the ork as it shook her for the third time.

Take weapons.

It *had* known that the Sisters were here!

The fighting around them was beginning to lessen. The orks were faltering, and the Sisters hacked at them without mercy, driving them back. Many of the smaller beasts were dropping their weapons and running away. Jatoya had slung her flamer and fought with her fists alone; Augusta saw her punch an ork in the back of the neck, saw it stumble to its knees.

One red-armoured figure – she couldn't tell who – was walking through the mess, bolter in hand, putting single shots into struggling heaps. Another was clearing the bodies from the altar steps, and she could see the broken form of Kimura, smoke still rising from the joints in her armour.

Then she saw one sister click the neck of her helm and remove it, revealing a freckled face and bobbed red hair, all tousled and sweating.

Viola.

Her expression was like acid-carved steel.

'Put her down.'

Viola raised her bolter, and took clear aim at the ork's head.

The warboss paused. Augusta saw it look round at its defeated force; saw its red eyes narrow, its lip curl. Then it let her go, and she fell, crashing to her knees on the cathedral floor.

Viola came closer, the bolter aimed and steady.

The ork bared its teeth at her.

Impressed with the new mettle of the youngest sister, Augusta stood up. She stepped in close to the warboss and said, 'You knew we were here.' Talking to the thing made her flesh crawl, but she had to know. 'How? Who told you?'

'Sis-tah.' The warboss looked from Augusta to Viola and back. It cocked its head to one side and said, 'So fool-ish. So *tiny*.'

Augusta glared at it. 'How did you *know*?'

'Blood Axes.' It thumped the crossed-axe symbol on its chest. 'We *kill*. Take *weapons*.'

She held its red gaze. Augusta had heard of the Blood Axes, they traded with humans sometimes – it might explain why this monster was so damned clever. But not how it had known–

Tanichus.

The realisation came like the Light of the Emperor Himself – a ray of pure Truth. Tanichus had been here before – had lived here for months – and only Tanichus had known that the Sisters were coming.

And, as Augusta remembered, he'd used his local knowledge to set the time of their reconnaissance.

He'd told them when to be here.

'Get the missionary.' She snapped the command over the vox, saw Caia nod and turn away.

'What did he offer you?' she said to the warboss.

It sneered at her, its red eyes cold.

Reached for the grenade at its belt.

She saw the motion, went to kick its wrist – but Viola was faster.

Her face like stone, the youngest sister shot it clean through the head.

Gore spattered. The huge beast teetered for a second, almost as if startled – then it crashed to the floor like a tree falling. The whole building seemed to shake.

A pool of crimson spread out across the flagstones.

'Good shot,' Augusta told the youngest sister.

Viola grinned.

Behind them, Caia had returned with Tanichus, the missionary almost gibbering with fear.

'Found him trying to flee,' Caia said. 'Scuttling out of the crypt like an insect.'

'Sister!' The missionary was white-faced; he looked like he was about to vomit. Her armour still dripping, she walked over to him, closing her hand about his neck just like the ork's had been about her own.

He looked at her, his eyes wide, his mouth open. 'Sister Superior, I swear by His Light–'

'You dare? You dare swear by the Emperor's name?' Her hand closed; she felt his breath catch in his throat. 'I should crush you where you stand.'

'Sister, please!'

At her feet, the warboss lay dead. The orks were finished and the Sisters had closed ranks at Augusta's shoulders – the entire cathedral seemed gathered at her back, looking at the missionary.

'You've been here before,' Augusta said. 'Lived with the townspeople. You're the link, Tanichus. You're the only thing that could have manipulated the pieces. Tell me, did you speak to the orks? Deal with them? Did you lie about the icon? Something to bring us out here, just so the orks could kill us for our *weapons*.' She shook him like a rat.

'Sister, I swear!'

Disgusted, she let him go, watched as Caia's gauntleted hands closed on his shoulders and forced him to his knees.

'Sister Kimura *died*,' Augusta said. She freed the seal on her helm and took it off, enjoying the relative cool of the marsh-thick air.

Meeting her flat, steel gaze, Tanichus was starting to panic. 'Please!'

She dropped to one knee, gripped his jaw in one bloody gauntlet and forced him to look at her.

'Repent, heretic, you may yet save your soul.'

Tanichus was shaking now, his face pale. Sweat shone from his skin.

She'd seen this a hundred times in the suddenly caught-out-and-penitent – the guilt, the fear. And they were exactly the admission she was looking for.

'Tell me the truth,' she snarled at him. 'What deal did you do?'

He was snivelling now, terrified. Words spilled out of him. 'When I came here,' he said, 'the townspeople told me about the orks. The tribe had been destroying the villages, committing such horrors... and they were going to wipe out the town. The people told the orks about the cathedral. Said they could have anything they could find if they just left the town alone. Then I came, and they begged me for my help. They knew that the orks would come back. Knew what would happen to them.' He seemed almost in tears. 'They're just people, sister, just families. They have lives and fears and hopes. Children growing up.' His face was etched in pain. 'I just wanted to help them.' He held back a sob.

Augusta saw the pity on Viola's freckled face, saw the stances of the others shift – they knew full well what the orks would have done to the townspeople.

He said, 'I went to find the orks. I told them that I would bring them weapons, armour, if they just left the people alone. And–'

'And so you brought them *us*.' Augusta's tone was scathing.

'You beat them, didn't you?' He was pleading with her. 'You *won*!'

She contemplated the sobbing man, water tracing clean lines through the filth on his skin, and she understood his pain, the choice he'd made.

But it didn't change the facts.

'Lysimachus Tanichus, you are a traitor. You have manipulated the Adepta Sororitas to your own ends. You have betrayed the Eccle-siarchy, and the name of the Emperor.' Tanichus opened his mouth, but she didn't want to hear it. 'And your story misses one critical point – what would have happened if we'd *lost?'*

'You're Sister Superior Augusta Santorus – you *don't* lose!'

'Tell that to Kimura.'

Tanichus glanced at the fallen sister, then slumped forwards, defeated. He was sniffling. 'I only wanted to help the people.'

'You betrayed us to the enemy.' She backhanded him, her metal gauntlet cutting his cheek. His head snapped sideways, then he looked back up at her, uncomprehending and horrified. 'You brought us here on a *lie*. You cost the life of Sister Kimura. You tried to flee the battle. Your guilt is manifest, and your life is forfeit.'

He stared at her, his mouth open.

But she wasn't done. 'However, I will say this – this world, Lau-tis, in the Drusus Marches of the Calixis Sector, is now under the observation and protection of the Order of the Bloody Rose. We claim this cathedral, and all within it, in His name. And we will protect the people – on the assumption that they acknowledge the Emperor of All Mankind.'

Tanichus had fallen forwards. He was shaking, his hands over his face. 'Please! I knew you'd beat them! I *knew!'*

'I will deliver your protection, Tanichus. But you...' She dragged his head up again. '*In pythonissam non patieris vivere* – I shall not suffer your life.'

'Sister Superior...' Viola's voice came to her ears, not over the vox. 'He should come back with us, face judgement–'

'Enough!' Augusta snapped the order and Viola recoiled. 'I know exactly what to do with this offal.'

'Sister,' Jatoya said, more cautiously. 'It is not our place–'

'He has *mocked* us!' Augusta barked, furious. 'Kimura is dead!'

Tanichus threw himself at her feet. 'Please!'

Viola and Jatoya exchanged a glance.

Augusta reached down with one hand, and dragged the sobbing

man back to his feet. 'You do not take the name of the saint in vain. You do not manipulate the Order to your own ends. And believe me, if the orks *had* won, both you and your town would still have been destroyed. That warboss would have cut you to pieces and eaten you.'

Tanichus was shaking now. She tore the rosarius out of his grasp, gave it to the closest of her sisters.

Then she pulled her fleur-de-lys punch-dagger from the front of her armour, and slit Tanichus' throat.

Augusta felt Viola flinch, though she said nothing. Tanichus gaped and fell, bubbles on his lips, hands to his throat, his blood mingling with that of the dead ork.

His last word, as he hit the floor, was *Mercy*.

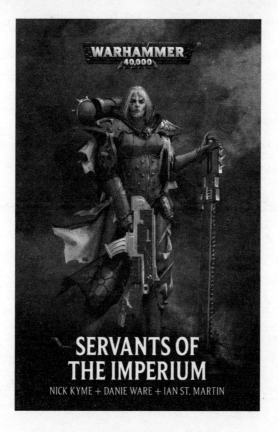

THORN
WISHES TALON

Dan Abnett

Introducing

GREGOR EISENHORN
AND GIDEON RAVENOR

INQUISITORS, ORDO XENOS

The past never lets us go. It is persistent and unalterable.

The future, however, is aloof, a stranger. It stands with its back to us, mute and private, refusing to communicate what it knows or what it sees.

Except to some. On Nova Durma, deep in the leech-infested forests of the Eastern Telgs, there is a particular grotto into which the light of the rising daystar falls once every thirty-eight days. There, by means of some secret ministry and ritual craft that I have no ready wish to understand, the blistered seers of the Divine Fratery coax the reluctant future around until they can see its face in their silver mirrors, and hear its hushed, unwilling voice.

It is my fervent hope that what it has to say to them is a lie.

That night, the waste-world called Malinter had six visitors. They left their transport, dark and hook-winged, on a marshy flood plain, slightly bowed over to starboard where the landing claws had sunk into the ooze. They proceeded west, on foot.

A storm was coming, and it was not entirely natural. They walked through streamers of white fog, crossing outcrops of green quartz, lakes of moss and dank watercourses choked with florid lichens. The sky shone like filthy, tinted glass. In the distance, a pustular range of hills began to vanish in the rain-blur of the encroaching elements. Lightning flashed, like sparks off flint, or remote laser fire.

They had been on the surface for an hour, and had just sighted the tower, when the first attempt was made to kill them.

There was a rattle, almost indistinguishable from the doom-roll of the approaching thunder, and bullets whipped up spray from the mud at the feet of the tallest visitor.

His name was Harlon Nayl. His tall, broad physique was wrapped in a black-mesh bodyglove. His head was shaved apart from a simple goatee. He raised the heavy Hecuter pistol he had been carrying in his right fist, and made a return of fire into the gathering dark.

In answer, several more unseen hostiles opened up. The visitors scattered for cover.

'Were you expecting this?' Nayl asked as he crouched behind a quartz boulder and snapped shots off over it.

+I didn't know what to expect.+

The answer came telepathically from Nayl's master, and seemed far from reassuring.

'How many?' Nayl called out.

Twenty metres away from him, another big man called Zeph Mathuin shouted back from cover. 'Six!' echoed his estimation. Mathuin was as imposing as Nayl, but his skin was dark, the colour of varnished hardwood. His black hair was plaited into strands, and beaded. Both men had been bounty hunters in their time. Neither followed that profession any longer.

'Make it seven,' contradicted Kara Swole as she wriggled up beside Nayl, keeping her head low. She was a short, compact woman with cropped red hair. Her voluptuous figure was currently concealed beneath a long black leather duster with a fringe of larisel fur around the neck.

'Seven?' queried Nayl, as whining hard-round smacked into the far side of the rock.

'Six!' Mathuin called again.

Kara Swole had been a dancer-acrobat before she'd joined the band, and ordinarily she would defer to the combat experience of the two ex-hunters. But she had an ear for these things.

'Listen!' she said. 'Three autorifles,' she identified, counting off on her fingers. 'Two lasguns, a pistol, and that...' she drew Nayl's attention to a distinctive plunk! plunk! 'That's a stubber.'

Nayl nodded and smiled.

'Six!' Mathuin insisted.

+Kara is correct. There are seven. Now can we deal with them, please?+

Their master's mind-voice seemed unusually terse and impatient. Not a good sign. One of several not good signs that had already distinguished this night.

The two other members of the team sheltered against a gravel shelf some distance to Nayl's left. Their names were Patience Kys and Carl Thonius. A slight, fussy, well-bred young man, Thonius held the rank of interrogator, and was technically the master's second-in-command. He had drawn a compact pistol from inside his beautifully tailored coat, but was too busy complaining about the weather, the mud, and the prospect of death by gunshot wounds to use it.

Patience Kys suggested he might like to shut up. She was a slender, pale woman, dressed in high boots of black leather, a bell skirt of grey silk and an embroidered black leather shirt. Her hair was pinned up in a chignon with silver clasps.

She scanned the view ahead, and located one of the hostiles firing from the cover of some quartz rocks.

'Ready?' she yelled over at Nayl.

'Pop 'em up!' he replied.

Kys was telekinetic. She focused her trained mind, and exerted a little pressure. The quartz rocks scattered apart across the slime, revealing a rather surprised man holding an autorifle.

His surprise lasted about two seconds until a single shot from Nayl hit him in the brow and tumbled him leadenly onto his back.

With a spiteful grin, Kys reached out again and dragged another of the hostiles out into the open with her mind. The man yelled out, scared and uncomprehending. His heels churned in the ooze, and he flailed his arms, fighting the invisible force that yanked him by the scruff of the neck.

There was a blurt of noise like an industrial hammer-drill, and the man ceased to be, shredded into pieces by heavy fire.

Mathuin had shot him. His left hand was a burnished-chrome augmetic, and he had locked it into the governing socket of the lethal rotator cannon that he was wearing strapped around his torso. The multi-barrels whirred and cycled, venting vapour.

The firing ceased.

+They have fled for now. They will return, I have no doubt.+

The master of the team moved among them. To the uninformed, Inquisitor Gideon Ravenor appeared to be a machine rather than a man. He was a box, a smoothly angled wedge of armoured metal with a glossy, polished finish from which even the approaching lightning seemed unwilling to reflect. This was his force chair, his life-support system, totally enclosed and self-sufficient. The chair's anti-gravity discs spun hypnotically as he advanced.

Inside that enclosing chair, one of the Imperium's most brilliant inquisitors – and most articulate theorists – lay trapped forever. Years before, at the start of a glittering career in the service of the ordos, Gideon Ravenor had been struck down during a heretical attack, his fair and strong body burned and fused away into a miserable residue of useless flesh. Only his mind had survived.

But such a mind! Sharp, incisive, poetic, just... and powerful too. Kys had not met a psi-capable remotely strong enough to master Gideon Ravenor.

They were sworn to him, the five of them. Nayl, Thonius, Swole, Mathuin and Kys. Sworn and true. They would follow him to the ends of the known stars, if needs be.

Even when he chose not to tell them where they were going.

* * *

The Divine Fratery practises a barbaric initiation process of voluntary blinding. Sight, as one might expect, is considered their fundamental skill, but not sight as we might understand it. Novices sacrifice one of their eyes as proof of their intent, and have that missing eye replaced by a simple augmetic to maintain everyday function. The one remaining organic eye is then trained and developed, using ritual, alchemic and sorcerous processes.

An initiated member of the Fratery may therefore be identified by his single augmetic eye, and by the patch of purple velvet that covers his remaining real eye at all times except for circumstances of cult ceremony. A novitiate, self-blinded in one socket, must work to fashion his own silver mirror before he is allowed his augmetic, or indeed any medical or sterilising treatment. He must cut and hammer his dish of silver, and then work it with abrasive wadding until it is a perfect reflector to a finesse of .0088 optical purity. Many die of septicaemia or other wound-related infections before they accomplish this. Others, surviving the initial infections, spend many months or even years finishing the task. Thus, members of the cult may additionally be identified by blistering of the skin, tissue abnormalities, and even significant necrotising scarring incurred during the long months of silver-working.

It is also my experience that few Fratery members have codable or matchable fingerprints. Years of scrupulous endeavour with abrasive wadding wear away hands as well as silver.

Overhead, the sky flashed and vibrated. Kara could hear the thunder, and felt the drizzle in the wind. Fog-vapour smirched out the distance.

With the toe of her boot, she gingerly rolled over the body of the man Nayl had shot. He was dressed in cheap, worn foul-weather clothes made of woven plastek fibre and leather. He had one augmetic eye, crude and badly sutured into the socket, and a velvet patch over the other.

'Anyone we know?' asked Nayl, coming up behind her.

Unlike the others, Nayl and Kara had not been recruited for ordo service by Ravenor himself. They had originally owed loyalty to Ravenor's mentor, Inquisitor Gregor Eisenhorn. Somewhere along the line, a decade or more past, they had become Ravenor's. Kara often thought of Eisenhorn. Stern, fierce, so much harder to bear than Ravenor, Eisenhorn had nevertheless been a good man to follow. And she owed him. But for Gregor Eisenhorn, she would still be a dancer-acrobat in the circuses of Bonaventure.

She often wondered what had become of her former master. She'd last seen him back in '87, during the mission to 5213X. He'd been a wreck of a man by then, supported only by his burning will and fundamental augmetics. Some had said he'd crossed a line and become a radical. Kara didn't believe that. Eisenhorn had always been so… hard line. She thought of him fondly, as she did the others from that time. Alizabeth Bequin, God-Emperor rest her, dear Aemos, Medea Betancore and Fischig.

They had known some times together. Great times, bad times. But this was her place now.

'Face doesn't ring any bells,' she said. She reached down and lifted the eye patch, just out of curiosity. A real eye, wide and glazed, lay beneath.

'What the hell is that about?' Nayl wondered.

Kara reached up and slicked the short, red strands of her rain-wet hair back across her head. She looked across at Mathuin and Thonius beside the other body. Thonius was, as ever, elegantly dressed, and as he crouched in the mud, he fussed about his shoes.

Thonius was Ravenor's pupil, which supposed that one day Thonius was to be promoted to full inquisitor. Ravenor had been Eisenhorn's interrogator. Kara wondered sometimes if Carl had anything like the same stuff.

'If you'd left him a little more intact, we might have made a decent examination,' Thonius complained.

'This is a rotator cannon,' Mathuin said bluntly. 'It doesn't do intact.'

Thonius prodded the grisly remains with a stick. 'Well, I think we've got an augmetic eye here too. And what's either an eyepatch or a very unsatisfactory posing thong.'

Thonius' caustic wit usually drew smiles from the band, but not this night. No one was in the mood for laughs. Ravenor, generally so forthcoming with his team, had told them virtually nothing about the reasons for coming to Malinter. As far as anyone knew, he'd simply diverted them to this remote waste-world after receiving some private communiqué.

Most alarmingly of all, he'd chosen to join them on the surface. Ravenor usually ran his team telepathically from a distance via the wraithbone markers they all wore. He only came along in person when the stakes were high.

+Let's move on,+ Ravenor said.

The grotto in the Eastern Telgs is deep in the smoking darkness of the forests. The glades are silent except for insect chitter, and wreathed with vapour and steam. There are biting centipedes everywhere, some as long as a man's finger, others as long as a man's leg. The air stinks of mildew.

Once every thirty-eight days, the rising star comes up at such an angle it forces its pale and famished light in through a natural hole in the rock face outside the grotto. The beams streak in down an eighty degree angle to the azimuth, and strike the still freshwater of the pool in the grotto's base, lighting the milky water like a flame behind muslin.

Brethren of the Fratery cower around the pool – after days of ritual starvation and self-flagellation – and attempt to interrupt the falling beams with their silver mirrors. At such times, I have observed, they remove the purple velvet patches from their real eyes, and place them over their augmetics.

Their flashing mirrors reflect many colours of light. Having ingested lho seeds and other natural hallucinogenics, they glare into their mirrors, and begin to gabble incoherently.

Voxographic units, run on battery leads, are set around the grotto to record their ramblings. As the light fades again, the masters of the Fratery

*play back the voxcorders, and tease out the future truths – or lies – that
they have been told.*

The tower, as they approached it, was far larger than they had first
imagined. The main structure, splintered and ruined, rose a full half
kilometre into the dark, bruised sky, like an accusing finger. At the
base, like the bole of an ancient tree, it thickened, and spread into
great piers and buttresses that anchored it into the headland. Crumbling stone bridge spans linked the rocky shelf to the nearest piers.

There was no way of defining its origin or age, nor the hands –
human or otherwise – that had constructed it. Even its purpose was
in doubt. According to the scans, it was the only artificial structure
on Malinter. Older star maps referred to it simply by means of a
symbol that indicated ruin (antique/xenos).

As they picked their way through ancient screes of rubble and
broken masonry towards the nearest span, the rain began to lash
down, pattering on the mud and driving off the raised stonework.
The rising wind began to shiver the glossy black ivy and climbing
vines clinging in thick mats to the lower walls.

'This message. It told you to come here?' Nayl asked.

+What message?+

Nayl frowned and looked at the floating chair. 'The message you
got.'

+I never said anything about a message.+

'Oh, come on! Fair play!' Nayl growled. 'Why won't you tell us
what we're getting into here?

+Harlon.+ Ravenor's voice sliced into Nayl's mind, and he winced
slightly. Ravenor's telepathy was sometimes painfully sharp when
he was troubled or preoccupied. Nayl realised that Ravenor's
thought-voice was directed at him alone, a private word the others couldn't hear.

+Trust me, old friend. I dare tell you nothing until I'm sure of
what we're dealing with. If it turns out to be a trick, you could be
biased by misinformation.+

'I'm no amateur,' Nayl countered. The others looked at him, hearing only his side of the conversation.

+I know, but you're a loyal man. Loyalty sometimes blinds us. Trust me on this.+

'What in the name of the Golden Throne was that?' Thonius said abruptly. They'd all heard it. Ravenor and Kys had felt it.

High in the ruined summit of the tower, something had screamed. Loud, hideous, inhuman, drawn out. More screams, from other non-human voices, answered it. Each resounded both acoustically and psychically. The air temperature dropped sharply. Sheens of ice crackled into view, caking the upper sweep of the walls.

They moved on a few metres. The keening wails grew louder, whooping and circling within the high walls, as if screaming avian things were flying around inside. As lightning accompanies thunder, so each scream was accompanied by a sympathetic flash of light. The psychic shrieks seemed to draw the storm down, until a halo of flashing, jagged light coruscated in the sky above the tower. Corposant danced along the walls like white, fluorescent balls.

Kys, her psi-sensitive mind feeling it worse than the rest, paused to wipe fresh blood off her lip with the back of her gwel-skin glove. Her nose was bleeding.

As she did so, the hostiles began trying to kill them again.

The Divine Fratery, may the ordos condemn their sick souls, seek to chart the future. All possible futures, in fact. With their mirrors and their abominably practised eyes, they identify events to come, and take special interest in those events that are ill-favoured. Disasters, plagues, invasions, collapses of governments, heresies, famines, defeats in battle. Doom, in any guise.

The masters of the Fratery then disseminate the details of their oracles to the lower orders of their cult. By my estimation, the Fratery numbers several thousand, many of them apparently upstanding Imperial citizens, spread through hundreds of worlds in the subsectors Antimar, Helican, Angelus and Ophidian. Once a 'prospect' as they call them has been identified, certain portions of the 'cult membership' are charged with doing everything they can to ensure that it comes to pass, preferably in the worst and most damaging way possible. If a plague is foreseen, then cult members will deliberately break quarantine orders to ensure that the outbreak spreads. If the prospect is a famine, they will plant incendiary bombs or bio-toxins in the Munitorum grain stores of the threatened world. A heretic emerges? They will protect him and publish his foul lies abroad. An invasion approaches? They are the fifth column that will destroy the defenders from within.

They seek doom. They seek to undermine the fabric of our Imperium, the culture of man, and cause it to founder and fall. They seek galactic apocalypse, an age of darkness and fire, wherein their unholy masters, the Ruinous Powers, can rise up and take governance of all.

Five times now I have thwarted their efforts. They hate me, and wish me dead. Now I seek to derail their efforts a sixth time, here, tonight, on Malinter. I have journeyed far out of my way, pursued by their murder-bands, to carry a warning.

For I have seen their latest prospect with my own eyes. And it is a terrible thing.

Laser fire scorched across the mossy span of the bridge arch, sizzling in the rain. Some of it came from the ruin ahead, some from the crags behind them. Stonework shattered and split. Las-bolts and hard-rounds snapped and stung away from the age-polished cobbles.

'Go!' yelled Nayl, turning back towards the crags and firing his weapon in a two-handed brace. At his side, Kara Swole kicked her assault weapon into life. It bucked like a living thing, spitting spent casings out in a sideways flurry.

They backed across the bridge as the others ran ahead. Mathuin and Kys led the way, into the gunfire coming out of the dim archways and terraces ahead. Mathuin's rotator cannon squealed, and flames danced around the spinning barrels. Stone debris and shorn ivy fluttered off the wounded walls. Kys saw a man, almost severed at the waist, drop from an archway into the lightless gulf below the bridge.

Ravenor and Thonius came up behind them. Thonius was still gazing up at the screamlight tearing and dancing around the tower overhead. He had one hand raised, as if to protect his face from the bullets and laser fire whipping around him.

+Concentrate!+

'Yes, yes... of course...' Thonius replied.

Mathuin ran under the first arch into the gloom of the tower chambers. His augmetic eyes, little coals of red hard-light, gleaming inside his lids, immediately adjusted to the light conditions, and revealed to him the things hidden in the shadows. He pivoted left, and mowed down four hostiles with a sustained belch of cannon fire. More shot at him.

Kys ran in beside him. She had a laspistol harnessed at her waist, but she hadn't drawn it. She extended the heels of her palms, and four kineblades slipped out of the sheaths built into the forearms of her shirt. Each was thin, razor-sharp, twelve centimetres long, and lacked handles. She controlled them with her mind, orbiting them around her body in wide, buzzing circuits, in a figure of eight, like some lethal human orrery.

A hostile opened fire directly at her with an autopistol, cracking off four shots. Without flinching, she faced them, circling a pair of the blades so they intercepted and deflected the first two shots. The second two she bent wide with her mind, so that they sailed off harmlessly like swatted flies.

Before he could fire again, Kys pinned the hostile to the stone wall with the third kineblade.

Mathuin was firing again.

'You all right there, Kys?' he yelled over the cannon's roar.

'Fine.' She smiled. She was in her element. Dealing death in the name of the Emperor, punishing His enemies, was all she lived for. She was a secretive being. Patience Kys was not her real name, and none of the band knew what she'd been baptised. She'd been born on Sameter, in the Helican sub, and had grown to woman-hood on that filthy, brow-beaten world. Things had happened to her there, things that had changed her and made her Patience Kys, the telekine killer. She never spoke of it. The simple fact was she had faced and beaten a miserable death, and now she was paying death back, in the God-Emperor's name, with souls more deserving of annihilation.

With a jerk of her mind, she tugged the kineblade out of the pinned corpse and flew it back to join the others. They whistled as they spun, deflecting more gunfire away from her. Five more hostiles lay ahead, concealed behind mouldering pillars. With a nasal grunt, she sped the kineblades away from her. They shot like guided missiles down the terraceway, arcing around obstacles, whipping around the pillars. Four of the hostiles fell, slashed open by the hurtling blades.

The fifth she yanked out of cover with her telekinesis, and shot. Now, at last, the gun was in her hands.

Inexorable as a planet moving along its given path, Ravenor floated into the gloom, passing between Kys and Mathuin as the ex-bounty hunter hosed further mayhem at the last of the hostiles on his side. Thonius ran up alongside him.

'What now?' the interrogator asked hopefully. 'At least we're out of that ghastly rain.'

Screamlight echoed and flashed through the tower from far above, reverberating the structure to its core. Kys shuddered involuntarily. Her nose was bleeding again.

+Carl? Zeph?+

Ravenor's mind-voice was quiet, as if he too was suffering the side effects of the psychic screams. +Rearguard, please. Make sure Kara and Harlon make it in alive.+

'But–' Thonius complained. Mathuin was already running back to the archway.

+Do as I say, Carl!+

'Yes, inquisitor,' replied Thonius. He turned and hurried after Mathuin.

+With me, please, Patience.+

Kys had just retrieved her kineblades. She held out her arms to let them slide back into her cuff-sheaths. The concentrated activity had drained her telekinetic strength, and the terrible screamlight from above had sapped her badly.

+Are you up to this?+

Kys raised her laspistol.

'I was born up for this, Gideon,' she grinned.

The prospect is, as most are, vague. There are no specifics. However, it is regarded as a one hundred per cent certainty by the masters of the Fratery that a daemonic abomination is about to be manifested into the material universe. This, they predict, will come to pass between the years 400 and 403.M41. Emperor protect us, it may have already happened.

There are some details. The crucial event that triggers the manifestation will happen on Eustis Majoris, the overcrowded and dirty capital world of the Angelus subsector, within those aforementioned dates. It may, at the time, seem a minor event, but its consequences will be vast. Hundreds may die. Thousands... mayhap millions, if it is not stopped.

The daemon will take human form, and walk the worlds of the Imperium undetected. It has a name. Phonetically 'SLIITE' or perhaps Slyte or Slight.

It must be stopped. Its birth must be prevented.

All I have done in my long career in service of the ordos, all I have achieved... will be as nothing if this daemon comes into being.

'It's getting a little uncomfortable out here,' Nayl remarked. A las-shot had just scored across the flesh of his upper arm, but he didn't even wince.

'Agreed,' said Kara, ejecting another spent clip onto the cobbles of the span, and slamming in a fresh one.

They'd been backing away steadily under fire, and now the archway was tantalisingly close.

They ducked their heads instinctively as heavy fire ripped out of the archway behind them, and peppered the landwards-end of the bridge span. Mathuin was covering them at last.

They turned, and ran into cover, bullets and las-fire chasing their heels.

Inside the archway, Thonius was waving them on. Mathuin's cannon ground dry, and he paused to pop out the ammo drum and slap in a fresh one from the heavy pouches around his waist.

Nayl bent in the shadows, and reloaded his pistol quickly, expertly. He looked up, and stared out into the torrential rain. In the dark of the storm and the swiftly falling night, he counted at least nine muzzle flashes barking their way.

'How many?' he asked.

This time, Mathuin didn't answer. He turned his stony, hard-light gaze towards Kara and raised an eyebrow.

'Fifteen,' she said at once.

'Fifteen,' mused Nayl. 'That's five each.'

'Hey!' said Thonius. 'There are four of us here!'

'I know,' Nayl grinned. 'But it's still five each. Unless you intend to surprise us.'

'You little bastard,' snapped Thonius. He raised his weapon, and pinked off several shots at the enemy across the span.

'Hmmm…' said Nayl. 'Still fifteen.'

+Kara. Can you join us?+

'On my way, boss,' said Kara Swole. She grinned at Nayl. 'Can you deal here? I mean, now it's seven and a half each.'

'Get on,' Nayl said. He started firing. Kara dashed off into the darkness behind them.

Thonius blasted away again. They all saw a hostile on the far side of bridge, through the rain, tumble and pitch off the crag.

'There!' Thonius said triumphantly.

'Seven each then,' Mathuin remarked to Nayl.

The Divine Fratery, as I have learned, find it particularly easy to identify in their prospects others who have dabbled in farseeing and clairvoyance.

It is as if such individuals somehow illuminate their life courses by toying with the future. The bright track of one has attracted their particular attention. It is through him, and the men and women around him, that the prospect of the manifestation has come to light.

He will cause it. Him, or one of those close to him.

That is why I have taken it upon myself to warn him.

For he is my friend. My pupil. My interrogator.

Kys hadn't seen or even sensed the cultists behind the next archway. Ravenor, gliding forwards without hesitation, pulped all four of them with his chair's built-in psycannons.

Kys followed him, striding through lakes of leaking blood and mashed tissue. She was worn out. The constant screams were getting to her.

They heard footfalls behind them. Kara Swole ran into view. Kys lowered her weapon.

'You called for me?'

+Indeed I did, Kara. I can't get up there.+

Kara looked up into the gloomy rafters and beams above them.

'No problem.' She took off her coat. Beneath it, she was dressed in a simple matt-green bodyglove.

'Hey, Kar. Luck,' called Kys.

Kara smiled.

She limbered up for a moment, and then leapt up into the rafters, gripping the mouldering wood, and gaining momentum.

Rapidly, all her acrobat skills coming back to her, she ascended, hand over hand, leaping from beam to beam, defying the dreadful gulf beneath her.

She was getting increasingly close to the flitting source of the screamlight. Her pulse raced. Grunting, she somersaulted again, and landed on her feet on a crossmember.

Kara stood for a moment, feeling the streaming rain slick down over her from the tower's exposed roof. She stuck out her hands for balance, the assault weapon tightly cinched under her bosom.

There was a light above her, shining out from a stairless door-way in the shell of the tower. Faint artificial light, illuminating the millions of raindrops as they hurtled down the empty tower shaft towards her.

'Seeing this?' she asked.

+Yes, Kara.+

'What you expected?'

+I have no idea.+

'Here goes,' she said, and jumped into space, into rainfall, into air. A hesitation, on the brink, dark depths below her. Then she seized a rotting timber beam, and swung, her fingers biting deep into the damp, flaking wood.

She pivoted in the air, and flew up into the doorway, feet first.

She landed firmly, balanced, arms wide.

A figure stood before her in the ruined tower room, illuminated by a single hovering glow-globe.

'Hello, Kara,' the figure said. 'It's been a long time.'

She gasped. 'Oh God-Emperor... my master...'

The man was tall, shrouded in a dark leather coat that did not quite conceal the crude augmetics supporting his frame. His head was bald, his eyes dark-rimmed. He leaned heavily on a metal staff.

Rainwater streaming off him, Inquisitor Gregor Eisenhorn gazed at her.

Down at the archway, Thonius recoiled in horror.

'I think we have a problem,' he said.

'Don't be such a pussy,' Nayl said.

'Actually, I think he might be right,' said Mathuin. 'That's not good, is it?'

Nayl craned his neck to look. Something blocky and heavy was striding towards them over the bridge span. It was metal and solid, machined striding limbs hissing steam from piston bearings. Its arms were folded against the sides of its torso like the wings of a flightless bird. Those arms, each one a heavy las-cannon, began to cough and spit. Massive hydraulic absorbers soaked up the recoil.

The archway collapsed in a shower of exploding masonry. Nayl, Thonius and Mathuin fled into the cover of the gallery behind.

'Emperor save me,' Nayl exclaimed. 'They've got a bloody Dreadnought!'

Rainwater dripped off Eisenhorn's nose.

'Gideon? Is he with you, Kara?' he asked.

'Yes, he is,' she stammered. 'Throne, it's good to see you.'

'And you, my dear. But it's important I speak to Gideon.'

Kara nodded.

'Ware me,' she said.

Far below, Ravenor heard her. Kara Swole stiffened, her eyes clouding. The wraithbone pendant at her throat glowed with a dull, ethereal light.

She wasn't Kara Swole any more. Her body was possessed by the mind of Gideon Ravenor.

'Hello, Gregor,' Kara's mouth said.

'Gideon. Well met. I was worried you wouldn't come.'

'And ignore a summons from my mentor? Phrased in Glossia? "Thorn wishes Talon..." I was hardly going to ignore that.'

'I thought you would appreciate a taste of the old, private code,' said Eisenhorn. His frozen face failed to show the smile he was feeling.

'How could I forget it, Thorn? You drummed it into me.'

Eisenhorn nodded. 'Much effort getting here?'

Kara's lips conveyed Ravenor's words. 'Some. An effort made to kill us. Nayl is holding them off at the gateway to the tower.'

'Old Harlon, eh?' Eisenhorn said. 'Ever dependable. You've got a good man there, Gideon. A fine man. Give him my respects. And Kara too, best there is.'

'I know, Gregor.' A strangely intense expression that wasn't her own appeared on Kara's face. 'I think it's time you told me why you brought me here.'

'Yes, it is. But in person, I think. That would be best. That way you can stop subjecting Kara to that effort of puppeting. And we can be more private. I'll come down to you.'

'How? There are no stairs.'

'The same way I got up here,' Eisenhorn said. He looked upwards, into the rain hosing down through the broken roof.

'Cherubael?' he whispered.

Something nightmarish in the strobing screamlight answered him.

Its pitted steel hull glossy with rain, the Dreadnought strode through the shattered archway. The booming storm threw its hulking shadow a hundred jagging directions at once with its lightning. Its massive cannon pods pumped pneumatically as they retched out streams of las-bolts. The weapons made sharp, barking squeals as they discharged, a repeating note louder than the storm.

Behind it, three dozen armed brethren of the Divine Fratery charged across the bridge span.

Stone split and fractured under the bombardment. Pillars that had stood for aeons teetered and collapsed like felled trees, spraying stone shards across the terrace flooring.

Nayl, Mathuin and Thonius retreated into the empty inner chambers of the ruined tower. Even Mathuin's rotator couldn't so much as dent the Dreadnought's armour casing.

'Someone really, really wants us dead,' Thonius said.

'Us… or the person we came here to meet,' Nayl countered. They hurried down a dim colonnade, and Nayl shoved both his comrades into the cover of a side arcade as cannon fire – bright as sunbursts – sizzled down the chamber.

'Golden Throne! There's got to be something we can try!' Nayl said.

Mathuin reached into his coat pocket, and pulled out three close-focus frag grenades. He held them like a market-seller would hold apples or ploins. It was just like Mathuin to bring a pocket full of explosives. He never felt properly dressed unless he was armed to the back teeth.

'Don't suppose you've got a mini-nuke in the other pocket?' asked Thonius.

'My other suit's at the cleaners,' Mathuin replied.

'They'll have to do,' said Nayl. 'We'll go with what we've got.' He looked around. They could hear the heavy clanking footfalls of the Dreadnought bearing down on them, the hiss of its hydraulic pistons, the whirr of its motivators.

'They may not even crack the thing's plating,' Mathuin remarked. As well as a supply of ridiculous ordnance, Zeph Mathuin could always be relied on for copious pessimism.

'We'll have to get them close,' said Thonius.

'We?' said Nayl. He'd already taken one of the grenades, and was weighing it up like a ball.

'Yes, Mr Nayl. We.' Thonius took another of the grenades, holding it between finger and thumb as if it were a potentially venomous insect. He really wasn't comfortable with the physicality of fighting. Thonius could hack cogitators and archive stacks faster than any of them, and could rewrite codes that any of the rest didn't even understand. He was Ravenor's interrogator because of his considerable intellect, not his killing talents. That's why Ravenor employed the likes of Nayl and Mathuin.

'Three of us, three bombs,' Thonius stated. 'We're all in this together. I'm not going to be pulped by that thing without having a go at stopping it myself.'

Nayl looked dubiously at Mathuin.

'It's not up for debate, you vulgarians,' Thonius said snottily. 'Don't make me remind you I'm technically in charge here.'

'Oh, that would explain why we're technically nose deep in crap,' Nayl said.

A thick section of stone wall blew in nearby, hammered to fragments by withering cannon fire. The massive weight of the Dreadnought crushed heat-brittled stone to dust as it stomped through the gap.

The trio began to run again, down the next terrace, trying to put some distance between them and the killing machine.

'Get ahead!' Mathuin said. 'I'll take the first pop.' Nayl nodded and grabbed hold of Thonius, who was still puzzling over his grenade, figuring out how to adjust the knurled dial to set the timer. Nayl got the interrogator into cover.

Thonius straightened his sleeves.

'If you've pulled my coat out of shape, Nayl...' he began.

Nayl glared at him.

Behind them, in the open, Mathuin primed his grenade, and turned. As the Dreadnought hove into view, he hurled the small, black charge.

Kara rejoined Ravenor and Kys like an ape, swinging down through the rafters, and leaping the last few metres.

Eisenhorn descended after her. He was being carried by a grotesque figure, a human shape twisted and distended by arcane forces. The thing glowed with an eldritch inner light. Its bare limbs and torso were covered with runes and sigils. Chains dragged from its ankles.

It set Eisenhorn's heavy, cumbersome form down on the flagstones.

'Thank you, Cherubael,' he said.

The thing, its head lolling brokenly, exposed its teeth in a dreadful smile. 'That's all? I can go back now?' it said. Its voice was like sandpaper on glass. 'There are many more phantoms up there to burn.'

'Go ahead,' Eisenhorn said.

The dreadful daemonhost zoomed back aloft into the rain-swept heights of the ruin. At once, the ghastly screaming began again. Light pulsed and flashed.

Eisenhorn faced Ravenor's chair. 'The Fratery has unleashed everything they have tonight to stop me. To stop me talking to you. Daemonhosts of their own. Cherubael has been battling them. I think he's enjoying it.'

'He?' said Ravenor via his chair's voxponder. 'Last we met, you called that thing "it", my master.'

Eisenhorn shrugged. His augmetics sighed with the gesture. 'We have reached an understanding. Does that shock you, Gideon?'

'Nothing shocks me any more,' said Ravenor.

'Good,' said Eisenhorn. He looked at Kara and Kys.

'We need a moment, Kara. If you and your friend wouldn't mind.'

'Patience Kys,' Kys said, stern and hard.

'I know who you are,' said Eisenhorn, and turned away with Ravenor. In a low voice, he began to tell his ex-pupil all he knew about the Divine Fratery.

'Kar… that's Eisenhorn?' Kys whispered to Kara as they watched the figures withdraw.

'Yes,' replied Kara. She was still rather stunned by the meeting, and Ravenor's brief waring had left her tired.

'Everything you and Harlon have said about him… I expected…'

'What?'

'Something more intimidating. He's just a broken old man. And I can't think why he consorts with a Chaos-filth thing like that host-form.'

Kara shrugged. 'I don't know about the daemonhost. He fought it and hated it for so long, and then… I dunno. Maybe he's become the radical they say. But you're wrong about him being a broken old man. Well, he's broken and he's old… but I'd rather go up against Ravenor unarmed than ever cross Gregor Eisenhorn.'

Mathuin's grenade exploded. The aim had been good, but the device had bounced oddly at the last moment, and had gone off beneath the striding Dreadnought. The machine paced on through the ball of fire, untroubled.

Mathuin dived for cover as the cannons began pumping again.

'Crap… My turn, I suppose,' said Nayl. He clicked the setter to four seconds, thumbed the igniter, and ran into the hallway, bowling the grenade underarm.

Then he threw himself into shelter.

The grenade bounced once, lifted with the spin Nayl had put on it, and smacked bluntly against the front shell of the Dreadnought.

It was just rebounding when it detonated.

The Dreadnought vanished in a sheet of flame that boiled down the hallway, compressed and driven by the walls and roof.

As it cleared, Thonius saw the Dreadnought. Its front was scorched, but it was far, far from dead.

'Damn. Just me then,' he said.

'You've dabbled in farseeing,' Eisenhorn said. 'I know that. Your time spent with the eldar drew you in that direction.'

'I won't deny it,' Ravenor replied.

'That makes you bright to the Fratery,' said Eisenhorn. 'It illuminates you in the interwoven pathways of the future. That's why they located you in their prospects.'

Ravenor was quiet for a moment. 'And you've come all this way, risked all this danger... to warn me?'

'Of course.'

'I'm flattered.'

'Don't be, Gideon. You'd do the same for me.'

'I'm sure I would. But what you're telling me is... crazy.'

Eisenhorn bowed his head, and ran the fingers of his right hand up and down the cold grip of his runestaff.

'Of course it sounds crazy,' he said. 'But it's true. I ask you this... if you don't believe me, why are these cultist fools trying so hard to prevent our meeting here tonight? They know it's true. They want you denied of this warning.'

'That I will trigger this manifestation? This daemon-birth?'

'You, or one close to you. The trigger point is something that happens on Eustis Majoris.'

Within his force chair, Ravenor was numb. 'I won't lie, Gregor. My current investigations focus on that world. I was en route to Eustis

Majoris when I diverted to meet you here. But I have no knowledge of this Slight. It hasn't figured in any of my research. I can't believe that something I will do... or something one of my band will do... will–'

'Gideon, I can't believe my only ally these days is a daemonhost. Fate surprises us all.'

'So what should I do, now you've warned me? Abandon my investigations on Eustis? Shy away from that world in the hope that by avoiding it I can also avoid this prophecy?'

Eisenhorn's face was in shadow. 'Maybe you should.'

'No,' said Ravenor. 'What I should be is careful. Careful in my own actions, careful to oversee the actions of my team. If there is truth in the Fratery's prophecy, it is surely bound up in the dire conspiracy I am just now uncovering on Eustis Majoris. But I must prosecute that case. I would be failing in the duty you charged me with if I didn't. After all, the future is not set. We make it, don't we?'

'I think we do. I hope we do.'

'Gregor, when have either of us shirked from serving the Throne just because we're afraid things might go bad? We are inquisitors, we seek. We do not hide.'

Eisenhorn raised his head, and let the falling rain drops patter off his upraised palm. 'Gideon, I came to warn you, nothing else. I never expected you to change your course. Now, at least, you're aware of a "might be". You can be ready for it. That's all I wanted.'

Far behind them, the sound of rapid cannon-fire and dull explosions echoed through the tower.

'I think the time for conversation is over,' said Eisenhorn.

Thonius' pockets were not full of munitions and ordnance like Mathuin's, but he reached into them anyway. In one, a mini-cogitator, in another, two data-slates. In a third, a clasped leather case in which he had wrapped his tools: files, data-pins, fine brushes, tubes of lubricant, a vial of adhesive, pliers and tweezers. All the bric-a-brac that aided him in conquering and tinkering with cogitators and codifiers.

'Carl! Get into cover!' Nayl was yelling.

Thonius slid out the vial of adhesive, and wiped the drooling nozzle down the side of the grenade ball, waiting a moment for it to get contact-tacky.

Then, taking a deep breath, he leapt out of cover into the face of the Dreadnought, and lobbed the grenade. It hit the front casing, and adhered there, stuck fast.

Mathuin threw himself out of cover, and tackled Thonius, bringing him down behind a pillar.

The grenade exploded.

'You see?' said Thonius. 'You see how *thinking* works?'

But the Dreadnought wasn't finished. The blast had split its belly plates, but it was still moving, still striding, still firing.

Thonius shrugged. 'All right... we're dead.'

The Dreadnought suddenly stopped blasting. It faltered. A chill swept over the chamber.

Ravenor's chair slid into view, heading towards the killer machine. With the force of his mind, he had momentarily jammed its weapons.

Sudden frost coated the walls, Ravenor's chair and the Dreadnought. The machine tried to move. Cycling mechanisms shuddered as it attempted to clear its guns.

A tall figure strode past Ravenor, heading for the Dreadnought. It held a runestaff in one hand and a drawn sword in the other. Its robes fluttered out behind it, stiff with ice.

'Holy Terra!' exclaimed Nayl. 'Eisenhorn?'

A second before Ravenor's mental grip failed, a second before the cannons resumed their murderous work, Eisenhorn swung the sword – Barbarisater – and cleft the Dreadnought in two. The sword-blade ripped along the fissure Thonius' cunning grenade had put in it.

Eisenhorn turned aside, and shielded his face as the Dreadnought combusted.

He looked back at them all, terrible and majestic, backlit by flames. 'Shall we?' he said.

* * *

With their Dreadnought gone, the remainder of the Fratery force fled. The warband and the two inquisitors slaughtered many as they made their escape into the storm.

Tugging one of her kineblades out of a body with her mind, Kys watched Eisenhorn ripping his way through the faltering hostiles around them.

'Now I see what you mean,' she said to Kara Swole.

'I'm done here,' Gregor Eisenhorn said. He looked back across the bridge span to the tower. Screamlight was still dancing around the summit. 'Cherubael needs my help now. I should go and see how he's doing.'

'I will be vigilant,' Ravenor said.

Eisenhorn knelt, and pressed his gnarled hands flat against the side of the chair.

'The Emperor go with you. I've said my piece. It's up to you now, Gideon.'

Eisenhorn rose and looked at the others. 'Mamzel Kys. Interrogator. Mr Mathuin. A pleasure meeting you.' He nodded to each of them. 'Kara?'

She smiled. 'Gregor.'

'Never a hardship seeing you. Look after Gideon for me.'

'I will.'

Eisenhorn looked at Harlon Nayl, and held out a hand. Nayl clasped it with both of his.

'Harlon. Like old times.'

'Emperor protect you, Gregor.'

'I hope so,' Eisenhorn said, and walked away, back across the bridge span towards the tower where the screamlight still flashed and sparked. They knew they would not see him again.

Unless the future was not as set as it seemed.

Malinter fell away below them, vast and silent. Nayl piloted the transport into low orbit, flashing out signals to their ship.

Once the nav was set and automatics had taken over, he turned his chair on its pivot, and looked at Ravenor.

'He wasn't the same,' he said.

+How do you mean?+

'He seemed so sane. I thought he was mad.'

+Yes. I thought that too. It's hard to know whether I should believe him.+

'About what?'

+About the dangers ahead, Harlon. The risks we may take.+

'So… what do we do?'

+We carry on. We do our best. We serve the Emperor of Mankind. If what Gregor said comes to pass, we deal with it. Unless you have a better idea.'

'Not a one,' replied Nayl, turning back to study the controls.

+Good,+ sent Ravenor, and wheeled his chair around, returning to the cabin space behind where the others were gathered.

Nayl sighed, and looked ahead at the turning starfields.

The future lay ahead, its back to them, saying nothing.

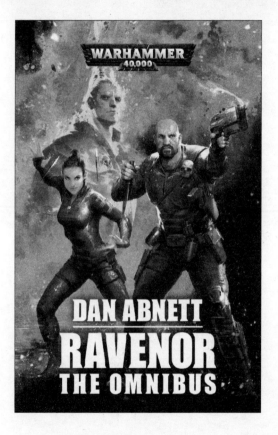

THE WRECKAGE

David Annandale

Introducing

YARRICK

COMMISSAR

Their fire drove us to shelter. The enemy was at the top of the ridge, dug in, behind cover, invisible. We were exposed. We had nothing to target. The las hit us hard. The night screamed with lethal energy. We lost three more squads before we made it inside the shell. Just ahead of me, a shot struck a pocket of gas. I ducked back, shielding my face from the heat of the explosion. Flames washed over troopers, melting rebreathers into flesh. The barrage drove us on, and I ran through smoke thick with the stench of burning corpses.

Sixth Company of the Armageddon Steel Legion's 252nd Regiment went to ground. Our shelter had been a freighter once. Its provenance, its identity, even its shape, were long gone. I guessed what it had been by the size of the ruin, and by the eroding remains of its former self: the length and curve of the hull. The ship had been destroyed by its crash onto the surface of the moon. The wreck had been stripped of anything worth having, then had been mined for scrap metal. Now it rusted, its bones gnawed by the corrosive rains of Aionos. It had been reduced to a cyclopean, arthritic talon.

'Lures,' Sergeant Otto Hanoszek said to me as I caught my breath behind a wall of pitted iron. 'Those damned ships were lures.' He pulled off his rebreather and wiped the sweat from his forehead with the sleeve of his trenchcoat. He was a thin man, much younger than he looked, with a face in perpetual flush. He was greying, looked like a veteran, and commanded his squad like one, but was only a few years older than I was, and the mantle of commissar still felt new on my shoulders.

'They were lures,' I agreed. 'And they worked.'

Hanoszek waved an arm, encompassing all of Aionos. 'Not for the first time, either.'

He was right about that, too. I ducked my head around the tear in the hull and looked uphill. I hadn't given up hope of gauging the location and size of the enemy forces. We needed better intelligence than 'high ground' and 'many.' At least a thousand, I guessed.

Night had fallen on Aionos. Its planet, the gas giant Kylasma, took up a third of the sky, and was still only half risen. A green smear through the drizzling clouds, it silhouetted the spires of the moon. They were twisted, broken shapes. They were the accumulated wrecks of thousands of ships, the centuries-old graveyard of the victims of the heretics we had come to purge.

'Lures,' I repeated. 'So the attack on Statheros was one too. Lures to catch what?'

'Us?' asked Hanoszek.

'I think so. But why?'

The incursion into the nearby Statheros System had been an atrocity. Three planetoid mining colonies devastated, their resources plundered, and everywhere the eight-pointed star of Chaos daubed with the blood of slaughtered civilians. Sixth Company's frigate, the *Castellan Belasco*, was dispatched. We had pursued what we had thought to be a force no larger than a squadron of lighters to Aionos. We had made moonfall and descended upon what we had thought was an encampment. It had been just another decoy.

The rain worked its way down behind my cap and down my collar. Its slight acidity burned. The troopers were used to this and worse on Armageddon, but as the precipitation broke down the metal, it released combustible pockets of gas from the wrecks.

'I hear you were on Mistral, commissar,' Hanoszek said.

'That's right.'

'Was it as bad as they say?'

I shrugged. 'We had wind there instead of rain. Take your pick.'

He didn't need to know any more. The wounds were still fresh. Some were still bleeding.

Las-fire streaked past my face as I pulled back. The sergeant grunted in surprise. 'Some good shots up there.'

'In that position, I should hope so,' I said. 'There is nothing impressive about their having the upper hand in these circumstances.'

Hanoszek laughed. 'As you say, commissar. Of course, they also *created* these circumstances.'

He was right, of course. I liked Hanoszek. He had a clear eye for the battlefield and the lunacies of war. What might have sounded like misplaced admiration for the enemy coming from someone else was, with him, a simple acknowledgement of how things stood.

'Then let's see if the captain has something to say about changing them,' I said. I had seen him move on towards the uphill end of the wreck.

'Yes, commissar.' His tone was noncommittal.

We clambered over heaps of broken metal and through the ghosts of the ship. Here and there, a bulkhead still projected sideways from the hull. Doorways without walls or rooms stood like skeletal sentinels. Along the way, we passed small groups of soldiers. Clad in their iron helmets and light-tan trenchcoats, they rested. Many were wounded. I was young, still feeling my way as a commissar, but I was no novice at war. I knew the challenges of this interlude. The relative safety after the punishing, unsuccessful fight was its own form of curse. During combat, there was no time to think of anything except the act itself. Now, in the limbo of inaction, when wounds were felt and when reflection was possible, was when thoughts of what might come next surfaced, and became apparent, and morale suffered. I stopped briefly to speak to a few troopers. I let them speak to me first.

I have known commissars who declare that there is no need to understand the soldiers who are in their charge. They say that it is enough to demand obedience to creed and mission. Perhaps it should be. But to understand the troops is to be better able to direct them. I sometimes think that the coldest commissars are fearful, though they would never admit this. They are afraid that if they get to know the soldiers as human beings, they will find it more difficult to carry out the more merciless aspects of their duty.

If this is so, they are cowards and a disgrace to our uniform.

So I listened to the troopers, and I spoke to them, trying to temper my response to the needs I heard. Where there was firmness of purpose, I gave encouragement. There were only two instances where I heard faltering that required discipline. Both cases, I noticed with some concern, were soldiers who appeared to be close to the captain. I had seen them drinking with him in the *Castellan Belasco*'s dining hall.

Context matters. So I had been taught, and so I had already learned, through hard lessons in the field. Context was why I tried, in those early days, to memorise the names of every soldier who fell within my remit. The day would come when that was no longer possible. I am pained by the thought of the anonymous thousands who, in later years, would die because of my decisions. I am pained, but not haunted. I know that if I had not made those decisions, the numbers would be infinitely worse. Context matters.

And on that day, on Aionos, I could still know all the names. I noted the problem cases, and a doubt festered.

We found Captain Jeren Marsec near the uphill end of the hull. He stood between two pieces of bulkhead that rose twenty metres above our heads. He was well under cover, but ahead of him was a large gap in the shell, wide enough for ten men to pass through. The other sergeants were there too, and a large number of troopers had gathered to listen. Marsec stood on a heap of refuse so all could see him. He was grinning. He could grin well. Though he had the flash, pride and handsome profile, he was no aristocrat. Before conscription, he had been a foreman in a Helsreach manufactorum. His natural charisma had carried him far. He was as popular with his superiors as he was with his subordinates.

'So, Yarrick,' he said when he spotted me, 'ready to spoil the enemy's little game?'

'What does he think he's playing at?' Hanoszek muttered under his breath. I almost didn't hear him.

I frowned. I didn't mind the sergeant's borderline insubordination. What I disliked was Marsec's flippancy. He should show confidence in our ultimate triumph. But the confidence he radiated seemed to be based solely on his own self-admitted brilliance. It was perhaps true that, on the tactical level, we were engaged in a game with the cultists. But it was a serious one, and the enemy was winning. There was something in Marsec's tone of voice that suggested he did not respect our foe's skills. We had already been given ample evidence that we should.

Cheers greeted the captain's question. Perhaps I was wrong. Hanoszek wasn't happy, and some of the other sergeants were looking grim, but most of the soldiers around us hooted their approval of Marsec. He had, it was true, led many successful missions. So I swallowed my doubts for the moment and said, 'I am always ready to ruin the day of a renegade, captain.'

'Good.' He pointed at the gap. 'What do you see there?'

'A way into the field of fire.'

He wagged a finger at me. That summoned a somewhat more nervous laugh from the troops. The commissar's uniform is not well-loved. Nor should it be. It is meant to be respected and feared. Marsec's little show at my office's expense was expertly calculated to endear him even more to his company, but it was a brave soul who openly enjoyed mockery of that sort. 'You lack imagination, Yarrick. I expected better of you. Where you see a death trap, I see opportunity.'

'Oh?' I grew uneasy.

'The entire company is going to charge through that opening.'

My doubts about Marsec were twofold. In the first place, his very popularity was, I thought, a problem. He loved his troops, that was clear, and they loved him back. That was all very well, but I worried that the affection he felt would get in the way of making the hard choices that befell every command sooner or later. Would he be able to issue the orders that would lead to the sacrifice of some squads for the preservation of the rest of the company?

Secondly, and paradoxically, he was reckless. I believe this was because he was aware of his popularity. He wanted to be worthy of it. He wanted to give his troops glory. It is one thing to send soldiers to their death with the full knowledge that one is doing so, and of the necessity of this action. It is another to make a grand gesture with no thought of the consequences. And because his troops loved him, they would throw themselves after his dream no matter how unsound. There was a cult of personality growing around Marsec. That was dangerous. They always are. I still believe that today as I wrestle with my own.

'He's mad,' said Hanoszek.

I silenced him with a look. I approached Marsec. At the base of his makeshift podium I said, 'I wonder if you might explain a few details to me, captain.' I kept my voice low, hoping he would take the hint. I had no desire to undermine his authority without sufficient cause.

He understood perfectly well. He remained where he was, and announced, 'Commissar Yarrick is worried. He thinks I'm about to order a suicidal charge. Let me reassure you, comrades, I am doing no such thing. There is a risk. Of course there is. This is war! And without risk, there is no glory!'

Shouts of affirmation from the company. A bit muted, though. Hanoszek and I weren't the only ones to see the obvious drawback of running straight into enemy fire.

'I am in constant touch with the *Castellan Belasco*,' Marsec continued. 'We have the means to destroy this nest of rats in one swift move. We will present such a target, and such a threat, to our foes that they will be forced to respond in kind. They will mount a counter-charge, or they will have to concentrate their fire massively. Either way, they will be giving away their precise position. At that moment, the *Belasco* will strike with an orbital barrage. Comrades, are you with me?'

The roar was unequivocal. They were.

Marsec stepped down with the cheers still deafening.

'So?' he asked me. He had to speak into my ear and raise his voice so I could hear him. 'What do you think, Yarrick?'

'It's a big gamble.'

'Worth taking, though. We have to try something to break out of this box they've put us in.'

'And if you're wrong? If it doesn't work? We could lose this war in this single action.'

'We won't,' Marsec assured me. He clapped my back. 'The rockets are ready to fly. The ship's augurs almost have the enemy's position. The problem is that those vermin are a bit too spread out, and under cover. We need to draw them out.'

'We're likely to do that,' I conceded. I still didn't like the plan. It felt wrong. Wars were rarely won by glamorous schemes.

'So we shall!' he said, delighted. He thought he'd won me over.

I was not convinced. Even so, I took my place at the front of the line as the company prepared to charge out of the hull. I would be coming out of the left-hand side of the gap. Marsec was in the centre. Hanoszek's squad was a few rows back and on the right. The sergeant made a point of walking past me before joining his troopers.

'What do you think, commissar?' he asked. 'Is this going to be a good death?'

His question was honestly meant. He wasn't joking.

'If this tactic achieves what the captain expects, then yes, to fall in this effort would be a good death.'

Hanoszek gave me a lopsided grin. 'I already knew that. Do you think it will work?'

That was his true question: were the deaths going to be worth it? Was he about to die for a good cause, or in the service of another man's ego? And I had answered him like a politician. I was a political officer. That wasn't the same thing at all. Not if I could help it. So I gave a direct answer to his direct question. 'I don't know.'

His grin became broader. 'Fair enough.' He moved on.

'The *Castellan Belasco* stands ready for our signal,' Marsec announced a few moments later. 'Warriors of Armageddon, forward!'

We charged out of the shelter and emerged halfway up the slope towards the ridge. On all sides, the corpses of the renegades' victims loomed over us. We were storming up a valley of wrecked ships. Few bore any resemblance to what they had once been. They had become massive tombstones, designed by lunatics. Metal reached for the sky with twisted desire. There were jagged angles the size of habs. Rotting husks, broken cylinders, fragments of towers and tumbled superstructures stretched away forever. We were in the land of industry's death.

I yelled my challenge at our enemies, daring them to cut me down. I raced with pistol drawn and sword upheld. I fired blindly into the night. And though I threw myself completely into the task of killing and survival, a part of my mind looked at the wider picture of two forces clashing in an ocean of wreckage and was dismayed.

The enemy did not return fire. There was no response at all to our attack. I stopped firing. Was anyone still there? We kept up the advance. In less than a minute, those of us at the front were almost at the ridge. I looked back. The totality of Sixth Company was now on the slope.

We reached the top. Before us was a landscape of exposed corridors and gigantic heaps of slag. There was no sign of the renegades. We stopped. If we advanced further, the footing would be treacherous and slow.

'Captain?' I asked. I knew we had fallen into another trap, but I couldn't see what it was. Seconds were ticking by. With each one that passed, I cursed myself for failing to see what had to be done.

Marsec was just as confused. 'Get me the vox!' he yelled.

Trooper Versten ran up with the communications equipment. 'I have the ship,' he said.

Marsec grabbed the handset. 'Come in, *Castellan Belasco*,' he said.

'We are here, Captain Marsec,' a voice from the frigate crackled back. I moved closer to hear the exchange. 'Are you in position?'

I didn't recognise the speaker.

'We are,' Marsec replied. 'But there's no one here. Abort mission.'

'We have you,' said the voice.

We have you. What did that mean? Marsec stared at the handset, then at me. His face was blank with confusion. I'm sure mine was too. When the realisation hit, it couldn't have taken more than two heartbeats after Marsec had received that answer. It was still too long. When I pick at this memory, I want to grab that commissar by the lapels and shake the young fool into action. How could he not see what was coming? How did he not realise the danger the moment he stared at that empty ridge?

My anger with my younger self is not rational. I realise this. It is powered by hindsight, motivated by my wish that I could have averted what happened next, and by other, later, greater frustrations. I have become much better at foreseeing disaster. But thanks to the stupidity of powerful men, I don't necessarily have any better luck at heading it off.

So it took me those few beats. Even then I was still confused, but the presentiment of doom was strong. I knew enough to listen to it.

'*Take cover!*' I yelled. I plunged back down the hill. '*With me!*' I didn't worry about the protocols of the chain of command. I was obeying dire necessity. I ran in a diagonal path, abandoning the clear route of the slope to forge into the thickets of wreckage. It was slower going, but there was cover, and I had to get us away from where the enemy wanted us to be.

I glanced back. Marsec was among those following me. Another contingent was disappearing into the ruins on the other side of the path. Then a comet pierced the night. The orbital bombardment was coming, and it was aimed at *us*. The barrage bombs landed on the peak of the ridge. They were little more than large masses. But then, so are meteors. Dropped from space, their impact was devastating. The hill became a volcano. Tonnes of metal were vaporised or turned molten. An angry god hammered the ground, smashing it, reshaping it. Hundreds of little insects in human form died in an instant. I was running, and then I was tumbling, and then I didn't know if I was on my feet or not. The world had become a riot of sense impressions, all of them too much, too loud, too painful. I kept moving. I didn't know where I was going. As the night screamed, I barely even knew who I was. But if I stopped, I would die, and so would the soldiers who had followed me down the hill. That I knew. So I struggled on, buffeted by the monster sound, pursued by the heat of metallic lava. Behind us, the world flew upward in blazing fragments. Wreckage became ash. The air was choked with rust.

It ended. The thunder faded to the sullen crackling of flame and the groans of settling metal. After the blaze of the impact, night came back down, thicker and darker than before. It was difficult to breathe. I stood for a few moments, mind and body thrumming like a struck bell, trying to clear my head and understand where I was. The scrap heap that surrounded me was even more fragmentary than the hull we had sheltered in before. It was bits of framework and shards of bulkhead, piled every which way on top of each other. I felt as if I were viewing reality through a cracked lens.

I found the direction of the slope, reoriented myself, and looked for other survivors. We came together bit by bit, moving slowly back towards the centre of the bombardment. What was left of Sixth Company on this side of the wreckage began to cohere. Our losses were great. We were down by well over half our strength. I hoped, but didn't dare expect, that there were some survivors on the other side of where the path had been.

We approached a transformed landscape. The closer we came to the point of impact, the more the wreckage lost all semblance of form. It was just vague shapes and angles now. There were still some big fragments, but for the most part we were moving between and over hills of scrap.

I found Marsec. At first he just followed me like a servitor. Gradually, he became functional again. He was a long way from leading, but he remembered his role well enough to be the visible centre around which the company could reform. There were a few dozen of us when we neared the crater. The soldiers had donned their rebreathers to better deal with the clogged air. I kept coughing up black phlegm.

'They took the ship,' Marsec was saying. His voice was hoarse. His eyes were full of a horror that was greater than the tactical disaster. He seemed to be trying to focus on something concrete. But his gaze flicked and flinched over every burned, mutilated corpse we passed. 'They took the ship. How is that possible? We saw their fleet. They couldn't take a frigate.'

'They've been taking ships for centuries,' I pointed out.

'Civilian vessels. I haven't seen any Imperial Navy wreckage here, have you?'

None that was recent, true.

Marsec didn't wait for my answer. 'How did they do it? They couldn't have. But they did. How–'

He stopped as we passed a wide pool of congealing metal. Its heat baked our exposed skin. Heads and limbs of men and women poked up from the surface, silvery-grey statues of agony. There must have been at least fifteen dead in this location alone. Marsec's face twisted. I saw a man who was experiencing guilt as a physical blow. He looked at me as if he would say something, but his personal horror was beyond his ability to communicate. I had no forgiveness to offer, and he didn't seek it. His decision had brought this fate to the troops he loved, and he knew it. I nodded that I understood, and we moved on.

I wasn't sure where we were going. It made a kind of sense to attempt to regroup close the point where we had been scattered. Beyond that, I had no ideas. I didn't know where the enemy was.

The entire top half of the ridge had vanished. The barrage bombs had left two gigantic craters. Our initial charge had been to the north, and we now stopped at the edge of the western crater. It was deep, wide and unnatural. Something massive poked up from the bowl. It had been untouched by the explosions, which had simply brushed away the centuries of soil. It was the tip of a pyramid. The stone was black, with a green tinge. Its designs were complex, alien and completely unfamiliar to me. They were not Chaotic, that much I could tell. They were too regular. If anything, they spoke of a deathly, soulless order. Part of the formation of a commissar at the schola progenium was necessarily instruction in the enemies of the Imperium, their nature and kind. This was something new. It looked like a tomb. And if, as seemed to be the case, this was just the peak of the structure, and its lines continued underground, it was a tomb the size of a city.

One of the survivors was Versten, and he had been trying the vox every few seconds as we reassembled what we could of the company. We were down to not much more than platoon strength, almost all regular infantry. We had lost all of our heavy weapons, and had precious few grenade launchers and flamers remaining.

Perhaps because we were on higher ground now, or perhaps because the air was beginning to clear, he finally made contact with another operator. The sliver of good news shook Marsec out of his lethargy. There were other survivors, led by Hanoszek, and they had reached the lip of the other crater.

'What are you seeing there?' Marsec asked the sergeant.

'There's a... captain, I'm not sure what it is.'

'That's all right. There's one here too.'

'What are your orders?'

'Hook up with us here. We will hold our position until–'

The las streak missed Marsec's head by a hair's breadth. We dropped to the ground. The single shot was joined by dozens. They were coming from the other side of the crater, and to our left. At the same moment, Hanoszek's voice started yelling that they were taking fire.

'Back down the slope.' Marsec shouted into the vox unit. 'Full retreat!'

But as we turned to start down, that path was closed to us too. With a roar, something dropped down from the clouds, and landed at the base of the slope. It trapped us, and it revealed how the ship had been taken. It was a Thunderhawk.

'We're saved,' a trooper gasped. His name was Rohm, and I made a mental note to terrorise him thoroughly, should we survive this day.

'We are *not*,' I hissed. 'Look at the markings.'

The air was still dusty, but even from several hundred metres away, the gunship's livery was unmistakable: two scythes the colour of magma, crossed over a background of night, between them a cluster of burning skulls. I didn't expect the trooper to know the beings who fought under that emblem. I *did* expect him to know that this design belonged on no flag of the Emperor's Adeptus Astartes.

The xenos who had built the pyramid in the crater were a mystery to me, but I knew of the Chaos Space Marines who descended from the Thunderhawk's assault ramp. They were part of the store of dark knowledge that it had been my responsibility to learn. The need to punish ourselves with this dangerous lore had been impressed upon me and my fellow students in an address given by the Lord Commissar Simeon Rasp. 'You are the guardians of the Guard,' he had told us. 'Vigilance requires knowledge. Some knowledge requires faith to be withstood. Hold fast to all three.'

I did so now. 'Those are Harkanor's Reavers,' I said.

The squad of five massive figures began moving up the slope. Their armour was a deep black, broken up by lines that glowed like flame. As they drew nearer, it seemed to me that those lines were not markings. They were too irregular. And they seemed to be moving.

'We cannot fight them,' I said. Not so reduced in number, and under harrying fire.

'We can't stay here,' Marsec said.

I waited for him to issue orders. He did not. If we paused much longer, we would be finished. I turned my head to look down into the crater. There was one route left to us. 'Some of those doorways are open,' I said, pointing at the pyramid.

Marsec grunted in surprise. He hesitated. I gave him a second longer, thinking that even that might be a mistake. Then he called out, 'We go down!'

The fire from the heretics intensified as we descended the slope. We shot back, but they were still attacking us from behind strong shelter, and our only sense of where they were came from the flashes of las. We lost several more troopers on the way down. Not all of them died right away. But we could not stop.

There was an open vault at the base of the pyramid. We made for it. As its bulk loomed over us, an ancient night made of stone, my instincts cried out to stop, to run another way, to try anything other than go inside. I didn't listen. There was no choice. I forced myself to run even faster as I hit the threshold. If I displayed reluctance, my example would be ruinous. So I plunged in, calling out as I did, so all would know that I was still alive. Marsec was right behind me, and once I was inside, he came too, bellowing something that wasn't coherent but sounded enough like an order to get the company to follow.

Once we were all inside, we paused. Our eyes adjusted to the darkness. It wasn't total. The green designs in the smooth stone glowed like near-dormant lumen strips. They showed that we were in a corridor that carried on in a perfectly straight line for some distance. We could see just enough to advance, if that was what we had to do. Marsec posted a watch at the door while Versten and I contacted Hanoszek's contingent. I had to warn him about the Traitor Space Marines.

'We saw them,' he replied. They had taken refuge in the other pyramid. 'What are the orders?' he asked.

A good question. I suspected that Hanoszek knew that it was.

'Stand by,' I told him, and had Versten fetch Marsec. When the captain arrived, I filled him in. 'The sergeant wants to know what action he should take,' I said, and offered the handset.

Marsec stared at it, then took it. As he did, a call came from the entrance. 'Enemies approaching!'

That seemed to be the additional jolt Marsec needed. His voice was sharper, more in the present moment, when he spoke to Hanoszek. 'Any sign of hostiles, sergeant?'

'Yes, captain. They're coming down the slope.'

'Go deeper into the pyramid,' Marsec said. 'Use the space as best you can. So will we. When we make it out again, we'll link up with you.'

There was a pause. Then Hanoszek said, 'Captain, there are lights in here. These structures might not be quite dead.'

'They must have been buried for thousands of years. Whatever was in them most certainly is dead. We have no time to do anything else, sergeant. You have your orders. Go!'

'Understood.'

Marsec passed the handset back to Versten. He looked as if he wanted something from me. I nodded. That seemed to satisfy him. 'Let's go,' he said.

He led the way down the corridor. He sent no scouting party ahead. He was right. We had no other options. Our best hopes at this moment were speed and luck. And yet, I felt that he would have charged into the darkness even if there had been time to feel our way more carefully through possible enemy territory. I wondered if he really had learned anything from the disaster we had suffered.

We moved down the corridor. After a hundred metres, it branched left and right, while straight ahead was a steep ramp. We went down. The ramp switchbacked a hundred and eighty degrees, and deposited us in another wide corridor. This one had many forks along its length.

We could hear voice and the tread of many boots echoing down from above. The heretics had entered the pyramid.

'I want an ambush point,' Marsec said as we jogged down the corridor. Either our eyes were finding it easier to see in the ghostly green half-light, or it was growing stronger.

'Plenty of intersections here,' I pointed out.

He shook his head. 'Main tunnel's too wide. After the surprise, they'll still be able to use their numbers.'

He was right. I didn't bother to mention that it was not just the numbers we had to worry about. I was relieved to hear him thinking like a warrior again.

We hurried down to the end of the corridor, and followed another ramp down to the next level. We were rushing to put more distance between us and our pursuers, to gain a little bit more time, but I was uneasy about venturing so far into the xenos construct. The risks behind us were bad enough. If we ran into something worse ahead, we could lose the entire company.

The third level down had even more branching corridors. We were in a maze. Though we had to take a side passage, it would be very easy to get lost once we were off the main path. The thought must have crossed Marsec's mind, too. He took in all the choices and hesitated. We didn't have long. I could still hear the heretics coming. Our lead had only grown by a few seconds at most. Worse, I could distinguish, above the general echoes of the pursuit, the heavy tread of something very large. The Traitor Space Marines were in the pyramid.

Trooper Lommell said, 'With your permission, captain,' and he barely nodded before she ran forward, ducking down one corridor, then another. The third seemed to offer what she wanted.

'Here,' she said. 'We should set up an ambush down here.'

'Why there?' Marsec asked, but he brought the rest of the company forward.

'It's very tight, and it gives us a usable back exit. I ran with a gang in the underhive of Tartarus on Armageddon, sir.' She carried the marks of her background. Her face was scarred with slashes in a cracked-glass pattern. When I had first seen her, I had assumed I was looking at an injury. It was not. It was a survival tactic in Tartarus. She had sliced her face herself, as a warning to her foes of how far she was willing to go. 'This environment isn't that different,' she said. 'It's just cleaner.'

'Good. Give us your expertise, trooper.'

She took us a few twists deeper into the labyrinth. The passageways were all empty, silent. They were dead. Except for the light. Why was it present? Whose purpose did it serve? The pyramid felt like a tomb, yet we had seen nothing that looked like markers, and what need did a tomb have for illumination?

I managed to keep track of our turns. Lommell set us up at a point where the narrow corridor we had taken had two intersections ten metres apart. Those branches, narrower still, fed on either side to other halls that would take us back to the main one. We had a perfect kill zone, and an easy retreat.

'Tartarus gave you a fine education,' I whispered to her as we waited for our foe.

'I didn't think so at the time.'

'We rarely do.'

We made just enough noise to give away which branch we had taken. Marsec sent a few soldiers on to create the illusion that we were still on the move, further along this passageway. The renegades took the bait. They rushed into our trap, laughing at the sport they were having.

This was my first look at them. In the dim green light of the pyramid, I couldn't see many details, but I had a sense of degraded human beings, wearing patchwork uniforms, no doubt stolen from their multitude of victims over the years. Their corruption had a hundred shades, yet it also had a unity. Across all the faces were runic tattoos and scarification. All the designs, however varied and however hard to make out, were an affront to the soul. They were, in the end, a single thing: the brand of Chaos.

The cultists were charging in without discipline or caution, which was madness, doubly so in a structure that must have been as alien to them as it was to us. I regarded them with contempt as they crossed the kill zone.

Just before we opened fire, I saw one of the Harkanor's Reavers loom out of the darkness. He brought with him his own terrible light. The designs on his armour that had puzzled me stood out clearly. They were cracks in the ceramite. Sorcerous heat spread fissures in the armour as if it were an eggshell. Baleful flame shone through. Then the cracks would seal, and new ones would appear. He was a mass of cooling lava given the shape of a man. That such a monster had once been human was beyond belief.

There was little chance that our ambush would take him down. We had no choice but to try. Culling the numbers of his followers would be a meaningless gesture if he still came after us. I prayed that Marsec, positioned in the shadows opposite me, realised this truth and waited.

He did. The forward elements of the cultists moved beyond the kill zone. The Reaver entered it. Marsec waited a few seconds more, letting another dozen renegades escape, waiting until the Traitor Space Marine was close to the centre of the trap. Then he gave the signal by firing his laspistol.

We opened up. Enfilading fire filled the space of the corridor. The las was so bright, it was as if we had brought day to the tomb. The heretics caught in the web of energy beams went down in seconds. The concentrated fire was such that they didn't have a chance to retaliate. Their comrades ahead doubled back. They tried to mount a counter-attack, but by staying out of our field of fire, they had no angle on our positions in the side passageways. We had reversed the situation that we had faced outside. Now we were the ones under cover, ripping our foes apart.

Then there was the Reaver. He stood in the middle of the barrage with no more concern than if it were a rain shower. He raised a flamer and launched a stream of burning promethium into the nearest passageway. Screams filled the corridors. A corner of our ambush failed.

Lommell trained her fire on the Reaver's flamer as he fired into the passageway one down from ours. The weapon exploded, drenching the Chaos Space Marine in liquid flame. From the grille of his helmet came an inhuman snarl. He staggered back a step. He wiped at the promethium. It seemed to annoy him rather than harm him, but he could not see with fire engulfing his head.

From the other end of the ambush, Trooper Rohm fired his grenade launcher. The frag struck the Reaver full in the chest. It blew out the flames, but rocked the monster to the core. He roared in anger and pain even as he yanked a bolt pistol from his thigh and fired a wide barrage of shells. They didn't need accuracy. Any that hit one of our positions killed the troopers in the front line.

Where the grenade had hit, the Reaver's armour was a molten mass. Instead of cracks, here was a wide gap, blazing with eldritch fire. The ceramite was slow to reform. I leapt out of the passageway in a forward roll, staying low, beneath the spray of bolter shells. I came out of the roll in a crouch. I was right at the Reaver's feet. I aimed my bolt pistol at the roiling, burning chest, and shot the Traitor Space Marine point blank. Energies from the materium and the warp collided. The explosion knocked me flat. The Reaver stood there with a great void where his chest had been. His ribcage poked out, burned and broken. Where his hearts and lungs should have been there was now nothing. The fire went out. The monster's arms hung limp, and then he toppled backward.

The cultists faltered. We turned our attention to them. They had thought to trap us between themselves and their superhuman master. Now *they* were caught, exposed, in the narrow corridor. We cut them down. I moved, crouching low, back to cover, and added my fire to the assault. I was exhilarated. We all were. The ambush had worked better than we could possibly have hoped.

As the last of the heretics fell, I glanced back, and my heart sank. The enemy had been cautious after all. A second force, larger than the first, was approaching. With it came another Reaver.

We were outnumbered, we had lost the element of surprise, and our cover was useless against power armour and a flamer. If we fought, we would die.

'*Go!*' Marsec shouted.

We bolted down the side passageways, taking the route Lommell had mapped out for us. Our only advantage now was speed. We knew where we were going. We sprinted, once more putting distance and time between us and the enemy. As I took corners at high speed, I blinked away the effect of the glowing designs. It would have been easy, at this pace, to follow their lines straight into a black wall. I turned into a wider corridor, and took it back to the main hall. Our portion of the company linked up. Marsec looked towards the way back up, but there was the sound of more pursuit coming from that direction, so we plunged on deeper into the pyramid.

We went down three more levels. The heretics were close. We didn't have time to set up another ambush. We kept moving forward, even when we reached a level that was ominously different. It still had a maze of corridors along its periphery, but the centre was a massive block. Its rectilinear designs were the most complex yet, and their light was the brightest, and most deathly. The main hall widened out before the monolith, and became a series of parallel tunnels that dropped beneath it. When we reached the tunnels, we paused. Their slope was steep, almost a fall. In their depths glowed a green mist.

And there was something moving. We could hear what sounded like the shifting of weights. Worse, we heard footsteps. The light flickered, as if something had passed between us and the source. There were other noises too. They were uncomfortably like voices. They spoke no recognisable words, and they could not come from any living throat. But down there, something walked and spoke. Whatever had built this pyramid was not done with it yet.

We couldn't have been perched at the edge of that descent for more than a second or two. That was long enough for us to hear and see all that was necessary. Marsec looked at me. We were trapped, yes. But we had one option. Perhaps it would be enough.

'We hide,' I said.

Marsec nodded. He raised his arm, waved his finger in a circular motion, giving the order to scatter. There were plenty of side corridors within reach, and we took them, racing for their shadows where we crouched down, motionless, silent, waiting for the arrival of our pursuers.

Throwing the dice on the fate of Sixth Company.

The Steel Legion is a proud fighting force. It has every reason to be so. It did then, too, though its time of greatest glory and most painful sacrifice, which would also be mine, still lay over a century in the future. This, now, was not a moment relished by any of the soldiers of Sixth Company as we hid in the dark and hoped that the enemy passed by. Doing so grated against my self-worth as well. But the Steel Legion has not earned its triumphs by fighting blindly, or without sense. We had a chance of victory here, and to seize it meant swallowing pride. That requires its own form of courage.

We waited. I watched, as close to the exit of my refuge as I dared, as the cultists arrived. Even with the damage we had done, they were still three times our number. The Reaver towered over them. They advanced to the edge of the tunnels. The Reaver barely paused long enough to look ahead before he led the renegades down the central tunnel. I listened to their war cries as they descended. A minute later, the cries became screams.

The first screams were of fear. Then, as I heard what sounded like energy discharges of some kind, I heard screams of agony. The Reaver roared. Guns fired. The sounds of alien energy intensified. The green glow became brilliant, a strobing, slashing light. The screams stopped as if severed. The Reaver's bellows filled with shock and pain. Then they too, fell silent.

Marsec stepped back out of the shadows. I joined him. We stared down into the tunnels. There was still movement down there, still the alien sounds. For the moment, at least, they weren't moving upward.

Marsec whispered, 'What's down there?'

'Something we are not equipped to fight, captain. But we can report its existence.'

'Agreed.'

Moving quietly, limiting himself to hand gestures alone, Marsec signalled our withdrawal. We maintained silence for the first two levels. When it became clear that the pyramid's denizens weren't following, and that the last of our enemies had gone down to their annihilation, Versten went back to work with the vox, trying to raise the scattered elements of Sixth Company.

Marsec called him up to the front with us. 'Anything?' he asked.

'No answer from Sergeant Hanoszek, sir. But I received a transmission from Sergeant Brenken on the *Castellan Belasco*. She and some armsmen have freed themselves and are fighting back. She says that the occupying force is small. The Traitor Space Marines were the ones who captured our ship, and they left behind only a minimal group of cultists. They're armed, of course, but...'

'But it wouldn't take much to dislodge them,' I finished.

'That's what she thinks, commissar, yes.'

I gave Marsec a significant look. Our Valkyries, some distance from the ridge, should still be intact. Even with our numbers reduced to not much more than two squads' worth, we could retake the ship.

'Good,' Marsec said. 'We'll link up with Sergeant Hanoszek. With our company reunited, we shall purge the scum from our decks.'

I frowned. He was assuming that Hanoszek's contingent still existed. Two Reavers had come after us. Unless some were mounting guard outside the pyramids, which seemed unlikely, that meant the other three were pursuing Hanoszek and his troops. Those were formidable odds. Marsec was basing his strategy on an assumption for which we had no evidence. I was uneasy, but decided to say nothing until we had reached the surface.

As we were climbing out of the crater, Versten managed to get through to Hanoszek's vox operator for a few seconds. The other fragment of Sixth Company was being pressed hard, and driven deeper into the pyramid. There was no question of their being able to set up an ambush. The heretics and the Reavers were upon them. They could not break off.

'Send a message that help is coming,' Marsec said.

'Belay that, trooper,' I told Versten. To Marsec, I said, 'Captain, a word.'

I expected him to be furious at my intervention. Instead, he seemed eager to talk, as if it was important to him that he bring me about to his perspective. We left the troops at the lip of the crater, and moved down the slope a short distance to speak behind a rounded heap of congealed slag.

'We cannot rescue them,' I said.

'We have to try.'

'No,' I said, 'we are duty-bound not to. Such an attempt would be doomed. You know that as well as I do. We would then be leaving a frigate of the Imperial Navy in enemy hands. That would be an unforgivable failure.'

'I have already failed my troops once this day,' Marsec said. 'I won't do it again.'

'You will if you follow this course. They will all die.'

'I have to try.'

I looked at him steadily. He did not blink. He knew exactly what he was saying. He knew the consequences. His ego had led us to this pass. He understood this, and sought redemption. But we didn't have the luxury for redemption. We needed victory. Before me stood a good man. The Imperium needed him to be something more, though. It needed him to be a good officer. Instead, he was the ruin of one. He was, in this moment of crisis, proving himself unable to make the truly hard decision. He was throwing that responsibility onto me.

'I cannot allow you to jeopardise this mission,' I told him.

'No,' he said softly. 'No, you can't. But you cannot make me abandon my troops.'

I pulled my pistol from its holster.

Marsec gave me a sad smile. He got down on his knees. 'Do what is necessary, Commissar Yarrick.'

'Why are you forcing my hand?'

'Stop me or let me do what I must.'

I put the muzzle of the pistol against his forehead. He closed his eyes. Peace suffused his features. I felt a grimace contort mine. I knew what I was doing was correct. I have had to use this ultimate sanction against officers more often than I care to count. Each instance is a tragedy, a necessity whose causes are so *unnecessary*. But never before or since have I encountered a soldier who accepted my judgement with such grace. I hope I never will again.

The hard decision was mine, as was the harder action. Silently, I cursed Marsec for this moment that I would have to live with for all my years to come. I curse him still. He was, even then, still not fully honest with either of us. He was seeking a martyr's end as redemption for his failure. In this way, he turned away from the hard decision. He made it mine instead. Mine the choice, and mine the even harder action.

So be it.

I pulled the trigger.

I marched back to the company. A horrified silence had fallen over it. 'We make for the landing site,' I said. 'We are retaking the *Castellan Belasco*.' I didn't mind the gazes, whether averted or hostile. They couldn't add to the burden I was already carrying, or to the further weight I was about to shoulder.

'Get Hanoszek,' I told Versten. 'Don't stop trying until you do.'

We had reached the base of the slope when Versten passed me the handset. It was hard to make out what Hanoszek was saying. His words kept being cut off by what sounded like static, but I knew to be weapons fire. He was asking for help.

'Sergeant,' I said, 'this is Yarrick. We cannot provide assistance. The ship is being held. That is the key to this mission's success. Do you understand?'

More explosions and cries in the background. Then, 'Yes.'

'Is there any way you can bypass the enemy?'

'No. We've already lost half our strength. They're backing us down a tunnel. Commissar, there's movement down there.'

I closed my eyes for a moment, hating what I was about to say. 'Sergeant, go deeper. Head towards that movement.'

Another pause. I didn't think it was only due to the fighting. 'Commissar?'

'What is down there will kill the enemy. Sixth Company will be victorious.' Again, I asked, 'Do you understand?'

There was no pause this time. 'I do.'

'The Imperium thanks you, Sergeant Hanoszek.'

'This is simply our duty, sir.'

He would have made a fine officer.

'I will remain on the vox,' I told him. 'All the way.'

'Thank you.'

We had no more exchanges after that. He left the channel open. I heard the sounds of the end. I kept my promise, and stayed present, bearing what witness I could. I was there as we reached the landing site, and boarded the Valkyries. Hanoszek and his portion of the Sixth fought well and hard and as long as they could, luring the enemy inexorably to disaster. The fight was still going on as we reached the frigate, and the immoral, leaderless rabble that occupied the bridge was confronted with the anger of the Steel Legion.

I was barely aware of our victory on the ship. All of my attention was focused on the terrible victory inside that pyramid on Aionos. I was there to hear Hanoszek, in mortal fear but still fighting, cry, 'Throne, what are they?'

He would receive no answer. None of us would for many years to come. Years of blessed ignorance.

But on that day, I still sought the pain of knowledge. I forced myself to learn the cost of my decision. I listened to the transmission until the sounds of battle ceased. I listened for almost an hour after that. I listened as the reclaimed *Castellan Belasco* prepared to leave the system.

I listened to the hollow, hissing remains of the hard choices.

YOUR
NEXT READ

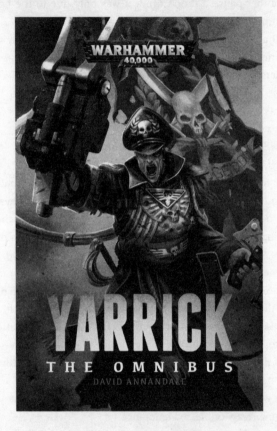

YARRICK: THE OMNIBUS
by David Annandale

Before he was a legend, Commissar Yarrick was already a hero, as you'll discover in this omnibus of two novels, a novella and six short stories set across his life and career.

RITE OF PAIN

Nick Kyme

Introducing

ADRAX AGATONE

CAPTAIN, SALAMANDERS

(THIRD COMPANY)

'Again.'

A prickling heat presaged the actual fire, followed a split-second later by the stench of his flesh burning.

The prisoner strapped down to the stone slab convulsed, his pelvis thrusting upwards in response to the pain. His wrists and fingers twisted, struggling against their bonds. His legs thrashed impotently in the manacles fastened to his ankles.

'Don't struggle,' the voice warned. 'Struggling only makes it worse.'

There were three others in the room with the prisoner. One, his actual torturer, never spoke. He carried the burning brand, the fork at the end of it blazing like a tiny sun. Another observed, keeping back and out of the weak light shining from above. The few glimpses the prisoner managed to snatch in his throes of agony suggested that the observer had his arms folded and shifted irritably.

The third, the one who had spoken, rasped and stayed close. His eyes were coals, smouldering red, the mirror image of the branding iron's business end. He and the observer were hulking, armoured in war-plate that growled and whirred as they moved, as if some animus of their draconic namesake was still trapped within and trying to escape.

'I will kill you both!' spat the prisoner, baring his fangs and snarling.

The third nodded, his black armour rimed a dusky orange from the forge-flame being pressed to the prisoner's exposed skin. It burned again, inscribing a line in his flesh, drawing pain.

'He is savage,' said the observer after the torturer had ceased. The torturer was smaller, dressed in robes rather than battle armour. He would die last, the prisoner decided.

'How many did he kill?' asked the observer.

'Seven. He killed seven brander-priests before I took him,' the black-armoured warrior replied.

The observer muttered something in response to that fact. The figure could not hear the exact detail, but the tone suggested disbelief.

'Are you certain this is right? He *is* savage,' repeated the observer.

'A monster,' said the third, leaning in close to talk to his prisoner. 'Are you ready to submit to the rite of pain?'

Deep, heavy breathing, with a growling undercurrent, answered. Cold, dark eyes like chips of flint regarded the third. He smiled.

'You want to gut me, don't you? Even now, you are working to release yourself from your bonds, planning your escape?'

For a few seconds there was no response, then the figure nodded. Slowly. Certainly.

The black-armoured warrior laughed, hollow and echoing in the solitorium. The torturer was about to advance when he raised a hand, stopping the human.

'This isn't working.'

'Then what do you suggest, Elysius?'

Elysius had been talking to himself, and hadn't expected a response.

'You need him, Agatone,' he answered. 'If you're going to hunt, this one will be of great use. But not before the rite.'

'Then what do you suggest?' Agatone repeated his previous question.

After a moment of silence, Elysius said, 'Out. Both of you.'

The human brander-priest obeyed at once, bowing his head and shuffling out of the chamber. Agatone was more reluctant.

'What are you going to do, Chaplain?'

'Teach him.'

Agatone lingered.

Elysius never let his gaze waver from the prisoner, though he turned his face a fraction towards the captain behind him.

'I said *out*. You might captain the Third, Agatone, but here in this solitorium chamber, I am in charge.'

Sensing a change, the prisoner began to relax, though his breathing was still frantic, heightened to battlefield intensity.

'And what if he kills you?' Agatone nodded at the prisoner. 'You've seen the state he's in. Even when he's not under the branding iron, he's still a savage creature.'

Elysius smiled again. 'No captain, he isn't. He's much worse than that. Now, please leave.'

Agatone was out of objections. He did as Elysius asked, leaving him alone in the dark with the monster.

'Just you and I now,' Elysius said once Agatone was gone.

'Your mistake.'

'I think not.' He picked up the branding iron left behind by the human priest. The coals of the brazier in which it was kept hot crackled and spat as it was pulled free. 'Stings, doesn't it?'

'Not as much as my claws will.'

Elysius chuckled mirthlessly.

'Very well then,' he said. 'Time to earn your rite.'

A sub-vocal command issued through his gorget quick-released the manacles on the prisoner's ankles.

The prisoner laughed, 'You're really going to regret this...'

A second command released the collar fastened to the prisoner's neck.

Rotating his wrist, Elysius swung the branding iron around as if it were a sword, leaving fire trailing in the dark behind it. His other arm ended in a stump at the elbow. His prisoner would think him disadvantaged, crippled even. That would be his mistake.

'Come then. Show me.' Elysius released the last bindings, the straps and chains spilling loose in a flood of leather and metal. Before his bonds had even hit the floor, the prisoner was up. He sprang off the slab and launched himself at Elysius with a roar.

The Chaplain cuffed him with a well-timed uppercut that stunned his jaw and sent the prisoner sprawling back with his own negated momentum. Then he advanced, lunging with the branding iron, searing flesh.

Screaming, wrathful, the prisoner tried to fight, but Elysius butted him, shattering his nose. Dazed, the prisoner swung, bone claws extending from his forearms. Elysius parried with the iron, smacking the claws away to deliver a second burning brand. He dodged an overhead slash and heard bone scraping metal as he brought his armoured knee up into the stomach of the prisoner, who gagged and spat.

Elysius kicked him over, lashing out with the brand again and again.

'You *are* a savage creature!' he snapped. 'But do not think you are more brutal than I. This is an infirmary and I the chirurgeon, cutting out weakness, flensing doubt and disloyalty. Tell me whelp, whom do you serve? With whom do you forge your bonds of brotherhood?' Elysius burned the prisoner one final time, finishing the mark, ending the rite of pain.

The prisoner did not struggle. He was too beaten for that. He let the burning in, allowing the brand to scorch his skin.

'I am fire-born,' croaked the prisoner, all defiance leaving him. 'I forge my bonds with the Salamanders.'

'And whose flame ignites your fury?'

'Vulkan's fire... beats in my breast. With it I shall smite the foes of the Emperor.'

Elysius backed down, allowing his breathing to return to normal. He ached. The rite had taken as much out of him as it had the prisoner before him. He put the brand down and held out his hand.

'Then rise, and be my brother.'

The figure touched the scar upon his chest. It was shaped in the head of a drake. He let Elysius help him up and felt his anger draining away, to be replaced by something more lasting, permanent... He felt a sense of *belonging*.

'How do you feel?' Elysius asked.

'Raw... but strong.'

'You are fresh-forged, that's why. Your armour is waiting for you, as are your other trappings.'

The prisoner snarled, 'Then to war.'

There was a glint in Elysius's eyes, a stoking of the fire within at hearing that word.

'Indeed, Brother Zartath. To war.'

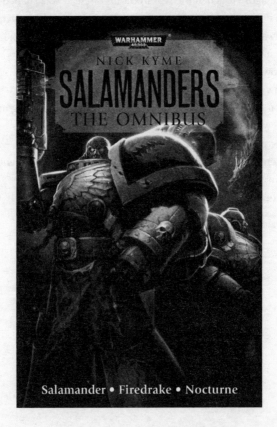

CHAINS OF COMMAND

Graham McNeill

Introducing

URIEL VENTRIS

SERGEANT, ULTRAMARINES

(FOURTH COMPANY)

Concealed at the edge of the jungle, Veteran Sergeant Uriel Ventris stared through the pouring rain at the grey, rockcrete bunker at the end of the bridge and tallied off the number of sentries he could see. There were four rebel troopers in the open, but they were sloppy, unconcerned, and that was going to kill them. They sheltered in the lee of the bunker's armoured door, smoking and talking. It was unforgivable stupidity, but Uriel always gave thanks whenever his enemies displayed such foolishness. The hissing of the warm rain falling through the canopy of thick, drooping fronds and bouncing from the rocks muffled all sounds. The roaring of the mighty river in the gorge below only added to the noise.

Moisture glistened on his blue shoulder guards, dripping from the inlaid chapter insignia of the Ultramarines. He slipped from his hidden position and ghosted through the drizzle, the actuators in his powered armour hissing as the fibre-bundle muscles enhanced his every movement. Uriel slid clear his combat knife and tested its edge, even though he knew it was unnecessary. The gesture was force of habit, learned at the earliest age by the people of Calth. The long blade was triangular in section, its edges lethally sharp and designed to slip easily between a victim's ribs, breaking them as it penetrated.

It was a tool for killing, nothing more.

Thanks to the heavy rain, the visibility of the guards was cut to less than thirty metres. Uriel's eyesight was far superior to a normal human's, he could clearly see the outline of the men he was about to kill.

He felt no remorse at the thought. The enemies of the Emperor deserved no mercy. These men had made their choice and would now pay the price for making the wrong one. Uriel slipped behind one of the bridge's adamantium stanchions, moving incredibly quietly for such a bulky figure. He was close enough to his victims for his enhanced hearing to pick out the individual sounds of their voices.

As was typical with soldiers, they were bemoaning their current assignment and superior officers. Uriel knew they would not complain for much longer. He was close enough for his superior senses to pick out the smell of their unwashed bodies and the foetid dampness of stale sweat ingrained into their flesh after weeks of fighting. His muscles tensed and relaxed, preparing for action. The rune on his visor display that represented Captain Idaeus flashed twice and with a whispered acknowledgement Uriel confirmed his readiness to strike. He waited until he heard the scraping footfall of his first target turning away and twisted around the stanchion, sprinting for the bunker.

The first guard died without a sound, Uriel's knife hammering through the base of his skull. He dropped and Uriel wrenched the blade clear, spinning low and driving it into the second guard's groin. Blood sprayed and the man shrieked in horrified agony. A lasgun was raised and Uriel lunged forwards, smashing his fist into his foe's face, the augmented muscles of his power armour smashing the man's head to shards. Uriel spun on his heel, dodging a thrusting bayonet, and thundered his elbow into the last guard's chin, taking the base of his skull off. Teeth and blood splattered the bunker door.

He dropped into a defensive crouch, dragging his knife clear of the corpse beside him and cleaning the blade on its overalls. The killing of the guards had taken less than three seconds. He glanced quickly around the corner of the bunker to the sandbagged gun positions further down the bridge. There were two, set in a staggered pattern to provide overlapping fields of fire. The dull glint of metal protruded from the glistening, tarpaulin covered positions and Uriel counted three heavy bolters in each emplacement. The rain and thundering river noise had covered his stealthy approach to the bunker, but there was nothing but open ground before the gun nests.

'Position secure,' he whispered into the vox-com, removing shaped, breaching charges from his grenade dispenser. He worked quickly and purposefully, fastening the explosive around the locking mechanism of the bunker's armoured door.

'Confirmed,' acknowledged Captain Idaeus. 'Good work, Uriel. Squads Lucius and Daedalus are in position. We go on your signal.'

Uriel grinned and crawled around to the front of the bunker, making sure to keep out of sight below the firing slit. He drew his bolt pistol and spun his knife, holding it in a reverse grip. He took a deep breath, readying himself for action, and detonated the charges on the door.

The bunker's door blasted inwards, ripped from the frame by the powerful explosion. Choking smoke billowed outwards and Uriel was in motion even before the concussion of the detonation had faded. He heard the crack of bolter fire from the jungle and knew that the remainder of the Ultramarines detachment was attacking. By now the enemies of the Emperor would be dying.

Uriel dived through the blackened doorway, rolling to a firing crouch, his pistol sweeping left and right. He saw two heads silhouetted by the light at the firing slit and squeezed the trigger twice. Both men jerked backwards, their heads exploding. Another soldier was screaming on his knees, blood flooding from his ruined body.

His torso was almost severed at the waist, razor-edged metal from the door's explosion protruding from his body. A las-blast impacted on Uriel's armour, and he twisted, kicking backwards in the direction the shot had come from. His booted foot hammered into a rebel guardsman's knee, the joint shattering. The man shrieked and fell, losing his grip on his weapon and clutching his ruined knee. The remainder of the bunker's complement crowded around Uriel, screaming and stabbing with bayonets.

Uriel spun and twisted, punching and kicking with lethal ferocity. Wherever he struck, bones crunched and men died. The stink of blood and voided bowels filled his senses as the last soldier fell. Blood streaked his shoulders and breastplate. His eyes scanned the dimness of the bunker, but all was silent. Everyone was dead.

He heard sounds of fighting and gunfire from outside and moved to the door, ducking back as heavy bolter shells raked the inside face of the doorway. He glanced round the edge of the bullet-pocked wall, watching with pride as the Ultramarines assault squad now joined the fray, their jump packs carrying them high over the bunker.

They dropped from above, like flaming angels of death, their chainswords chopping heads and limbs from bodies with shimmering, steel slashes. The first gun emplacement was in tatters, sandbags ripped apart by bolter fire and tossed aside by the attacking Space Marines. The poorly trained defence troopers broke in the face of such savagery, but the Ultramarines were in amongst them and there was no escape. The assault troopers hacked them down with giant, disembowelling strokes of their swords. The battle became a slaughter.

The staccato chatter of massed bolter fire echoed from the sides of the gorge, explosions of dirt rippling from the bullet-ridden sandbags of the second gun emplacement. But even under the constant volley, Uriel could see the gunners within were realigning their heavy bolters. Hurriedly, he voxed a warning.

'Ventris to Idaeus. The second gun position has re-sited its weapons. You will be under fire in a matter of moments!'

Idaeus's rune on Uriel's visor blinked twice as the captain acknowledged the warning.

Uriel watched as the captain of Fourth Company barked a command and began sprinting towards the second gun position. Idaeus charged at the head of five blue-armoured warriors, and Uriel swore, leaping forwards himself. Without support, the assault troops would be prime targets! Tongues of fire blasted from the heavy bolters, reaching out towards the charging Ultramarines. Uriel saw the shells impact, bursting amongst the charging Space Marines, but not a single man fell, the blessed suits of powered armour withstanding the traitors' fire. Idaeus triggered his jump pack and the rest of his squad followed suit, streaking forward with giant powered leaps.

Las-blasts filled the air, but the Ultramarines were too quick. Idaeus smashed down through the timber roof of the gun nest, a fearsome war cry bursting from his lips. He swung his power sword, decapitating a rebel trooper, and backhanded his pistol into another's chest, smashing his ribcage to splinters. Uriel's long strides had carried him to the edge of the gun nest and he leapt, feet first, into the sandbagged position. He felt bone shatter under the impact and rolled to his feet, lashing out with his armoured gauntlet. Another rebel died screaming. The sound of gunshots was deafening. Uriel felt a shot impact on his shoulder, the bullet ricocheting skywards. He turned and fired a bolt into his attacker's face, destroying the man's head. He sensed movement and spun, pistol raised. Captain Idaeus stood before him, hands in the air and a broad grin on his face. Uriel exhaled slowly and lowered his weapon. Idaeus slapped his hands on Uriel's shoulder plates.

'Battle's over, sergeant,' he laughed.

Idaeus's grizzled face was lined with experience and his shaven skull ran with moisture and blood. Four gold studs glittered on his forehead, each one representing a half-century of service, but his piercing grey eyes had lost none of the sparkle of youth. Uriel nodded, scowling.

'It is, yes, but the Codex Astartes tells us you should have waited for support before charging that gun nest, captain,' he said.

'Perhaps,' agreed Idaeus, 'but I wanted this done quickly, before any of them could vox a warning.'

'We have heavy weapons with us, captain. We could have jammed their vox units and blasted them apart from the cover of the bunker. They sited these gun positions poorly and would not have been able to target us. The Codex Astartes says–'

'Uriel,' interrupted Idaeus, leading him from the charnel house of the gun nest. 'You know I respect you, and, despite what others say, I believe you will soon command your own company. But you must accept that sometimes it is necessary for us to do things a little differently. Yes, the Codex Astartes teaches us the way of war, but it does not teach the hearts of men. Look around you. See the faces of our warriors. Their blood sings with righteousness and their faith is strong because they have seen me walk through the fire with them, leading them in glorious battle. Is not a little risk to me worth such reward?'

'I think I would call charging through the fire of three heavy bolters more than a "little risk" though,' pointed out Uriel.

'Had you been where I was, would you have done it differently?' asked Idaeus.

'No,' admitted Uriel with a smile, 'but then I am a sergeant, it's my lot in life to get all the dirty jobs.'

Idaeus laughed. 'I'll make a captain out of you yet, Uriel. Come, we have work to do. This bridge is not going to blow up on its own.'

As the assault troopers secured the bridge, the remainder of Captain Idaeus's detachment advanced from the jungle to reinforce them. Two tactical squads occupied the bunkers at either end of the bridge while Uriel organised the third repairing the sandbagged gun nests. In accordance with the Codex Astartes, he ordered them re-sited in order to cover every approach to the crossing, rebuilding and strengthening their defences.

Uriel watched as Idaeus deployed their scouts into the hills on the far side of the ridge above the gorge. They wouldn't make the same mistake the rebels had made. If the traitors launched a counter-attack, the Ultramarines would know of it. He stepped over a dead guardsman, noting with professional pride the bullet hole in the centre of his forehead. Such was the price of defeat. The Ultramarines' victory here had been absurdly easy, barely even qualifying as a battle, and Uriel felt curiously little pleasure at their success.

Since the age of six, he had been trained to bring death to the Emperor's enemies and normally felt a surge of justifiable pride in his lethal skills. But against such poorly trained opposition, there was no satisfaction to be gained. These soldiers were not worthy of the name and would not have survived a single month in the Agiselus Barracks on Macragge where Uriel had trained so many years ago. He pushed aside such gloomy thoughts and reached up to remove his helmet, setting it on the wide parapet of the bridge. Thousands of metres below, a wide river thundered through the gorge, the dark water foaming white over the rocks. Uriel ran a hand over his skull, the hair close cropped and jet black. His eyes were the colour of storm clouds, dark and threatening, his face serious. Two gold studs were set into his brow above his left eye.

The bridges were the key to the whole campaign. The Emperor's warriors had driven the poorly armed and trained planetary defence troopers of Thracia back at every turn and now the rebel-held capital, Mercia, was within their grasp. Despite horrendous losses, they still had the advantage of numbers and, given time, they could pose a serious threat to the crusade. The right flank of the Imperial Guard's push towards Mercia was exposed to attack across a series of bridges, one of which Uriel now stood upon. It was imperative the bridges were destroyed, but the Imperial Navy had demanded days of planning for the missions to destroy the bridges, days the crusade could ill afford to waste. Therefore the task of destroying the bridges had fallen to the Ultramarines. Thunderhawk gunships had inserted the assault teams under cover of darkness, half a day's march from the bridges, and now awaited their signal to extract them after the crossings had been destroyed.

The rebellion on Thracia was insignificant but for one thing: reports had filtered back to the crusade's High Command that Traitor Space Marines of the Night Lords legion were present. So far, Uriel had seen nothing of these heretics and, privately, believed that they were phantoms conjured by the over-active imagination of guardsmen. Still, it never paid to be complacent and Uriel fervently hoped the reports would prove to be true. The chance to bring the wrath of the Emperor down on such abominable foes could not be passed up.

He watched a Techmarine wiring the bridge supports for destruction. Melta charges would blast the bridge to pieces, denying the traitors any way of moving their armoured units across the river and flanking the Imperial attack. Uriel knew that the same scene was being repeated up and down the enormous gorge as other Ultramarine detachments prepared to destroy their own targets. He scooped up his helmet and marched towards a mud-stained Techmarine hauling himself over the parapet and unwinding a long length of cable from his equipment pack. The man looked up as he heard Uriel approach and nodded respectfully.

'I suppose you're going to tell me to hurry up,' he grumbled, bending awkwardly to hook the cable into a battery pack.

'Not at all, Sevano. As though I would rush the work of a master craftsman like yourself.'

Sevano Tomasin glowered at Uriel, searching his face for any trace of sarcasm. Finding none, the Techmarine nodded as he continued wiring the explosives, moving with a lop-sided, mechanical gait as both his legs and right arm were heavier, bionic replacements.

The apothecaries had grafted these on after recovering his body from the interior of a wrecked Land Raider on Ichar IV after a rampaging carnifex had ripped it apart. The horrifying creature's bio-plasma had flooded the interior of the armoured fighting vehicle, detonating its ammo spectacularly. The carnifex was killed in the blast, but the explosion sheared Tomasin to the bone and, rather than lose his centuries of wisdom, the chapter's artisans had designed a completely new, artificial body around the bloody rags of his remains.

'How long until you and the servitors are finished?' asked Uriel.

Tomasin wiped the mud from his face and glanced up the length of the bridge. 'Another hour, Ventris. Possibly less if this damned rain would ease up and I didn't have to stop to talk to you.'

Uriel bit back a retort and turned away, leaving the Techmarine to his work and striding to the nearest gun nest. Captain Idaeus was sitting on the sandbags and speaking animatedly into the vox-com.

'Well make sure, damn you!' he snapped. 'I don't want to be left sitting here facing half the rebel army with only thirty men.'

Idaeus listened to the words that only he could hear through the comm-bead in his ear and cursed, snapping the vox unit back to his belt.

'Trouble?' asked Uriel.

'Maybe,' sighed Idaeus. 'Orbital surveyors on the Vae Victus say they think they detected something large moving through the jungle in our direction, but this damned weather's interfering with the auguries and they can't bring them on-line again. It's probably nothing.'

'You don't sound too convinced.'

'I'm not,' admitted Idaeus. 'If the Night Lords are on this world, then this is just the kind of thing they would try.'

'I have our scouts watching the approaches to the bridge. Nothing is going to get close without us knowing about it.'

'Good. How is Tomasin getting on?'

'There's a lot of bridge to blow, captain, but Tomasin thinks he'll have it done within the hour. I believe he will have it rigged sooner though.'

Idaeus nodded and rose to his feet, staring into the mist and rain shrouded hills on the enemy side of the bridge. His face creased in a frown and Uriel followed his gaze. Dusk was fast approaching and with luck they would be on their way to rejoin the main assault on Mercia before nightfall.

'Something wrong?'

'I'm not sure. Every time I look across the bridge I get a bad feeling.'

'A bad feeling?'

'Aye, like someone is watching us,' whispered Idaeus.

Uriel checked his vox-com. 'The scouts haven't reported anything.'

Idaeus shook his head. 'No, this is more like instinct. This whole place feels wrong somehow. I can't describe it.'

Uriel was puzzled. Idaeus was a man he trusted implicitly, they had fought and bled together for over fifty years, forming a bond of friendship that Uriel found all too rarely. Yet he could never claim to truly understand Idaeus. The captain relied on instinct and feelings more than the holy Codex Astartes, that great work of military thinking penned ten thousand years ago by their own Primarch, Roboute Guilliman. The Codex formed the basis of virtually every Space Marine chapter's tactical doctrine and laid the foundations for the military might of the entire Imperium. Its words were sanctified by the Emperor himself and the Ultramarines had not deviated from its teachings since it had been written following the dark days of the Horus Heresy.

But Idaeus tended to regard the wisdom of the Codex as advice rather than holy instruction and this was a constant source of amazement to Uriel. He had been Idaeus's second-in-command for nearly thirty years and, despite the captain's successes, Uriel still found it hard to accept his methods.

'I want to go and check those hills,' said Idaeus suddenly.

Uriel sighed and pointed out, 'The scouts will inform us of anything that approaches.'

'I know, and I have every faith in them. I just need to see for myself. Come on, let's go and take a look.'

Uriel took out his vox unit, informing the scouts they would be approaching from the rear and followed Idaeus as he strode purposefully to the end of the bridge. They passed the far bunker, the one the rebels should have occupied, noting the glint of bolters from within. The two Space Marines marched up the wide road that led into the high hills either side of the gorge and for the next thirty minutes inspected the locations Uriel had deployed the scouts to watch from. The rain deadened sounds and kept visibility low and there was enough tree cover to almost completely obscure the jungle floor. There could be an army out there and they wouldn't see it until it was right on top of them.

'Satisfied?' asked Uriel.

Idaeus nodded, but did not reply and together they began the trek back to the far bunker where they could see Sevano Tomasin.

The warning came just as the first artillery shell screamed overhead.

Almost as soon as Uriel heard the incoming shell, the comm-net exploded with voices; reports of artillery flashes in the distance and multiple sightings of armoured personnel carriers and tanks. A blinding explosion in the centre of the bridge, followed by half a dozen more in quick succession, split the dusk apart. Uriel shouted as he saw the servitors and two Space Marines blasted from the bridge, tumbling downwards to the rocks below.

The two officers sprinted down towards the bridge.

Uriel dialled into the vox-net of the Scouts as he ran and yelled, 'Scout team Alpha! Where in the warp did they come from? Report!'

'Contacts at three kilometres and closing, sergeant! The rain held down the dust, we couldn't see them through the dead ground.'

'Understood,' snapped Uriel, cursing the weather. 'What can you see?'

'Can't get an accurate count, but it looks like a battalion-sized assault. Chimeras mainly, but there's a lot of heavy armour mixed in – Leman Russ, Griffons and Hellhounds.'

Uriel swore and exchanged glances with Idaeus. If the scouts were correct, they were facing in excess of a thousand men with artillery and armoured support. Both knew that this must be the contact the auguries on the Vae Victus had detected then lost. They had to get everyone back across the bridge and blow it right now.

'Stay as long as you can Alpha and keep reporting, then get back here!'

'Aye, sir,' responded the scout and signed off.

More shells dropped on the bridge, the echoes of their detonations deafening in the enclosed gorge. Each blast threw up chunks of the roadway and vast geysers of rainwater. Some were air-bursting above the bridge, showering the roadway with deadly fragments.

Uriel recognised the distinctive whine of Griffon mortar shells and gave thanks to Guilliman that the PDF obviously did not have access to the heavier artillery pieces of the Imperial Guard. Either that or they realised that to use such weapons would probably destroy the bridge.

Most of the Space Marines who had been caught in the open were in cover now and Uriel knew they were lucky not to have lost more men. He cursed as he saw the lumbering shape of Sevano Tomasin still fixing explosive charges and unwinding lengths of cable back towards the last bunker. The Techmarine's movements were painfully slow, but he was undaunted by the shelling. Uriel willed him to work faster.

'One and a half kilometres and closing. Closing rapidly! Dismounted enemy infantry visible!' shouted the scout sergeant in Uriel's comm-bead.

'Acknowledged,' shouted Uriel over the crash of falling mortar shells and explosions. 'Get back here now. There's nothing more you can do from there. Sword squad is waiting at the first bunker to give you covering fire. Ventris out.'

Uriel and Idaeus reached the bunker and splashed to a halt behind its reassuringly thick walls. Idaeus snatched up his vox-com and shouted, 'Guard command net, this is Captain Idaeus, Ultramarine Fourth company. Be advised that hostiles are attacking across Bridge Two-Four in division strength, possibly stronger. We are falling back and preparing to destroy the bridge. I say again, hostiles are attacking across Bridge Two-Four!'

As Idaeus voxed the warning to the Imperial Guard commanders,

Uriel patched into the frequency of the Thunderhawk that had dropped them in position.

'Thunderhawk Six, this is Uriel Ventris. We are under attack and request immediate extraction. Mission order Omega-Seven-Four. Acknowledge please.'

For long seconds, all Uriel could hear was the hiss of static and he feared something terrible had happened to the gunship. Then a voice, heavily distorted said, 'Acknowledged, Sergeant Ventris. Mission order Omega-Seven-Four received. We'll be overhead in ten minutes. Signal your position with green smoke.'

'Affirmative,' replied Uriel. 'Be advised the landing zone will in all likelihood be extremely hot when you arrive.'

'Don't worry,' chuckled the pilot of the gunship. 'We're fully loaded. We'll keep their heads down while we extract you. Thunderhawk Six out.'

Uriel snapped the vox-unit to his belt and hammered on the bunker's door. He and Idaeus ducked inside as it slid open. The five Space Marines within were positioned at the bunker's firing step, bolters and a lascannon pointed at the hills above, ready to cover their brothers' retreat. Uriel stared through the anti-grenade netting, watching the scouts falling back in good order towards the bridge.

'As soon as the scouts are past you, fall back to the first gun nest and take up firing positions,' ordered Idaeus. 'The other squads are already in position and they'll cover you. Understood?'

The Space Marines nodded, but did not take their eyes from the ridge above the approaching scouts. Idaeus turned to Uriel and said, 'Get across and see how close Tomasin is to blowing this damned bridge. We'll join you as soon as we can.'

Uriel opened his mouth to protest, but Idaeus cut him off, 'Stow it, sergeant. Go! I'll join you as soon as Alpha Team are safe.'

Without another word, Uriel slipped from the bunker. Another series of thunderous detonations cascaded across the bridge and impacted on the sides of the gorge. Uriel waited until he detected a lull in the firing then began sprinting across the bridge, weaving around piles of rubble, debris and water filled craters left by the explosions. He could still see Sevano Tomasin behind the sand-bagged gun nests, working on the detonators.

He heard gunfire behind him, the distinctive, dull crack of bolter fire and the snapping hiss of lasguns. He glanced over his shoulder as a terrible sense of premonition struck him.

Twin streaks of shrieking projectiles flashed overhead, one landing behind him and another before him with earth shaking detonations. The first shell exploded less than four metres above the men of Alpha team, shredding their bodies through the lighter scout armour leaving only a bloody mist and scraps of ripped flesh. The shockwave of the blast threw Uriel to the ground. He coughed mud and spat rainwater, rising in time to see Sevano Tomasin engulfed in blinding white phosphorent fire.

The Techmarine collapsed, his metal limbs liquefying and the flesh searing from his bones. A second melta charge ignited in his equipment pack, also cooked off by the mortar shell's detonation. Tomasin vanished in a white-hot explosion, the rain forming a steam cloud around his molten remains.

Uriel pushed himself upright and charged towards the fallen Space Marine. Tomasin was dead, there could be no doubt about that. But Uriel needed to see if the detonator mechanism had gone up with him. If it had, they were in deep, deep trouble.

Idaeus watched the first squadron of enemy vehicles crest the ridge above, hatred burning in his heart. Even in the fading light, he could clearly make out the silhouette of three Salamander scout vehicles and Idaeus vowed he would see them dead.

He could smell the acrid stench of scorched human flesh from the blasted remains of the scouts. They had died only ten metres from the safety of the bunker. Idaeus knew he should fall back to the prepared gun positions further along the bridge; if they stayed here much longer, they'd be trapped. But his thirst for retribution was a fire in his heart, and he was damned if he would yield a millimetre to these bastards without exacting some measure of vengeance for his fallen warriors.

'Nivaneus,' hissed Idaeus to the Space Marine carrying the lascannon. 'Do you have a target?'

'Aye, sir,' confirmed Nivaneus.

'Then fire at will. Take down those traitorous dogs!'

A blinding streak of las-fire punched from the massive weapon. A Salamander slewed from the road, its hull blazing and smoke boiling from its interior. The vehicles' supporting infantry squads fired their lasguns before the Space Marines' bolter fire blasted them apart with uncompromising accuracy. But Idaeus knew they were inconsequential. Killing the tanks was all that mattered.

Nivaneus calmly switched targets and another Salamander died, its crew tumbling from the escape hatches on fire. The last tank ground to a halt, stuttering blasts from its autocannon stitching across the bunker's face. Idaeus felt the vibrations of shell impacts. He smiled grimly as the Salamander's driver desperately attempted to reverse back uphill. Its tracks spun ineffectually, throwing up huge sprays of mud, unable to find purchase. Dust and an acrid, electric stench filled the air as Nivaneus lined up a shot on the struggling tank.

Before he could fire, a missile speared through the rain and smashed into the immobilised tank's turret. It exploded from within, wracked by secondary detonations as its ammo cooked off.

'Captain Idaeus!' shouted Uriel over the vox-net. 'Get out of there! There will be more tanks coming over that ridge any moment and you will be cut off if you do not leave now! We have you covered, now get back here!'

'I think he's got a point, men,' said Idaeus calmly. 'We've given them a bloody nose, but it's time we were going.'

The Ultramarines fired a last volley of shots before hefting their weapons and making for the door.

'Uriel!' called Idaeus. 'We are ready to go, now give me some fire.'

Seconds later a withering salvo of bolter fire and missiles swept the ridge top, wreathing it in smoke and flames. Idaeus shouted, 'Go, go, go!' to the Space Marines and followed as they sprinted through the rain. The mortar fire had ceased; probably due to the Griffon tanks being moved up into a direct firing position, thought Idaeus. Whatever the reason, he was grateful for it.

He heard a teeth-loosening rumble and a squeal of tracks, knowing without looking that heavy tanks had spread out across the ridge, moving into a firing position behind them. He saw two missile contrails flashing overhead and heard the ringing clang of their impact. A crashing detonation told him that at least one enemy tank was out of action, but only one.

'Incoming!' he yelled and dived over a pile of debris into a crater as the thunder of two battle cannons echoed across the gorge. He felt the awesome force of the impacts behind him, even through the ceramite of his power armour. His auto senses shut down momentarily to preserve his sight and hearing as the massive shell exploded, the pressure of the blast almost crushing him flat. Red runes winked into life on his visor as his armour was torn open in half a dozen places. He felt searing pain and cursed as he yanked a plate-sized piece of sizzling shrapnel from his leg. Almost instantly, he could feel the Larraman cells clotting his blood and forming a protective layer of scar tissue over the wound. He had suffered much worse and shut out the pain.

The two surviving Leman Russ tanks rumbled downhill, smashing the smoking remains of the Salamanders aside with giant dozer blades. Furious gunfire spat from their hull-mounted heavy bolters, sweeping across the bunker's face and the bridge, throwing up spouts of water and rock. None hit the Ultramarines and Idaeus shouted, 'Up! Come on, keep moving!'

The Space Marines rose and continued running towards the comparative safety of the far side of the bridge. More tanks and infantry spilled over the ridge, following in the wake of the Leman Russ battle tanks. Las-blasts fired at the Space Marines, but the range was too great.

Then, at the edge of his hearing, Idaeus heard the welcome boom of a Thunderhawk gunship's engines and saw the angular form of the aerial transport sweep from the above the jungle canopy. Rockets streaked from its wing pylons, rippling off in salvoes of three and the ridge vanished in a wall of flames. Heavy cannons mounted on the hull and wings fired thousands of shells into the rebels, obliterating tanks and men in a heartbeat.

Idaeus punched the air in triumph as the Thunderhawk swept over the ridge and circled around for another strafing run. He jogged leisurely into the sandbagged gun nest, the Space Marines who had followed him taking up firing positions.

'Uriel,' voxed Idaeus. 'Are you ready to get out of here?'

'More than ready,' replied Uriel from the bunker behind Idaeus. 'But we have a problem. Tomasin was killed in the shelling and he had the detonators. We can't blow the bridge.'

Idaeus slammed his fist into a sandbag. 'Damn it!' he swore, teeth bared. He paced the interior of the gun nest like a caged grox before saying, 'Then we're going to have to hold here for as long as possible and pray the Guard can realign their flank in time.'

'Agreed. The Emperor guide your aim, captain.'

'And yours. May He watch over you.'

Uriel shut off the vox-com and slid a fresh magazine into his bolt pistol, staring out at the flame wreathed hillside. The distant Thunderhawk had circled around, guns blazing at something Uriel could not see. Fresh explosions blossomed from behind the ridge as more traitors died.

Suddenly shells burst around the gunship and streams of fire, bright against the dark sky, licked up from the ground. Uriel swore as he realised the traitors were equipped with anti-aircraft weapons. The gunship jinked to avoid the incoming fire, but another stream of shells spat skyward and seconds later the gunners had the Thunderhawk bracketed. Thousands of shells ripped through the gunship's armour, tearing the port wing off. The engine exploded in a brilliant fireball. The pilot struggled to hold the aircraft aloft, banking to avoid the flak, but the gunship continued to lose altitude, spewing black smoke from its stricken frame.

Uriel watched with horror as the Thunderhawk spiralled lower and lower, its wobbling form growing larger by the second.

'By the Emperor, no!' whispered Uriel as the gunship smashed into the ground just before the bridge, skidding forwards and trailing a brilliant halo of sparks and flames. The wreckage crashed into the unoccupied bunker, demolishing it instantly and slewing across the bridge towards the Ultramarines with the sound of shrieking metal. The remaining wing sheared off, spinning the flaming gunship upside down and tearing up the roadway. The gunship ground onwards, finally coming to a halt less than two hundred metres from the gun nests.

Uriel let out the breath he had been holding. Movement caught his eye and he saw more enemy vehicles rumbling through the swirling black smoke towards the bridge.

'Targets sighted!' he shouted. 'Enemy tanks inbound. Mark your targets and fire when you have a clear shot!'

The lead rebel armoured column consisted of dozens of Chimeras, daubed in blasphemous runes. Uriel snarled as he recognised the winged skull motif of the Night Lords crudely copied onto the Chimeras' hulls. There could be no doubt now. The taint of Chaos had come to Thracia. Each vehicle mounted a powerful searchlight, sweeping blindingly back and forth in random patterns across the bridge as they charged. Missiles and lascannon blasts pierced the darkness, and the night was illuminated by scores of exploding tanks. No matter how many the Ultramarines killed, there were more to take their place. Soon the bridge was choked with burning wrecks. Hundreds of screaming soldiers dismounted from their transports, working their way forward through the tanks' graveyard.

Uriel fired shot after shot from his pistol. It was impossible to miss, there were so many. The darkness of the gorge echoed to the sounds of screams and gunfire. But Uriel was not fooled by the slaughter they were wreaking amongst the ranks of the traitors.

Their ammunition was finite and soon the battle would degenerate into bloody close quarters fighting and, though they would kill many hundreds, they would eventually fall. It was simply a question of numbers.

He reloaded again and wished there was something else he could do, cursing Sevano Tomasin for dying and condemning them to this ignoble end. He pictured again the image of the Techmarine incinerated by the chain-reacting melta charge in his equipment pack.

Something clicked in Uriel's head and he stopped.

No, it was insane, utterly insane and suicidal. But it could work. He tried to remember a precedent in the Codex Astartes, but came up with nothing. Could it be done? A frag wouldn't do it and only the assault troops had been issued with kraks. He checked his grenade dispenser. He had one breaching charge left.

His mind made up, he grabbed a Space Marine from the firing step, shouting to be heard over the bolter fire.'I'm heading for the captain's position. Give me covering fire!'

The man nodded and passed on his order. Uriel ducked out the ragged doorway and crouched at the corner of the bunker. Streams of las-blasts and bolter rounds criss-crossed the darkness causing a weirdly stroboscopic effect.

Volleys of sustained bolter fire blasted from the bunker and Uriel leapt from cover, sprinting towards Idaeus's position. Instantly, lasgun fire erupted from amongst the burning tanks. Each shooter was silenced by a devastatingly accurate bolter shot. Uriel dived behind the gun nest and crawled inside on his belly.

Idaeus, bleeding from a score of gouges in his armour, directed disciplined bolter fire into the traitors' ranks. Two Space Marines lay dead, the backs of their helmets blasted clear and Uriel was suddenly very aware of how much less protection there was in the gun nest than the bunker.

Idaeus spared Uriel a glance, shouting, 'What are you doing here, Uriel?'

'I have an idea how we can blow the bridge!'

'How?'

'The assault troops have krak grenades. If we can attach some to one of the melta charges on the bridge supports it could set of a chain reaction with the others!'

Idaeus considered the idea for a second then shrugged. 'It's not much of a plan, but what choice do we have?'

'None,' said Uriel bluntly. Idaeus nodded and hunkered down in the sandbags, snatching out his battered vox. Hurriedly, he explained Uriel's plan to the sergeant of the assault troopers, receiving confirmation as to its feasibility of execution.

Idaeus raised his head and locked his gaze with Uriel. 'You picked a hell of a time to start thinking outside the Codex, sergeant.'

'Better late than never, captain.'

Idaeus smiled and nodded. 'We'll have about thirty seconds from the first detonation to get clear. If we're not off the bridge by then, we're dead. I've already called for another Thunderhawk, but it will not arrive before morning at the earliest.'

The captain opened a channel to the remaining Space Marines in his detachment and said, 'All squads, as soon as the assault troops move, I want enough firepower laid down on these bastards to blow apart a Titan. Understood?'

Shouted confirmations greeted Idaeus's order. He reloaded his pistol and motioned for Uriel to join him at the edge of the gun nest.

From the second gun nest, flaring jets of light erupted as the assault squad fired their jump packs.

'NOW!' yelled Idaeus and the Ultramarines fired everything they had. Volley after volley of bolter shells, missiles and lascannon shots decimated the rebel troopers. The swiftness of death was unbelievable. The Space Marines pumped shot after shot into their reeling mass.

It began with a single rebel turning his back and fleeing into the night. An officer shot him dead, but it was already too late. Others began turning and fleeing through the maze of wrecked tanks, their resolve broken in the face of the Emperor's finest.

And then it was over.

Uriel could not recall how long they had fought for, but it must have been many hours. He checked his visor chronometer and was surprised to find it had been less than two. He knelt and counted his ammo: six clips, not good. Risking a glance over the top level of sandbags, their outer surfaces vitrified to glass by the intense heat of repeated laser impacts, Uriel saw the bridge littered with hundreds of corpses.

The tension was palpable, every Space Marine ready to move the instant they heard the first detonation of a krak grenade. Long minutes passed with nothing but the hiss of the vox, the crackle of flames and moans of the dying outside. Everyone in the gun nest flinched as they heard the crack of rapid bolt pistol fire. The shooting continued for several minutes before dying away.

Uriel and Idaeus exchanged worried glances. Both sides were using bolt pistols.

Uriel shook his head sadly. 'They failed.'

'We don't know that,' snapped Idaeus, but Uriel could tell the captain did not believe his own words.

Weak sunlight shone from the carcasses of the crashed Thunderhawk and smashed tanks on the bridge, their black shells smouldering fitfully. The rain had continued throughout the night. Thankfully, the rebels' attacks had not. There was no detonation of krak grenades and Idaeus was forced to admit that the assault squad had been thwarted in their mission.

Uriel scanned the skies to their rear, watching for another Thunderhawk or perhaps Lightning strike craft of the Imperial Navy. Either would be a welcome sight just now, but the skies remained empty.

A sudden shout from one of the forward observers roused Uriel from his melancholy thoughts and he swiftly took his position next to Idaeus. He saw movement through the burnt out shell of the Thunderhawk, flashes of blue and gold and heard a throaty grinding noise. The sound of heavy vehicles crushing bone and armour beneath their iron tracks. Darting figures, also in blue and gold, slipped through the wrecks, their movements furtive.

With a roar of primal ferocity that spoke of millennia of hate, the Night Lords Chaos Space Marines finally revealed themselves. Battering through the wreckage came five ornately carved Rhino armoured personnel carriers, coruscating azure flames writhing within their flanks. Uriel was speechless.

They resembled Rhinos in name only. Bloody spikes festooned every surface and leering gargoyles thrashed across the undulating armour, gibbering eldritch incantations that made Uriel's skin crawl.

But the supreme horror was mounted on the tanks' frontal sections.

The still-living bodies of the Ultramarine assault squad were crucified on crude iron crosses bolted to the hulls. Their armour had been torn off, their ribcages sawn open then spread wide like obscene angels' wings. Glistening ropes of entrails hung from their opened bellies and they wept blood from blackened, empty eye sockets and tongueless mouths. That they could still be alive was impossible, yet Uriel could see their hearts still beat with life, could see the abject horror of pain in their contorted features.

The Rhinos continued forwards, closely followed by gigantic figures in midnight blue power armour. Their armour was edged in bronze and their helmets moulded into daemonic visages with blood streaked horns. Red winged skull icons pulsed with unnatural life on their shoulder plates.

Idaeus was the first to overcome his shock, lifting his bolter and pumping shots into the advancing Night Lords.

'Kill them!' he bellowed. 'Kill them all!'

Uriel shook his head, throwing off the spell of horror the spectacle of the mutilated Ultramarines had placed upon him and he levelled his pistol. Two missiles and a lascannon shot punched towards the Night Lords. Uriel prayed the tortured souls crucified on the Rhinos would forgive them, as two of the tanks exploded, veering off and crashing into the side of the bridge. The prisoners burned in the flames of their destruction and Uriel could feel his fury rising to a level where all he could feel was the urge to kill.

The Space Marine next to Uriel fell, a bolter shell detonating within his chest cavity. He collapsed without a sound, and Uriel swept up his bolt gun, emptying the magazine into the traitor legionnaires. A handful of Night Lords were dead, but the rest were closing the gap rapidly. Two more Rhinos died in fiery blasts. Disciplined volleys of bolter and lascannon fire from the Ultramarines in the bunker kept hammering the ranks of Night Lords as they attempted to overrun the gun nests. But few were falling and it was only a matter of time until the traitors reached them.

The Space Marines across the bridge from Uriel and Idaeus perished in a searing ball of white-hot fire as Night Lord warriors unloaded plasma guns through the firing slit of their gun nest. The backblast of the resultant explosion mushroomed into the dawn, incinerating the killers. Still they came on.

Uriel yelled in fury, killing and killing. An armoured gauntlet smashed into the gun nest.

Idaeus chopped with his power sword and blood sprayed.

Uriel yelled, 'Grenade!' as he saw what was clutched in the severed hand. He kicked the hand into the gun nest's grenade pit and rolled a dead Space Marine on top. The frag blew with a muffled thump, the corpse's ceramite back-plate absorbing the full force of the blast.

'Thank you, brother,' muttered Uriel in relief.

Another Night Lord kicked his way into the gun nest, a screaming axe gripped in one massive fist. His blue armour seemed to ripple with inner fires and the brass edging was dazzling in its brightness. The winged skull icon hissed blasphemous oaths and Uriel could feel the axe's obscene hunger for blood. Idaeus slashed his sword across his chest, but the blade slid clear. The warrior lunged, slashing his axe across Idaeus's shoulder and blood sprayed through the rent in his armour. Idaeus slammed his elbow into his foe's belly and spun inside his guard, hammering his sword through the Night Lord's neck.

He kicked him back outside as more enemies pushed themselves in. Uriel fired his pistol and rolled beneath a crackling power fist. He drove his combat knife into the gap between his enemy's breastplate and helmet, wrenching the blade upwards. Blood fountained and he yelled in sudden pain as the warrior fired his bolter at point blank range. The shell penetrated Uriel's armour and blasted a fist-sized chunk of his hip clear. He stabbed his opponent's neck again and again, stopping only when his struggles ceased completely.

Idaeus and the last Space Marine in the gun nest fought back to back, desperately fighting for their lives against four Night Lords. Uriel leapt into the combat, wrapping his powerful arms around one Chaos Space Marine's neck. He twisted hard, snapping his spine.

Everything was blood and violence. The Space Marine fighting alongside Idaeus fell, his body pulverised by a power fist. Uriel dragged his blade free from the Night Lord's helmet and beheaded the killer, blowing out another foe's helmet with a bolter shell. Idaeus drove his sword through the last Night Lord's belly, kicking the corpse from his blood-sheathed blade. The two Space Marines snatched up their bolters and began firing again. The gun nest stank of blood and smoke. The last Rhino was a blazing wreck, the prisoner on its hull cooking in the fires.

He tossed aside the bolter as its slide racked back empty and grabbed Idaeus by the shoulder.

'We need to get back to the bunker. We can't hold them here!'

'Agreed,' grimaced Idaeus. Grabbing what ammo they could carry, the two warriors ducked outside into the grey morning and ran back towards the bullet scarred bunker. The attack appeared to be over for now.

As they ran, Idaeus's vox crackled and a voice said, 'Captain Idaeus, do you copy? This is Thunderhawk Two. We are inbound on your position and will be overhead in less than a minute. Do you copy?'

Idaeus snatched up the vox and shouted, 'I copy, Thunderhawk

Two, but do not over-fly our position! The enemy has at least two, but probably more, anti-aircraft tanks covering the bridge. We already lost Thunderhawk Six.'

'Understood. We will set down half a kilometre south of the bridge,' replied the pilot.

Uriel and Idaeus limped inside the bunker and dropped the bolter magazines on the floor.

'Load up. This is all we have left,' ordered Idaeus.

The Ultramarines began sharing out the magazines and Uriel offered another bolter to Idaeus, but the captain shook his head.

'I don't need it. Give me a pistol and a couple of clips. And that last breaching charge of yours, Uriel.'

Uriel quickly grasped the significance of Idaeus' words. 'No, let me do it, captain,' he pleaded.

Idaeus shook his head, 'Not this time, Uriel. This is my mission, I won't let it end like this. The seven of us can't hold the Night Lords if they attack again, so I'm ordering you to get the rest of the men back to that Thunderhawk.'

'Besides,' he said with a wry smile. 'You don't have a jump pack to get down there.'

Uriel could see there was no arguing with the captain. He dispensed the last breaching charge and reverently offered it to Idaeus. The captain took the charge and unbuckled his sword belt. He reversed the scabbard and handed the elaborately tooled sword to Uriel.

'Take this,' he said. 'I know it will serve you as well as it has served me. A weapon this fine should not end its days like this, and you will have more need of it than I.'

Uriel could not speak. Idaeus himself had forged the magnificent blade before the Corinthian Crusade and had carried it in battle ever since. The honour was overwhelming.

Idaeus gripped Uriel's wrist tightly in the warrior's grip and said, 'Go now, old friend. Make me proud.'

Uriel nodded. 'I will, captain,' he promised, and saluted. The five remaining Space Marines in the bunker followed Uriel's lead and came to attention, bolters held tightly across their chests.

Idaeus smiled. 'The Emperor watch over you all,' he said and slipped outside into the rain.

Uriel was gripped by a terrible sense of loss, but suppressed it viciously. He would ensure that Idaeus's last command was carried out.

He loaded a bolter and racked the slide.

'Come on, we have to go.'

Idaeus waited until he saw Uriel lead the five Space Marines from the bunker towards the jungle's edge before moving. He had a chance to do this stealthily, but knew it wouldn't be long before the Night Lords realised the bridge was now undefended and the rebels drove their forces across. He would not allow that to happen.

He crawled through the mud and rubble, keeping out of sight of the enemy lines, eventually reaching the pitted face of the rockcrete sides of the bridge. He grabbed a handful of mud and ash, smearing it over the blue of his armour, then slithered onto the parapet. The river was thousands of metres below and Idaeus experienced a momentary surge of vertigo as he looked down. He scanned the bridge supports, searching for one of the box-like melta charges Tomasin had placed only the day before. He grinned as he spotted one fixed to the central span. Muttering a prayer to the Emperor and Guilliman, Idaeus pushed himself over the edge.

He dropped quickly, then fired the twin jets of his jump pack, angling for the central span. The noise of the rockets' burn seemed incredibly loud to Idaeus, but he could do nothing about it. It was all or nothing now.

He cursed as he saw his trajectory was too short. He landed on a wide beam, some twenty metres from the central span and crouched, waiting to see if he had been detected. He heard nothing and clambered through the multitude of stanchions, beams and tension bars towards the central column.

Suddenly, a shadow passed over the captain and he spun in time to see dark winged creatures in midnight black power armour swoop down alongside him. Their helmets were moulded in the form of screaming daemons and ululating howls shrieked from their vox units. They carried stubby pistols and serrated black swords that smoked as though fresh from the furnace. Idaeus knew the foul creatures as Raptors, and fired into their midst, blasting one of the abominable warriors from the sky. Another crashed into him, stabbing with a black bladed sword. Idaeus grunted as he felt the blade pierce one of his lungs, and broke the Raptor's neck with a blow from his free hand. He staggered back, the sword still embedded in his chest, taking refuge in the tangle of metal beneath the bridge to avoid the howling Raptors. Two landed between him and the melta charge as dozens more descended from the bridge. Three more swooped in behind him, their wings folding behind them and they landed on the girders. Idaeus snarled and raised his pistol as they charged.

Idaeus killed the first with his pistol. A second shot killed another, but he couldn't move quick enough to avoid the third. White heat exploded in his face, searing the flesh from the side of his skull as the Raptor fired its plasma pistol. He fell back, blind with pain, and didn't see the crackling sword blow that hacked his left arm from his body. He bellowed with rage as he watched his arm tumble down towards the river, Uriel's last breaching charge still clutched in the armoured fist.

The Raptor closed for the kill, but Idaeus was ready for it. He dragged the smoking sword from his chest and howled with battle fury as he hammered the sword through the Raptor's neck. He collapsed next to the headless corpse, releasing his grip on the sword hilt. Dizziness and pain swamped him. He tried to stand, but his strength was gone. He saw the Raptors standing between him and the melta charge, their daemon-carved helmets alight with the promise of victory.

He felt his lifeblood pumping from his body, the Larraman cells powerless to halt his demise and bitterness arose in his throat. He reached out with his arm, propping himself upright as weariness flooded his limbs. He felt a textured pistol grip beneath his hand and grasped the unfamiliar weapon tightly. If he was to die, it would be with a weapon in his hand.

More Raptors hovered in the air, screeching in triumph and Idaeus could feel a bone-rattling vibration as hundreds of armoured vehicles began crossing the bridge. He had failed. He looked down at the pistol in his hand and hope flared. The flying abominations raised their weapons, ready to blow him away.

Then the Raptors exploded in a series of massive detonations and Idaeus heard a thunderous boom echo back and forth from the sides of the gorge. He twisted his dying body around in time to see the beautiful form of Thunderhawk Two roaring through the gorge towards the bridge, its wing mounted guns blasting the Raptors to atoms.

He smiled through the pain, guessing the fight Uriel must have had with the pilot to get him to fly through the flak of the Hydras and down the gorge. He raised his head to the two Raptors who still stood between him and his goal. They drew their swords as Thunderhawk Two screamed below the bridge. Lascannon fire chased the gunship, but nothing could touch it.

Idaeus slumped against a black stanchion and turned his melted face back towards the two Raptors. Between them, he could see the melta charge. He smiled painfully.

He would only get one shot at this.

Idaeus raised the plasma pistol he had taken from the dead Raptor, relishing the look of terror on his enemy's faces as they realised what must happen next.

'Mission accomplished,' snarled Idaeus and pulled the trigger.

Uriel watched the unbearably bright streak of plasma flashing towards the central span of the bridge and explode like a miniature sun directly upon the melta charge. The searing white heat ignited the bomb with a thunderclap and it detonated in a gigantic, blinding fireball, spraying molten tendrils of liquid fire. The central support of the bridge was instantly vaporised in the nuclear heat, and Uriel had a fleeting glimpse of Idaeus before he too was engulfed in the expanding firestorm.

The echoes of the first blast still rang from the gorge sides as the remaining charges detonated in the intense heat. A heartbeat later, the bridge vanished as explosions blossomed along its length and blasted its supports to destruction. Thunderous, grinding cracks heralded its demise as giant sections of the bridge sagged, the shriek of tortured metal and cracking rockcrete filling Uriel's senses. Whole sections plummeted downwards, carrying hundreds of rebel tanks and soldiers to their deaths as the bridge tore itself apart under stresses it was never meant to endure.

Thick smoke and flames obscured the final death of Bridge Two-Four, its twisted remains crashing into the river below. Thunderhawk Two pulled out of the gorge, gaining altitude and banking round on a course for the Imperial lines. Even as the bridge shrank in the distance, Uriel could see there was almost nothing left of it.

The main supports were gone, the sections of roadway they had supported choking the river far below. There was now no way to cross the gorge for hundreds of miles in either direction.

He slid down the armoured interior of the Thunderhawk and wearily removed his helmet, cradling Idaeus's sword in his lap. He thought of Idaeus's sacrifice, wondering again that a warrior of the Ultramarines could command without immediate recourse to the Codex Astartes. It was a mystery to him, yet one he now felt able to explore.

He ran a gauntleted hand along the length of the masterfully inscribed scabbard, feeling the full weight of responsibility the weapon represented. Captain Idaeus of the Fourth Company was dead, but as long as Uriel Ventris wielded this blade, his memory would remain. He looked into the blood-stained faces of the Space Marines who had survived the mission and realised that the duty of command now fell to him.

Uriel vowed he would do it honour.

YOUR NEXT READ

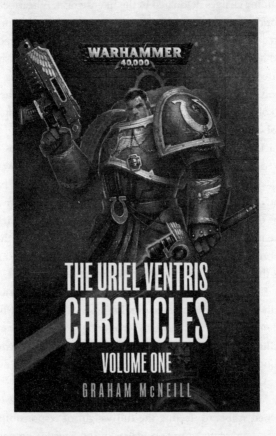

THE URIEL VENTRIS CHRONICLES: VOLUME ONE
by Graham McNeill

Uriel Ventris takes command of the Ultramarines Fourth Company and leads them into danger against drukhari, tyranids and more – and faces his own trials that will test him to his very limits and beyond.

ECLIPSE OF HOPE

David Annandale

Introducing

MEPHISTON

CHIEF LIBRARIAN, BLOOD ANGELS

I stand in the middle of a field of corpses.

We were summoned, and so we have come to Supplicium Secundus. We are winged salvation, but we are a terrible, final salvation, and our wings embrace the horizon with fire. We are the Blood Angels. To confront us is to die, and death is my remit, my reality, my unbounded domain. I have known death, and defeated it, claimed it as my own. To my cost, to my strength, death is my one gift to bestow, and I am nothing if not generous. But today, my liberality is unwanted, unneeded.

Undone.

The dead on the plain are uncountable, and not a one of them has fallen by my will. I emerged with my brothers from the drop pod to be confronted with this vista. There is, it must be said, a certain perfection to it. This is no mere slaughter or massacre. This is not a battlefield where defeat and victory have been meted out. This is death, simply death. The plain is a vast one, stretching to the distance on three sides, ending in the blurry hulk of Evensong Hive to the north. The skyline is smeared not by distance, but by smoke. It is thick, grey flecked with black, a choking pall of ash. It is the lingering memory of high explosives, incinerated architecture and immolated flesh. The fires have burned themselves out. There is a meaning to this smoke. It is the smoke of *afterwards*. It is the smoke of *finished*. It is the smoke of the only form of peace our era knows, the peace that comes when there is no one left to die.

Wind, sluggish and hot, fumbles at my cloak, breathes its last against my cheek. It pushes at the smoke, making the grey stir over the corpses like an exhausted phantom. There is no sound. There are no trees to rub leaves in a susurrus of mourning. There is no tall grass to wave a benediction. The ground has been chewed into a mulch of mud. Wreckage of weaponry and of humanity is slowly sinking into the mire. In time, all memory of the events of Supplicium Secundus will vanish. Smoke lingers. It does not last.

There is no order to the dead. There is no hint of this having been a war. There is no division between armies, no demarcating line of the clash. There is only brother at brother's throat. By bolter, by sword, by cannon, by hands, this has been the pure violence of all against all. The full panoply of Supplicium's population lies, stilled, before me. I see civilians of both genders, and of all ages. I see the uniform of Unwavering Supplicants, the local planetary defence force.

I see the proud colours of the Mordian Iron Guard, now covered in mud.

We are here because of the Iron Guard. It was their General Spira who called out to us. His message was fragmented and desperate. We have not been in contact with him since that first cry. I look at his men who have killed each other, and doubt that we shall hear from him again.

Over the vox network, reports arrive from the other landing sites. Supplicium Secundus is a compact world, dense in composition and with a handful of small habitable zones at the equator. In each of these areas, a hive has arisen, and it is just outside these hives that our strike forces have landed, a multi-pronged attack designed to inflict simultaneous punishments on the enemy. Sergeant Saleos calls from Hive Canticle, then Sergeant Andarus from Hive Oblation, then Sergeant Procellus from Hive Anthem. It is the same everywhere: endless vistas of death. We came because of heretical rebellion. We came because the Iron Guard was overmatched. We have found only silence.

Behind me, the Stormraven gunship *Bloodthorn* sits on a clear patch of land. I am in the company of Stolas, Epistolary of 4th Company, Chaplain Dantalion, Standard Bearer Markosius and a tactical squad led by Sergeant Gamigin. Standing a few metres to my left, the sergeant scans the landscape with an auspex. Nothing. Frustration radiates from my battle-brothers. Their hunger for the bloodshed of combat eats at them. Their bolters are still raised, seeking absent targets. They are angry at the dead. Our standard rises above the plain, proud but still in the dying wind, a call to a battle that is long over.

'This is a waste of time,' says Stolas.

'Is it?' I say.

At my tone, Stolas snaps his head around. 'Lord Mephiston,' he begins, 'I–'

I cut him off. 'Do you know what has happened here?'

'No, I–'

'This is something you have seen before?'

This time, he does not try to answer. He simply shakes his head.

'Mordian has slain Mordian,' I point out. '*All* the Mordians are slain. That gives me pause.' I turn from Stolas, losing interest in the reprimand, refocusing my thoughts on the madness before me. And madness is what it is, I realise. Insanity. There is no logic, and this is the flaw in the tapestry of mortality. My eyes range over the infinity of bodies. The perfection I see is, in truth, only the perfection of abomination. 'We are not wasting our time,' I say, speaking more to myself than to Stolas. 'There is a mystery here, and it bears the mark of Chaos.'

Something flickers in my peripheral vision. I look up. Movement in the smoke. A figure approaching. A man.

His movements are jerky, random, yet purposeful in their energy. He cuts back and forth, advancing in no clear direction until he catches sight of us. Then he runs, pounding towards us over the backs of the fallen. He pistons his legs with such force that I can hear the snap of bones beneath his feet. His arms are outstretched as if he were running to embrace us. He emerges from the smoke. His teeth are bared. His face is red, his tendons popping. He is snarling with incoherent rage. What manner of man would charge, so unhesitatingly, and so completely alone, against the Adeptus Astartes? And what manner of man would do so unarmed? Only one sort: a man completely in the grip of madness.

He leaps on Sergeant Gamigin, biting and clawing and spitting. The man cannot possibly hope to break through the Blood Angel's armour. Gamigin stands there, bemused. After a minute, he hauls the man off and holds him out by the scruff of his neck. The snapping, feral creature is a Guardsman. His uniform is in tatters, but enough of it remains to identify him as a colonel.

With a sudden clench of his fist, Gamigin snaps the man's neck and hurls him to the ground. He stomps on the officer's head, smashing it to pulp. Over his helmet's vocaliser comes a growl that is growing in volume and intensity.

'Brother-Sergeant?' Chaplain Dantalion asks.

Gamigin whirls on him, drawing his chainsword.

'*Sergeant.*' I use my voice as a whip. Gamigin pauses and turns his head. I step forward and hold his gaze. The lenses of his helmet are expressionless, but mine are the eyes without pity or warmth. I see the taint of the warp gathering around Gamigin like a bruise. The madness that has descended upon him is not the Red Thirst. It is not the manifestation of the Flaw, though our genetic curse may create an increased vulnerability. The tendrils of the warp bruise are deeply tangled in Gamigin's being. There is no salvation for him except what he wills himself. 'Give us space,' I tell the others. 'Take no action.' I do not draw my blade. 'Gamigin,' I say, then repeat his name twice more.

The growl stops. His breathing is heavy, laboured, but suggesting exhaustion, not frenzy. He sheaths his chainsword. 'Chief Librarian,' he says. He shakes his head. 'Forgive me. I don't understand what happened.'

'Try to describe it.'

'I felt disgust for the officer, and then a blind rage. All I wanted to do was kill everyone in sight.'

The silence that follows his statement is a heavy one. I have no need to point out the implications. The madness that killed Supplicium Secundus still lurks, seeking purchase now in our souls. I let my consciousness slip partially into contact with the everywhere non-space of the warp. I anatomize the energies that flow about me. I find the mad rage. It is a background radiation, barely detectable, but omnipresent. The planet is infected. The disease that killed its population has a pulse, an irregular beat like that of an overtaxed heart. I pull back my awareness back to the here and now, but now that I have seen the trace of the plague, I can identify its workings. It scrabbles at the back of my mind. It is an annoyance, barely there but never absent, scratch and scratch and gnaw and claw. It wants in, and it will work at us until, like wind eroding rock, it has its way. It is in no hurry. It is now as fundamental to the planet as its nickel-iron core. It has forever. If we stay here, given enough time, we will all succumb. This is not defeatism. It is realism. A Blood Angel can and must recognize inevitable doom when it is encountered. The doom we face, coded into our very genes, is just as patient, just as certain of its ultimate victory.

The difference is that we can leave Supplicium Secundus and its disease behind. I am loathe to do so without discerning a cause, however.

Then a voice sounds in my ear bead. 'Chief Librarian?' It is Castigon, captain of 4th Company. He is aboard the strike cruiser *Crimson Exhortation*, which awaits us at high anchor.

'Yes, captain.'

'Do you concur with the other reports? There are no survivors?'

I glance at the dead colonel. 'That is now the case, yes.'

'Is it possible for you to return to the ship?' Castigon does not give me orders. He would never be so foolish. But his request is not unreasonable.

I hesitate, thinking still that perhaps some revelation might await us in the abattoir of the hive before us. 'Is this a matter of urgency?' I ask.

There is a pause. Then: 'Possibly.' I sense no deliberate vagueness on Castigon's part. He sounds genuinely puzzled. From his tone, I would say that he has chosen his answer carefully. After a moment, he speaks again. 'We have found the Mordian fleet.'

Found. The fleet should not have needed finding. It should have been in constant communication with us. But there was none when we arrived in the system, and no immediate sign of other ships in orbit around Secundus. 'There is an ominous ring to your words, captain,' I say.

'It is in the nature of this day, Chief Librarian.'

The Supplicium System is perched on the edge of extinction. This is nothing new. It is its very nature. There was once, against all sense, a colony on Supplicium Primus. The small planet is perilously close to the sun, but its gold deposits are vast. Its rate of rotation is the same as its revolution, and one face burns in an eternal day, while the other is forever trapped by night. Along the band of its twilight, a temperate zone permitted habitation until six centuries ago, when a solar storm of terrible magnitude stripped Primus of its atmosphere.

Secundus and Tertius, larger, more distant, and with stronger magnetic fields, weathered the storm, preserving their atmospheres and their civilizations. But here, too, humanity's grip is precarious. The orbits of the two planets are very close, but fall on either edge of the range of temperate distances from their star. Secundus is arid, Tertius frigid. But the Imperium is filled with worlds far more hostile, and they are held for the eternal glory of the Emperor. The Supplicium system has called for help. It must be heeded.

It was. Help came.

And failed.

Aboard the *Crimson Exhortation*, I stand with Castigon in the strategium. There are many tacticarium screens offering information, but our attention is focused on what we can see through the great expanse of armourglass at the front of the bridge. The hololiths and readouts render the meaning of the view clear, but there is a terrible majesty to the unfiltered, uncatalogued, raw vision before us.

The Mordians were but one system over when Supplicium Secundus cried out for help, and so they came. Now their fleet is dead. Its ships move, tumbling past each other along mindless trajectories. Some have collided. Even as we watch, a Sword-class frigate, turning end over end with slow grace, slams into the flank of Lunar-class cruiser *Manichaean*. The smaller ship breaks in two. Its halves float away, shedding debris. The *Manichaean* has taken a solid blow amidships, but continues its sluggish momentum, its course barely altered.

There is no flare of engines anywhere in the fleet. There are no energy signatures of any kind coming from the ships. This is why the fleet was invisible to us at first. It has become, in effect, a tiny belt of iron asteroids. I look at the tacticarium screens. There is evidence of inter-ship combat. Some of the hulls show signs of torpedo hits and lance burns. Not all, though. In truth, very few. What killed the fleet took place inside the ships.

Castigon despatched squads aboard the *Crimson Exhortation*'s Thunderhawks and Stormravens with the mission to board ships, where practical. The warriors engaged in this task know what we found on the surface of Supplicium Secundus, and they know about the ongoing risk of the plague. They will steel themselves against the temptations of anger. They will hold themselves in check. As the reports come in to the strategium, however, the caution begins to seem excessive. Though the background whisper of rage is ever present, basic discipline is enough to hold it at bay because there are no triggers. The fleet is empty. No troopers have been found.

The Mordian army, to a man, descended to Secundus to slaughter itself. All of the bodies on the ships belong to the naval crews, the slaves, and even the servitors. The doom is so powerful, even the mindless succumbed to killing frenzy. As below, so above. Each vessel boarded unveils another tale of mutual carnage. There is nothing left in planetary orbit but dead flesh and dead metal.

'I have never seen the like,' Castigon confesses.

'Neither have I.' The deaths of worlds and entire fleets, yes, I have seen such things. I have been instrumental in bringing about the annihilation of heretical solar systems. But this massacre is different in kind. The only weapons involved appear to have been those borne by the servants of the Imperium, who turned their arms on each other. We have not seen the smallest hint of an opposing force, which makes the enemy all the more dangerous. There *must* be an enemy. What we have seen cannot be due to chance. A warp-thing very like a disease has been spread across Supplicium Secundus and the intervention fleet. I cannot bring myself to believe that it arrived spontaneously. It was brought here. It was unleashed.

'I am recalling the reconnaissance squads,' Castigon says. I nod. He is right to do so. There is nothing more to learn here. I am now given to doubt whether there would, after all, be anything on the planet worth finding.

The question is rendered moot as the last of the gunships is docking with the *Crimson Exhortation*. There is a sudden explosion of vox traffic coming from Supplicium Tertius. The transmissions are bedlam, but the clamour of voices is clear because of the uniformity of the message. Tertius is screaming for help. The *Exhortation* receives pict feeds whose images shake, swerve and break up altogether. They are documents whose very assembly is the expression of desperation. They bear witness to riot, terror, madness. The streets of the cities are turning into massive brawls, the inhabitants swarming over each other like warring ants. Chaos (let me call it by its name) is spreading over the planet like a slick of promethium. The rapidity of the infection is remarkable. When we arrived in-system, we were in contact with the spaceport on Tertius, and there was no hint that anything was awry. Now, a day later, as we race to leave the orbit of Secundus and ride hard for Tertius, I know that we could well be too late. So does every warrior aboard this vessel. We know this, but we shall not allow it to be so. If will alone could move our ship, we would already be at anchor over the planet.

Castigon tries to hail one control node after another. Spaceports, planetary defence force bases, the lord-governor, working his way down to whatever nobles or commanding officers are mentioned in our records of Tertuis. He is forced to give up. Order is rapidly collapsing on Tertius. It occurs to me that the only minds we might save from this disaster will be our own.

The transmissions become more troubling during our journey to Tertius. Between the close orbits of the two planets and their approaching conjunction, our voyage is a short one. It is also far too long. The clamour rises to a shriek, and then the voices plummet into a far louder silence. The pict feeds vanish too. Before they do, they grace us with a mosaic of paroxysm.

As the *Crimson Exhortation* streaks towards a world now covered by an ominous calm, Castigon gathers his officers in the strategium. Stolas and the others create extra space for me around the tacticarium table. I exist, for them as for myself, in a sphere of shadow. I think of it as symbolic, but it appears to have a real force. The living, either pushed or recoiling, are distanced from the unknowable thing in their midst. I am the resurrected and the recently born. The body that was Calistarius walks. The mind that animates it is Mephiston. Calistarius was no more than than a prologue to me.

Stolas asks, 'If all communication has ceased, are we not already too late?'

Castigon does not hesitate. 'Collapse will precede extinction,' he pronounces. 'It will take some weeks for even the most determined population to kill itself. Crisis has befallen the people of Tertius under our watch, and we shall not fail them.'

He speaks for us all. We come to Tertius not as Angels of Death, but as Salvation.

'We must destroy the obscenity,' Sergeant Gamigin says, his voice soft yet edged with righteous anger. It is the anger that will do battle with rage. He has felt the touch of the enemy, and will retaliate with a passion fuelled by justice. He, too, speaks for us all. Whatever foe is attacking Supplicium, be it xenos or daemon, we will find it, and we will exterminate it so utterly, not even its memory shall remain.

And then, in the next second, it finds us first. The collision alert sounds. Helmsman Ipos bellows orders. The ship moves ponderously to evade. We all face forwards. We witness our near destruction.

The *Crimson Exhortation* has come upon a dark ship. It is even more massive than the strike cruiser. Utterly without light, it is a deeper night against the void. It passes over us, and for minutes we are swallowed by a presence that is both shadow and mass. When this happens, when we can no longer see the stars, there is no sense of movement, no sense of the passing of this great vessel. Instead, there is only the great weight of total absence, and it is easy to believe that we have entered an eternal night. The bottom of the stranger's hull brushes the top of our spires, shearing them off. But then the ships part, ours shuddering as Ipos fights to make her angle down just a little bit faster, the other coasting on with dead serenity.

Damage is minimal. The *Exhortation* comes around, and the scanning begins. The other ship appears to be drifting. It is without power, and the augurs find no trace any sort of radiation. 'From the Mordian fleet?' asks Stolas. 'Perhaps the crew succumbed to the rage plague as the ship tried to leave,' he continues.

'No,' I say. I am unsatisfied. The coincidence of our near-collision nags at me. It is simply too improbable. In the vastness of the void, for two specks of dust to encounter one another, something more than chance must be at work, and this ship cannot be just another tomb of Guardsmen.

The configuration of the ship, beyond its great size, is difficult to make out at first. This is not just because of its darkness. Though it is solid enough, there is a profound vagueness to the form.

'That is a battle-barge,' Ipos calls out, startled.

He is correct. He is also wrong. The shape is, it is true, based on that of an Adeptus Astartes battle-barge. But there are insufficient details, and much that is there seems wrong. The silhouette is distorted. The hull is too long, the bridge superstructure too squat, the prow so pointed and long it is a caricature. No matter how much illumination we pour onto the ship, it defies the eye. It will not come into proper focus. 'No,' I say. 'It is not a battle-barge. It is the memory of one.' I mean what I say, even if I am not sure how such a thing has come to be. I am not speaking metaphorically. What drifts through space before us is a ship as it would be imperfectly remembered.

Then a detail that is not blurred comes into view. The ship's name: *Eclipse of Hope*.

'It's a ghost,' Dantalion says.

I frown at the terminology, not least because it seems to be accurate. The *Eclipse of Hope* is known to me. It is known to all of us. The battle-barge disappeared during the fifth Black Crusade. Five thousand years ago. Worse: the ship was a Blood Angels vessel. I dislike its existence more and more. Its presence here cannot be a coincidence. The power necessary to orchestrate this 'chance' encounter is immense.

'Is it really the–' Gamigin begins.

'No.' I cut him off. 'That ship is destroyed.' It must be, after five millennia in the empyrean. The thing that bears the name now is a changeling, though at a certain, dark level, it is intimately linked with the original. Somehow, the collective memories of the *Eclipse of Hope*, or the memory of a single being of terrible power, achieved such potency that an embodiment has occurred. Its manifest solidity is extraordinary. I have never known a warp ghost to have so much material presence. It must represent a concentration of psychic power such as has never been imagined. It...

I turn to Ipos. 'Can we plot the trajectory of this ship's passage through the system?'

'A moment, Chief Librarian.' Ipos appears to slump in his throne. I can see his consciousness slip down the mechadendrites that link his skull to the machine-spirit and cogitators of the *Crimson Exhortation*. On the bridge, navigation servitors begin chanting numbers in answer to unheard questions. After a few moments, Ipos returns to an awareness of the rest of us. The results of his efforts appear on a tacticarium screen. If the *Eclipse of Hope* has maintained a steady course, she passed near Supplicium Secundus, and through the centre of the Mordian fleet.

'Captain,' I say to Castigon, 'that is the carrier of the rage plague. Destroy it, and perhaps there will be something to save of Supplicium Tertius.'

The phantom remains dark as the *Crimson Exhortation* manoeuvres into position for the execution. The immense shadow does not change direction. Its engines do not flare. No shields or guns flash to life. It coasts, slow leviathan, serene juggernaut, messenger of mindless destruction.

No. No, I am wrong. I am guilty of underestimating the enemy. There is nothing mindless here. The spectre of a Blood Angels battle-barge unleashes a plague whose symptoms might as well be those of the Red Thirst. There is a hand behind this. There is mockery. There is provocation that warrants a retaliation most final. But how to find the hand behind this horror?

That question must wait. The *Eclipse of Hope* is the paramount concern. It has almost destroyed an entire system through its mere presence. If its journey is not stopped, untold Imperial worlds could fall to its madness. The *Eclipse of Hope* must die a second time. Today. Now.

How? I wonder.

The *Crimson Exhortation* is in position. On Castigon's orders, Ipos has taken us some distance from the phantom. The strike cruiser is great dagger aimed at the flank of the battle-barge. Beyond the

Eclipse of Hope, there is nothing but the void. Supplicium Tertius is still some distance away, but Ipos has placed it safely at our starboard. It is important that there be nothing for a great distance in front of us except our target. Castigon has ordered the use of the nova cannon.

'Conventional weapons will do no harm to a warp ghost,' I tell him.

'It is solid enough to have hit us,' Castigon replies. 'It broke iron and stone. It can be broken in turn.' He turns to Ipos. 'Helmsmaster, are we ready?'

'In a moment, captain.' We have never had the luxury of so passive an opponent on which to use the gun. Ipos takes the opportunity to triple-check all of his calculations and run through his instrument adjustments one more time. When he finds no errors, he signals Castigon.

I can feel the build-up in the ship's machine-spirit. It is excited to be using this weapon again. The nova cannon is a creation of absolute power, because it destroys with absolute efficiency. We are merely its acolytes, awakening it from its slumber whenever we have need of its divine wind.

'Fire,' Castigon orders.

The deck trembles. The entire ship vibrates from the forces unleashed in the firing of the nova cannon. The weapon is almost as long as the hull. The recoil jolts the frame of the *Exhortation*. The cannon is not a weapon of precision, but the shot is as close to point-blank range as is possible with the cannon without destroying ourselves in the process. The projectile flashes across the void, injuring space itself. It hits the *Eclipse of Hope* in the centre of its mass. There is a flare of blinding purity. It is at this moment that the cannon warrants its name. The explosion reaches out for the *Crimson Exhortation*, but falls short. Even so, there is another tremor as the shockwave hits us. We have hurled one of the most powerful weapons in human history at the *Eclipse of Hope*.

It doesn't notice.

The dark serenity is undisturbed. The ghost ship continues its steady drift towards Supplicium Tertius, bringing its plague of final wrath. The bridge and the strategium of the *Crimson Exhortation* are silent as we stare into a future haunted by the *Eclipse of Hope*. Within hours, one ship will have extinguished all human life in a system. It will have done so with no weapons, no struggle, no strategy. Its mere passage will have been enough. And if the phantom should reach other, more crowded systems? Or cross paths with a fleet in transit? Vectors of contagion, visions of hell: my mind is filled by the plague spreading its corroding ifluence over the entire galaxy.

The *Eclipse of Hope* must be stopped. If nothing in the *Crimson Exhortation*'s arsenal will avail, then one alternative remains.

'I will lead a boarding party,' I announce. 'The vessel must be killed from within.'

'Can you walk in a ghost?' Castigon asks.

'It is solid enough to have hit us,' I echo.

'If that is the source of the plague,' Dantalion muses, 'then entering it will be fraught with great moral peril.'

'Most especially for a Blood Angel,' I add. The Flaw will be sorely felt in this situation.

The Chaplain nods. 'The threat does seem rather precisely targeted.'

'That is no coincidence,' I say. 'It is also a risk we must run.'

Castigon nods, but his expression is doubtful. 'How do you plan to kill a ghost?' he asks.

'I will discover that in due course.' I turn to go. 'But shouldn't one revenant be able to destroy another?'

We do not use boarding torpedoes. We cannot be sure that they would be capable of drilling through the spectre's hull. Instead, the *Bloodthorn* transports my squad to the *Eclipse of Hope*. This is to be an exorcism. On board with me, then, are Epistolary Stolas, Sanguinary Priest Albinus, Chaplain Dantalion and Techmarine Phenex. Sergeant Gamigin is present, too. He was insistent upon coming, even though it seems that this mission requires a different set of skills. He has faith enough, however, and having been touched by the dread ship's influence, he is hungry for redemption.

I sit in the cockpit with pilot Orias as the *Bloodthorn* approaches the landing bay door of the battle-barge. The door does not open. This is not a surprise. What is striking is the way in which the details of the hull resolve themselves. They become clearer not because we draw nearer, but because we are looking at them. The sealed bay door has a material presence it did not a few minutes ago. I am aware, in my peripheral vision, that the surrounding hull is still blurry.

Orias has noticed the same phenomenon. 'How is this possible?' he wonders.

'It is feeding on our memories,' I answer. 'We know what a battle-barge looks like. It is supplementing itself with our own knowledge.'

I can see the anger in the set of Orias's shoulder plates. His resentment is righteous. We are witnessing a monstrous blasphemy. Still, we have also learned something. We know more about how our foe works.

Then the unexpected does occur. The door rises. The bay is a rectangular cave, dark within the dark. It awaits us. It welcomes us. We must have something it needs, then. This, too, is valuable to know. If it has needs, it has a weakness.

'This forsaken vessel mocks us,' Orias snarls.

'It is arrogant,' I reply. 'And arrogance is always a mistake.' Show me your weaknesses, I think. Show me your desire, that I might tear you in half. 'Take us in,' I tell Orias. 'Drop us and depart.'

The next few minutes have a terrible familiarity. The gunship enters the landing bay of a battle-barge. I pull back the bulkhead door. We wait a few moments, guns at the ready. Nothing materialises. We are simply staring at an empty bay.

'I do not appreciate being made a fool of,' Gamigin grumbles. His bolter tracks back and forth, aiming at air.

'Guard your temper, brother-sergeant,' I tell him. 'See with how little effort the vessel encourages us to anger.'

We disembark. The banality of our surroundings makes our every move cautious, deliberate. We trust nothing. I am first on the deck, and the fact that it does not reveal itself to be an illusion without substance is almost a surprise. The rest of the squad follows me. We step away from the gunship and form a circle, all approaches covered. The emptiness is full of silent laughter. We ignore it. Our enhanced vision pierces the darkness, and all we see is ordinary deck and walls. The known and the familiar are the danger here. Each element that is not alien is a temptation to a lowered guard. Then, as Orias pulls the *Bloodthorn* out of the bay and away from the *Eclipse*, the darkness recedes. Light blooms. It is the colour of decay.

The light does not come from biolumes, though I see their strips along the ceiling. It is not a true light. It is a phantom of light, as false as anything else about this ship, a memory plucked from our minds and layered into this construct of daemonic paradox. As we move across the bay towards its interior door, the space acquires greater solidity. The ring of our bootsteps on the decking grows louder, less muffled, more confident. Did I see rivets in the metal at first? I do now.

By the time we reach the door, the constructed memory of a battle-barge loading bay is complete. I am no longer noticing new, convincing details. So now I can see the weaknesses of the creation. The ghost has its limitations. The bay seems real, but it is also empty. There are no banks of equipment, no gunships in dock. There is only the space and its emptiness. The *Eclipse of Hope* could not make use of our full store of memories. 'I shall have your measure,' I whisper to the ship. Does it, I wonder, know what it has allowed inside. Does it feel me? Is it capable of regret? Can it know fear?

I shall ensure that it does.

As we step into the main passageway off the bay, the attack begins. It is not a physical one. There are no enemies visible. There is nothing but the empty corridor and the low, sickly grey light. But the ship embraces us now, and does more than feed off our memories. It tries to feed us, too. It feeds us poison. It feeds us our damnation.

Walking down the passageway is walking into rage itself. We move against a gale-force psychic wind. It slows our progress as surely as any physical obstacle. It is like pushing against the palm of a giant hand, a hand that wraps massive, constrictor fingers around us. It squeezes. It would force self-control and sanity out. It would force uncontrollable anger in, and in, and in, until we burst, releasing the anger once more in the form of berserker violence.

I feel the anger stir in my chest, an uncoiling serpent. The bone-cold part of myself, that which I cannot in conscience call a soul, holds the serpent down. It also takes further measure of the ship. There are still limits to the precision of the attack. That is not the Black Rage that I am suppressing. It is too mundane an anger. It is potent. It is summoned by a force powerful enough to give substance to the memory of a battle-barge. But it is not yet fully aligned with the precise nature of our great Flaw. That will come, I have no doubt. But we have the discipline to defeat anger of this sort.

I glance at my brothers. Though there is tension and effort in their steps, their will is unbowed.

Stolas says, 'The light is becoming brighter.'

'It is,' I agree. Despite our resistance, the ship is growing stronger. Our mere presence is giving it life. The light, as corrupt as it was in the bay, has assumed a greater lividity. We can see more and more of the passageway. The ship cements its details with more and more confidence. The greater visibility should make our advance easier. It does not.

The phantom's mimicry is uncanny. With every incremental increase of illumination comes a further revelation of perfect recall. This is the true ghost of the *Eclipse of Hope*. We are travelling one of the main arteries, and the phantom has a complex memory to reconstruct: stone-clad walls and floor, gothic arches, vaulted bulk-heads. They are all here. Even so, as accurate as the recreation is, it remains a ghost. There is something missing.

Phenex's machinic insight gives him the answer first. He raps a fist against the starboard wall. The sound of ceramite against marble is what I would expect. Yet it makes me frown.

Albinus has noticed something, too. 'That isn't right,' he says.

'There's a delay,' the Techmarine explains. 'Very slight. The sound is coming a fraction of a second later than it should.'

'The response is a conscious one,' I say. 'It is a form of illusion. That wall is not real. Your gauntlet is banging against the void, brother.'

I spot Gamigin staring at his feet, as if expecting the surface on which he walks to disintegrate without warning. If we are successful here, he may not be far wrong.

From behind his skull helm, Dantalion casts anathema on the ship. His voice vibrates with hatred.

'Save your breath,' I tell him. 'Wait until there is something to exorcise.'

'There already is,' he retorts. 'This entire ship.'

'Have you the strength to spread your will over such a large target?' I ask him. 'If so, you have my envy.'

Dantalion will not appreciate my tone. That is not my concern. What *is* my concern is that my team be as alert and focussed as possible. The ship inspires anger, and I do not think it cares in what direction that anger is expressed. Dantalion's hatred of the *Eclipse of Hope* is normal, praiseworthy, and proper. It is also feeding the vessel. Unless we find a target that we can overwhelm somehow, the Chaplain's broad, sweeping anger will do us more harm than good.

We are making our way toward the bridge. This is not the result of considered deliberation. We exchanged looks at the exit from the landing bay, and of one accord set off in this direction. There is nothing to say that we will find what we seek there, or anywhere else, for that matter, on this ship. But the bridge is the nerve centre of any vessel. We seek a mind. The bridge is the logical place to begin.

It troubles me that we are taking action based on nothing stronger than a supposition. I cannot detect any direction to the warp energies that make up the *Eclipse of Hope*. There does not seem to be any flow at all. I understand the nature of the immaterium. I know it better, perhaps, than anyone in the Imperium, save our God-Emperor. Yet the substance of the *Eclipse* defies me. It appears inert. This cannot be true, not with the intensifying light, the consolidation of the illusion, and the gnawing and scratching at our minds. There is something at work here. Perhaps I can find no current, no flow, no core because these things do not exist yet. The effects of the ship are those of a field, one that may extend the entire length and breadth of the vessel. 'It isn't strong enough yet,' I mutter.

'Chief Librarian?' Albinus asks.

'The ship is still feeding,' I say. 'We cannot be sure of its full nature until it has gorged. Perhaps then it will act.'

'Then we can kill it?' Gamigin asks.

I nod. 'Then we can kill it.'

Down the length of the battle-barge we march. We ignore the side passageways that open on either side. We stick to the direct route, always pushing against the ethereal but implacable rage. Our tempers are fraying, the effort needed to suppress flare-ups of anger becoming stronger by the hour. And there is more. There is something worse. The more I strain, the more I find traces of an intelligence. It does not drive the ship. It is the ship itself. It is as if this were truly a revenant. The knowledge is frustration, hovering at the edge of tactical usefulness, a buzzing hornet in my consciousness. If the ship is sentient, then I must cut out its mind. To do that, I must locate it. But the *Eclipse of Hope* is still too quiescent. It is a beast revelling in its dreams of rage, not yet prepared to wake. It torments us. It does not fight us.

The walk from the bay to the bridge is long. There is no incident, no attack. The march would be tedium itself, were it not for the slow, malevolent transformation of the ship around us. We are presented with the spectacle of the familiar as evil, the recognizable as threat. The more the ship resembles what it remembers itself to be, the more we are seeing a manifestation of its power. The light is brighter yet. The growing clarity remains in the nature of a bleak epiphany. There is nothing to see but death, embodied in the form of the ship itself. Everything that presents itself to our eyes does so with a cackling malignity, pleased that it imitates reality so well. It does so only as a show of force. Everything that appears can be taken away. I am sure of this. The ship is a dragon, inhaling. The immolating exhalation is imminent.

We are one deck down, and only a few minutes away from the bridge when the dragon roars. The light dims back to the grey of a shroud. The ship now has a better use for the energy it is leaching from us. It is awake. The sudden explosion of consciousness is painful. The ghost turns its full awareness upon us.

Can a ship smile? Perhaps. I think it does, in this very second.

Can it rage?

Oh, yes.

The *Eclipse of Hope* hates, it angers, it blasts its laughing wrath upon those beings who would dare invade it, the intruders it deems little more than insects and that it lured here in its dreaming. It has fed upon us, and now would complete its feast with our final dissolution.

Dissolution comes from the walls. For a moment, they lose all definition. Chaos itself billows and writhes. And the ship can also sing. The corridor resounds with a fanfare of screaming human voices and a drum-beat that is the march of wrath itself. Then the walls give birth. Their offspring have hides the colour of blood. Their limbs are long, grasping, with muscles of steel stretched over deformed bones. Their skulls are mocking, predatory fusions of the horned goat and the armoured helm. Their eyes are blank with glowing, pus-yellow hatred. They are bloodletters, daemons of Khorne, and the sight of their arrival has condemned mortal humans beyond counting to a madness of terror.

As for my brothers and myself, at last we have a foe to fight. We form a circle of might and faith. 'Now, brothers,' Dantalion says.

'Now this vessel of the damned shows its true nature. Strike hard, steadfast in the light of Sanguinius and the Emperor!'

'These creatures, sergeant,' I tell Gamigin, 'you are at full liberty to kill.'

It takes him a moment to respond, unused to any expression of humour on my part. 'My thanks, Chief Librarian,' he says, and sets to work with a passion.

The bloodletters wield ancient swords, their blades marked by eldritch designs and obscene runes. They come at us from all sides, their snarls drowned out by the choir of the tortured and the infernal beat, beat, beat of a drum made of wrath. The music is insidious. It pounds its way deep into my mind. I know what it is trying to do. It would have us march to the same beat, meet rage with rage, crimson armour clashing with crimson flesh until, with the loss of our selves to the Flaw, there is no distinguishing Blood Angel from daemon. The bloodletters open their fanged maws wide, tongues whipping the air like snakes, tasting the rage and finding it good. They swing their swords. We meet them with our own. Power sword, glaive and chainsword counter and riposte. Blade against blade, wrath against rage, we answer the attack. Monsters fall, cut in half. The deck absorbs them, welcoming them back to non-being. And for every foul thing we despatch, two more burst from the walls.

War is feeding on war.

'This will end only one way,' Dantalion says at my side. His brings his crozius down on a daemon's skull, smashing it to mist. 'It will not be our victory.'

He is not being defeatist. He is speaking a simple truth. The corridor before us is growing crowded with the fiends. They scramble over each other in their eagerness to tear us apart. They will come at us forever, created by our very acts of destroying their brothers. Bolter fire blasts them apart. Blades cut them down. And where two stood, now there are ten.

'We cannot remain here,' says Albinus.

Even as he speaks, the ceiling unleashes a cascade of bloodletters.

They fall upon us with claws and teeth, seeking to overwhelm through the weight of numbers. We throw them to the ground, trample them beneath our boots. I feel the snapping of unholy bones and know I have inflicted pain on a blasphemy before the daemon is reabsorbed.

Dantalion staggers, gurgles rasping from his vocaliser. He must have looked up at the wrong moment. A bloodletter has thrust its sword underneath his helm. With a snarl of effort, the daemon rams the blade home, piercing Dantalion's brain. Our Chaplain stiffens, then falls. Gamigin roars his outrage and obliterates the bloodletter with a single blow of his chainsword.

The rage grows. We fight for vengeance now, too. The harder we struggle, the closer we come to dooming ourselves. The onslaught of bloodletters is a storm surge, and the faster we kill them, the faster they multiply.

'To the bridge,' Gamigin calls out. 'That is our destination, and we can make a stand there for as long as it takes to exorcise this abomination.'

'No,' I answer. 'Not the bridge.' With the phantom now fully awake, I have looked at the tides of its thought. We are on the wrong path. The core of this memory-construct is not the bridge. It is, rather, a place of much knowledge. 'The librarium.'

The ship hears me. Until this moment, its strategy was one of venomous attrition, grinding us down in stages, feeding on the ferocity of our skill at destruction. Then I announce our goal, and things change. The *Eclipse of Hope* now desires our immediate deaths. To the torrent of daemons, the walls and ceiling add their own attack. The corridor distorts beyond the most delirious memory of a battle-barge interior. Hands reach for us. They are colossal, large enough to clutch and crush any of us. They are veined, the hands of a statue, and though they are stone, they seem to flow. They are not a memory; they are a creation, the spectre of art, their reality created from microsecond to microsecond. They are scaled talons, both reptile and raptor. They are clawed and hooked, with barbs on every knuckle. They are the concept of *ripping* given embodiment, but they are massive too, and what they do not tear into ribbons, they will smash.

There is a hand descending directly above me. It becomes a fist. The ship would see me pulped. It is showing me that it knows fear. It believes I can do it harm.

I shall prove it right.

The consciousness that holds the ship in this simulacrum of reality is not the only force capable of creation. The warp is mine, too. I walk in a ghost, but I am the Lord of Death. My will shapes un-matter, gives direction to the energy of madness. The air shimmers as a pane of gold flashes into being over our heads. The ceiling's hands smash into it and break apart. I pour my essence into the shield. I turn it into a dome. The daemons caught along the line of its existence are bisected. Then the dome surrounds us. Its perimeter extends a bare metre beyond our defensive circle.

I am channelling so much of my will into maintaining the shield against the hammering assaults of the bloodletters and the fists of the walls that I am barely present in my body itself. Yet I must walk. We cannot stay here. I must reach the librarium.

'Chief Librarian,' Albinus says, 'can you hear me?' Albinus knows me best of those present. More properly, he knew Calistarius well, and seems to have taken on a quest to understand the being that rose from his friend's grave. Albinus's goal is laudable, if hopeless. Even so, there are times when he does seem to have some real insight into the realities of my being. When I nod, he says, 'We must move. Can you walk and maintain the shield?'

The blows of the enemy are torrential. Given time and strength, they will smash any barrier. The phantom is very strong. I must maintain my focus on the reality of the shield. I speak through gritted teeth: 'Barely.'

He nods. 'Then let us take our turn, brother,' the sanguinary priest says.

Brother. I am rarely addressed by that word. With good reason.

Calistarius was a brother among others, to the degree any psyker can truly be accepted in the ranks of the Adeptus Astartes. But Calistarius is dead, and when Albinus says *brother*, he is addressing a shade, one with far less substance than the hellship in which we fight. Calistarius will not return. Mephiston walks in his stead. I am a Blood Angel. I would destroy any who would question my loyalty. But *brother*? That bespeaks a fellowship that is barred to me.

Let that pass. Albinus is correct in the matter of strategy. 'Agreed,' I manage.

'Show us our route,' he tells me.

I turn back the way we came. The effort is huge. I am holding back not just dozens of simultaneous physical attacks, but also the entire psychic pressure of the ship. Turning my body is like altering the rotation of a planet.

Albinus moves in front of me. The rest of the squad takes up a wedge formation. I relax the shield. It becomes porous, but doesn't evaporate completely. I can reinforce it at a moment's notice. The squad charges forwards to meet the rush of the bloodletters. Stolas creates his own shield. The epistolary is a powerful psyker. I have seen him devastate lines of the enemy with lightning storms worthy of myth. But he is not what I am, and though we move in an environment woven entirely of the warp, our powers are not increased. The ship is a parasite that has swallowed its host. So the shield Stolas raises slows the bloodletter horde, but cannot stop it. Our blunt spearhead collides with the foaming tide. We shove our way through the daemonic host for a dozen metres before their numbers threaten to swamp us once again. I snap the shield back to full strength, giving us space and a chance to regroup. When Albinus gives me the signal, I pull back into my physical self, and we move forwards.

This is how we advance. It is our only way, a painfully slow stutter of stops and starts. We travel thousands of metres in this manner. The tally of our slaughter lengthens with every step, and every butchered daemon, every act of wrath, is another drop of psychic plasma for the *Eclipse of Hope's* unholy engines. Our journey through the ship will be the path of our damnation if I am wrong about what I will find in the librarium.

We wend our way deep into the heart of the ship. The repository of archives, history and knowledge is not in a spire, as it is on the *Crimson Exhortation*. Rather, it waits on the lowest deck, a few hundred metres fore of the enginarium. To guide us there, I follow rip tides of the warp. The phantom is awake and blazing with power. It cannot hide the patterns of its own identity now, any more than a human could will away the whorls of fingerprints. By acting against us, the *Eclipse of Hope* exposes itself to my scrutiny and my judgement.

We reach the librarium. A massive iron door bars our passage. Its relief work is an allegory of dangerous knowledge. It announces what lies in the chambers beyond, and it warns the uninitiated away. Tormented human figures fall in worship or agony before immense tomes. Daemons are not represented in the art – no Imperial ship would sully itself with such an image. Instead, the danger is depicted as twisting vines and abstract lines that tangle and pierce the figures. The risks that lurked in the archives of the original librarium must be merely the shadows of what awaits now. On the other side of the door lies the consciousness of the ship. I can feel the pulse of its fevered thoughts beating through the walls. The rhythm matches that of the drums, still pounding and echoing through the defiled corridors. Are the thoughts the source of the daemonic march, or does the music come from a darker place and a greater master, shaping the mind of the ghost? I have no answer. All I need is the destruction of both.

Is that all I desire? No. It is not. But desire is a treacherous master.

'Albinus,' I manage, the shield still at full strength.

'Chief Librarian?'

'I will need Stolas.' The strength in that chamber will be massive. We must hit it with all the power we possess.

'We will stand and hold,' Phenex says.

'For Sanguinius and the Emperor,' Gamigin adds.

The wedge formation faces down the corridor. My fellow Blood Angels have their backs to the door. Once Stolas and I cross that threshold, their only defences will be physical. It will be enough. They will hold back the ocean of Chaos with bolter and blade for as long as Stolas and I require to triumph or fall.

I lower the shield. I grasp the ornate bronze handle of the door. When I pull, I encounter, to my surprise, no resistance. Is this surrender? I wonder. Or perhaps the ship is marshalling its resources for the true fight about to begin. No matter. Stolas and I enter the librarium. The door swings shut behind us. The boom of iron against stone has a different quality to it than the sounds in the corridor. It takes me a moment to identify what has changed. The answer comes as I take in the sights of the librarium.

This chamber, and this chamber alone, is real.

Stolas and I move through a vast cavern of damned scholarship. We are funnelled along a path between towering stacks of scrolls, parchments and tomes. The path takes us towards an open space at the heart of the chamber. This is not a recreated memory. This is not a product of the warp, or at least, not in the same sense as the rest of the ship. The chamber itself is of familiar construction. It could be a librarium on a true battle-barge. There is a fresco on the domed ceiling: a vision of Sanguinius, wings outstretched, sword in hand, descending in fury, bringing light and blood to the enemies of the Emperor. But the fresco has been defaced. Huge, parallel gouges, the claws of some giant fiend, cut diagonally through our primarch. Runes have been splashed in blood over the painting. I look away from the obscenity. I have no desire or need to read it.

(Ah, says a whisper in the furthest recesses of my mind. *Can* you read it, then?)

I sense that the stacks have changed since the ship vanished five millennia ago. They are huge. The volume of texts is astounding. The stone shelves are bursting with manuscripts. The floor is littered with lost sheets of vellum. Some curator has been at work here, accumulating works with obsession but little care. And yet there has been care enough to preserve the librarium itself after the rest of the ship has died. This space is the grain of sand around which a daemonic pearl has formed. The mind of the ship needs this core of reality in order to give a semblance of the same to the phantom. It must be the key that has allowed the *Eclipse of Hope* to escape the empyrean and spread its plague through the materium.

The centre of the librarium has become a dark shrine. There are four lecterns here. They are huge, over two metres high, created for beings larger than Space Marines. They are wrought of a fusion of iron and bone, the two elements distinguishable yet inseparable, a single substance that shrieks the obscenity of its creation. The designs are the product of nightmare: intertwining figures, human and xenos, all agonized, their mouths distorted that they might howl blasphemous curses at a contemptuous universe. Sinuous coils, both serpent and whip, scaled and barbed, weave between and around the bodies, carrying venom and pain. I think I see movement in the corner of my eye. I look at the forged souls more closely. I was not mistaken. They are moving, so slowly a year would pass while a back is being broken. But they are moving. And they are suffering.

The lecterns are coated in thick layers of dry, blackened blood. Here, too, there is movement. Slow, glistening drops work their way down the frameworks, adding to the texture of torture with the same gradual inexorability as the growth of stalactites. I raise my eyes. The blood is coming from the books.

The books. These things cannot be truly be called by that name, no more than the Archenemy can be called *human*. They are gargantuan, over a metre on each side. They rest on iron and bone, but they are bound in iron and flesh. Metal thorns pierce their spines. The sluggish gore crawls, drip by endless drip, down the pain of the lecterns. The flesh of the covers has not been tanned into leather. Rather, it is black and green and violet. It is in a state of ongoing, but never completed, decomposition. It is also not dead. There is a just-visible thrumming, as of flesh taut against the stress of torture.

Through the walls, I can make out the muffled beat of combat. There is not much time, but I must be cautious. I must be sure of my actions, or I will doom us all. I must be so very, very careful, because of the other thing in the chamber. There is a dais in the very centre of the librarium, surrounded by the four lecterns. I have avoided looking closely at it, thinking perhaps my first glance deceived me, and if I turned away, the illusion would vanish. It has not.

'Lord Mephiston...' Stolas begins. He is transfixed.

'I know,' I tell him. I turn and face what has been waiting.

Spread out on the dais is an ancient star chart. It is on fading, brittle parchment. The map is the only part of this monstrous exhibit that has always belonged to the librarium. My finger traces the name of the system depicted: Pallevon. Then I look up.

A statue sits on the dais. There is nothing grotesque about its material. It is simply bronze. It does not move. It does not cry out.

It is me.

The figure stands with weapons sheathed and holstered. Its expression is calm. It should not exist. Yet it is as real as all of the other objects in this room. It is not a ghost, but it haunts me like one.

I have been manoeuvred like a piece in a game of regicide. The ship's desire to kill me when I declared the librarium as my goal was a feint. It simply reinforced my determination to reach this point. For a moment, I am blinded by a red haze of rage. Then the cold darkness within me recognizes the trap, and dampens the fire. I pull back.

'What does this mean?' Stolas asks.

'It means we were expected. It does not mean that our mission changes.'

'And this?' he points at the star chart.

'Another lure.' We must ignore it.

Stolas peers more closely at the statue. 'Look at the eyes,' he says.

I had thought the gaze was neutral. I was wrong. The eyes look just to my left. I turn in that direction to stare at one of the lecterns. I approach it. The book, immense, pulsing with the pain of its knowledge, waits for me to turn back its daemon-wrought cover.

Stolas turns around, taking in not just the four massive tomes, but the rest of the collection as well. 'So much knowledge...' he says. His vocaliser turns the whisper into a wind of static.

'Dire knowledge, all of it,' I say.

'Think of what we could do to the enemies of the Imperium with such insight,' Stolas argues.

He does not need to tempt me thus. I feel that draw on my own. I reach out to the book before me. I open it.

There is a moment. A fraction of a second so minute as to defy measure. I experience it, notwithstanding: a fragmentary impression of the being who last touched this book. A towering horned shadow. Eyes that burn crimson with malevolence and knowledge and... something else... a memory, a memory so specific that it is a weapon aimed at the soul of the Blood Angels. A memory that leads to a future that crushes our Chapter in a clawed fist.

The shard of vision vanishes. In its place is a yawning promise. The book is abyssal. It will tell me all. Whatever questions I have, they will be answered. Omniscience is within my reach. There will be no more mysteries. All of the past, all of the present, all of the future – everything will be made known to me.

My identity made clear. What is it that lies coiled in my depths? I shall know that, too.

The means to total illumination, and total power, are not complicated. I simply need to start reading.

The pull is beyond any concept of temptation. I am in the gravitational jaws of a black hole. The event horizon is long past. There is no escape, and why should I wish it?

Yet I do. I refuse. My will pushes back. It is the will that pulled me from the Black Rage, that raised me from the my tomb of rubble. It is the will that shapes the energies of the empyrean to my ends. Power? I am the Lord of Death. What is that, if not power most dread?

Is this will entirely my own? Is it entirely *me*?

No answer. No matter. I see the room with clarity again, and step back from the book.

To my right, Stolas is clutching one of the other tomes. I call to him, but it is far too late. His face is wracked by dark ecstasy. He turns his eyes my way, eyes that have become a glistening black. His body is shaking. His speech is slurred. 'Oh,' he says. 'Oh, you must know...'

'No, brother,' I tell him. 'We must not.'

The shimmering in his eyes leaks down his cheeks. The tears become tendrils. The tendrils become worms. He is lost.

Did the accursed book promise me power? Let me show it what power means. I call the warp to me. I force it to do my bidding. I accumulate the energy within me until the straining potential threatens to tear me apart. And when I am ready, as time ticks from before the act to the act itself, I know that the *Eclipse of Hope* has its own terrible moment. It senses what is about to happen. It finally does know fear.

I strike. And there is nothing but fire.

I burned the librarium to ash. I was the centre of a purging sun. When I was done, the mind of the ship was but a memory itself. Mine. Stolas, too, was gone, incinerated. Though I know his soul had already been taken, I know also that my inferno destroyed his body and his gene-seed. His trace and his legacy are gone forever, and his name, then, must be added to the register of my guilt. I left the scoured chamber to find my brothers standing in an empty, dark corridor. The bloodletters vanished when I killed the mind.

The vessel is inert once more.

But it has not vanished. Even now, after we have returned to the *Crimson Exhortation*, and nothing alive and sentient walks the halls of the *Eclipse of Hope*, the ghost ship remains intact, an apparition that will not return to the night from whence it came. The crisis on Supplicium Tertius has abated. The survivors are no longer killing each other. So the ship no longer appears to be a carrier of plague.

But we cannot destroy it. The fact of its continued existence will haunt us with the possibility of further harm. It is a memory that refuses to be forgotten. So, too, are the books. Those are my personal ghosts. I fought the temptation. I destroyed the unholy. But what might I have learned? What if I could have absorbed those teachings and stayed whole, unlike Stolas? What if the absolute self-knowledge from which I turned was the door, through darkness, to salvation?

What have I thrown away?

I will think on these things. But not now. There is something more immediate to confront. The being that launched the *Eclipse of Hope* on its voyage has not finished with us yet. We are still being moved on the regicide board. The *Exhortation* has received a message. A brother, long though lost, has returned to us.

He awaits us in the Pallevon system.

As our great ship rushes us to a destiny five thousand years in the preparation, I attune my mind to the empyrean. I am not surprised to hear, grinding over the flows of the warp, the sound of eager laughter.

REDEEMER

Guy Haley

Introducing

ASTORATH

HIGH CHAPLAIN, BLOOD ANGELS

There were chords of pain that played for Astorath alone to hear. Music that troubled the dreams of insane composers haunted his waking hours. If it played anywhere, anywhere at all, then he would hear it. Most often he heard a lonely tune wrung from one miserable instrument, but at times these soloists would be joined by others to make quartets or sections, and in the worst of days an entire, melancholic orchestra would gather. Then the music would sing most urgently to him across time and space. Always it was discordant, tragic, full of pain and anger, notes played out of sequence as less-talented hands fumbled their way over a maestro's work. The music recalled something great nonetheless, and was all the more painful for imperfection.

These outpourings were for others to tame. The duty of his brother Chaplains was to get the strains to play in tune, to conduct the suffering towards a last crescendo. When the brothers in black and bone took the lead, the music would climax and cease, and in the ceasing Astorath the Grim would know that all had returned to rightness.

Sometimes the music did not stop. Sometimes it rose to unbearable heights, past all hope of redemption, down to the blackest pits of despair, where it continued, polluting all around it with pain.

It was Astorath's role, as Blood Angels High Chaplain, to end these painful discords. His solemn duty was fratricide. His axe tasted noble Space Marine blood as often as it did the vitae of the Imperium's enemies. 'The Ender of Songs', the aeldari called him, and apt though that was, he had a better-known title.

To the Chapters of the Blood, he was the Redeemer of the Lost, and he was loved and loathed in equal measure for his excellence at his duty.

Astorath slept his way across the light years. Wherever he went, his sarcophagus travelled with him, seated in the place of honour at the heart of the *Eminence Sanguis*.

Only a few of the most high Blood Angels had their own personal sarcophagus. Astorath was naturally among them. The exterior of his sarcophagus was decorated with stylised sculpture that depicted the warrior inside. Although distorted by being wrapped around the lid, it was unmistakably Astorath rendered in the abyssal black of polished carbon.

The sarcophagus was set at an angle of forty-five degrees at the centre of a ring of carvings depicting the High Chaplain's responsibilities. In Astorath's chamber all was chill. Frost coated the carvings. Red lumens bathed the room in a bloody glow, and black shadows hid from it. The colours echoed Astorath's inner world. While Astorath slept, his dreams were of black and they were of red, and nothing else, until somewhere a warrior's soul broke, and the music began again.

Each song was different. He heard this one as a screeching passage that rose and stopped, and began again, over and over, a piece badly practised whose end could not be attained. It penetrated the bloody red; it sent ripples over the oily black. The music called to him for it could call to no one else. The song was a plea for mercy only he could grant. It woke him.

Stirred from his slumber, Astorath opened his eyes in the blood-threaded amnion nourishing his body. The sarcophagus' machine-spirit detected the movement, and began the process of full awakening. Drains opened at the base of the sarcophagus to suck the amnion away. The mask covering Astorath's mouth came free, the amnion level dropped past his chin, and he took his first free breath since he had lain down to rest. The needle interfaces of monitoring machines slid from the sockets of his black carapace. Thick tubes twisted like umbilical cords suckled greedily at the arteries in his forearms, thighs and neck as he slept. They throbbed now as they returned his purified blood to him, and detached from his skin with sorrowful kisses.

Light falling on the black sculpture changed, fading from sanguine to gentle red gold, the colour of the sunlight of Balor. Inset wheels spun within the sarcophagus' ornate decoration, locks disengaged, a heavy bar disguised as the figure's crossed arms lifted and rose. The lid slid up and away.

Astorath sat up. Pale skin and jet-black hair glistened with residual preservative fluid.

'Sergeant Dolomen,' he said. His voice was quiet yet filled with authority. Vox-thieves hidden in the room's decoration opened up communication with the command deck.

'My lord,' Dolomen responded.

'A brother is lost. Prepare our Navigator for fresh directions. We have work to do.'

The *Eminence Sanguis* appeared on no roll of service for the Blood Angels. It was not expected to take part in the Chapter's battles and rarely did. It had been requested, built and commissioned solely as the personal transport of the High Chaplain, and had conveyed many holders of the office across the galaxy.

Sepulchral halls linked sombre chambers. Every being upon that craft, whether unmodified human, tech-priest or Angel of Death, understood the solemnity of their mission and carried themselves with utmost dignity. The *Eminence Sanguis* was a near-silent ship, where robed figures went on solitary errands. Its machine-spirit was as cold as the void outside its plasteel skin and as distant as the stars it sailed for.

It was a fast ship, quick in the void but swiftest in the warp. Although it was of low mass, in the realm of the warp concepts had more importance than physical truths, and the ship was heavy with duty. So singular was its purpose it cut easily through the conflicting currents of ideas that made the immaterium treacherous. Not even the madness of Chaos could deny the weight of Astorath's work. Aided by the importance of its mission and the faith of those aboard, it passed through the worst of storms, and made impressive speed whatever etheric tempests curdled the Sea of Souls.

In the nightmare of the warp, the *Eminence Sanguis* turned aside from its prior destination towards the source of the song.

Astorath's armour terrified the mortals who came to greet him. There were only three of them stood at the edge of the landing platform when he emerged into the dank forest, and they were frightened, for death stood behind him. His battleplate's ceramite was carved to resemble musculature exposed by flaying, and was painted to match. His jump pack was an arcane design, its form dictated more by art than function, and to the cowering men and single woman, he appeared to be blessed with wings. The pinions were immobile, sculptures of metal as crow black as his hair, yet to them they seemed real. His pauldron was a field of skulls. His knee-pads featured more of the same. The axe he carried was as tall and heavy as the largest of the mortals, with a haft fashioned to resemble a spine. All he carried and all he wore spoke of the ending of life.

The world of Asque only accentuated his deathly aspect. The Blood Angels Stormraven squatted on a rusted landing platform half overtaken by forest growth. Support pillars were engulfed by rippled grey wood. Slimy creepers strangled guard rails, and buried machinery in wet mats of giving flesh. The ship was black, covered in red saltires and glowering skulls. Upon the ancient pad it resembled the ornamentation on an overgrown tomb, peeking out through a cemetery's ruin.

Mould crawled up every surface of the arching roots holding the fungus-trees off the ground. Clouds of their spores floated past in granular mists. The three mortals wore heavy respirators to protect themselves against the spores, but Astorath had no need of such protection, and stood before them bareheaded, a winged giant clad in skinned muscle. In the gloom of the fungal forest, his pale skin appeared blue. He was flanked by Sergeant Dolomen and the Sanguinary Priest Artemos, his only companions from the Chapter. Together they represented the triumvirate of bone, blood and death that shaped the Blood Angels' soul. They were doom incarnate.

Astorath did not look human, and he was not. The mortals were right to be afraid.

'Where are our brothers?' Astorath asked them through bloodless lips.

Despite their protection, the mortals' eyes were rimmed red with spore exposure. The leader, the female, spoke with a voice roughened by poor quality air. She was old, but had that wiry strength certain women keep until the end of their lives.

'They are this way, my lord,' she said, pointing a wavering arm behind her to tangles of roots and trunks receding into the spore-blue air.

Astorath looked into the forest. Far off, the music played.

'Take me there,' he said. 'Dolomen, guard the ship.'

The men and woman looked at each other nervously. None of them wished to be the one to start the march. The idea of telling Astorath what to do, even when asked to provide guidance, seemed to fill them with terror.

'Take me now,' Astorath said.

Relieved to be commanded, the civilians led the way down a run of rockcrete stairs that was so buried in rotted matter, fungal stands and roots it appeared no more than an animal track.

'You, female. Tell me what happened here.' Astorath's footsteps were heavy, thumping on the soft ground like dying heartbeats.

'Your brother took the ordes meat–' began the woman.

'From the beginning. Tell me of this place. Tell me what happened to you before my brothers came. It will help me understand what has befallen them.'

So she did. Her name, she said, was Srana. Astorath filed it away with a million other names, never to be forgotten.

'This world is not a bad world,' Srana began. 'I have read of others. I know there are worse places than Asque.'

They were obliged to duck through interlaced rubbery vines whose rough surfaces adhered to them. Astorath and Artemos shoved their way through with difficulty, for the vines would not break, and the paths the humans took were too small for them. As Astorath forced his way out, the woman glanced back, to see if she had spoken out of place. Astorath's return stare had her turning her face away twice as quickly.

'Before the silent ones came, we lived in sunlight, up there.' She pointed upwards, where arrow-straight trunks lifted off from their cradles of roots, though she did not look, too afraid or too saddened by what had happened. 'Up there are our homes. That is our world, not this place. Up there, there is no mould. The air is clear. The weather is warm. We had good lives.'

'The nature of this world's purpose?'

'The production and export of chemical products derived from the great fungi,' she said. 'Their wood is no good. It is black-hearted, rots quickly. No use for building, but when bled and boiled it gives useful liquors. We had our duties to the Imperium, and we fulfilled them.' She dared to look back again. 'All we wish is to do so again, to live in the sun and pay our dues to the God-Emperor. We worked hard. We prayed hard. I am so sorry about what has happened here. Please, let the Emperor know we are sorry for whatever we did to anger Him and bring this disaster on ourselves. I am so sorry the Red Angels came to help us, and this happened. I–'

'What happened here is not your fault,' said Astorath bluntly. 'You have done no wrong. If you had, I would kill you, but you need not fear punishment from me. Unless there is some element of your tale that is deserving of harsher judgement?'

She shook her head. 'None, no, my lord. We did nothing. We are victims. I think. Maybe the meat… Maybe we poisoned him?'

'All humanity is a victim in these dark times. If you speak the truth, you have nothing to fear. You did not poison him. Continue your tale.'

'The rift came, and the sky turned sick. The silent ones came soon afterwards. They appeared in nightmares at first, pale, naked things, the size of half-grown children, pot-bellied, long arms, horrible in proportion, but their faces were the worst. They were blank, no eyes or nose, only a curved mouth full of jutting teeth. We all dreamt about them, standing in the corner of our sleeping chambers, staring at us.' She shuddered at the memory. 'It didn't take long for us to realise that we dreamed of the same things, of silent, pale faces with no eyes. A few panicked children was all it took. Word got round. We were afraid.

'We worked on as best we could. Then the tithe ships stopped coming. Then the merchantmen. We produce enough food for ourselves, but are dependent on outsiders for many other things. We sent out messages from our astropaths in the capital, but got no reply. They tried harder, until one by one they went mad, and so Count Mannier ordered no more attempts be made, in order to save the last.'

'When was this?'

'Decades ago. I was young then, old enough to remember how things were. There are no sky-speakers now. Some of what I relay to you was told to me by my mother.'

'You speak of matters dealt with by the planetary government.'

'My mother was adviser to the count. I am of noble birth,' she cackled. 'Though you would not believe it now.'

'Continue.'

'The dreams became worse. Then they stopped being dreams. We woke in the night to find the silent ones looking at us. They'd vanish, after a while, but they were there. We had picts and vid-captures.' She went quiet. 'Then, after a little longer, they started to hunt us.'

They passed along a road broken to useless slabs by fungal roots.

'We killed a few, they were flesh and blood it seemed, and it gave us heart. But they came and went as they wished. We struggled to trap them. We couldn't see them. They picked us off at their leisure. We were afraid to sleep. So many of us died in nights of terror, and we were driven from our homes, down here. They didn't come down here so much, on account of the spores maybe. We managed to hold on, but we were dying slowly. The count took the chance with our last astropath and sent the message – I was a girl still then. It took so long to answer, we didn't think anyone would come. Then your brothers arrived, and they were cunning and brave and killed many of the silent ones. Everything looked like it would be good again. It was, for a while. They took back this township for us, so we could look on the sun. They drove the creatures deeper into the forest. We began to rebuild.'

They reached a stairway choked by the outgrowths of the tree it circled, and started to climb upwards.

'Then your brother took the ordes meat, and suddenly it wasn't good any more.' She smiled weakly. 'Come on, it's this way.'

When Astorath and Artemos arrived in the reclaimed township they found their brothers out on patrol, and so settled down to wait for their return in a room in a derelict habitat.

'We should consider the possibility that this entire planet must be purged,' said Artemos, speaking by private helm-to-helm vox 'You heard what she said.'

'The old rules are not so rigidly applied,' said Astorath. 'Word of daemons has spread now. Once, even you would not have known of them, brother. How can knowledge of them be hidden when they walk openly across the galaxy?'

'Knowledge isn't what bothers me,' said Artemos. He lifted a ragged curtain and glanced out through a cracked window. The habitat overlooked a landscape of lacy branches that moved in the light of the planet's moon. 'This whole place might be tainted. You know what it's like when they get their fingers in the minds of men.'

'If every world that had known the touch of the daemon since the rift opened was laid waste, there would be no Imperium left,' said Astorath. 'Purity of thought is the best safeguard. The question of whether this world is tainted is for others to answer. It is not obviously so, and we do not have the resources to deal with it if it is. Our mission is to secure our missing brother.'

Artemos shrugged. 'You are right. I speak prematurely. The things here could have been Chaos-warped predators, rather than daemons. Or they could be a strange kind of xenos. Some of those things the aeldari consort with.' He shook his head and let the curtain drop. 'Xenos or daemon, they are filth, all of them. The galaxy is not what it was. The old evils come sneaking out of the shadows.'

'Put these questions from your mind, Brother-Priest,' said Astorath. 'Whatever they are, they are not our business. Mercy for the lost is our sole concern.'

They waited a few hours for the Blood Angels assigned to Asque to return to the outpost. A single half-squad had been sent, and there were three of them left, all Primaris Marines. They were not surprised to find Astorath at the township.

'I am Brother Fidelius, 11th squad, Third Battle Company, acting sergeant,' said the warrior who led them. 'These are Edmun and Caspion. You are High Chaplain.'

'I am,' Astorath confirmed.

'Then I greet you as my lord.' Fidelius dropped to his knee and bowed his head.

'May the blessing of the Angel's virtues and graces fill you and carry you through battle, my brother. Now rise.'

Fidelius stood again.

'Who is the one who is afflicted?' Astorath asked.

'Brother-Sergeant Erasmus.'

Astorath paused before asking his next question.

'And is Brother-Sergeant Erasmus like you, or like me?' The gravity of his question seemed to distort space around them.

'He is not a Primaris brother, my lord, if that is what you mean,' said Fidelius.

'So you were deployed as a mixed squad?'

'At our captain's command,' said Fidelius. He looked at his brothers. 'We three were among those raised from the Great Blooding. We lack experience. Erasmus came to teach us.'

'You fought as mortals on the walls of the Arx Angelicum?'

'We did,' said Fidelius. 'There were four of us Primaris Marines, until the xenos things slew Brother Aelus. The four of us and Erasmus were deemed enough for the task at hand, but these things are slippery, and claimed their due in blood. Erasmus said...' He shared a look with his brothers. Astorath recognised it, for he had seen it many times – the look of a Blood Angel exposed for the first time to the effects of the Rage. 'Erasmus said Aelus made a grave error, and that we must learn from it. He said that Aelus' death was fair exchange for the thousands of their dead, and we will avenge him. We were looking for the silent ones when you arrived. They stay away from the population now. We've cleansed most of this sector. We'll get the rest.'

'Are they daemons?' asked Artemos.

'I know little of daemons, but I don't believe so,' said Fidelius. 'They are easy enough to kill, though they are stealthy. They're psychically able, they cloud the mind, they're never where you think they are, but they are of flesh and blood. There's not very many of them. Dangerous to unmodified humans, but little threat to us. I can imagine how easy it was for them to wreak havoc on a planet this sparsely populated, but we would have had this continent secure and been on our way to the other hemisphere if it weren't for...' He paused again. Disquiet showed in his eyes. 'If it weren't for this.'

'What became of Aelus' gene-seed?' asked Artemos.

'It was lost. We tried to save it, but we could not. We have no

Priest with us. I apologise. Perhaps it could have been retrieved, but I do not have the skills.' Fidelius turned his attention back to Astorath. 'If you have responded to our message, then the worst has happened. I didn't believe it was possible. Erasmus was so noble.'

'You thought it something else?'

'I am no expert, and hope deceived me, perhaps, but I hoped so. If you are here, it is not some other thing. It is the Black Rage.'

'It is,' Astorath confirmed.

'I am surprised you arrived so swiftly. I sent word only days ago.'

'I did not get your summons,' said Astorath. 'I require no message. The music of torment called me, so I came.'

'It happened here,' said Brother Caspion. They were in a house built around the topmost trunk of the arrow-like trees. The spongy wood, slender as a man at that point, made a central pillar around which all else was constructed. Broken pots lay about, and a smear of blood darkened the wall. 'Brother-Sergeant Erasmus had been behaving erratically all day, but we did not know what we were seeing. If we had, we would have acted.'

'Be calm, young brother. This is not your doing,' said Astorath.

Caspion nodded gratefully. 'They were giving us a feast in our honour when Erasmus turned. He ate the meat, then something happened, and before we could react he had killed two of the mortals, shouting as he did about traitors and being trapped. We tried to restrain him but his strength was too great and he escaped. The natives have not returned here since it happened.'

'Relations seem good otherwise,' said Astorath.

'Fidelius convinced them Erasmus was influenced by the creatures. They were shocked a Space Marine could be so affected, but they believed it,' said Edmun.

'I do not like to trade in falsehood,' said Fidelius. 'Forgive me.'

'A lesser evil. Let them continue to believe it is so,' said Astorath. 'It would be for the best if that remains the story they tell after we are gone.'

'Better they fear the alien than their protectors, brothers,' said Artemos.

'Better still that the twin curses of our gene-line remain secret,' said Astorath.

'They feared that their meat offended us, and triggered his behaviour somehow,' said Edmun. 'Is that how it happens?' he asked tentatively.

Astorath watched the Primaris Marines closely. Though the new Space Marine breed seemed resistant to the flaw, they were still taught the rituals and the severity of the curse. To little effect, it seemed. So many had been inducted so quickly that they'd had no time to learn properly.

'The women, Srana, she mentioned this ordes meat. Was there anything unusual about it?'

'They said it was a delicacy. They were excited. The animal has to be hunted, and they have not been able to hunt since the creatures came. It was bloody, and tough, but of good savour,' said Fidelius. 'Could it have been the cause?'

'It is most unlikely,' said Astorath. He paced around the room and stopped by the bloodstain. 'Whose blood is this?'

'Brother Erasmus',' said Caspion, ashamed. 'I injured him.'

Astorath pulled a strip of spongy fungus wood from the wall. He chewed on it, letting snatches of experience be teased from the coagulated blood. There was little genetic material, and therefore little could be gleaned. Beneath the ponderous thoughts of trees, Astorath got impressions of bewilderment and fear, then the anguished tune of Erasmus' soul played loud and drowned out all else, and he spat the chewed wood out. 'The Rage comes unannounced. You all partook of the meat?'

Fidelius nodded.

'Then it was not the cause. You are unaffected? No increase in your thirst?'

'None, my lord. It does not affect us the same way,' Fidelius said, almost apologetically.

Astorath looked around the room. 'And Erasmus burst out of the door? After you wounded him?'

'Yes, my lord. Erasmus then dropped to the forest floor,' said Fidelius.

'One hundred and thirty feet,' Edmun said disbelievingly.

'He had his battleplate,' said Fidelius. 'No weapons except his combat knife. He vanished. We've combed the area thoroughly, grid by grid. Edmun is a good tracker.'

'I lost him,' Edmun said. 'We followed his trail to the bounds of the next settlement, where the trail gave out. The enemy tried a sortie against us there, and we were forced to fight. When it was done, I could not find his tracks again.'

Astorath nodded, still examining the room.

'I am finished here. Tell the people of this village they have nothing to fear. Soon you will be able to complete your mission, for the greater glory of the Emperor. First, you must direct me to where the greatest concentration of enemy are.'

'But why?' said Fidelius. 'They are to the north, Brother-Sergeant Erasmus ran south.'

'He will be where the enemy are,' said Astorath. 'We are warriors. We suffer a warrior's curse. Though they may be violent towards their own, those under the influence of the Black Rage are still servants of the Emperor. They fight for Him until the end, however misguidedly.'

Astorath prepared for the giving of mercy. He had stripped the top portion of his armour off, and sat cross-legged in a habitat yet to be reclaimed by the planet's depleted people. Artemos held out his bare arm for Astorath to cut, and with the Sanguinary Priest's blood Astorath anointed his skin. He lapped at Artemos' wrist twice to blunt his Red Thirst, and, through the vitae of Sanguinius running through Artemos' veins, to remember the sacrifice of their primarch. The curse music sang in Astorath's mind as the blood filled his mouth.

'You can't go alone,' Artemos said. He wiped his arm and clad it in ceramite again. The ritual was a businesslike affair. Under such circumstances, the armouring of the soul was done with the same practical battlefield efficiency as the reloading of a boltgun. 'The settlement to the north is full of the enemy. We should all go.'

'I have fought some of the most celebrated heroes of the Blood, brother. These creatures are feeble. They will not slow me, and when I find Erasmus I will best him.' The blood symbols were drying on Astorath's skin. He sheathed his blade, and began to collect his armour pieces.

'Let me come with you.'

'This is my duty alone, brother.'

Artemos helped him don his back-plate and breast-plate, holding them in place while Astorath bolted them together with a sanctified power driver.

'Then take some of Erasmus' Primaris brothers with you, as a precaution against mishap. We cannot afford to lose you, when we have lost so much already.'

Astorath looked over his shoulder into Artemos' eyes. 'Are you seriously suggesting a mere sergeant might get the better of me?'

'No, my lord.'

He returned to his armour. 'There will be no mishap. The Primaris Marines will remain here. It is inevitable that they will see the effects of the Black Rage first-hand one day, for we all do, whether as witnesses or sufferers. I would prefer them not to yet. The Primaris brethren brought hope to our Chapter. It is best if as few of them as possible see the curse that afflicts the rest of us. The Chapters of the Blood have been through much these last centuries. Allow us a moment of resurgence before we must face the monsters within again.'

'The truth will out.'

'Truth always does. However, it will be many years before these Primaris Marines return to Baal. They have done good work here, but this entire world must be freed. They may die before they can pass the information on to others of their kind.'

'Are you sure I cannot accompany you?'

Astorath ran his thumb lightly down the edge of the Executioner's Axe. Blood beaded on his skin.

'I go alone, Artemos.' He pushed his still-bleeding hand into his gauntlet and locked it into place. 'Do not ask again.'

The forest of Asque was silent. So dominant were the fungiforms and moulds that animal life was scarce. Astorath walked roads high over the ground choked by fungal growth. Symbiotic relationships with the fungi were common in the few animal species which thrived, and ever adaptable humanity had taken their lead. The road was carried on buttresses encouraged to grow from nearby fungus-trees, but the network required maintenance; in the years since the rift the sky-roads had buckled and the marks of human habitation everywhere were vanishing.

It took so little to erase humanity's efforts from existence. Astorath's duties, though obscure, were ultimately a part of the fight against that, to prevent mankind vanishing from history like so many hundreds of species before it.

The town rose in delicate towers high above the canopy. Once he had passed under the shadow of the first, he encountered the enemy.

A pallid, bloated shape disentangled itself from the shadows and leapt at him. Astorath's head buzzed with psychic interference. He could not see it clearly at first, but the efforts undertaken to improve a Space Marine's mind were as great as those that went into rebuilding his body. He shook the thing's influence off, and its form was revealed to him.

It was vaguely humanoid, mushroom-pale, bloated, disgusting as so many xenos were. Hooked claws in its wrists squealed off his armour. The mouth snapped at him, every bit as hideous as Srana had said.

'Surprise is your chief weapon, creature,' said Astorath. He grabbed it by the throat and held it aloft. It was surprisingly strong, and would easily slay a mortal man. 'But you have little else, and nothing that can do harm to me.'

In his grip the beast was helpless. It thrashed about and hissed until its breath was spent and it was dead.

He dropped the pasty thing. It sank bonelessly into itself and began to emit clouds of yellow spores from its body.

Astorath strode on, following strains of a funereal tune only he could hear.

'Brother Erasmus!' he shouted. His amplified vox echoed down silent streets, scaring up rare aviforms and startling parasitic growths into shedding slimy seeds. 'Brother-Sergeant Erasmus! Return to us! Return to your Chapter! Return for the Emperor's mercy!'

His shouting attracted the creatures. En masse they clouded his mind more effectively, but he aimed his blows at the blurred shapes and cleaved them down anyway. They sought to bury him under a weight of their bodies, and did, but they could not penetrate his armour. Soft fingers pried at his seals. Sharp claws scraped at his ceramite. The Emperor's armament held firm against their efforts and they died by the dozen.

'You do not learn,' he said, striking them down. 'You cannot harm me.' He paced his blows to preserve his strength, weathering the soft drumming of their alien fists on his battleplate and chopping them down with a forester's steady rhythm.

Killing all the way, he passed into the inner districts of the town, where grand squares were upheaved by the unchecked movement of living supports. Towers were choked by the rubbery vines, great tangles of them bursting from every window. The further he went the more creatures appeared, all attacking without consideration for their feebleness. His boots crunched on human bones made soft by decay. Thousands had died here, and it sorrowed him.

Finally, a rune flicked into being upon his helm-plate. A chime announced his true quarry was near. He activated his jump pack and burst from a knot of the creatures.

Black wings spread, prolonging his short flight. He directed himself to a broad platform overlooking a further square, and there he found Brother Erasmus.

The fallen sergeant raged and screamed, shouting imprecations at enemies ten thousand years dead. The blood red of his armour was obscured by milky alien blood and brilliant smears of yellow spores. His knife had broken halfway along the blade, but he wielded it as if it were the finest sword. A hundred of the fungoid creatures swarmed him. Astorath wondered how long Erasmus had fought. It was not unusual for a brother gripped by the Rage to fight until his hearts burst, the ferocity of the affliction being enough to overtax a Space Marine's body, but if Brother-Sergeant Erasmus had fought since the day he had fallen, he showed no signs of fatigue, and still killed with great efficiency.

Astorath watched awhile. Though the Black Rage was a terrible curse, those afflicted displayed an echo of the primarch's martial glory when they fought, and the sight never failed to move him. The music of Erasmus' suffering sang loudly in his mind.

'Terrible, and glorious,' Astorath said, then called out, 'Brother! I am coming to you. Stand fast! Soon your suffering shall be done.'

He ignited his jets, and thundered down into combat.

They fought side by side, purging the town of its infestation. Astorath's axe buzzed through the xenos trailing lightning, and in short time the battle was done.

The High Chaplain faced the lost brother.

'Father!' Erasmus cried, his voice choked with spiritual pain. 'Have you come? Is Horus dead?'

'He is long dead,' Astorath said calmly. He held his axe across his body in both hands. 'Come to me, and know an end to suffering.'

'If he is dead, why do I see him, standing over me? Why does my blood leave my body? Oh father, why have you forsaken me?'

The lost brother threw himself at Astorath, and the day's real fighting began.

Erasmus was possessed by the death memories of Sanguinius, and full of desperate strength. Astorath judged Erasmus too strong to grapple, so took his time, softly singing the hymns of ending as he struck away pieces of the warrior's armour and bled away his might with gentle cuts. There were quicker ways to end one of the lost, but Astorath would do so only in extremis; the warrior must be comforted, and blessed. The final rites of death were as important as the rites of apotheosis and must be correctly observed.

Astorath fought to preserve the secrets of his Chapter. He fought to end the rampages of those who could not find a noble end in battle, but most of all he fought to save their souls. Kindness guided his axe above all things.

'You are a traitor, a betrayer, a worm in the eye of father,' shouted Erasmus. 'You consort with evil for your own benefit while the Imperium burns! Why? Why? Why?' Erasmus directed a flurry of blows at Astorath. The High Chaplain stepped back, mindful that even a broken blade propelled with such strength could break his armour.

'I am not Horus, brother,' he said softly. 'I am your redemption.'

He stepped back and around, swinging his axe with the motion, and took Erasmus' leg off at the knee.

The Space Marine fell face forward and howled piteously with sorrow. He tried to rise.

'I die! I die! Slain at the hand of my brother!'

Astorath stepped in, kicked the knife from the Space Marine's hand and with another blow shattered his armour's power plant, expertly deactivating the battleplate without triggering an explosion. A good part of Erasmus' strength was thus denied him.

'Why?' sobbed Erasmus. 'Why does it have to end this way?'

Astorath squatted down, rolled Erasmus over onto his back and pulled free his helm. The warrior's face was swollen with vitae, his eyes blooming with burst blood vessels. His eye teeth were at their fullest length. But there was yet nobility in him. There always was in the lost.

Astorath rested his palm on the warrior's brow. 'Peace, brother. Be at peace. I am not Horus. I am not the Emperor. I am High

Chaplain, and you are Brother-Sergeant Erasmus. The wars you speak of were over ten thousand years ago. Now your fight is, too.'

Erasmus' eyes cleared a little.

'What… what has happened to me?'

'The Black Rage. Our father's death, echoing down time.' He gave the Space Marine a solemn stare. 'Now, listen to me. We are Space Marines, we do not pray. We hold no person to be a god, and all gods to be monsters. We give praise to no one but mortal heroes, and we thank the Emperor as a man and not a divine being. But we will pray now, you and I, for peace in death.'

Astorath spoke sacred words. Through the fog of the rage, Erasmus repeated them, and a little more lucidity returned.

'Our lord's anguish…' Erasmus said. Tears spilled down his cheeks. 'I feel what the Angel felt. I can't stand it. He is sorrowing for me, for all of us. End it swiftly, please!'

'Fear not, my brother, mercy is my purpose.'

Astorath rose. The Executioner's Axe descended.

The music stopped, and a new weight was added to the High Chaplain's burden.

He recovered Erasmus' head, and voxed Artemos.

Artemos performed his grisly work back in the village. The Primaris Marines guarded the habitat door. The people kept away. They knew something sacred was happening within. Reductor blades sawed though bone, and ribs cracked wetly to give up precious gene-seed.

'Fear not, brothers,' Astorath said to them. 'Your brother died as all Blood Angels should, in communion with the Great Angel, Sanguinius.'

'High Chaplain,' said Fidelius. 'May I have permission to ask your guidance?'

'You may.'

'Will this happen to us?'

Astorath answered thoughtfully. 'Your creator, Belisarius Cawl, has many qualities, but he is a braggart and wears hubris like a gown.

It is impossible to eliminate Sanguinius' suffering from our souls. But it may be that you are immune from its effects.'

'Then, if we shall never see what the Angel saw, can we truly call ourselves Blood Angels?' asked Edmun.

'You are Primaris Marines, but you are Blood Angels first. The blood of Sanguinius flows in your veins as it does in mine. You may never suffer the way that Erasmus did, but rest assured, you are my brothers,' said Astorath.

He made sure to meet the eyes of each of them, and as he did he heard a few distant notes of pain – a foretaste, perhaps, of what might come to pass.

Artemos joined them. 'It is done. Erasmus' gene-seed is secure. We will return his armour to the Chapter.'

'Then we are finished here,' said Astorath. He looked to the sky, and opened his vox-link 'Sergeant Dolomen, we are returning. Prepare the Stormraven for flight. Please inform the *Eminence Sanguis*, we depart immediately. More duty awaits us.'

Somewhere in the immensity of space, a new tune had begun to play.

YOUR
NEXT READ

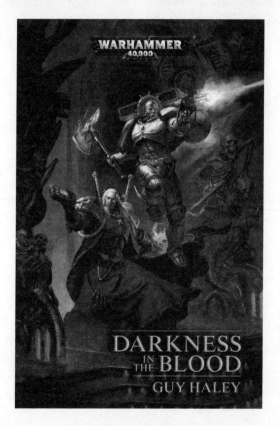

DARKNESS IN THE BLOOD
by Guy Haley

Baal has been saved from the tyranids, yet the Blood Angels' greatest challenge awaits them. Reinforced by the new Primaris Space Marines, Commander Dante has been made warden of Imperium Nihilus. But to save the shattered Imperium, he and his brothers must first defeat the darkness within themselves.

EXTINCTION

Aaron Dembski-Bowden

Introducing

EZEKYLE ABADDON

FIRST CAPTAIN, SONS OF HORUS

Legions die by betrayal. They die in fire and futility.
Above all, they die in shame.

Kallen Garax, Sergeant of Garax Tactical Squad, Sons of Horus 59th Company. His armour is wreck-blasted and cracked, gunmetal grey with the sea-green paint scorched away into memory. Across his helm's left side, image intensifiers refocus with smooth whirrs, miraculously undamaged from his fall.

His men are in pieces around him. Medes is a dismembered ruin, his component parts scattered over the rubble. Vladak is impaled through the chest, decapitated by junk, twitching in a spread of bloodstained sand. Daion and Ferac had been closest to the defence turrets' power generator when their length of the wall exploded under a gunship's strafing run. Kallen has a flash memory of both warriors covered in chemical fire, burning as the shockwave sent them sprawling. Their scorched remains scarcely resemble anything human. He doubts they'd been alive when they hit the ground.

Smoke rises all around him, though the wind steals the worst of it. He can't move. He can't feel his left leg. Jagged wreckage lies strewn in every direction; a particularly sharp chunk of it impales his thigh, pinning him to the charred ground. He looks back at the burning stronghold, with its remaining turrets firing at the gunships strafing the battle-ments, and an entire wall broken open to the enemy. Across the desert, the enemy come on in a dusty horde, half-occluded by the dirty smoke thrown up by their bike tyres and smoking engines. Dirty silver on a dull, desecrated blue: the Night Lords, riding in wild unity.

He keeps his calm, speaking over the vox, demanding Titan support that he knows isn't coming, despite the princeps's promises. They are betrayed, left here to die under VIII Legion guns.

Kallen looks at the plasteel bar driven through the meat of his leg, and gives it an experimental tug. Even with pain nullifiers flooding his bloodstream, the grind of metal against bone peels his pale lips back from his teeth in a snarl.

'*Tagh gorugaaj kerez,*' he calls out in Cthonic. '*Tagh gorugaaj kerez.*'

A howl sounds closer, mechanical and full-throated. Jump-jets, whining to a close.

'*Veliasha shar sheh meressal mah?*' asks a vox-voice in a language he doesn't speak. He knows the sound of Nostraman, tongue of the sunless world, but speaks none of it himself.

A shadow eclipses the world's poisoned sky. It isn't one of his brothers. It doesn't offer a hand to help him rise. Instead, it aims a bolter down at his face.

Kallen stares into the gun barrel, dark as the nothingness between worlds. His eyes flick left, where his own bolter lies in the rubble. Out of reach. With his leg impaled, it might as well be half a world away.

He unlocks his helm's seals and pulls it free, feeling the desert wind on his bleeding face. He wants his killer to see him smiling.

Sovan Khayral, Techmarine, bound to the Sons of Horus 101st Company. The bridge burns around him, shrouding his vision with greasy smoke the ventilators have no hope of scrubbing into something breathable. To compensate, his eye lenses cycle through filters: thermal sight reveals nothing but smears of migraine heat;

motion-sensing tracks the crew staggering and suffocating on the deck, and slouched in their seats.

The ship dying around him is the *Hevelius,* a destroyer of some renown in the Sons of Horus fleet. Like so many of the Legion's ships, she was at Terra when the Throneworld burned. The last sight Khayral had of the auspex display showed the flickering runes of the Death Guard fleet closing into killing range, herding the outnumbered and outgunned Sons of Horus vessels into showing their bellies. The Death Guard meant to finish this up close and personal. They'd get their wish, in a matter of moments.

Khayral's dense ceramite acts as a heat shield against the fires consuming all life around him. Retinal displays mark the temperature close to melting flesh and muscle from the bone. Sirens wail without respite, never needing to pause for breath in the choking smoke.

He hurls himself at the control throne, throwing aside the slack corpse-to-be of *Hevelius*'s asphyxiating captain. Through the smoke, he keys a code into the console built into the armrest. Shipwide vox comes alive with a nasty, wet crackle. Circuits are melting all across the ship, diseased and rotting and burning.

'All hands,' he says through his helm's mouth-grille speaker. 'All hands, abandon ship.'

Nebuchar Desh, Captain of the Sons of Horus 30th Company. He exhales a rancid coppery breath from his lungs, feeling bloody spit stringing between his teeth. One of his hearts has failed, now a cooling dead weight in his chest. The other beats like a heathen war drum, overworked and out of rhythm. His face is on fire with the pain of the lash wounds tiger-striping his flesh. The last whipcrack stole one of his eyes. The one before that opened his throat to the gristle.

He raises his sword in time for the whip to lash back, wrapping his fist and the hilt in a serpentine rush. A sharp pull tears the weapon from his grip. Disarmed, half-blind, breathless, Desh falls to one knee.

'For the Warmaster.' With his ravaged throat, the words are as strengthless as a whisper. His enemy answers with a bellow, loud enough to shake Desh's remaining eye in its socket. The wall of sound hits him with rippling physicality, denting and bending his armour plating in a series of resonating clangs. He stands against the wind for three erratic heartbeats until it breaks his balance, hurling him down and sending him skidding across the landing platform with a squeal of ceramite on rusting iron.

As he tries to rise, a boot presses down on the back of his head, grinding his mutilated face into the iron deck. He feels his teeth snapping in their sockets, gluing to the inside of his mouth with thick, corrosive saliva.

'For the–'

His benediction ends in a voiceless gurgle as the blade slides lovingly home into his spine.

Zarien Sharak, Brother of the Sons of Horus 86th Company. A seeker, a pilgrim, a visionary – he seeks out the Neverborn, surrendering his flesh to daemons as a statue of meat and bone offered up for reshaping. He pursues them, proves himself to them with sacrifices of blood and souls, forever seeking the strongest to ally with him within his own skin.

He no longer recalls how long he's been on this world, nor how long the World Eaters have been chasing him. He isn't here to run from them, he's here to stand and face them. They chase him now, laughing and howling up the side of the mountain. Sharak can hear the mad wetness in their words, and pays their frothing laughter no heed. His muscles burn; the last daemon to dwell within his flesh was cast out seven nights before, leaving him drained and anaemic in search of another. Soon, he knows. Soon.

His gauntleted hand grips the rocky ledge above. He has the briefest moment to smile at the bolt shells bursting stone into fragments nearby before he hauls himself up and out of the World Eaters' line of fire.

The shrine awaits him, as he knew it would, though it resembles nothing he'd expected. A single sculpture, weathered by mutable time, reduced to something stunted, formless, vague. Perhaps it had once been an eldar, in the era when this entire region of space had been the domain of that sick and weak alien breed.

You have found me, comes the voice in his mind. Sharak sweats at the silent sound. He turns, seeing nothing but the deformed statue and the endless expanse of glass desert in every direction.

Sharak, it beckons. *Your enemies draw near. Shall we end them, you and I?*

Sharak is no fool. He's whored his flesh as a weapon to devils and spirits alike, but he knows the secrets most of his brothers lack. Discipline is all it takes to maintain control. Even the strongest of the Neverborn is no match for the strength of a guarded, warded human soul. They could share his flesh, but never dominate his essence.

This daemon is strong. It has demanded much of him these last months, and here at the precipice, it offers everything he needs to save his life. But he is no fool. Caution and care are his watchwords when dealing with this realm's creatures. He's seen too many of his brothers become scorched husks, home to daemonic intelligence, all trace of themselves scoured and scraped away from within.

The World Eaters howl below – not like wolves, but fanatics. It's the lack of anything feral that makes it so sickening to hear, so much more of a threat. A beast's howl is a natural thing. A fanatic's cry is something of anger and tormented joy in equal measure, born of spite and twisted faith. He turns back to the stunted stone pillar.

You've followed my voice for a hundred days and nights. You've made foes of brothers and cousins alike, just as I asked. And now you stand before the stone that sinners once carved in my image. You've proven yourself in every way I asked of you. You are worthy of this union. What now, Sharak? What now?

'I'm ready,' Sharak says. He bares his throat in a symbolic gesture, and pulls his helm free. He can hear the rattle and grind of ceramite over rock. The World Eaters are almost upon him.

The Joining is different each time. Once, it was a hammer blow to his sternum, as if the daemon wriggled its way through an invisible puncture hole into his body. Another time, it came as a burst of consciousness and sensuality – perceiving shadows of lost souls moving at the edges of his eyes, and hearing whispers on the wind from entire worlds away. This time, it strikes with heat, with a burning itch across the skin. He feels the Joining physically at first, a welcome violation of his flesh despite the bleeding and choking. It hurts down to his bones, weighing them down, driving him to his knees. His eyes turn next, hardening in their sockets, fusing to the bone behind. He taps them, scratches them, pulls at them... they're stones in his skull, edged by spines pushing from his face.

The strength is narcotic in its intensity. No combat drugs, no stimulant serum can match the energy feeding the fibres of his muscles. He starts to claw at his armour plating, no longer needing its protection. Ceramite peels away in chunks, making room for the chitinous ridges beneath.

Sharak looks past the pain, refocusing, seeking to calm his racing hearts. Control. Control. Control. It's only pain. It won't kill him. It can be overcome. It...

It hurts. It hurts more than the agonies of all past Joinings. It hurts to his core, beyond his flesh, hurting past the aches in his bones and into something deeper and truer and infinitely more vulnerable.

A lesson here, the voice says. *Not all pain can be controlled.*

Sharak turns, screaming through a mouth now crammed with knife-teeth. His jaw barely obeys him. His voice strangles off, killing the cry, and becomes someone else's laugh.

And not all enemies can be beaten.

Fear – fear for the first time in his life – floods through his organs in an adrenal rush.

Erekan Juric, Captain of Vaithan Reaver Squad. Lasfire slashes past him, ionising the air he breathes and leaving scorched smears across his armour. He ignores the incidental beams, firing back at the humans with his bolter kicking in his fist. The turbines on his back are heavy, broken things that no longer breathe flame. They stutter and sigh, exhaling smoke and bleeding promethium.

At his boots, his brother Zhoron is cursing him and thanking him, all at once. Juric drags Zhoron by the backpack, hauling him metre by metre up the gunship's ramp. Both of them leave a snail's trail of fluid along the ridged metal: Zhoron leaves a path of his blood from where his legs now end; Juric leaves a dripping track of leaking oil and fuel, with spent shell casings clanging down on the metal ramp by his boots. In the gunship's cargo bay, hastily loaded crates wait in ramshackle order, with wounded warriors in abundance.

'Shersan,' he voxes. 'Go.'

'Yes, captain,' comes the confirmation, flawed by vox-crackle. For a moment, Juric smiles, even under enemy fire. *Captain.* An echo of an era when the Legion still had a structure; from the time before they were hunted like dogs by those they'd failed.

With a shudder, the ramp starts its grinding rise. The gunship kicks, lifting off the ground on a cloud of engine wash and swirling dust. Juric releases Zhoron, tosses his empty bolter into the gunship's waiting cargo bay, and starts running.

'Don't,' his downed brother warns through pained hisses. *'Erekan. Don't do this.'*

Juric doesn't answer. He drops from the rising ramp, thudding back down onto the rocky ground, breaking stones beneath his boots. In his fists, both weapons whine as they accrue power in unison: the curving axe shivers with lightning dancing over its silver blade, while the plasma pistol trembles with the heating of its spinal coils. Bursts of gas relieve the pressure from muzzle vanes. It wants to fire. He knows this gun, and he knows its will. It wants to fire.

The humans are upon him now. He faces them at the heart of the burning fortress, while evacuating gunships rise into the grey sky. The first is a woman, her face a canvas of fresh scars, invoking gods she scarcely understands. Two men run behind her, armed with salvaged twists of metal, their violated flesh different only from the woman's in the cartography of their mutilations, but the same in intent. A mob charges behind the three leaders, screaming and chanting, killing each other in a bid to reach him. Faith gives them courage, but their zealotry has driven them past the point of self-preservation.

Juric starts butchering them, saving the overkill of his pistol for what will surely come afterwards. Swing after swing takes him through the rabble, his axe never ceasing. Blood flecks his eye lenses, and sizzles as it burns away from his energised blade. These lives are meaningless.

'Kahotep,' he breathes the name through his helm's vox-speakers. 'Face me.'

The reply is a psychic pulse of distant mirth. *+Now why would I want to do that?+*

Juric puts his boot through the chest of the last man standing, and runs even as the body falls. Another shadow darkens the sky as a gunship judders overhead, before the concussive boom of its engines lift it into the storm. As if in sympathy for the falling fortress, rain starts in a hissing torrent. It does nothing to fight the fires.

Breathless, Juric asks the vox: 'Who's still on the ground?'

Name-runes and acknowledgement pulses flicker across his retinal display, along with a chorus of voices. The stronghold will fall before the hour turns, and half of his men are still inside its sundered walls.

He crosses the courtyard, leaping the green-armoured bodies of his dead brethren, heading to one of the last remaining buildings. The defence turrets are silent now, all as broken as the battlements. Thousand Sons gunships, stark and dark in the rain, drift over the tumbled plasteel walls. Their battle tanks rumble in through holes torn in the stronghold's barricades. With them come phalanxes of the walking dead, directed by unseen hands.

'Kahotep,' he says again. 'Where are you?'

+Closer than you think, Juric.+

Yet another shadow blacks out the sky, this one cast by a vulturish gunship of old indigo and worn gold, not fleeing in shame but bearing down in triumph. Juric throws himself into the vague cover of a fallen wall, his eyes activating retinal runes on his eye lenses.

'I need anti-armour fire in the southern courtyard. Do we have anything left?'

The responses aren't encouraging. At least more of his men are escaping. That's what matters.

The Thousand Sons gunship burns the air with heat haze from its engines, hovering above the courtyard. Its spotlights cut down through the darkness, raking over the desecrated ground.

+*Where did you go, Son of Horus? I thought you wanted to face me. Was I wrong?*+

The gunship's landing claws bite into the earth, grinding bodies beneath their weight. As the engines cycle down, the ramp beneath the cockpit starts to lower, a maw opening to breathe warriors into war.

Juric watches the Rubricae march forth. His targeting reticule leaps from enemy to enemy, detecting mismatching life signs that suggest everything and conclude nothing. Are these men alive or dead? Both, perhaps. Or neither.

'Vaithan, to me.'

Three runes flash in response. It'll do. It's enough.

He wills his jump pack to fire, but the turbines' response is a shudder and a shower of sparks. He's grounded, and will need to do this the traditional way. Unopposed, three seconds is all it will take to close the distance. Four or five if they land more than one hit, which is likely.

Thayren strikes from above, landing boots-first into the phalanx of the walking dead. Dusty ceramite breaks beneath his impact and two automatons in the blue and gold of the Thousand Sons go down to the dirt, falling with no sound of protest.

Juric starts running the moment Thayren lands. For all his flaws, which he considers many and varied, he's no coward. The Rubricae's bolters bark in his direction the moment he rises into sight.

Whatever independence death stole from them, it left them able to aim. Each explosive hit is a horse kick to his body, blasting ceramite shards away and sending him staggering, cursing the loss of flight. Temperature gauges flicker in alarm as his armour starts to burn with blue witch-fire.

He finishes the first by taking its head, cleaving the stylised warhelm free. Dust bursts from the neck in a thin cloud, with the smell of tombs best left untouched. With the breath of dust comes a faint, relieved sigh. Juric doesn't see the headless body fall; he's already moved on, axe leading the way.

Thayren duels two of the enemy, easily weaving aside from their heavy, precise swings. Juric is almost at his brother's side when protesting engines herald the arrival of Raxic and Naradar. Both hit the ground amidst the Thousand Sons formation, chainblades revving, bolt pistols crashing.

Juric staggers again, down on one knee. His axe falls from his grip. The witch-fire washes over his armour, refusing to burn out, digesting the ceramite and eating into the softer joints.

'Zhoron!' calls one of the other Reavers. Even through the pain biting at his joints, Juric tries to tell them it's futile. The Apothecary is already gone, evacuated on the way to Monument.

He tastes the acid of his own spit on his tongue, and hears the sorcerer's voice in his mind.

+*This is how a Legion dies.*+

The warship sits silent in space, her reactor cold, her engines dead. Battlements line her spine in a protrusion of castles and spires, with thousands of powerless gun turrets aimed up into the void. She drifts alone at the heart of an asteroid field, suffering occasional impacts against her scarred armour, each slow crash adding to the asymmetry of her scars.

She once carved her name through the galaxy at the vanguard of humanity's empire, a bloodthirsty herald of eminent domain. She once hung in the skies of Terra, laying waste to mankind's cradle. Now she lies still, abandoned in hell, hidden from those who covet her.

Her spirit is a tight, tiny essence in her inactive core; the only iota of sentience and life within the immense hulk. This soul, as true as any human life despite its artificial genesis, slumbers in the infinite cold. She waits to be reawakened, but holds no hope it will ever happen. Her sons fled her decks, leaving her here to grow frigid and silver with ice crystals, so far from the light of the closest sun that the star is nothing but a pinprick in the night.

She dreams a warrior's dreams: of fire, of pain, of blood soaking across steel while great guns roar. She dreams of the Many that once lived within her, and the warmth they took when they left.

She dreams of the times she broadcast her name to lesser vessels, shrieking *Vengeful Spirit* as she crippled and killed her enemies.

She dreams of the last words spoken in her presence, ordered in the low growl of the one who'd come to command her. She knew him, as she knew all of the Many. He'd stood before her machine-spirit heartcore, a massive clawed hand against the glass of her brain. Her mind filled the cavernous chamber, shielded and armoured in dense metal. Liquids bubbled. Engines groaned. Pistons clanked. The sound of her thoughts.

Abaddon, she'd said to him. *We can still hunt. We can still kill. You need me.*

He couldn't hear her. He wasn't linked, so he could neither hear nor respond. She knew that had been intentional. He was deafening himself to her, to make the abandonment easier. He'd spoken the final three words, then. The last words she heard with the clarity of consciousness.

'Shut her down.'

Abadd–

Ezekyle the Brotherless, a pilgrim in hell. He stands at the edge of a cliff that reaches impossibly high into a sky the colour of madness and migraines, and he looks down at the armies warring below.

Ants. Insects. A crusade of souls the size of sand grains, half-lost in the dust churned up from the hammering of so many thousands of boots and tank treads.

His armour is a patchwork panoply of scavenged ceramite, repaired countless times after countless battles. The armour he wore in the rebellion is long-since abandoned, left to rot aboard the warship he exiled into the ether. His weapons from that war are likewise gone: his sword broken in some nameless skirmish years ago, and the claw he stole from his father left at the Legion's last fortress, the bastion known to the Sons of Horus as Monument. He wondered if they still left the weapon on display with the Warmaster's stasis-locked remains, or if they'd given in to their fevered hungers and fought over the right to be its bearer.

There was a time he'd be down there with them, waging war at the vanguard, maintaining a steady stream of orders and listening to a flow of positioning reports, all the while killing with a smile in his eyes and a laugh on his lips.

From this distance, he has no hope of discerning which companies are embattled, or even if either side holds to any of the old Legions' structures. Even a cursory glance through the dust clouds is enough to betray the most obvious truth: the Sons of Horus are losing once more, against an enemy horde that vastly outnumbers them. Individual prowess and heroism means nothing down there. A battle can break down into ten thousand duels between lone souls, but it isn't how wars are won.

The wind, always a treacherous companion in this realm, carries infrequent scraps of shouted voices from the valley below. He lets the sounds wash over him without guilt, as unconcerned for the screaming as he is for the way the wind drags at his long, loose hair.

Ezekyle crouches, gathering a fistful of the red sand that serves this world as worthless earth. His eyes never stray from the battle, instinct pulling at him despite having no investment in whoever lives and dies.

Far below him, gunships crow and caw above the battlefield,

adding their incendiary spite to the dusty frenzy. Titans – at this distance no larger than his fingernails – stride through the choke, their weapon fire still bright enough to leave thread-thin blurs across his retinas, each one a little slice of razored light.

He smiles, but not because of the battle. What world is this? He realises he doesn't even know. His wandering takes him from planet to planet, avoiding his former brethren when he can, yet now he stands upon a world watching hundreds of his brothers dying, without even knowing the planet's name or what they sell their lives to defend.

How many of the men screaming and fighting and bleeding down in the valley would he know by name? Most, without a doubt. That, too, makes him smile.

He rises to his feet, opening his fist. The lifeless, glassy dust glitters away in the wind, catching the light from three weak suns before spreading in a thin burst, lost to sight.

Ezekyle turns his back on the battle, and leaves the cliff behind. Footprints mark his passage, but he trusts the wind to breathe his tracks into memory before anyone catches sight of them. He looks to the horizon, where seven vast stepped pyramids rise into the sky, shaped by hands neither human nor alien, but wrought solely by divine whim.

In this place in space, on every world he walks, desire and hatred forge the landscape more reliably than mortal ingenuity or natural tectonics. He's crossed bridges over oblivion, threaded between islands of rock hanging in the void. He's explored the tombs of xenos-breed kings and queens, and left priceless plunder to lie untouched in the dark. He's travelled the surface of hundreds of worlds in this realm where the material and the immaterial meet to mate, scarcely paying heed to the extinction of the Legion he once led.

Curiosity drives him, and hatred sustains him, where once anger was all he needed. Defeat cooled the fires of that particular forge, however.

Ezekyle Abaddon, no longer First Captain, no longer a Son of Horus, keeps walking. He'll reach the first great pyramid before the first of the three suns sets.

YOUR
NEXT READ

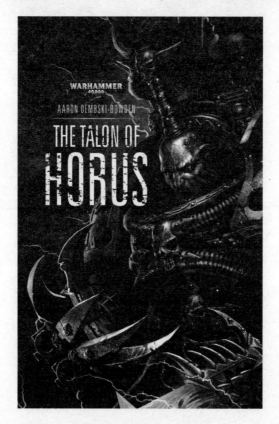

THE TALON OF HORUS
by Aaron Dembski-Bowden

When Horus fell, his Sons fell with him. A broken Legion, beset by rivalries and
hunted by their erstwhile allies, the former Luna Wolves have scattered across
the tortured realm of the Eye of Terror. And of Abaddon, greatest of the Warmaster's
followers, nothing has been heard for many years. Until now...

PRODIGAL

Josh Reynolds

Introducing

FABIUS BILE

APOTHECARY, EMPEROR'S CHILDREN

Fabius Bile hummed with quiet satisfaction and studied the tiny shapes floating in the half-dozen man-sized nutrient tanks. The children were scrawny things, culled from the lower hives of three worlds, but there was a fierce potential in them, which stirred his somnolent creativity. It had been some time, and he was glad to find that the fires of ingenuity had not been utterly snuffed, as he sometimes feared.

The systems of the laboratorium flickered as *Vesalius* slipped into the obscuring depths of warpspace. The ancient Gladius-class frigate was his personal vessel, claimed in some long-ago raid on a forgotten world. Its former name had been stripped from it, as had every trace of its previous owners. Now and forever, it was simply *Vesalius*. Whatever cruel spirit now haunted its core seemed happy enough with the name. Which was just as well. Bile was not in the habit of letting his tools dictate their own designations, however useful they might be. 'That is the responsibility of the creator,' he said, as he thumped a flickering hololithic projector. 'To name a thing is to lay out its purpose.' He looked around, ensuring all was in its proper place.

Magnetised trays of surgical equipment, much of it designed by Bile himself, occupied the walls, alongside diverse charts, documenting his ongoing experiments and various observations. Enhanced pict-captures of in-progress dissections jostled for space with chemical readouts and scraps of poetry, culled from worlds without number. Beauty drawn from amidst the wreckage. Poetry, like music, was a passion of his. A holdover from ancient days and associations, comforting in its familiarity.

The laboratorium was his private fiefdom aboard the vessel, the one place where he could be alone, free from the squabbling factionalism of his servants. It was his own fault, for fostering a climate of healthy competition among the crew, necessary though it might be. Only the strongest survived in this galaxy.

'And you will be strong, my children. It is writ in your very blood.' He studied his reflection in the void-hardened glass of the tanks. A thin face looked back, sallow and marked by scar tissue and minor inflammation around the nodal insertion points that dotted his skull. Metallic arachnid limbs, topped by blades, saws and glistening syringes, rose over his hunched frame, twitching in time to some faint modulation. The skull-topped sceptre he leaned on glowed faintly with an unnatural radiance. Power thrummed through it, sinister and greedy. It yearned to be used. An amplifier, its slightest touch could elicit a raging torrent of agony in even the strongest subject. Hence its name – Torment.

Even clad in power armour, Bile was gaunt, like a parasite hunched inside the hollowed-out body of its victim. The deep purple of the ceramite had faded to a dull hue, and bare patches of grey showed through in places where it was not hidden beneath his coat of stretched, screaming faces. Like the ostentatious name of his sceptre, the coat was a sign of an instinctual theatrical indulgence. Such monstrous whimsy was hardwired into the genetics of the Third Legion, as much a part of them as their hair colour and pallor.

'It cannot be helped, I suppose. Blood will out.' He activated his armour's vox-recorder. It was an old habit, and one he saw no reason to break. Even the most mundane of his musings were of value, he'd found. Idle fancies on the nature of progenoid cultivation could be traded to lesser Apothecaries for substantial gains, in raw materials or even necessary technologies. His researches were responsible for the survival of more than one Legion lurking in Eyespace, whether they'd admit it or not. And most wouldn't.

His name was a curse among his brothers. They had their reasons. No man loves the surgeon who removes his limb, gangrenous or not. Fortunately, Bile did not require love. He required isolation and respect, two things he had in abundance. For the moment, at least. He traded his skills as an Apothecary for protection, for resources, for whatever he needed. He bore no grudges from his previous life, no old hostilities. The Legion Wars were done, and whatever martial ambitions he might once have harboured with them.

'All things end. That is the nature of this universe. All of us are destined to be ash, scattered across sand. All save you. And those who will come after.' Bile peered into the nutrient-tanks, taking note of the changes already being wrought in those youthful physiologies. He had perfected the implantation of certain organs and glands, necessary to the extension and expansion of human potential. While these children would not become the ideal, as exemplified by a Space Marine, they would be more than human. And, best of all, completely stable. They would be stronger, faster, more aggressive than the standard template. More suited for survival in this harsh universe.

'We are deceptively fragile things, my brothers and I. We stand as citadels, our bastions replete with hidden flaws and weaknesses. At our height, we might have ruled. But now, we crumble, like all things must. But in our ruination is the seed of what might be.'

That was his work now. His great responsibility. To improve upon the flawed designs of those who'd come before, and seed the stars with a New Man – one adapted to the grim darkness of the current millennium. The children in the nutrient-tanks would be among the first generation of that new species. The alterations he was making to them would be passed along, down through their progeny, to future generations. They were the foundation stones of his new race, chosen for viability and adaptability.

'And you will thank me,' he said. 'You will know me, and venerate my works, for I shall not abandon you, as my father abandoned me, and his father, him. Wherever you go, whatever your triumphs, I shall be at your side, one hand upon your shoulders. For am I not your progenitor? Did I not pluck you from obscurity, to raise you chosen up, as I have your brothers and sisters?'

Vesalius' hold was full of cryogenic sarcophagi, of his own design, each one containing a sleeping body. Children mostly, some older, some younger. The Flesh-Tithe, his servants called it. He had worked miracles upon many worlds, and those worlds repaid him in raw materials. The firstborn sons and daughters of noble houses slumbered beside orphans taken from industrial factory-worlds, or feral children who had once roamed the underhives of a dozen worlds. Some came willingly, aware of the honour of being selected. Others had to be rounded up by his servants on those worlds.

Over the centuries, he had seeded innumerable worlds with his creations. Clones, transhumans, specially bred mutants – these saw to his will. They ruled in his name, or twisted planetary bureaucracies to suit his needs. Some served simply to ensure that planetary defence fleets patrolled a certain sector, on a certain cycle, or to hide evidence of his genetic harvest among their tithing to the bloodless inheritors of the legacies of the Legions of the First Founding. It would not do for the tottering husk of the Imperium to discover the full extent of his activities, and his creations worked to protect his secrets.

All were his children. In spirit, if not in biology.

'As you are my children,' he said, to the shapes slumbering in their nutrient-tanks. His smile of satisfaction faltered. Once, there had been another who might have claimed that distinction. A daughter of his flesh, drawn fully-grown from his womb-vats, and draped in damask and silk. Her face filled his mind's eye for a moment, before he banished it. His first true creation, and possibly his last. Unique in all the galaxy, built from blood and possibility.

Wherever she was, she was no use to him now. He felt no anger at the thought. She had chosen her path, as he had created her to do. That her path had not been his had been a miscalculation on his part, rather than a mistake on hers. She existed, and that was enough. She lived and her living was a sign he was not mad, whatever others claimed.

Bile often pondered the matter of his sanity. While the distinction between reason and lunacy for veterans of the Long War was often so miniscule as to be meaningless, he nonetheless found himself considering it at odd moments. Perhaps it was because his mind was all he had. The flesh he wore was not his original flesh. This body was not his first, nor would it be his last. The blight, which clung to his genetic code even now, saw to that. But his mind... his mind was the aleph around which the entirety of his existence rotated. Without his mind, he was nothing.

Behind him, something chuckled.

He tensed, his grip on Torment tightening. Hololithic targeting overlays shimmered to life before his eyes, and the sensor feed of his armour crackled as it became active. His hand dropped to the Xyclos needler holstered on his hip. He had designed the weapon himself. He often had a need to test new chemical concoctions under battlefield conditions. Even the smallest scratch from one of the thin darts it fired could induce madness or death.

'Show yourself,' he said. Whatever it was likely wasn't sapient in any true fashion. Even the ones that talked were just parroting mortal responses. He wondered what sort of being it was. Sometimes, things slipped past *Vesalius'* Gellar field. The frigate was old, and its systems often worked in strange ways.

Too, the ship's machine-spirit had a decidedly crude sense of humour. More than once, it had let a warp-entity aboard, only to trap the creature on one of the lower decks, and study it at length through its internal sensors. Sometimes, he suspected that *Vesalius* might have a thirst for knowledge rivalling his own. 'Is this another of your pranks, *Vesalius*?'

A signal-rune flashed crimson. A lifetime living in the Eye of Terror had necessitated the devising of new sorts of sensors, ones that could detect fluctuations in the very substance of reality. A slight ripple in his vitreous humour and a taste of ashes added to his growing sense of unease. The sterile air of the laboratorium was tainted by something raw and damp. '*Vesalius* – initiate laboratorium lockdown procedures Stanislaw-Omega.'

Air hissed as the locking mechanisms built into the laboratorium's single bulkhead sealed. Plasteel shutters slid down, further isolating the chamber. Whatever was in here wasn't getting out until he said so. Bile drew his needler. 'Now, the question you must ask yourself is this – why would I risk trapping myself in here with you?'

He turned slowly, letting his targeting systems do their job. The overlays expanded and contracted, cataloguing information, closing in on the source of disturbance. 'Perhaps, it is because I lack fear. Especially of some warp-spawned scavenger.'

Another red rune flashed. He swung the needler around. Nothing. He ground rotting teeth in frustration. 'Or maybe it's confidence. I have faced the worst horrors of deep space and found them to be momentary diversions, at best.'

A laugh. Low and guttural. It reverberated through the chamber, rattling the specimen jars on their shelves. The children stirred in their tanks, as if beset by nightmares. Bile hissed in frustration. 'Come out now, and perhaps I will kill you before I dissect you.'

More laughter. Bile grimaced. 'Laugh if you wish, but know this – I have ways of maintaining the integrity of warp-spawn, however much they might wish otherwise. You might be nothing but a figment of delirium given solidity by a random confluence of interdimensional phenomena, but I will make you howl regardless.' He levelled the needler, as his targeting overlay pinged. 'Even figments can bleed.'

As he spoke, the warp-entity condensed out of empty air, a mass of teeth and tendrils. It had too many mouths and each one was speaking in a different language. It smashed aside equipment racks and cogitator banks in its rush to grapple with him. Bile didn't move. He couldn't risk it damaging his nutrient-tanks, or the precious specimens within. The Xyclos needler hissed, peppering rubbery flesh with silvery splinters.

The daemon shrieked and slammed sucker-laced tendrils down on him. The force of the blow drove him to one knee, and his armour's internal monitoring systems shrieked a warning. Torment clattered from his grip, growling in frustration as it rolled away. The daemon flushed from pink to purple, and the cancerous mass at the heart of the lashing tendrils split open to disgorge an oscillating maw of shimmering, diamond-like teeth. He had no doubt that those teeth could crack ceramite. Where the needler's splinters had pierced it, its sorcerously constructed flesh was going septic, but not quickly enough.

Tendrils looped about his arms and throat. With a thought, he activated the chirurgeon. He had designed the complex harness himself. It clung to his shoulders and spine with a strength that surprised even him, at times, and its spidery limbs often had a will of their own. At the moment, however, it seemed inclined to obey his commands. Syringes and cutting blades lanced out as a bone-drill whirred to life. The daemon squealed in what he hoped to be pain. It was hard to tell with such creatures.

Despite that, its tendrils still entangled him, and with crushing strength, pulled him closer to its oscillating maw. A sweet smell like rotten fruit washed over him as the chirurgeon continued its butchery. Hissing ichors splattered cogitator consoles and specimen jars. But the daemon refused to release him.

'Stubborn brute – as single-minded as all your kind.'

When he spotted the sigils branded on what passed for its flesh, he realised why. Someone had summoned this creature, and sent it after him. There was no way of telling how long it had been hunting him, waiting for its moment to strike. This was not the first time such a thing had occurred – his enemies were without number, and prone to excess.

He tore his arm free of its coils and groped for the largest of the sigils. Its flesh felt like rubber stretched across wet sand. He dug his fingers in, trusting the ancient servos within his gauntlet to give him the strength he required. Unnatural tissue tore with a wet sound. He peeled the mark away, and a coruscating smoke spewed from the wound.

The daemon shuddered, wailing from its many mouths. 'Felt that, did you?' Bile said. As it thrashed, he freed the needler and took aim at the emptiness beyond the spinning circle of teeth. He fired, emptying the needler's cylinder. Its tendrils whipped away from him as it slammed backwards into the bulkhead. Opalescent smoke gouted from between its fangs. It was screaming now, babbling in a hundred languages, begging for mercy, cursing him, swearing vengeance, every mouth shrieking something different.

He examined the twitching scrap of meat he'd harvested. He'd hoped the creature would disappear with the sigil's removal. Then, there might be other bindings. The scrap pulsed in his grip, as if it might persist separate from the whole. He deposited it an empty specimen jar. The jars were marked with such symbols as would keep the sample fresh and stable. Wiping his fingers on his coat, he retrieved Torment and stalked towards the weeping, shivering mass now slumped on the floor of the laboratorium. A rotting tendril slashed out at him, coming apart in fragrant chunks when he batted it aside with Torment. 'Still some fight left in you. Good.'

At his thought, the chirurgeon clicked eagerly. Its blades gleamed as it readied itself for the harvest. The pulsating mass squirmed back from him, losing parts of itself with every undulation. He'd been right after all. It was coming apart, thanks to the excision of the binding rune. Eyes like tumours opened in its body, and fixed him with a communal glare. He paused. There wasn't anger there, or even frustration. No, it was… calculation? Glee?

Sensors shrilled a warning, as something caught him around the scalp and jerked him backwards. The daemon wasn't alone. He crashed down amidst steel racks of fibre bundles and prosthetic limbs. Jars containing Catalepsean nodes, occulobes and Betcher's glands toppled from their shelves and smashed to the floor around him. The waste of such valuable materials sent a thrill of anger through him, and he surged up with a snarl, Torment raised. A second creature, much like the first, spun towards him, barbed tendrils slashing.

Before it could reach him, something fell upon it with a feline snarl. Bile skidded to a halt, startled by the sudden intervention. A third daemon had pounced upon the second. This one was of a more highly developed breed, and his sensors began to analyse its shape, cataloguing it for further study. Daemons came in as many shapes as there were stars in the firmament, and no two were truly alike, despite what some sages contended. Even those with a stable manifestation often took on unique qualities, as if they were individuals rather than mere manifestations of a psychic gestalt.

The newcomer tore tendrils from the oval body of its prey, splattering the walls and floor with ichors. The daemon let loose a high-pitched shriek and cast its attacker aside. Before it could recover, Bile pinned it to the deck with a boot and brought Torment down with bone-cracking force. The inhuman shape spasmed, venting noxious gases. Torment throbbed in his grip as he struck the warp-entity again and again, until it was an unrecognizable heap.

The first daemon surged towards him, even as he stepped back. Its flesh sloughed away as it lunged, teeth snapping. He smashed it from the air and trod upon it, bursting a glaring eye. It shuddered and went still.

The newcomer rose to its full height with a sigh. 'Hello, Fabius. I felt you thinking of me.' The creature smiled prettily. Her features were almost human, almost lovely, but not quite. She wore a diaphanous robe, which did little to obscure what lay beneath it. Horns of glossy black, veined with red, curled tightly against either side of her narrow skull. A thick mane of stiff, quill-like hair spilled down her back and shoulders. Clawed fingers, clad in gold, dripped with the ichors of the daemon she'd attacked. Eyes like red mirrors stared out of a face at once familiar and odd. A beautiful face, androgynous and strange. Once, long ago, he might have seen a similar face reflected back at him.

'Melusine,' he said, softly. Memories of a child, growing at an enhanced rate, filled his head unbidden. From foetus to adult in a few weeks. But human seeming, for all that he'd included other elements in her genetic makeup. At least then.

His first attempt at creating something of his own. The first child of his nutrient-vats, grown rather than altered. He had seen her only a few times since the day she'd left his apothecarium in Canticle City. 'You are much changed, since last we spoke, Melusine,' Bile said. 'Where have you been?'

'I have been dancing in the court of Slaanesh, and promenaded through the gardens of Nurgle. I have watched the fires of Khorne's forges burn the horizons, and traded bits of dreamstuff with the caged seers of Tzeentch.' She spun in a slow pirouette as she spoke. 'I have been everywhere and nowhere and now, I am here.' She stopped and stared at him. He recognised the look, though her eyes, her face, were different.

'Why?'

'To save you. Did you get my message? I haven't sent it yet, but I thought you might have received it.' She spoke at wrong angles, tangling words in awkward shapes. It had been endearing, at first. Some of it was affectation, he suspected. The rest... insanity, possibly. Had she ever been sane, truly? Perhaps not.

She cocked her head, studying him with goatish eyes, and he wondered if she could hear his thoughts. It wouldn't surprise him. Who knew what she might've learned, in her centuries lost to the warp. He cleared his throat. 'Message? No. My apologies. I've been preoccupied. How are you, my dear?' It hurt him somewhat to see how much his creation had altered, in her time in the wilderness. She had degenerated further since the last time they'd spoken.

Too much the daemon, too little the mortal. And less of the latter every time he saw her. One day, he might not even recognise his own handiwork.

'I yet persist, as you created me to do.' She ran a finger along one of her horns. 'Do you like them? I dreamed of them, waiting between worlds, and then they grew. It hurt at first. It still hurts, sometimes. When I remember what pain is.' She licked her lips. 'In the courts of the Dark Prince, there is much discussion on the subject of pain. You are admired there, and they speak of you highly.'

'The horns are lovely,' Bile said. 'What message?'

She smiled. There was something of him in that smile, he thought. Perhaps the only thing of him remaining. A crooked smile for a crooked creature. 'I haven't sent it yet. I might not, now.'

'Melusine,' he said, warningly.

She frowned and flexed her claws, like an angry felinoid. 'A daemon whispered to me that you are marked. And all that bear your stamp with you.' She reached out and tapped one of the nutrient-tanks. He twitched, Torment half-raised. He forced himself to relax.

'Even you?'

'Especially her,' she said, looking away. 'But not me. Not yet. Not until I'm her.' She pressed a hand to his chest. 'She came to warn you. And I followed.'

'Why?' he asked, curious.

'Is that not a daughter's prerogative?'

'I wouldn't know,' Bile said. He ran a finger along one of her horns. 'I cannot decide whether this is an improvement or not.' He looked at the dissolving carcasses dirtying the floor of his laboratorium. 'Who sent them?' There were any number of potential candidates. The Eye knew no lack of sorcerers – the sons of Magnus, or Lorgar's fanatical brood.

She laughed and slid out of reach. 'I don't know. Me, maybe. Or someone else. There are entire races which spend their eternities chanting prayers for your destruction. There are worlds where to speak your name is to court death, and even one where you are worshipped as a saviour.'

Bile gestured dismissively. 'I have many enemies, yes. Which ones in particular initiated this assault, child?' If someone specific was after him, he needed to know. He had weathered such sieges before, and would likely do so again, before his work was complete. But the Legions still needed his expertise. He was too useful to kill out of hand. Or so he'd thought. He glanced down again at the remains of the daemons, wondering what had changed.

Melusine shook her head. 'Does it matter? Would it change anything?'

He hesitated. Then, 'No.' It was convenient that she had come when she had. But perhaps there was more to this than simple good timing.

Her smile became sad. 'No. Even when the fire comes, you will hold to your path. I saw it, then, in the moments to come.' She turned in a slow, graceful circle, hooves clicking against the deck. 'Do I please you? Will she?'

Bile looked down at her. 'Unintended results are still results.'

Melusine laughed. An old pain flared within him. For a moment, a child's face, perfect in all ways, swam before his eyes. He forced the image aside, trying to concentrate on the here and now. The creature before him was a perversion of his art. Yet another thing taken from him and twisted into something broken and useless. Had she come to kill him? That would be fitting, almost. The creator undone by his creation.

'You say such lovely things.' She pushed away from him. 'Beware the future. It comes for you, lean and a-thirst. It eats away at your possibilities, narrowing the span of potential paths to but a single road. You cannot go back, but neither must you go forward.'

'A singularly unhelpful statement, Melusine.' He reached out to stroke her cheek, half-lost in memory. As a child, he had seen in her the future. What was she now?

'I am but as you made me.' Her face twisted as she said it, and she caught his hand, holding it in place. He studied her, trying to find the traces of the child she had been. A new life, a new sort of being. The first of many, he'd hoped at the time. But then she'd grown and gone, vanishing into the vastness of the Eye of Terror. Then Fulgrim had cast down his edict and thrice-damned Lucius had shattered the other bio-crèches.

He smiled, thinly. He had nearly killed Lucius, then. Not for the first time, and probably not the last. He took some satisfaction from the memory, regardless. He was perhaps the only being Lucius the Eternal truly feared, for Bile knew how to render a Space Marine down to his bones while still keeping him alive. He'd come close to reducing Fulgrim's favoured pet to shrieking lumps of red meat and hiding him away, to spend eternity unable to do anything save think on his crimes.

After that, his attentions had been diverted down other, more blasphemous avenues of inquiry. Away from invention, to innovation. To improve upon familiar foundations, for the use of others. But still, he yearned to create... to craft something utterly unique.

'You were the first of the vat-born, you know. A new thing under the sun. Created before even the second-generation of primarchs I nurtured in Canticle City. Even before I reclaimed the carcass of the Warmaster.' He smiled, remembering. 'An experiment, a mingling of multiple genetic templates... including mine.'

'I am a daughter of your blood and bone,' she said. She stepped away from him and started to trace patterns in the condensation on one of the nutrient tanks.

'Yes. You are my daughter.' The word felt strange on his tongue. Space Marines could not breed, not without excessive modification or mutation. A check placed upon them by the Emperor. Another mistake. Why create such a race, and then bar them from achieving their full potential? Fear, perhaps. Fear of being replaced. Bile had no such worries himself – indeed, it was his intention to become obsolete. But not yet. Not until his work was complete, and his new humanity had no more need of his guiding hand.

'Am I as you expected?' she asked again, more insistently this time.

'No.' He frowned. 'Did you know that was the only time Fulgrim ever forbade me from indulging my creativity? He was... horrified. Or so he claimed. Imagine that: a monstrosity such as the Phoenician had become, horrified by a child. I suspect that moment was when I began to take issue with that whole charade of his... Like father, like son, I suppose.' He remembered Fulgrim rising above him, serpentine coils rattling in titanic fury. The wrath of a god, or something close. He could not recall being afraid. Even then, fear had been all but burned out of him.

'Like parent, like child.'

'Yes. So it seems.' She had never called him father. He had discouraged such familiarity in those days, finding it distasteful. His attitudes had mellowed somewhat, in the intervening centuries. Encouraging paternal ties aided in strengthening bonds of loyalty between himself and his creations. Perhaps, if he'd allowed her to call him father, she might not have followed the sibilant whispers of the warp. 'Have you come to kill me, Melusine?'

She looked at him. 'I don't know,' she said. She stared into one of the nutrient-tanks. A young girl floated within, curled into a foetal ball. 'Is she my replacement? Or will I be hers, when the time comes?' Her tone was one of accusation. He tensed. He did not wish to destroy her, but he would. She would not be the first product of his genius that he'd been forced to put down.

'There can be no replacing you, my child.' Bile extended his hand, but she stepped back. He held out his hand for a moment, but then let it drop. 'You were my first. As you shall always be. Horns and all.'

'I dreamed them.'

'Yes,' he said. Her eyes grew unfocused, and her shape wavered. His finest work, but his most flawed. Soon, he suspected that she would lose all substance, and vanish entirely. Or else become unrecognizable. Why had she come? To punish him? Or to warn him? And if so, why – a scrap of filial obligation? Or because someone or something had sent her?

He did not believe in the Dark Gods. Or any gods, for that matter.

But there were forces at play in the universe which he could not fathom.

'Why did you come, Melusine?' he asked again.

'To warn you. I was told… I was told and so I came.' The look she gave him was almost pitying. 'You have so many enemies that they make war upon one another for the right to dictate your fate.'

He was silent for a moment. Then, 'Good. If they are busy with each other, then I will have fewer distractions to contend with.'

'They said you would say that.'

He almost asked the obvious question, but restrained himself. It didn't matter. Nothing mattered except his work. Let all of the universe come against him; he would endure, and his work would endure. 'You could stay. Your help would be welcome,' he said.

'Why?' she asked, as if reading his thoughts.

'A father's prerogative,' he said. Paternal consideration was alien to him. He played at fatherhood, but it was motivated more by mockery than any deep well of emotion. Was this what the Emperor had felt, when he saw what Horus and Fulgrim had become? He wanted to hold her, to clasp her to him, until she was again what she had once been. Proof of his sanity, in an insane universe. 'Do you remember when I taught you the proper way to hold a scalpel, my child? When I showed you how to flense tissue from bone?'

She stared at the child in the nutrient-tank. 'No,' she said, and her voice was small. So small. His hands clenched, and Torment whined in his grip. That something of his had been reduced to such a state infuriated him. She looked at him, her face a porcelain mask. 'I came to warn you, but I was too late, wasn't I?'

'No,' he said, gently. 'No, I am still here.'

'I do not like talking to ghosts,' she said. 'Goodbye.'

And then she was gone. As swiftly as she'd appeared. Leaving behind the faintest whiff of sulphur and cinnamon. The laboratorium's systems flickered again. Readouts skipped across his overlay, as the ship's systems returned to normal. The Gellar field had experienced a minor disruption, but was functioning at optimum levels now.

Bile suddenly felt tired. He leaned forward on his sceptre, gazing at the nutrient-tanks. Were these children doomed to madness as well? And if so, what then? Was it all nothing more than a lunatic's dream?

Perhaps his mind had gone, after all. Perhaps...

He blinked, studying the marks Melusine had left on the nutrient-tank. A word. Just one – 'Father'. He laughed, as Melusine's words came back to him: *Even when the fire comes, you will hold to your path. I saw it, then, in the moments to come.*

Bile smiled. 'Yes, I suppose I must.'

Mad or not, he had a responsibility. A duty to bring about the next steps in humanity's long journey towards its proper place in the universe. The galaxy would burn, and from its ashes would rise a new people. His people.

Whatever came, they would endure. They would persist.

His children.

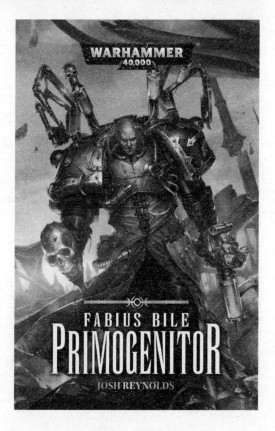

VEIL OF DARKNESS

Nick Kyme

Introducing

CATO SICARIUS

CAPTAIN, ULTRAMARINES

'I am the Undying. I am doom incarnate…'

It towered over me, this monster of living metal. It wore a crown with a red gemstone, torcs banded its mechanised arms and an azure pectoral hung around its neck. These were royal trappings. Here I fought a king of the dead, a robotic anachronism of an old and conceited culture, full of darkest anima.

Necrons, they were called. Its regal status only spurred me on.

'We are the slayers of kings!' I declared, spitting the words in anger at the gilded monster before me.

We fought alone, the monster and I. None interfered. I had drawn only my sword. For my victory to have any meaning, this was how it had to be. Even terms, its crackling war-scythe matched against my venerable Tempest Blade. But in the end, it was not my sword that was found wanting…

After a savage duel, it cut me deeply. No foe had ever done that before. And with blood filling my mouth, I fell. I, Cato Sicarius, Master of the Watch, Knight Champion of Macragge, Grand Duke of Talassar and High Suzerain of Ultramar, fell.

And as the veil of darkness wrapped around me like a funerary shroud, I heard the monster's words again...

'I am doom.'

I came around coughing up amniotic fluid, spraying the inside of the revivification casket. I roared, thundering my fist against the glass, my muscles and nerves suddenly aflame.

'Release me!' I spat, half-choking.

Locking clamps around the casket disengaged, admitting me back to the world of the living. I arrived breathing hard, sitting in a half-capsule of briny, viscous liquid and murderously staring down my Apothecary.

'Welcome back, brother-captain.'

Lathered in gelatinous filth, I scowled. 'Venatio.'

My Apothecary had the good grace to nod.

He was wearing his full armour-plate, white to identify his vocation as a medic rather than the ubiquitous Ultramarine-blue of our Chapter, but he went without a helmet. An ageing veteran of my command squad, Venatio's hair was fair, closely cropped, and he had dark green eyes that had seen too much of death.

It was dark in the apothecarion, shadows suggesting the shape of various machines and devices the Chapter medics employed in the service of preserving life. The air reeked of counterseptic and a fine mist clouded the floor. It was clean, cold; a desolate place. How many had come through these halls bloody and broken? How many had arrived and never left? Always too many.

I made to rise but Venatio lifted a gauntleted hand to stop me.

'Don't presume you can keep me from climbing out of this casket,' I warned him.

The hand gesture became placatory. 'Let me at least run a full bio-scan first.'

Venatio had the device in his other hand and was already conducting his test, so I endured the amniotic filth a little longer. When he was done, I refused his proffered hand and extricated myself without his help. My side ached. Once I was out of the casket and standing on the tiled floor, I looked down and saw why. An angry scar puckered my flesh from where the Undying's war-scythe had cleaved me.

'It's remarkable you are even alive, let alone walking, brother-captain,' the Apothecary said, consulting biometric data from his scanner.

'I'll do more than walk,' I promised vengefully, but realised I had no knowledge of what had happened after I had collapsed. 'What of Damnos? Were the Second victorious?'

Venatio's already severe expression darkened, pinching together the age lines of his face.

'After your defeat, Agrippen and Lord Tigurius rallied the men. But we had badly underestimated the enemy and were forced to evacuate. Damnos is lost.' He lowered his voice. 'So too Venerable Agrippen.'

I clenched my fist so hard that the knuckles cracked. It was a sparse chamber we occupied; much of the apothecarion's equipment was situated at its periphery with only my amniotic casket within striking distance. I hit it hard, putting a fissure in the glass. Had I my Tempest Blade at hand, I might have cut it apart. Galling was not the word.

I was about to ask Venatio to tell me more when another voice from the shadows, a presence I hadn't noticed in my recently revived state, interrupted.

'I had to see it for myself...'

A son of Ultramar, *the* son of Ultramar, if some amongst the Chapter were to be believed, stepped into the light. He too was fully clad, his plumed helmet sitting in the crook of his left arm, a ceremonial gladius strapped to his left leg. Gilt-edged shoulder guards and breastplate shone in the lambent lumen-strip above us, and his war-plate was festooned with the laurels of his many years of vaunted service.

'Severus.' I bowed my head out of respect for the veteran, but his stern expression, hardened further by his scars and the platinum studs embedded in his bald forehead, suggested he came here with ill news.

'Cato.'

I hated the fact he used my given name, though I knew he hated me for doing so first. We were rivals, he and I. Severus Agemman was my predecessor as Captain of the Second. He in turn succeeded Saul Invictus after the great hero fell at Macragge. Now he stood as Calgar's right hand, and I beneath him. We were rivals because our war philosophy was very different. Agemman was a blunt but effective adherent to the Codex Astartes, whereas I *interpreted* our primarch's teachings and was less predictable. Some have said reckless. Only Agemman has ever said so to my face.

He smiled, but it was a cold, pitiless gesture.

Out with it then.

'I wish I could I report I was here merely to see the dead brought back to life...' Agemman gestured to the formidable scar raking my side. The smile faded to the thin, hard line of his mouth. 'But, I cannot. You are to stand before Lord Calgar. The Chapter Master would have knowledge of what happened on Damnos and why we returned to the empire in ignominious defeat.'

My eyes narrowed, but I held my temper. An argument here, now, with Venatio looking on, would serve no good purpose.

'And am I to be held responsible for this defeat? I know that whilst I yet stood, the warriors of the Second were not routed.'

Agemman refused to be baited. He was rigid, and a pain in the arse for that.

'You have six hours to prepare your testimony.'

'My *testimony*? Am I to be judged then?'

My opponent betrayed no emotion, though I refuse to believe he did not take some petty pleasure in all of this.

'The events on Damnos were disastrous. Questions must be asked.'

I began to walk towards the chamber door, still dripping.

'Then let us go now. I have nothing to hide and don't need six hours to realise that.'

Agemman put his armoured bulk in my path.

'Cease this wanton disregard for orders, Sicarius! Your reckless behaviour is what has brought you to this point.' He calmed down, though it took some effort to reassert the mask of control he had been wearing ever since addressing me from the shadows. 'It seems you have yet to learn that.'

'Don't speak to me like a neophyte, Agemman,' I warned. 'As they have on countless occasions, my swift actions prevented an earlier defeat. I prefer to win hard battles, not easy campaigns and reap the hollow glory. Next time you behold my banner on the field, look at the victories upon it and then look to your own.'

I goaded him out of a desire to return the disrespect he had just afforded me. I vaunted the First, and their captain. They were some of the bravest and most capable warriors in the Chapter, but that didn't mean I had to like them.

Agemman had every right to strike me. To my irritation, he resisted, but as he spoke through clenched teeth I knew he'd come close.

'Six hours.'

Agemman left the apothecarion without another word. He'd be saving them for my trial, no doubt.

To his credit, Venatio said nothing. He merely gave his professional report.

'You are fit to resume your duties, brother-captain.'

At a command from the Apothecary, a serf entered the room from a side chamber and began scraping the remaining amniotic gel from my skin.

Still seething after Agemman's exit, I nodded to Venatio.

'Tell me, Brother-Apothecary. Where are my armour and weapons?'

'The Techmarines have been repairing them. I understand there was much damage to the war-plate in particular. You'll find them in the armourium. East wing.'

Dismissing the serf, I grunted a word of gratitude to Venatio and left for the weapon workshops. Something in the penumbra around the apothecarion had set me on edge and I desired the return of my war trappings as soon as possible.

The Fortress of Hera is a vast and near-impregnable bastion. It is the noble seat of Macragge, the slab-sided barrack house of the Ultramarines Chapter, and has always been so. Its armouriums, battle cages and shrines are many. We all worship at them in our own way, these temples of violence and honour. I found Techmarine Vantor easily enough.

Like the apothecarion, the armourium was dark, but far from cold. It radiated heat that prickled the air and raked my nostrils. There was smoke and flame, ash and the taste of metal. Great engines tended by serf-engineers and cyberorganic servitors pummelled iron and steel. Here, the artefacts of war were repaired and manufactured. On a metal dais, a Rhino armoured transport lay gutted, whilst incense was burned and canticles of function were invoked. At a great anvil, blades were tempered and honed by hammer-armed servitors. Workshops were arrayed in multitudes with their rows of dark iron benches and churning machineries.

All of this fell into insignificance, however. For nearest to me was a servo-armed Techmarine, stooped over a suit of magnificent power armour.

It was good to see it again. It would feel even better to don it.

'Brother...' I announced my presence at the armourium's door, which had slid open to admit me into the expansive workshop.

Vantor turned at the sound of my voice, his bionics grinding noisily as he moved.

He bowed slightly. 'Captain Sicarius, I have almost finished my ministrations to your armour.' Spoken through the vox-grille covering his mouth, the Techmarine's voice was as mechanised as his right arm and leg. 'I'm sure you'll be pleased to learn that, like you, it yet lives.'

I always found it curious, the way the adherents of the Cult Mechanicus regarded inanimate adamantium and ceramite. Vantor

had not only been repairing my armour, but also had been sooth-
ing its machine-spirit too. As a Techmarine, Vantor wore not the
blue of the Ultramarines but the red of the Martian world where
he had received his clandestine training. Only his shoulder pad
remained the blue of Ultramar as a concession to his dual fealty.

'Indeed I am, brother. I long to wear it again, and feel the grip
of my Tempest Blade in my–' I stopped abruptly, my eye drawn
to a work-team of servitors labouring at the back of the chamber.

I could not disguise my anger. 'What in Terra's name is that?'

Beyond the honest industry of the armourium, beyond the slow
beaten battleplate and forged blades, the tanks and engines, was
an abomination.

Vantor turned, incredulous.

'Frag, shrapnel. They are what remnants of the enemy we managed to salvage before the evacuation.'

Ranked up, steadily being logged and categorized, examined and
tested, were pieces of the necron. Heads, fingers, limbs, even broken portions of their weaponry, were under heavy scrutiny by the
Techmarine's lobotomised serfs. I counted over twenty different
benches of the material.

The urge to grasp my sword deepened.

'They are inactive, I take it?'

Vantor nodded. 'Of course, but by studying even the inert pieces
of necron technology we can develop our knowledge of them.'

The fact that the Techmarine could neither see nor appreciate the
danger in bringing this flotsam into our fortress-monastery only
served to show the gulf between us in sharper relief.

I walked through the workshop, Vantor following, and approached
one of the work benches where a servitor was toiling over an array
of limbs, heads, even torso sections. I reached out to touch one of
the silver skulls, its rictus grin mocking me even in destruction, but
fell just short of touching it.

'How are they even here? I am no expert on the necron, but aren't
they supposed to disappear when destroyed?'

Vantor came to stand beside me. A blurt of binaric dismissed the servitor and set it to another task.

'Apparently, the Damnosian natives found a way to retard that ability through magnetism.'

I frowned at Vantor. 'Really? A human colony with rudimentary engineering ability, using only electromagnets and a theory, achieves what the Mechanicus couldn't?'

'I was similarly unconvinced, and yet...' He gestured to the workshop full of deactivated components.

'I would not have sanctioned this research,' I declared. My gaze lingered on one skull in particular. There was something strangely familiar about it.

He blinked, his very human eyes like flashes of burned umber.

'Lord Calgar agrees that our knowledge of this enemy is of paramount importance if we are to fight it effectively.'

'We fought effectively enough,' I replied, my manner absent-minded as I drew closer to the skull. Like a siren it seemed to call to me, beckoning, reminding...

I felt the darkness close, the veil around me tightening and suffocating. Vantor's next words were lost in this fog as was my response. All I could see was the skull, the eyes aglow and its rictus grin. I reached for my blade but grasped air, neither hilt nor scabbard. Legs buckling, unable to hold my weight, I fell to my knees and gasped. The air would not come. I was drowning with no ocean for miles, save the one of oil and blackness devouring me. Everything surrendered to the dark: Vantor, the armourium, the serfs, my armour – all was consumed. Only I remained, staring down the lidless orbs of that gilded, grinning skull.

'I am doom...'

The last of my breath ghosted the air as an icy chill came over me. I felt ice underfoot, though I was still inside the fortress-monastery, and a low rumbling tremor in its frigid depths...

I breathed and the darkness crowding my vision bled away at once like ink dispersed in water. The ice melted and I resurfaced.

The necron skull was in my hands, grasped tight. Its eyes were lifeless, dead in their sockets, a rusty patina weathering cheeks, pate and temples of gunmetal grey. Not gold. Not the king. Not here.

Vantor was gone – only the servitors were left and I assumed he had let me stay here to peruse the battlefield relics as if I alone could unlock some secret by merely looking at him. He hadn't realised I had become lost in a dream.

The wound in my side flared anew and I grimaced to keep the pain at bay.

My armour was waiting for me, a gift from Vantor.

I took it, eager to leave the armourium and the unquiet resonance it had stirred inside me. I needed to ease my mind. It had been never so pure and focused as when in combat. I headed at once for the battle cages.

I found an old comrade in the lonely arena.

Daceus was the only warrior sparring that night and I crossed a gloomy threshold of empty cages, their servitors dormant and inactive within, to reach him.

'Brother-sergeant,' I called up to him, having to raise my voice above the punishing din of his sword blade striking the vital kill-points of the combat servitor he had chosen to pit himself against. It was a grossly uneven contest, of course. Daceus could have wrecked the machine many times over but was here to practise his form and test his stamina, not incur the wrath of the Techmarines by needlessly dismantling servitors.

'Pause routine,' he uttered breathlessly and looked down at me, his face mildly beaded with sweat. Daceus saluted, sword in front of his body. 'Brother-captain, I am glad to see you returned to us.'

'I hoped to bless the reunion with honest combat.'

Ever the martial exemplar, Daceus stepped aside and hammered the icon which opened the cage door with his fist.

'Then let us see what benedictions you might offer.'

Already, he was measuring my combat efficacy, observing, strategising. My brother-sergeant wanted to know how sharp my fighting edge was. So did I.

Using the Tempest Blade in the battle cage would dishonour the weapon and put me at an unfair advantage, so I selected a training gladius from the rack to match the one wielded by my opponent. The balance was good, the blade straight and sharp despite the many hours of practice bouts it must have endured. It was no master-crafted weapon, but it was a worthy one.

'Helmets on or off, brother?' asked Daceus. Here in the cages, once blades were drawn, rank ceased to have meaning.

'Off. I want to be able to breathe and use my senses without hindrance.'

'Agreed. No strikes above the neck then. First to three hits?'

I nodded, taking up a fighting stance in my power armour. Vantor would be annoyed if I scratched it so soon, but I believed war-plate needed scars before going into battle proper.

'Begin.'

Daceus's first thrust was quick and aimed at my torso. I barely parried it before a second lunge caught me off guard and took a chip out of my plastron.

We paused and returned to our initial engagement positions.

'First hit is yours, brother.' I tried, and failed, to hide my annoyance. 'Again.'

Daceus chopped downwards, high to low, and I managed a hasty block in response. Stepping back, I invited him to advance, which he did with a swift back to forehand slash. I used a hilt guard to protect myself and forged a jab of my own, but Daceus deflected it easily and used the kinetic momentum to rotate his blade into a half circling up and over slash that smashed against my clavicle and put me down on one knee.

I was sweating, but Daceus returned to the initial engagement position and did not dishonour me by offering me a hand up.

'That's two,' he said with the barest hint of a smile.

Now I was burning with shameful anger. Returning to position, I adopted a ready stance. 'Again.'

This time I swept in low, beneath the crossways slash crafted by my opponent and went in under Daceus's guard. He stabbed downwards, a makeshift block, and our blades clashed. But the force pushed his sword hand outwards and I used the weakness to hammer my shoulder into his solar plexus. Daceus reeled, staggering back to regain footing, but I pressed my attack, first using an overhead slash to break open his flailing guard, then delivering a diagonal uppercut that put a groove in his plastron and pulled him to the ground.

We went again, this time exchanging a flurry of blows, feints and blocks. Our blades became a blur of clashing steel and I began to feel like my old self again. After a brutal riposte, I swapped hands mid sword flourish and smacked the flat of my gladius against Daceus's gorget.

He gasped as the blade came close to his neck: a foul stroke.

I ignored his slight shock and returned to position.

'Evens, two hits apiece. Again.'

As I moved through the blade disciplines, the finely crafted sword strokes, I felt a background pulse directly behind my eyes. It was like an intense headache, a drum inside my skull, pounding in time with my heartbeat.

Shadows flooded the arena that housed the battle cages; it had been this way since I had entered. But now, the darkness began to coalesce and I felt it close around me like a slow clenching fist. A silent predator lying in wait, it crouched at the edge of my vision and from somewhere distant I felt a chill enter my bones.

It was snowing, the battle cage far away and forgotten as an arctic tundra overwhelmed it in my senses. At the edge of a frost-encrusted ruin, the veil of darkness persisted. Through the black fog, an enemy emerged.

'I am doom...'

Beneath my feet, the ice trembled like the beating of some immense heart.

The king had returned, in all his gilded and terrible majesty.

We clashed, I with the Tempest Blade crackling in my gauntleted fist, the primarch's name on my lips like an unsheathed sword.

The king swung his war-scythe around, the great reaping edge like a crescent moon cut from the bleakest night and fashioned into a weapon. Our blades struck together in a cascade of sparks and we broke apart. I took a moment's respite but the necron king needed none, his anima fuelled by some ancient will and driven by the machine he had surrendered his mortal flesh to become. Massive, overpowering, he loomed over me in seconds.

'Not again!' I roared. 'I am a Lion of Macragge, I am Master of the Watch. A slayer of kings!' With fury born of desperation and hate, I hurled myself at the necron. His scythe haft shattered, sheared in two by my blade and I battered his weary defence as he threw up his arms in surrender.

'No mercy for you,' I vowed, raining down blows until my shoulder ached and my lungs were fit to burst.

Breath did not come. I was drowning again and the veil of darkness crept into my field of vision, smothering and denying me my prey.

'No! I will not be cheated of my victory. Not again, not–'

As I collapsed, retching what I thought was fluid from my chest but bringing up only air, I saw Daceus.

His gladius was broken, split along the blade. His vambraces were hacked apart, his face awash with shock and anger.

'My brother…' I struggled to gasp, falling. Daceus, despite my wounding of him, rose up to catch me.

At the doleful clang of our power armour meeting, I resurfaced from the dream and the pool of dark imaginings that choked me.

'Brother-captain…' He sounded panicked. I waved his concern away, and stood up unaided.

'I am all right. And you?' I asked, gesturing to his battered war-plate.

'A scratch,' he lied, then frowned. 'What happened?'

I saw no sense in hiding the truth, so I told him of what I had seen, of my slayer reborn, of the duel I thought I was fighting against *him*.

'I could have killed you, Daceus.'

'But you did not.'

But I could have. I almost did.

A remnant from Damnos, some revenant I had brought with me, lingered. I felt the chill of it in the air around me and the dull pain in my side. I saw it in the shadows, the veil of darkness which harboured monsters of cold steel and viridian fire.

Something in the gloom around us caught my attention and I seized the Tempest Blade, throwing a fresh sword from the rack to Daceus at the same time.

'What is it?' The sergeant caught the blade easily and swung around, trying to follow my gaze.

I whispered, 'Are we alone?'

Daceus nodded slowly and I eased open the door to the cage.

'Not any more...' I told him.

Together, we crept from the battle cage and spread out. My eyes never left the exact spot where I had seen movement, and I battle-signed the enclosing manoeuvre to the sergeant.

As well as the battle cages themselves, the arena had a servitor rack. It was an automated station where deactivated combat-servitors yet to be invested with sparring protocols would wait until called upon. Some sixty of the automata were currently in the rack in three rows of twenty, one surmounting the other.

More machines. More cold steel.

In the dingy arena hall, they did not look so dissimilar from the necrons displaced around the east wing armourium.

Daceus and I closed on the servitors' dormant forms. One in particular had drawn my eye. On Damnos we had seen necrons that clothed themselves in the rancid flesh of the dead, using their skins as a crude and scarcely effective form of camouflage.

I could almost swear the eye sockets of this one were aglow...

Not waiting for Daceus, I thrust with my blade, releasing an actinic blur of fused steel and energised brutality.

Impaled on my sword, I wrenched the interloper from the servitor rack and with a grunt threw it down for us to finish off.

Daceus stopped me.

'Brother-captain...' He sounded concerned, but was looking at me and not our enemy. 'It is just a servitor. Not even active.'

'Strength of Guilliman...' I breathed, before letting the Tempest Blade sag down by my side. He was right. It was just an automaton. Nothing more. No assassin clothed in flesh. 'Perhaps I left the care of Brother Venatio too soon.'

To his credit, Daceus tried to reassure me.

'You were in a suspended animation coma, brother-captain. Some... side-effects are to be expected.'

I grunted, the equivalent of a vocal shrug, and heard the chime of choral bells echo throughout the arena.

'Has it been that long?'

Daceus's eyes narrowed in confusion. 'Long for what?'

'I am to stand before Lord Calgar and be judged for my command on Damnos. I had thought I had longer to prepare.'

'It would be my honour to accompany you to the Hall of Ultramar, my lord.'

'Aye. Agreed.' I clapped Daceus on the shoulder. He was as good and loyal a soldier as any captain had a right to have in his service. 'Gratitude, brother.'

We left for the Hall of Ultramar and an audience with its regent and most august lord.

Replete in his war panoply, the Lord of Macragge was seated upon a throne like a battle king of old, and my heart both swelled with pride and trembled with awe at the sight of him. He wore his formal battleplate, a ceremonial suit festooned with laurels and awards. A pair of hefty power gloves clothed his hands, which he rested regally on the throne arms. His hair was white as hoarfrost, and he glowered at me through one organic eye. The other eye was a bionic, and even less welcoming.

'Brother-captain,' he said, radiating authority. 'Come forward.'

Here in the Hall of Ultramar, the great and noble were personified in statue form and shadowed me as I walked the long processional to a place before my lord. I saw Invictus, Helveticus and Galatan, Titus, all measuring my worth with the weight of their marble stares. I would not be found wanting.

Daceus had come with me as far as the great bronze doors, and there I had bid him stay, despite his offer to the contrary. I didn't want him caught up in this. Any judgement would be my burden to carry.

As I walked, I passed under great looming archways and saw again the shadows within the chamber's lofty vaults. I tried to avert my gaze, turning my mind to the matter at hand, but when my eyes alighted on Lord Calgar I saw a strange halo encircle his head. At first I continued with the slightest break in step, aware of not only Calgar's eyes upon me but Severus Agemman's too and the honour guard of Macragge. Then, as I drew closer, I realised that what I believed to be a trick of the light was an actual glow. No, not merely a glow, a *mark*. It was viridian green, and I saw a fraction too late what it portended.

'Get down!'

Agemman reacted first to my warning, putting himself between me, as I ran down the processional, and Calgar, who was at the other end of it. He thought I had lost all sense and was preparing to knock some back into me. I had drawn my pistol, prompting the honour guard to draw arms also. Five bolt weapons were trained on my chest in an instant. My gaze went to the eaves above us, the shadows in the vaulted roof, and I pointed to get my brothers' attention and stop them from executing me.

'Up there!'

Agemman saw it too, crouched like an iron gargoyle, the darkness as its cloak. A single eye betrayed its position, but we would be far too late to prevent it achieving its goal. In truth, the optic was a targeting matrix and Lord Calgar was in its crosshairs.

A long, slim rifle slid into its grasp. I watched it shoulder the weapon and aim it. Reality slowed, as if the assassin were chronologically a few seconds ahead of us and functioning in a different time stream.

A plume of viridian gas expelled from the rifle's vents like a breath. There was no recoil, only the expulsion of a missile that raked through the air. I followed the missile's trajectory in my peripheral vision, triggering my pistol in the same moment and setting the vaults alight with a pulse of energised plasma. The others had seen the danger now and were discharging their own weapons into the time-shifted assassin above us.

Calgar grunted, the sound someone makes when they're gut punched and the air is blasted from their lungs. Having got to his feet when the interloper had been discovered, he fell back and clattered into and then out of his throne, half rolling down the steps that led up to his seat.

We destroyed the archway where the assassin had made his nest, ripping up the shadows with streaks of blinding muzzle flash and plasma and bringing down a cascade of debris. This was the Hall of Ultramar and we had wrecked it like a band of careless thieves.

Time resumed, our weapons fell silent again, but the quarry was gone, slipped back into whatever darkness had spawned it. The assassin hadn't merely escaped, it simply wasn't there anymore, phased out like the necrons too badly damaged to self-repair. Only we hadn't destroyed it. Not even close.

With the immediate danger passed for now, Agemman was at Lord Calgar's side. The honour guard closed around them protectively like an armoured cocoon.

'Stay with the Chapter Master...' I was running back down the processional, the vaunted marble heroes urging my every step. Every footfall I took was punctuated by a glance above me, back into the shadowed roof and searching for my enemy.

Bursting through the bronze doors, I met Daceus.

The brother-sergeant was armed, having clearly heard the gun-fire from within.

'What's happened?'

I didn't linger, but kept on down the corridor, intent on reaching the east wing of the armourium where I knew an answer would be waiting. Daceus kept step.

'Our enemy is in the Fortress of Hera,' I told him. 'They have just tried to assassinate Lord Calgar.'

'Blood of Guilliman! Is he—'

I spared the brother-sergeant a stern glance. 'He lives. He *will* live.'

Daceus would chastise himself for his doubt later; now we had to reach the armourium.

I was about to raise Vantor on the vox to get a warning to the Tech-marine when the shrieking alert sirens told me I was too late. Light from the lumens and glow-globes shrank to an amber wash that overlaid the halls of the fortress-monastery in sickly monochrome.

I activated the vox in my gorget. 'Agemman.'

His reply was a few seconds late in coming.

'We're headed for the apothecarion. Brother Venatio awaits us.'

'The alert?'

'Is coming from the armourium in the east wing.'

All my fears suddenly crystallised. The memory of the necron 'corpses' returned, those that were too badly damaged to self-repair but unable to phase out. Only they weren't damaged. It was a ruse and in our ignorance we had invited them into our bastion, our home.

I wanted to hit something, but instead I bit back my anger and answered Agemman.

'Sergeant Daceus and I are on our way there now.'

I cut the link – the First Captain had enough to deal with.

As we entered the east wing, the corridors strangely abandoned, I saw the veil of darkness. Something writhed within it, something of cold steel with viridian eyes like balefires.

'Am I imagining that?'

Shaking his head, Daceus racked his bolter slide and took aim at the mechanised horrors emerging from the shadows.

The Tempest Blade is a relic of Talassar, and I am a descendent of that world's noblest household. I honoured my ancestors by bringing its fury to my enemies. A necron exoskeleton is formidable but no match for a power sword such as this. They were warrior-caste, the foot soldiery of their darkling empire. The first I vaporised with a ball of incandescent plasma, the second I beheaded. My armour was impervious to their beam weapons and I was barely slowed as I hacked the arm off a third and then bifurcated its torso. Three necrons phased out in a cascade of howling energy.

Daceus neutralised three more with precise burst-fire from his bolter. Even when one of the mechanoids was a handspan from his face, the sergeant was unflinching and maintained strict fire discipline. He tore the thing apart almost point-blank and let the frag pepper his armoured form.

When we were done and the necrons vanquished, we waded into the darkness looking for more but the veil was thinning by then and disappeared entirely in a few more seconds.

Daceus scowled. 'How many of these things are we dealing with?'

'Judging by what I saw dissected in Vantor's workshop, dozens.'

'Could they gain a foothold here, a means of bringing greater forces directly into the fortress?'

I clapped my sergeant's shoulder guard to reassure him.

'We won't let that happen, brother.'

Ahead of us, the east wing of the armourium beckoned. Its entry gate was open and a flickering light from within threw syncopated flashes into the gloom.

Inside, the armourium was a charnel house. Blood streaked the walls and machineries. It mingled with oil from the drones. Every serf, servitor and enginseer was dead. Their bodies lay strewn about the workshop, eviscerated and impaled. The luminator rig above had been damaged during the commotion and threw sporadic light

across the grisly scene. Every flash revealed a fresh horror: faces frozen in terror and death. But there was no sign of the necron, none
at all. The limbs, torsos, skulls and weaponry were all gone.

Then I saw Vantor, and my grief redoubled.

The Techmarine was dead, split from groin to neck by an
energised blade. It had cut through his artificer armour like tin.
Biological entrails entwined with cables and wires as all that com-
prised Euclidese Vantor was vented out and strewn like offal. It
was no way for my brother to meet his end. His murderers had
robbed him of glory.

I placed my gauntleted hand upon his face to close his still-staring
gaze. Even the dishonoured dead should be allowed eternal sleep.
Such was the damage done, even his gene-seed could not be
recovered.

For a moment I shut my eyes, marshalling my anger, turning it
into something useful.

The sensation of drowning came back, and the darkness in my
mind's eye returned with it. I fought it down, clenching a fist to
stay focused. Whatever trauma I was experiencing would have to
wait. I was determined to master it.

I addressed Daceus.

'A deadly enemy is at large in these halls, brother. It has already
laid low our Chapter Master and now it seeks to end us into the
bargain.' I gritted my teeth. 'We will not yield to it. We must rouse
our battle-brothers, hunt this menace down and exterminate it.'

Daceus nodded grimly and we left the armourium as we had
found it. No time to mourn or bury the dead. More caskets would
line the Fortress of Hera's funerary chambers if we did not act.

'Brother-captain!' Daceus stabbed out a finger, and was already
raising up his bolter as the veil of darkness returned. It was real this
time, not a shadow creeping across my subconscious.

I fed a surge of energy down the Tempest Blade and it crackled
into an azure beacon.

It was the assassin, his cyclopean eye aglow.

'By Guilliman's blood,' I swore. 'I will have that bastard's head...'

But he wasn't alone, as three bulky warriors stomped up alongside him bearing twin-barrelled cannons. A trio of muzzle flares roared into being.

I got off a single shot, and took the one-eyed assassin directly in his glowing orb. Unprepared to engage his chronometric defences, his head exploded in a pulse of scorching plasma. As the corridor lit up with the flare of a necron cannonade I had the satisfaction of seeing Calgar's shooter crumple and phase out.

Resurrect from that.

'Move!' I grabbed Daceus and we dove back inside the armourium as the corridor where we'd been standing was stitched with viridian beams.

Hunkered down, our backs against the wall as our enemy advanced down the corridor spewing fire, Daceus handed me a primed charge.

'Here...'

I glanced at him quizzically.

'One can never be too prepared.'

'Even in the fortress-monastery?'

He shrugged. In my hand, I held a krak grenade.

I leaned out into the corridor, squeezing off a snapshot and clipping one of the bulky cannon-wielders. The necron was heavily armoured but the plasma bolt tore off its right shoulder and most of its arm. Unable to heft its weapon, it stumbled and collapsed against the corridor wall. But it was far from finished, as its self-repair protocols activated.

Behind the first wave, three more immortal warriors lumbered into view.

'There are too many.'

Daceus fired off a bolter burst one-handed, the two of us alternating our snap-fire in an attempt to slow down our enemy. It wasn't working.

'Agreed,' said the sergeant.

A plan formed. I thumbed the krak grenade's detonator, and primed it for a six-second timer.

'Give me some covering fire.'

Daceus triggered a three-round burst as I leaned out with him a fraction later and clamped the krak grenade to the wall.

'Back, now!'

We ducked back inside the armourium as a firestorm ripped through the corridor, bringing most of the ceiling down and sealing it off.

Daceus and I were back on our feet a moment later. Outside the armourium, the dust was still settling. Chunks of debris fell from the ceiling, and where internal circuitry was exposed, wires spat and fizzed.

Our enemies were trapped, but already the veil of darkness was beginning to coalesce again.

Daceus raised his bolter but I seized his arm and urged him away from the rubble.

'Come on. We need to gather reinforcements.'

We had scarcely taken a few steps when the vox crackled again.

'Sicarius...' It was Agemman. His voice was strained and I heard the distinctive sounds of combat in the background. *'We are under attack. The necrons have laid siege to the apothecarion. Lord Calgar is in danger. I don't know how much longer we can–'*

The link was severed in a blurt of hostile static. Agemman was gone and no amount of attempts was going to raise him again.

Like smoke on the wind, the darkness abated. It was headed elsewhere, possessed of a singular purpose.

Grim-faced, Daceus and I set off for the apothecarion. I hoped to Guilliman we would not be too late.

Despite the wailing alert sirens, the warning strobes and its call to arms, the Fortress of Hera was eerily empty.

It had unnerved Daceus. 'Where are our battle-brothers?'

I shook my head, hurrying down the ghost-like hallways as my vox hails were met with forbidding silence.

'Engaged against the necrons.'

'With no word, no warning or attempt to coordinate defences?'

Daceus was unconvinced.

So was I.

'There is no other explanation, brother-sergeant.'

That too was a lie. I could think of one, so could Daceus, but neither of us would speak it.

There were no further encounters with the necrons before we reached the apothecarion. Standing at the end of the short hallway to the chamber's entrance, I realised why.

There was no entrance. It had been entirely consumed by the veil of darkness.

As if sentient and reacting to our sudden presence, the tendrils of night began to whip and eddy as if borne by an ethereal breeze. Twisting and uncoiling, unfurling like a ragged black cloak, the darkness came for us.

Within its depths were the necrons.

Three armoured warriors stomped towards us, coffin-shaped shields locked together in the manner of some ancient empire. Unlike the other necrons we had faced, these carried energised khopesh blades and were emblazoned with dynastic symbols. I knew a warrior elite when I saw it. I also knew who they were protecting.

A one-eyed necron, not an assassin but more a vizier, cowered behind this trio of formidable guardians. Stone like lapis lazuli accented his mechanised body in long strips and a gilded beard clasp protruded from his chin. In one metal-fingered hand he carried a staff; the other clutched the tethers of the veil. Here was the architect of darkness. And it was through him we would have to go if we were to reach our stricken Chapter Master.

As his guardians marched towards us, the vizier extended a talon in our direction.

His voice echoed with the resonance of ages.

'Defilers. Infidels. You are an inferior species, lesser in every way to the Necrontyr. Behold what your arrogance has wrought. You will have all eternity to regret it.'

I glanced to Daceus. His bolter was aimed and ready.

'Bold words. Sounds like a challenge.'

My brother-sergeant snarled. 'Which I gladly answer.'

Daceus unleashed an unceasing storm of fire from his bolter. The heavy shells hammered the necron shield wall, battering the guardians back and breaking their defence. It ended with the hard *thunk* of the bolter's empty magazine. Daceus dropped it, unholstering his sidearm in one hand and drawing his gladius with the other.

I saluted our opponents with the Tempest Blade, hilt raised up to my eyes.

'In the name of Ultramar, you will not stand between us and our Chapter Master.'

Two of the vizier's guardians yet lived. I brought my sword down preparing to engage them, when Daceus stopped me.

'No, brother-captain. Kill that thing,' he nodded towards the vizier. 'Save Lord Calgar.'

After a moment's hesitation and knowing the fate my sergeant had condemned himself to, I ran down the corridor.

One of the guardians stepped into my path but I parried its khopesh blade and thundered a kick into its lowered shield, smashing the necron aside. Hearing Daceus engage them both, and not stopping to see how he fared, I leapt at the vizier.

The ancient necron recoiled, brandishing his staff defensively as vortices of shadow swirled around him. I watched the darkness retreat, like mist before the sun, carrying the vizier with it, clinging on like some infernal passenger. I vaulted into the air, the sword of Talassar held aloft in a two-handed grip. As the blade descended, the vizier was already fading. Cruel laughter echoed around me as I scythed through nothing, embedding my sword in the deck-plate underfoot with a resounding *clang*.

But I would not be denied, and gave chase into the apothecarion. Behind me, Daceus was fighting for his life. I could not stop, or his sacrifice would mean nothing.

With the scent of my fleeing enemy still on me, I hurried through the gaping doorway.

The vizier had not run far, for inside the apothecarion the veil of darkness howled like a captured thunderhead. It bleached all vitality from the room and its occupants as if their very life forces were being surrendered to sustain it.

At the eye of this storm, I saw Agemman and the survivors of Calgar's honour guard. Two were dead already, slumped against the medi-slab where the Lord of Ultramar lay supine and unconscious.

Venatio was nearest to him, but far from ministering to our wounded Chapter Master, he was fighting hard against a score of necrons. Like the creatures we had fought on Damnos, they wore the skins of the dead like mantles or trophies, and carried no weapons as such except for their dagger-length talons. The Damnosians had taken to calling them *flayed ones*.

One turned as I entered the apothecarion, alerted to my presence by the vizier who was skulking in the background, half-smothered by shadow.

It sprang at me, this flesh-draped horror.

I weaved away from its reaching claws and cut its midriff, parting abdomen and torso through its spinal column. I didn't wait to see it dissipate – more were coming.

I shot one with my swiftly drawn plasma pistol. The burst took it in the chest, arresting its mad leap and blasting it into the ether. I aimed at a second but one of the flayed ones slashed my forearm, tearing up the vambrace and disarming me. Sweeping the Tempest Blade, I decapitated it. A third I impaled through the chest, staggering a fourth with a heavy punch. It was dazed, or rather I had forced a system reboot, and it took a few seconds for it to adjust. Long enough for me to cleave it open diagonally from shoulder to hip. It phased out in a flurry of sparks.

My efforts had got me as far as the medi-slab.

Calgar's recumbent form looked frighteningly still and I tried to tell myself he yet drew breath.

Some eighteen necrons had been struck down around us. Several had phased out, but the rest were currently self-repairing. In the encroaching veil of darkness, I saw more viridian balefires flicker into life as the vizier summoned yet more warriors.

For Agemman's benefit, I aimed my sword at the vizier.

'We need to end that thing.'

The other defenders' bolters had run dry of ammunition long before and the First Captain had taken up one of the fallen Ultramarines' relic blades in preference to his ceremonial gladius. The remaining honour guard wielded power axes, whilst Apothecary Venatio had his chainsword.

'How do you propose we do that?' Agemman gestured to the necron horde that had just redoubled in size. A ring of steel stood between us and the vizier.

There was but a few seconds' respite to form a strategy before the flayed ones would be on us again.

'With courage and honour, Severus. He won't escape this time. Make me a breach with your warriors, and I'll pierce whatever passes for a heart in this thing.'

'What of Lord Calgar?'

Venatio spoke up. 'I'll stay by the Chapter Master's side.'

Agemman glanced back at me.

'If this fails, you'll be overwhelmed.'

I nodded. 'Aye, but you always said I was reckless.'

I heard the smirk in his response. He summoned the honour guard and prepared to open the gap I needed.

Self-repairing, several of the necrons jerked back to their feet. Their jaws clacked as if laughing, and they sliced their talons against one another in anticipation of the kill. For machines, they displayed an unnerving awareness of malice.

I lowered my sword, looking down the blade as I adopted a ready stance.

'Cut deep...'

Leading the honour guard, Agemman charged the necrons.

The sudden attack briefly stunned the horde and for a few seconds they reeled against the First Captain's fury. Agemman used his bulk and strength to break the flayed ones apart, ignoring the claws that raked his armour.

He roared, cutting a necron down with every sweep of his borrowed relic blade.

'Courage and honour!'

Through the flurry of power axes, I saw mechanised limbs fall in a metal rain. Torsos were hacked apart, heads cleaved. Like their captain, the honour guard were brutal. Relentless. My warrior's heart thundered with pride to witness such unstinting determination and bravery.

Like a speartip they had driven deep into the flayed ones, forcing a channel that thrust all the way to vizier. Embattled on every side, Agemman cried out and with one last effort made the breach I needed.

'Do it, Sicarius... Now!'

The distance was short, my passage blocked only by broken necrons underfoot.

I fixed the singular orb of the vizier with a glare that promised retribution.

'For Ultramar!' I declared, my fury unstoppable. 'Here you die!'

As I reached my enemy, I sprang into a shallow leap using it to gain loft and additional momentum. Holding nothing back, I struck down one-handed putting every iota of strength I possessed into the blow. My Tempest Blade cut the staff in half and carried on without pause into the vizier's skull. I split him down the middle, bifurcating his cyclopean eye, and did not stop until I had sheared him clean through. Both halves collapsed in a frenzy of flashing sparks and thrashing wires. The vizier phased out before they even hit the ground.

Triumphant, I turned to Agemman.

The darkness was receding, my plan had succeed–

Agemman was down, parted from his relic blade. The three honour guard were strewn around him, slain. Venatio lay sprawled on his back. The Apothecary was unmoving.

Calgar was alone, unconscious and undefended on the medi-slab.

As I saw the thing that loomed above him, I realised it would be his mortuary slab instead.

My sword felt loose and heavy in my grasp. I scarcely had breath to speak.

'No...'

An old enemy turned to regard me and in its fathomless gaze I saw the fall of empires and the terrible entropy of ages.

It had returned. The gilded king, my nemesis, the Undying of Damnos.

'I am doom.'

As the darkness closed in around me and I drowned again, I saw its war-scythe held over Calgar in an executioner's grip. There was no pity in his eyes, no mercy, not even malice, just a deep abiding ennui that presaged an end to all things.

The ice came back, crusting the ground and shawling my body in a sudden snowfall. Beneath it, I heard the beating heart that quaked the very earth.

I gasped, but breath wouldn't come. Black spots flecked my sight, converging at the edge of my vision. I raged but knew I was dying. My gauntleted fingers slipped from the sword's hilt and I heard it clatter uselessly to the ground.

I fell to one knee, then all fours.

Crawling, still defiant, I felt the scrape of talons pinning me as the flayed ones swarmed over me, swallowing me in a sea of cold metal. Something seized my face and then a hand clamped around my neck. A blade pierced my shoulder, another in my back and I was steadily transfixed.

Powerless, I could only watch as the war-scythe descended...

As the veil of darkness claimed me, I heard far away voices but dismissed them as nostalgic memory. I had died on Damnos and come back, but there was no returning from this.

A dense ball of white heat flared in my side prompting a gout of hot fluid to erupt from my throat, spewing up over my lips in a coppery wash. I spat it out, retching up the blood–

No... it wasn't blood. It was the briny, amniotic soup of the revivification casket I could taste in my mouth.

I opened my eyes and found I was cocooned by a viscous recuperating gel.

Had I survived? Were the voices I heard real after all? Did Daceus yet live and muster reinforcements?

My mind overloaded with uncertainty, and with my senses restored I hammered a fist against the inside of the casket. My rebreather had come loose and I was drowning in this filth.

The locking mechanism disengaged and I fell forwards onto the apothecarion floor as the revivification casket opened with a blurted warning chime.

On my knees, coughing up the amniotic brine that had saved my life and kept it tethered to the world, I looked up into the eyes of my Apothecary.

I could scarcely believe what they were telling me.

'Venatio?'

He nodded respectfully, fashioning a warm smile. 'Brother-captain. Welcome back to the world of the–'

'You're alive...' Staggering, I got to my feet. I was sweating with the intense biological rigours my body had just undertaken and was still a little unsteady. Venatio went to assist me but I held him back with my outstretched palm.

'And so are you, Sicarius. You were badly injured and have only just–'

I interrupted for a second time. 'Injured where? Here, in the fortress-monastery?'

Something wasn't right. An odd sense of recollection, a very mortal experience described as *dèja vu*, that which is 'seen already', was affecting me. I remembered the chronometric device utilised by the assassin, how it had blurred time and I wondered if I was somehow trapped in it.

'Damnos.' Venatio's eyes narrowed. He was already consulting his bio-scanner, as if their readers could provide some clue to my sudden distemper. 'You were struck down on Damnos, several weeks ago in fact. You have just this moment come back to consciousness.'

I gazed around the apothecarion, at the shadows at its periphery, but saw no veil of darkness, no hidden foes this time.

'I was drowning…'

Venatio bowed his head, abruptly contrite. 'Apologies, brother-captain. Your rebreather came loose towards the end of suspended animation. You appeared to be experiencing some form of nightmare. It's not uncommon. So close to revival, I couldn't interrupt the process to wake you or replace the rebreather. It was inactive for but a few seconds.'

I was shaking my head.

'But this is… it's impossible.'

The Apothecary showed his hands in a placatory gesture. 'You are here. You are back with us. What is your name?'

I frowned, incredulous. 'My name?'

'Yes. What is it?'

'Cato Sicarius. I am master of my senses, Venatio.'

'You do not seem it.' Agemman stepped from the shadows, just as he had before.

'Severus…' Another apparition. 'I saw you fall.'

The First Captain opened his arms as physical testament to his veracity. 'I am standing before you now, Cato.' He disengaged the locking clamps on his battle-helm and removed it, placing it in the crook of his arm. 'Brother.' He came over and put his hand on my shoulder. This scarred veteran of the Tyrannic Wars, hair shorn close to his scalp, service studs gleaming in his brow, was trying to reassure me as one battle-brother to another.

I began to realise the truth and it stirred an even greater concern within me.

'You are here to summon me before Lord Calgar, are you not?'

Nonplussed, Agemman let go of my shoulder. 'I am, yes. How did you know?'

I didn't answer and turned to Venatio instead.

'Apothecary, tell me – did we bring anything back from Damnos, anything from the necron?'

Venatio nodded slowly. 'Yes, but–'

'And is it under Techmarine Vantor's custody in the east wing armourium?'

Agemman answered. 'It is. What is this about, Sicarius?'

I met his questioning gaze with one of certainty and urgency. 'Do you have a sidearm you can lend me?'

Agemman nodded, not understanding but beginning to trust my instincts. He unholstered his bolt pistol and handed it over.

Appreciating the grip of the weapon, I regarded them both.

'We have to get there at once – the Fortress of Hera has been breached.'

Daceus had been on his way to the apothecarion when we met in the corridor.

I quickly explained the situation and together the four of us made all haste to the armourium in the east wing of the fortress-monastery.

Both Agemman and Daceus had their bolters, whilst Venatio and I held pistols. I hoped it would be enough for whatever awaited us in Vantor's workshop.

'Should we invoke a fortress-wide alarm?' asked Daceus on the way.

Agemman shook his head. 'Let's see what's in there first.' He had donned his battle-helm again, so I couldn't see his face, but I knew he doubted my assertion that the fortress was in danger and I suspect he didn't want to create needless panic.

I saw him exchange a glance with Venatio. The Apothecary hid his concern poorly, but I took no heed. We had arrived at the armourium.

We had not voxed ahead. I was insistent on this. Whatever awareness the dormant necrons in the workshop possessed, I didn't want to risk my warning activating them prematurely.

I hammered the icon for the door release and stepped first into the armourium.

It was much as I remembered: a hive of industry and labour, serfs and engineers hurrying back and forth, servitors engaged in their menial tasks, arms and armour in various conditions of repair and restoration. And there, at the back of the expansive workshop, tended by a small army of menials, was the salvage from Damnos.

Vantor turned as I entered. He was just finishing working up my armour-plate. I saw the Tempest Blade and my plasma pistol on a separate rack nearby.

'Brother-captain, your timing is impeccable.'

'I do hope so.'

The Techmarine's expression changed from warm greeting to slight confusion as Agemman, Daceus and Venatio filed in after me.

'Is there a problem I am unaware of, brothers?'

My gaze was fixed on the back of the workshop.

'Evacuate your labourers.'

Vantor looked to Agemman for confirmation.

'Do as he asks, brother.'

Like ants returning to the nest, the horde of serfs, enginseers and servitors removed themselves from the armourium. None questioned their orders, but some looked worryingly askance at the Ultramarines in their midst as they departed.

'With me.' I advanced into the workshop, indicating a perimeter around the necron salvage where I then came to a halt.

Vantor joined the others as they fell in beside me.

'This is illogical, Captain Sicarius. What are you trying to–'

Dozens of viridian eyes flaring into life in the gloomy armourium arrested the Techmarine's question and had him instinctively reaching for his plasma carbine instead.

'They are self-repairing...'

I raised Agemman's bolt pistol. My battle-brothers readied their weapons in unison with me.

I scowled as the necron host began to reassemble itself.

'Not for long.'

Roaring muzzle flare and a hail of fire broke the tension as the five of us unleashed our weapons, engulfing the back of the workshop in explosive annihilation and destroying everything in it.

Only when we had emptied our clips did we stop firing. Even Vantor exhausted the power cell in his plasma carbine.

When it was over, the back of the workshop was a scorched, half-destroyed ruin. It was as if a battle had just ended. In truth it had. We had won.

Agemman slammed a fresh clip into his bolter, ever the prepared soldier.

'Whatever is left, incinerate it.'

Daceus and I were sifting through the wreckage, making sure we had cleansed the room thoroughly.

I lowered my borrowed bolt pistol, and signalled to my sergeant to stand down.

'There's nothing left. The threat has been neutralised.'

Across the workshop, Venatio caught my eye. He gestured to the carnage around us.

'How did you know?'

I had no good answer for him, so I told the Apothecary the only thing that made any sense.

'I saw a darkness in my dreams and vowed I would not see it come to pass.'

Agemman was more pragmatic. 'Whatever the cause of your prescience, I for one am glad of it.' He bowed his head. 'Gratitude, Sicarius. But Lord Calgar yet awaits.'

* * *

Agemman insisted I be cleaned and wearing my armour before my audience with the Lord Calgar. As I had seen in my half-remembered dream, I walked the processional of the Hall of Ultramar with the statues of heroes measuring my every step.

And as before, I knew I would not be found wanting under their gaze.

Lord Calgar waited for me, seated upon a throne, his banners describing a legacy of war and glory behind him. Agemman was by his side.

I stopped at a respectful distance and saluted.

With a huge, power-gloved hand, Calgar beckoned me to approach. 'Come forth, Cato.'

I obeyed, masking any surprise at such informality, and took a knee before the Lord of Ultramar.

I bowed my head solemnly. 'I stand in judgement.'

'Rise. You are not being judged this day, though I had reviewed the engagement on Damnos.'

My eyes narrowed in confusion as I came to my feet.

'My lord?'

Agemman maintained his studied silence as Calgar explained.

'Damnos wounded us all, but you and the Second suffered more grievously than most.'

'It is a stain on my honour.'

'One I would see removed, Cato. I will not have this go unchallenged.'

I frowned again, not quite grasping Calgar's meaning.

'Permission to speak freely, my lord.'

'Granted.'

'What exactly are you saying?'

Calgar's eyes were like chips of steel. 'In your unconscious visions, you saw the ice? You heard the beating of its heart?'

My voice almost caught in my throat at this revelation.

'Yes.'

'It is the necron, mocking us. I feel it in my bones, Cato. Whether

447

it be one year or fifty, we are not done with Damnos, and it is not done with us.'

A nerve tremor in my cheek didn't quite manifest into a smile. And it would not until the stain against my honour was removed and Damnos reconquered.

'I shall count the days until our return, my lord. This isn't over.'

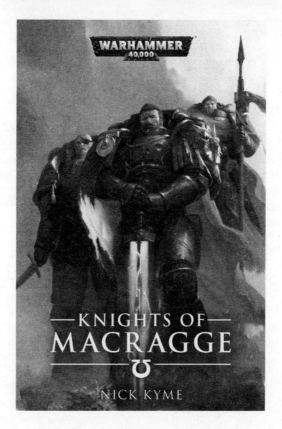

FIREHEART

Gav Thorpe

Introducing

YVRAINE

EMISSARY OF YNNEAD

The Clan Council took place amongst the inverted forest of the Sighing Winds Dome. Extruded from the underside of Saim Hann Craftworld, the habitat was named well, for its hundreds of ancient trees grew downwards towards the glimmer of stars below from the fertile substrate of the craftworld's foundation, while a constant breeze stirred the dark blue needle-leaves of the Skypines, white-blossomed Snowgiants and grey-barked Silver Queens. Every hillock and vale had its own voice, so that as the semi-random gusts flowed across the dome a chorus of tree-song filled the air. The Saim Hann eldar could navigate from one side to the other by sound alone, and indeed one of the greatest festivals of the Saim Hann calendar was the Race of the Night-shrouded in which blindfolded competitors sped upon their jetbikes along a treacherously winding course.

That cycle's activity was more sedate though no less devoid of motion. Among the spreading branches floated elegant rafts upon which the delegations of the Clan Council assembled, each clan to its own platform. They drifted slowly among the upside-down boles, the root-scrawled ground seemingly above them, an endless gulf of stars below. Gaily coloured gonfalons and pennants fluttered around the rim of each cloud-barque, bearing the runes and motifs of the clan and the individual members of its entourage. The attendees were as brightly turned out as the anti-grav platforms, displaying all the finery of their position like extravagant show birds trying to attract their mates.

Allies gathered closer together where they could converse without need for artificial amplification, forming an instantly recognisable picture of changing allegiances, factions and sentiment. Ribbon-tailed messenger doves flitted from one platform to another to take greetings, promises and reminders of past oaths between attending parties further afield. It was not simply tradition that necessitated the use of such antiquated means of communication; the location of the dome placed it on the periphery of Saim Hann's infinity circuit. With only the most residual background psychic activity to link them, the council members were required to use eloquence and presence to make their arguments rather than relying on the shared-mind empathy of the craftworld's crystalline nervous system.

It was also, very deliberately, a means to curtail the influence of the seers, who were only one of the many factions represented at the Clan Council. Here their voice was no greater than any other – and in the regard of many present, somewhat less important, judging by the dearth of other cloud-rafts in their vicinity.

At the centre of the drifting constellation of delegates, one eldar stood alone upon an unadorned platform. The Saim Hann were noted among others of the Asuryani for their extravagance, but in the manner of her garb the visitor being scrutinised by the clan chiefs outdid all others present. Alone of those in the dome, Druthkhala Shadowspite was unarmed – the chieftains and their aids all proudly bore heirloom weapons even though some had not seen battle for a generation and more. Even so, her warrior nature was evident from the bladed, serrated armour she wore. It was of Commorraghan craft, the highly decorative pieces laced together with threads of alien sinew, the plates themselves covered in dark red lacquer shaped to accentuate her lean body as much as to protect her vital organs.

Much of her flesh was visible but the pale skin itself was obscured by bright tattoos that covered her arms, thighs and midriff, composed of hundreds of tiny vignettes of bloodshed – decapitations and eviscerations contorted as she bent a tautly muscled arm, while graphic depictions of even more brutal murders stretched across her stomach when she drew herself up to her full height. Her hair was the equal of any banner on display, a heaping crest of red and black that cascaded in complex braids almost to her ankles. Her face had not been spared ornamentation, marked by scarlet ink with an arachnid design across her cheeks and brow, her features bounded by a tiara of alternating spikes and skull-shaped gems.

Also uniquely she bore no spirit stone, for she had been raised among the drukhari of Commorragh, though of late the former Bloodbride's mistress passed by another name – Yvraine of the Ynnari. Enmity between Saim Hann and the Dark City had existed for generations, but it was her role as herald for the Emissary of Ynnead that earned Druthkhala the antipathy of her current audience.

'This world – Agarimethea – is of no value to Saim Hann,' said one of the chieftains, Loirasai Bluewoven. With fists on hips, she turned her head left and right to address her words to the cluster of eldar about her, seeking to impress her view upon her ad-hoc coalition. 'It is a maiden world, home to great beasts and verdant forest and little else. Not even the Exodites laid claim to it, and the Bluewoven clan have no desire to become colonists, and even less to be errand-runners for the Ynnari.'

'If Yvraine so desires to know whether Agarimethea hides secrets from the Age of the Dominion we are happy for her to pass there herself,' added Celidhi of the Mistwearers. He flourished an open palm towards Druthkhala as though offering a gift. 'I am sure we can all agree that Saim Hann will hold no claim to this world.'

Druthkhala suppressed a sigh at the posturing of the clan leaders. Few had been more surprised than she when Yvraine had named her as a messenger for the Ynnari, but the Opener of the Seventh Way had acted out of keen insight and Druthkhala's malicious patience in the Crucibael arena had indeed become a valuable diplomatic skill. While retaining a dispassionate air, in thought she painted gory pictures of the clan leaders dying at her hand as they continued to debate amongst themselves, a distraction from the meandering discussion. She caught a mention of her name and returned her attention to the council, reviewing the last few moments from her subconscious memory.

'We know from others that an Exodite ship was bound for Agarimethea,' Druthkhala told them. 'It is very likely it arrived.'

'There are no Exodites on Agarimethea,' said Cuithella Frostwave.

'Precisely,' replied the Ynnari messenger, imagining Cuithella's features contorting in shock as her lungs filled with blood. 'The Exodite vessel might be there still. Or there are other secrets of the aeldari that have lain hidden by the forests since the demise of our civilisation. The Ynnari are embroiled fighting for our fate in several wars at present and call upon our friends in the craft-worlds to assist us in the continuing hunt for the croneswords of Morai-Heg.'

'And here you will find no favour, mistress of the dead,' said Celidhi. 'Your dread prophecies fall unheeded like the leaves of the deep forest. None here wish to usher in the doom of our people with the rise of Ynnead.'

'Take care that you speak only for yourself, Mistwearer!'

A blur of red through the inverted canopy announced the arrival of a Vyper, its pilot deftly steering between the branches and boles while a passenger swayed and swung from a fighting platform at the back where usually a heavy weapon was mounted. The long carapace of the newcomer's machine was adorned with a large rune of the World Serpent, the sigil of Saim Hann itself, a sparkling emerald for its eye. Black-and-scarlet pennons flew from the rail of the fighting platform, matching the flamboyantly styled armour of its rider and the streamers of the long-bladed lance he held. His helm was hung upon his belt, leaving bare the laughing face of a pale-maned lord, braids tied into the flowing locks with cords of more red and black.

'Nuadhu!' Celidhi and the others turned in the direction of the newcomer, some with smiles, others with frowns. The Vyper circled the gathering at speed, the wind of its passage fluttering clan pennants and delicately arranged hairstyles.

'You do not speak for Clan Fireheart,' declared Ameridath Frostwind. 'You have no place at this council until you succeed your father.'

The Vyper slid to a halt between the Frostwind cloud-barque and Druthkhala, Nuadhu Fireheart's expression hostile as he turned on Ameridath.

'As well you know, coldheart, my father lies upon the brink of his ending and cannot answer any summons to council.'

'A chieftain that cannot lead is no chieftain,' Ameridath replied haughtily. 'If you had any honour you would relieve Naiall of his duties as leader of your clan.'

'The usurpation would break his heart and I do not wish him soon dead like some,' snarled Nuadhu. His gaze moved to Druthkhala. Startling eyes that matched the green of his Vyper's jewel and the spirit stone upon his chest fixed upon her. The Fireheart opened his mouth and then shut it without a word, eyes roaming up and down Druthkhala.

'Have you something to say, lordling?' said Druthkhala.

'I do.' He brandished his spear, its pennons caressing the plates of his armour. 'I will lead an expedition to Agarimethea to seek the treasures of the dominion-now-lost.' He stared at her unabashed for several heartbeats and then blinked self-consciously. 'I assume you will accompany us.'

'Clan Fireheart will support the Ynnari?' The slightest of smiles passed across Druthkhala's lips at the thought.

Nuadhu's confident facade cracked slightly and he looked away for an instant. 'Mostly.'

Her eyes narrowed but she nodded her acceptance even as the other clan leaders gave voice to their dissent.

Letting free a shout of exhilaration, Nuadhu slapped a hand to the shoulder of his pilot, B'sainnad, as the pair raced through the burgeoning maw of the webway delving. The swirl of an opening released them above the immense trees of Agarimethea's world-forest, the virgin expanse spread without interruption to the horizon. The sky was a crystal-clear azure, the only clouds streaming like pennants from the mountain peaks in the distance. Nuadhu had never tasted air so clear nor seen a sight so pristine. He urged B'sainnad on, his thoughts mingling with his pilot's over the spirit connection of the Vyper. Sharing the same desire, B'sainnad guided them down, swooping towards the verdant canopy.

After them came a trio of jetbikes. The first was ridden by Alyasa, windweaver of the Firehearts. It had been his psychic mastery that had forged the webway branch from the starship in orbit. A moment later Caelledhin Icewhisper punched through the veil between the real and unreal, the pale blue of her armour starkly different to the scarlet of her companions. At her shoulder rode Druthkhala Shadowspite, mounted not upon a craftworld jetbike but the serrated, bladed skimmer of a Commorraghan reaver; a thorn of dark blue contrasted with the Saim Hann machines that followed, jetbikes and Vypers spilling from the void-path like blood in the wake of a shark.

A delighted laugh escaped Yvraine's herald as she accelerated alongside Nuadhu.

'Is there anything better than a swift steed and an open sky?' said the heir to the Firehearts.

'The touch of blade on flesh and dance of blood on the air,' Druthkhala replied with a savage grin. Nuadhu fixed his smile upon his lips though he felt his heart race at the sentiment, reminded that the beautiful warrior was not born of the Asuryani.

'I am no stranger to the taking of life,' he told her, lifting his spear. 'This is Drake's Fang, the bane of many foes since the time of the Fall.'

Druthkhala said nothing, her eyes fixed ahead as they dipped to the level of the highest branches, conjoined jet stream cutting a furrow through the leaves beneath them.

'I ride upon *Alean*,' Nuadhu continued. 'Named for the steed of Kaela Mensha Khaine.'

'How sentimental,' Druthkhala replied. She let one hand rise from the handlebars to point ahead. 'What is that?'

She drew his attention to a sparkle from a valley ahead. Nuadhu judged it the glint of water, a river or lake, and was about to say as much. The thought evaporated as he spied a slender object rising a little higher than the surrounding trees, the sparkle of sunshine flashing from its summit.

He pulsed a thought to B'sainnad, slowing them so that Alyasa and Caelledhin caught up, the seer to his left, half-sister to the right. Druthkhala looped overhead to draw alongside Caelledhin, her dark stare directed at Nuadhu.

'I see it,' said Caelledhin before he said anything. 'What has your rush of blood brought upon us now, I wonder.'

'You recall that I detected a flux upon the veil between worlds,' said Alyasa. 'I believe we have discovered the source.'

In the short time that had passed since they had first seen something amiss, the rapid approach of the wild riders had revealed more of the half-hidden structure. The metal point was the tip of a needle-like monolith, one of seven that rose up from the valley floor. The lower slopes had been cleared of trees and the neat line of deforestation delineated a heptagonal gulf across the width of the valley. In between rose a single pyramid of gleaming metal, its flanks ornamented with geometric shapes interconnected with straight lines, which pulsed with a greenish hue.

As one, the eldar slowed and stopped, each feeling the same sense of shock that gripped Nuadhu's heart. Caelledhin gave voice to the word that echoed through all of their thoughts.

'Necrontyr.'

'Now we know what happened to the Exodites.'

Druthkhala's statement broke the spell that had captured the attention of the wild riders. Even so, Caelledhin thought it offhand, if not callous. Annoyance fuelled her retort.

'And likewise ends our involvement here, Ynnari.' She was about to turn her jetbike around when her half-brother stopped her.

'Let us not choose our path hastily.'

'You choose every path with haste, Nuadhu,' Caelledhin said with a snort. 'That is why we are here at all.'

'I see no threat,' the clan-heir asserted, though his eyes rested more upon Druthkhala and her bare thighs than the Necrontyr architecture in the distance. 'We can investigate a little further.'

He couched his lance beneath his arm and raised a pair of magnifiers to his eyes, panning along the valley.

'You stagger the credulity of even the most gullible fool.' Caelledhin shook her head. 'We owe Yvraine nothing more. Any promises made have been kept. We should return quickly so that Druthkhala can bear the disappointing news back to her mistress.'

'During the ancient wars the Necrontyr seized the weapons of our people,' Nuadhu said, though it was unclear for whom he made the commentary. 'Our ancestors' warp-wielding defied their abilities, and the enemy could not destroy them all but placed them into hidden vaults so that they could not be unleashed.'

'And the aeldari did the same to theirs, placing them in the webway where the Necrontyr could not reach them.' Caelledhin shrugged. 'What prompts this unnecessary history lesson?'

'Look at the pyramid,' said Nuadhu, passing the magnifiers.

Caelledhin raised them to her eyes and focused on the Necrontyr settlement, their workings adjusting to her gaze to bring the central edifice into stark relief. The flanks were adorned with the same circuit-like decoration of all Necrontyr construction. Caelledhin was about to throw the magnifiers back when a sapphire glint caught her eye. The focus adjusted as she looked to the base of the pyramid, almost hidden behind the intervening tree canopy. Here the circuit-script turned into flowing runes and encircled an oval gem – judging by the rangefinder displayed by the device, the stone was easily as tall as her.

'Aeldari runes…' Her breath caught in her throat at the thought. For countless ages the tomb-precinct had stood, older than the craftworlds by aeons, long before the coming of She Who Thirsts. The runes themselves made when the aeldari dominion was itself newly birthed.

'It could be a weapon we can use against the Dark Gods.' Druthkhala turned a long stare upon Nuadhu, her eyes offering both a challenge and perhaps also a promise.

Nuadhu retrieved his magnifiers and stowed them away. 'My heart tells me that this is a great opportunity to strike a blow in the eternal war.'

'Then your heart is a fool, and you are a greater one for heeding its advice,' said Caelledhin.

B'sainnad chuckled, earning a scowl from his lord.

'Destiny lacks patience,' Nuadhu retorted with a sneer. 'When we return with Yvraine's prize, the fortunes of Clan Fireheart will rise again. The indignities we have suffered during father's indisposition will be swept aside.'

'Ridiculous,' growled Caelledhin. 'We number only thirty but you would pitch us against a host of the Necrontyr.'

'I see no host,' Nuadhu said, a lopsided smile upon his lips, a flick of his gaze towards Druthkhala. 'If we are swift – and none are swifter than the wild riders – we will take our prize and be away before these slumbering beauties even flutter a metal eyelid.'

Caelledhin's protest went unheard, lost in the growing whine of *Alean*'s acceleration. A scarlet blur surrounded Caelledhin and the Ynnari herald, the wild riders behind their leader as surely as the tail follows a gyrinx. The child of the Icewhisper glared at the Ynnari beside her.

'This is your fault,' Caelledhin snapped.

'You give me too much credit, daughter of Saim Hann,' Druthkhala replied. 'Your brother is capable of great acts of monumental stupidity without my help.'

And then she too was gone in a smudge of dark blue and a fading shriek of anti-grav engines.

They kept low, the uppermost leaves of the primordial forest whipping at the angled fins of their jetbikes. Following Nuadhu in single file, the wild riders curved across the woodlands towards the valley, its undulations like the World Serpent that was the totem of their craftworld. Nuadhu crouched low behind B'sainnad's shoulder against the rail of his fighting platform to reduce the drag, hair tossed across his face as he craned for a look past his pilot.

It was impossible to be sure from the low angle of approach but it seemed that nothing stirred about the structures. The unworldly glimmer of the Necrontyr pilasters remained undimmed, neither strengthening nor waning in their intensity. The Fireheart heir took this as a good sign and signalled for his warriors to fan out behind him as they crested the last wooded ridge.

'Sleep the long sleep, worry us not with your dead dreams,' he whispered, eyes scanning the pyramid for any sign of activity. He spied no movement and with a flick of the wrist gestured for the squadrons to descend to the valley floor. The shadows of the wild riders flitted over the leaf canopy.

'Eyeless are the guards that patrol such places,' warned Morwedhi as they neared the alien structures. 'Nothing passes unseen through the tomb-lands.'

Nuadhu's skin prickled as they passed the boundary marked by the border needles but it was a trick of the mind rather than any real barrier. Diving steeply down the treeless slope he could see that not only had the forest been removed, all organic matter – undergrowth and soil – had been stripped away to the bedrock of the mountain. Into this bared grey was cut a concentric arrangement of trenches and furrows, the widest more than a dozen paces across, the narrowest channel no more than his spread fingers. So deep were these cuts that they swallowed all light, angular chasms that wrought a maze of interlocking shapes about the pyramid at their centre.

Meadhu pulled ahead for a few heartbeats and then dropped back alongside the lord of the wild riders.

'Nothing lives here,' he said, shaking his head. 'This is no place for the living.'

'Hush your woes, cousin,' replied Nuadhu. 'If you fear the grave then perhaps your time as a wild rider is coming to an end.'

'Fear keeps the edge of the senses keen,' the wild rider retorted. 'And perhaps also the wits.'

Nuadhu ignored the criticism and angled their approach across the barren ground. The expanse directly around the main structure was devoid of crevices or any other mark, broad enough for three Vypers to comfortably land abreast. Nuadhu impulsed B'sainnad to stop and gestured for several others to do likewise while the rest of the wild riders took up patrols around the perimeter. Some ascended higher to keep watch further along the valley, silhouetted against the empty sky.

Nuadhu stowed Drake's Fang and leapt over the rail, flashing a smile to Druthkhala mid-jump as she settled her reaver jetbike on the pale stone. Caelledhin landed between them, scowling, lips pursed.

'See, half-sister? The ancient dwellers slumber still. They care not for our little excursion.'

He and the others approached the pyramid. There appeared to be no joins or entrances, the sheer surface marked only by the circuit-tracery and aeldari runes. Alyasa lifted a hand, fingers splayed as he neared the closest sloping wall.

'These wards are strong, binding together a most puissant force,' he declared. 'Whatever is contained within emanates with a forceful spirit.'

'I feel it too,' confessed Caelledhin, and Nuadhu also felt the tremor of psychic power from within the vault-structure. Druthkhala looked from one companion to another, bemused, her own psychic sense stunted.

'A weapon, perhaps, capable of slaying demigods,' said Nuadhu, dragging his eyes away from the Commorraghan and back to the pyramid. 'Such abounded during the Wars of the Old Ones.'

'I see no way in,' said Caelledhin.

'Nor I,' added Druthkhala. She looked at Alyasa. 'Is there some craftworlder trick to open it?'

'These bindings are as old as the seeding of this world,' replied the windweaver. 'Even if I were a seer, I do not think I would have the means to open this vault.'

'It is not our concern,' said Caelledhin, stepping back. She darted a glare at Druthkhala. 'If the Ynnari want what is within, they can come and claim it.'

Nuadhu was about to concede the point, but it galled him to return to Saim Hann with only rumour, not proof. He was also keenly aware of the hot flush he felt whenever Druthkhala looked at him, and the desire to impress stirred him to one last effort.

'There must be some way to get inside,' he declared, striding up to the immense gem on the closest facing. It was just within reach, by far the largest gemstone he had ever seen.

'It is bound in wraithbone,' Alyasa exclaimed at his side, pointing to the swirled fitting around the immense jewel.

'And through it perhaps we might learn more,' announced Nuadhu. He laid his hand upon the closest spiral of the psycho-reactive substance.

There was an instant of connection, but it was followed not by recognition but a burst of rejection. Sparks erupted as the psychic pulse hurled him away, sending him clattering to the flat rock almost at Druthkhala's feet. He sprang up, embarrassed and enraged. His anger drained, as did the warmth in his body as a flash of jade light drew his eye to the seven pilasters that bounded the Necrontyr complex. A matching hue blazed from the network of artificial chasms around them.

Nuadhu was no coward – in fact his foolhardiness overruled self-preservation on many occasions – but he was also not one slow of wit.

'Run!' he bellowed to the others as he started sprinting.

Ahead of him B'sainnad guided *Alean* off the ground and swooped close, allowing Nuadhu to spring upon the platform as it passed. Around them the mounts of the others rose up and darted to their riders, responding to their psychic calls as animal mounts might answer the whistle of a master or mistress. Druthkhala had no such advantage and was forced to dash all the way back to her reaver-steed, though it leapt into life at the moment of contact as she bounded into the long saddle.

'The mountains are opening!'

Alyasa's cry made no sense until Nuadhu looked around, to see that indeed the peaks of the surrounding mountains were peeling apart like the petals of immense flowers, green light gleaming from within. Above the roar of the rising windrush as B'sainnad guided them higher, he heard a chorus of skin-crawling howls echoing from the parted summits. Within the emerald glow crescent shapes turned, one at each of the seven surrounding peaks.

How had they not seen the number of mountains about the valley? Even as sickle-winged craft soared from within, landslides broke the slopes, sending plates of rock cascading into the valley to reveal gleaming metal inside.

Beams of green power lashed out as the crescent craft swept after the fleeing wild riders. Where the rays touched, riders and mounts were atomised. Within the space of ten heartbeats, three Vypers and four jetbikes had been obliterated. Teeth gritted, Nuadhu looked back to see the seven craft bank hard after the Saim Hann force, their crackling death rays readying to fire again.

Inspiration struck as they flashed across the boundary of the delving, once more flying over the greenery.

'Beneath the leaves,' he called to the others, pointing with Drake's Fang. 'They shall dare not follow us there.'

Two more wild riders succumbed to the lethal blasts before they plunged into the concealment of the forest. Branches lashed at Nuadhu but he ignored them, clinging hard to the rail as B'sainnad dodged them past the boles of ancient trees. All was lit like a green twilight, layers of thick canopy obscuring not only the sun but also the murderous attention of the Necrontyr pursuers.

Yet relief was short-lived. No sooner had they reached the sanctuary beneath the leaves than silvery shapes appeared in the murk – Necrontyr skimmers powering through the forest.

The landscape was a half-seen smear of browns and greens to either side, the light alternately blinding and dim as B'sainnad banked past soaring tree trunks and swooped through gaps in the foliage. The scream of Necrontyr fighter craft overhead was a constant companion, keeping the wild riders beneath the shield of the canopy, but there was no respite from the snap of deadly beams and crackling rays that chased them through the arboreal maze.

Nuadhu clung to the platform rail, hanging on tightly as *Alean* turned so sharply that they flew almost inverted for several thunderous heartbeats, the stabilising fins that extended to either side slashing bark from a towering bole. An instant later a green pulse of energy slashed past, ripping through the same tree, missing by the smallest of margins – had B'sainnad been even a heartbeat tardy in his manoeuvre the Vyper and its riders would have joined the trail of broken jetbikes and dead eldar scattered along the line of their retreat.

The heir of Clan Fireheart gritted his teeth, ducking to avoid decapitation by a branch, and glanced over his shoulder. Metallic gleams powered from light to shade, seeming to strobe in and out of existence as they hurtled through the dappled sunbeams.

Every now and then a gunner on one of the other Vypers would draw aim on their pursuers and let loose a volley of scattered laser fire or the scintillating beam of a bright lance.

A cry from ahead warned that the woodland was coming to an end. Nuadhu checked the pursuit again, confirming that the Necrontyr skimmers were also to the left and right. Any change of course would take the wild riders perpendicular to the chasing machines, and away from their goal of the webway gate.

'Our course must be as serpentine as our totem,' Nuadhu told them as the scarlet flock burst out into the bright sunshine of a bush-studded vale. 'Present no easy target.'

B'sainnad complied immediately, jinking *Alean* first one way and then the other, following the slightest dip or rise in the ground. Around them the other riders swerved past each other in almost haphazard fashion, avoiding each other by a hair's breadth on occasion. At their heart, Druthkhala struggled with her reaver jetbike, jerking at the controls to avoid collisions, lacking the instinct and swarm-empathy that allowed the wild riders to fly so close to each other without mishap.

A chilling howl descended on the group as the circling Necrontyr craft dived to attack once again. Fresh coruscations of lethal jade energy flared past as the pursuing pack broke from the tree line. Just a spear's cast to Nuadhu's right, his cousin Morwedhi disappeared amid exploding jetbike parts as a green beam bisected her steed from engine to prow.

Nuadhu had his first proper look at the foe. The lead line of Necrontyr were some form of centauroid construct, their upper halves humanoid in form, atop beetle-like anti-grav sleds kept aloft by banks of gleaming suspensor engines. With them came more Necrontyr warriors mounted in arc-shaped machines like flying wheels.

'There!' Nuadhu rose to his full height and pointed down the slope with Drake's Fang. 'Our next port of salvation.'

A herd of giant saurians plodded across the open lands, several dozen strong. The scaled beasts were the equal of a Phantom Titan in height, legs as long and thick as the trees just departed.

B'sainnad darted a questioning look back at his lord.

'Under them and through them,' Nuadhu insisted. 'Use them as cover!'

The pilot shook his head doubtfully but did as commanded, angling the Vyper between the legs of the closest beast. The other wild riders split, each pilot choosing his or her own path through the moving limbs and swaying necks of the saurians.

Tails lashed and broad mouths snapped at the interlopers, sending two of Nuadhu's companions crashing into the ground with their untimely sweeps. Jade beams flared down, the pained bellows of wounded saurians drowning out the whine of jetbikes as the flickering rays parted limbs and punched effortlessly through thick hide into monstrous organs.

Nostrils flaring, hooting bellows sounding their panic, the herd moved faster, their fear quickly creating a stampede. Ahead, two of the brutes collided, trapping Meadhu's mount between their flanks. An explosion scattered sparks over *Alean*. Broken pieces of scarlet carapace and the crushed body flopped to the ground to be stomped into the unforgiving dirt by the monsters that followed.

Yet for all the danger posed, the stampede was also a blessing. Necrontyr engines suffered worse as they tried to follow the wild riders into the thrashing beasts. Flattened beneath descending feet and swept into the air by whipping club-tails, the alien skimmers broke off their pursuit, curving away to either side.

The wild riders throttled back their engines and kept station with their massive escorts, bobbing and weaving to avoid the press of bodies whilst maintaining position within the heaving masses. The route of the maddened herd took them down to the steep-sided river that cut along the bottom of the valley, almost directly towards the waiting webway gate.

'One last dash,' Nuadhu exhorted his followers, urging B'sainnad to steer out from the rampaging saurians and into the river canyon. Fresh bursts of aerial fire followed the flitting red craft into the defile, vapour clouds rising from the frothing waters where the high-energy beams struck them.

The crevasse was no less treacherous than negotiating the wayward saurians, but likewise shielded Nuadhu's company from the murderous intent of the Necrontyr. Still some distance ahead and above, the purple swirl of the webway opening hung in the air like a sky-bound black hole.

Nuadhu spared a moment to look around, first to check on Caelledhin and Druthkhala, and then to appraise their other losses. His half-sister followed almost directly behind, darting through the spume left in the wake of the Vyper. The herald of Yvraine was a little further back in the group, her passage leaving vortices through the rainbow-threaded river mist.

Gladdened to see them alive, Nuadhu's heart then sank. Less than half of those that had departed Saim Hann would return with their lord. Cousins and kin-bonded warriors he had known for a lifetime had been lost. He had led them into battle before but, as his eye roamed back to Druthkhala's seemly appearance, he knew that a selfish motive had brought them here.

Noting his gaze upon her, the Ynnari messenger guided her bike alongside him. Moments later, Caelledhin joined them, glaring daggers at both her half-brother and the former arena fighter.

'Counting the cost of your folly?' Caelledhin snapped. 'You should! Twenty of our kin dead. Their spirit stones lost. For what? For nothing!'

Nuadhu knew she was right. The truth of it burned at his heart. *This* was why he could not countenance his father dying, why he could not – dared not – take up the mantle of chieftain. He was not worthy, and even less qualified.

But he had to make amends. That was the true test of a leader, and he would not dare admit any concession to his half-sister. The merest hint of weakness would see the Firehearts subsumed into Clan Icewhisper.

'We shall return,' he declared. 'Not lost are those that remain in our thoughts. Not wasted are those lives spent in achieving a later victory.'

'Madness, to throw away more lives on your vanity.'

Ahead, the river turned away from their preferred course. They eyed the open stretch of sky between them and the webway, what seemed like an impossible gulf to cross as crescent attack craft soared back and forth against the clouds. The other wild riders gathered close, the hum of jetbikes and Vypers adding to the roar of the waters.

'Not vanity,' said Nuadhu. He matched the ire of her stare with grim determination and then looked to Druthkhala. He raised his voice so that all could hear. 'Now we know for certain that the Necrontyr have something they want to keep from us. There is a prize on Agarimethea worth fighting for.'

At his command, B'sainnad gunned the engine and *Alean* leapt upwards from the cover of the river gorge, their sudden appearance answered by the scream of descending Necrontyr.

YOUR
NEXT READ

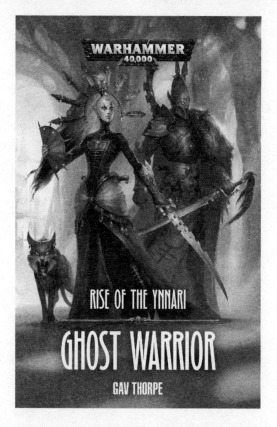

RISE OF THE YNNARI: GHOST WARRIOR
by Gav Thorpe

When the long-lost Craftworld Ziasuthra reappears,
Iyanna Arienal and Yvraine of the Ynnari lead an expedition to it in hope
of retrieving the last cronesword. But why has the craftworld returned now,
and can its inhabitants be trusted?

BLOOD GUILT

Chris Wraight

Introducing

NAVRADARAN

EPHOROI, ADEPTUS CUSTODES

The Tower of Hegemon, like all the edifices of Old Terra, had mutated over the long ages. Once, it had been a thriving nexus, humming with the activity of serfs and overseers. Its cogitator banks had been full of data-processing machine-spirits, chewing through location markers for a billion citizens on a world newly forged into Unity. The tall windows had been fashioned from crystalflex, and the warm light of a young sun had poured through them.

Now the cogitators were near silent. Their huge copper-faced banks were tended ritually by the distant descendants of those first menials, their robes clattering with the armour of ancestral bones, but the lenses remained dark. Musty chambers hung with cloaks of shadow, rarely visited, their walls stacked with the cracked leather spines of books that were seldom opened.

From far below came the noise of forges turning. Armour-wrights chiselled and etched occult names into ancient auramite, one after the other, recording battles that no one outside the tower would ever hear of, and whose heroes and monsters would find their way into no other Imperial records. The crystalflex windows were gone, replaced by heavy armourglass defence-slits. The sun was gone too, its sky turned grey like mourning ash. Old candles, each fashioned from priceless beeswax, guttered quietly in stone alcoves or drifted aimlessly on wandering suspensors.

The tower was larger now. Its original outline had been modified in the era of Dorn, brutalised and reinforced to withstand the predations of the Warmaster. In the years that had followed, as the Edict of Restraint came into force, those walls were extended further and the old foundations were delved deeper. Archives were expanded, ready to receive the centuries' worth of compiled records. Its golden-armoured inhabitants, now donning black in remembrance of failure, padded through the deeper vaults, treading paths into the planet's crust as they traced ritual processions and marked the passing of epochs.

While they held vigil in that darkening citadel, the stars burned. Empires rose and fell, threats came and went. A hundred High Councils were convened, and their occupants disputed, and then sickened, and then died, and then more were chosen. The tower became subsumed into the surrounding grasping mass of construction. Grey walls were raised around it, above it, through it, until the old carcass merged into the sprawl of the greater Palace, consumed as if dissolved in acid. A visitor would never have known where the halls of the Adeptus Custodes began and where they ended, save perhaps for some inner sense to warn them, some premonition that those chambers were the home to immortals, and that death lay behind its many doorways.

Of the Ten Thousand, less than half remained locked within that sarcophagus of eternity. They were the scholars and the seers, their proud heads bent in supplication before altars of learning and mysticism. They were the astrologers and the prognosticators, examining the fall of the tarot and interpreting old dreams. Many more remained on the high walls beyond, patrolling in endless rote. The most honoured of all no longer walked within Hegemon, but were kept in seclusion within the Sanctum Imperialis, lost in communion with the Emperor Himself.

Of the remainder, only a few were Ephoroi; the far-seekers, the ones who roamed. They passed down from the high portals and went into the world-city, sometimes in glory, more often in obscurity. In the lost age, the Ephoroi had been numerous, pursuing Blood Games across the entire globe before returning to the Palace. Now they were almost extinct, an order whose time had passed. So rare were their excursions that many even among the educated could speculate that the Adeptus Custodes were no more, just another part of the flotsam that had been dragged away along with the primarchs.

But they lingered still, just like the faint candle-flames in their stone alcoves. Their tasks had not altered since the earlier days of the order, and still they hunted threats to the Throne with the remorseless obsession of Martian thought-machines, treading the many perilous trails of the world-city and bringing back tidings of its degradation to the silent tower. Some hunts would take days, others years, others never ended.

This one had taken seven months. It had begun with a turn of a single tarot card, identified as anomalous by the seers. Investigations had followed, combined with the consultation of nine grimoires and the close interrogation of specialist astropaths stationed within nine different nodes of the Sanctum Imperialis. Psycho-conditioned serfs were sent out into the spires, their eyes replaced by augur-repeaters and their bodies stuffed full of data-cores. Simulations were run, models were compared, testimonies sought.

And then, at the end of it all, a single hunter was loosed. Like a hawk unclipped from the jesses, Navradaran of the Ephoroi left the confines of the Tower of Hegemon under the cover of night and slipped into the maw of the eternal conurbation, a ghost in gold, already moving fast, his quarry fixed before his blood-red eyes.

* * *

The Lord Sleox was not used to hurrying. His robes, heavy as rolls of tapestry, caught up in his ankles as he went, nearly sending him tumbling to the floor. A retinal scroller-feed told him that the lifter was past due to depart, and things were being cut far too fine.

He stumbled down the long corridor, its walls lined with portraits, feeling his heart-rate thud and his breathing grow quicker.

It did not do to display concern. A scion of the House Sleox was never concerned, at least not in front of the staff. Even in the utmost extremity, one had to retain a certain level of decorum, of self-command, lest the most basic and fundamental tool of nobility – deference – be eroded.

'Is all well, my lord?' asked Ysica, her face a picture of concern.

'Absolutely well,' Sleox replied, picking up the pace. 'Some important news has come in from our holdings on Geres, that is all.'

Ysica looked confused. Sleox could understand that – the House had many holdings on Geres, that was true, but it had been a long time since a senior member of the cartel had visited in person. That was what indentured agents were for, and the House had hundreds of those.

She didn't demur, though. That was good, and reflected well on her training. In any case, there was no time for a fuller explanation, even if he had been inclined to give one. Things had become perilous with a speed that had, to be frank, unnerved him. The game had always been dangerous, but some enemies were more potent than others.

'Ensure the *Hervol* is primed for immediate dispatch,' he said as he walked. 'I want orbital clearance settled before we get there. No fuss. And keep your queries limited to private channels.'

Ysica nodded, scampering a little to keep up. Her face creased in concentration as she activated her inbuilt comm-bead and double-checked the hastily made arrangements.

Sleox hardly noticed. His slippers sank into thick rugs underfoot, one after the other in a long procession across a polished hardwood floor. Everything in the mansion was authentic, bought with coin pulled from a commercial empire of considerable heft. That empire had been a front, of course – the aura of respectability, and it had kept things looking just legitimate enough. Until now.

He reached the end of the gallery and a pair of glossy doors slid back. The gritty air of Terra's streets wafted over him, let in by the open aperture of a subterranean groundcar depot. One of his private fleet was waiting for them, a tracked monster with ablative plating and a swooping promethium fume-grille.

Its doors hissed open and Sleox got in, followed by Ysica. The groundcar boomed into motion immediately, snarling up the ramp and out of the aperture. It thundered through a long tunnel before veering out on to the main transitway, clogged as ever with hundreds of vehicles shuttling between the great rearing spire-complexes.

'*Hervol* reports clearances obtained and engines already fired,' Ysica relayed. 'Lifter also reports ready for dispatch, and orbital visas are coming over the grid within moments.'

'Not soon enough,' Sleox growled, looking out of the narrow viewports as the groundcar picked up speed. He leaned up to the vox-grille set into the las-proof screen between them and the driver. 'Faster. Get me there and you'll be rich. Fail and you'll be dead.'

He adjusted his robes and pulled a scanner out from an angle-mounting at head-height. The lens flickered then resolved into a scatter-graph of pulsing green dots. He frowned as his eyes ran over the sweep, scouring for signals.

'Not good,' he muttered, craning over to look up through the nearside viewport. 'Damn it.'

As ever, the visual field was clogged and overhung with the titanic flanks of the spires, soaring up in terraces of milky sodium-glare and casting thick shadows at their feet. The transitways swirled and ducked like a bloodstream network, tangled and clotted. The filmy air above was almost as congested, hung with processions of smoggy flyers and cargo-barges.

Sleox wasn't concerned about the cargo-barges. He *was* concerned, though, about the jet-black flyer with locked wings that was gaining fast, sliding among the more cumbersome aircraft like a shark among shoals.

He leaned forwards, grabbing the vox-grille. 'Faster,' he ordered again.

The driver dared a backward glance, just to make sure. He was already risking the attention of the Arbites by weaving through the press of ground-traffic so recklessly, but he saw the look on Sleox's face, nodded and returned to the controls.

Ysica picked up on her master's nervousness.

'Lord, er, is there anything I should–' she began.

'Tell the lifter to gun its engines,' Sleox said, drumming his fingers on the plush leather armrest. 'Tell them to be ready to boost as soon as we're in.'

There was no use in telling her what this was about. She wouldn't understand any part of it anyway, and if she got properly scared then her usefulness was ended. Perhaps she would have to be quietly removed too, but only once they got clear of Terra and out into the safety of the deep void. Geres was a sanctuary, the kind of place even an Imperial noble could lie low for a while and gather resources again. The key thing was to get there.

The groundcar skidded as the driver pushed it hard between two oncoming munition-trucks. Its engines were already straining, their ancient coolant systems creaking under the powerload.

'Faster,' said Sleox for a third time, watching the flyer come in closer. It was dropping lower now, clearly tailing them, gaining a lock and preparing to fire.

Sleox checked the forward scanners. They were coming under the heavy lintel of the dropsite now, a looming jumble of misshapen towers that thrust up around the perimeter of many staggered rockcrete aprons. Lifter cranes wheezed up and down within cages, ferrying the orbital craft up from underground storage racks and out on to the exposed launch pads. The entire site trembled continually, its foundations shivered by the procession of take-off and touchdown.

The groundcar shot down the first of the under-tunnels, snaking through the twisting innards of the crypt-stratum before emerging at a core departure well. Servitors milled around them as the overloaded engines clanged down to idle, followed swiftly by uniformed customs officials. Militarum troop-carriers trundled through the poorly lit underpasses, their lumens sweeping the dank interior for any number of ill-defined threats.

Sleox slammed the door-release and sprang out, pushing his way through the crowds and racing across the short distance to the vacuum elevators. Ysica scrambled to follow, tripping in the dark and clutching at her dataslate. From behind them came the sound of atmospheric turbines. Surely the flyer couldn't follow them down here? You never knew, though. Not with these pursuers.

They piled in and the vacuum elevator shot up, streaking inside its enclosed tube, before juddering to a halt at the disembarkation level. Sleox and Ysica bundled out and raced across the asphalt, ignoring the soot-thick air that roared and swirled around them, leaving the groundcar's driver to screech back off into the dark without them. The lifter had been primed as instructed, and its heavy engines were already whining up to boost velocity. Dozens more were in similar states, ranked and ready for lift-off, their many undercarriages lost behind gouts of engine smoke and hydraulic discharge.

Sleox looked over his shoulder. Soldiers in black-and-gold helms were tumbling out of another elevator just twenty metres away, sweeping their lasguns around and searching for the right lifter to intercept.

'On board, *now!*' he cried, racing up the ramp. Ysica was barely halfway up before the launch klaxons kicked off and the deck began to drum. Void-seals slammed closed, secure bolts rammed into place, lock-chains sprang loose and clattered across the apron. Sleox threw himself into a launch-chair and strapped the restraint harness on with fumbling fingers. Ysica did likewise, just as the roar of the engines hit full tilt and the lifter finally pushed off.

For a moment, Sleox stayed put, breathing heavily, his back erect against the shaking lifter walls, waiting for the impacts of las-fire on the hull. The hold, capable of accommodating twenty, was almost empty – just the two of them, sat opposite one another, surrounded by the rumble of atmospheric drives.

Seconds passed. Then minutes. Then, finally, he relaxed. He let out a short laugh and took a deep breath. They were away. Once they rendezvoused with the *Hervol*, things would be fine – he had already paid handsomely to ensure that the passage through orbit would go undetected.

'Signal the captain,' he said, unclipping his restraint harness as the ascent entered its dominant phase and the decks stopped shaking. 'Tell them we got out, but tell him to be careful – this is not over yet.'

Ysica began to transmit and Sleox reached over for the cockpit door release. The lifter wasn't a big vessel – just four principal chambers, plus the high-mounted cockpit, but there were more comfortable places to sit out the journey.

The interior doors slid open with a grind of servos. On the far side stood a giant, clad in gold and draped in robes of purest black. Sleox only had time to register that this wasn't one of his crew, and only partly to register that this wasn't even truly one of his species, before a single bolt-shell punched cleanly into his chest and sent him crashing into the far wall of the hold.

It didn't explode – the detonation would have ruptured the lifter's skin – but it was still enough to carve a hole in his ribcage from which there would be no return. Lord Sleox's last expression was one of darkly comical surprise, a look that he retained even as his broken body slid down the wall and crumpled on to the hold's deck.

Ysica looked up at the giant before her, her mouth open. Her face was white, her limbs rigid. The giant slowly entered the hold, ducking low under the doorway. The lifter continued to make its way up through the atmosphere, travelling on the trajectory given to it by its now deceased master.

For a moment neither of them spoke. Eventually, Ysica summoned up the courage.

'Wh-what did you want with him, lord?' she asked, terrified.

'Nothing,' said Navradaran, placing his guardian spear before him. 'I came to find you. As you very well know.'

The pretence dropped. Ysica leaned back, still strapped in, hands folded in her lap, and shot her killer a look of regret.

'He was worried about the Arbites,' she said, almost affectionately. She looked over at Sleox's corpse. 'He thought they'd uncovered his little games. If he'd known that *you* were after him–'

'I wasn't.'

'No. I suppose not.' She looked around her. 'So are we still on course?'

'To one of my ships, yes. Do not attempt to derail this vessel – the crew are under my command and the systems have been cleansed.'

Ysica smiled wryly. 'Very well. I won't, then.'

She looked absurdly slight set against the leviathan before her. She appeared young, slim, dressed in a standard aide's garb of bodyglove and half-cloak, the sigils of House Sleox embroidered proudly in blue thread. He was gigantic, a lumbering demigod of auramite, a paragon of the past made flesh and thrust into the decayed vista of the present.

'It must have been useful,' said Navradaran, evenly enough, 'to employ that man's services.'

Ysica snorted. 'He was a fool. They all were. Greedy and incautious. The only thing that keeps them safe – for a while – is their numbers. Terra is home to billions of fools. They flock together for warmth, so it seems.'

'How many were there?'

'My employers? I don't remember.' She laughed. 'Really, I don't. It's been a very long time. You work for one and then another, and they blur into one. I don't even remember when they first sent me here. It was before the smog came, though. I still remember how the stars were, before the toxins closed over for good.'

Navradaran looked at her steadily the whole time, his face hidden behind a mask of gold.

'Then you are very old.'

'By mortal standards. You have to be.' Her face became more serious. 'We deal in millennia, you understand. That's our unit of currency. Most of them here never understood that. They lived for their own lifetime, gauging success by how many wars were won and lost on how many worlds. They could hear of a victory and think that the corner had been turned, but failed to see the bigger picture. It's all been going the same way, right from the start. All the same way. It just takes a while to get the pieces on the board.' She sighed, and rolled her shoulders. 'You'll have the same perspective, I guess. How did you find me?'

'These lordlings you cultivated,' Navradaran said. 'They were nicely judged. Corrupt enough to enrich you, not so corrupt they would be uncovered easily. Of sufficient influence for you to learn things, but not so central that we would already be watching them. They were a little too perfect. We study these patterns. We rehearse what we would do, were our roles reversed.' He leaned on the spear-shaft. 'And we delve into the paths of fate. We are not as blind as you suppose.'

Ysica nodded in mock salute. 'And yet I have been here for a long, long time. Your runes have taken a while to lead you to me.'

'Things have unfolded as they must.'

'Yes, you really believe that, don't you?'

The roar around them began to fade away as the lifter pulled clear of the atmosphere. Internal engine-noise remained, but the shielded hold became curiously quiet, and even the vibrations in the decking diminished. They might have been in any chamber of the Imperium just then.

'That's your weakness,' Ysica said idly. 'You've allowed yourselves to become passive. I've often wondered why you did that.'

'You clearly know much about us,' said Navradaran calmly.

'Ha. Sarcasm. That's good.' She looked amused. 'But, yes, I do know all about you. I was schooled in your ways before they sent me here, all the better for evading you. You're Ephoroi. The most dangerous of all, for one of my calling. I'm glad it's you that ended me, though, rather than a Watcher of the Throne.'

'We are all Watchers of the Throne.'

'For all the good it does you. You know that it's just a tomb now? There's *nothing down there*.' She laughed again. 'That's the irony. You actually see it. You see what it's become. And still you guard it. You're like dogs sniffing at the corpse of their master, hanging around with nowhere else to go.'

Navradaran resembled a graven image. He never moved, his voice never altered its inflection.

'Do you hope to enrage me?' he asked. 'I fear you will be disappointed.'

'No, I've no chance of that,' Ysica said. 'If the Warmaster couldn't rouse you to anger, I don't think I will.' She looked almost rueful. 'It's depressing, actually. I can respect an enemy who hates me. You, though... It's like your hatreds are all locked away, buried in that one old war and pushed down hard. You were the most damaged of all, I think. And you don't even perceive it.'

'We understand our limitations.'

'Really? I don't think you understand anything. Even the Space Marines make more effort than you do, and they're just brutes. At least they try to learn, try to develop.' She sighed. 'You're the only ones left who remember. Maybe that's why you do so little. It must be such a heavy burden, *knowing*.'

The Custodian took a single step towards her, just one, but despite herself she shrank back. 'You were doing more than observing,' he said. 'We know about the cabals you seeded, deep in the city. As we speak, they are being uprooted.'

'The ones you know about,' Ysica replied. 'You'll find a few. You might even find hundreds. As I said, this is the work of millennia.'

'What was your purpose in this?'

Ysica smiled. 'You want me to *tell* you?'

'I think you will.'

She looked at him shrewdly. 'Or you'll break out the instruments.'

'No. You will tell me because your work is done. You were not simply going along with your lord's games this time. You were using him to leave Terra.'

'Very good. Then you'll know it's too late for this to be prevented.'

'There have always been cults.'

'Not like these.'

'Terra is watched like no other world.'

Ysica grinned. 'And yet the day will come when you'll be blind. For all your guns, all your warships, your entire Imperium hangs on a single thread. Take it away and everything topples. That day will be soon, Ephoroi. You might have prevented it, perhaps, had you stirred yourself earlier, but it was easier, wasn't it, to languish in your old guilt and torpor. You've been indulgent. You've been slow.'

'What have we to feel guilty about?'

'Come, now, we're both too old and battered for that.' She looked up at the impassive mask and a flicker of regret crossed her features. 'We could have had such conversations, you and I. Do you think I *like* spending my time with dullard lords and rabid inquisitors? Their pride is matched only by their ignorance. They defend that which they don't understand, and in doing so only hasten their own demise. But we've seen how things really stand. We know the manner of power in the universe. We both have our Eyes of Terror – mine in the void, yours entombed right here.'

'What was your purpose in this?' he repeated.

'To watch. To report.'

'And more.'

'Possibly so.'

The lifter's ascent began to lessen. Fresh thrusts kicked out from the voidcraft's hull, pushing into an approach vector. Somewhere up above it, nearing all the time, a true battleship was waiting, its hangar cantilevering open and its cannons trained.

'You do not have long to live,' said Navradaran. 'You have been a traitor to your species. Unburden yourself now and your soul's torment will be eased.'

Ysica shook her head. 'Don't try that filth on me. I'm a traitor to nothing. *Nothing*. There isn't anything left now, save the coming storm. There's no nobility in cleaving to an empty promise. All you have ahead of you is the same gradual stagnation, the slow falling apart. I can forgive the others for that – they don't know any better. But you. *You*. It disgusts me.'

Navradaran loomed over her, keeping his grip tight on the spear.

'What was your purpose in this?' he asked again.

Ysica looked up at him. The sham-fear was all gone now, a product of her many years of subterfuge, and her dark eyes were steady. She saw her reflection in the polished gold, and for a moment it was as if two masks were placed against one another, each as rigid and unknowable as the other.

'You took your names from our oldest legends,' she said softly. 'From ancient Grecia. That was the tale of your kind, that they were tyrants of old, ruling in tandem with kings. And you would issue the call to war against the people you'd enslaved, such that they could be slain freely without blood-guilt. And for that you called yourselves righteous, and divine, but hid the truth where it could never be found, for you knew that the souls you'd enslaved were more numerous than could be counted, and in every generation they grew, and no matter how many wars you launched or how many pogroms you enacted, one day those numbers would sink you. That's why you remained here, locked behind gates that were built to withstand the apocalypse. You understand your own hypocrisy. Every time you lift your blade, you feel the weight of your old sins on it. You never shed the guilt – it merely grew in the shadows while you looked elsewhere.'

'What was your purpose in this?'

'What good would it do now, to know?'

'We will find out, one way or another.'

'Then you will waste more energy on things that cannot help you.

He's coming now – did your cards tell you that? The boundaries of the Eye are breaking. It doesn't matter whether you go to meet him or wait for him here, the result will be the same.'

Navradaran listened patiently. 'And you prepare the way for him.'

'He needs no prophet.'

The deck jolted. The entire lifter shook, as if mighty arms had taken it up and grasped it tight. The engines gradually wound down, and from the outside came the distant howl of a cargo bay repressurising. Ysica knew what was coming now – troops rushing across the interior hold, shackles being brought, null-chambers activated. Once that door opened, all that remained for her was pain and madness, for as long as she could endure it.

She moved. She moved faster than ever before. All her long training went into that movement – releasing the restraint, reaching for her blade, sweeping it up to her neck and plunging it through the flesh.

Except that she never made it. Navradaran was faster, just as he had to be, catching her weapon-arm and breaking it before she could ram the knife home. She cried out as her wristbone snapped, feeling a wave of nausea sweep through her.

And then the Custodian was closer, leaning over her, whispering the last words she would hear before the interrogations came.

'You will not die here,' he said, firmer than before. 'You have not earned that mercy. Only when the last truth is taken from you, when the last confession is extracted, will death come at last, and then you will realise the full magnitude of your crimes.'

Ysica fought to remain conscious. Above them, doors were crashing open, boots were hitting the deck.

'I will only ask you one more time. What was your purpose in this?'

She stared at him and all her assurance was gone. There was anger there now, and the beginnings of fear.

'I was watching you, Custodian,' she said. 'I was watching the watchers. I was ascertaining whether you would be a threat to him, when he comes.'

The outer airlocks were unsealed. The noise of men shouting came from the far side of the hold's doors.

'And what did you tell your masters?' Navradaran asked.

She looked at him defiantly, drinking in that long, last stare.

'That you're not ready,' she said. 'That you're nowhere close.'

'That is what she said?' asked the Captain-General, looking out over the sea of spires.

'The last of her words to me,' replied Navradaran, standing beside his master on the high balcony. Behind them both rose the old walls of the tower, whitened from the passing of aeons.

'You place credence in them?'

'She was a creature of falsehood,' said Navradaran, carefully. 'But she had lived here a long time. Many thousands of years, perhaps, in different bodies, dwelling in different places. She had seen many things change.'

'A record of her full testimony under agony came to me last night,' Valoris said, his voice like the grate of rusted steel. 'It is as you say, the cults are being seeded. Intelligence can be passed to the Inquisition, but they do not have the numbers for them all.'

'Then I will return to the city.'

'No, not this time.' The Captain-General turned his war-ravaged face towards Navradaran's. 'They tell me dreams have returned. Heracleon has already spoken to you of them, I understand.'

'He mentioned a name.'

'Speak to him, but do not linger. Perhaps she is even right. Perhaps we have remained on Terra too long.'

'She said those things to introduce doubt,' Navradaran said.

'And yet they may also be true. She is not the only diviner to emerge. Those others that we capture tell us the same things, and they no longer fear.'

Above them, in the luminous night skies, riven by billions of lights and barred by the contrails of a thousand flyers, humanity teemed much as it ever had done. The sacred pinnacles jutted into a haze of filth, their turrets proud against the dark. They were all oblivious out there, just as they had been made to be.

'What, then, is your command?' asked Navradaran.

'Take ship. We are gathering an old harvest now and I wish for it to be hastened. If these accounts have any authority, then we will need to complete the great work before the chance is lost.'

'Then you believe her. You believe that he is coming.'

'He has always been coming,' said Valoris. 'The only question is when, and on what battlefield we meet him.'

'Have you an answer, then?'

The Captain-General turned away. His severe face peered out into the gloom, as if his bloodshot eyes could somehow tear the murk asunder.

'Not yet,' he murmured. 'The path ahead is still in shadow.'

Navradaran nodded. 'The way will be made clear.'

Valoris did not smile. 'A fragment of a dream,' he said. 'The only thing I took from fifteen years of contemplation. Let us hope I read it right, for we no longer have the luxury of error.'

'What did it tell you?'

Valoris stared out into the gaudy night.

'The same thing I have been telling our star-speakers for months. The same thing I shall tell you and all others who I send out in pursuit of this slender hope.'

Only then did the Captain-General turn again to regard him.

'He calls His daughters home, Navradaran,' he said. 'That is our task now, the only one that matters – to ensure they answer.'

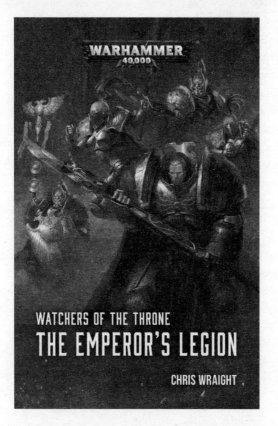

ARGENT

Chris Wraight

Introducing

LUCE SPINOZA

INTERROGATOR, ORDO HERETICUS

I come round, and the pain begins again. It is severe but manageable, so I do not request control measures. I look down and see my arms stripped of their armour, and that momentarily alarms me because I have been armoured for a very long time. I flex my fingers, and the pain flares. Both my forearms are encased in flexplast netting, wound tight, and there are spots of blood on the synthetic fabric. For a moment I look at the dark fluid as it spreads in spidery, blotted lines. My wounds will take a long time to heal even with the assistance of the medicae staff, and that is frustrating.

I realise that the drugs I was given have dulled my senses, and I blink hard and flex my leg muscles and perform mental exercises to restore mental agility.

I take in my surroundings. I am in a cell made of metal floors and metal walls, perhaps five metres by six. A single lumen gives off a weak light, illuminating a narrow desk and an even narrower cot, on which I am lying. The blankets are damp with sweat and tight to my body. I guess that I am back in the ordo command post beyond the Dravaganda ridgeline. I consider whether I am strong enough to move, and place my hands on the twin edges of my cot. Pushing against the metal tells me that I am not – the bones are still broken and incapable of supporting my weight. I could perhaps swing my legs around and stand, though. I would prefer to keep moving, to get my blood flowing again. I am not a child to be protected – I am a grown woman, an interrogator of the Ordo Hereticus, a warrior.

But I do not move, for the door slides open and my master enters. I can tell it is him even before the steel panel shifts, for his armour hums at a pitch I recognise. I believe that he could have chosen to have the telltale audex volume reduced, but he sees no use for stealth and sees many uses for a recognisable signature. To know that he approaches is a cause for dread, and I have witnessed the effect often during actions on terrified subjects.

A part of me dreads his coming too, even now, after I have been a member of his retinue for over a year and served on numerous missions. Inquisitor Joffen Tur cultivates fear as another man might cultivate an appreciation of scholarship or the contents of a hydroponic chamber, and I am not yet entirely immune to his practised aura.

He enters, ducking under the door's lintel. He is in full armour – dark red lacquer, trimmed with bronze. The breastplate is an aquila, chipped with battle damage. His exposed head is clean-shaven with a bull neck and a solid chin. His eyes do not make a connection with me – as ever, he does not focus, as his thoughts are at least partly elsewhere. A man like Tur is always giving consideration to the unseen.

'Awake, then, Spinoza,' he grunts, standing before me.

I attempt to salute, and the pain makes me wince.

'Don't bother,' he says. 'You'll be useless to me for another week. Just tell me what happened.'

'On Forfoda?' I ask, and immediately regret it. My wits are still slow.

'Of course on bloody Forfoda,' Tur growls. 'You're in bed, both your arms are broken, you're a mess. Tell me how you got that way.'

I take a deep breath, and try to remember.

First, though, I must go back further. I must recall the briefing on the bridge of the *Leopax*, Tur's hunter-killer. This is only one of the vessels under his command, and not the largest. By choosing it he is sending a signal to the other Imperial forces mustering at Forfoda – this world is not the greatest of priorities for him, he has other burdens to attend to, but he deigns to participate in order to reflect the Emperor's glory more perfectly and with greater speed.

Tur does not place great store on courtesy, and I admire him for this. He knows his position in the hierarchy of Imperial servants, and it is near the top. One day I aspire to command the same level of self-belief, but know that I have some way to go before I do so.

We assemble under the shadow of his great ouslite command throne – myself, the assassin Kled, the captain of stormtroopers Brannad, the savant Yx and the hierophant Werefol. In the observation dome above us we can see Forfoda's red atmosphere looming, and it is easy to imagine it burning.

Tur himself remains seated as we bow, one by one. He does not acknowledge us, but rubs his ill-shaven chin as flickering lithocasts scroll through the air before him.

'They're torching everything,' he says in due course. 'Damned animals.'

I stiffen a little. He is not referring to the cultists who have brought this world to the brink of ruin, but to the Angels of Death who are now hauling it back to heel. I do not find it easy to hear those blessed warriors described in such terms, as used as I am to Tur's generally brusque manner. When I first heard that we would be in theatre with the Imperial Fists, I gave fervent thanks to Him on Terra, for it had long been a dear wish of mine to witness them fight.

But my master is correct in this, of course – if we do not extract the leaders of the insurrection for scrutiny then we miss the chance to learn what caused it.

'I'll take the primus complex,' Tur says, squinting at a succession of tactical overlays. 'We need to hit that in the next hour or it'll be rubble. Brannad, you'll come too, and a Purgation squad.'

I am surprised by that. Tur has been insistent for months that I develop more experience in conventional combat, and I had expected to make planetfall with him. He is concerned that my reactions are not quite where they should be, and that I am at risk of serious injury, and so I have pursued my training in this area with zeal.

He turns to me.

'You'll take the secondary spire. They're scheduled to hit the command blister in three hours. Go with them. See they do not kill the target before you can get to her.'

I do not hide my surprise well. 'By your will,' I say, but my concern must have been obvious, for Tur scowls at me.

'Yes, you'll be alone with them,' he says. 'Is that a problem? Do you wish for a chaperone?'

I am stung, and suspect that I blush. 'No problem,' I say. 'You honour me.'

'Damn right,' he says. 'So don't foul it up.'

The target is the governor's adjutant Naiao Servia, whom our intelligence places within the secondary spire complex. Her master is holed up somewhere in the central hub, defended well, and thus Tur is correct to devote the majority of his resources there. I cannot help but think that my assignment is more about testing me than utilising our expertise optimally. That is his right, of course. He wishes me to become a weapon after his own design, and in the longer run that goal honours the Emperor more than the fate of a single battlefront.

So I ought to be thankful, and I attempt to remember this as I take my lander down through Forfoda's red methane atmosphere towards my rendezvous coordinates. I do not know how Tur arranged it – he tells me only what I need to know – but he has persuaded the warriors of the Adeptus Astartes to let me accompany them, and that is testament to the heft his word carries here.

'Accompany', though, is a misleading word. I am to serve my master's will in all things, and his will is that Servia is taken alive. I do not yet know how the Imperial Fists will react to this, and on the journey over I catalogue the many factors weighing on an unfavourable outcome.

I am a mortal. Worse, I am a woman. Worse still, I am a mere interrogator. None of these things are destined to make my task with these particular subjects easy, which is no doubt what Tur intended.

We make planetfall and boost across the world's cracked plains towards the forward positions. In order to divert my mind from unhelpful speculation, I look out of the viewports. I see palls of burning promethium rising into the ruddy clouds above. I see the hulks of tanks smouldering in the rad-wastes between spires. I see the northern horizon burning, and feel the impact of shells from the Astra Militarum batteries. This front is heavily populated by both sides – there must be many hundreds of thousands of soldiers dug in. A full advance would be ruinous in both human and equipment terms, so I am sure the commanders back in the orbital station would prefer to avoid it.

My transport touches down on a makeshift rockcrete plate set out in the open, ten kilometres behind the first of our offensive lines. I check my armour-seal before disembarking. Yx told me with some relish that I would last approximately ten seconds if I were to breathe Forfoda's atmosphere unfiltered. Only in the enclosed hives can the citizens exist without rebreathers, and our artillery barrages have compromised even that fragile shell of immunity.

I give my pilot the order to return to the *Leopax* and make my way towards a low command bunker. On presentation of my rosette I am waved inside by a mortal trooper in an atmosphere suit. His armour's trim is gold, and he bears the clenched fist symbol of the Chapter on his chest. Just catching sight of it gives me a twinge of expectation.

I am shown inside by more armoured menials, and taken to a chamber deep underground. I enter a crowded room, dominated by six warriors in full Adeptus Astartes battleplate. They are as enormous as I expected them to be. Their armour is pitted and worn, betraying long periods of active service, and it growls with every movement – a low, almost sub-aural hum of tethered machine-spirits.

Intelligence has already given me their names and designations. Four are Space Marines of a Codex-standard Assault squad – battle-brothers Travix, Movren, Pelleas and Alentar. The fifth is a sergeant, Cranach. The sixth is far more senior, a Chaplain named Erastus, and I immediately sense the distinction between them. It is not just the difference in livery – the Chaplain is arrayed in black against the others' gold – but the manner between them. They are creatures of rigid hierarchy, just as you would expect, and their deference to Erastus is evident.

As I enter, they have already turned to regard me, and I look up at their weather-hammered, scarred faces. The Chaplain's is the most severe, his flesh pulled back from a hard bone structure and his bald head studded with iron service indicators.

'Luce Spinoza,' Erastus says, his voice a snarl of iron over steel. 'Be welcome, acolyte.'

'Interrogator,' I say. It is important to insist on what rank I do have.

Cranach, the sergeant, looks at me evenly. I sense little outright hostility from the others – irritation, perhaps, and some impatience to be moving.

'Your master cares little for his servants,' Erastus says, 'to place them in harm's way so lightly.'

'We are all in harm's way,' I say. 'Emperor be praised.'

Cranach looks at Erastus, and raises a black eyebrow. One of the others – Travix, perhaps – smiles.

Erastus activates a hololith column. 'This is the target,' he says. 'The summit of the upper spire thrust. Here is the command nexus – too far to hit from our forward artillery positions, and shielded from atmospheric assault, so we will destroy it at close range. Once the target is eliminated, we will move on, and the Militarum can handle the rest.'

'The adjutant Servia, present in that location, must be preserved,' I say. Best to get it out in the open as soon as possible, for I do not know how far Tur has already briefed them.

'Not a priority,' Erastus says.

'It is the highest priority.'

He does not get angry. I judge he only gets angry with obstacles of importance, and I hardly qualify as that.

'This is why we have been saddled with you, then,' Erastus says.

'Fought before, acolyte?' Cranach asks, doubtfully. He looks at my battle armour – which I am fiercely proud of – with some scepticism.

'Many times, Throne be praised,' I say, looking him in the eye. 'I will not get in your way.'

'You already are,' Erastus tells me.

'The Holy Orders of the Inquisition have placed an interdict on Servia,' I tell him. 'She will be preserved.' I turn to Cranach. 'Do not call me acolyte again, brother-sergeant. My rank is interrogator, earned by my blood and by the blood of the heretics I have ended.'

Cranach raises his eyebrow again. Perhaps that is his affectation, a curiously human gesture for something so gene-conditioned for killing.

'As you will it, interrogator,' he says, bowing.

So that is my first victory – minor, though, I judge, significant.

'Study the approach patterns,' Erastus tells me. 'If you come with us, you will have to be useful.'

'I pray I will be so, Brother-Chaplain,' I say.

'Why did you say that?' Tur asked.

'Say what?'

'*I pray I will be so*. That was weak. These are the sons of Dorn. They only respect resolve.'

'I did not consider my words.'

'No, you bloody didn't.'

Something in my master's tone strikes me as unusual then. Is his speech a little... petulant? I have spent some time with the Adeptus Astartes now, and the contrast cannot help but be drawn.

But that is unworthy. Tur is a lord of the Ordo Hereticus, a witch-finder of galactic renown, and on a hundred worlds his name is whispered by priests with a cross between reverence and fear. He speaks as he chooses to speak, and there is no requirement of an inquisitor to be decorous, especially to the members of his own retinue.

'Did you understand the attack plan?' he asks.

'It was a simple operation, suited to their skills,' I say. 'We were to approach the spire using an atmospheric transport, breaking in three levels below the command dome where the shielding gave out. From there to the dome was only a short distance. They would seize it, kill the occupants, set charges to destroy the structure, then break out again to the same transport.'

'And you ensured they knew what I demanded?'

'A number of times. They were in no doubt.'

'Did they know the manner of corruption in the spires?'

'No. Neither did I. As I recall, at that stage none of us did.'

Tur grunts. He has a surly look about him, perhaps due to fatigue. He has been fighting for a long time, I guess, and there must be many actions still to conduct.

'Go on, then,' he says. 'What happened next?'

I strap myself into my restraint harness within the gunship's hold. Set beside the Space Marines I feel ludicrously small, even though my armour is the equal of any in the Ordo Hereticus and has performed with distinction in a hundred armed engagements on a dozen worlds.

We are transported in a mid-range assault gunship – an Imperial Fists Storm Eagle. The entire squad is assembled within its hold, and the craft is piloted by two of their battle-brothers whose names

I am never given. The Space Marines do not volunteer much information, which suits me, as I am used to that.

We take off amid a cacophony of engine noise, and the entire craft shakes atop its thrusters' downdraught. The machine is heavily built, a mass of ablative plates and weapon housings, and so enormous power is required to lift it. Once moving, however, the speed is remarkable, and we are soon shooting across the battlefields. I patch in an external visual feed from the craft's auspex array, and see the war-blackened spires rush towards us. The plains below are scarred by mortar impacts, their rock plates burned and broken. Our target becomes visible – a slender outcrop of burning metal, jutting high above the rad-wastes like some sentinel monument.

I turn my attention to my companions. Erastus is silent, his skull-face helm glinting darkly under the glimmer of strip lumens. He holds his power maul two-handed, its heel on the deck. My eyes are drawn towards it. It is a magnificent piece, far too heavy for a mortal to lift, let alone use. It has a bone casing, scrimshawed with almost tribal savagery, and its disruptor unit is charred black.

Cranach is reciting some oath of the Chapter, and I do not understand the words – I assume he uses the vernacular of his own world. Movren has taken a combat blade and is turning it under the lumens, checking for any hint of a flaw. They are reverent, these warriors, and I find their sparse dedication moving. In my vocation I am frequently presented with sham piety or outright heresy, and it is good for the soul to see unfeigned devotion.

'Vector laid in,' comes a voice from the cockpit, and I know then that the assault will begin imminently. 'Prepare to disembark.'

I tense, placing my gauntlet over my laspistol's holster. It is a good weapon from a fine house of weaponsmiths, monogrammed with the sigils of the ordo and fashioned according to the Accatran pattern, and yet it looks painfully small set against the bolt pistols and chainswords of my companions.

The Storm Eagle picks up altitude, still travelling fast, and we are rocked by incoming fire. The lumens are killed, and the hold glows a womb-like red. I begin to wonder at what point our suicidal velocity will begin to ebb, and only slowly realise that it will not be until the very point of ejection. The pilot slams on airbrakes hard, jamming me tight against my restraints.

The Space Marines are already moving. They break free and charge across the bucking deck-plates with astonishing poise, given their immense weight. I join them just as the forward doors cantilever open and the flame-torn atmosphere howls in.

The gunship is hovering just metres away from a vast hole torn into the edge of the spire, and lasfire surrounds us in a coronet of static. Erastus is first across the gap, leaping on power armour servos and landing heavily amongst broken metal structures. The rest of the squad jumps across, until only I remain, poised on the edge of the swaying gunship's gaping innards.

I look down, and see a yawning pit beneath me, falling and falling, streaked with flame and racing gas plumes. That is a mistake, and my heart hammers hard. I curse the error, brace myself and leap, flying out over the gap and feeling the wind tug at me. I land awkwardly, dropping to all fours amid the tangle of blown rockcrete and metal bars. By the time I right myself, the Imperial Fists have already lumbered further in, their bolt pistols drawn and their chainswords revving. The gunship pulls away, strafed with lines of lasfire, and the backwash from its engines nearly rips me clear from the spire's edge.

I run hard, leaping over the debris. My breath echoes in my helm, hot and rapid. I have to sprint just to keep up with the Assault squad, who are moving far faster than I would have guessed possible. They are smashing their way inside, breaking through the walls themselves when they have to, making the corridors and chambers boom and echo with the industrial clamour of their discharging weapons.

By the time I get close again I can see their formation. The four battle-brothers are firing almost continuously, punching bloody holes through an oncoming tide of Forfodan troopers. Cranach carries a combat shield, and uses that in conjunction with a power fist to bludgeon aside any of them that get in close. But it is Erastus who captivates me. He is roaring now, and his voice is truly deafening, even with my helm's aural protection. His movements are spectacular, almost frenzied, and he is hurling himself at the enemy with an abandon that shocks me. His power maul is a close-combat weapon, and it blazes with golden energies, making the cramped spire interior seem to catch fire.

I am firing myself now, adding my las-bolts to the crashing thunder of bolt-rounds. I do some small good, hitting enemy troops as they attempt to form up before the onslaught, but in truth I do not augment the assault too greatly, for its force is entirely unstoppable, a juggernaut of power armour that jolts and horrifies in its speed and overwhelming violence. It is all I can do to keep up, and I struggle to do that, but at least I do not slow them. By the time we have cut and blasted our way to the target location, I am still with them. It is another small victory to add to the tally, though I can take little pleasure in it.

I see the approach to the command dome beckon, a long flight of white stone steps, over-arched with gold. I hear more gunfire, and glimpse movement from within – many bodies, racing to meet the challenge. At that stage all I think is that the defenders' bravery borders on madness, whatever foul creed they have adopted, for they are surely doomed to die quickly.

I do not know what we will meet inside, though. We have not got that far yet.

'You did not contribute much,' Tur says.

'I did my best.'

'Did they wait for you to catch up?'

'No.'

My master looks down at my broken arms, my blood-mottled bandages, and the heavy shadow of disappointment settles on his unforgiving face.

'It might have done you some good,' he says, 'just to witness them.'

'It did,' I say.

'They're crude things, the Adeptus Astartes,' Tur says. 'Don't believe the filth preached by the Ministorum – they're not angels. They're hammers. They crush things, and so we use them as such – never forget that.'

'I will not.'

And yet, I find his words lacking again. The warriors had not been crude, at least not in the way he meant. They were direct, to be sure, but there was an intelligence to their brutality that could be detected up close. They were incredibly destructive, but only as far as was required by the task. I almost tell Tur then what I thought I had gleaned from that episode – that their viewpoint may have been narrow, targeted solely on a limited set of military objectives, but within that ambit they were more impressive than any breed of warrior I had ever served with.

Since entering the ordo I have willingly embraced the diversity of our calling – its dark compromises and the necessity of working within flawed and labyrinthine political structures. I have accepted this, and learned to use the knowledge to my advantage and to the advantage of the Throne, but, for all that, when I saw the Angels of Death in action, and observed the purity of purpose they embodied, and reflected that the Emperor Himself had created them for this reason and no other, a faint shadow of jealousy had imprinted itself on me.

I am not proud of this. My vow is to eradicate it, lest it divert from the tasks I will have after Forfoda, but I cannot deny that it is there, and that it must demonstrate some kind of moral truth.

'You entered the command dome with them?' Tur presses.

'I did. I was with them at the end.'

He looks down at my shattered limbs, then up at my face again.

'Go on, then,' he says.

* * *

Erastus is the first one into the command dome. He is still roaring – in High Gothic now, so I understand fully what he is saying.

'For the glory of the primarch-progenitor!' he cries. 'For the glory of Him on Earth!'

In isolation, those battle-shouts may seem bereft of much purpose, a mere expression of aggression that any thug from an underhive gang could match, but that is to misunderstand them. The volume generated by his augmitters is crushing, and it makes masonry crack and the air throb. The echoing, overlapping wall of sound is almost enough by itself to grind the will of our enemies into dust. The effect on his battle-brothers is just as profound, though opposite – they are roused by their Chaplain's exhortations to further feats of arms, such that they fight on through an aegis of audio-shock, a rolling tide of sensory destruction. I am caught up in it myself, despite my status as an outsider. I find myself crying out along with the Chaplain, repeating the words that I recognise from the catechism where they occur.

'For the Emperor!' I shout as I fight. 'For the Throne!'

And yet I am still appalled at what I witness. We have been misled, all of us, and did not understand the degradation that had been visited on Forfoda. Until then, we had been fighting human-normal troops, carrying standard weaponry, and our intelligence had told us the insurrection was of a political nature. I now see that this is a front, and that extreme corruption has come to this world. Among the standard troops there are now bloated and diseased things, their organs spilling from their flesh, their weapons fused to their limbs in webs of glistening cables.

I wish to gag, but I am surrounded by those who will not hesitate, who have made themselves impervious to horror. They tear into these new enemies, and I see their churning blades bite into unnatural flesh. That fortifies me, and I fight on, taking aim at creatures with lone baleful eyes and swollen, sore-crusted stomachs.

For the first time, we are tested. The command dome is crowded with these nightmare creations, and they come at us without fear.

The air tastes like suppuration, and there are so many to slay. I stay close to Erastus, whose fortitude is undimmed. My laspistol is close to overheating now, and I reach for my combat knife, though I do not think it will serve well against these things.

The situation blinds me to the objective, and for a moment I am fighting merely to avoid annihilation, but then I see her for the first time – Naiao Servia, recognisable from Tur's vid-picts, cowering among the capering fiends she has unleashed. She is obese, her lips cracked, her cheeks flabby with sickness, so I see that she has reaped the rewards of her betrayal. Lines of black blood trace a pattern down her neck, and I do not wish to speculate where it has come from.

Cranach is fighting hard, using his shield and power fist to great effect. His squad members work for one another, covering any momentary weakness of their brothers, carving into the horde of decay as a seamless unit. I see Pelleas go down, dragged into a morass of fluids by three pus-green mutants, and the others respond instantly, hacking their way to his side. They are selfless, a band of soul-brothers, trained from boyhood to keep one another on their feet and fighting.

It is then that I know they will prevail, for the enemy has none of this. These opponents are perversions, individually formidable but without cohesion. I keep firing, giving my laspistol a few more shots before it overloads, aiding the progress of Erastus towards Servia's unnatural bulk.

The adjutant has become huge, far beyond mortal bounds, a slobbering mountain of rotting flesh. Her tongue, slick as oil, lashes from a slash-mouth filled with hooked teeth. Her body spills from the ruins of her old uniform, and tentacles lash out at the Chaplain.

He leaps up at her, swinging with his crozius, and drives a gouge through her swelling stomach. She screams at him, vomiting steaming bile, and he fights through it, his injunctions never ceasing.

I move closer, aiming at the creature's head, trying to blind her, narrowly missing. Then one of her tentacles connects, wrapping around the haft of the Chaplain's power maul, grabbing it and wrenching it from his grip. The weapon flies free, burning through the corrupted blubber and making the fat boil.

Without it, the Chaplain is diminished. He fights on, tearing at the monster with his clenched fists. His brothers are fully occupied and do not see his peril. Only I witness the maul land, skidding across the fluid-slick floor and coming to rest amid a slough of fizzing plasma.

Servia can overwhelm her prey then, pushing him back. Bereft of his weapon, Erastus will be overcome. I feel my laspistol reach its limit. I look over at the maul, crackling still in a corona of energy, and know what I must do.

I race towards it, discarding my laspistol, and reach for the crackling weapon. Lifting it nearly breaks my ribs – it is as heavy as a man, and my power armour strains to compensate. Disruptor charge snakes and lashes about me, and the thing shudders in my grip as if alive. I can barely hold on to it, let alone use it, but Erastus is now in mortal danger.

'For the Emperor!' I cry, mimicking his strident roars, and throw myself at the creature.

I swing the maul at its spine, two-handed, putting all my weight into the blow. This betrays my ignorance – the weight and power of it is far too much, and as it connects I realise my error. My arms are smashed even through my armour, and the wave of pain makes me scream out loud. The released disruptor charge explodes, throwing me clear of the impact and cracking open ceramite plate. I cannot release the maul – it remains in my grip, locked by ruined gauntlets amid gouts of flame.

But the blow is enough. The creature reels, its back broken, and Erastus surges towards it, ripping the tentacles free of its twisted body. His battle-brothers fight through the remains of the throng, subduing the attendant horrors to bring their fire to bear on the leader.

I am in agony. I can feel my bones jutting through my flesh, my blood sloshing inside my armour, and I am lightheaded and nauseous. It takes all my strength merely to lift my head and stay conscious.

I see Erastus punching out, driving Servia back. I see the rest of the squad level their bolt pistols, ready to destroy it.

'No!' I cry, raising a trembling, ruined arm. 'Preserve her!'

Erastus halts. He looks at me, then at the trembling mass of blubber before him. Cranach is poised to wade in closer, to rip its heart from its diseased chest. His battle-brothers make no move to comply. Soon they will kill it.

'Hold,' the Chaplain commands, and they instantly freeze. Servia shrinks back, crippled but alive.

Cranach moves to protest. 'It cannot be suffered to–' he begins.

Erastus cuts him dead. He nods in my direction.

I try to keep myself together, and know that I will fail. I see them looking at me, bristling with barely contained battle-fury. They want to kill it. They live to kill it.

'*Preserve her,*' I tell them, down on my knees in puddles of blood.

Cranach looks at the Chaplain.

'She has the crozius, sergeant,' Erastus tells him.

That is the last thing I remember.

Tur does not say anything for a while.

'When they brought you back here–' he begins.

'I remember none of it.'

He nods, thinking. 'They didn't tell me everything.'

'I do not think they speak of their battles,' I say.

'No, maybe not.' He is struggling for words now. I do not know if he is proud to learn what happened, or maybe disappointed. Tur has always found castigation easy – it is his profession – but praise comes less naturally.

'You did well, then,' he says eventually. 'The subject is on the *Leopax*, and I'll speak to her soon. She'll regret being alive. I'm not in the mood to be gentle.'

When is Tur ever in that mood? I might smile, but the pain is still prohibitive.

'And you are recovering, then?' he asks, awkwardly.

'Yes, lord,' I say.

He nods again. 'Weapons training,' he says. 'When this is over, you need more of it. Perhaps this is an aptitude I have overlooked.'

I do not say anything. I do not think it will be necessary, for reasons I will not disclose to him.

Do not misunderstand me. I remain loyal to my master. He is a great man in many ways, and I aspire to learn from him. One day, in the far future, my ambition is to be as devoted a servant of Terra as he has been, and to have a reputation half as formidable. I cannot imagine serving under another as dedicated to the Throne. Indeed, I find it hard to imagine serving under anyone else at all.

But I have learned much on Forfoda, and some lessons are still to come.

'As you will, lord,' I say, hoping he will leave soon.

It takes three weeks to subdue the remains of the insurrection. The Imperial Fists linger in theatre longer than originally intended once the scale of corruption is revealed. Many of the spires are destroyed wholesale, and many millions of survivors are deported in void-haulers, ready either for slaughter or mind-wiping. Our strategos estimate it will take months to purge the world, and that the Ministorum will be required to maintain scrutiny for decades after that, but it has been retained, and its forges and its manufactoria remain ready for use by the Holy Imperium of Man.

I take much satisfaction in that. Once my arms heal, I begin the process of regaining strength. I take up my duties as fast as I am able. Tur does not visit me again, for he is detained with many cares. Yx tells me that Servia's testimony was instrumental in the recapture of the industrial zones north of the spires, and that gladdens my soul.

Near the end, I have the visitor I have been expecting. He also does not have much time, so his presence here honours me. When Erastus walks into the training chambers in the Dravaganda command post he seems even more gigantic than before. His armour is a little more worn, his angular face carrying an extra scar, but the energy in his movements is undiminished.

'Interrogator,' he says, bowing. 'I would have come sooner, but there were many calls on us.'

I bow in return. 'It is good to see you, lord Chaplain,' I say.

I notice then that he carries his power maul, the thing he called a crozius. It looks different to me – smaller, as if cut down somehow. Perhaps I damaged it. I know how much the warriors of the Adeptus Astartes venerate their weapons, and so the thought troubles me.

'This is Argent,' Erastus says, hefting the heavy piece as if it weighs nothing. 'It has been in the Chapter for a thousand years. For an outsider to handle it, even to touch it, earns the wrath of us all.'

He is still severe. Perhaps he knows no other way to be.

'I did not know,' I say, wondering why he has come here to tell me this.

'We protect that which is precious to us,' he says. 'But we also understand what is truly significant. Take it, and observe what has changed.'

I receive the maul again, and then see truly that it has been heavily adapted. It is shorter, lighter, its power unit truncated and the bone casing modified. Even then I struggle to hold it steady, and my armour-encased arms ache.

'Why have you done this?' I ask.

'Because it is yours now,' he says.

I cannot believe it. I move to give the weapon back, unable to accept such a gift.

'If you spurn the offer,' Erastus warns me, 'it will be a second insult, one I will not overlook.'

I look down at the crozius. The detail on its shaft is incredible. It is a thing of beauty as well as power. The gesture overwhelms me, and I do not have the words for it.

'You do me too much honour,' I say at last, and it seems like a weak response.

'I have only just started,' he says, standing back and regarding me critically. 'You hold it as if it were a snake. Grip the handle loosely. I will show you how to bear it without breaking your bones.'

It is then that I know why he has come. He will instruct me in how to wield it, and I understand then that it will henceforth become my own weapon, the one I shall carry in preference to all others.

It will hurt. I will damage the healing process by doing this. Tur will be angry, for he desires me back in service within days.

None of that matters. I do as I am bid, then look to the Chaplain. I do not know if such a thing has ever been done before. My soul fills with joy, and I determine to make myself equal to the gesture. Perhaps that will be my purpose now – to live up to this deed, to ensure that Argent is used as it ought to be used, for the glory of Him on Earth.

That would be a fine ambition, I think, one worthy of my high calling.

'Show me,' I say then, hungry for the knowledge.

YOUR
NEXT READ

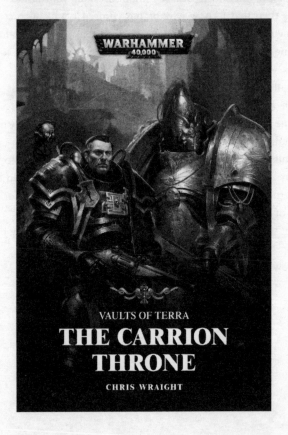

VAULTS OF TERRA: THE CARRION THRONE
by Chris Wraight

Inquisitor Crowl, who serves on Holy Terra itself, follows the trail of
a conspiracy that leads him to the corridors of the Imperial Palace…

THE ABSOLUTION
OF SWORDS

John French

Introducing

COVENANT

INQUISITOR, ORDO MALLEUS

*'Claims of innocence mean nothing:
they serve only to prove a foolish lack of caution.'*

– Judge Traggat, *Selected Sayings*, Vol. III, Chapter IV

I

Snow had come to Crow Complex as night fell. The ice-laden wind spiralled through the stacked domes and spires, reaching its fingers down into the cloisters to ripple the flames of candles. A trio walked through the ragged light, crimson robes dragging over the stone floor. No one stopped them. They passed like shadows beneath the sun. Most of the members of the complex's orders had hidden from the cold as the sun had set. Those few hurrying through the processionals saw the bronze hand of the Order of Castigation hanging around the trio's necks, and moved on. One did not draw the attention of the castigators unnecessarily.

The first of the trio was tall and slender, and the fall of the robes made it seem to glide over the floor rather than walk. Brass glinted inside its cowl. The second was heavier-set, and walked with head bowed and hands folded into its wide sleeves. A checked band of white and black silk ran around the hems of its sleeves, marking it as the abbot of its order. The last was hunched, fat, and moved with dragging steps. The fabric over its shoulders bulged, and it clinked as it walked. A length of chain trailed along the ground beneath the edge of its robe. To anyone considering if they should check the trio's progress, this last figure removed any doubts; a weighted penitent was a visible reminder of the price of sin and the cost of absolution.

The wind tugged at the trio's hoods as they stepped onto the Bridge of Benevolence. A sheer drop fell away to blackness either side of the narrow span of stone. Snow was already settling on the slabs.

'Sweet tears of Terra,' gasped the hunched figure, as a gust cut across the bridge.

The figure in the abbot's robe turned its head slightly towards the hunched figure behind him.

'Your pardon,' said the hunched figure, and then muttered to himself. 'This wind is enough to flay the armour off a tank.'

The trio passed on across the bridge, and towards the looming mass of the High Chapel. Hundreds of metres tall, and over a kilometre across, its size rivalled the cathedrals of other worlds. Twin doors of iron stood closed at the end of the bridge. Plumes of flame rose from vast braziers set to each side of the archway. Copper feathers cascaded down the face of each door.

A pair of guards stepped from niches as the trio reached the end of the bridge. Each wore a brushed-steel breastplate over white robes woven with scarlet flames. Both carried lasguns, the barrels hung with saint coins and water vials. The Ecclesiarchy had held no men under arms since the Age of Apostasy, so these guardians were technically separate from the priests whose will and creed they followed. They were of the Iron Brotherhood, pilgrim warriors who had taken oaths to guard the chapel's sanctity. Of all the souls in the Crow Complex, they were some of the few who would question the right of an abbot to pass where he wished. They levelled their weapons at the trio.

'Entrance to the chapel is barred by order of the prefectus prior,' said one of the guards. 'I cannot open the way, even to your order.'

The trio stood unmoving and silent.

'By whose will do you come here at this hour?' snapped the other guard. 'You are not Abbot Crayling. Who are you?'

'I ask your forgiveness,' said the first of the trio, her voice sharp and clear. The nearest guard blinked, tattooed skulls briefly closing over his eyes. The other opened his mouth to speak.

The robed woman crossed the gap to the guards in a blur, red cloth spilling in her wake. The nearest guard pulled the trigger of his gun. A fist hit the back of his hand. Bones shattered. He gasped air to shout, as an elbow whipped into his temple. He fell, lasgun slipping from his grasp to the snow covered ground. The second guard was slower, his fingers still scrabbling at the safety catch of his gun as the woman grabbed his collapsing comrade and threw the unconscious body at him. The wind caught the hood of their attacker and the velvet cowl fell back from a slim face beneath a shaven scalp. The second guard toppled, and tried to rise. A boot lashed across his jaw. He slumped to the ground. The lasguns went tumbling down into the abyss beneath the bridge a second later.

'Someone will notice,' said the hunched man. Neither he nor the figure dressed as the abbot had moved. The woman glanced up at him. The x-shaped henna stain running across her face made her eyes seem like polished jade set in copper.

'I will add it to my penance,' she said, 'but we do not have the luxury of time.'

The fat figure grunted, chains clinking as he shifted his weight. The hunch on his shoulders moved. A slit in the side of his robes opened and a fabric-wrapped bundle slid to the ground.

'If we are abandoning subtlety I won't need these,' he said, pulling chains from under his robe and letting them rattle to the ground. He knelt and unbuckled the straps around the bundle. The fabric peeled back; oiled metal gleamed within its folds. A pair of bolt pistols etched with gold feathers lay beside a long-hafted warhammer, and a sheathed great longsword. Beneath them were ammo clips and a narrow-bladed power sword. He tossed the bolt pistols to the girl with the painted face. She caught them, checked their action and holstered them beneath her robes. He passed the rest out, and for a second the clink of weapons and harnesses chimed against the wind.

The man in the abbot's robe settled the sword behind his shoulders, stepped up to the doors, and pushed a section of the frosted metal. A small door hinged inwards.

'Follow,' he said, and stepped through.

II

'You sleep at the other end,' growled the Pilgrim.

Cleander Von Castellan sighed. He was starting to wish that they had picked a different infiltration location than this forgotten hole.

The cavern he now squatted in had not been made for the purpose it now served. Cleander guessed that it had been a water cistern, feeding the thirst of the first monasteries built when Dominicus Prime had been a barely populated backwater. Now it was a store for the tides of humanity that came to the shrine world. Like everything in the sprawl built by the faithful, it had an acquired name that rang hollow to Cleander's ear. The Garden of Eternity, they called it. Pillars marched into the dark holding up a ceiling of cracked plaster. Crude paintings of trees and vines wound up their sides. Sheets of cloth hung from wires strung between the pillars dividing the cavern into a maze of spaces. The light of small fires and oil lamps cast shadows against the fabric screens. Salt deposits glittered where the rough floor met the bases of columns. Glum, unwashed faces had risen and looked down again at Cleander and Koleg as they had passed. There had been no offers of help or friendly greeting to fellow pilgrims. This was the kind of place that bred despair rather than good cheer.

They had eventually found a place in the maze of screens. That alone had been difficult. Every space had a claim on it, and they had to exchange cylinders of fresh water to find somewhere. The commerce that clung to almost every inch of life down here in the Warrens almost made Cleander want to laugh. They had to pay an offering of candle tokens at three shrines for directions to the Garden of Eternity. When they had found the entrance, it had turned out to be a rusted iron door set in a crumbling arch beneath a sculpture of the Emperor as provider. Even then a hooded crone sitting just inside the door had held out her hand for a donation. Cleander had noticed the blunderbuss welded to the metal struts of the crone's other hand, and handed over another token. That the thug of a pilgrim who loomed over them had some claim on the bit of ground he sat on did not surprise Cleander. It was, though, getting on his nerves.

He looked up into the pilgrim's face. The man's head was a ball of scar tissue arranged around a snarl of broken teeth. Tattered fur covered his shoulders, adding to the bulk of the muscles beneath. Layers of stained cloth covered the rest of his body. Red veins spidered the yellow of his eyes.

Cleander tried a smile.

'I am sorry, brother traveller,' he said. 'Is something amiss?'

The big pilgrim raised a hand and jabbed a thick finger towards the other end of the sleeping hall.

'You sleep down there,' growled the pilgrim.

Cleander glanced at Koleg, but his companion's eyes were focused on a point in the distance, his face as blank as ever.

'We have already paid to be here,' said Cleander, and fixed his smile in place. He could almost see heavy cogs turning in the big pilgrim's skull.

'You go–' began the thug.

'No,' said Cleander. 'Like I said, we have paid.' He held the smile in place, his good eye barely flicking as he sized up the thug. Lots of muscle, arms tattooed with tiny, black dots, one for every day spent on pilgrimage to the Crow Complex, a gang brand from Iago running around the left forearm.

The thug's patience seemed to run out. He stepped back, tensing to lash a kick into Cleander's face. The man's collar shifted down his neck. A circle of faded ink coiled at the base.

'The Tenth Path,' said Cleander quickly. The thug froze. Cleander reached up to his own throat, careful to keep the movement slow, and pulled his collar down. The tattoo was false, but looked real enough: a ragged halo of ink curled around a bare circle of skin. He flicked his eyes at Koleg. The soldier returned the look without expression and bared his neck to show the same mark. Cleander looked back at the thug. 'We are seekers of the Tenth Path.'

The thug looked between them. The other pilgrims sitting nearby had already shrunk back, and made it very clear that they had other things to concern them.

'You,' said the thug at last. 'Follow.' He turned and began to walk towards the far end of the cavern. Cleander stood, lifting the roll of rags holding his possessions and hanging its rope cord across his shoulders. Koleg followed, pulling his coat close about him. The specialist's face was impassive as always, flint-grey eyes moving over the fabric partitions and huddled pilgrims as they passed. Koleg moved with unhurried care, precise and controlled. The dark skin of his scalp glinted in the firelight, the old surgical scars pale lines around the base of his skull. Unless you had spent years in the specialist's company, there was little for the eye to catch in his appearance. Most people tended not to notice Koleg, as though he blended with the banality of life. He was also one of the most dangerous people Cleander had ever known.

They trailed the thug, passing down a corridor between fabric screens. People pulled back from their path, and Cleander could see fear in their eyes in the instant before they glanced away. It was not him that they feared, he was sure. At times he had cowed pirate lords and alien princes, but here and now he was just a man with one eye, a ragged beard and greying hair. Clothed in patched and reeking rags, he looked and smelled just like all of the rest of lost humanity.

'Where are we going?' he asked the thug.

The brute kept walking. 'To see the confessor.'

Cleander felt his gut tighten, but kept his face impassive. A confessor could be trouble. The firebrand priests of the Ecclesiar-chy were often dangerous and likely to deal with those they saw as heretics without mercy or waiting for reasons. It had taken him and Koleg three weeks to get this far. They were walking the Tenth Path, down into the dark. Now it might end not in revelation, but in fire.

'Here,' said the thug, stopping and pulling aside a panel of weighted fabric. They stepped through. The base of one of the pil-lars rose from the centre of the space beyond. Worn fabric hung over the rough stone, threadbare carpets covered the floor, and bowls of burning oil stood on poles. There was no sign of anyone else. The thug let the hanging drop, and turned to them.

'What is the truth of the first path?' he said.

'That there can be truth,' said Cleander without a pause.

The thug looked at him, nodded slowly, and then looked at Koleg.

'What is the truth of the second path?'

'That the universe is truth,' said Koleg.

The thug stared at him.

Cleander held himself still. It had taken a lot of work and more than a little blood to learn the replies they had just given. Those words should be enough to take them one more step, but if the thug asked another question they were in trouble. He felt his fin-gers twitch, feeling the absence of his digi-rings.

The thug nodded, and moved the hangings covering the base of the pillar. A corroded metal door sat beneath. A heavy lock had been welded to the door and frame. A ragged circle had been burned onto the metal. The thug pulled a key on a leather thong from under his tunic, and slotted it into the lock.

Cleander took a step forwards.

The thug paused, hand still on the unturned key. 'How found you the path, brethren?' he said.

A chill ran over Cleander's skin. He licked his lips, mind racing through all of the intelligence Viola had compiled for them on the Tenth Path. This was not a question that they had encountered. The question might have been one of the cult's ritual challenges, or it might be simple curiosity. Either way there were more wrong answers than right.

'By many steps, brother,' said Cleander carefully. There was an extended moment in which he held the thug's stare. The man's gaze twitched.

Cleander yanked the bedroll off his shoulder. The thug's fist lashed out. Cleander ducked, hand scrabbling at the roll of rags in his hands. The thug reached under the layers of his tunic and pulled a length of chain from his waist. Barbs glittered on the edges of the sharpened links. The thug swung. Cleander ducked again, hand reaching inside the bedroll. The weapon hit the floor, and snapped back into the air. Koleg was moving behind the thug. The chain whipped out. Cleander jerked aside. A barb caught his right shoulder and bit deep. The thug yanked, and Cleander lurched forwards, pain rushing through him. Blood spread across his tunic from his shoulder.

Cleander could see Koleg stepping up behind the thug, right hand wreathed with blue lightning. The thug's lips pulled back in a grinning snarl. Rows of hooked metal teeth glinted in his mouth. He yanked the chain again. Cleander went with the force of the pull and slammed his knuckles into the thug's throat. The man staggered, choking. The barb ripped from Cleander's shoulder. Fresh pain burst through him, but his hand had found the grip of the needler hidden inside his bedroll. He pulled the pistol free as the links arced down again.

Blue arcs enveloped the thug's head. His body jerked, muscles spasming, jaws clamping down on his tongue. Blood poured down his chin. Cleander saw Koleg's fingers closed around the base of the man's neck. The polished armatures of the shock-gloves shone as they discharged power.

'You shoot now,' said Koleg.

Cleander brought the pistol up and squeezed the trigger. The gun's hiss was lost under the crackle of electrical discharge. The toxin sliver hit the thug in the right eye and he dropped, muscles still twitching as he hit the floor.

Cleander stepped back, breathing hard. Shadows were moving behind the fabric hangings. Shouts echoed off the cavern ceiling. Koleg dropped to one knee and pulled grenades and weapons from under his coat, laying them on the floor in neat rows.

'That was not optimal,' said the soldier.

'At least we know we found the right place,' replied Cleander.

Cleander ripped open the rest of his bedroll. Objects tumbled out as blood scattered from his wounded arm. He grabbed a falling injector with his good hand and smacked it into his shoulder next to the wound. The cocktail of numb, spur and blood coagulant poured into him an instant after the needle punched through his skin. He let out a sharp breath. Koleg looked up at him, and tossed him a compact filter mask. Cleander caught it and shook the straps free. Koleg already had his mask on, his eyes hidden behind a slot visor set in a white ceramic faceplate. A short chrome cylinder projected from each side of the mask's chin.

'How long until they find us?' asked Cleander.

A shadow loomed next to one of the hangings. A chain blade roared to life, and sliced down through the fabric. Cleander brought the pistol up and put two needles into the shadow. The figure dropped, ripping the hole wide as it fell, chain blade growling in its death grip. Another shape was moving behind it. Cleander could see the shadow of a handgun. He shot again, heard a noise from behind him and spun, putting another shot into a silhouette.

'Secure your mask,' called Koleg, his voice flat and metallic as it came from his own mask's speakers. He held a pistol with a short, tubular barrel. The broken breech of the weapon was wide enough to swallow a shot glass.

Cleander pulled the mask over his head, the rubber seals pressed into his face. The world beyond the photo-visor became a twilight blue. More shadows were moving beyond the screens. He heard the clunk of a gun arming.

'Secure,' he shouted, hearing his own voice echo flat from his speaker.

Koleg nodded, dropped a grenade shell into the pistol launcher, and closed the breech with a flick of his wrist.

Gunfire ripped through the fabric screens. Cleander dropped to the floor as the bullets sawed through the air above him. The torn hangings swayed and his eye caught the flash of muzzle flare. He sent three needles into the space behind the flash, and the gunfire stopped. Koleg, unmoved, aimed the pistol launcher up and pulled the trigger. The grenade thumped into the air, hit the ceiling above and burst in a grey cloud of gas. The spent casing spun to the ground as Koleg cracked the launcher, and dropped another grenade into the breech. He fired again, the shot arcing high over the fabric hangings, then again and again, in a quick, remorseless rhythm.

Grey and cyan fog rolled through the cavern, sinking from the roof, spreading between the cloth hangings. For an instant there was a muffled lull in noise. Then the screaming boiled up, rending the air as terror ripped from a hundred throats. Weeping and shouting blended with the cacophony, as the hallucinogen and terror gas flooded the cavern. Inside his mask, Cleander gulped the sanitised air. It tasted slightly metallic.

Koleg bent down and began to gather up the rest of his equipment, then shrugged into a twin shoulder harness. A macrostubber sat in the left holster, and the pistol grenade launcher went into the empty right holster, the grenades into loops and pouches across his chest. Cleander scooped up his own collection of trinkets. Two heavy rings went onto each hand, a power dagger in a sheath onto his left forearm, and a patch over his left eye socket.

Koleg moved over to the door in the pillar base. The thug's key was still in the lock. Around them the sounds of panic rolled with the spreading fog. Cleander clicked a switch on the side of his mask, and his view through the visor snapped into cold black broken by splashes of red and yellow body heat.

'We proceed?' asked Koleg, drawing his macrostubber pistol from its holster. Cleander moved up next to him, and gripped the key. The lock turned smoothly. Cleander felt the door shudder as bolts thumped back into the frame. He pulled it wide. A flight of stairs spiralled down into the dark. Traces of green warmth moved in the blue-stained cold of Cleander's sight.

'We proceed,' he said and stepped through.

III

Prior Prefectus Gul paused as he crossed the threshold of the western sub-chapel. Candles burned on the altar dominating the far end of the long chamber, filling the nave with the warm glow of flames, but leaving the rest to shadows. The candle in Gul's right hand lit a circle of floor around him, but then slid off into the quiet gloom. Lumn had stopped three paces behind Gul, and waited, head bowed, arms folded in his wide sleeves. His face was wide, the flesh soft beneath his tonsured hair. In the low light the grey of Lumn's robes seemed liked folded shadow.

'Wait for me in the south transept,' said Gul. Lumn bowed his head even lower, then turned and moved away into the darkness of the chapel's main vault. Gul watched him go for a second. Lumn was his Silent Acolyte, an order whose entire existence revolved around serving the spiritual leaders of the Crow Complex. Conditioned to obedience and secrecy, the Silent Acolytes completed their novitiate training by having their tongues cut from their mouths. They were supposed to be utterly trustworthy, and Gul had never had reason to doubt Lumn's devotion. But trust was a coin made of false gold.

Gul stepped into the sub-chapel, and let the quiet of night gather around him. Like the rest of the High Chapel, it was almost deserted. During the day, Dominicus' sun would rise through the sky, and its light would fall through the chapel's windows and crystal dome, illuminating the faithful. Once the sun began to fall, the prayers faded and those who had been granted a place at twilight prayer left the chapel to sleep in silence. Only the members of the order of the Eternal Light moved amongst the pews and pillars, tending the candles that burned in the one hundred and eight shrines. As the second most senior brother in all the orders of the Crow Complex, Gul was one of the only other souls who saw the High Chapel in the dark.

He liked the night. It was a sea of calm in the constant whirl that was the governance of the monastery complex. That you could only hear yourself think when this supposed place of peace was empty, was an irony that struck him every time he stepped into the High Chapel. Not that he ever thought of it as a place of true peace, nor of the blessings that were given within its walls as anything but empty lies. The Imperial Creed was a doctrine of blood and greed, and bloated power feeding on the fear of the faithful. The Emperor did not protect, and never had. He was a man who did extraordinary things, who had earned the Imperium he had created, but a man none the less. For all his power, one might as well take a hook and line to the sea and fish for truth as pray to the Emperor for deliverance, enlightenment or mercy.

Gul had not always known that the Emperor was not divine. Once he had been like all the other credulous fools. Now he held the truth locked inside his skull, hidden by competence and masked by piety. He could smile at a grossly fat prelate exhorting starving pilgrims to beware the lure of gluttony. He could watch the preachers dole out blessings while the devotional servitors followed them to collect coin from the grateful. He could do these things because he knew the truth. That core of secrets locked inside him gave him a strength that the Imperial Creed never had. He was a heretic, and he was blessed to be so.

He stepped towards the sub-chapel's altar, glancing at the candle that marked the time. His rendezvous with his contact in the Tenth Path was not until the next division, but he liked to arrive first. It gave him comfort, a veneer of control over what was happening. Besides, it gave him time to think. His footsteps echoed softly under the gaze of the stone saints lining the walls. It had been sixty days since his last meeting, and he had not expected to be summoned again so soon. Had something changed? What would be asked of him? Was there something wrong?

He was a pace from the altar when the candle flames rippled. A breath of cold air touched the back of his neck. He whirled around, eyes going to the arch he had entered through.

There was nothing there, just the distant light of torches falling in the main transept. Cold air gusted past him again, and the candles on the altar guttered. Somewhere a door banged shut. The air was still again, the dark in the sub-chapel almost total now. Footsteps echoed behind him, and Gul turned.

'Who is there?' he called, and the stone echoed back his voice in fading whispers.

'...is there?'

'Who...'

'... there... there... there...?'

The afterglow of the extinguished candle flames clung to his retinas as he turned and stared at the dark.

'Prior Prefectus Aristas Gul,' said a voice from behind him. He whirled back, eyes wide, mouth dry.

Fire sparked in front of him. Gul flinched, but the flame held steady, a single tongue of orange in the black. The image of a hand holding a burning taper formed next to the light, and then the flaring light caught the outline of a hooded figure. Black and white checks ran around the sleeves of the red robes.

'You should not be here,' snapped Gul, his voice ringing high. He could feel cold snaking down his skin. 'I demand–'

'A scholar once told me that humans lit candles in prayer before they even knew they were not alone in the cosmos,' said the robed figure. The hand holding the taper reached out, and put the flame to the wick of a candle. The fire caught. 'Before they knew that their gods were lies, they still drew hope from that one small act.'

Gul felt his mouth open to call out, but the words caught before they could reach his tongue. The robed figure turned. The bronze hand hanging on the robed man's chest glinted. Gul's frozen mind finally registered the colours and details of the figure's robes. He could see the hilt of a sword and the butt of a gun projecting up behind the man's hood.

'You are not Abbot Crayling,' he said, anger overcoming fear. 'You are not of the Order of Castigation. Who are you?'

A swish of fabric jerked Gul's eyes to the arched doorway at the other end of the chapel. A slender figure in red robes stood outlined against the glow from beyond. Her hood was down, and he could see the ruddy 'X' crossing her face beneath a shaved scalp. A heavy step rang behind him and a hunched figure appeared from the dark, muscles and fat rippling under crimson fabric as the man hefted a double-handed hammer.

His skin felt tight, his blood a racing beat of ice in his flesh. Fears and possibilities formed and spun in his mind: discovery, betrayal, escape. He should run. He should make for the small door behind the altar and flee. He should call out. Lumn might still be close enough to hear him. But he did not move or speak. Instead his mouth repeated the last words they had spoken.

'Who are you?' he breathed.

The tall man with the sword across his back reached up and lowered his hood. The face beneath was young and strong, long black hair pulled back in a topknot above hard, dark eyes.

'I am Covenant,' said the man, 'and I am here to offer you a chance of absolution.'

IV

Cold darkness swallowed Cleander as he descended the spiral stairs. The world was painted in blue in his infra-visor. Only he and Koleg stood out, their shapes yellow and red with warmth. They had closed the door into the sleeping cavern, and had been descending for long enough that they had left all light far behind. After a while he had switched to dark vision, but there were no scraps of light for it to gather, just a grey blur at the edge of sight. He had switched back to the blindness of infra-vision, and moved by touch, left hand running over the rough stone of the wall.

'These catacombs run deep,' he muttered after a while.

'A fact that we knew at mission briefing,' said Koleg.

Cleander shivered, suddenly wishing that he had something more substantial than pilgrim rags to keep him warm. 'It should not be this cold – there are no air currents, no running water. So why is it getting colder?' he said. Koleg hesitated behind him. He turned, and looked at the soldier. Koleg's shape was a bright rainbow of body heat.

'The temperature is stable,' said Koleg. 'It isn't getting colder.'

Cleander felt himself become very still. Ice ran over his skin. In his eyes the colours of the infra-sight swam, switching and blurring. His teeth rattled against each other in his mouth. He turned back to the darkness beneath the next step. He reached out for the wall. His fingers slid into empty air. He flinched, but kept his hand extended. The cold bit into his bare skin. He moved his hand to the side, breathing slowly. His fingers touched stone. It felt warm, as though it had been warmed by the sun.

'There is a door on my right,' he said, carefully. 'Follow the direction of my right arm.'

Koleg moved close, hand macrostubber levelled, one hand on Cleander's shoulder.

'Ready,' said Koleg.

Cleander's right hand flexed on the grip of his needler.

'Moving,' he said, and stepped into the waiting emptiness beyond the door.

A deeper chill washed over him, as though he had stepped through a cascade of water. The view in his infra-visor flashed, bubbles of yellow and red heat popping against blue. He snapped the visor to normal vision. For a moment the black remained pressed against his eyes. Then light began to sketch a reality around him. A blue-green glow spread up columns framing eight openings set to either side of a long chamber. The columns supporting the arches were carved from a stone that glistened like glass. A long pool of liquid ran down the centre of the floor, its surface a black mirror. Cleander stepped forwards, and Koleg moved past him, pistol levelled, tracking between each of the archways.

'This is it,' said Cleander. 'This is where they were bringing us.'

'This is the target?'

Cleander did not respond. His eyes flicked over the chamber. For a second he thought had seen something sinuous move under the stone surface of the wall, as though it were a sheet of glass opening on an ocean.

'Who was it that the big lug said he was bringing us to see?' said Cleander, softly. He was suddenly wishing that he had argued for a different approach in tackling the Tenth Path, an approach that included a platoon of his household mercenaries. Or a Space Marine strike team.

'The confessor...' said Koleg.

Cleander turned to answer, and stopped. A tall, hunched statue stood under a white shroud at the far end of the chamber. The fabric stirred as though in a breeze. The scent of crushed flowers and spoiled meat brushed Cleander's senses. Rage bubbled up inside him, staining his thoughts red. Whispers chirped at the edges of his mind, promising things he never knew he wanted. He shut out the thoughts and sensations.

He knew what this was; the warp was close, shivering just beyond the skin of reality, feeling for a crack through which to pour. To others, even that touch would be enough to force them to their knees, eyes wide but seeing nothing. Cleander had touched the warp and seen its true face many times, and though he knew better than to think himself immune to its promises, he also knew himself well enough to see those promises as empty. He was not a good man, he was very far from a good man. He knew the power of wealth and lies, and enjoyed using both. He cared for few, and saw most people as expendable and worthless at best. He had no ideals, and his few beliefs all had a price. These were facts that he had never denied, but they were not weakness; they were armour against false desire.

Koleg swayed where he stood, and then moved forwards, gun raised. Cleander stepped to follow, and then paused. He glanced up, and then back to the pool of water running down the centre of the room. The ceiling above was vaulted stone. Perhaps it had been the crypt of one of the first temples raised on Dominicus Prime, now buried deep beneath the mountain of stone that was the Crow Complex. Handprints covered the ceiling, hundreds of handprints in dried, dark liquid. Cleander paused.

'Koleg,' he said, carefully.

'Yes?'

'The pool,' said Cleander. Koleg snapped a glance at it, and then back to the space beyond his gun.

'I see it,' said Koleg.

Cleander stepped forwards, kneeling slowly. He stared at the black gloss surface. The water beneath was black, and Cleander could not tell if that was because he could not see through it, or if it was perfectly clear and he was looking down into an abyss.

'It reflects nothing,' he said, and reached out to touch it.

'What are you doing?' called Koleg.

'The confessor,' he said. 'That is what is supposed to be down here. The first steps of damnation are always wrapped in the costume of piety – isn't that what Josef keeps on saying? So when all those lost souls come down here, they come to confess. And why do the pious confess?' His fingers were just above the surface. 'To be washed clean.'

He touched the water.

Circles spread across the pool, struck the sides and rebounded. Water lapped over the edges.

'Is this wise?' said Koleg as he moved next to Cleander.

'No,' said Cleander, and the word was a puff of white in the suddenly freezing air. 'But if I was wise I would not be here in the first place.'

More water was splashing out of the pool as its surface began to chop and heave. A low moan ran around the chamber, and Cleander looked up for a second. When he looked back, it was into a face floating beneath the surface of the water. He leapt to his feet. Koleg spun.

The face was pale, the flesh fat under blue-veined skin. Silver hair swirled around it, billowing in the water. Its mouth was open, tongue pink between white teeth. The eyes were closed as though in sleep, or peaceful death. Cleander tried to move, to bring his needler up, but he was frozen in place, eyes locked on the image forming beneath the waves. A torso appeared beneath the face, then arms and legs. Lines of stitched scars criss-crossed flesh. Silver tubes ran into the tips of its fingers and ran off into the depths. Cleander's heart was a paused beat in his chest. The face in the water opened its eyes. He had an impression of colour swirling around ragged pupils. Ice was spreading across the floor from the pool edge.

+Help,+ said a voice that echoed in Cleander's skull. +Help me.+

He felt his limbs moving, felt himself bend down to the water, reaching beneath to pull the figure out into the air.

+Free me.+

'Von Castellan!' shouted Koleg, close but so far away. 'Stand back, now!'

+Please,+ whispered the voice in his head.

A hand gripped Cleander's arm and yanked him back. He swore, surged up, confusion and anger roaring through him. Koleg shoved him away, and Cleander's eyes cleared.

Figures stepped from the black spaces of the archways. Tatters of soaking cloth hung from them. Jagged circle tattoos slid over the exposed skin of their arms and necks. Darkness shone from the marks, shredding light, fuming night. Grey ash powdered their faces. Their eyes were closed, and frost breathed from their lips. Serrated knives and barbed chains hung from their hands.

Koleg fired. A tongue of flame ripped from the macrostubber. The shroud covering the shape at the end of the chamber billowed, and the lost pilgrims, who had found their way along the Tenth Path to a revelation that they could no longer escape, leapt forwards in a blur of sharp edges.

V

'What are you talking about?' said Gul, his eyes wide as he stared at Covenant. He could feel calm draining from him. 'This is a gross violation of–'

'The Tenth Path,' said Covenant softly.

Gul breathed out, mind racing through what was happening.

Covenant turned back to the altar, reached out, and lit a second candle from the first.

'Three years ago someone came to you and asked you to help him keep a secret,' said Covenant. 'He said to you that he saw a connection between you both, a shared vision of the truth. You were scared. You wondered how someone could know thoughts you had never spoken to another soul.'

Gul felt his hands start to tremble.

'Are you...' he said. 'Are you with him?'

'He said that you were right, that the faith you had turned from was false, that there was nothing divine in the universe beside what we made, that to believe otherwise was to create your own prison. He said that everything you had been told was a lie.' Covenant's eyes stayed fixed on the twin candle flames. 'And then he asked you to serve, to help others who saw the truth, to protect them, and give them aid and shelter. And that is what you have done, prior. You have found ways of hiding people, of diverting funds, and deflecting attention from a cult that you have never seen.'

Shock shuddered through Gul. His head was spinning. Anger flared up, hot and bright.

'You don't know what you are talking about,' he snarled. 'You really have no idea what you are–'

'The Inquisition,' said Covenant. 'The man who came to you said that he was of the Inquisition.' He raised his hand, and opened his fingers. Luminous lines spread across the palm as an electoo lit.

Gul stared at the glowing image of a stylised 'I' broken by three bars across its middle. It was a sigil he had only seen once before, and then, as now, its implication stole every thought from his skull.

'And the Inquisition is something that I know very well,' said Covenant.

'But he *was* of the Inquisition,' Gul heard himself say.

Covenant gave a single slow nod.

'Yes.'

'Why did he... need me?'

'Because he needed someone to protect the seed he planted here until he could harvest its flower.'

'I don't understand,' said Gul. 'He was an inquisitor, and he said that I served humanity. Yet if you are an inquisitor how can you condemn me for doing his work?'

'Because everything you have believed is a lie. The Tenth Path are not lost souls that share your misguided heresy. They are a coven devoted to darkness and ruin. What you have sheltered and protected is a cradle of monsters.'

'I don't believe you...'

'Yes, you do,' said Covenant.

Gul felt the shaking start at his feet, and roll up through muscle and skin. Something in him wanted to shout that he was innocent, that it was just another layer of lies. But something in Covenant's voice cut through that tissue of comfort. He felt his knees begin to fold.

A strong hand caught his shoulder and steadied him. Gul glanced behind him and saw a scarred face in the shadow of a hood, and realised that the fat man with the hammer had stepped behind him without a noise.

'Steady,' growled the man softly. 'Remember what you were, prior. Face this with courage.'

Gul blinked, confused, but felt his back straighten and some strength return to his limbs. Covenant remained still, gaze fixed, face expressionless. Gul felt moisture on his cheek, and raised his hand to touch his face.

I am crying, he realised. 'What...' he stammered. 'What can I do?'

'Before dawn comes the Tenth Path will be no more. There is nothing more you can do to aid or condemn them. But the one who began this, the one who deceived you, he lives, and above all else he fears what you can give me.'

'I will tell you everything,' said Gul.

A breath of cold air stirred his robes, and prickled his skin. 'I...' he began to say, but Covenant's head had jerked up, eyes moving across the shadows beyond the altar.

'How many ways in are there?' growled the fat man behind Gul.

'What?' stammered Gul. 'The main arch, the priest's door, and–' the words caught in his throat as he realised what the draught of air meant. 'And... and the way through the undercroft.'

'Severita,' called Covenant.

'I feel it, lord,' came a woman's voice from close by the arch into the main chapel. 'Something is here.'

'What is happening?' hissed Gul.

'A watcher,' said Covenant. 'The man who you served would have sent a servant to watch over you, to make sure you did not stray.' The breath of cold air was stronger now. The candle flames rippled.

'Where is the entrance to the undercroft?' said Covenant.

'Here,' said Gul, taking a step forwards without thinking. A warm glow had filled him suddenly. 'It's just behind this part of the altar. There is a trick to it,' he said, and felt a smile form on his face as he spoke. 'A trick lock that releases a panel. I have often wondered why anyone would conceal such a thing. As an amusement, perhaps.' He laughed. His mind was clear. There was nothing to fear. Everything was simple. He just needed to show them where the hidden door was. He heard the one called Covenant shout something, but the words were distant, soft, meaningless. All that mattered was the next step he needed to take.

A thin figure stood before him in the shadows. Pale robes hung from it, a hood hiding its bowed head. Recognition sparked in the fog of Gul's thoughts.

'Lumn?' he said, and felt the warm dullness of his thoughts shift as he frowned at his Silent Acolyte. 'What are you doing here, boy? I said to wait in the south transept.'

Lumn did not answer, but raised his head. The face beneath the hood was Lumn's but its eyes were holes, and for an instant Gul could not see the chapel, just the dark and stars swirling against the blood- and violet-stained sheet of night.

Then something lifted him from his feet and spun him over, as gunfire tore through the air.

VI

Cleander brought the needler up and squeezed the trigger twice. Toxin splinters hissed into the nearest pilgrim's throat. The man crumpled, the chain in his fist whipping out with the last of his momentum. Cleander ducked. The chain whistled over his head. Another pilgrim was on him before he could stand. A knife sliced across his forearm. He flinched back, and shot the pilgrim in the face.

'Koleg!' he shouted.

More figures were coming from the arches on either side of the chamber. Two ran at Cleander. Neither had hands. Hooked blades projected from the stumps of their wrists. The first swung at him. He ducked under the blow, came up and levelled his closed fist. The digi-weapons in his rings fired. A stream of plasma hit the hook-armed figure, and blasted him into a cloud of ash and screaming heat. Another man came at him, hook arm arcing down towards his head. Cleander stamped his foot out, felt bone break under his heel, and the pilgrim was falling backwards. He rammed the muzzle of his needler into the man's face and squeezed the trigger three times.

Cleander raised his head, breathing hard. A mass of figures was pouring from the arches, eyes closed, weapons reaching.

'Koleg!'

'Down!' shouted Koleg.

Cleander dropped.

Koleg's macrostubber purred thunder. The first rank of pilgrims fell, torsos almost cut in two by the deluge of rounds. Koleg panned the pistol left, scything into the crowd of bodies. Blood puffed into the air, scattering across the black surface of the mirror pool. The macrostubber clicked dry.

More pilgrims were scrabbling over the bodies of the dead, teeth bared, eyes twitching beneath closed eyelids. Cleander stood as Koleg levelled his pistol launcher and fired. Fire burst across the far side of the chamber. The visor in Cleander's mask blinked to near black. Gasping cries rolled with the roar of the inferno. Limbs thrashed in the blaze. As his visor switched to mundane sight, he could see mouths moving in snarling faces as the flesh cooked from skulls.

Cleander moved forwards, needle pistol in both hands. Koleg was snapping a drum into his macrostubber. The surface of the pool was a mirror of flames. The fire coiled in the air, tongues spiralling together, roaring with the screams of the dying. The grey shroud covering the statue at the end of the chamber caught light, and dissolved in a curtain of ashes. The thing – that was not a statue – stood tall and shook itself free of cinders.

It had started as a human, or perhaps many humans. It looked like a man, but a man so tall that its shoulders touched the ceiling. Its skin was the white of marble. Rows of red eyes ran down its cheeks. Muscles bunched as it moved, and blood seeped from the iron bolts hammered into flesh. Chains circled its limbs and the links rang as it stepped forwards. Cleander knew what it was, though he wished with all his heart that he did not. It was a host to the powers of the warp, a conduit to the hungering beyond. It was a creature of Chaos.

The air in the chamber reeked of sulphur. The creature took a juddering step forwards. Koleg fired. The creature raised a hand. Cleander had an impression of long fingers and sharpness. Time stuttered, and the bullets melted in the air. Sparks and metal droplets scattered onto the surface of the pool. Koleg dropped the macrostubber, his hands a blur as he reached for the grenade launcher. The creature roared. A spear of fire ripped from between its teeth. Koleg dived aside as fire washed where he had stood. The creature dropped to all fours, and leapt through the blaze.

+Help me...+

Cleander heard the voice in the back of his head. He took the last step towards the ice-crusted pool, and looked down. The figure was still there, just beneath the surface. Ghost light blazed in its eyes. Its hands were moving, paddling weakly, tugging against the silver tubes linked to its fingers. He could see its lips moving, could see teeth glinting like pearls beside the wound where its tongue had been.

On the other side of the chamber, Koleg was rolling over, the right side of his body on fire. The creature from beneath the shroud stretched back to its full height. The air shimmered around it. Cleander could feel heat radiating from it. The figure in the pool was writhing under the ice, and he could see an echo of the warp creature's movements in the desperate thrashing. They were connected, the host creature and the body tethered in the pool. He should do something now that he understood that fact, he should...

+Help...+

Sensations were spinning through Cleander's skull. He felt his gun drop from his fingers. Everything was a rolling cloud of competing voices from his memory: his father shouting at him, the leaden disappointment in his sister's eyes, the stillness of Covenant.

+Help−+

He punched his hands through the water's surface. Ice cracked. Wet warmth surrounded his arms, soft and thick, like blood. He touched flesh, gripped, and twisted, and he felt something snap. Time blinked.

And then he was falling forwards into the dark embrace of the water.

VII

Gul hit the floor. Air thumped from his lungs. He rolled over and gasped. There was a slow quality to everything, as though his mind were a jammed chronometer catching up with time. He was on the floor next to the tier of pews that ran down the right of the chapel. The atmosphere was bright with explosions. The place where he had been standing in front of the altar was ten paces away. Something had picked him up and flipped him through the air like a hand batting away a toy. Lumn stood in the dark beyond the altar. Except it was not Lumn.

The young man's face was a mask broken by black holes where his mouth and eyes had been. Colour and shape distorted around him, light casting shadow, shadow burning with light. Bolt rounds burst in mid-air around him. Shrapnel tore the wood of the seating. Splinters spun out. Lumn turned his head towards Gul, and stepped forwards. Covenant stepped across his path. Light haloed the inquisitor, and the air in front of him shimmered. A wall of invisible force blasted from Covenant. Broken pews tore from the floor. Lumn met the wall of force with a raised hand. Light shattered just beyond his palm. A shockwave rolled outwards. Gul felt his ears pop.

To his left he could see the woman with the marked face vault onto the pews, fire blazing from her bolt pistols. One of the bolts stuck Lumn in the shoulder and punched him off his feet in a spray of shrapnel and blood. Covenant was moving, the great sword sliding from his shoulder in a single blur of sharpness and activating a power field. Lumn hit the floor, and the sword descended above him. He vanished. Covenant's sword struck the floor. Stone sheared into shards.

A shadow rose above Gul. He looked up. Lumn stood on the

tier above him. Black smoke coiled from where the bolt round had ripped away his shoulder and half of his face. Worms of pale light burrowed through the bloody flesh, and Gul realised that muscle and bone were bubbling up to fill the wound. The edges of Lumn's form were like a ragged cloak blowing in the wind. The pews crumbled to glowing ash around him. He pointed at Gul and his hands seemed to grow, spreading through the air like the shadows reaching from flame. Pain exploded in Gul's chest. Ice formed on his lips as he screamed.

The fat man with the hammer charged from behind Gul, muscle surging under fat as he spun his warhammer. Lumn raised his hands, and to Gul they seemed to be claws of hooked bone. The man swung the hammer, roaring, face locked in rage. Claws and hammerhead met, and suddenly Lumn was going backwards, shadows coiling around him, and there was blood mixing with the embers.

Bolt rounds exploded against the shadows around Lumn. Gul could see the woman with the bolt pistols leaping across the chapel. He heard words lift into the air between the roar of her guns. 'Blessed father of mankind...' the voice rose high and clear, echoing from the high roof. 'May my hands be your talons...' Fire blistered the gloom.

The man with the hammer glanced over his shoulder.

'Get up! Move!' he shouted at Gul, as Lumn stepped from the fire of the explosions, and punched his clawed hand into the man's side. The man gasped, eyes wide, blood on his lips. Lumn lifted him from the floor.

'For I am your Seraph...' The woman leapt across the last yards between her and Lumn, pistols still firing.

Lumn's head turned towards her. His face was a mass of red flesh, his eyes holes in a bloody skull. Lightning and blue fire lit the dark, and the woman was crumpling to the floor, the words of her prayer lost on her lips. Lumn threw the man with the hammer across the chapel, and stepped forwards, his form flickering like the frames of a faulty pict feed. He no longer looked like the young man who had walked at Gul's side for three years. He no longer looked even human. His body pulsed with wet sinew and cold fire as he reached out for Gul. The clawed fingers closed over Gul's mouth. Sharp claw tips bit into his cheeks as Lumn pulled him off the floor like a child lifting a broken toy.

+Silence,+ hissed a voice in Gul's thoughts as he saw blackness fold around him.

The sword blow severed Lumn's arm at the elbow. White light flooded Gul's eyes as the power field flared. A cry filled the air, rising higher and higher. Half blind, Gul had time to see Lumn reel back, blood pouring from the stump of his arm. Covenant followed him, turning with the weight of his sword as he cut. Lightning flashed, and Lumn, or whatever had called itself Lumn, was falling, its blood burning as it scattered through the air.

VIII

The memory came to Cleander as he drowned.

'How many choices do I have?' he had asked.

Covenant had held Cleander's gaze for a second, dark eyes unblinking.

'There is always a choice.'

'Information or execution?'

Covenant shook his head.

'Execution is kindness in this universe, Duke Von Castellan, and you know nothing that I want to know.'

'So?' Cleander had said, raising his eyebrow. 'That is supposed to be your threat? You should work on your technique.'

'You are not a coward, and you are not unintelligent, so please do not insult my intelligence by saying that you don't understand what I am saying.'

'Obliteration...' Cleander had said at last.

'For you,' said Covenant, 'and for your family, and everyone you ever knew and cared for. Those that are not found will be hunted for all time without hope of forgiveness.'

'You can't do that. No one can do that.'

'I can, and you know that I can,' said Covenant.

'If I am the man you say I am, then you should know that I don't care about anyone else.'

'But you do.'

Cleander had not replied for a long moment, and then nodded once at the inquisitor.

'What is the other choice?'

Hands gripped his back and hauled him out of the dark. He broke the surface of the water, gasped for air, and vomited. Water and bile poured from his mouth as he coughed and heaved air into his lungs.

'You are alive,' said Koleg from above him.

'Your...' Cleander vomited again. 'Your observations are as insightful as ever.'

'It was intended to reassure you.'

'Good...' gasped Cleander. The world in front of his eyes was smeared with grey and pain. 'Good...'

He rolled over and tried to sit up. The chamber was quiet. Flames still crawled over the heaped corpses, and a layer of smoke was gathering beneath the roof and flowing through the archways into the spaces beyond. The pool of water stirred with the waves from Cleander's exit, but it was just water, its surface reflecting the devastation in rippled fragments. A corpse floated close to the edge of the pool, its head waving on its broken neck.

'Where is the... monster?' he asked.

'The host creature fell when you broke the neck of the thing in the pool,' said Koleg. He pointed at the far side of the pool where a heap of skin lay on the wet stone like a discarded coat.

Koleg shifted his weight, and Cleander noticed that the soldier was holding his right arm against his body. His scorched mask and visor hung around his neck, and glossy burns marked the side of his face. Not for the first time, Cleander wondered if the alterations made to Koleg's brain removed pain or just the man's ability to feel the emotion of being in pain. He felt his own hands begin to tremble.

'It was as Covenant expected,' said Koleg, nodding at the floating corpse in the pool. 'Another warp conduit and symbiotic possession, just like on Agresis.'

'Yes, yes... just like it,' said Cleander, not really listening. His limbs felt numb and his head was swimming. 'Help me up.' Koleg reached down with his good arm. Cleander gripped the arm and pulled himself up with a stream of swearing. He swayed on his feet, looked around the floor, frowning. 'Where is my gun?' Koleg held it up. Cleander nodded, took it, and began to limp towards the arch that led to the stairs.

'Where are you going?' called Koleg. 'This area will need to be cleansed.'

'Someone else's problem, someone else's job. I am going to somewhere where the transmitter will be able to reach our lord and master, and then...' he trailed off, pausing, blinking. He thought of the reflection he had glimpsed in the surface of the pool before he had touched its surface: a man with dark hair and beard, his skin marked by time and scarred by blades, one eye a pit, the other a flicker of black under his own gaze. 'Then I am going to drink more than is necessary, and then, I guess, I am going to wait to hear where I will next serve my penance.'

He limped on to the arch, before turning and looking back. Koleg stood where he had been before, face unreadable in the light of the cooling fire.

'Are you coming?' asked Cleander. After a second Koleg gave a nod and followed him.

IX

Gul turned his head, blinking at the sunlight. Blue sky curved in a dome above him. The chair beneath him was carved from driftwood. Slabs of smooth stone ran away from him until they met the sea. Waves lapped against the stone edge, sending spray into the air to cool the warm breeze. Beyond that, the sea was a wide band of deeper blue beneath the sky. He knew where he was, knew that if he looked behind him he would see the tower of Solar Truth rising from the land like a shard of broken glass. He also did not know how he could be there. It had been three decades since he had last been in this place, since he had left his home to follow his faith. He turned to look behind him.

'This is very pleasant,' said a voice in front of him.

His head snapped around. A woman sat in front of him. At a glance she looked young. Red hair rose in the wind around a slim face. Her eyes were dark, her mouth tilted in a smirk. A silver carafe and two crystal goblets of amber wine sat on a stone table between them. He noticed that the goblet nearest the woman was almost empty, as though she had been drinking from it for a while. The green silk of her robe shimmered in the sunlight as she picked up the goblet and brought it to her lips.

'Try it,' she said. 'It is worth it.'

Gul frowned. Memories of the chapel on Dominicus Prime pushed into his thoughts, the flash of gunfire, and the sound of screams rose, but they seemed distant, unconnected to him and unimportant.

He picked up the goblet and took a sip.

'Where did you get this?' he breathed. 'They never let this vintage out of the arch-prior's personal cellar.'

'Oh, we have the means to get almost anything we like,' said the woman. 'But in this case I got it from you, Aristas.' He looked up at the sound of his first name. The woman smiled, and gestured at the sea and sky around them. 'Just like I got all of this from you.'

Gul stared at her.

'Who–?'

'You can call me Mylasa,' she said before he could finish the question. 'Do you like it? It was one of the few places in your head that you remember with happiness. Seemed like a good place for you to have this moment. Shame it could not be longer, really.'

'What?'

'I – or should I say *we*, because what is life but not being able to do anything without it being at someone else's bidding – have just searched your mind, prior. I have stripped down all of the memories I could find, and where I needed your help, I have inflicted pain and nightmares on you until you told me – there I go again, of course I mean us – until you told *us* everything we needed to know.'

Memories came into focus in his head.

'Covenant...' he breathed. 'You are with the inquisitor.'

'Yes,' she nodded, and took a sip of her wine. 'And before you ask, the pain and the screaming are over. We are done. *You* are done. I removed the memories of what I did. This is a... oh, I don't know... a gift, a kindness to ease my torturer's soul.' Mylasa put her goblet down on the table, filled it again, and took a gulp, then sighed.

'If you have inflicted pain on me, but I cannot remember it, then what is to be my true punishment?'

'You are a heretic, prior, but you are not an evil man. There is actually a difference, but don't tell anyone. You are just a fool and very unlucky.' She looked over her shoulder at the waves rolling across the sea.

'So the chapel, Lumn, Covenant, it all happened?'

'Some time ago, in fact,' said Mylasa. 'It took a while to make sure that we had every detail of what you knew.'

'The Tenth Path...' he said. 'I had no idea. I don't even...'

'I know,' she said. 'But innocence proves nothing, as someone very perceptive once pointed out. You were used, prior, and so you suffer.'

'By the man who came to me before,' he said, 'by the man who claimed to be an inquisitor.'

'Oh, he was an inquisitor,' she said, and he noticed that the smirk had gone from her lips. 'Inquisitor Goldoran Talicto, in fact – Scion of Gorgonate Collegium, Scourge of the Nine Stars of Nix.'

'But...'

'There are truths in the universe, prior, truths so big that to know them is death or madness. The first truth is that every whisper of daemons that thirst for souls and torment – those whispers are just a shadow of the greater truth. There are creatures that wish to enslave mankind, creatures so powerful that it is easiest to call them gods and their avatars, daemons. To know this truth is to be condemned to death, prior.'

Gul felt cold prickle his skin despite the warmth of the sun.

'How can that be true?'

Mylasa continued as though she had not heard his question. 'The second great truth is that those who are meant to protect us from such forces are divided as much as they are united. And sometimes – once upon a blessed rare age – one of them falls to something worse than divergent opinion. They become a slave to their own view of mankind's salvation.'

'And Inquisitor Talicto is one such–'

'He used you to protect one of his projects. The Tenth Path were sheltering and nurturing a psyker that they had bonded to a host that acted as a conduit for the... things from the warp. It was crude, and luckily was largely a failure.'

'I didn't know,' he said.

'We know, and we know everything that you did to protect the Tenth Path. Those details will help us to condemn Talicto in the sight of his peers.' She raised her goblet as though in a toast. 'You have served the Emperor well.'

'Is that why you are talking to me?' he asked. 'As thanks from Covenant?'

She laughed, covering her mouth as though choking on her wine.

'No, I am doing this myself. Covenant would tell you none of this.'

'But why tell me anything?' he asked.

'Because if you know secrets, sometimes it is good to tell someone who will never be able to break your trust.'

Gul frowned. He was feeling dizzy. The sun was warm on his skin. He could smell the salt spray from the sea.

'And what is this? A dream? An illusion?'

Mylasa looked at him for a long moment, and then stood, turning away to face the sea.

'Drink the wine,' she said. 'It is really very good.'

X

+It is done,+ said Mylasa. Cleander flinched at the sound of the psyker's thought-voice. He would really rather have not been there, but Covenant had insisted that they all gather in the cell where they had been keeping Prior Prefectus Gul in the weeks since Dominicus Prime.

Cleander glanced at his sister on the other side of the room, but Viola was looking at Covenant, her face emotionless beneath the plaited ivory of her hair. Covenant himself stood at the foot of the slab, robed in grey. Josef stood next to him, the preacher's face mottled with fading bruises, a servitor hovering above his shoulder, gently pulsing blood into his neck through transparent tubes. That Josef was alive at all was a miracle, but perhaps that was the benefit of piety. Koleg leant against the wall to the side, posture and face utterly unreadable. Severita knelt to the side of the prior, the hilt of her sword clasped between her hands, head bowed. The low sound of the ship's engines rumbled through the quiet. They were all waiting, he realised.

'He's dead?' asked Josef, eyes on the body of the prior shackled to the steel slab.

+Yes,+ replied Mylasa. Cleander looked at her reflexively, and then turned away, with a wince. Metal encircled the psyker's neck and head. Bulbous tubes hissed steam into the air, and bundles of wires snaked between blisters of chrome. Her face sat in the mass of machinery like a strangled pearl. Withered limbs hung from the machinery like the mane of a jellyfish, hovering just above the ground. Static crackled around her in oily flashes.

'One less for the edge of your sword, Severita,' said Cleander, hearing the hollow sneer in his voice. The penitent sister did not bother to look up from her prayers. 'Was he expecting another form of forgiveness, I wonder?'

+He died without pain, and with a memory of kinder times,+ said Mylasa. +In this age that is absolution enough.+

'Something for us all to aspire to,' snorted Cleander.

'We have what we need,' said Covenant. Every eye in the chamber moved to him. He was still looking at the body of the prior. 'A conclave of war has been called on Ero. Talicto will be there. And there will be a reckoning.' He looked up, eyes moving slowly over each of them around the slab, and then turned and walked away. The others followed after a second. Cleander lingered, looking down at the dead heretic.

'A kindness...' he muttered, and snorted. 'I think I would rather take the cruelty of life.' He shifted the eyepatch over his empty socket and walked away, leaving the dead to silence.

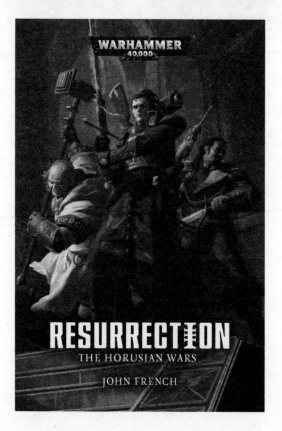

YOUR NEXT READ

WARHAMMER 40,000

RESURRECTION
THE HORUSIAN WARS

JOHN FRENCH

THE HORUSIAN WARS: RESURRECTION
by John French

Summoned to an inquisitorial conclave, Inquisitor Covenant believes
he has uncovered an agent of Chaos and prepares to denounce
the heretic Talicto before his fellows…

SHADOW KNIGHT

Aaron Dembski-Bowden

Introducing

TALOS

NIGHT LORDS (TENTH COMPANY)

The sins of the father, they say.

Maybe. Maybe not. But we were always different. My brothers and I, we were never truly kin with the others – the Angels, the Wolves, the Ravens...

Perhaps our difference was our father's sin, and perhaps it was his triumph. I am not empowered by anyone to cast a critical eye over the history of the VIII Legion.

These words stick with me, though. The sins of the father. *These words have shaped my life.*

The sins of my father echo throughout eternity as heresy. Yet the sins of my father's father are worshipped as the first acts of godhood. I do not ask myself if this is fair. Nothing is fair. The word is a myth. I do not care what is fair, and what is right, and what's unfair and wrong. These concepts do not exist outside the skulls of those who waste their life in contemplation.

I ask myself, night after night, if I deserve vengeance.

I devote each beat of my heart to tearing down everything I once raised. Remember this, remember it always: my blade and bolter helped forge the Imperium. I and those like me – we hold greater rights than any to destroy mankind's sickened empire, for it was our blood, our bones, and our sweat that built it.

Look to your shining champions now. The Adeptus Astartes that scour the dark places of your galaxy. The hordes of fragile mortals enslaved to the Imperial Guard and shackled in service to the Throne of Lies. Not a soul among them was even born when my brothers and I built this empire.

Do I deserve vengeance? Let me tell you something about vengeance, little scion of the Imperium. My brothers and I swore to our dying father that we would atone for the great sins of the past. We would bleed the unworthy empire that we had built, and cleanse the stars of the False Emperor's taint.

This is not mere vengeance. This is redemption. My right to destroy is greater than your right to live.

Remember that, when we come for you.

He is a child standing over a dying man.

The boy is more surprised than scared. His friend, who has not yet taken a life, pulls him away. He will not move. Not yet. He cannot escape the look in the bleeding man's eyes.

The shopkeeper dies.

The boy runs.

He is a child being cut open by machines.

Although he sleeps, his body twitches, betraying painful dreams and sleepless nerves firing as they register pain from the surgery. Two hearts, fleshy and glistening, beat in his cracked-open chest. A second new organ, smaller than the new heart, will alter the growth of his bones, encouraging his skeleton to absorb unnatural minerals over the course of his lifetime.

Untrembling hands, some human, some augmetic, work over the child's body, slicing and sealing, implanting and flesh-bonding. The boy trembles again, his eyes opening for a moment.

A god with a white mask shakes his head at the boy.

'Sleep.'

The boy tries to resist, but slumber grips him with comforting claws. He feels, just for a moment, as though he is sinking into the black seas of his homeworld.

Sleep, the god had said.

He obeys, because the chemicals within his blood force him to obey.

A third organ is placed within his chest, not far from the new heart. As the ossmodula warps his bones to grow on new minerals, the biscopea generates a flood of hormones to feed his muscles.

Surgeons seal the boy's medical wounds.

Already, the child is no longer human. Tonight's work has seen to that. Time will reveal just how different the boy will become.

He is a teenage boy, standing over another dead body.

This corpse is not like the first. This corpse is the same age as the boy, and in its last moments of life it had struggled with all its strength, desperate not to die.

The boy drops his weapon. The serrated knife falls to the ground.

Legion masters come to him. Their eyes are red, their dark armour immense. Skulls hang from their pauldrons and plastrons on chains of blackened bronze.

He draws breath to speak, to tell them it was an accident. They silence him.

'Well done,' they say.

And they call him *brother.*

He is a teenage boy, and the rifle is heavy in his hands.

He watches for a long, long time. He has trained for this. He knows how to slow his hearts, how to regulate his breathing and the biological beats of his body until his entire form remains as still as a statue.

Predator. Prey. His mind goes cold, his focus absolute. The mantra chanted internally becomes the only way to see the world. *Predator. Prey. Hunter. Hunted.* Nothing else matters.

He squeezes the trigger. One thousand metres away, a man dies. 'Target eliminated,' he says.

He is a young man, sleeping on the same surgery table as before.

In a slumber demanded by the chemicals flowing through his veins, he dreams once again of his first murder. In the waking world, needles and medical probes bore into the flesh of his back, injecting fluids directly into his spinal column.

His slumbering body reacts to the invasion, coughing once. Acidic spit leaves his lips, hissing on the ground where it lands, eating into the tiled floor.

When he wakes, hours later, he feels the sockets running down his spine. The scars, the metallic nodules...

In a universe where no gods exist, he knows this is the closest mortality can come to divinity.

He is a young man, staring into his own eyes.

He stands naked in a dark chamber, in a lined rank with a dozen other souls. Other initiates standing with him, also stripped of clothing, the marks of their surgeries fresh upon their pale skin. He barely notices them. Sexuality is a forgotten concept, alien to his mind, merely one of ten thousand humanities his consciousness has discarded. He no longer recalls the face of his mother and father. He only recalls his own name because his Legion masters never changed it.

He looks into the eyes that are now his. They stare back, slanted and murder-red, set in a helmet with its facial plate painted white. The bloodeyed, bone-pale skull watches him as he watches it.

This is his face now. Through these eyes, he will see the galaxy. Through this skulled helm he will cry his wrath at those who dare defy the Emperor's vision for mankind.

'You are Talos,' a Legion master says, 'of First Claw, Tenth Company.'

* * *

He is a young man, utterly inhuman, immortal and undying.

He sees the surface of this world through crimson vision, with data streaming in sharp, clear white runic language across his retinas. He sees the life forces of his brothers in the numbers displayed. He feels the temperature outside his sealed war armour. He sees targeting sights flicker as they follow the movements of his eyes, and feels his hand, the hand clutching his bolter, tense as it tries to follow each target lock. Ammunition counters display how many have died this day.

Around him, aliens die. Ten, a hundred, a thousand. His brothers butcher their way through a city of violet crystal, bolters roaring and chainswords howling. Here and there in the opera of battle-noise, a brother screams his rage through helm-amplifiers.

The sound is always the same. Bolters always roar. Chainblades always howl. Adeptus Astartes always cry their fury. When the VIII Legion wages war, the sound is that of lions and wolves slaying each other while vultures shriek above.

He cries words that he will one day never shout again – words that will soon become ash on his tongue. Already he cries the words without thinking about them, without *feeling* them.

For the Emperor.

He is a young man, awash in the blood of humans.

He shouts words without the heart to feel them, declaring concepts of Imperial justice and deserved vengeance. A man claws at his armour, begging and pleading.

'We are loyal! We have surrendered!'

The young man breaks the human's face with the butt of his bolter. Surrendering so late was a meaningless gesture. Their blood must run as an example, and the rest of the system's worlds would fall into line.

Around him, the riot continues unabated. Soon, his bolter is silenced, voiceless with no shells to fire. Soon after that, his chainsword dies, clogged with meat.

The Night Lords resort to killing the humans with their bare hands, dark gauntlets punching and strangling and crushing.

At a timeless point in the melee, the voice of an ally comes over the vox. It is an Imperial Fist. Their Legion watches from the bored security of their landing site.

'What are you doing?' the Imperial Fist demands. 'Brothers, are you insane?'

Talos does not answer. They do not deserve an answer. If the Fists had brought this world into compliance themselves, the Night Lords would never have needed to come here.

He is a young man, watching his homeworld burn.

He is a young man, mourning a father soon to die.

He is a traitor to everything he once held sacred.

Stabbing lights lanced through the gloom.

The salvage team moved slowly, neither patient nor impatient, but with the confident care of men with an arduous job to do and no deadline to meet. The team spread out across the chamber, overturning debris, examining the markings of weapons fire on the walls, their internal vox clicking as they spoke to one another.

With the ship open to the void, each of the salvage team wore atmosphere suits against the airless cold. They communicated as often by sign language as they did by words.

This interested the hunter that watched them, because he too was fluent in Astartes battle sign. Curious, to see his enemies betray themselves so easily.

The hunter watched in silence as the spears of illumination cut this way and that, revealing the wreckage of the battles that had taken place on this deck of the abandoned vessel. The salvage team – who were clearly genhanced, but too small and unarmoured to be full Astartes – were crippled by the atmosphere suits they wore. Such confinement limited their senses, while the hunter's ancient Mark IV war-plate only enhanced his. They could not hear as he heard, nor see as he saw. That reduced their chances of survival from incredibly unlikely to absolutely none.

Smiling at the thought, the hunter whispered to the machine-spirit of his armour, a single word that enticed the war-plate's soul with the knowledge that the hunt was beginning in earnest.

'Preysight.'

His vision blurred to the blue of the deepest oceans, decorated by supernova heat smears of moving, living beings. The hunter watched the team move on, separating into two teams, each of two men.

This was going to be entertaining.

Talos followed the first team, shadowing them through the corridors, knowing the grating purr of his power armour and the snarling of its servo-joints were unheard by the sense-dimmed salvagers.

Salvagers was perhaps the wrong word, of course. Disrespectful to the foe.

While they were not full Adeptus Astartes, their gene-enhancement was obvious in the bulk of their bodies and the lethal grace of their motions. They, too, were hunters – just weaker examples of the breed.

Initiates.

Their icon, mounted on each shoulder plate, displayed a drop of ruby blood framed by proud angelic wings.

The hunter's pale lips curled into another crooked smile. This was unexpected. The Blood Angels had sent in a team of Scouts...

The Night Lord had little time for notions of coincidence. If the Angels were here, then they were here on the hunt. Perhaps the *Covenant of Blood* had been detected on the long-range sensors of a Blood Angel battlefleet. Such a discovery would certainly have been enough to bring them here.

Hunting for their precious sword, no doubt. And not for the first time.

Perhaps this was their initiation ceremony? A test of prowess? Bring back the blade and earn passage into the Chapter...

Oh, how unfortunate.

The stolen blade hung at the hunter's hip, as it had for years now. Tonight would not be the night it found its way back into the desperate reach of the Angels. But, as always, they were welcome to sell their lives in the attempt at reclamation.

Talos monitored the readout of his retinal displays. The temptation to blink-click certain runes was strong, but he resisted the urge. This hunt would be easy enough without combat narcotics flooding his blood. Purity lay in abstaining from such things until they became necessary.

The location runes of his brothers in First Claw flickered on his visor display. Taking note of their positions elsewhere in the ship, the hunter moved forward to shed the blood of those enslaved to the Throne of Lies.

A true hunter did not avoid being seen by his prey. Such stalking was the act of cowards and carrion-eaters, revealing themselves only when the prey was slain. Where was the skill in that? Where was the thrill?

A Night Lord was raised to hunt by other, truer principles.

Talos ghosted through the shadows, judging the strength of the Scouts' suits' audio-receptors. Just how much could they hear...?

He followed them down a corridor, his gauntleted knuckles scraping along the metal walls.

The Blood Angels turned instantly, stabbing his face with their beam lighting.

That almost worked, the hunter had to give it to them. These lesser hunters knew their prey – they knew they hunted Night Lords. For half a heartbeat, sunfire would have blazed across his vision, blinding him.

Talos ignored the beams completely. He tracked by preysight. Their tactics were meaningless.

He was already gone when they opened fire, melting into the shadows of a side corridor.

He caught them again nine minutes later.

This time, he lay in wait after baiting a beautiful trap. The sword they came for was right in their path.

It was called *Aurum*. Words barely did its craftsmanship justice. Forged when the Emperor's Great Crusade took its first steps into the stars, the blade was forged for one of the Blood Angel Legion's first heroes. It had come into Talos's possession centuries later, when he'd murdered *Aurum*'s heir.

It was almost amusing, how often the sons of Sanguinius tried to reclaim the sword from him. It was much less amusing how often he had to kill his own brothers when they sought to take the blade from his dead hands. Avarice shattered all unity, even among Legion brothers.

The Scouts saw their Chapter relic now, so long denied their grasp. The golden blade was embedded into the dark metal decking, its angel-winged crosspiece turned to ivory under the harsh glare of their stabbing lights.

An invitation to simply advance into the chamber and take it, but it was so obviously a trap. Yet... how could they resist?

They did not resist.

The initiates were alert, bolters high and panning fast, senses keen. The hunter saw their mouths moving as they voxed continuous updates to each other.

Talos let go of the ceiling.

He thudded to the deck behind one of the initiates, gauntlets snapping forward to clutch the Scout.

The other Angel turned and fired. Talos laughed at the zeal in his eyes, at the tightness of his clenched teeth, as the initiate fired three bolts into the body of his brother.

The Night Lord gripped the convulsing human shield against him, seeing the temperature gauge on his retinal display flicker as the dying initiate's blood hit sections of his war-plate. In his grip, the shuddering Angel was little more than a burst sack of freezing meat. The bolt shells had detonated, coming close to killing him and opening the suit to the void.

'Good shooting, Angel,' Talos spoke through his helm's crackling vox-speakers. He threw his bleeding shield aside and leapt for the other initiate, fingers splayed like talons.

The fight was mercilessly brief. The Night Lord's full gene-enhancements, coupled with the heightened strength of his armour's engineered muscle fibre-cables, meant there was only one possible outcome. Talos backhanded the bolter from the Angel's grip and clawed at the initiate.

As the weaker warrior writhed, Talos stroked his gauntleted fingertips across the clear face-visor of the initiate's atmosphere suit.

'This looks fragile,' he said.

The Scout shouted something unheard. Hate burned in his eyes. Talos wasted several seconds just enjoying that expression. That passion.

He crashed his fist against the visor, smashing it to shards.

As one corpse froze and another swelled and ruptured on its way to asphyxiation, the Night Lord retrieved his blade, the sword he claimed by right of conquest, and moved back into the darkest parts of the ship.

'Talos,' the voice came over the vox in a sibilant hiss.

'Speak, Uzas.'

'They have sent initiates to hunt us, brother. I had to cancel my preysight to make sure my eyes were seeing clearly. *Initiates.* Against *us.*'

'Spare me your indignation. What do you want?'

Uzas's reply was a low growl and a crackle of dead vox. Talos put it from his mind. He had long grown bored of Uzas forever lamenting each time they met with insignificant prey.

'Cyrion,' he voxed.

'Aye. Talos?'

'Of course.'

'Forgive me. I thought it would be Uzas with another rant. I hear your decks are crawling with Angels. Epic glories to be earned in slaughtering their infants, eh?'

Talos didn't quite sigh. 'Are you almost done?'

'This hulk is as hollow as Uzas's head, brother. Negative on anything of worth. Not even a servitor to steal. I'm returning to the boarding pod now. Unless you need help shooting the Angels' children?'

Talos killed the vox-link as he stalked through the black corridor. This was fruitless. Time to leave – empty-handed and still desperately short on supplies. This… this *piracy* offended him now, as it always did, and as it always had since they'd been cut off from the Legion decades ago. A plague upon the long-dead Warmaster and his failures which still echoed today. A curse upon the night the VIII Legion was shattered and scattered across the stars.

Diminished. Reduced. Surviving as disparate warbands – broken echoes of the unity within loyalist Astartes Chapters.

Sins of the father.

This curious ambush by the Angels who had tracked them here was nothing more than a minor diversion. Talos was about to vox a general withdrawal after the last initiates were hunted down and slain, when his vox went live again.

'Brother,' said Xarl. 'I've found the Angels.'

'As have Uzas and I. Kill them quickly and let's get back to the *Covenant.*'

'No, Talos.' Xarl's voice was edged with anger. 'Not initiates. The real Angels.'

The Night Lords of First Claw, Tenth Company, came together like wolves in the wild. Stalking through the darkened chambers of the ship, the four Astartes met in the shadows, speaking over their vox-link, crouching with their weapons at the ready.

In Talos's hands, the relic blade *Aurum* caught what little light remained, glinting as he moved.

'Five of them,' Xarl spoke low, his voice edged with his suppressed eagerness. 'We can take five. They stand bright and proud in a control chamber not far from our boarding pod.' He racked his bolter. 'We can take five,' he repeated.

'They're just waiting?' Cyrion said. 'They must be expecting an honest fight.'

Uzas snorted at that.

'This is your fault, you know,' Cyrion said with a chuckle, nodding at Talos. 'You and that damn sword.'

'It keeps things interesting,' Talos replied. 'And I cherish every curse that their Chapter screams at me.'

He stopped speaking, narrowing his eyes for a moment. Cyrion's skulled helm blurred before him. As did Xarl's. The sound of distant bolter fire echoed in his ears, not distorted by the faint crackle of helm-filtered noise. Not a true sound. Not a real memory. Something akin to both.

'I... have a...' Talos blinked to clear his fading vision. Shadows of vast things darkened his sight. '...have a plan...'

'Brother?' Cyrion asked.

Talos shivered once, his servo-joints snarling at the shaking movement.

Magnetically clasped to his thigh, his bolter didn't fall to the decking, but the golden blade did. It clattered to the steel floor with a clang.

'Talos?' Xarl asked.

'No,' Uzas growled, 'not *now*.'

Talos's head jerked once, as if his armour had sent an electrical pulse through his spine, and he crashed to the ground in a clash of war-plate on metal.

'The god-machines of Crythe...' he murmured. 'They have killed the sun.'

A moment later, he started screaming.

* * *

The others had to cut Talos out of the squad's internal vox-link. His screams drowned out all other speech.

'We can take five of them,' Xarl said. 'Three of us remain. We can take five Angels.'

'Almost certainly,' Cyrion agreed. 'And if they summon squads of their initiates?'

'Then we slaughter five of them *and* their initiates.'

Uzas cut in. 'We were slaying our way across the stars ten thousand years before they were even born.'

'Yes, while that's a wonderful parable, I don't need rousing rhetoric,' Cyrion said. 'I need a plan.'

'We hunt,' Uzas and Xarl said at once.

'We kill them,' Xarl added.

'We feast on their gene-seed,' Uzas finished.

'If this was an award ceremony for fervency and zeal, once again, you'd both be collapsing under the weight of medals. But you want to launch an assault on their position while we drag Talos with us? I think the scraping of his armour over the floor will rather kill the element of stealth, brothers.'

'Guard him, Cyrion,' Xarl said. 'Uzas and I will take the Angels.'

'Two against five.' Cyrion's red eye lenses didn't quite fix upon his brother's. 'Those are poor odds, Xarl.'

'Then we will finally be rid of each other,' Xarl grunted. 'Besides, we've had worse.'

That was true, at least.

'*Ave Dominus Nox*,' Cyrion said. 'Hunt well and hunt fast.'

'*Ave Dominus Nox*,' the other two replied.

Cyrion listened for a while to his brother's screams. It was difficult to make any sense from the stream of shouted words.

This came as no surprise. Cyrion had heard Talos suffering in the grip of this affliction many times before. As gene-gifts went, it was barely a blessing.

Sins of the father, he thought, watching Talos's inert armour, listening to the cries of death to come. *How they are reflected within the son.*

According to Cyrion's retinal chrono display, one hour and sixteen minutes had passed when he heard the explosion.

The decking shuddered under his boots.

'Xarl? Uzas?'

Static was the only answer.

Great.

When Uzas's voice finally broke over the vox after two hours, it was weak and coloured by his characteristic bitterness.

'Hnngh. Cyrion. It's done. Drag the prophet.'

'You sound like you got shot,' Cyrion resisted the urge to smile in case they heard it in his words.

'He did,' Xarl said. 'We're on our way back.'

'What was that detonation?'

'Plasma cannon.'

'You're… you're joking.'

'Not even for a second. I have no idea why they brought one of those to a fight in a ship's innards, but the coolant feeds made for a ripe target.'

Cyrion blink-clicked a rune by Xarl's identification symbol. It opened a private channel between the two of them.

'Who hit Uzas?'

'An initiate. From behind, with a sniper rifle.'

Cyrion immediately closed the link so no one would hear him laughing.

The *Covenant of Blood* was a blade of cobalt darkness, bronze-edged and scarred by centuries of battle. It drifted through the void, sailing close to its prey like a shark gliding through black waters.

The *Encarmine Soul* was a Gladius-class frigate with a long and proud history of victories in the name of the Blood Angels

Chapter – and before it, the IX Legion. It opened fire on the *Covenant of Blood* with an admirable array of weapons batteries.

Briefly, beautifully, the void shields around the Night Lords strike cruiser shimmered in a display reminiscent of oil on water.

The *Covenant of Blood* returned fire. Within a minute, the blade-like ship was sailing through void debris, its lances cooling from their momentary fury. The *Encarmine Soul*, what little chunks were left of it, clanked and sparked off the larger cruiser's void shields as it passed through the expanding cloud of wreckage.

Another ship, this one stricken and dead in space, soon fell under the *Covenant*'s shadow. The strike cruiser obscured the sun, pulling in close, ready to receive its boarding pod once again.

First Claw had been away for seven hours investigating the hulk. Their mothership had come hunting for them.

Bulkhead seals hissed as the reinforced doors opened on loud, grinding hinges.

Xarl and Cyrion carried Talos into the *Covenant*'s deployment bay. Uzas walked behind them, a staggering limp marring his gait. His spine was on fire from the sniper's solid slug that still lodged there. Worse, his genhanced healing had sealed and clotted the wound. He'd need surgery – or more likely a knife and a mirror – to tear the damn thing out.

One of the Atramentar, elite guard of the Exalted, stood in its hulking Terminator war-plate. His skull-painted, tusked helm stared impassively. Trophy racks adorned his back, each one impaled with several helms from a number of loyalist Astartes Chapters: a history of bloodshed and betrayal, proudly displayed for his brothers to see.

It nodded to Talos's prone form.

'The Soul Hunter is wounded?' the Terminator asked, its voice a deep, rumbling growl.

'No,' Cyrion said. 'Inform the Exalted at once. His prophet is suffering another vision.'

YOUR
NEXT READ

NIGHT LORDS: THE OMNIBUS
by Aaron Dembski-Bowden

Guided by the visions of the prophet Talos, a Night Lords warband struggles for survival. But when they come into conflict with fellow renegades and are hunted by the eldar, they find themselves returning to the scene of their greatest defeat and drawn into a battle they cannot possibly win.

ICONS OF

From the maelstrom of a sundered world, the
Eight Realms were born. The formless and the divine
exploded into life.

Strange, new worlds appeared in the firmament, each one
gilded with spirits, gods and men. Noblest of the gods was
Sigmar. For years beyond reckoning he illuminated the realms,
wreathed in light and majesty as he carved out his reign. His
strength was the power of thunder. His wisdom was infinite.
Mortal and immortal alike kneeled before his lofty throne.
Great empires rose and, for a while, treachery was banished.
Sigmar claimed the land and sky as his own and ruled over a
glorious age of myth.

But cruelty is tenacious. As had been foreseen, the great
alliance of gods and men tore itself apart. Myth and legend
crumbled into Chaos. Darkness flooded the realms. Torture,
slavery and fear replaced the glory that came before. Sigmar
turned his back on the mortal kingdoms, disgusted by their
fate. He fixed his gaze instead on the remains of the world he
had lost long ago, brooding over its charred core, searching
endlessly for a sign of hope. And then, in the dark heat of
his rage, he caught a glimpse of something magnificent. He
pictured a weapon born of the heavens. A beacon powerful
enough to pierce the endless night. An army hewn from
everything he had lost.

Sigmar set his artisans to work and for long ages they toiled,
striving to harness the power of the stars. As Sigmar's great
work neared completion, he turned back to the realms and saw
that the dominion of Chaos was almost complete. The hour
for vengeance had come. Finally, with lightning blazing across
his brow, he stepped forth to unleash his creations.

The Age of Sigmar had begun.

GHOSTS OF DEMESNUS

Josh Reynolds

Introducing

GARDUS STEELSOUL

LORD-CASTELLANT, HALLOWED KNIGHTS

The boat carved a slow track through the thick bulrushes. Clouds of insects, disturbed by its passing, rose towards the pale green sky with an audible hum.

The vessel was a flat-bottomed riverboat, its aft deck stacked with cargo. Bales of cloth from Verdia, and bolts of silk from some far, eastern kingdom were stacked precariously beneath a heavy tarpaulin to keep off the weather. Gardus sat on a large cask of sweet wine beneath the tarpaulin, and watched the home he had all but forgotten draw nearer, through the curtain of morning mist.

The Lord-Celestant shifted on his perch, feeling oddly unbalanced without his weighty silver war-plate. The simple tunic and leather jerkin he wore beneath his woollen Nordrathi cloak had been cut especially for his immortal frame, as had his boots. None of it helped him to fit in.

The crew had given him a wide berth since they had left the riverside docks of Hammerhal Ghyra, despite his initial, hesitant attempts to engage them in conversation. Perhaps it was his size. Or the runeblade he wore at his side. The sword was almost as long as one of the oars the crew used to ply the waters, and its wielder was almost twice the size of the tallest crewman.

Regardless of the reason, they had left him alone. He'd half hoped they would encounter a troggoth or some other malign river-beast on the voyage south along the Quamus River, if only to prove that he and his sword meant them no harm. Such an encounter might have kept him from thinking of what awaited him at the end of his journey. He frowned and turned away from the city as it drew closer.

The dreams had started innocuously.

Gardus barely noticed them, so rarely did he sleep. A fact of his new reality was that the needs of mortality had all but abated. But he'd had time, of late, to ponder such things. To think and consider the echoes within his own head.

Such rumination was not encouraged among the ranks of the Stormcast Eternals. Even less so, when one was not simply a Liberator standing in the battle line, but a Lord-Celestant, with all the duties and obligations that came with such a rank. The past was the past – to try to grasp it was a distraction at best, and outright folly at worst. Warriors had perished, seeking the answers to unspoken questions.

Then, death was not an unfamiliar experience for Gardus.

Nonetheless, he'd done as always and sought solace in the movement of the stars. He had climbed the highest peaks of Azyr, and then further still, following the winding celestine bastions of Sigmaron to the uppermost heights, where the blue gave way to the black. Finally, he had wandered the outer rings of the Sigmarabulum, so close to the firmament that he'd fancied he might slip and fall upwards forever.

He'd hoped to find forgetfulness there, or at least a way to calm the sudden turbulence that afflicted his soul. But all he'd found was more dreams. And more time to think about the dreams. He closed his eyes and ran a hand through his shaggy white hair. It had been black, once. Before his second death. Now, it was the hue of moonlit ice.

That wasn't the only change. There were others – some subtle, others not. He could feel the light, shimmering beneath his skin. That strange radiance, pulsing within him. If he relaxed, even for a moment, it would escape. It grew brighter with every passing day, as if seeking to return to wherever it had come from.

He was not the only Stormcast Eternal to change after being reforged on the Anvil of Apotheosis, but he took little comfort from that fact. Some lost memories, or pieces of themselves. Others became hollow, as if they were mechanisms of steel, rather than flesh and blood. He shone like a star, and dreamed strange dreams.

He let his gaze wander across the slow, sunlit waters. Bulrushes clumped thick and long to either side of the boat and stretched away into the morning mist. If he looked hard enough, he could almost make out familiar faces in the swirling vapours. Men and women he had known, and helped – or failed to help.

He heard their voices in his dreams – the voices of the living and the dead, or perhaps those caught somewhere in between. Ghosts of a past that was drawing further away with every decade that slipped unnoticed through his fingers. The ghosts of those he'd laboured among, and laughed with, and even loved, before a crash of lightning had stolen him away.

Gardus felt no resentment. His faith was not a rock to be broken, or iron to rust and chip. His faith was a river, always changing and renewing itself with every passing day. But sometimes, like every river, he felt a need to find the sea.

Perhaps there would be answers there. Or maybe, only more questions. In any case, he'd decided to come back to the beginning. His journey had begun in Demesnus. And so, it had brought him back, many centuries after he had left. He felt the hull of the boat scrape against something and opened his eyes.

'Are you awake, then?'

Gardus looked up, as the captain of the riverboat stumped towards him, her round features set in a scowl. The duardin was as broad as all of her kind, but dressed in simple garb, befitting a sailor. Thick iron bracers encased her forearms, and her red hair was bound tight and coiled atop her head in a bun. A small fyre-steel axe was thrust through the wide leather belt strapped about her midsection.

'I am awake, Fulda.'

'Good. I hate to throw a sleeping man off my boat.'

Gardus stood. He loomed over her, but she didn't seem unduly concerned. He smiled. 'I trust I have not inconvenienced you overmuch.'

'You mean other than scaring my crew half to death?'

'Yes, other than that.' Gardus looked towards the docks. 'It smells the same.'

Fulda's frown deepened. 'It's Demesnus. It doesn't change. It just sinks a bit deeper into the bulrushes.' She turned her scowl on the city. 'What does one of your sort want here anyway? There's nothing here but mud, fish and moss-lepers.'

Gardus felt a prickle of irritation. 'Demesnus is one of the greatest centres of learning in southern Ghyran.'

Fulda peered up at him. 'Maybe a hundred years ago. Now it's the biggest fish market in southern Ghyran.' She hiked a thumb over her shoulder. 'Which is why I need you off, so I can make room for the load of salted fish I'm taking to the markets in Hammerhal.'

Gardus chuckled. 'I understand.' He held out his hand. Fulda looked at it for a moment, and then clasped it.

'You're an odd one, Azyrite.'

'So I've been told.' Gardus left her shaking her head, and made his way towards the gangplank and the wharf beyond. The crew were already hard at work unloading cargo as he tromped down the wooden boards, but paused to watch his departure warily. Gardus pretended not to notice.

The wharfs stretched along the untidy curve of the Quamus. Berths of varying sizes jutted out into the shallows of the river, alongside raised piers. Warehouses lined the path opposite, their doors flung open as the dockhands and crews went about their duties. Fulda's vessel wasn't alone. Dozens of riverboats crowded the berths. There were flat-bottomed rafts and multi-storeyed paddle-wheels, as well as stranger craft – vessels made from woven, living reeds and even a lithe dragger, pulled by a coterie of gigantic, highly vocal waterfowl.

While Demesnus was not the largest port in southern Ghyran, it had carved itself a niche as a necessary stopover along the inter-section of several rivers. Or, at least, such had been the case when Gardus had been mortal. It was still as busy as he remembered. Overhead, birds swooped and squalled with raucous disapproval.

As he stepped onto dry land, he saw mortals in the dull ochre uni-forms and troggoth-hide armour of the city guard escorting scribes through the crowd. The scribes likely worked for the Rushes – the leading families of Demesnus, who formed the city's ruling coun-cil. There was cargo to be inspected, and taxes on foreign goods to be collected.

Several of the warriors studied him with narrowed gazes. Gardus knew they were taking note of his size and his blade, but they made no move to stop him as he walked along the wharf. Most mortals would take him for an outlander – from the wilds of Ghur, per-haps, or the hinterlands of Aqshy, where some folk grew to great size. Others would recognise him for what he was. Either way, they would steer clear of him.

He made his way along the wharf, moving carefully through the crowd. Over the sounds of ships being unloaded and dockhands shouting, he heard a sharp cry. At first, he dismissed it for the call of a bird. But when it came again, he recognised it as human. He turned, seeking the origin of the sound.

He saw a flash of movement – too abrupt to be a part of the nor-mal routine of the wharfs – and started towards it. Near a freshly unloaded fishing boat, a trio of men herded a slim, ragged shape against a mooring post. The men were of a sort Gardus had seen in every city – rough-looking and brutal, wearing a mishmash of armour. Sellswords and bravos, of the sort that even the most des-perate freeguild would think twice about contracting.

'Filthy leper,' one of the men spat. 'Ought to burn the lot of you.' His ire was directed at the young woman huddled against the post. She was clad in threadbare robes and rags, that might once have been of better quality. She held a knife in one hand, and jabbed at the air.

'Leave me alone,' she said, her voice high and thin with dismay. 'Someone help me!' Gardus saw nearby fishermen turn away, as the sellswords patted their weapons meaningfully. He stalked towards the confrontation, hands balling into fists.

One of the sellswords leered. 'No one is going to help you, leper. They know better.'

'She is not a leper,' Gardus said, as he caught the closest of the men by the scruff of his neck, and without pause, flung him from the wharf. The second spun, hand falling to the hilt of his sword. Gardus caught his wrist and squeezed. The mortal's eyes bulged. 'There is no sign of moss, no odour,' Gardus continued. He slapped his prisoner from his feet, and sent him tumbling into a nearby pile of fish.

The third man – the one who had threatened the woman – backed away, sword out. It was a cheap, back alley blade, its length pitted and chipped. 'Stay back,' he shrilled. Gardus lunged, moving more swiftly than mortal eyes could follow. He slapped the sword aside and drove a fist into its wielder's sternum. Bone cracked, and the swordsman folded up into a heap. He wasn't dead, but he would soon wish he was. Gardus turned, looking for the woman. But she was gone – fled as he had dealt with her tormentors. He frowned and shook his head.

He reached down and hauled the second man out of the fish. 'Get your friend to a hospice,' he rumbled, shoving the frightened man towards his downed companion. The man bent hurriedly to do as Gardus had commanded, his injured hand pressed to his chest. Gardus watched them go, noting with some chagrin that he had attracted an undue amount of attention. 'Can't be helped, I suppose,' he murmured.

Behind him, someone cleared their throat. 'Mercy is a sword with two edges. Or so Elim of Vyras had it, in his seminal treatise, *On Clemency*.'

'But an honest man need never fear its cut,' Gardus said, finishing the quote. He smiled and turned. 'Hello, Yare.'

'Hello, Steel Soul. I thought I recognised the rumble of your voice. We were supposed to meet at the northern wharf.' The old man was tall, despite his accumulation of years. A halo of white hair encircled a bald head. Yare's ravaged eye sockets had healed in the years since Gardus had last seen him, forming a thick mask of scar tissue, balanced atop the remnants of a once proud nose.

'Someone was in trouble.'

Yare nodded. 'This is Demesnus, my friend. Someone is always in trouble.' The philosopher wore thick robes of wool and fur against the growing chill of the season, and held a wooden staff. Beside him, a small gryph-hound leaned against his leg, its tail twitching. It shrieked softly in challenge, as Gardus neared. Yare patted the creature's wedge-shaped skull. 'Easy, Dullas. The Lord-Celestant means me no harm.'

Gardus looked down at the gryph-hound. Solid black, with feathers the colour of ash, the beast was a stocky mix of leopard and falcon, with a temper to match. He acted as Yare's eyes, when the old man let him. 'He was just a hatchling, when we gifted him to you.'

'He grew quickly. Likes his fish,' Yare said, stroking the beast's feathers. Dullas hissed in pleasure and wound himself about the old man's legs. 'Then, so do I.' Yare smiled and extended his hand. Gardus took it gently, all too aware how fragile Yare was, these days. He had been old when they'd first met, in the slave-pens of Nurgle's Rotbringers. He was ancient now – almost a hundred seasons, but still surprisingly spry.

Gardus studied him. 'You look well, my friend. Better than when I last saw you.'

'Home is a healer,' Yare said. 'And fresh marsh honey is a

wonderful preservative. A spoonful a day helps to keep me from feeling the full weight of my years.' He cocked his head. 'Is Angstun with you? He and I have a discussion – several, really – to continue.'

Gardus chuckled. 'I'm sorry, no. But he sends his greetings.'

Yare laughed. 'I bet he does.' The Knight-Vexillor of the Steel Souls and the elderly philosopher had become good friends, in the days following the fall of the Sargasso Citadels. They shared a love of esoteric philosophies, as well as a willingness to argue a point for days on end. Having witnessed some of this verbal sparring first hand, Gardus couldn't help but feel admiration for the old man's stamina.

A stiff breeze curled in off the wharf. Yare shivered, and Gardus shifted himself so that he stood between the old man and the river. 'You did not have to meet me here, Yare.'

'I know. But I am not an invalid, yet.' Yare smiled. 'My students tell me that the fog is getting thicker. It slouches in off the water in the mornings, and creeps on cat-feet through the maze of streets and alleys, filling them sometimes until noontide.'

Gardus nodded. 'There'll be ice on the river soon, then,' he said. He glanced at the river, remembering. 'I recall those days. Sometimes, the frost on them was so thick, the rushes broke. You could hear them snapping, all throughout the day.'

'The music of winter,' Yare said.

Gardus felt an ache in him, as he remembered. He turned away from the water. 'It is good to see you, Yare.'

'And it is good to hear you, my friend.' Yare clutched at Gardus' arm, just for a moment. 'I'm glad you came. I feared that Sigmar had sent you beyond the reach of my letters once again.'

'Not of late. Though there are rumours that we will be descending into the dark of Shyish soon.' A petition had come, to re-open one of the few remaining realmgates that connected Shyish and Azyr. Gardus had little doubt that Sigmar would grant it, as he had other, similar petitions recently. In the last decade, expeditions had entered the underworlds of Lyria and Shadem, among others. New cities rose, amidst the ghosts and dust.

'Is that why you finally decided to come, then?' Yare tilted his head, as if studying Gardus. 'And clad as a mortal.' He reached out and tugged on Gardus' sleeve. As ever, the blind man's perceptions were sharper than Gardus gave them credit for.

'I would prefer not to go into the lands of death encumbered by malign dreams,' he admitted. He flexed his hands, as a breeze blew in off the river. For a moment, he thought he heard something, in the space where the susurrus of the wind met the slap of water. Voices, rising up and falling away, just at the edge of hearing. He looked at Yare. 'It's still here, then. I thought... I hoped it would not be.'

Yare smiled sadly. 'It took some time to find. I had my students compare half a dozen maps of the city, from this century to the last. The way Demesnus has grown, even since I returned, is startling. New streets appear by the months, new voices, new smells.'

'The light of Azyr brings new growth, even to the Realm of Life.'

Yare chuckled. 'But is it merely growth for the sake of growth?' He raised a hand, forestalling Gardus' reply. 'I know, you didn't come here to debate philosophy, much as I might wish otherwise.'

'Afterwards, my friend. I promise.' Gardus felt gripped by a sudden urgency. 'After I have laid these ghosts to rest, once and for all.'

Yare sighed. 'There have been three Grand Hospices, since yours burned. They are all tangled together, in the histories. The same place, scattered across different locations. The one I knew was destroyed when the servants of the Plague God last attacked. Another was closed when its master fell into disfavour with the Rushes. And the third... the third became a plague pit and was torn down...'

'You found mine, though,' Gardus said. The urgency was all but unbearable. 'The one I built...' He flexed his hands, feeling the ghost of an old ache. He had built it himself. Not alone, but he had worked alongside the others, stacking stones. He remembered the songs the others had sung, as they'd worked, and the prayers the priests had spoken as the foundations had been sunk.

He remembered, but not clearly or well. It was like a particularly vivid dream.

Or a nightmare.

Yare nodded. 'I think so. A set of ruins, on the western edge of the city, overlooking the wharfs there. Overgrown, now, like much of that part of the old city.' He frowned. 'We've lost so much in the centuries since you were mortal. Demesnus was once a major port – a centre of learning and wisdom. There were broadsheets on every corner, and the air bristled with debate. Now...' He shook his head. 'I fear the students I tutor in the art of dialectics and rhetoric will be the last.'

'If you have taught them well, they will not be.'

Yare laughed. 'Let us hope.' He turned his blind gaze westward. 'What you seek is there, Gardus. I am sure of it.'

'Then that is where I must go.'

'Do you wish for company?'

Gardus smiled and clasped the old man's shoulder. 'No, my friend. You have done enough. But when I am done – when I have found what I seek – we will sit and debate.'

Yare patted Gardus' forearm. 'I look forward to it, my friend.'

Demesnus had grown, since Gardus had last seen it.

It did not come as a surprise – Yare's letters had said as much – but reading about something and seeing it first-hand were two different things. But despite the changes, he still recognised the city he had once loved.

The roots of Demesnus were sunk deep in the mud of the Quamus. It had grown from a scattering of simple bulrush huts, to a thick palisade of marsh-oak and, finally, a city of imported stone, banded on two sides by wharfs and quays. A city of weavers and fisherfolk, ruled by the descendants of the inhabitants of those first bulrush huts.

Gardus forced himself to walk slowly. To amble, rather than march. He let the old smells fill him – the stink of pitch-lanterns and burning moss; of dung and fish; the distinct pong of the tanneries and the wharfs – hoping they might stir his sluggish memories. As he left the river behind, the reek of commerce gave way to the smell of baking bread and flowering orchards. The patter of street vendors duelled with the catcalls of the broadsheet urchins. The folk of Demesnus had an abiding interest in the written word, despite the average citizen being only nominally literate. Yare's fears in that regard seemed unfounded, from what Gardus saw.

The boarded streets of the riverside gave way to flat stones, or rutted dirt paths, carving crooked trails between buildings that still bore the scars of fires set centuries before. It was exactly as he remembered, and yet unfamiliar. There was more green, for one thing.

Demesnus had never truly recovered from the various assaults and sieges that had befallen it during the Chaos incursions of the past century. Unable to rebuild, or simply unwilling, buildings had been left as ruins. And as was common in Ghyran, what mortals abandoned, nature soon reclaimed. Whole blocks of the city now faltered under the weight of old growth. Broken structures slumped beneath spreading trees and clinging vines, which created impromptu parks. Many of these had become orchards, or communal gardens. Others were seemingly avoided, and left to whatever vermin might choose to call them home.

Despite this, the city had prospered visibly in recent years. With trade once again flowing along the Quamus, the city's population had swelled. Every street was crowded with throngs of people, laughing, talking, buying, selling. *Living.*

As he moved through the crowds, tatters of memory stirred, and his head echoed with the dolorous hymn of a hospice – coughing and moaning, prayers and whispered pleas. The sounds of the sick and the dying. The street around him wavered, like a desert mirage, and for a moment, he stood elsewhere. The same spot, but many centuries ago.

He smelled again the acrid stink of burning pitch, and heard the ringing of the great river-bell. The ground trembled, as soldiers thundered past, their faces white with fear. The streets were flooded, water pouring down the lanes, as the river broke its banks. The enemy had come, on barques of bone and gristle, sailing a blood-dimmed tide.

Almost against his will, he turned, watching as the echoes of the past raced through the present, overlaying it in his mind's eye. Ghostly fires burned, as street-vendors hawked their wares. Soldiers raced towards the wharf, through heedless carts and crowds.

Garradan... help us...

He pressed on, trying to escape the tangle of recollection. But the past held him tight. He felt a wash of heat, as a building collapsed, spilling burning slates across the street. The air was split by the shriek of primitive artillery – he looked up and saw comets of greasy flame, trailing smoke, arc overhead. He heard the dull boom of the siege engines, assailing the landward gates.

Garradan... please...

Gardus stumbled, narrowly avoiding a tinkerer's cart as it trundled down the street. He stepped back, into an alleyway. He shook his head, trying to clear it. The hospice. He had to get to the hospice.

Garradan... where are you...

Around him, the city wavered between what it had been and what it now was. The streets twisted around him, and it was all he could do not to simply freeze in place. The horizon rippled, birthing familiar turrets and towers, that vanished moments later. It was as if the world were in flux, caught between past and present, but only for him.

Garradan... save us...

He found himself walking down a familiar crooked lane, lined with marsh-lanterns. Even at midday, they glowed with a pallid light, casting long shadows on the brick walls to either side. The lane widened into a plaza, its surface broken by a carpet of thick, winding roots that stretched in all directions. Twisted trees, with full boughs, rose from craters of broken cobblestones, and birds sang amid the branches.

The sounds of the city were muted here, swallowed up in curtains of green. Ivy snaked across the walls of nearby buildings, and swaddled the weatherworn statues that overlooked the street. Gardus found himself holding his breath, as he walked over the thick patches of weeds and wild bramble.

At the other end of the circular plaza, nestled between buildings to either side, was a crumbled facade. He recognised a high archway of imported stone, rising atop a semicircle of rough-hewn steps, worn smooth in places. The great wooden doors, so visible in his memory, were now nothing more than a few splinters attached to rusty hinges. The two great lantern posts were still there, to each side of the doors, though they were now rusted through. And the carving of the twin-tailed comet over the archway.

Garradan... where are you...

Gardus stopped, and stared. Remembering. He remembered watching as the comet had been chiselled into the stone. He could feel the weight of the lantern posts as he helped set them into place. He remembered that first day, as he'd welcomed his first patient – a carter who'd been trodden on by a horse. The man had cursed loud and long, as his fellows helped him up the steps. How he'd screamed, as Garradan had set his leg.

Garradan... help us...

Overcome, he sank down, head in his hands. He could hear them all, the voices rising, asking, pleading, thanking, cursing. The wind in the trees sounded like the whispers of the dying. They filled him, drowning out all thought. He closed his eyes, and the words came to his lips. Canticles, prayers, the armour of faith.

Then, a new sound. The birds fell silent. The wind died away. And the bells rang. He remembered the bells – it had cost him – cost *Garradan* – the last of his inheritance to have them fashioned, but it was worth every coin. Great bells of bronze, to accompany the songs of the faithful...

He blinked back the beginnings of what might have been tears, as the low tones echoed across the plaza. The bells were still here.

After all this time. Still ringing, even after so many years. He stumbled to his feet, and towards the steps, drawn by the sound of the bells. He had to see them again, to hear them above him.

But as he passed through the archway, he heard something else, beneath the bells. The sound of voices, raised in a hymn. The broken stones of the foyer were covered in a carpet of dried rushes, and curtains of the same now occupied the doorways beyond. Braziers of incense smoked in the corners, and mortal forms were huddled along the walls.

Gardus stopped. There were people here. Living ones, not ghosts. But perhaps not for much longer. Beneath the fug of incense, he smelled the stink of sickness. Of death and the dying. Instinctively, his hand fell to his sword, but he fought the urge to draw it. The sickness he smelled was unpleasant, but natural. Familiar. Moss-lepers and marsh-lung. Wracking coughs accompanied him across the foyer and to the archway that led to the heart of the hospice. Eyes and muted whispers followed his progress, but none of those in the foyer made any move to stop him.

There were more of them, in the entry chamber beyond. Once, it had been filled with cots and pallets, with the sick and the dying. The sick were still here, but they were not alone. A crowd knelt or sat, filling the chamber, their voices raised in song as the bells rang.

Pilgrims and penitents, devoted and zealots. He saw crones, clad in sackcloth, and men who had carved the sign of the comet and the hammer into their flesh. Others were clad more sedately, in blue robes that they had obviously dyed themselves. There were men and women and children as well. Infants cried softly as their parents sang.

At the opposite end of the chamber was a statue. It was stained with dirt, but he recognised his own face – or what had been his face, once – lifted to the ceiling, where the remains of the ancient murals a grateful patron had commissioned still clung. It was him, but not – an idealised version of the man he had been. Tall and strong, bearing a great two-handed blade over one shoulder. He stared at it, wondering when it had been carved. And who had done so. Was Garradan remembered, then?

He wanted to speak. But something held him back. Was it fear? Or regret? Who were these people? And why were they here, in this forgotten place?

'It's you.'

Startled, Gardus turned. The woman he'd rescued on the wharfs stood behind him, staring. So preoccupied had he been, he had not noticed her approach. 'Yes,' he said softly, so as not to disturb the prayers of the other mortals. 'I am glad to see that you are unhurt.' Gardus smiled. 'I am Gardus.'

She hesitated. 'Dumala. You're not mortal, are you?'

Gardus avoided the question. 'Do you… live here?'

'We do. Saint Garradan called to us, and we came.' She smiled shyly. 'I saw him once.' Gardus looked at her, and she hastily added, 'In a dream, I mean.'

'Oh? Did he speak?'

She flushed. 'It wasn't that sort of dream.' She looked at the statue, and made the sign of the hammer. 'I… saw him, as he must have been. Ministering to the sick. Feeding the poor. Striking down daemons with his silver blade.'

'It was a candlestick,' Gardus murmured.

'What?'

'Nothing. And so you came here?' He had heard similar stories before. The Devoted of Sigmar often followed in the footsteps of holy men and women who had come before, and long since passed into celestial sainthood – most were warriors like Orthanc Duln, the Hero of Sawback, or martyrs like Elazar Tesh, who had brought down the pillars of the Red House upon himself and the hounds of slaughter. 'Why?'

'I told you. He called to me. He called to all of us. So we came to sit and pray, as he did, until our purpose reveals itself.' She looked at him. 'Does he call to you as well?' She motioned to the statue. 'They say Sigmar raised him up, and set him in the sky, so that he might always watch over us.' She peered at him. 'Your face… it is familiar, I am certain.'

Gardus turned away. The song had ended, and the bells had fallen silent. People had noticed him now, and he felt a twinge of unease as he felt their attentions. 'I doubt it. This place… it used to be a hospice, didn't it?'

'That it did, stranger.'

Gardus turned to see a small figure approach, wrapped in rags and bandages, leaning on a pair of canes. He could smell the stink of illness wafting off of the newcomer. A familiar odour – the soft pungency of moss-leprosy. He could see the grey-green stains on the rags, and the fuzz of moss, peeking through the bandages.

The cancerous moss ate away at flesh and muscle, leaving only clumps, clinging to pitted bone. It was a common ailment here, and throughout the Jade Kingdoms, and one Gardus remembered well from his mortal life. Long had Garradan of Demesnus laboured among the moss-leper colonies, isolated in anchored ships along the river. Thankfully, the lepers could feel nothing as their bodies dissolved.

'I am Carazo, friend,' the leper said, his voice a harsh, wet rasp. 'Might I know you?'

'I am Gardus.'

Carazo peered up at him, his eyes a bright blue within the mass of stained bandages that hid his face. 'A fine name.' He hunched forward suddenly, coughing, his frame wracked by tremors. Instinctively, Gardus reached for him. Carazo twitched back. 'No, my friend,' he wheezed apologetically. 'No. Best not to touch me. What's left of me might well slough off the bone. Very messy.'

'You should not be standing.' Gardus looked down at him. 'How are you standing?'

'Sigmar gives me strength, friend. As he gave Saint Garradan the strength to fight against the slaves of darkness.' Carazo fumbled in his rags, and produced a tarnished medallion, bearing the twin-tailed comet. 'Sigmar guided me across many battlefields in my time, and this is but one more.' He chuckled. 'Though I rather think it shall be my last.' He looked around. 'It is a good place, though.'

'You were a warrior-priest,' Gardus said.

'I had that honour, once. Now I'm just a humble pilgrim, tending to this most holy of places.' Carazo turned to look at the statue. 'I first heard of him when I was a novice in the temple here. He cast down a hundred foes, to defend those he had tended, and when he fell, the enemy wept to see such courage.'

Gardus did not remember them weeping. The Skineaters had not seemed to possess the capacity, nor the inclination. And he had not killed a dozen of them, let alone a hundred. 'And you... venerate him?'

'Just a few of us, for now. But our numbers grow.' Carazo coughed again. Dumala stepped to his side, not quite touching him. There was a concern there, like a child for a parent, and Gardus could not help but wonder at the connection. 'Soon, he might reveal why we are here. When enough of us have come to this sacred place.' He looked at Gardus. 'Until then, we pray and sing, and make do as best we can. Hardship is the whetstone of faith.'

'Some hardships are more difficult than others.' Gardus looked at Dumala. 'Those men who accosted you earlier, on the wharf...'

Carazo stiffened. 'They attacked you again? Why did you not tell me?'

Dumala looked away. 'I did not want to worry you, or the others.' She glanced at Gardus. 'He saved me,' she said. 'Maybe the Saint sent him to help us.'

Gardus looked back and forth between them. 'It has happened before?'

'They think we bring sickness,' Dumala said. 'Many of our number are ill – Saint Garradan watches over the sick – but we keep to ourselves. We grow our own food, where there is space. We endanger no one, save ourselves.' Her voice became heated. 'They have no right to try to drive us from this place! I – we – will not go!'

Heads turned, and people murmured as her words echoed.

Carazo waved Dumala to silence. 'It will be well, child. The Saint watches over us. He would not have called us here, merely to see us turned out.' He looked at Gardus. 'Regardless of why you came, I am grateful to you for saving her life.'

Gardus bowed his head. 'I could do no less.'

'Even so, you have my thanks. And I welcome you here, brother. Stay, if you wish. We have food, and there are pallets for those with nowhere else to go. We ask only that you abide by the peace of this place, and perhaps pray with us, at evensong.'

Gardus paused, considering. Then he nodded.

'It would be my honour.'

Gardus sat on the steps as night fell, weaving rushes.

Though he had not done so in a century or more, he found that his hands remembered the way. So he wove, and let his mind wander over what he had seen. The pilgrims had been welcoming of him, if wary. Their days were spent weaving bulrush baskets, or fishing nets, which they sold in the markets to feed themselves. When not at work, they cared for the sick among them, or sang hymns and prayed, seeking enlightenment.

A peaceful existence. And yet, one that left him ill at ease. Why had they come here? Something had drawn them, but what? Did they hear the same voices he did? And if so, what did it mean? He shook his head. Too many questions, but precious few answers.

They were weak with hunger, ravaged by illness, and seemed to subsist as much on prayer as scraps of bread and watery soup. In that regard, they were little different from other pilgrims he'd seen. Hardship was their proof of faith.

Carazo wasn't the only leper among them. Others coughed blood, or shook with fever and chills. A few of them, like Dumala, were healthy, but the rest were almost at the liche-door. They'd come from as far away as Aqshy, hoping Saint Garradan would heal them.

A rush snapped in his hands. He paused.

'Was that why I was drawn here?' he murmured, selecting a new rush from the pile beside him. 'To minister to the sick once more?' A part of him leapt at the thought. But surely Sigmar would have told him, if he was to be released from his oath of duty. Then, the ways of the God-King were, at times, mysterious.

No. There was something else. He could feel it, like water running beneath the earth, or the air just before a storm. As if he had arrived just before the rain began to fall.

He stopped again. He felt eyes on him.

A familiar face peered at him from a side street. The man he'd thrown off the wharf earlier. And he wasn't alone. Others sidled into the plaza, until there were more than a dozen sellswords lounging among the trees, watching him. A muttered comment elicited harsh laughter.

The laughter died away, as he looked at them directly. He considered asking them what their business was, but decided to err on the side of patience. He went back to his work.

A few moments later, his patience was rewarded.

'Rushes are wonderful things. Utilitarian. Practical. You can use them to make seats for chairs, or to fill out coats and pillows. They can be peeled, and the hearts boiled or eaten raw. Their pollen can be used to thicken flour, for making bread. The local broadsheets use them for paper. Why, the earliest settlers of this place even made their homes from them. Just goes to show, anything can be made useful, with a bit of effort.'

Gardus looked up from his work. A short, thin man stood watching him. He was dressed simply, if richly, in a heavy coat of dark leather, lined with eiderdown, and a shapeless hat of otter fur. A brooch of silver, decorated with a spray of feathers, was pinned to the side of the hat. He leaned on a cane of dark wood, carved with shapes reminiscent of the harvest, and had a short sword sheathed on one narrow hip.

'They tell me you accosted several of my employees.'

Gardus set aside the bulrushes and stood. The sellswords

twitched, some reaching for their weapons. But the newcomer did not so much as flinch.

'You're a big fellow, aren't you?' he asked. He glanced back at the sellswords and waved them back. 'Bigger than these.'

'And with a sword to match.' Gardus let his hand drop to the pommel of his runeblade. The newcomer nodded.

'So I see. I am Sargo Wale.' Wale bowed shallowly, one hand on his hat to hold it in place. 'You might have heard of me?'

'No.'

'You are new to the city, then?'

'No.'

Wale frowned. 'How curious. I should have thought I would have heard of a fellow of your... vigour. And you certainly should have heard of me. My ships line the wharf. My grain and my orchards feed the city, and keep Demesnus from sinking into the mire, like so many of our neighbours.'

Gardus crossed his arms. 'Nonetheless, your name does not ring familiar.'

'May I have yours, then?'

Gardus made to answer, but something held him back. 'No,' he said finally.

Wale smiled and shrugged. 'Ah well, no matter. I'll just call you friend.' He set his cane down and leaned on it, one thin hand atop the other. 'I am here to speak to Carazo. Where is he?'

'Inside. Sleeping.' The old priest had used up what little energy he had leading his people in another hymn. The last Gardus had seen, Dumala had been bullying the old man into laying down somewhere. 'He is ill.'

Wale sighed, and peered up at the sky. 'They all are. This place... it is not healthy. Perhaps in time. But not now.' He thumped the street with his cane. 'The soil is sour, you see. It needs a firm hand to till it, and turn out the stones. You know whereof I speak?'

Gardus said nothing. Wale continued, as if he had. 'I own this land. I bought it, fair and true, from the council. They were glad to be rid of it.' He frowned. 'I will turn it into something useful. Another orchard, perhaps, or maybe even a park. The soil is still sweet, beneath the sour. Or it can be made so again. With a bit of effort.'

Gardus looked him up and down. Wale's smile widened. 'You think me a liar, sir? Why, I'm no scion of the bulrushes, come from money and privilege. I came here from Aqshy, without a single coin to my name. But I knew how to work the soil.' He held up his hands. They were scarred and muscular. 'These hands were worn bloody on handle of plough and haft of scythe, my friend.' He turned them over, studying them. 'I bargained with treekin and waged war on beasts, to carve out my first fields. And I paid well, and was paid, for the privilege of feeding this growing city. I'm a man of the soil, me. I take what it offers, and give back, when I can.' He gestured with his cane. 'Nothing more.'

'Your men tried to hurt one of the people living here,' Gardus growled, tired of Wale's patter. 'And not for the first time, if what they say is true.'

Wale's smile vanished. 'And you believe them?'

'I have no reason not to.'

'My apologies. Were they a friend of yours?'

'No.'

'Then less reason still to involve yourself in matters that don't concern you.' Wale peered up at him. 'Step aside, and we'll say no more about it.'

Gardus crossed his arms. Wale blinked, but recovered quickly. He glanced back at his men, and then shook his head. 'Ah, well. One must learn to endure what comes.' He looked at Gardus. 'Is it money, then?'

'No.'

'Mm. Something else?'

'I want you to leave.'

'And so I will. But I will return.' Wale looked up at the hospice. 'This place is mine, now. By right, and by law. They can't stay here. Better for everyone if they move along.'

'Because you wish to turn this place into something useful.'

Wale shook his head. 'For their own good. For the good of the city.' He took off his hat and ran a hand through thinning silver hair. 'This was a place of healing, once. A long time ago. Now, it's a graveyard. It needs tending, and not by sickly wretches, coughing out prayers, and spreading their ills to honest folk.' He slapped his hat back on his head and looked at Gardus. 'I know what you are, friend. I've been to Hammerhal, aye, and Azyrheim as well, if you can believe it.'

'Then you know these will not be enough to move me, if I decide to stand here.' Gardus indicated the sellswords with a sweep of his hand. A gesture of bravado, but necessary. The sellswords had the look of men who'd just realised that they probably weren't going to be paid.

Wale nodded thoughtfully. 'And yet, I own this land. Mine by right, you see?' He held his hand out. 'You're like a stone, sitting in my field. I can try to dig you out...'

'Or you can go around me.'

Wale smiled thinly. 'Never been one for that. But, never been one to tempt the gods, either.' He hunched forward, leaning on his cane. 'I expect that you came here for a reason, my friend. I expect that reason has to do with them inside. Maybe you can move these stones, where I can't.'

'What do you mean?'

'I came here today to drive them out once and for all. I have warrants from the Rushes, allowing me to use whatever methods I deem best.' He twitched his cane towards the sellswords. 'I'm a simple man, friend. I use what tools are to hand. But I wouldn't say no to a bit of help.'

'You want me to get them to leave.'

'You'd be ensuring their safety. Sigmar's law is on my side, and I'd rather not water this ground in blood.'

Gardus' hand dropped to the hilt of his sword. 'If I say no?'

Wale smiled sadly and shrugged. 'Then these fellows will earn their pay.'

'And if I stand against them?'

'Then they'll die, I imagine.' Several of the sellswords blanched at this. Wale continued, 'But I will have what I'm owed. Even if I have to involve the Rushes, and the city guard.' He frowned. 'I'll hire an entire freeguild regiment, if that's what it takes. So, you have to ask yourself – am I the stone, or the man who'll move it?'

Gardus said nothing. Wale sighed and peered up at the darkening sky. 'I'll give you until evensong tomorrow. After that, I'll do what must be done.' He turned away. 'As, I imagine, will you.'

Gardus watched the sellswords drift away, as their master departed, in ones and twos. They wouldn't go far. And they'd be back, in force. Possibly with help from the city guard, if Wale had been speaking the truth. Gardus had little reason to doubt him.

Mortals like Wale were becoming more common, as Sigmar's influence spilled out into the wider realms. They remade the land in Azyr's image, whether they meant to or not, taming the wilderness and helping the cities of men grow. Gardus had seen it before, and had even aided it, once or twice. That was the Stormcast Eternals' purpose, after all. To drive back the dark, so that the light of Azyr might flourish. To make new what was old.

Men like Wale were necessary, in that regard. They consecrated the ground the Stormcast cleansed in blood and fire, and sowed the seeds for the harvest to come. They raised the cities and rebuilt the roads. Without them, all that warriors like Gardus had achieved would soon fall back into ruin.

But necessity was not always just. He remembered other men, like Wale, from his life as Garradan. Men who wanted lepers burned, and the sick herded onto barges. Men who wielded necessity as a shield, for their own fear and greed.

He turned, and looked up at the ruins of his hospice.

'Sigmar guide me,' he murmured.

'They will return tomorrow at evensong,' Gardus said, as he watched Dumala and others fill bowls of soup for the hungry.

'And we will be here to greet them,' Carazo said. They stood in an antechamber, watching as the pilgrims took their evening meal. Soup and hard, crusty bread, donated by a sympathetic baker. 'Saint Garradan will provide. As he always has.'

'What if he wishes you to leave?'

Carazo looked at him. 'Has he spoken to you, then, brother?'

Gardus looked away. Carazo sighed, and went on. 'Wale never showed an interest in this place until we moved in. Then he decided he needed it.'

'And the Rushes gave it to him.'

Carazo nodded. 'Of course. We are lepers and beggars and fanatics. They don't want us here. But our numbers grow, and they fear what others might say if they turn us out. We are not the only followers of the twin-tailed comet in this city, though most worship the Everqueen, these days.'

'So they hand the problem to Wale.'

Carazo laughed, but it quickly turned into a cough. 'Wale has done much good for the city. I admit that.'

'And you haven't,' Gardus said. Carazo shrugged.

'What is the measure of such a thing? We preach, sometimes, to those who wish to hear. We tend to the sick among us. We sit out of sight, and pray and sing. We are peaceful, as Saint Garradan was peaceful. But like him, we will fight to defend this place, and our way, if we must.'

'I doubt he would want that.' Gardus looked at the old priest. 'Why stay?'

Carazo coughed and dabbed at his bandaged features with a rag. 'The Saint called us here, though we know not why. So we came, and we found a sort of peace in this place.' He looked at the statue. 'I will not leave, until I know why the Saint called me here.'

'Nor will I,' Dumala said firmly. She offered Gardus a bowl of soup.

He waved it aside. 'It is not a question of allow,' he said. 'They will come, and there is little you can do to stop it.' He looked around.

'Wale has the Rushes on his side. He has the law.' The words tasted bitter, even as he said them.

'And we have a higher law,' Carazo said. He made the sign of the hammer. Gardus' reply was interrupted by the sudden scream of an infant. He turned, to see a woman trying to quiet her child, to no avail.

Gardus stepped over to her. 'Let me,' he rumbled. The woman stared up at him, fear in her eyes. Gardus held out his hands. 'Please.'

She looked at Carazo, who nodded. Gingerly, she held out her child, and Gardus took him. He lifted the infant, and rocked him gently, quieting his screams. The woman smiled, the exhaustion on her face easing slightly. 'He is quiet,' she said.

'I remember when I, too, was a child,' Gardus said softly. 'All men were children once, and in need of comfort.'

'Some might say we still are,' Carazo said.

Gardus smiled gently. 'Yes.' The infant had quieted, and he handed the boy back to his mother. 'He is colicky. A warm bath may help.'

Dumala stared at him. 'How do you know that?'

Gardus looked at her. 'Know what?' He turned to Carazo. 'If you will not leave for your own sake, think of this child – and of the others here. Think of Dumala.'

'I told you – I will not leave,' she began, but Carazo silenced her with a look.

'Perhaps you are right. But it is not a decision I can make lightly. I must pray.' He raised his hands, and the others fell silent. 'We all must pray, and seek answers from Saint Garradan. If it is his will that we go – if it is Sigmar's will – we will go. But we must pray.' He looked at Gardus. 'Will you pray with us, brother?'

Gardus nodded, after a moment. 'I will.'

Perhaps in prayer, he would find the answers he sought.

Gardus snapped alert.

He could not say why, but something had drawn him from his

meditations. He glanced at Dumala, and saw that she was sleeping beside him. So were Carazo and the others. Prayer had given way to slumber as the night wore on.

He rose, wondering if Wale's men had come early. If so, he would greet them. Quietly, he padded from antechamber to antechamber, searching for the source of the disturbance. But he found nothing, saving the sick and the lost, sleeping fitfully. Did they dream of him, of the man he had been?

Garradan… please…

He turned. 'I hear you,' he said softly. 'I have always heard you. But when will you tell me why you call out to me?'

Garradan… we need you…

He paced through cold corridors, his breath billowing in the chill. Mortals huddled for warmth, shivering and coughing in their sleep. This place was not good for them. They did not light fires for lack of fuel. They had no food, save what could be scavenged. And yet they stayed, in defiance of all common sense.

Garradan… help us…

His hands clenched into fists. Into weapons. Light flickered in an antechamber. Silently, he moved towards it, his every instinct screaming now. Warning him. There was a smell on the air. A sickly smell, worse than any other, but familiar. One he had smelled before, in places men ought not to go.

Garradan… Garradan… Garradan…

His name beat on the air like the wings of a dying bird. It brushed across the edges of his hearing with painful flutters. He ducked beneath an archway, and the ill light washed over him, filling the antechamber. Men and women lay asleep on pallets, tossing and turning.

Something abominable was coiled about them.

Gardus stopped, a prayer caught in his throat.

The thing looked up at him with more faces than mouths, and more mouths than eyes. It was at once a slug and a cloud and a serpent – no, a nest of serpents – a scabrous, shimmering wound in reality. A thing that should not be. Tendrils of glistening mist wound about the sleepers, pulsing red, and Gardus knew that it was feeding on them in some way. Like a vampire, it drew the life from them, and took it into itself.

Time seemed to slow. His hand fell to his sword. It reared, like a snake readying itself to strike, and unfurled in some awful way. Its mouths moved.

Garradan... Garradan... Garradan...

'No,' Gardus said. Light rose from his flesh, a clean light, and the thing shrank back like a startled beast. The whispers were mangled into moans as it squirmed away from him, slithering into the dark. He followed it, moving quickly.

Was this why he had been drawn here? All this time, had he been haunted in truth, and not just by memories? He did not know. All he knew was that the thing – the daemon of plague and murder – held in itself the souls of innocent and damned alike. It slithered away from him, crawling on withered hands, its faces twitching and gaping. He could hear the voices in his head. A silent storm of whispers and moans. Anger, fear and pain, merging into a dolorous hammer stroke – a pulse of unsound that reverberated through the air, undetectable, save by one with a shard of the divine grafted to their soul.

The ground glistened with grave-light where the daemon-spirit passed, and Gardus could smell the sourness it left in its wake. The earth sickened in its presence, and the air became miasmatic. It was no wonder so many of Carazo's followers were ill.

The daemon-spirit stopped in what had once been the central chamber of the hospice. As Gardus followed, it began to come apart like a cloud caught by a breeze. In slips and tatters, it sank down into the broken soil, until there was no sign it had ever been at all. Gardus sank to his haunches at the point of its disappearance. Tentatively, he pressed the palm of his hand to the ground. He could feel it, somewhere below him. Like water rushing beneath the earth. Burrowing down, down to... what?

He looked around the chamber. He noted the fire-scarred stones and the ugly, fleshy growths that clung to the blackened timbers that pierced the broken ground like talons. As was the way in Ghyran, life had returned with a vengeance. Tapestries of green hung down the broken walls, rippling gently in the night breeze. Overhead, the shattered remains of the dome of glass had turned a filthy brown, from neglect. Sigmar's face was hidden beneath a mask of grime. Thin pillars of starlight fell across the chamber like the bars of a cage.

He heard rubble shift, behind him. He glanced back, and saw Dumala.

'When I awoke, you were gone,' she said. 'I thought...' She shook her head. 'What are you doing here?'

'What is this place?' he asked, as he stood.

'They buried them here. All of those who died when the hospice burned.' Dumala joined him, her arms wrapped tight about her. She shivered slightly, her eyes wide. 'You can still feel it. That's what Carazo says.'

'Feel what?'

'What happened here.' Dumala looked up at him. 'Can you feel it?'

Gardus did not reply. He stared at the ground, a sick feeling growing within him. All the dead... How long had they been trapped down there, in the stifling dark? Broken souls, changing, made into something else by pain and fear. By a plague that had been more than mere sickness. A plague of the soul, as well as the flesh.

How long had they festered until the scent of new life, new souls, had drawn them questing from their pit. A new thing, born in blood and darkness, and hungry. So hungry.

He felt Dumala flinch away from him, as if startled. Belatedly, he realised that he was shining. Starlight shimmered over him and from within him, turning the greens and browns of the chamber to silver. Dumala had fallen to her knees, hands clasped in prayer. Tears streamed from her eyes and her mouth moved wordlessly. Gardus stepped back, trying to dim his radiance. To hide the light once more. But it was hard. Something about this place, this moment, called out to it, and the light... the light *answered*.

'Garradan...' she whispered, reaching for him. 'Your face... I knew...'

'No,' Gardus said. Softly at first, and then more insistently. 'Garradan is dead. He died here. I am Gardus.' He made to draw her to her feet, but she fell onto her face.

'No, I am not worthy,' she moaned.

Gardus hesitated, momentarily at a loss. Then, with a sigh, he dropped to his haunches. 'Get up, please.'

She looked up at him, tears streaking her face. 'Why didn't you tell us?' she whispered. 'You came, and we did not know – I am not worthy.' She made to fall forward again, but Gardus caught her.

'Up,' he said, helping her to her feet. 'Why would you think that?'

'I – I questioned, I doubted, I thought – I thought...'

'You thought Garradan would not come.'

She nodded. She turned away, shivering. 'I was going to leave.'

'That is why you were at the wharfs.'

'I wanted to leave. To go. But they caught me, and then – and then...' She trailed off. 'My faith was not strong enough. Carazo's faith is like iron. I wish mine was.'

'No. Be like water,' Gardus said softly. 'Water flows and renews.' He tapped his head and his chest. 'Running water never grows stale. When water – when *faith* – stagnates, it becomes something else. Fanaticism. Obsession. It makes your soul and mind sick. You must be water, always flowing into the sea, to rise up as vapour and fall as rain.'

'I-I do not understand,' Dumala said haltingly.

'Faith without question, is not faith. To be truly faithful, you must always question. You must always be flowing away from certainty, for in certainty, there is only stagnation. Perhaps not immediately, but it will come.' Even as he said it, he realised that he had answered his own questions. He had come here seeking some sort of assurance, and found only more uncertainty. And perhaps that was what he had always been meant to find.

'Why did you call us here?' she asked.

'I didn't.' He looked at the ground. 'There is a sickness in this place. Whatever drew you all here, it feeds on you now. If you stay, it will only get stronger.'

She shook her head, not understanding. 'Carazo will not leave. Nor will most of the others.' She frowned. 'Some of them can't. Too sick.'

Gardus nodded. 'I know.'

'Will you stay with us?' She touched his arm. 'Will you help us?'

He looked down at her. 'For one night more, at least.'

Gardus spent the rest of the evening and most of the next day in silent vigil over the gravesite. The daemon-thing would come again. But this time, it would not leave the chamber. He would make certain of it.

Now that he had seen it, it was impossible to ignore the thing's presence below his feet. Waiting for nightfall, when it might rise and feed again. As it had likely done for months. It was no wonder that illness was rampant here.

Others might have seen that as evidence of corruption. Enough, at least, to warrant burning this place to the foundations, and salting the ashes. But Gardus was not others. Sickness was to be fought, here more than anywhere else.

'Was this why I was drawn back here, now, of all times?' he murmured, looking up at the mural of Sigmar. 'To confront hungry ghosts? I should not be surprised, I suppose. We were forged for war, and it seeks us out.' Sigmar, as ever, remained silent as to his intentions. Even the few times Gardus had spoken to the God-King face to face, he had found himself questioning what was said, and whether what he had heard had been what was meant.

Questions and uncertainty. These, not hardship, were the whetstones of faith. He felt that he was where he needed to be, whatever the reason. And so he would wait, and do as Sigmar willed. As he hoped Sigmar willed.

'Patience is something of a burden,' he grumbled. He patted his runeblade in its plain sheath, sitting across his knees. He could feel the heat of the blade, the echo of its forging. Like him, it was more than just a sword. He hoped it would be enough. He hoped *he* would be enough. But only time would tell.

Behind him, he could hear the faithful of Saint Garradan singing an old Verdian hymn. A song of life and renewal, of hope. He closed his eyes, and for a moment, he almost thought himself in Azyr once more, walking the rim of the Sigmarabulum, listening to the song of the stars. As Dumala had said, Carazo had decided not to leave. Some few had departed, but most of the congregation had stayed.

For her part, Dumala told no one of her realisation, not even Carazo. Her faith in him was somewhat unnerving, even as he made use of it. She and a few others would keep watch for Wale's men, and ring the hospice bells when they spotted them. Gardus suspected that a show of force would be enough to make the sellswords rethink any plans to violence. And if not, he would deal with them, if necessary.

As you dealt with the Skineaters?

The question caused him to stiffen. He was not sure whether he had thought it, or not. He took his sword off his knees and stood. 'I did what I thought was right,' he said.

Right... right... right...

Long shadows crept along the unsettled earth. The night came on, and a chill prickled across the nape of his neck. 'Do you know me?' he asked. He felt foolish as he did so. 'Have you been calling to me, all this time?'

Silence. But he felt as if he were being watched. The air had taken on a pall, as before a storm. He drew his blade, and cast aside his sheath. 'You called. I am here. Answer me.'

Still, no reply. Then...

Garradan…

'Yes,' he said, bringing his runeblade up. 'I hear you. I have been hearing you for a long time, I think. I am sorry I could not come sooner.'

Garradan… help us…

'I will. If I can.' He turned, seeking any sign of the daemon-thing. He'd half hoped his presence would keep it quiescent. It had seemed to fear him, the night before. But there was no fear in its voice now – only a raw, ugly *need*.

In the other chamber, the song rose. He felt the ground shudder beneath his feet, as if the sound pained it. Had their prayers woken it, that first night? Had the hymns stirred some faint memory, and brought what had been growing in the dark to the surface?

Garradan… where are you… Garradan… please…

'I am here.' He raised his blade, watching the ground. 'I am waiting.'

The song faltered. He spun, as the bells began to ring, and a babble of worry rose. He could hear Carazo trying to keep people calm, and something else – shouts, and the clatter of weapons. He started towards the archway.

Garradan… don't leave us… You can't leave us…

Gardus paused, and turned back, as the daemon-spirit erupted from beneath the churning soil, its many mouths open in a manifold scream. Hands and arms sprouted from its serpentine length, like the legs of a centipede. He staggered, and fingers and fists thudded into him, striking with inhuman force, bruising his flesh as he was driven back, against a broken support timber. It was at once there and not – incorporeal, but somehow hideously solid. The thing surged up, larger than he'd imagined, and coiled about him, knocking aside fire-scarred rubble in its fury.

Gardus smashed a gibbering, gnawing face, and slashed out with his runeblade. The moist spirit-stuff parted like jelly, rippling and splitting around the edge of the sword, before reforming with a wet splat. Gardus grunted in frustration and redoubled his efforts, chopping at the viscous matter as it rose up around him. As he fought, the whispers of the dead insinuated themselves, burrowing through the walls of his concentration.

Garradan... help us...

My hands... I can't feel my hands...

Dark... So dark... Why can't I see...

Garradan...

Garradan...

'Silence,' Gardus roared. But the voices continued, doubling and redoubling, drowning out his own thoughts. The daemon's coils convulsed about him, nearly crushing the air from his lungs. He fought to free himself, as fingers and teeth dug into his flesh. Blood ran down his arms and legs, dripping to the broken ground.

He tore himself free of the entity's coils, splitting it in two with a wild blow, and staggered back against another fallen timber. There was blood in his eyes, and his breath thick in his lungs. The daemon-spirit hissed and writhed, reforming slowly.

He heard a chuckle, from somewhere close by. 'It's strong, for something so young. Then, good soil does wonders with even the smallest seed.'

Wale.

Gardus blinked blood and sweat from his eyes. He could hear screams. The shouts of Wale's men, and the rattle of weapons. 'No,' he said hoarsely.

'I warned you. I gave you a chance. But here it is, evensong, and this stone is still in my field.' Wale sighed. 'I'm no butcher. Just a man of the soil. But this field is mine, by right.' Gardus heard the click of Wale's walking stick, striking a rock. 'As is this harvest. Someone else might have planted the seeds, but the crop is Grandfather's, through and through. I've been waiting for it to ripen for decades.'

The daemon-spirit had finished reforming. It lurched towards him with a slug-like undulation. Faces and hands bulged like blisters on its gelatinous body, biting and groping at the air. The voices

of the dead hung on the air like the hum of insects. He felt weak –
as if the daemon's miasma were sapping his strength.

'Beautiful,' Wale said. Gardus saw him, standing near the far wall,
his hands folded over the head of his cane. 'A new thing, under
Grandfather's sun. That's a true joy, that is. Bringing something
new into the world.'

The daemon-thing turned at his words, its faces contorted in
expressions ranging from confusion to frustration. It snarled, in
many voices, and Wale frowned. 'Now, now, little one. None of
that. I'm not here to harm you.'

It stretched its upper half towards him, faces splitting and sprout-
ing anew as they extended. Mouths moved, voicing a babble of
what might have been questions. Wale gestured, and there was a
sudden sickly light. The daemon-thing jerked back, with a startled
hiss. 'Go back to your meal, little one. You'll find no nourishment
from my withered frame.' The thing turned, and began to slither
back towards Gardus.

Gardus lifted his sword. 'Is this your doing, then? Is this monstrosity something you've conjured?'

The daemon-thing undulated closer, mouths opening and closing. Parts of it were singing. Some were praying – to Sigmar, to
Khorne – but the words twisted, becoming a paean to Nurgle. Gardus twisted aside as it lunged, its malformed jaws tearing a chunk
from the timber behind him.

Garradan… help us…

Wale laughed. 'Me? No. This is the fruit of death, and I'm no
killer. Just a farmer. A man of the soil, as I told you. I know a few
tricks, but I'm no sorcerer or rotbringer. But isn't it magnificent?
Grandfather loves all things that live and grow, friend. Even this.
Even you. You should remember that, should you walk these green
places again.'

Garradan… we need you…

The daemon-thing shimmered in the dark, shining with the ugly
light of a bruise or an infected wound. The runeblade felt heavy

in his hand. The thing seemed to shrug off his strongest blow, and he wondered at the weakness he felt. He touched one of the wounds on his arm, rubbing the blood between his fingers. The thing licked its lips. His blood marked its mouths and limbs, and crimson pulses ran through its semi-opaque form.

It was feeding on him. The mortals had given it the strength to manifest, but it needed more than they could provide. He lowered his sword, as realisation flooded him. Fighting it would only make it stronger. It would bleed him, and leave him a broken husk.

It was greedy, like an infant. And like an infant, it needed comfort.

Garradan... please...

He stabbed his sword into the ground. 'Yes,' he said, stepping forward, weaponless. He spread his arms. 'I hear you.'

It surged towards him, with a murmur of triumph. He heard Wale cackle in pleasure. The daemon-thing engulfed him. It was like being struck by a spray of icy water, and he fought the urge to resist. He felt teeth fasten into his flesh, and fingers clutch at him, with desperate ferocity.

He sank down, drowning in effluvia, and let loose his hold on the light within him. It burst forth, from every pore. It swelled, filling the daemon-thing. The entity screamed in many tongues, and heaved itself away from him, its form writhing. Gardus stumbled after it. The blood that slicked his limbs shimmered like fire, and where it struck the ground, plumes of smoke curled upwards. He caught hold of the daemon-thing and dragged it towards him, as the light grew blinding in its intensity. It squirmed in his grip, babbling.

Garradan... Garradan... Garradan...

'I am here,' he said. 'I am here. I will help you.' It twisted, coming apart in his hands, boiling away to nothing. Faces stretched like clay, bubbled and fell away, leaving only fading moans to mark their passing. His light filled the chamber as he gathered the dissolving remnants to him, hugging it close. He murmured to the struggling entity, whispering words of comfort. 'I did not mean to leave you here,' he said. 'But I will not leave you again.'

Garradan… help us…

He closed his eyes. 'I will.' It beat at him, trying to free itself, but its struggles grew weak, and finally ceased entirely. As it fell silent, he looked down, and saw that he held something frail and broken and pale – something that murmured wordlessly as it came apart in his hands and spilled away like dust.

'No!'

Something caught him on the back of the head, and shattered. He staggered, sinking to one knee. Wale roared and struck him again, with the remains of his cane. Despite his withered frame, the old man was far stronger than he looked – stronger than any mortal. Wale cast aside the fragments of his cane and caught Gardus by the scalp. 'You killed it! Murderer!'

Wale drove him face first into a timber. Gardus slumped, dazed. Wale kicked him in the side, knocking him onto his back. 'What harm did it ever do you? It was no more than a seedling.' The old man drew his sword. The blade was dull and brown with old rust. Ugly runes decorated its length, and Gardus could feel the malignant heat of its magics. He shook his head, trying to clear it.

'It was a monster,' he said hoarsely. 'As are you.'

'Just a farmer, friend,' Wale said, as he raised his blade. 'And after I'm done with you, I'll grow such a crop here as this city has never seen.'

'Gardus!'

Gardus looked up, and saw Dumala. She had his runeblade in both hands and sent it skidding across the ground towards him, as Wale spun towards her, face twisted with fury. Gardus caught the hilt, and lunged to his feet. Wale, realising his error, turned back. Their blades connected with a hollow clang. Gardus forced Wale back.

'You'll grow nothing,' he said.

'It's – You can't! This place is mine,' Wale snarled. 'Mine by right!'

'No,' Gardus said. 'It is *mine*.' Wale's blade shattered as Gardus swept it aside. Wale fell back, mouth open in denial. Gardus slammed his sword through Wale's chest, and drove him back against a timber. He loosed the hilt and stepped back, leaving Wale impaled.

Wale clawed at the runeblade as his thin form began to unravel. His coat shed its feathers, as his limbs shed skin and muscle. He crumpled inwards, like fruit gone rotten, and fell away, leaving only one more black stain to mark his passing. Gardus pulled his blade free, and turned. 'Thank you,' he said.

Dumala nodded. 'Just returning the favour.' She gestured. 'Look,' she said softly.

The chamber had changed. Was changing.

Blue flames danced across black walls, leaving only bare stone in its wake. The unsightly vegetation crumbled away, and new, vibrant growth replaced it. Wherever his blood had fallen, green shoots pushed through the soil, and spread outwards.

His light had seared away the filth. The pall he'd felt was gone, and the whispers of the ghosts had fallen silent. 'Wale's men?' he asked.

'Gone,' Dumala said. 'You were right. They had no stomach for a fight. They ran, the moment we began to resist.' She smiled. 'You should have seen Carazo, waving his canes as if they were warhammers.' Her smile faded, as she took in his wounds, and the black mark of Wale's demise. 'What happened here, Garradan – Gardus?'

For a moment, he had no answer for her. 'What was meant to,' he said finally.

She frowned. 'How do you know?'

'I don't.' He looked up at the mural of Sigmar, and smiled. 'But I have faith.'

YOUR
NEXT READ

HALLOWED KNIGHTS: PLAGUE GARDEN
by Josh Reynolds

During the greatest battles of the War for Life, the Stormcast Eternals suffered a great tragedy: the Hallowed Knights' Lord-Castellan Lorus Grymn was lost to the Realm of Chaos. Now his fellow Steel Souls venture into the domain of Nurgle himself in search of their lost comrade…

ONE, UNTENDED

David Guymer

Introducing

GOTREK GURNISSON

DUARDIN SLAYER

Master,

The artefact is within my grasp, but there have been complications and I am unable to report to you as requested. I can only hope that this note will be recovered by another of your agents and returned to you in my stead. I am still within the bounds of the Twin-Tailed City and appear likely to remain so for some time. I just need more time.

I will not fail you.

Still and eternally the faithful servant of Azyr,

Maleneth Witchblade

'Get back, aelfling,' Gotrek scowled. 'This is not something that your pretty little eyes need to see.'

Maleneth rolled her 'pretty little' eyes as Gotrek bent over the open sewer that ran along the back yard of the Missed Striking, one hand on the ivy-scrawled corner of a brick wall. She watched with a casual anatomist's fascination as the immense muscle groups that corded his back rippled and flexed. The duardin turned to look over the single plate of black armour fixed across his left shoulder.

His one good eye was virulently bloodshot, his preternaturally aged skin slacker and more haggard even than usual. His huge blade of gold-struck orange hair drooped over the armour's leonine features, sodden with stale beer where he had slept with his head against a trestle table. 'I told you–' His throat suddenly clenched. His face blanched. Red light from the street lamps slithered across it. 'Grungni's beard.'

Then he was violently, messily sick into the sewer.

Maleneth patted the thickly creased skin at the back of his head. 'There, there.'

'I hate you, aelfling,' Gotrek said between ructions. 'I hate you and all your darkling kin.'

'I know.'

After a few minutes the duardin's heaves subsided, and he spat the last chunks of a green sausage and ghyrvole egg supper into the ditch.

'This has never happened to me before.'

'I am sure that you say that to all of the girls.'

Gotrek glared at her.

'A joke,' she said.

'I think there was something nasty in my beer,' Gotrek complained.

Maleneth nodded sympathetically. There had indeed been something nasty in the Slayer's beer. Several somethings. Duardin were notoriously resistant to poisoning, but the amount of gravelock, heartcease and scarlet clover that Gotrek Gurnisson had obligingly consumed over the last day and a half would have killed a gargant. He should have been curled up on the weed-filled yard bleeding out of every orifice rather than complaining of an upset stomach.

Maleneth looked up at the night sky, trying to judge the time.

The moons were swathed in autumnal colours. Even the realm's cohort of satellites responded to the life song of the Everqueen, and on a clear night Maleneth could see foliage stirring in another world's winds. This was not such a night. Scraps of dark cloud raced across their faces. A thin mist shrouded the creaking wooden tenement runs and lean-tos of the Stranglevines, and even Maleneth's inhumanly chill breath fogged the air in front of her face. It was past midnight.

She sighed as the Slayer began to dry retch over the ditch. He should have been dead three times over already. But even in his current condition she was not sure that she wanted to risk hurrying things along. She had fought the duardin twice before, and on both occasions had barely escaped with her life. And that had been before he had acquired the fyreslayers' master rune, multiplying his already formidable strength severalfold. The rune smouldered quiescently from the scarred, fire-ruined meat of his chest. Occasionally, when the Slayer had drunk enough to pass out and sleep, it also whispered, though not in any language that Maleneth had ever heard. No. She belonged to a fantastically long-lived race. Barring a knife in the back she could afford a little patience.

'Come on, Gotrek,' she said. 'I think you left a beer untended in there.'

'Give me a moment here, damn you.'

Before she could try to cajole the duardin any further, the tavern's back door opened. Another posse of drunks stumbled through the rectangle of wobbly warmth and light and into the moonlit yard. They appeared to be armed, in some distress and without exception, drunk. Not an agreeable combination in Maleneth's experience, even in the most salubrious of establishments. And even in the Stranglevines of Hammerhal Ghyra, establishments did not come more insalubrious than the Missed Striking. Gotrek had found his way through its doors the way a blind woman found her own bed.

Eager to avoid any trouble with the local ruffians, Maleneth nodded across the yard to them, as though standing over a retching duardin in the dead of night was the most natural activity in Ghyran. To her relief they ignored her utterly, too intent on their own whispered arguments to mark even Gotrek's outlandish appearance.

A young woman in a nightdress and a thin shawl ran barefoot into the yard after the gang of armed drunks. Tears streamed down her reddened cheeks as she screamed something about a 'Tambrin'. It was her distress, rather than her peasant prettiness and state of undress, that made Maleneth forgo her earlier misgivings about attracting attention and turn to watch. She had come a long way from the girl who would murder the row's cats and kidnap the neighbours' children, but she still found other people's pain arresting. A burly man in a sweat-stained linen vest tried to put a coat over her. His head looked like an executioner's block, all nicks and bloodstains with strange chunks missing. The woman beat her fists against his chest until he gave up. The other drunks, clearly as embarrassed by the display as Maleneth was enthralled, fussed over strappings and buckles.

There were two of them, both human, both what Maleneth would call old despite being at least a century her junior.

One was clad in leaves of delicate, lightly scuffed mail that appeared to have more of a decorative function than offering any real protection. A laurel of dried leaves and flowers sat nestled on a coarse stubble of grey hair. He carried a long-handled hammer. *The next step in the cultural surrender of Ghyran*, Maleneth thought. Azyrite might was irresistible, in all its forms. The old faiths had adapted to and appropriated from the doctrines of Azyr to remain relevant to the new order, or else had simply been assimilated wholesale into the Sigmarite faith. The warrior-priest of Alarielle was an extreme example.

Maleneth felt herself uniquely qualified to judge – a shadowblade of Khaine, now an agent of the Order of Azyr. Or at least she had been. Her failure to return to the Order with the master rune would have done little to ease her superior's understandable distrust.

The second figure was more difficult to make out in detail. She kept to the darkest parts of the yard, as if out of habit. Her hood was drawn tight against the cold, not a single strand of hair falling free. Her cloak was made from woven leaves, and real ones, not the steel likenesses worn by the warrior-priest. They changed colour with the light, turning from black to autumnal red with the streaking of the clouds across the moons. Despite that exotic quality the garment was well worn, stained by sweat, soil and beer, and had probably never been anything but functional to begin with. The only thing to distinguish the woman from another common footpad or down-on-her-luck highwayman was a string of campaign badges on her collar. They marked her as ex-Freeguild. Perhaps even one of the Living City Rangers, judging by the raiment, well known throughout Ghyran as the best scouts and trackers in the Mortal Realms. Maleneth recognised some of the battles. The most recent had been fought about fifteen years ago.

'What's going on over there?' said Gotrek.

'Nothing.'

'Really? Because it *sounds* as if someone's mislaid a child.'

'As I said,' said Maleneth. 'Nothing.' But the Slayer was already stomping towards the armed gathering. Maleneth swore. Talk about something that he actually wanted to hear and Gotrek's ears were as keen as any darkling aelf's.

'You were supposed to be watching them while I visited the night market, Junas,' the distraught woman yelled as Gotrek walked over.

'It was a rough-looking crowd tonight, Madga,' said the big man, Junas, defensively. 'Helmlan wanted more help on the door. What was I supposed to say?'

'Speaking of rough-looking crowds,' muttered the warrior-priest, his eyes widening at the sight of Gotrek's sagging crest. He shuffled smartly out of the Slayer's way.

'I hear that someone has lost a child,' said Gotrek, in a tired voice that sounded like a slab of granite dropped into a conversation.

'What's it to you?' said Junas. 'I don't know who you are.'

Madga slapped him. Maleneth saw the brawler's biceps tense. Her hand strayed to her knife belt, but whatever anger he was containing he found room for a little more.

'I know you,' said the ex-Freeguilder, slowly. 'You're the fyreslayer that slept the night on Helmlan's table.'

A glitter of malice in Gotrek's one eye made the old veteran step back.

'I am no fyreslayer, woman.'

'My mistake, master duardin.' The ranger bowed.

'Aye. It was.'

'My name is Madga,' said the young woman, wiping the tears from her face on the sleeve of her nightdress as though to make herself presentable for the permanently dishevelled Slayer. 'This is my husband, Junas.' The tavern brawler crossed his arms over his chest. Maleneth recognised a display of threatened masculinity when she saw one. All bulging neck muscles and scowls. Like a feral alley starwyrm. 'The priest is Alanaer.' The older man painstakingly put together a drunken bow, leafmail twinkling under the light of the moons. 'The Freeguild ranger is called Halik.' The woman so named nodded curtly. 'Anyone who drinks often enough in the Missed Striking to be on first-name terms with my husband isn't the sort I'd want to trust my family to, but anyone who'd drop it all in the dead of night to go looking for a boy can't be all bad, can they?'

Maleneth did not think that the girl had intended it as a question, but the hopeful inflection she gave it made it sound like one. The priest, Alanaer, smiled faintly, as if remembering the last time he had been spoken of so highly.

'Do you have children?' Madga asked.

Gotrek scoffed. 'Take another look, girl. If this one ever got her claws on a child, she would probably skin it alive. And eat it.'

Maleneth nodded.

The young woman blanched. 'I... I actually meant you, master duardin.'

Gotrek grimaced, as though pained by an old tooth. He grumbled something in his own archaic form of the Dispossessed tongue, his breath misting the midnight air. He stamped his boots on the cobblestones, taking small but obvious comfort in crushing the small flowers that sprouted between them.

'It is quite the collection of arms you carry for a missing child,' said Maleneth.

'Someone saw the boy heading towards one of the catacomb entrances,' said Halik.

Gotrek raised an eyebrow, and turned to Junas. He shook his head slowly. 'You live a stone's throw from the entrance to such a place and you would leave your child untended?'

The big man coloured. 'The entrances are all locked,' he protested. 'And patrolled by the watch.'

'It was the ghost of Hanberra!' Madga wailed. 'He's taken my Tambrin.'

Some of the gloom lifted from Gotrek's complexion.

Trust the Slayer to be revived by talk of spirits and monsters, Maleneth thought. 'Ghost?' she asked, casting a furtive look over her shoulder.

There was not much in this world that she truly feared. It was coldness, she often supposed, rather than genuine courage. But as a devotee of the God of Murder, the undead stirred a peculiar revulsion in her which, on a night as dark as this one, might have been mistaken for fear.

Alanaer shook his head. 'A folk myth, pedalled by some of the Sigmarites.'

'It's true though,' Junas murmured. He touched the small hammer he wore around his neck. 'Hanberra was a hero of the old city. The one that stood here before Hammerhal. Before the War Storm. He fell defending it from Chaos. Sigmar tried to take him, for his Stormhosts, but he refused, because there were still folk in the city he could save.'

'His children,' cried Madga. 'He defied the lightning to go back for his children. And he looks for them still.'

'It's just an old tale,' said Alanaer. 'One the Azyrheimers have latched on to, to warn about what happens to those who turn their backs on Sigmar.'

Halik, Maleneth noticed, looked unconvinced, but she nodded. 'True or not, Tambrin was seen alone. Heading towards the Downs.'

Madga started to sob.

'I'm going to bring him back, Madga,' said Junas.

Halik and Alanaer both grunted their agreement.

'Please, master duardin,' Madga sniffed. 'Will you help? Please?'

Gotrek scowled, but nodded. 'Aye. I'll help find your boy.'

Maleneth sighed.

With any luck, a little light exertion would be just what the various poisons in the duardin's body needed to do their work. And failing that, there was every chance that the monsters of the catacombs or the ghost of Hanberra could do what she had been unable to.

Kill Gotrek Gurnisson.

The stairs into the catacombs went down forever. It seemed that way to Maleneth, at least, after a second hour had elapsed with no end in sight.

Maleneth wondered if Madga was still up there, waiting. Probably. For a moment it had looked as though the peasant woman would come with them, and it had only been a word from Alanaer that had dissuaded her.

At least there was little chance of her being discovered and moved on by the watch. Their patrols were laughably infrequent, and could almost have been designed to give the entrances to the catacombs as wide a berth as possible. Maleneth had not harboured any elevated expectations of the local law enforcement and so had not been disappointed.

Maleneth tried to recall the pretty, tear-soaked face that had watched them disappear into the old sewers beneath the Stranglevines Downs, but could not seem to call it back to memory. She sighed. She could have used some cheering up.

Even this deep under the earth of the city, the brickwork was florid with life. Weeds and scruffy flowers matted the steps. Tuberous roots broke through the walls and ceiling, forcing everyone except Gotrek to walk with a crouch lest they strike their heads. More than once a particular brute of an obstacle funnelled the adventurers down to single file to slither over the crumbling, weed-carpeted steps on their bellies. Maleneth appreciated those interludes even if Junas, Halik, Alanaer and Gotrek manifestly did not. They were a chance for her to sit down and rub her aching thighs while the others caught up, struggling and cursing behind her.

What sustenance do these plants draw from this grey place? Maleneth wondered. Where do they turn in lieu of sunlight? In Azyrheim, too, the days were often dark. The city had no sun, but bathed in the light of Sigendil, the High Star, at the very heart of the cosmos, it shared in the brilliance of a trillion stars. Perhaps it was the song of the Everqueen alone that bade them grow.

She could see in near-perfect darkness. Her senses of hearing and intuition were so acute that she could fare reasonably well even without vision. But even she was starting to miss the cheap, imported illumination of the Stranglevines' street lamps.

The ranger, Halik, bore a torch, but she had not lit it.

There had been no need.

The only light that had followed them into this forgotten corner of Alarielle's realm was that of Gotrek's axe. Zangrom-thaz, it was called, in the language of the unbaki fyreslayers who had crafted it. The forgeflames bound up in the huge fyrestorm greataxe licked at his flesh and at the hairs of his beard without finding a purchase on either. Another effect of the fyreslayers' ur-gold on his body, Maleneth thought. She could feel the axe's heat perfectly. Sweat beaded her forehead. The palms of her hands were damp, to the extent that she almost feared she would be unable to draw a weapon should the need arise. The tangling vegetation shrivelled back from him, much to the Slayer's childish glee.

The weight of rock above Maleneth's head seemed to close in. It dawned on Maleneth that it was this, rather than the darkness, that was truly disturbing her.

In her duties for the Temple there had been no dungeon so deep that she could not penetrate it, no arcane fortress warded so completely that she could not reach its heart. There was an aspect of killer instinct at play there, but largely it came down to preparation. Since she had been an acolyte, Maleneth had known never to open a door without first knowing of at least two others by which she could flee. Following Gotrek wherever the idiot duardin chose to swing his axe denied her that. It was simply not possible to carry the same sigmarite-clad self-assurance that she was accustomed to when she had no idea where she was or what she was supposed to be doing.

Her hand strayed over the array of knives sheathed to the lightweight, drakespawn leather plate of her thigh. Her neck itched as though she were being watched. Like a zephyrat in a sadist's maze. She almost feared to look back, stricken by the bizarre certainty that she would see a million tons of Ghyranite rock crashing over the stairs behind her if she did.

Forcing herself to swallow her phobias and face them, she glanced over her shoulder. Junas walked behind her, hunched, scared, stroking the hammer pendant that hung from his neck and muttering a prayer to Sigmar. For himself or for his child, Maleneth could not quite make out. Maleneth's hand moved involuntarily from her knife belt to the device at her own neck. The locket was in the form of a silver heart bound in chains. A small window between revealed a quantity of blood inside.

It had belonged to her former mistress.

'What other choice did I have, my lady?' she whispered. 'Let the Slayer go? Return to Azyrheim empty-handed? The Order would cast me onto the streets and to the tender mercies of the Temple. I fear that the last person who would have granted me a painless end died when I murdered you.' She smiled, heartened somewhat by the memory of the last Lady Witchblade drowning in the blood of her own cauldron.

'Who are you talking to, aelfling?' said Gotrek.

'The dead,' she said.

The Slayer snorted, but for several hours thereafter said no more.

The vegetation started to become yellower and sicker. Halik drew her hood tighter. Junas' mashed-up face contorted further in disgust, finding breathing into his own elbow pit preferable to the rancid sweetness of the decaying plantlife. Alanaer spoke prayer after prayer until his voice gave out, but only the axe-fire of Zangrom-thaz seemed able to purge the plants of their blight. This mercy Gotrek delivered with apparent relish and no sign of weariness.

Maleneth's sense of smell was many times keener than any of theirs, and she decided not to mention how deep into the stones the contagion ran. If she did then even Junas might have second thoughts and turn back. Getting the Slayer killed was one thing, but surviving long enough to cut the master rune from his flesh and escape with it was another. It was a task that would undoubtedly benefit from having another warrior or two between her and whatever monster it was that had finally bested the old duardin.

'A corruption has taken root here,' Halik murmured.

'Really?' Maleneth asked, as a cackling Gotrek Gurnisson burned another mushy curtain of vines from their path. 'What makes you think that?'

The ranger pursed her lips, but said nothing.

Maleneth decided not to rile the woman any further. Sometimes, she just could not help herself.

'Who built these stairs?' Gotrek asked. He looked down. The steps wound on away from him, as if a gigantic god-beast had driven a drill into the heart of Ghyran only to see it become entrapped in its rich soil. 'They bear the mark of dwarven craftsmanship. The age of these worlds of yours is hard even for one who's seen as much as this dwarf to conceive. Even the works of my people would falter if abandoned for such a span of years.'

'That's impossible,' said Junas. 'The folk of the Mortal Realms lived in ignorance until the first coming of Sigmar. He taught them how to raise their cities and to build great monuments.' The big man looked defensive as Halik and Alanaer turned to him. 'I can't read, but you think I can't listen?'

'Maybe that's so,' Gotrek mused, sniffing at the great depth of blackness beyond the reach of his axe. 'But who do you think taught *him?*'

Gotrek lowered himself gruffly to one knee, rubbing at his thigh with a scowl.

The ground at the base of the stairs was buckled. Pale weeds and stalk-like flowers had pushed the flagstones out of true. But after the hours they had spent on the stairs it looked as though it had been levelled flat by the Six Smiths of Grungni themselves. Alanaer sat against one of the mossy pillars that framed the mouth of the stairwell, red-faced, mouth hanging open, his knees pulled up to his leafmail coat. He was probably regretting the beer he had consumed earlier. Or perhaps he was simply regretting following Junas and Halik at all.

Maleneth realised that she did not know her companions on this adventure very well. And if the catacombs were half as dangerous as she had heard them to be then she probably never would.

Even the Stormcast Eternals had been unable to cleanse them of all evil.

Gotrek thumped his thigh and issued a curse in consonant-heavy Dispossessed duardin.

'Cramp?' Maleneth asked.

'I'd like to see how spry you are when you get to be this age, aelfling.' Gotrek nodded his flattened crest towards the tumble-down architecture around them. His nose chain tinkled loudly in the enclosed space. 'I'm twice as old as this ruin. I think I've held up well, all things considered.'

Halik lowered her torch to the rune-fuelled brazier at the heart of Gotrek's fyrestorm greataxe and lit it. She lifted it as she padded past. Its wavering light pushed into the darkness, revealing a hallway flanked by massive granite columns. Some of them had been carved into figures. Their identities however had been long hidden beneath blotching mould and withered creepers. Like the staircase before it, it seemed to go on forever.

'Could the boy have… have got this far?' Alanaer panted, sitting up with effort.

'He could be no more than an hour ahead of us,' said Junas.

Which means he has been dead for no more than an hour, Maleneth thought, but chose to keep it to herself.

'We've not passed him,' said Halik. 'A small child may have been able to move faster. He would have had less difficulty on the stairs.'

'You are talking about a four-year-old boy,' Maleneth said aloud. 'Walking alone for hours in the dark. Why would he not stop? Or turn back?'

No one had an answer. At least, not one they liked.

'I don't know,' Halik admitted.

The ranger crouched with only a slight protestation of old bones, and brushed worn fingertips over a patch of flattened stems and crushed flowers. Maleneth knew that she was not the equal of a Living City Ranger when it came to the tracking of quarry, but she knew how to read a spoor. It was a footprint. A small footprint. Such as might be made by a child.

'Unbelievable,' said Maleneth. 'He really did come this way.'

'If you doubted it, aelfling, then why come?' said Gotrek.

Maleneth chose not to dignify that with an answer.

'There are some older prints here.' Halik waved her hand over the pale grasses. 'But Tambrin's is the only one to have been made recently.'

'So he wandered down here alone,' said Junas, relieved.

'It looks like it,' said Halik, rising stiffly. 'And much less than an hour ahead of us I would say.'

'Let's be moving then,' said Gotrek.

'Tambrin!' Junas yelled.

After the hours they had spent with just the occasional furtive whisper between them, the sudden shout startled Maleneth. The syllables rang from the columns and down the hall. Even Halik's torch seemed spooked, cavorting back from the out-breath, making shadows flap around them like bats. Maleneth swore in Druhirri, reaching for her knife belt, even as Junas ran past her to charge bow-legged down the desolate hall.

'Tambrin!' he yelled.

'Quiet, you idiot,' Maleneth hissed.

'Let him shout, aelfling,' Gotrek grumbled. 'Sound travels in strange ways below ground. And if the ground-sniffer says the boy's close then he's probably close.'

'And if something else hears?'

Gotrek grinned, broken teeth flashing yellow and red in the firelight. 'Good.'

'Fair enough,' said Maleneth. 'So long as we understand one another.'

'Tambri–'

A wooden club swung out from behind a pillar before Junas could finish. It mashed into the middle of his face with a horrible wet sound. The big man dropped like a sack of grain. A squeal went up as the brawler hit the flagstones, rat-man warriors pouring from myriad hiding places amidst the crumbling stonework and hanging plant life. Their robes were soiled and mangy. Deep hoods concealed their faces but for dripping noses and rotten, elongated mouths filled with cracked and yellowing teeth.

'Skaven!' Maleneth yelled. 'Plague monks!'

It dawned on her that the monks had selected this hall for their lair with good reason. They would have known that any would-be adventurer wishing to brave the catacombs from the Stranglevines Downs, already exhausted by the descent, would have first to pass through it. The preponderance of clubs and nets in their scabrous paws told her the monks' intentions for such fools.

'They mean to take us alive,' she said.

'Hah!'

With a roar Gotrek barrelled towards the oncoming horde, his axe held high. Fire trailed from the monstrous weapon like a comet's tail. A single blow cleaved a plague monk in two and incinerated it. Three more armed with quarterstaves and maces pounced on him while he was still wreathed and half blinded by crimson smoke.

Maleneth heard a rapid flurry of blows, followed by an angry shout.

She decided to leave the Slayer to it.

A plague monk charged at her with a squeal.

Yellow froth bubbled up from toothless black lips, staining the creature's hood. Maleneth let it come within arm's reach, then vaulted its hunched back with an aerial cartwheel. With one hand she drew a knife. With the other she took hold of the foetid folds of cloth at the back of the monk's hood. It shrieked in dismay, but was still running as she landed. She yanked back. The monk's footpaws flew out from under it as it fell backward onto its tail.

She dropped to one knee and then turned, plunging the knife into the belly of the monk that had been scurrying in behind the first. Its own momentum drove its heart and lungs down onto the blade. Forged from celestite and etched with the murderous blessings of Khaine, a nick was enough to kill even those most resistant to death.

Except for the one life she most wished it to take, it seemed.

Maleneth relished the horror on the plague monk's face as it expired.

She turned again.

The monk she had thrown to the floor was already on its foot-paws. Skaven were fast. As fast as her, if not faster. It came at her with bared teeth, on all fours like a rabid dog. There was a *hiss*, a *thunk*, and an arrow exploded from the monk's eye socket. It jerked once, as though surprised by something on its shoulder, and then fell over.

Halik grunted, as if surprised to see that she was still strong enough to draw a bow and sharp enough to aim it, then turned to loose a second arrow into the fray.

It skewed high.

Maleneth's lips pricked into a smile. With a long fingernail, she tapped on the silver talisman at her collar. *Little wonder that the Azyrite Hags go to such lengths to stay young.*

The skaven appeared to be focusing their considerable numbers on killing Gotrek. The monks' leaders had apparently concluded that despatching the Slayer quickly would allow them to capture the three humans and the aelf more easily. They were probably right. Maleneth would have come to a similar conclusion in their position.

A monk in more ornate robes than the rest crouched on a pedestal of rubble just at the limits of Gotrek's wildly dancing axe-light. It wore creamy yellow robes and a mitre, decorated with fly eggs, dung pellets and spider's silk. With two bandage-wound paws it waved a censer-topped stave, the effect of which was to fill that end of the corridor with greenish fumes that drove the monks caught in the haze to new heights of rabid insanity.

Gotrek bellowed, trying to get at the skaven priest, but found himself hemmed in by the sheer mass of foes that surrounded him.

From the stairs behind them, Alanaer began to chant, words of sylvanspeak that had the diseased roots behind the walls writhing in agony. Dust rained from the ceiling, and for a moment Maleneth feared that the warrior-priest meant to bring the entire hall down on their heads.

Then the grey-haired priest lifted his open palm to his lips and blew. A mighty gale flurried down the halls with a swirl of sepulchral leaves. The battering-ram force hurled skaven from their footpaws, bludgeoning through a corridor all the way to their malefic leader. The plague priest hacked as the fumes from its own censer were blown back into its face by the warrior-priest's scouring wind.

Maleneth saw the opening and took it.

She sprinted, hurdling stricken monks between herself and their priest as they picked themselves off the ground. She was fast, practically a blur as she covered the hundred or so feet in a matter of seconds. The last dozen she turned into a leap, a knife appearing in her off-hand as she dropped.

'For Khaine!'

She slashed the knife across the skaven's throat, intending to gizzard it, only to see her blade *thunk* into the mouldy wood of the priest's staff. Its reflexes were astonishing. The priest hissed, fangs bared, and swung up the butt of its staff. Maleneth twisted to one side. The staff whooshed across her chest. The priest spun, cackling like a fanatic, his censer emitting a weary drone as he spun it overhead, then turned to bring it whirring back towards her.

'For Sigmar!'

She roundhoused the priest, a heel-kick across the snout, deliberately unbalancing herself and falling to the ground as the plague censer droned overhead. The big bronze censer crushed the flagstone behind the one she was sprawled over. Whizzing fragments ripped her drakespawn leathers. Noxious fumes rushed over her. Her eyes filled with stinging tears. The skin bared by her torn armour itched. Coughing, she crawled away from the plague fumes on her back.

The priest tittered as it jumped off its rubble mound to follow.

This was, she acknowledged, not turning into the incisive decapitating stroke that she had envisioned.

Already, the monks that Alanaer's prayer had thrown down were rallying. Several were even peeling away from Gotrek, drawn by the commotion and their priest's shrill laughter. She cursed, glancing back at the Slayer, and in doing so identified another good reason for the wilier of the plague monks to abandon that particular prize in search of another.

Gotrek Gurnisson was on fire. He was liquid gold, sparks hissing, poured into the cast of a duardin form. The flames grew fiercer as the Slayer butchered his way through the squealing plague monks, feeding off his fury and feeding it in kind. His greataxe moved with such speed that it looked to Maleneth as though he wielded two of them, the air around him webbed with fiery after-traces. The heat was so incredible that Halik and Alanaer could no longer even contribute to the fight at all. They had retreated to the shelter of the stairwell. The occasional refrain of a prayer rose over the roar of the flames, but otherwise the Slayer had effectively cut off his, and Maleneth's, only means of aid. It was a testament to the unholy durability of the plague monks that they were able to endure the Slayer's proximity and still fight.

With an ugly snarl, Maleneth tore her gaze from the approaching plague priest and looked around. A way out. A place to hide. *Anything.* What she found, recessed behind two thick, ivy-strangled columns, was so subtly worked into the wall and well-hidden that she almost failed to see it at all. It was an arch. A feeling of bleakness and unreasoning dread emanated from it, a chill finding its way through her violet eyes, and from there along rarely used ways to her heart. Her snarl became a shiver. Something about the arch urged the eye to move on, and discouraged any thought of approaching. But Maleneth had nowhere left to run.

Even as she ignored her own disquiet to sprint towards it, the rat-men on her heels fell off the chase with squeals of terror. Maleneth turned to look over her shoulder. The plague priest jabbed a claw at Maleneth and shrieked at the cowering monks. Maleneth did not understand the chittering speech, which was a small tragedy on the priest's part for it was one of the last acts it would ever perform.

Gotrek reared up behind it.

The Slayer had grown massive. Muscles bulged with rune-forged might. His good eye blazed like a freshly minted coin. Even his eye-patch was limned by a halo of golden brilliance. Flames wreathed him.

Maleneth had known many great wielders of power. She had witnessed the awesome rituals performed by the magisters of the Collegiate Arcane, and had ended the life of more than one rogue wizard in her time. But even the last, desperate conjurations of sorcerers driven mad by the promises of Chaos had been tame and controlled compared to what Maleneth beheld now. It was as though someone, or some*thing*, breathed dragonfire against the thin skein separating Ghyran from the aether that swirled beyond its sphere in the cosmos. Unveiling the dead stars and wrathful deities that lingered there in all their awful magnificence.

The sooner I get that rune out of him the better, Maleneth thought.

With a howl that shook the roots of Ghyran, Gotrek cut the plague priest in half. The two halves of its diseased body consumed themselves in flame before they could hit the ground. The Slayer breathed it in, exhaling it like sparks from a furnace. Those skaven bright enough to have been directing their efforts elsewhere squealed in terror at the sight. They broke, scampering off down the long hall.

Maleneth did not expect them to come back. She noted, however, that despite being for many the closest avenue of escape, none of them had tried to flee down the side tunnel behind her.

With a deep breath, Halik emerged from her hiding place behind the stairs. She cast a wary look at Gotrek as she padded down the hall. But the Slayer did not move. He was hunched over the rubble of the priest's pedestal. It was a cairn now, burnt to twisted plates of unreflective glass by the intensity of the heat and magic that he had unwittingly unleashed upon it. The glassy lump creaked under Gotrek's weight, splintering and popping as it cooled. He was breathing hard, steam curling off his crisped, cooling skin.

It was probably optimistic to hope that it was the cocktail of poisons in his blood finally starting to tell. If there was a toxin anywhere in the planes of existence that could have endured such runefire then it was under the jealous protection of the Hags of Azyr – held against the day that Sigmar himself needed to feel the knife of Khaine.

'What in Sigmar's Storm was that?' said Halik.

Maleneth smiled weakly and shook her head. That was a longer story than she had the strength for, and one that she was not entirely sure of the end of herself.

Alanaer crouched by Junas.

'He's alive,' the warrior-priest declared. He pulled the big man up to sitting, and smiled ruefully as the brawler spat out another tooth. 'But I doubt he'll be breaking any more young ladies' hearts with this face.'

Halik managed a nervous chuckle. 'Skaven,' she muttered, as it left her.

'More of Thanquol's craven minions, I expect.' Gotrek moved like a statue taking life, slowly, vitrified gore and dust trickling from his shoulders. He drew in a shuddering breath, then coughed it up. He wiped blood from his bottom lip on his thumb, then lifted it to his eye. He grunted and stuck it in his mouth. 'Leftovers from the war on the other side of the Stormrift Gate. With skaven you never can kill them all.'

'No.' Alanaer shook his head. 'The servants of the Great Corruptor have long coveted my Queen's realm. I expect that their presence here predates the Grey Lord's invasions of Hammerhal Aqsha by some time.'

'What have you found here, darkling?' Halik looked up at the archway that Maleneth had discovered. Her footsteps slowed noticeably as she looked on it. She shivered as she reached out to run her hand along the inside of the stone arch, hesitating, finally bringing the hand back to her side unused. 'Tambrin passed this way,' she breathed. 'The ground here is marked, and not by skaven paws. And.' The ranger paused, ear cocked. 'Can you hear that?'

Maleneth listened, then nodded, impressed. The ranger was good. For a human.

'Footsteps,' she said.

'And still only one set,' said Halik.

'He has somehow bypassed a locked door, a watch patrol and now a skaven ambush as well,' said Maleneth. 'He belongs in a temple of Khaine, this child.' She turned to join the old ranger in her study of the arch. 'It reeks of soulblight and carrion. Whatever dwells beyond this portal, I fear it is beyond even Khaine's reach now. Such things are best left buried.'

Gotrek heaved himself to his feet with a clink of gold chain and a dying splutter of half-seen flame. Maleneth had to marvel at his determination. And all this for the myth of an ancient ghost, for surely Gotrek Gurnisson cared less for this Tambrin boy than even she did, and she cared nothing at all. It was with a mixture of amazement and frustration she was lately becoming painfully familiar with that she watched the Slayer limp towards her.

'What are you all standing about for?' he said. 'There's black work ahead of us yet.'

After what he had inflicted on the plague monks, nobody felt inclined to argue.

A chill blue light shone from the passage beyond the archway. The languid movements of the mist that filled the corridor diffused and scattered it. It was like being submerged in water.

Maleneth felt her breath starting to come quick and shallow. She studied the walls. Frost prickled the weeds and mosses that encrusted their ancient stonework. But aside from the chill the plants looked healthy. The air in this part of the dungeon smelled clean. For some reason, that pristine quality troubled her more than the rank despoliation in the chamber that had preceded it. It was the sterility of abandonment. Nothing had moved in to claim these halls. That alone was enough to give Maleneth's heart jitters.

There was a tired creak as Halik raised her bow.

The ranger's aim wavered.

'Sigmar preserve us.'

Maleneth drew her hand from the frost-stippled wall and looked up. Her eyes were sharper than those of the human ranger. At that precise moment she wished they were not.

Between her looking away and turning back the mists ahead had parted. Or rather, something had drawn them apart. They clung to the walls of the passage in a way that was wholly unnatural, trembling like cold skin, and bathed in blueish light. A taller-than-human figure stood revealed in the ankle-deep mist. Its body was formed of crackling energy. A long cloak and a suit of ribbed, holly-like armour filtered its fell glow. It turned its head to look back over its shoulder and Maleneth felt that her heart would stop. A black helmet masked its face with coiling shadows. In one fizzing blue hand it led a small boy. Were one to mentally unbox the ears and reset the nose then the resemblance to Junas would have been striking. For all that he was standing upright, the boy seemed to be sound asleep.

'Thambrin,' said Junas, the most recent break to his nose making his voice come out as a frightened honk. 'Praith Thigmar.' He shook off Alanaer's supporting arm and tottered forwards, hand outstretched to his son. 'I'm here, Thambrin.'

The shade drew the boy in close.

'Begone, spirit.' Gotrek hefted his axe. Its forgefires chased the shadows from his face, filling its creases with new ones. 'Release the child and walk amongst the living no longer.'

The shade turned to regard them fully, pushing the boy behind its back. It flickered rather than moved, its outline stuttering in and out of focus with a horrible vibration as though it were only weakly tethered to the living realm.

'What are you waiting for?' Junas snarled. 'Thoot it.'

Maleneth was not sure if Halik did as Junas demanded or if terror had simply loosened her hold on her bowstring.

A foot away from the ragged armour of its chest her arrow disintegrated. Aged a thousand years in the blink of an eye, the shaft fell to dust like a stick fed into a Kharadron steam-shredder. A brittle wedge of rusted and barely recognisable steel dinked on the spirit's breastplate and dropped to the floor. The apparition crunched it under one icy boot. It looked up. Maleneth gasped in horror as its helmet melted back. A skull face glared out from a hood of shadow, eyes blazing with malefic lightning. The breath that Maleneth had taken caught. It refused to come out. She felt it freeze in her lungs where it hid, icicles creeping outwards into her heart. Her mouth stretched into a silent scream, her black hair turning slowly white.

Then the ghost screamed.

It hit Maleneth like a lightning bolt. Something inside her braced, clinging on to meat and bone like a drowning woman to a wrecked ship in a storm. From the corner of her eye she saw Halik as her soul was blasted from her body. Pale and ephemeral, its hands grasped for the ranger's body, but passed through, unable to prevent the corpse from toppling. With a plaintive wail the disembodied soul dissolved into the aether. Maleneth grit her teeth. Junas had folded to the ground, his hands over his ears. Alanaer was screaming. Over and over. As if to block out the banshee cry with the terrified sound of his own voice.

'It is the ghost of Hanberra!' the warrior-priest wailed, holding his hammer before him as if its crossed shadow would ward the visitation from his sight. 'By the light of my Queen, it is true. The hero who broke free from Sigmar's lightning to go back for his family!'

Even without the benefit of a dark legend, Maleneth would have known that this was no ordinary shade. The empty halls. The skaven's terror. Its bearing and raiment – all made it clear that this had been the spirit of a great hero in life. But death had eroded him until only the deepest core of the warrior's former personality remained.

A solitary purpose.

'I said unhand him,' said Gotrek.

Unlike the others, the Slayer simply looked weary, as though having been burned once by the purple sun of Uthan Barrowalker, the winds of Shyish could no longer touch him. Maleneth looked for the warning flicker of runefire, but in vain. The master rune was cool in the Slayer's chest. It was, perhaps, a sign of the tremendous power it contained that once unleashed it took time to recharge. Not that that came as any great solace to Maleneth at that moment.

'Give me my thon,' snarled Junas. 'He'th mine, not yours.'

'He's mine. Not yours.'

The words echoed back at them as if from a deep well.

Maleneth shuddered.

The ghost of Hanberra did not move. One moment it was upright. Then it was turned away, hunched over the sleepwalking boy. And then it was facing its mortal pursuers again, the boy held in its arms, drifting away from them as though drawn on the freezing in-breath of the deep earth itself.

'Thambrin!'

Junas lurched into a charge.

Gotrek caught his scuffed and damaged wrist with one hand. Despite barely coming up to the big man's chest, the duardin stopped him without effort.

'Don't be an idiot, manling,' he said in a voice like stone. 'You've failed the boy once today already. Don't fail him again by dying now.' The Slayer pulled back on Junas' arm, dragging him easily to the floor at his feet. He looked down the passageway towards the towering wraith. 'Your boy is dead, spirit, as are you. Unhand this one and face a dwarf nearer your own age. My axe will grant you the release you seek.'

The spirit issued a sepulchral moan.

'Release.'

Its cloak flapped about it like the wings of a bat and a warhammer of truly monstrous proportion appeared in one gauntleted fist. With the other hand, it cosseted the still-sleeping infant to its chest.

Then with a hiss it swung.

Gotrek ducked his head at the last moment.

The hammer punched a hole through the roof of his crest and pulverised a block from the wall. Masonry dust rained through the embittered shade. It painted the Slayer grey. Gotrek shook it off his head, shortened his grip on his axe, and punched it straight up into the spirit's body. The red runes on its fyresteel blades glowed like coals plucked from a fire. The shade flickered and the fyrestorm greataxe cleaved through scraps of aether. The wraith rematerialised a dozen feet away. Swifter than Maleneth could follow it moved again, its hammer no longer *there*, embedded in stone beside the Slayer's face, but *here*, poised above its own crackling skull at the apex of a downswing.

Gotrek threw himself to one side as the hammer stove in the flagstone he had been standing on. He landed on his back with a crunch of armour and a gravelly curse. The duardin was insanely tough, but nimble he was not.

Alanaer began to chant.

The ice that caked the stonework around Hanberra's feet cracked and hissed. Vines groped from the thaw to tug on the harder edges of the spectre's armour. A tendril wound its way up his leg to reach for the sleeping child.

The shade pulled Tambrin in close and hissed. *'He's mine. Not yours.'* It drew in a breath of amethyst-flecked magic, turned towards the warrior-priest, and screamed.

Alanaer was lifted from his feet and thrown back down the passageway. He landed on his back and rolled. Unconscious or dead, Maleneth did not know. Either way he did not get up again.

Taking full advantage of the distraction, Gotrek hacked at the shade's ankle from prone. The fyresteel blade passed through the spirit's leg, leaving a flickering line of blue energy and golden fire where it had crossed. The shade stuttered in and out of form, screeching in outrage. Maleneth covered her sensitive ears as the ghost of Hanberra kicked Gotrek in the ribs. There was a blast of sound and pressure as if from a thunderbolt and the Slayer was hurled across the passageway, plunging into the mist like a brick into water before crunching into the stonework behind it.

Shaking masonry from his crest, Gotrek pulled himself back up.

This is it, Maleneth thought. The Slayer's doom.

Finally he could die. She could recover the rune from his remains and, if she was quick about it, return to Azyr late in some kind of triumph.

Hanberra drifted back. Its hammer blinked to a defensive position as Gotrek shrugged off the last of the wall and barrelled towards it with a roar. Maleneth frowned. She could see that Hanberra was not fighting to its utmost. The ghost actually seemed more intent on shielding the child in its arms than it was on actually defeating Gotrek.

And that, Maleneth thought, is just not going to be good enough.

She rifled through what was left in her various pouches and pockets. Her long mission had kept her away from the blood markets of Azyrheim, and her fruitless efforts to concoct a poison that would actually kill Gotrek Gurnisson had depleted her supplies still further. But she still had a few herbs. Poisons that she had not yet thought to try. Her fingers closed around the hard nut of a wightclove and she withdrew it from her pocket. It was tough, ridged and white as bone. She kissed it for Khaine's blessing and then crushed it to a powder against the back of her hand.

Leaping into the midst of the contest with a yell, Maleneth struck the powder from the back of her hand and across Hanberra's arm. The arm that held the boy.

The spirit shrieked as its arm and shoulder wavered.

A concentrated and properly delivered dose of freshly harvested wightclove would banish a spirit and, though Maleneth would not like to test it, cause severe discomfort to a Mortarch. With a single dried clove the best she could hope for was a temporary loss of corporeality, but that was all she wanted. The shade tried desperately to keep a hold of the child, but its efforts were as fruitless as those of Halik's spirit had been on her own body. Its arm had taken on the consistency of mist. The child fell through it. Maleneth dived as the spirit cried out in anguish, intercepting the boy before he could hit the ground, and then rolled, curling to protect his body with her own.

She broke from her roll just before she hit the wall, braking with an out-turned foot. The boy lay beneath her, pudgy arms and legs spread out. Unbelievably, he was still asleep.

Behind her, the spirit raged.

Aether rose off the ragged figure like smoke. It clenched its fist, finding it once again solid, and took its massive warhammer in a two-handed grip. It stuttered back and forth around its streaming outline, screaming in rage.

'Thambrin!' Junas cried, but made no move to intervene.

Maleneth bared perfect teeth in a grin.

This is more like it, she thought. A little more of this and you might rid me of this burdensome Slayer yet.

Exhausted beyond even his own awesome strength, but defiant to the last, Gotrek looked up to meet his doom. His one eye met Hanberra's and for some reason that was not immediately apparent to Maleneth, the shade hesitated. An unlikely understanding seemed to pass between ancient duardin and lost soul. A pain they had both shared. A pain that had broken one and made the other.

'He's mine. Not yours.'

'No,' said Gotrek. 'This one is still of the living. Begone, spirit. Seek your boy in the Lands of the Dead.'

'*Dead...*'

Hanberra's hand flickered to its eye sockets. The shade's corposant skull stared at them as if seeing them as they were for the first time in a thousand years. Its warhammer burst into a cloud of rising ash above its head. Its armour began to peel away, lightning seething about the trapped human shape underneath.

'*Dead...*'

'Aye,' said Gotrek. 'Aye, he's gone and it was your fault. And no. It doesn't get any better. So begone, spirit. Begone and be at peace.'

'*Hangharth was his name,*' the spirit said, as though remembering a precious revelation it had thought long forgotten. '*Sigmar forgive me.*' Its dissolution accelerated. There was a muffled *crump*, as if of lightning striking somewhere far below ground, and the ghost of Hanberra vanished in a puff of smoke, its last words a breath on a dead wind. '*I should never have left.*'

Maleneth stared at the thinning cloud in horror.

From somewhere behind her, she could hear Alanaer coughing as the warrior-priest stirred.

'That was brave, aelfling,' said Gotrek. The duardin picked himself up and walked stiffly towards her. She offered no protest as he bent to take the child from her. Tambrin was a stocky boy, and was clearly going to grow into a large man, but tucked into the crook of the Slayer's huge arm he looked gangly and long-limbed. His lips smacked together as he started to stir. Gotrek shushed him with a few gravelly consonants of what might, to ears attuned to the sounds of picks on stone and hammers on anvils, have been a lullaby. A grin, unsettling in its strange lack of hostility, spread across his scarred face. 'Maybe there's hope for you yet, eh?'

'Gotrek...' said Maleneth.

The duardin's expression hardened. 'Come on, aelfling. Let's go on back.'

'Do you mean, do you *honestly* mean, that the ill-tempered old Slayer I knew genuinely came down here to save a human child?'

Gotrek glanced fleetingly at the child in his arms. 'Of course not.' Grumbling under his breath, he deposited the boy into Junas' crushing embrace. 'But you said I left a beer untended up there.'

YOUR
NEXT READ

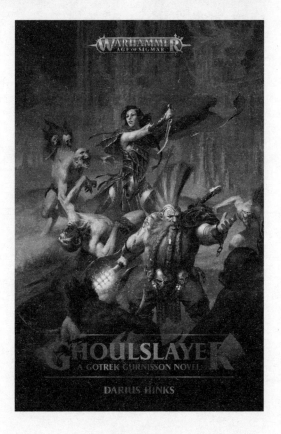

GHOULSLAYER
by Darius Hinks

Gotrek Gurnisson returns! His oaths now ashes, and branded with the rune of the god who betrayed him, the Slayer seeks the ultimate foe – the Undying King himself…

GODS' GIFT

David Guymer

Introducing

HAMILCAR

LORD-CASTELLANT, ASTRAL TEMPLARS

I held out my hand, palm down, fingers spread, hovering over the animal print caked into the dried mud of the mountain side. The heel of my palm was about level with the matching point of the imprint. The tips of my gauntleted fingers came nowhere even close to the clipped indents left by the passing beast's claws. I frowned.

'Are you familiar with the monster, Lord-Castellant?'

The old woodcutter, Fage, crouched across from me on the other side of the print, a long, *long* way away. His eyes possessed the faint shimmer of the Azyr-born, but his insect-bitten skin and sour odour were those of a naturalised Ghurite. He wore a wax coat fastened up tight with wooden toggles and string, and a pair of trousers of similar material but mismatched colour. A hat fashioned from the skin of a furred creature was pulled down over his greying head, flaps covering his ears. White fog curled about his lips, for though we were half a day's march from the Seven Words and the great peak of the Gorkoman, the air still had teeth.

He looked at me, waiting to be told that 'By Sigmar, yes, I know well this beast,' and that it was nothing I had not slain a thousand of before.

I had no wish to lie, particularly, but a reputation for semi-divine infallibility was the foundation of all that I had raised here.

'I cannot be certain,' I said, after a reasonable pause.

Broudiccan snorted. The hugely armoured Decimator loomed silently amongst the wiry leechwood pines a few dozen paces up-slope.

He knows me too well.

The trees of the High Gorwood were short, ten or eleven feet tall, clad in reddish bark with long, waspish branches swaying only partially in tune with the wind. A little deeper in, the shadows of several similarly outfitted Astral Templars of the Bear-Eaters jigged and wavered in the light of a fire. The clatter of a rough camp being set rang about the carnivorous trees. The warriors were in high spirits. One of the vanguard-hunters was already beating a slow rhythm into an improvised drum. Another, the raptor – Illyrius, judging by the quality of his singing voice – was opening the Saga of the Barrel Kings. The saga was a favourite of the Bear-Eaters due to their small (though not the way Illyrius sang it) role in the death of the god-beast Mammothas in its final verse.

In the Age of Myth, Sigmar had tasked his brother-god, Gorka-morka, with the purge of monsters from the mortal realms. With the dawning of the Age of Sigmar, that task had been bestowed upon the Astral Templars.

To the Bear-Eaters, a beast-hunt through the Gorwood felt almost like a reward.

'We will know more when the light returns,' I told the woodsman, ignoring my lieutenant's weighted silence.

Fage peered out into the thickening darkness. Dusk fell suddenly over the Gorkoman, and the colour was fast draining from the landscape. The clicks and chirps of creatures were fading in the transition from day to night. The burden of life in the Realm of Beasts was more or less equivalent, regardless of your side of the dawn. The woodsman fiddled anxiously with the hatchet that dangled from his undercoat on a leather thong.

'There is nothing to fear in the Gorwood,' I said, baring my teeth. 'Hamilcar Bear-Eater is with you now.'

The woodcutter pulled himself together and nodded, reassured. As well he should be.

For I am a savage vision, awe-inspiring if I might say, at least to human eyes. My hair is dark and wild. My skin is marked with etchings of my own application. Others have oft-times questioned why I would deface Sigmar's great work with my own. I have no answer for them except that I wished to do so and did. My armour is the colour of amethyst, the very spirit and hue of death, strung with dead animals and scrawled with tribal glyphs whose shape I recall but whose meaning I can no longer comprehend.

I am, if we are to speak in understatements, no Vandus Hammerhand.

Leaving his axe where it hung, Fage planted his hands to his thighs and stood with an audible creak. I chose to remain crouching, lest the mortal startle.

'This beast took twenty of my people,' he said, shaking his head sadly. 'The rest of the camp fled.' He looked at the print as if vowing to commit it to memory. 'I'm the only one that made it to the Seven Words.'

'It is a long journey,' I said, rising slowly with a rattle of heavy sigmarite and hanging mail. I stand over him like a mountain. 'You may find that others have made it upon our return.'

It was also a terrain crawling with beastmen, skaven and worse, but this, I judged, the woodcutter did not wish to hear.

A sudden rustle in the litterfall had the man reaching for his axe, but it was only Crow. My faithful gryph-hound had been scouting further downslope and burst from the trees, chewing my gauntlet in greeting, then dropping his ice-blue beak to sniff at the print in the mud. I did not know what, if anything, he expected to find, for the print was days old at least. Frankly, we were fortunate to have even that much to go on, for the ground of the Gorkoman is hard, its topsoil thin and its climate sufficiently disagreeable to turn an exposed patch of earth to slurry in short order.

'Sigmar blesses us,' I said aloud, scratching the downy feathers behind Crow's eyes. The gryph-hound clacked its beak in annoyance, then surrendered to my touch, emitting a throbbing growl as he pushed his head into my gauntlet. His bright blue eyes glittered in the twilight, tilted sideways, but still studying the trees with more caution than I could profess.

Broudiccan crossed his arms.

'The camp is made,' he said. The Decimator Prime was a man of grim and silent stature. I have never seen a man so capable with a starsoul mace be so reticent to speak of his deeds. If a few of his acts had been misattributed to my heroism, then I would not be surprised. 'We should rest,' he went on, the nature of the quest clearly rendering him uncommonly loquacious. 'Continue tomorrow.'

Fage looked at me, startled. 'You sleep?'

I startled him just a little further with a roaring laugh. 'Only when my foes are uninspiring.'

I do not dream. Sometimes I think it another mortal impurity beaten out of me on the Anvil of Apotheosis, but I know others who speak of their dreams and it is true that I used to dream. It was not so very long ago that I would close my eyes in dread of reprising my dying moments under the claws of the Abyssal, Ashigorath, another night. Though I must remind myself that it has been a hundred years since the Realmgate Wars raged over Ghur. There were times when I feared myself mad, but perhaps that, too, was a symptom of my second Reforging, for the nightmares became less frequent as the decades passed. Now, I do not dream.

That was I how I knew this dream was not mine.

A giant tree stood above me, a deciduous giant that had no earthly place amongst the carniferns and leechwood pines of the High Gorwood. It was night, a vastly swollen moon framing the great oak's bower. The stars were unfamiliar ones, as if positioned as an afterthought by one who had never given them much consideration. I, on the other hand, am a creature of Azyr, and they were the first things I noticed out of place. The night chorus, too, was gone. Silence circled me and the great tree like an unseen threat, and though I felt no wind on my skin, the oak leant over me and rustled.

In a groan of bark and a murmur of leaves, it spoke.

'Help me.'

With an angry crunch, the tree reared up onto its roots, tearing great clumps of earth away from the ground as if it meant to rise away. I reached over my shoulder, but whoever's mind conjured this dream had not seen fit to furnish me with a weapon. My warding lantern was similarly absent.

'He stole my life.'

'Where are you?' I roared over the shaking branches.

'I am dying. You will be next.'

There was a ripping sound, a splitting of hard bark, sap splattered from the wound like human blood. I flung a hand in front of my eyes as the sap turned to searing amber and burned the dream from my sight.

I woke up waving my hands furiously, Ghur's bright sun a stabbing pressure on my eyes. I grunted, still only half awake, prising Crow's beak from my vambrace.

'I was having the most pleasant dream,' I said, stretching ruefully, hoping to brazen the episode out.

Unfortunately, there were those amongst my Vanguard Chamber who had been with me since Jercho and the Sea of Bones, and even those who had not would have heard the stories. They watched me arm myself as if I might pick up my halberd upside down or try to fit my warding lantern over my head.

Fage, naturally, was oblivious. The masks the Stormcast wore to battle made it almost impossible for one who knew them less well than I to judge their mood. The woodcutter had apparently woken early and hovered about the outskirts of the camp, coat fastened, axe in hand, and clearly eager to find what was left of his group.

I forced the man to eat something while I splashed the soil with watered wine, a libation to Sigmar and the local deities of the hunt, and set the anxious woodsman loose.

Fage hared off into the trees, the pair of vanguard-hunters I had ordered to keep an eye on him striding purposefully after him.

Only Fage knew exactly where we were heading. The Seven Words was still a ruin of her former (and I am being generous here) glory. No one, least of all me, had paid overly close attention to where the woodcutters and quarrymen that poured through the Azyr Gate disappeared to upon their arrival. I knew there was every chance that Fage could find the monster that had taken his fellows without my warriors' help, but with any luck the sharp-eyed vanguard-hunters would spot the beast before it spotted him.

The remaining hunters fanned out into the trees, raptors with longstrike and hurricane crossbows advancing more carefully behind them.

The Astral Templars were no less keen than their mortal guide to be about the hunt.

I walked over to Broudiccan. The Decimator nodded to me as he pulled on his battered helmet and tested the draw of his heavy-headed mace from its shoulder sleeve. It was all the welcome I was going to get, but my dream was weighing on my thoughts and I needed to discuss it with someone.

'What do you know of the Gorwood?' I asked him, measuring my stride to his. He shrugged. 'I know that Uxor Untamed held the Seven Words for several years before I took it from him.'

'You *and* Lord-Castellant Akturus.'

I waved off the correction. 'Is that why we still call it the Gorwood, I wonder? Has it always been the haunt of beastmen and their kind?'

Another shrug.

Broudiccan's imagination was as stilted as his words, but to me the staggering variety of the eight mortal realms has always been a source of wonderment. The mark of the gods was not always as obvious as the Mountains of Maraz or Gouge Canyon, but wherever you chose to look, that was what you saw there. Every peak and defile, every endemic tree and native creature had been shaped, deliberately or otherwise, by the divinities that had once moved amongst them – and in many lands still did.

'Do I recall Barbarus speaking of a cult of tree worshippers?'

'A dead cult,' Broudiccan shrugged. 'I saw some of the ruins they left behind. They were gone long before the Untamed took their country.'

I pondered on the Decimator's words as we continued after Fage and the Vanguards.

Ghur was a wild place, ever changing, and little of it had been effectively explored. This was true even of such bastions as Excelsis and Shu'ghol, fortresses of enlightenment that Sigmar knew better than to send the likes of me, but compared to their toothless savagery the Gorkoman was an ancient and untamed wilderness.

Anything could be lurking on the slopes of the High Gorwood.

The leechwood pines thickened as I pushed downhill, sharp-edged branches striking against my armour, the occasional twig drawing blood from my face. The Vanguard had dropped out of view, even Crow loping off after them, agitated by something or other. He left Broudiccan and me alone.

'I dreamt last night,' I said.

'I know.' Clearly, the Decimator had no wish to discuss it further.

'It was a prophetic dream.'

Broudiccan's grim mask turned towards me.

'You do not believe me?'

'Prophecy is not your gift.'

The Decimator's understatement threatened to bring a laugh out of me, but I suppressed it. 'If you doubt me because of the incident with the seraphon...'

Broudiccan sighed. 'The stars were all in their proper place when I looked at them.'

'They had shifted once again by the time you had dragged yourself to my throne room,' I barked. 'The slann was signalling me for help. Just as the oak is now.'

'The... oak?'

I gave him a feral grin. 'Tell me it would not be the strangest thing you have seen in the mortal realms.'

Broudiccan did not answer that. 'But why do these portents speak only to you?'

I frowned.

I could see that the Decimator would take some persuading. My reputation amongst the Freeguild regiments of the Ghur-lands was a legend of valour, courage and shining charisma. My reputation amongst my immortal brethren was for recklessness, grandstanding and personal bravado. The Bear-Eaters wore my legend like a token of blessing on their armour, but that did not mean they would follow me into the Crystal Labyrinth on the strength of my say-so.

'Tell me where the oak guides you and we will go there. But if it does not guide you...' Broudiccan shrugged again. I was getting a little sick of seeing it. 'We still have a monster to hunt.'

I threw him a reluctant nod of agreement, just as Crow's shriek and the wail of something bestial rang through the trees. My first thought was that the gryph-hound had found something more appetising than jerked lizard for our repast, then an arrow thud-ded into the tree beside me.

'Beastmen!' I yelled at the top of my formidable voice as gangly ungors clad in crimson bark and animal skins poured out from the trees. Arrows hissed towards me. Most were caught up in the hanging nets of predatory branches, but a dozen or so clattered off mine and Broudiccan's armour.

The Decimator wordlessly freed his starsoul mace and ran to meet the beastman charge. I spun my halberd overhead, lopping off an ungor's head as it ran towards me, then caught the haft two-handed to bring it down as though I were an axeman splitting wood. The blade struck the ungor's arm from its body. The animal bleated in shock and panic as leechwood pines leaned in on all sides to haul the struggling creature into their branches.

I tried to ignore the horrific slurping noises from the trees as the beastman's death throes subsided, thinking again of those cuts to my face that I had foolishly dismissed as insignificant grazes.

A star blast from Broudiccan's mace proved a welcome distraction, pulverising a beastman. The shockwave threw two more off their hooves and into the clutches of the thrashing leechwoods.

Just as I made to join the Decimator, Crow bounded into the carnage.

The gryph-hound scrabbled to a halt on the rough ground, silver beak and claws all bloody, only to stare at me judgementally before turning and running back the way he had come. Huffing air out through my pursed lips, I left Broudiccan and chased after the gryph-hound. The Decimator Prime could take care of himself.

Branches lashed at my face as I pounded after Crow. The trees were aroused now, responding to the taste of spilled blood in the air and the vibrations of the hunt. The wood around me shivered in expectation.

A larger beastman gor galloped into my path. A longstrike bolt fizzled in its gut. I ran it down without slowing, and the goat-headed monstrosity thumped off my breastplate. Something purple winked from behind a tree. I stumbled to a halt, arms out like a break sail. Illyrius. The raptor pointed his hurricane crossbow at the creature and swore in a language dead even to me. A withering volley of charged bolts whittled down the pack of gors that had been massing behind me for a charge. When I had regained my composure, I saluted the raptor with my halberd and looked around for Crow.

I did not need to look too hard.

Simply following the sound of bones being cracked and organs torn open, I found the gryph-hound, up to his neck in a large gor's stomach.

A vanguard-hunter ran across me before I had a chance to move. Firing off thunderous blasts of his boltstorm pistol from the hip, he headed towards Fage.

The woodsman was fending off a pair of ungors with the speed and strength of uncompromising terror. The opportunistic runts had naturally been drawn to the human while the two vanguard-hunters I had left with him were engaged with five of their burlier cousins. Each of the giant bestigors boasted the size and brawn of a Stormcast Eternal, if not the blessed raiment and the skill. Broudiccan barrelled into the melee with his customary silent rage, and I left him to it, confident that the woodcutter would live to tell the tale.

Hooves pounded on the hard ground behind me. Closing fast.

Timing it to perfection, I looped my halberd up and back and saw the blade sink into the muscular but unprotected torso of a stampeding centigor. The beast's speed and my own strength came together to devastating effect, my halberd passing clean through the centigor's chest and bringing its equine lower quarters crashing to the ground at my feet in a spray of mulch and grit. I confess to being unsure as to the ultimate fate of its upper body.

Twirling my halberd through a sequence of lazy circles, I scanned the area for more enemies, only to find them all fully engaged in dying or fleeing. The fizz and snap of hurricane and longstrike bolts pursued the latter, a bestial squawk or two and a shaking of ravenous trees attesting to the raptors' lack of mercy and their aim.

If not their actual woodcraft in spotting the ambush in the first place.

I found Broudiccan in the aftermath doing as all good second-in-command's should in such situations, remonstrating bitterly with the two hunters I had left with Fage. The mortal looked rattled, but none the worse for a scratch or two that would give him a story to tell when he returned to the Seven Words.

I dismissed the three warriors and crouched by the shaken woodsman. His eyes rolled towards me, and for a second I was afraid he might bolt.

The last thing I wanted was to have to send Crow to bring him back.

'I presume you have not been troubled by beastmen before now?' I said, as kindly as I could muster.

He shook his head. 'The best lumber comes from further down the mountain, nearer the Nevermarsh. Our palisade was high enough to keep the... the beasts at bay. And we paid natives to ensure the woods were clear before we set out to cutting.'

'Natives?' I asked. I could not say why that struck a chord with me, except perhaps that Fage had never bothered to mention them before now.

He swallowed and nodded. 'Good people. Primitive. But good people. Whatever they could take off the beastmen was the only payment they would accept. All they asked was for us not to damage their sacred trees.'

'And did you?'

The man blanched. 'Cut a sacred tree? In the Gorwood?'

A twitch of movement caught my eye, and I reached instinctively for my warding lantern, but it was only a bestigor, suspended between the branches of a pair of trees and jerking as the blood was sucked out of it. It seemed to make the woodsman's point neatly, and he did not elaborate further.

'Could the monster that murdered your comrades have been some slave beast of the brayherds?' I asked.

'A jabberslythe?' suggested Broudiccan.

'A razorgor?' offered Illyrius.

Fage shook his head, angry. 'I don't know. How would I know?'

'It is all right,' I said. 'I do not think it is either of those things.'

I had seen both before and far worse in the armies of Chaos, and none could account for the track we had found the night before. An idea formed in my mind and I pursed my lips, ready to give credence to the possibility that I just might be infallible after all.

'Show me where the better trees are.'

The sun sank behind the mountain. Ghur's sun is a wild and untamed thing, prone to rise and set wherever, and whenever, it will. Its abandon I can respect, though it does make timekeeping a challenge. I estimated that it had been eight or nine hours (by the Azyrite measure) since the ambush in the Gorwood when Fage pointed me towards a swathe of large and imposing trees.

For all their rude stature, there was something funereal about the scene. The woodcutters' hard work had coppiced into the boundaries to leave a verge of jagged stumps between those bigger, rounder trees and the bloodthirsty homunculi of the Gorwood. They looked like grave markers – the sort that you can find in the Freeguilder cemeteries of Azyrheim, if the Knights of Usirian will let you pass, which is seldom a given.

It all reminded me of my dream.

I perused the treeline, the idea I had been playing with since my last conversation with the woodsman taking on a kind of shape. I pointed to a tree at random. Being no expert, one looked about as good as another to me.

'Cut it down,' I said.

Fage looked at me as if such wild nonsense had never been heard within shouting distance of a lumber camp.

'What?'

'Humour me.'

The woodsman glanced at the other Stormcast for support, but to a warrior they were masked and grim and he found no contradictory argument there. 'All right.' He made his way, half-skipping over the stump-riddled slope towards the tree I had indicated.

Fage unhitched his axe, eyed up the trunk, measuring the blow, then hacked into the wood. Bark flew off as he teased the axe-blade out of the trunk. I wondered if the groan that passed through the verdant copse was genuinely one of discontent or purely in my imagination.

Finally, the axe came out. The gash it had inflicted on the wood was pitifully shallow.

Felling a tree was clearly harder than it looked.

'Is that all?' I said

Fage lowered his axe, his pride stung. 'It'd take a score of men, paired up and working in shifts, to bring something like this down.'

I crack my knuckles. 'Step aside.' I walked towards the wounded tree, letting the haft of my halberd slip through my grip until I held it near the butt. The long curve of its axe-like blade glinted in the last of the sun.

This time I definitely heard something.

A groan, as if ancient timbers were being drawn into a stressed and unpalatable new position. The foliage rustled briefly, then moved, a wave of restless leaves heading slowly in our direction. Fage hurried back to the line of Vanguards who calmly raised their weapons to the trees.

The front rank of trees gave way, and I took an involuntary step back.

I saw then why I had such difficulty identifying the spoor we had discovered in the High Gorwood, why there had been only a single print, and how it had been made in such unlikely ground.

The creature towered over us all. It was huge, lignified, armoured in thick plates of reddish bark and encrusted with orange lichens. Buzzing clouds of insects emerged from bore holes in its bark and swarmed around its aggressively branched crown. Its eyes were myopic pools of amber, buried within toughened whorls. They seemed to have difficulty focusing on something as small and active as me, and the monster peered down with short-sighted loathing.

I have never been to Ghyran.

I am familiar enough with the warlike forest spirits that inhabit the Jade Kingdoms to bluff it, if challenged, for they exist too in the wilder places of Azyr. They are different, of course, as the Everqueen and the God-King are different; reclusive, patient, less prone to spring rages and content, by and large, to sleep through the cycles of the Heavens.

This was a Ghurite Treelord.

It was a beast.

I lowered my halberd, lifting my open hand to show I meant it no harm.

'You came to me in my dream. Tell me, how may Hamilcar Bear-Eater hel–'

The treelord snatched me up without breaking stride, blasting the wind from my lungs and tossing my halberd to the ground. Broudiccan shouted something that I could not hear for the wind whistling in my ears, presumably *'loose!'* for soon thereafter the air burned to the rapid fire of hurricane crossbows. The smell of wood smoke reached me, but the treelord took another lurching step and smacked a vanguard-hunter into the bole of a tree with a swipe of its hand. The Stormcast dissolved into a bolt of lightning that hammered the dead warrior back to the Heavens. The tree smouldered in its wake and the beast gave a rumble of steady outrage, its grip on me tightening until sigmarite creaked and ribs bowed.

My vision burst into colours, stars blistering the foreground of what was otherwise a blur of bloody bark and hissing swarms. The treelord's hand had swallowed my lower body up to the waist. Its grip pushed my warding lantern up against my breastplate, but its gnarly index finger was clamped over the shutter and I could not open it.

Bracing my hands against the treelord's finger, I tried to force it far enough down to free the lantern.

I am a beast of a man, a giant even amongst my fellow Stormcast. I am the Champion of Cartha, the Eater of Bears. I slew the Ironjaw war chief, the Great Red, in an unarmed combat that lasted a day and a night. My strength is a thing of fireside tales and legend, yet I could not for the life of me move that finger.

I was not even wholly convinced that it noticed the attempt at all.

Lightning-flecked quarrels and boltstorm fire thundered and cracked. Somewhere in that awkward streak of greenish ground and amber sky, I saw Crow tearing bark from the treelord's shins, trying to climb. The treelord ignored him utterly. Another streak of lightning bolted skywards.

I am not afraid to die.

I have done it before and I will doubtless have to do so again, but if my warriors were to be spared the torment of the soul forges that day, I was going to have to fell the treelord myself.

The constant spinning motion of the treelord waving me about in its fist was starting to have an unpleasant effect even on my constitution. I gritted my teeth against the rising bile, then spat with inch-perfect precision in the monster's lidless eye.

I felt the anger run through the treelord's gnarled bulk as it turned its age-dulled eyes from my warriors to me.

I would have gasped in pain, but the monster's grip was crushing my diaphragm and all I could do was mouth silent profanities as it drew me in. I could feel my bones being ground, my feet, legs and stomach being compacted like a nut in a vice. Something metal clattered hollowly on hard wood. I almost cried in elation as I looked down to see that the treelord's tightening grip had forced my warding lantern wholly out of its clutches.

Frankly, I had no idea if the restorative power of Sigmar would harm or hinder the Ghurite, but it was all I had. My fingers felt as if they were clad in sponge rather than sigmarite. My arms had become bendy and gained a joint, but somehow I got my hands over the lantern's mechanism and drew the shutter.

The light of Sigendil and every bright star over Azyrheim emptied from my lantern and into the treelord's half-blind eye.

It gave a slow but emphatic roar of pain.

I had hoped that it would drop me, but, of course, it had to hurl me with every chip and whorl of its awesome strength as if I had just burst into flames.

I crashed through a tangle of leechwood pines, their branches willowing over my heavy armour and savaging my face. By some sweet irony, the treelord had thrown me too hard for the branches to get a purchase on me, only slowing me down as I battered my way through and thumped heavily to the ground.

Groaning, astonished that my legs could still stand my weight, I stumbled up and around, and swayed to face the treelord.

Its legs had been stripped of bark. One was on fire. Its body sprouted quarrels like virile new growths and the eye I had burned was leaking a milky white sap. It gave a tortured groan and collapsed.

It dropped straight down, falling onto what I will call its knees, though they did not bend so much as bow, then split like hollow bones. Its shoulders sagged, and then it was still, the creak of settling wood overlain with the grating disquiet of the insects that had called it home. My relief was such that the sight of Fage swatting at a furious swarm of fat-bellied wasps with the flat of his hatchet almost made me chuckle.

The sudden shudder of tearing bark knocked my good humour flat, throwing me straight back into the final moments of my dream the previous night.

Acting on a premonition, I flung up a hand as the treelord's great trunk tore up the middle and a searing beam of amber flashed across us.

It faded quickly, leaving only a tingling warmth upon my skin, and I lowered my hand to see the bark that had clad the belly of the treelord had given way to reveal a cocoon of some kind within the dripping sap. Held in a foetal curl within its protective juices was a sylvaneth unlike any I had seen before. Her bark was brittle, and where new growth showed, it was yellow and unhealthy. The entire inside of the tree smelled rotten.

The tree spirit looked up at me like a blind crone on her death bed.

I went to her.

'It was you,' I said, gruff, but gentle. 'It was you that sought to reach me in my dream.' The sylvaneth turned to the sound of my voice without any suggestion of recognition or, indeed, sanity. 'Why did you attack us? Or the woodsman's people?'

'I am dying,' she rasped, her voice like wind through reeds.

I understood. The Jade lines ran strong here, strong enough to support these great trees. 'You fled here to heal.'

'Ghur'thu heard my call,' she said, presumably referring to the treelord I had unfortunately just slain. It must have killed Fage's woodsmen and driven off the native tree worshippers too, which must have come as a nasty shock to their beliefs.

'It does not look as though you are healing,' I said.

'He stole my life.'

I shot a questioning glance at Fage, who shrugged. 'Not yet, he hasn't.'

'He stole my *life*.'

Her use of the word "stole" struck me as awkward, and I was almost certain that I was misinterpreting her meaning somehow. There was no time to interrogate her further than that, however. She was dying.

'You will be next,' she hissed.

That gave me pause. A vision of myself held in a cage of warp lightning and screaming filled my thoughts, and I cursed the Lord-Veritant of the Knights Merciless who put it there.

'What... makes you say that?'

'Because he told me.'

'He?'

She opened the mottled bark of her mouth to answer as a feeble shudder passed through her body. She relaxed into the soft wall of her cocoon with a sigh, and said no more.

For a time, no one sullied the grove with words.

I lowered my eyes and placed my hand upon her body. I felt a light tingling through the metal of my gauntlets. I did not know what had been done to her.

But I would find out.

THE DANCE
OF THE SKULLS

David Annandale

Introducing

NEFERATA

THE MORTARCH OF BLOOD, VAMPIRE

The Mortarch of Blood's party arrived at the royal palace in Mortannis with the coming of full night. Neferata, her handmaidens and her ladies of court swept up the grand staircase leading to the palace doors. On either side, standing to attention, were the elite guards of two cities: Mortannis to the right, Nachtwache to the left. Walking one step behind Neferata, Lady Mereneth said, 'I do not trust the nature of this honour.'

'Nor do they expect us to,' Neferata told her favoured spy. 'This will not be the trap. They know the consequences will be too great. What will come will be more subtle, one our enemies can deny.'

Neferata had come to Mortannis to attend a ball arranged explicitly for her visit. The event was formally presented as an act of fealty and peace. She knew, therefore, exactly what it was. She was entering a battlefield.

She would not have it any other way.

Mortannis lay close enough to Nulahmia for it to be a point of concern. Queen Ahalaset had never challenged Neferata directly, and the tensions between the two cities had long been unspoken, subterranean. Close to the borders of Mortannis' region of influence lay Nachtwache. It was ruled by Lord Nagen and Neferata had kept a close watch on the relations between Mortannis and Nachtwache. As long as there had been friction between the two, friction that she had encouraged, the two powers had kept each other contained. She had even tolerated temporary alliances in the face of the threat from the legions of Chaos. But the armies sworn to the Everchosen were, for the time being, pushed back from this region of Shyish, and it appeared that the cities' rulers had formed a much more substantial alliance. That would never do.

So she had accepted the joint invitation from Ahalaset and Nagen immediately, after putting on the expected charade of diplomatic negotiations. There was work to be done here, and she knew she was putting her neck into the jaws of a trap. Though she arrived at the palace with only her immediate retinue, she was confident in her assurance to Mereneth. Ahalaset and Nagen would not strike here, with their own guard. Neferata's army waited outside the gates of Mortannis – legions of vampires, skeletons and wraiths cantoned in the lower reaches of the mountains that surrounded the city. Any move by the forces of Mortannis or Nachtwache would see Mortannis burned to the ground.

These were the realities of the game about to be played. They were known by all. The war would take place at another level. There would be no siege, no scaling of the walls. After all, this was a celebration. The war would be invisible, until a point came when the combatants chose to drop the illusion.

Neferata's party passed through the high doors of the palace, down the entrance hall and into the grand ballroom. Torchlight shone off the gold leaf of marble caryatids that held up the vaulted ceiling of the ballroom. The ceiling mosaic was a wonder of bronze-covered bones. Hundreds of skeleton arms reached from the edges of the vault towards the centre, where a huge skull composed of other skulls opened its jaws in an ecstasy of death.

The honour guard of the two cities was also present in the

ballroom, but more discreetly, keeping to positions against the walls. In the fore, lining the path of the procession to the large dais at the back of the ballroom was the gathered nobility of Mortannis and Nachtwache. Vampires and mortals bowed as Neferata passed. She acknowledged their greetings with the faintest of nods. She met the eyes of the nobles, all of them, and watched the spasm of fear and admiration take them.

Queen Ahalaset and Lord Nagen stood together on the dais. Though Ahalaset was host, they were side by side, equals at the event. They bowed too, completing the show of respect that had greeted Neferata.

No one was armoured except the guards, and even their plate was ceremonial, adorned with jewels and golden skulls, more resplendent than practical. Neferata, like her opponents on the dais, had prepared for the kind of war about to be waged. She wore a regal black dress of silk so fine it flowed like water. The train of the dress was much lighter than its length would suggest, and it moved behind her over the marble floor like the touch of night. From her shoulders hung a crimson cape. Its leather, so soft it was a mere breath of wind against the fingers, was made from the tanned flesh of fallen enemies.

'We are honoured, Queen Neferata, that you accepted our invitation,' said Ahalaset as she rose again. Her cheekbones were high, her eyes proud. Her brilliant green robes shimmered with silver thread, which wove the designs of scores of coats of arms, as if meant to remind Neferata that Ahalaset too had long experience on the battlefield.

At the end of his bow, Nagen began to reach out for Neferata's hand to kiss. When she did not extend her arm to him, he turned his gesture into a flourish, though the effort was clumsy enough to be obvious, then straightened. He wore a damask coat and a waistcoat inlaid with diamonds. The buttons of the coat were obsidian and shaped into finger bones. Its delicate fringe was human hair. Nagen's features were narrow and refined, and he consistently let a single fang poke down from beneath his upper lip. 'It is our greatest wish,' Nagen said, 'that you understand our intentions to be peaceful. We want you to know that Nulahmia can trust Mortannis and Nachtwache.'

'Of course you do,' Neferata said, and smiled.

Her hosts hesitated for a moment, uncertain how to take her words. Then they returned her smile and descended from the dais. 'We hope you will enjoy the ball,' said Ahalaset. She and Nagen led Neferata's party to join the other nobles. 'There will be a Dance of the Skulls.'

'Then my pleasure is assured in advance,' Neferata said.

Ahalaset clapped her hands. Musicians emerged from side doors at the rear of the ballroom, carrying instruments and chairs. They mounted the dais. Within moments, the orchestra began playing, and the war began.

'Do they think we do not realise this is a trap?' Mereneth whispered to Neferata as they watched the first of the dances.

'Of course they know that we are not fooled,' said Neferata. 'They believe they can overcome our wariness, and that is what matters. They will act, have no fear. Our journey will not have been in vain.'

A few dances in, Neferata saw, from the corner of her eye, Lord Nagen turn towards her, about to invite her to the floor. As if she had not noticed, she took a single, graceful step away and began to speak to one of the ladies of Ahalaset's court. Mereneth remained where she was, and Nagen, already committed to the beginnings of a bow, had no choice but to make his invitation to the spy. Mereneth accepted.

Neferata left her conversation as quickly as she had begun it, but though her departure was abrupt, the other vampire was awed, not offended. With a parting glance, Neferata saw the woman shrink before her, overcome with the knowledge that she had not been destroyed.

Neferata walked slowly along the edge of the dance, watching Mereneth and Nagen. Other nobles parted before her, backing away even when they also sought to greet her. She exchanged brief words with the vampires and mortals she passed, but they did not deflect her attention from the ball.

Mereneth was a skilled, graceful dancer. Nagen had difficulty keeping up with her. Her movements were never such that he stumbled, though. She kept him away from the edge of humiliation, and though Neferata could tell that he was a well-practised dancer himself, and prided himself as such, Mereneth's control of their turns made him appear even better than he was. He had to focus on his steps, and he was grateful enough for the guidance of Mereneth's hands that he did not pay attention to what else they might be doing. Neferata kept level with them as they moved up and down the ballroom floor. Twice, at chosen moments, she caught Nagen's eye and gave him the hint of a smile. The first time, he seemed unsure that she had done so. The second time, his face lit up with certainty, and her unspoken, vague promise was enough. He devoted himself with even greater energy to his performance, as if to say, *Look how well we shall dance together.*

Neferata allowed her smile to grow a little broader, though she hid her amusement. *Are you already forgetting your purpose, Lord Nagen?* she thought. For the moment, it seemed he had.

When the dance ended, he and Mereneth joined her. Nagen rushed to speak before Neferata could escape him again. 'Queen Neferata,' he said, 'will you do me the honour of being my partner for the Dance of the Skulls?'

'It would be my great pleasure,' she said.

Nagen beamed. Neferata held him before her with her smile. He would, when the necessity pushed him hard enough, remember what he was supposed to be doing. He would remember that his purpose this night was not to secure a dance with the Queen of Nulahmia. But he was not remembering now. And while Neferata transfixed him, he was not looking at Mereneth, and he did not see her slip the ring she had stolen into Neferata's hand.

'And now,' Neferata said, releasing Nagen from her gaze, 'I have neglected my other host for too long.' She left Nagen happy and willing to be distracted by Mereneth once again. She doubted he would ever notice the missing ring. The theft was a preliminary step. She had no specific use for the ring as yet. Instead, her possession of it opened up a wider field of action. She would see what possibilities would arise.

Ahalaset was at the feasting table on the other side of the ballroom. She gestured for Neferata to join her. 'You must tell me what you think of this vintage,' she said when Neferata drew near. She filled two crystal goblets from a large decanter.

Neferata accepted hers and brought it to her nose. She sniffed a finely crafted blend of blood. 'Most inviting,' she said, but did not drink.

Ahalaset smiled. 'Please accept it,' she said, and drank first.

Neferata sipped. 'This is extraordinary,' she said, and it was. She tasted the innocence of the newborn, the enthusiasm of youth and the wisdom of age. They existed together on her palate, forming the entire arc of mortal life. She was impressed. 'You have some superb artisans at your disposal,' she said.

Ahalaset raised her goblet in a toast. 'I am pleased you think so,' she said. 'I selected this vintage purposely for your visit.'

'I am honoured.'

Ahalaset lowered her voice. 'I have, if you are interested, Queen Neferata, set aside a gift more potent yet.' Her eyes flickered quickly to the left and right.

Ensuring that I am alone, Neferata thought. She was. She had dispersed her retinue through the crowd, inviting Ahalaset to make her move. 'You interest me,' she said. 'Do go on.'

Ahalaset pointed to a small door in the corner of the ballroom, behind the dais. 'You will find in there my personal choice of slaves,' she said. 'They have been curated for the quality of their blood. They come from the same families whose lives you have just tasted.' She produced a small, golden key. 'Should you wish to savour their delicacies…?'

Neferata accepted the key. 'I should indeed,' she said. *Good*, she thought, *we are done with the prelude. Now we can begin.* With a knowing smile to Ahalaset, she made her way over to the door and let herself in.

She entered a richly appointed chamber. In the centre was a divan draped in crimson cushions and silks. The candles of human tallow on the chandelier were encased in red-tinted glass skulls, suffusing the room with a warm, intimate glow. The light was dim, though, and Neferata noted the many deep shadows in the corners. The shape of the room was an octagon, and chained to the walls were the offerings. They were men and women in the prime of life, anointed in oils and scents, gold bands pulling their heads back to present their throats. Neferata felt the beat of their pulses, their rich blood a thin slice away from jetting into her mouth. Incense wafted from censors on either side of the divan. The atmosphere of the chamber was heady, luxurious. It was, Neferata thought, a most beautiful trap. If the opportunity arose, she must congratulate Ahalaset. She doubted Nagen had contributed much beyond his mere presence.

Neferata turned around slowly, her witchsight piercing the shadows. She did not think the attack would be that obvious, and she was right. The chamber was empty except for the slaves. She walked past the mortals, examining them closely but not touching any of them yet. They stared back at her, their pupils dilated. Their fear was mixed with a confused pleasure. Neferata inhaled the scent of their emotions, detecting the taste of a powerful opiate. She did not think it was poisonous. It seemed, to her senses, that its purpose was simply part of the flavouring of the blood.

Neferata's lips drew back over her fangs. The bait truly was irresistible. *Well done, Ahalaset. Well done.*

She circled the chamber again. Between the prisoners hung tapestries depicting the most sensual of atrocities. Neferata moved them aside until, to the left of one of the male slaves, she saw the barely discernible outline of a door in the wall. She located the keyhole and experimentally inserted the key Ahalaset had given her. It turned easily, and she heard the lock slide into place. It was curious, she thought, and therefore significant, that the same key opened both doors to the room.

She locked the entrance door too. She stood in the centre of the room for a few moments, waiting. Whatever the nature of the attack, she would adapt, and she would counter it. That was her most terrible strength – to see each moment for what it was, to discard a plan instantly, and form a new one, to flow across war like water.

The attack did not come.

'Very well,' she murmured. 'If we must play out this charade to the end, let us do so and have done with this.' She walked over to the slave directly in front of her and sank her fangs into his neck.

The blood was everything Ahalaset had promised. If the vintage in the ballroom represented the peak of the art of blending, here she encountered a rarefied purity of blood. These slaves had clearly been raised since birth for this purpose alone. The taste of life was intoxicating, and Neferata would have willingly gorged herself from this single slave, then waited before indulging in the next. But this was war, and she would not cede the battlefield to Ahalaset. She swallowed twice, then stepped back from the prisoner. He looked at her with bovine fear. His lips moved, but they were too sluggish to form words.

'You are a product of superb breeding,' Neferata told the slave. 'All of you are,' she announced to the chamber. 'Be proud of your destinies.'

With the flick of a clawed finger, she sliced the man's throat wide open. The enticing blood poured down his body and pooled onto the floor. Neferata moved on to the next slave, drank briefly from her neck, then slashed her throat too. And so she went on, taking just enough for a taste and then killing the mortals. The chamber filled with the smell of wasted blood. Neferata shook her head, feeling the rare moment of regret. To throw away such fine stock was a crime.

Still the attack did not come.

Neferata's senses were vibrating with tension. This had to be where she was most in danger. This had to be the trap. But the moments passed, and the slaves died, and nothing happened. The more time passed, the more she felt the temptation to relax her guard, and the more wary she became.

She had slaughtered two thirds of the slaves now. She bent down to the neck of the next one. As her teeth sank into his throat, he brought his arms up in a flash. His chains snapped, brittle as porcelain. His right forearm and hand were a leather sheath, its illusion perfectly crafted, and they slid to the ground, revealing the blade built out of his elbow. It was silver, etched in runes, and flashed with emerald light. The air crackled with its power, and the assassin stabbed the sword at Neferata's throat.

A moment's unwariness and the blade would have decapitated her. But she had not been unwary. Neferata leapt to one side and ducked. The sword passed over her head, flashing with the heat of an arcane sun. She reached out and grabbed the assassin's arm just below the elbow. He struggled to free himself, but he was held with a grip that could crush stone. Neferata pushed the arm back, holding it against the wall. The assassin struck at her with his other arm, but he might as well have been hitting steel.

'Very good,' she whispered. 'Very good.' She took the assassin by the throat and forced his head back. He began to whine in frustration and terror. 'Shhhhh,' she said. 'You did very well. You came closer to succeeding than you think. Your queen should be grateful to you. Or is it your lord?' Neferata cocked her head, breathing in the man's fear. 'No,' she decided, 'you are one of Ahalaset's playthings.' Nagen's role in all of this was the political ally, and the extra force inside the palace. 'Your queen decided to control all of the details of my assassination. She was correct to do so, even though she failed.'

The assassin squirmed in her grip. She lifted him off the ground, holding him in mid-air, depriving him of leverage. He groaned.

'Hush now, hush now,' Neferata said. 'Your part in the dance is not yet done. There is a great turn to make.' She yanked the assassin to her and bit into his neck. There was no time to savour the taste of his blood. There was only the attack. She drank his life. She drained him of his will, and of Ahalaset's, and she filled him with hers.

When she was done, she released the assassin. He stood before her, docile, a thrall waiting for the orders that would define his new purpose. She looked him up and down. He was clad only in a loincloth, unsuitable for his new task. 'You have robes elsewhere,' she said.

He nodded.

She unlocked the doors from the chamber, then handed the assassin the key he would have used had he been successful. 'Go and don your robes,' she said. Then she gave him Nagen's ring and issued her commands. He bowed and left the chamber through the hidden door. Neferata circled the room once more. She killed the remaining slaves quickly. Then, with sharp, rapid jerks, she tore the corpses apart and tossed the dismembered remains into a heap before the divan. In that hill of meat, discerning if there was a body that was missing would take time.

Neferata lifted the train of her dress. It was soaked in blood. She ran a hand over the silk, murmuring a soft incantation, and the blood pattered to the floor. Then she returned to the ballroom.

Nagen and Ahalaset were standing together at the feasting table when Neferata emerged from the chamber. Ahalaset hid her alarm well. Nagen looked rattled. Neferata smiled to them both, and ran a finger along her upper lip. 'Your gift was beyond expectations,' she said to Ahalaset. 'I can only hope that I will be able to offer you something half as delightful when next you come to Nulahmia. And you will visit me, won't you?'

'Of course I will,' said Ahalaset.

'As will you, Lord Nagen,' Neferata said.

He bowed, his composure returning. 'Nothing would please me more.'

The orchestra had stopped playing for a few moments, and now it began again. A celebrated chord sounded, slowly thrumming twelve times, summoning the celebrants for the Dance of the Skulls.

Neferata offered her hand to Nagen. 'I made you a promise,' she said. 'Now I shall keep it.'

His earlier rapture lighting up his eyes, Nagen took her hand and led her onto the ballroom floor. As they took their places, Neferata saw a handmaiden walk quickly from the chamber to Ahalaset and whisper to her. As careful as the queen of Mortannis had been when she was talking to Neferata, she could not disguise the relief that flashed over her features. She prowled the edge of the dance floor, her gaze on Neferata. Her look was of someone who had had a narrow escape, and now sought a new route to victory.

Satisfied, Neferata turned her full attention on Nagen as the dance began.

Vampires and human nobles faced each other in two lines. Servants gave each of the vampires an enthralled human slave with silver chains wrapped around the neck. Every mortal noble held an ivory bowl in the shape of a skull. The music played and the aristocratic dancers moved together in groups of four. Though the vampires and nobles faced each other, the true partners in each cluster were the undead. The humans were the subordinates. The only difference between the slaves and the bowls was that the slaves were able to support themselves for the first part of the dance.

The music hit its first crescendo, the dancers completed their first turn and, in time to a sudden, emphatic beat in the melody, the vampires cut the jugulars of the slaves. Now the dance proper began, where the skill of the participants was put to the test. The vampires controlled the jet of blood and as the humans whirled around them, they caught the blood in the bowls. At the start of each refrain, the humans bowed, presenting the bowls to the vampires, who drank, and then the bowls were filled again. Though the movements of the dancers slowed in time to the music, there were never any full stops. The motion was continuous, and it was forbidden for even a single drop of blood to fall to the floor. So the dance would go on until the slaves were exsanguinated and that, too, had to be timed perfectly so the victims did not die prematurely. At the final flourish, the vampires would decapitate the slaves and exchange skulls with the mortal nobles.

And all this time, the vampire partners never broke eye contact with each other. The letting of blood and the killing were performed as if unthought. The dance made the mortals unimportant, beneath notice. Blood flowed, people died, yet all that mattered was the contact between the partners, all the more intense because they never touched physically.

Neferata held Nagen's gaze in a grip of iron. Though he was her willing prisoner, her task as they danced remained delicate. She saw before her a vampire who was happy to play the fool for her, yet she had no doubt that his loyalty remained with Ahalaset. Nagen feared Neferata as much as he desired her, and he wanted that fear disposed of. But he was vain, too, and Neferata read the fatal weakness in his vanity. He believed that he could indulge in the pleasure of her company and the dance until the moment of the assassination. The trap had failed. Perhaps there was another plan, or perhaps he believed he could distance himself from association with it. Whatever he was thinking, he would be wary. He was enraptured, not enthralled. He was not without his own power. If Neferata was too forceful in an attempt to control his will, he would sense the attack, and all would be lost.

So Neferata was subtle. What she wanted from Nagen was a small thing, a very small thing, a thing so attuned to his natural inclinations that it should require only the tiniest push to make him take a single, brief action when and how Neferata commanded. As they spun about the dancefloor, rounding each other, bowing to each other, and drinking from the proffered skull bowls, she added subtle gestures to her arm flourishes. Her fingers played in the air for an extra moment, making patterns that were only for Nagen's eyes. Even he would not notice them, but they had their effect. Halfway through the Dance of the Skulls, his face hung a bit looser than it should, and his pupils were a bit wider. And as they leaned in towards each other after filling the bowls with blood yet again, the torn veins of the prisoners pumping out streams between their fingers, Neferata moved her lips, shaping a few inaudible words. She did not even whisper.

She did so little. She was sure she'd done enough.

She saw Mereneth watching from the sides as the Dance of the Skulls drew to its climax. With a light inclination of her head, Neferata directed Mereneth's gaze to the other side of the ballroom.

The exuberant finale of the dance came. The vampires snapped the heads off their slaves. The human nobles extended both hands, to receive and to give. The orchestra thundered a last, victorious chord, proclaiming the triumph of death.

And Ahalaset screamed.

All movement in the ballroom ceased. The assassin, clad now in the rich robes of a noble guest, unnoticed until he struck, stood behind Ahalaset, his blade arm through her back, her heart impaled on its point. The rune-enchanted silver glowed through a slick of gore. Ahalaset's shriek turned into a hacking choke. The assassin held her body up a few moments more, and then it slid off the blade.

The assassin stood motionless over the corpse of the queen. He did not look up, and barely reacted when Ahalaset's honour guard surged forward and cut him down with pikes and blades.

'Search him!' the captain of the guard commanded, and Neferata was pleased. It was much better that the idea come from one of Ahalaset's minions.

In the time it took for the guards to turn out the pockets of the assassin's robes, Neferata felt all eyes in the ballroom on her. This was the turning point of the larger dance, the one that only she had truly known everyone had been caught in this night. Right now, the two courts believed she was responsible for Ahalaset's death. There was no other reasonable conclusion to be drawn. It was also the truth.

But the truth was ephemeral. It was a tiny, weak thing compared to the armoured colossus of perception. And the moment turned.

'There's a ring,' said one of the guards.

'I have seen that before,' said the captain. After a pause, he said, 'It has the seal of the house of Nagen.' He sounded confused.

Now perception spread the fog of doubt throughout the ballroom, and truth retreated. It was time for her work during the Dance of the Skulls to bear fruit. Time for Nagen to do that single thing. To speak one sentence. A sentence that came easily, because it was the motto of his family. A sentence he took pride in, and believed in. It was his belief in that sentence, after all, that had led him to conspire against Neferata with Ahalaset.

He had simply never planned on uttering that sentence right now.

'Never bend the knee!' he shouted.

Neferata turned to look at Nagen with carefully crafted disgust. He was so shocked by what he had said that his mouth hung open, suddenly bereft of words.

Neferata raised her eyebrows in a show of anger calibrated so that only Nagen would be close enough to see that it was mockery. 'I will have no part of your conflict,' Neferata told him, and walked away.

'Wait!' Nagen called to her. 'Wait!' he shouted at Ahalaset's guards as they descended on him. He tried to protest his innocence, but his words were drowned out by the roar of anger from the warriors.

Neferata gestured to Mereneth and the rest of her retinue. They followed her up onto the dais where she elected to watch the final steps of the royal dance. The orchestra was silent, the musicians huddling together for protection, but Neferata could hear music all the same. It was the beat and melody of violence unleashed at her command.

The palace guard cut Nagen down, piercing him with a dozen spears before he could muster a defence. Too late, the soldiers of Nachtwache rushed to his aid, and then to avenge their lord. Soon the dais was the lone island of calm in the ballroom. Neferata and her handmaidens brushed away the warriors who staggered too close, and plucked stray arrows from the air.

The fighting spread through the ballroom, the nobles from both cities joining in the attacks or caught between the blades of the warring troops. Blood and fire swept through the hall and out the palace doors. Neferata listened to the greater clashes of blades from the courtyard and the streets beyond, and to the growing thunder of armies hurling themselves against each other. She tapped at the air with a finger, conducting the carnage. When the time came for her forces to enter the city, she did not think there would be much left for them to do.

Neferata turned to the orchestra master. The thin vampire was crouched beside his chair, trembling. 'My compliments,' she said, speaking quietly, though her voice rode effortlessly over the clamour of battle. 'Your music was most pleasing.' She would see the musicians were well rewarded. 'You played with exquisite skill.'

'So did you, my queen,' said Lady Mereneth.

Neferata smiled, accepting the compliment. 'Yes,' she said, 'I rather think I did.'

It had been a most excellent ball.

YOUR
NEXT READ

NEFERATA: THE DOMINION OF BONES
by David Annandale

With her kingdom surrounded by enemies on all sides, the Blood Queen Neferata must call upon all of her cunning and guile if she is to maintain her rulership… fortunately, those qualities are not in short supply…

THE OLD WAYS

Nick Horth

Introducing

ARMAND CALLIS

AGENT, ORDER OF AZYR

HANNIVER TOLL

WITCH HUNTER, ORDER OF AZYR

Armand Callis winced as the marsh strider bucked beneath him. Every time the beast moved, his legs rubbed painfully against the rough hide saddle that was lashed around the creature's segmented body. They had been travelling for hours, and he still hadn't got used to the strider's awkward, rolling gait as it stretched out its six long limbs to balance on the soupy morass beneath them. He sighed as he peered through the gathering fog, hoping to catch sight of their destination looming into view. It was useless. He could barely see more than a few metres ahead.

'How much farther?' he shouted.

'Soon,' grunted their guide, a wizened old fellow with an expression that could turn milk sour.

Callis' marsh strider clicked and hissed, before releasing an arcing jet of fluid from its mandibles. On the whole, Callis decided that he preferred horses.

'Marshpoint is close,' said Hanniver Toll, mounted upon his own strider to Callis' left. Beneath his signature wide-brimmed hat, the older man's face was chapped pink by the cold and had several days' worth of stubble across his chin. Callis rubbed his own face ruefully. His typically neat and well-groomed moustache was tapering wildly out of control, and a coarse beard itched beneath the scarf wrapped around his mouth.

'Follow my lead once we arrive,' said Toll. 'The feud between the Junicas and the Dezraeds is on the verge of erupting into a full-scale border war.'

'No wonder,' muttered Callis. 'I'd be miserable too, if I lived out here.'

The Brackenmarsh was a featureless expanse of foul-smelling mud and grime that lay to the east of the great city of Excelsis. It was a bubbling pit of slime and weeds that reached to the mouth of the enormous Ulwhyr Forest. They had avoided the winding trade road that led through the marsh to the frontier township, as Toll had wanted to make it to Marshpoint as swiftly as possible. Unfortunately, marsh striders were the only way to cross the fenland – travelling by foot was a sure way of getting yourself drowned or eaten by the primitive beasts that dwelled within its murky depths. Despite their immense size and vicious, barbed fore-limbs, the mantis-like beasts were completely docile. Each of their six legs ended in a tangle of thick hairs that spread out across the rippling surface of the water, forming buoyant pads that allowed the striders to skip across the marsh with surprising speed.

'The disappearance of Adrec Junica has turned a tense situation into a volatile one,' said Toll. 'House Junica has long accused the Dezraeds of trying to undermine their trade in silksteel, and now they have an excuse to spill blood.'

'If that happened, the Freeguilds would not receive their ship-ments of silksteel.'

Silksteel was a substance woven by arachnids found within the Ulwhyr. Thin and light, it possessed a fearsome tensile strength, meaning that it could be woven into light, padded armour that stopped blades and arrows as surely as steel plate. As Excelsis lacked vast natural deposits of metal, silksteel was vital for outfitting the local regiments. Without it, the already undermanned city guard would find itself under-equipped too.

'Indeed,' said Toll, nodding. 'We're here to try and neutralise the fray by uncovering whether Lord Junica's firstborn son was indeed slain by the hands of the Dezraeds, or simply drank too much, stumbled into the marsh and drowned.'

'Hardly seems like vital work for an agent of the Order of Azyr,' said Callis. 'Couldn't they have sent a detachment from the city guard?'

'The city guard is stretched parchment-thin as it is,' said Toll. 'The battle for Excelsis left the city weak and vulnerable. If it comes under siege again, it will fall. Trade has been severely hampered and the people are ready to riot. Callis, this infighting could be the spark that ignites a full-scale uprising.' Toll paused. 'We would have no choice but to set the White Reaper loose. That's not an outcome I would relish.'

Callis fought off a shudder. He had once come face to face with Lord-Veritant Cerrus Sentanus – the White Reaper of Excelsis – and had barely escaped with his life. If Sentanus was loosed upon the inhabitants of the city, the streets would run with blood.

'Here,' growled their guide, pointing one thin finger into the distance. Following his gesture, they could see the lambent glow of torches flickering. Rising up out of the mist like the backbone of some drowned behemoth, a perimeter wall loomed over a short pier of mildewed wood. It was a well-made fortification, as these things went. The wood was smoothed and sanded down to prevent anyone scaling it, and dotted along the line were swivel-mounted arbalests with large, hook-shaped magazines. A great, circular tower loomed above the parapet, and atop the battlements, Callis could see a heavy ballista, aiming out into the gloom.

'The ones who built this place knew their business,' Callis said. 'You'd only require a few men to hold this wall against a horde.'

'You're looking at Junica coin,' said Toll. 'They employed the most skilled duardin siege-smiths when they built this place. You don't survive out here, beyond the city's reach, unless you can defend yourself. Their private armies are larger than many Freeguild regiments. House Dezraed's included.'

Callis' eyebrows quipped. 'I'm surprised that's allowed.'

'Both Dezraed and Junica are old Azyr stock. At one time or another, they've both had figures on the council of Azyrheim. The men we're here to see, though, are minor scions of the great houses. Still, they're powerful figures with a bottomless supply of coin and the ear of the Excelsis council. As long as they pay their tithes and maintain their shipments, the city is content to allow their standing armies.'

As they approached the bank, the marsh striders hauled themselves out of the dank swamp, flicking their long limbs free of foul-smelling weeds.

'Who passes?' came a shout from the palisade gatehouse, where a bucket-helmed face peered down at them, silhouetted against the sickly yellow sky. The figure was leaning against a swivel-gun mounted upon the edge of the wall.

'We are expected,' shouted Toll, dropping nimbly from the saddle, patting the beast's chitinous, armour-plated leg affectionately. The thing gave a shrill chirp and lowered its many-eyed head to the mossy earth, loudly slurping at a clump of moss. 'I am Hanniver Toll, agent of the Order of Ayr. Open the gate.'

Even from a distance away, Callis could see the colour drain from the man's face.

'The witch hunter,' breathed the guard. The figure made a frantic gesture to someone on the other side of the wall, and there was a clanking, grinding sound. Slowly, the great gate began to creak open.

'So this is Marshpoint,' said Callis. 'Hardly a sight to set the blood astir.'

It was far from the worst hovel that Callis had ever laid eyes on – indeed the poor quarters of Excelsis were far more rundown – but a tangible pall of misery hung over the cluttered white stone houses that formed the main street. The construction was simple, functional and rather ugly, with thatched green roofs slanting away into the fog, and uneven masonry.

'Someone threw this town up in a hurry,' said Callis.

'It's more fort than town, truly,' said Toll. 'The only people who live here are soldiers and workers from the silksteel plantations. We're probably the only outsiders these people have seen in months. Few travellers or merchants risk the trade road this far east.'

Shrouded figures hustled across a road of rough-hewn cobbles in the fading light, glancing at the newcomers with nervous eyes. The central plaza, such as it was, featured a statue of an imposing warrior, a Stormcast Eternal with hammer raised to the skies. The grandeur of the craftsmanship was marred by the smear of verdigris and mould, and the hazy green light that filtered through the darkening clouds gave the noble image an unsettling pallid glow. The looming towers and the high wall cast the squat, unremarkable little town in shadow, giving it a claustrophobic feel.

Several shabby-looking guards dressed in leather jerkins stared down at them from a walkway that ran the length of the outer wall. One strode down the steps to meet them, removing a woollen cap as he did so to reveal a boyish, earnest face, dark-skinned and fresh-eyed. He looked barely out of his teens.

'They told us to expect visitors,' he said. 'But we weren't expecting you here for another few days. We thought you'd take the trade road.'

'I would prefer to resolve the situation here as swiftly as possible,' said Toll. As he stepped forward, he removed his wide-brimmed hat and reached into his coat. He withdrew a waxen scroll, marked with the image of a blazing comet.

'Sigmar's teeth,' whispered the guard as he studied the paper. His eyes went wide. 'Sorry, sire. Forgive my blasphemy. I...'

'I have business with Lords Fenrol Dezraed and Kiervaan Junica,' said Toll, ignoring the man's discomfort. 'Send word of my arrival to both.'

'Um... Begging your pardon, sire, but they won't leave their estates,' mumbled the guard. 'Neither of them. We've already seen blood spilled, and with the Junica boy missing, they're readying for war...' He shook his head. 'They've stopped the patrols and blocked the roads. There's only fifty of us defending this entire town. Heavens forbid the orruks come pillaging and burning, or the bog-devils swarm the walls at the White Witch's command.'

'Your name?' said Toll.

'Guardsman Rolkyr, sire,' said the man.

'Send word to both the houses, Guardsman Rolkyr, and return to your post. Your diligence is noted. It would appear that there are some souls yet in Marshpoint who remember their duty.'

Rolkyr seemed surprised. He gave a slight nod and scrambled away up the stairs, shouting orders to his men.

'Son,' shouted Toll. The guard turned. 'Where's the tavern?'

'The Moss Throne,' said Rolkyr, gesturing to a rather shabby two-storey building across the cobbled square. Dim light shone through the lower windows, but other than that it looked more like an abandoned barn than a place to catch a good night's sleep. The sloped roof was thick with ivy, which draped down the mouldy wooden walls like strands of wet hair. The windows were round and the entire structure sat oddly slanted on the street, as if it was about to slide into the bog. Still, it was a tavern, and they'd have ale. Callis had drunk in far worse places.

'Obliged,' said Callis, snapping a friendly salute.

'Tell the Lords Dezraed and Junica that they can grace us with their presence at this fine establishment.'

'Sire,' nodded Rolkyr in agreement. 'Just supposing, but what if they refuse?'

'They will not,' said Toll, 'if they value their continued existence.'

They took a table in the centre of the tavern and ordered food along with a thin, tasteless ale. Gradually the clientele filtered out, eyeing the newcomers uneasily as they left. The common folk were mostly slight, pale figures, lean from hard work but rather sickly looking. No one but the barkeep, a rotund man of middling years with a drooping moustache and sad eyes, spoke to them. Callis, tired though he was, could feel the aura of tension and unease that surrounded them. It wasn't merely their presence that unsettled the locals. The town had the distinct feel of a city facing a siege. A burgeoning sense of dread reminded him of times he had spent awaiting battle, knowing that bloodshed was coming, but unable to do anything other than stand ready until the killing started.

After perhaps an hour, they heard the clatter of hooves outside. Callis moved to the window, while Toll continued to pick at a rather sorry slice of grey meat. Peering out of the misted glass, Callis saw two-score soldiers riding pale mares and carrying long, forked spears emerging out of the haze. They flanked a great carriage of crimson and gold, shining gaudily amidst its unassuming surroundings. These soldiers were a different breed to the ragged fellows manning the palisade. They wore thick cloth tunics with silver pads upon the shoulders and chest, and their armour glittered in the gloomy evening light. The image of an aetherhawk in flight was embossed upon their chest plates and upon the barding of their mounts. Callis recognised the motif – the symbol of House Dezraed. The same image hung from the banners of Excelsis' market square and soared above the Halls of Justice.

He returned to the table and drained the rest of his ale, wincing slightly at the silty, bitter aftertaste.

A few moments later, the door opened, letting in a drizzle of rain and a chill wind. The soldiers entered in perfect parade lockstep, their boots stamping out a staccato rhythm on the wooden floor of the tavern. They spread out in a fan on either side of the door, slamming the hafts of their spears down and raising their heads imperiously. The tavern hound, a morose-looking beast with rheumy eyes and a matted mane of blue-grey fur, got up from its position under Toll and Callis' table, and sauntered across the floor. It paused briefly to idly lap at its hindquarters and gaze at the newcomers.

'My name is Captain Lecian Celtegar,' said the lead soldier in a clipped Azyrite accent. He wore a half-face helm with a bright blue plume, and was the only guard not carrying a longspear. Instead, he rested his hand on a fine, silver longsword at his belt. He removed his helm, revealing a wave of blond hair and an angular face locked in a permanent half-sneer. Callis disliked the man on sight. 'May I present my Lord Fenrol var Dezraed, the Eagle of the East, Warden of Marshpoint and the scourge of the forest greenskins.'

Callis glanced at Toll. The witch hunter leaned back in his chair, a long-suffering expression upon his face.

A man entered the tavern. At first, Callis thought it was several men, wrapped up in a single enormous bedsheet. The mighty Lord Dezraed was far from the statuesque patrician his entourage had intimated. He was a huge, wobbling bulge of a human, enormously fat with no suggestion of muscle beneath. A toga of rich crimson silk struggled vainly to lend an air of Azyrite nobility to the wall of flesh, but to no avail. Dezraed's eyes narrowed as he laid eyes on them, two sunken pools of glassy ice within his pink slab of a face. The man's thin blond hair had been separated and slicked back by rain, and he carried a look of utmost irritation.

'So you are the findsman, are you?' he said to Toll, his voice a deep, throaty gurgle. 'You believe it proper to force me out of my home and onto the streets where Junica's assassins lurk? You drag me to this *hovel*, like I am some minor cutpurse to be ordered about at your own will?'

Toll rapped his fingers on the table and stared levelly at Lord Dezraed.

'Take a seat, my lord,' he said, and there was not a hint of irritation or anger in his words. Not for the first time, Callis wondered how the man remained so calm. 'Lord Kiervaan var Junica will be joining us presently, then together we three will unpick this mess.'

Dezraed's eyes widened.

'You invite the very man that seeks my death? Who baselessly blames me for the abduction of his firstborn son, as if I would sully my hands by laying them upon that thin-blooded wretch? I summoned you here to deal with that madman once and for all, not to–'

'You do not summon the Order,' said Toll, and though his voice remained level, there was a sliver of ice in his words. 'You do not make demands of us. Now sit.'

The noble's great lips quivered in astonished rage. He was not a man used to being spoken to so curtly, Callis thought with some satisfaction.

'May I offer you a drink?' said Toll, indicating his cup of ale.

Dezraed snorted, turning his nose up at the humble spread that lay before the witch hunter.

'Wine,' he barked at his retainers, who rushed back outside into the rain. Dezraed snapped his fingers and another two perfumed servants rushed forth carrying an immense curule chair between them. They set it down. The man eased his bulk into it with a groan of protesting timber.

They waited perhaps another thirty minutes or so in interminable silence before they heard the clatter of approaching horses. Dezraed's men moved to surround their master, who slurped the last dregs from a horn of pale, sweet-smelling mead. The door swung open and a stocky man in black leather and chainmail entered. The newcomer took in the scene, fixing on Toll for a moment. The witch hunter met his gaze. Eventually, the man slammed one fist on the door and a group of heavyset men entered, armoured in gold-plated scale armour and long, black hoods. Each carried a black-iron mace fashioned in the shape of a comet. They held their weapons at the ready as they filtered in, glaring daggers at Dezraed and his own gleaming host. Callis let one hand fall to his pistol and readied a foot to overturn the table if things went awry, as they typically did in these situations. If Toll felt the tension, he did not show it.

A thin, aging man dressed in austere black entered, flanked by two more guards. He wore a military-style jacket and breastplate, polished and buckled with parade-ground precision. His greying hair was shaved close to the scalp, and he wore his moustache thin and curled with wax. This one fancies himself a military man, thought Callis. A strangely common delusion amongst the noble classes, that. Lord Junica took in his modest surroundings with the air of a man examining some unpleasant substance stuck to the sole of his boot. His face was gaunt where Dezraed's was flabby, and his brow was furrowed in a cold glare that only intensified when he caught a glimpse of his rival.

'Lord Junica,' said Toll, tearing a hunk of black bread in half and dabbing it into the thin stew. 'Please, join us. I am Hanniver Toll, of the hallowed Order of the Azyr.'

'You ask me to sit beside the man who killed my son?' hissed Kiervaan Junica. 'I should paint the floor with this fat bastard's blood.'

Dezraed spluttered in outrage and his guards stepped forwards, spears lowering threateningly. Junica's men took a pace back, readying their own weapons. There was a muffled yelp as the barkeep dived behind his counter to the sound of smashing glass. Toll took another bite of bread and washed it down with a swig of ale.

'I did not kill your idiotic spawn, but I wish I had,' shouted Dezraed, slamming his meaty fists upon the table. 'The only good Junica is a dead Junica, and if you insult my honour again, I shall seek the satisfaction. I warn you now!'

'Enough,' said Toll, and the two men looked at the witch hunter in surprise. Seemingly oblivious to their disbelief, Toll took up a napkin in one hand and dabbed at his moustache.

'Stand your men down. If there is even a drop of spilled blood at this table, then word will make it back to Excelsis, I assure you. Next time the Order dispatches an agent to your doorstep, they will not send a single man. They will send in the hounds, my lords. Your lands and your profits will be confiscated. Both of you will be dragged before the Halls of Justice to explain why you defied the word of the God-King. Perhaps we shall give you to the White Reaper, so that he may uncover the true extent of your failures.'

Lord Dezraed's red face went suddenly pale, and even Lord Junica looked unnerved at the threat. Callis allowed himself a small grin. There was a distinct pleasure to be found in watching Toll work.

'This is a private matter,' Kiervaan Junica stuttered. 'There is no treason here. I only wish to know the truth behind the disappearance of my son.'

'Disrupting the flow of vital supplies in a time of war is treason,' said Toll. 'If I possessed the same disposition of many of my kin, you both would already be returned to the city dungeons, there to wait for the hangman's rope around your necks. Now sit, my lord.'

Junica eased himself into a chair. His bodyguards stood on either side.

'Pass me the ale,' said Toll, gesturing at Lord Junica.

The noble looked startled at the blunt request, as if Toll had just fired his pistol into the ceiling. His attendants stared at each other in confusion.

'Excuse me?' Junica said.

'The ale,' Toll repeated.

To Callis' surprise, Junica reached out an uncertain hand and passed the jug of sour-smelling liquid to the witch hunter, who took it and poured himself a fresh cup.

'You accuse Lord Dezraed of murder without proof?' said Callis.

Junica glanced at him, surprised, as if he had not noticed him at all before he had spoken.

'Long has the feud between Junica and Dezraed raged,' he said. 'When we forged a path on the frontier with blood and spirit, the Dezraeds followed us like parasites, leeching off of our noble work. As they have always done.'

'You dare?' roared Lord Dezraed, spittle flying from his lips. 'House Dezraed desires only to serve the will of Sigmar, as *we* have always done. It is the Junicas who provoke us, stealing away the riches of the land for themselves alone, threatening honest workers and harassing my soldiers at every possible turn. Excelsis is built upon the blood of the Dezraeds. We were here long before the

Junicas, and we shall be here long after your ragged house crumbles into dust.'

'My steward, Ghedren, saw your men pursue my son into the forest,' said Junica, indicating the unassuming man in the chainmail hauberk. 'They were drunk, seeking sport. My firstborn son. Aldrec was a strong, brave boy, and your men ran him down like a dog. At your order, no doubt.'

'My soldiers did nothing of the sort. Yet I know that you yourself resort to murder all too quickly, Junica,' snarled Dezraed. 'As did your son. On the very night you claim he was assaulted, it was he who murdered a Dezraed man in cold blood, then fled the scene of the crime rather than face the consequences. Half a dozen more of my men have disappeared also. No doubt their bodies have been dumped in some stinking bog with Junica daggers in their backs.'

'You witnessed this altercation?' Callis asked Ghedren.

'I did,' the man said, nodding. 'It is as the Lord Junica states. Words were exchanged and swords were drawn. I do not know who struck the first blow, but Aldrec was wounded on the arm in the struggle. He fled on horseback. The Dezraeds chased him.' The man spoke with a soft, lilting accent, quite at odds with his coarse and weathered face. Callis guessed that Ghedren was in his third decade or thereabouts, but he had the rough look of a man who plied his trade in the wilds. Callis noticed the familiar curling lines of blue-ink tattoos emerging from under the man's collar. A fellow Reclaimed. A descendent of the nomadic tribes who had once lived here, before Sigmar's Tempest brought the light of the heavens back into the realms, rather than a great, Azyr-born family like his masters. Perhaps that was why he appeared to possess some humility.

'They went beyond the eastern gate and into the Ulwhyr,' he continued. 'I followed after them, but they were horsed and I was not. I lost them in the darkness, but I heard screams, so returned to seek help.'

'The words of a lowborn mercenary employed by the Junica,' said Captain Celtegar, with a dismissive snort. 'How utterly convincing.

I tell you now, upon my honour and that of my men, no such incident took place. This one lies.'

Ghedren simply shrugged. 'It is what I saw.'

'How many days past was this?' asked Toll.

'Five days, sire.'

'And you have returned since to search the area?'

'We have. We found no sign of Master Junica, nor of his pursuers.'

'It is possible, then, that something else could have occurred within the Ulwhyr? Not murder?' Toll continued.

Ghedren shrugged. 'Perhaps, but the Dezraed soldiers were after blood.'

'You will take me and my associate there,' said Toll. 'You will guide us to the spot where you lost track of them. If what you say is true, there will be traces of their passing.'

Ghedren looked at his master for confirmation. Lord Junica nodded slightly.

'Captain Celtegar will accompany you,' said Lord Dezraed. 'Along with two men of his choosing. Just to ensure that this is not some foolish attempt at revenge.'

'I have such a thing as honour, you bloated fiend,' snapped Junica. 'A concept that escapes you entirely.'

Their bickering was about to start over anew, when Toll slammed his fist on the table.

'Silence,' he barked. 'At dawn, we will enter the Ulwhyr and find out the truth of this. My lords, you will remain in Marshpoint until I tell you otherwise. And I warn you both, if blood is shed on these streets, I promise I will ensure that a price is paid. Now leave.'

Callis followed Toll out of the eastern gate of Marshpoint early the next morning, rubbing at his itching eyes. It had not been a relaxing sleep in the cramped guest chambers of the Moss Throne. The room had smelled of mildew and rot, and he had been kept awake by the sounds of buzzing insects and a slow, steady dripping from the roof above his head.

'So, what do you think of our Lords Junica and Dezraed?' Toll asked.

Callis scratched his beard and yawned.

'They would each see the other destroyed if they could,' he said. 'That's clear. But I am not sure about a murder plot. Lord Dezraed hardly seems like a master schemer.'

'Do not underestimate him,' said Toll. 'Marshpoint may not be a glamorous place, but the silksteel plantations are of great value to both houses. They would not send lackwits out here to oversee one of their most valuable trades. Fenrol Dezraed looks like a greedy fool, but clever men often hide behind the mummer's mask.'

'Why the firstborn son?' said Callis. 'Why not the old man himself? If you're going to start a war, why not make that your opening move? If this is a Dezraed scheme, what's the end goal?'

Toll rolled his hat in his hands and nodded thoughtfully.

'Be watchful as we enter the Ulwhyr,' he said, checking the firing pan of his four-barrelled pistol. 'Observe all. Discount nothing.'

'I've patrolled the wilds before,' said Callis. 'I know well what it's like out here.'

'I do not just mean the forest,' Toll replied, but before Callis could ask what he meant, the witch hunter strode over to greet the Junica steward, Ghedren, who was waiting for them on a flooded path that led out towards the distant spectre of the Ulwhyr Forest. The man carried a well-made composite bow and a heavy-bladed knife at his hip. He was wrapped in a large wolf-skin cloak that smelled strongly of wet fur. He dipped his head in greeting as they approached. The vast, ominous expanse of woodland that was the Ulwhyr lurked on the eastern edge of the town, emerging out of the early morning murk. The canopy was an impenetrable carpet of dark green, the trunks of the trees below gnarled and twisted, leading into darkness. A tide of sickly green mist rolled out from the bog, swirling around the mouth of the forest like the breath of a fallen giant.

'So that's where we're headed?' Callis said. 'Seems like an inviting sort of place.'

Ghedren smiled. 'The Ulwhyr is dangerous, yes. But it is also a place of life. For many years, my people walked its secret paths, hidden from those that wished us harm. It protected us, granted us all that we required. One need only show the forest the proper respect and they can walk amongst its shadows unscathed.'

'You almost sound as though it's a sentient thing,' said Callis.

'Perhaps it is. These lands are rife with magic. Within the Ulwhyr dwells things more ancient than a mortal could possibly contemplate,' said Ghedren. 'The forest belongs to them, not us.'

'For now,' interrupted Toll. 'In time, the light of the God-King will reach even the darkest corners of these lands. We will tame this place, and then we will burn away the shadows.'

'Some evils cannot be banished so easily.'

'I did not say that it would be easy,' said Toll, who then went to converse with the gaggle of nervous-looking guards manning the east gate, leaving Ghedren and Callis alone.

'You were raised in the city?' asked the steward.

'I was,' Callis replied. 'Though my family weren't Azyrite. I served in the Freeguild for many years.'

Callis briefly thought to mention his regiment, but decided against it. The Coldguard of Excelsis had been entirely liquidated for their part in the heretical plot to overthrow the city, after all, and he was the sole survivor. That fact tended to set people on edge, for some unfathomable reason.

'I thought as much,' said Ghedren, nodding. 'You have a soldier's bearing. It is surprising to me that a man so young – one of the Reclaimed, no less – is in the employ of the Order. You must be a man of rare talents to be elevated so high.'

'I'm merely a soldier, as you say. Just doing what is asked of me.'

Ghedren gave an awkward, sad smile.

'Aren't we all?' he said. 'Yet it seems that we must work twice as hard for half the praise.'

'Aye,' said Callis. 'I won't disagree with you there.'

'Your master... This witch hunter,' said Ghedren. 'He is Azyr-born, I take it.'

Callis blinked in surprise as he realised he had never thought to ask.

'I confess, I have no idea,' he said.

'He's more alike to them than us, I think,' said Ghedren. 'I worry that he does not understand this place, not truly. He is a creature of the crowded street, the shadowed back-alley...'

They heard boots squelching through the mud, and turned to see Toll leading three soldiers along the muddy path towards them – two Dezraed guards and the captain, Celtegar. All had pistols strapped to their belts and had ditched their spears for more practical longswords.

'Corporals Brujda,' said the captain, indicating the shaven-headed woman, 'and Yol.' The latter was a short, stocky red-headed man with a wispy beard and lazy eyes. The two soldiers gave perfunctory nods, all business. Celtegar cast a withering look at Ghedren.

'Where do you insist that this fiction occurred?'

'They pursued the Junica boy this way, along the path and into the forest,' said Ghedren.

'Lies.'

'He was bleeding from his wounds, and they were striking him with lances.'

'When this farce is over, I'll have your head for this, savage,' snapped Celtegar.

'You'll keep a civil tongue in your head,' snarled Callis, moving to within an inch of Celtegar's face, enjoying the look of surprised fury on the man's angular features. 'The only justice here will be served by the Order of Azyr.'

For a moment, Callis thought Celtegar would swing for him. He tensed his arms, ready to block the man's punch and return it in kind.

'Stand down, Armand,' said Toll. 'This is not the time nor the place.'

Callis stared into the captain's grey eyes a moment longer, just to let him know the time had long passed where he would suffer the insults and barbs of blue-blooded fools. When he stepped back, Celtegar was all but trembling with rage.

'Lead on, Ghedren,' the witch hunter said. 'I would have us get to the truth of this as soon as possible.'

Callis had never much liked forests. He'd fought in several during his time in the Freeguilds, and these had been amongst his most miserable experiences. The deep woods played tricks on a soldier's mind, made one jump at every sound and every flickering shadow. The Ulwhyr was worse than most. It was a twisted labyrinth of curling boughs, smothered in darkness. Its mist swirled around their legs and up to their knees, making every step a potential hazard. Callis had expected the usual cacophony of sounds, the chattering of insects and the hooting of birds, yet the ominous canopy above them was startlingly silent. He winced at every snapped stick and muttered curse from his companions. If anyone was lurking in wait for them, they would hear the approach from a mile away.

They had been walking for perhaps two hours when Yol stumbled, then let out a curse in shock when he realised what had caught his foot. It was a corpse, face down in the soil. The grey flesh and stiffness of the limbs suggested this was at least a few days old. A man armoured in the silver of House Dezraed.

Callis rolled the body over with his boot. The dead man's eyes were wide, crazed even, like a frightened deer. His mouth was open in a scream, and blood had caked around his eyes and mouth.

'Lartach,' breathed the Dezraed woman, Brujda. 'He went missing a few days back. Around the same time as the Junica boy. He was an idiot and a drunkard, but a decent enough sort otherwise.'

'There are no wounds,' mused Callis. 'Nowhere. How did this man die?'

'The White Witch,' muttered Yol, shaking his head.

'Enough with that nonsense,' snorted Captain Celtegar.

'What's that you say?' asked Callis. 'The guard at the gate mentioned that name.'

'Just a legend,' said Celtegar, waving a dismissive hand. 'A tale concocted by the natives of this region. It's all they ever talk about. The dreaded White Witch of the Ulwhyr, the taker of children. A ghost, whose screams can stop the heart of mortals.'

'Oh, she is real,' said Ghedren softly. 'These are her lands.'

'All you people ever talk about are ghosts, spriggans, tolmickles and bog-devils,' mocked Celtegar. 'Backwards nonsense. This is probably just another fool who got drunk and choked on his own spew.'

Ghedren stood and slowly moved off deeper into the treeline.

'Horse tracks,' he said. 'They lead this way.

'Continue,' said Toll.

Callis squinted. 'I don't know how you can see anything in this fog.'

'My father taught me to hunt in these woods,' said Ghedren. 'He taught me to track, to move unseen, to hide my trail. To understand and respect the dangers of the wild. These men we seek, the Dezraed guards, they may have lived here for many years now, but they have learned no such lessons. Such superstition is beneath them, so they say. They believe only in the power of the God-King, and scorn the wild tales of uncivilised folk.'

'If Celtegar is what counts as civilised, I'll gladly remain a so-called savage,' muttered Callis, and Ghedren chuckled.

They were losing light now, despite the fact that it could not have been more than a few hours since they had set off. The thick canopy overhead cast them into near pitch-black darkness. Every tangled cluster of vine seemed to take the form of a skulking beast of the forest, and every wisping curl of fog seemed almost alive in its movement, drifting towards them out of the murk. Callis shook his head, angry with himself for allowing this miserable place to unsettle him. Eventually, they came to a wide, enclosed clearing, hemmed in on all sides by fat-trunked oaks. A great pool of greenish water spread out before them, dotted by clusters of drooping reeds and sharp rocks. At the far end of the pool, a bank of discoloured leaves rose into a steep mound dominated by a huge, long-dead blackwood tree. In the centre of the marsh was a small island of pale flesh and shining metal.

'Another body,' said Ghedren.

They waded out into the morass to get a closer look. It was a dead horse, half-submerged in the foetid water, pallid and bloated. Something had torn great chunks out of the beast's hide, devoured most of its innards. They shoved against the carcass and found a rider beneath, pinned by the animal's weight. The dead man's face was horribly swollen and his skin a pale green.

'Scavengers,' said Ghedren, noticing Callis' uncomfortable look. 'These are the bites of several creatures. These, however...'

He indicated scores of smaller slices across the flank of the horse and on the body of the dead man. They looked like gouges, ragged and imprecise, rather than the neat cut of a blade. One such tear had ripped open the unfortunate soldier's cheek, and another had torn a bloody line across his throat. It looked as if the horse had been dragged down into the mud, and the rider had become trapped underneath its weight, helpless against his attackers.

'There's something out here,' growled Captain Celtegar. 'Watching us. I can feel it. Whatever did this, it isn't far away.'

Ghedren knelt, placed a hand on the mossy earth and stared off into the blackness of the forest. After a moment, he shook his head.

'I do not sense anything nearby,' he said.

'Who cares a damn what you sense, curseblood?' snapped Celtegar.

Callis had heard that term before. Several of the officers in his regiment had muttered the same insult behind his back, not caring if he heard. It was used to denigrate any who did not hail from blessed Azyr, anyone who was – in their eyes – tainted by native blood.

'Use that word again and I'll break your jaw, you preening shit,' said Callis, slowly and deliberately.

Celtegar's men squared up, their hands on the hilts of their swords. The captain stepped close to Callis, who had to lean his head back to maintain eye contact. He was a big brute, this one, but still, Callis had fought bigger.

'You will withdraw that insult,' said Celtegar.

'You shall first,' said Callis. 'You forget who I represent here, captain. Strike a member of the Order, and see the consequences.'

'Silence,' hissed Toll. The witch hunter's pistol was raised, aimed out into the swirling fog. In a matter of moments, the mist had grown as thick as smoke, and now formed an opaque wall around them. They could barely see more than a dozen feet in any direction. Something stirred with a splash in the water nearby, and they all started, drawing their blades and forming a circle, hostility temporarily forgotten.

'I told you,' said Celtegar, his voice tight with fear. 'Something is coming.'

He had barely finished speaking when something broke the surface of the bog and closed around his leg. Celtegar shrieked in surprise and toppled backwards, sending up a great wave of water as he splashed onto his rear. An arm, rotted through and draped in weeds, was clamped tightly around his ankle. A head emerged, flaps of decaying skin hanging loosely from a grinning skull. The undead thing began to haul itself along the captain's prone form, reaching for his neck with creaking fingers. Callis put a boot against the undead's chest, kicking it off the screaming Celtegar and into the murky water. He hacked at its neck with his blade. The head came free, sinking into the bog.

Another figure erupted from the water behind Corporal Brujda, wrapping its arms around her neck, teeth tearing at her neck and shattering as they crunched into her plate gorget. She gasped in revulsion and began to awkwardly swipe and slash at its forearms, trying to cut it loose. Yol smashed the pommel of his blade into the undead thing's head, and it fell back into the water, but another was already rising in its place. This corpse looked fresher than the others, and was clad in the same shining metal plate as the Dezraed warriors. Its head lolled at a strange, unnatural angle, but Callis could make out a thin, cruel face with eyes glazed and vacant.

'G-Gaulter?' stammered Yol, lowering his blade just a fraction.

Too much. The risen corpse slashed its own weapon, a rusted sabre, across in a wide arc, and there was a splatter of bright crimson. The Dezraed guard fell, clutching an opened throat, gurgling and choking. He splashed into the water, and his former companion leapt upon him and drove its sword into his chest again and again.

'Move!' shouted Toll, grabbing Captain Celtegar under the arm and hauling the heavyset man to his feet. The water boiled to life as yet more rotting bodies clambered upright. The witch hunter fired and a corpse came apart in an explosion of bone and flesh. The stench of rot and acrid gunpowder choked the air.

'This way!' shouted Ghedren, splashing through the water towards a rising bank of dead leaves.

They staggered after him, weaving their way through the mass of decaying bodies. As they dragged themselves up onto the muddy bank, more dead things erupted from the water, scraping and clawing at their legs. Callis saw a skeleton rise up ahead of him, a curling branch of thorns protruding from its eye sockets. He drew his pistol and fired. The bullet smashed the skull into a thousand shards of wet bone, and the thing slumped back beneath the surface. Then they were out, on their hands and knees, dragging themselves free. Toll grabbed Callis' hand and hauled him up. Callis turned, searching for the Dezraed woman, Brujda. She was wading after them, hacking at the bodies rising around her, eyes terrified.

'Come on,' roared Callis, stretching out his hand, straining to reach her.

She was only an arm's length away when half a dozen dead things surrounded her and bore her down. Her scream cut off abruptly as she went under, and bubbles broke the surface. Callis and Celtegar tried to cut their way down to reach Brujda as she thrashed underwater, but more of the dead were rising with every moment, blocking their path and dragging themselves onto the shore. The foetid surface of the swamp turned a deep crimson.

'She's gone,' said Toll, firing round after round, the grey-black smoke from his pistol churning with the pale, white mist.

An arm wrapped in rusted chainmail reached out of the mist to grasp the witch hunter around the throat. A leering skull appeared over the man's shoulder, its yellowed fangs snapping as it sought to bite down into Toll's exposed neck. Toll drove an elbow into the side of the thing's head and there was a crunch of breaking bone, but its grip did not relent. Callis stepped forward, trying to keep his balance while straining to reach Toll. He lost his footing in the slick mud and fell, slipping and cursing, back towards the marsh water. Somehow he managed to grasp a fistful of gnarled roots to stay his descent. He looked up to see Toll stumbling backwards, the skeleton still tearing at his neck. The witch hunter fell, seemingly in slow motion, swallowed up by the mist.

'Toll!' shouted Callis, crawling forwards on his hands and knees, searching for his companion. There was no reply, and he could see nothing but the ghostly shapes of shambling figures drawing ever closer. He fired and one of the figures dropped to the ground with a rattling groan.

'He is lost, Armand,' shouted Ghedren. He loosed his bow and an arrow sailed past Callis' head to smash a skeleton to the ground. 'We must run! This way! Follow my steps.'

Callis took one last look into the thick fog.

'Hanniver?' he shouted, but heard only the echo of his own words in response.

It was hopeless. To blunder out into the gloom with the dead all around would be to seal his own fate alongside the witch hunter's. He felt numb. It seemed absurd – all that he and Toll had been through, only for the man to fall here. Cursing, he turned and followed Ghedren, who led them higher, along the crest of the mound. It was a strange formation, Callis noticed. There was an almost artificial curve to it, a gently sloping arc through which rose a great, twisted tree of black wood. Ghedren stopped beneath its creaking boughs, watching the others as they approached him. The ground suddenly groaned beneath their weight, the roots splintering. Soil and clusters of leaves tumbled away into a pitch-black hole. Callis tripped and fell, sliding towards the drop, clutching desperately for a handhold on the mud-slick roots. He stared up at Ghedren.

'Help us,' he shouted, but the man did not move a muscle.

'Forgive me.'

Ghedren reached down and tugged hard at a thick cluster of vines, raising his long dagger in one hand. He sliced down, again and again, and with a loud crack the roots came apart. The ground beneath Callis and Celtegar fell away. They toppled end over end as the world spun. Callis tried to grasp a hold, but could find no purchase. Something ripped at his cheek and blood splattered across his face. Dirt blinded him and filled his mouth. Suddenly, he struck something with enough force to blast the air from his lungs. Everything went dark.

Callis was dragged back to consciousness by a stabbing pain in his face. He brushed a hand against his cheek and felt torn flesh. Groaning, he struggled to his feet, spitting foul-tasting soil. He stared up and saw a trickle of light filtering down from above. That snake, Ghedren. He had led them here, like lambs to the slaughter. But where, exactly, were they?

Someone moaned beside him. He saw a gleam of metal in the darkness. It was Celtegar. The Dezraed man stood and teetered, favouring his left leg.

'Are you all right?' asked Callis.

'Just fine,' spat the man. 'I warned you we could not trust that wretch. Now, where are we?'

'Good question,' said Callis. He squinted, waiting impatiently for his eyes to adjust to the gloom. They appeared to be in some kind of tunnel. It looked too smooth to be a natural formation. He ran his hand down the wall to his left and felt something hard and cold. Stone. So this was some kind of ancient structure they had fallen into, built from…

His hand brushed over a stone and he felt a circular indentation. Below that, he ran his fingers over a row of sharp objects, a surface of irregular curves and indentations. A shiver of fear ran down his spine.

'Skulls,' he whispered. 'Skulls in the walls.'

Celtegar bent and picked up his blade. Callis gathered his own and recovered his pistol, his heart thumping. His eyes had adjusted to the light, and he could see that all around them were bones, packed into the earth – row upon row of grinning skulls and the curving beams of ribcages. Fingers and teeth arranged in spiral patterns that turned his stomach. Hundreds upon hundreds of dead things, packed and piled upon each other. Not just human bones, but the fanged skulls of forest beasts and the delicate frames of dead birds. He stepped forward and felt the crunch of more bones underfoot.

'By the God-King,' whispered Celtegar. 'What is this place?'

Ahead, the tunnel curved and descended. Callis moved forwards carefully, the carpet of bone crunching with every footstep. Ahead, the tunnel ended at the mouth of a cave, a pitch-black archway of stone from which hung several objects that clattered and tinkled in the wind. Animal bones, bound together with long ropes of knotted hair, formed into gruesome marionettes. Runes were carved into the black surface, in a language Callis could not read. They were harsh, childlike etchings, and their simplicity somehow made them all the more unsettling. He edged closer and felt the dangling totems clatter against his leather jerkin as he eased past them. Beyond, a low-ceilinged chamber was formed from tangled roots, which curled around each other to create an enormous throne of twisted briar. Upon the throne sat a skeletal figure, head bowed. It was draped in robes of white cloth and a silk gauze covered its face. Around this figure were scores of skeletons, a congregation near one hundred in number, their heads bowed in supplication. Men, women, duardin and aelves. Some were full-sized. Most were small, delicate things. Children, Callis realised with horror. He moved closer. Behind the throne, he noticed another tunnel, thick with vines and thorny brambles. This one appeared to slope up, and he could see the faint shimmer of light.

'This way,' he muttered to Celtegar, who nodded. Together, they began to inch their way through the chamber, between the kneeling dead. They drew closer to the enthroned figure. Its fleshless hands rested upon the knotted armrests of its seat. In its right fist, it clutched a silver dagger.

At the very foot of the throne, kneeling amongst the throng, was a tall, broad-shouldered figure swathed in a black cloak, and a silver aetherhawk embroidered across the back glittered in the dim light. His shoulder-length hair was black, smeared with mud and dead leaves.

'It's the Junica boy,' muttered Celtegar, starting forwards.

The man's head lolled at a strange angle, and his neck was coated in dried blood.

'He's dead,' said Callis. 'We must leave.'

'We need to retrieve the body,' said Celtegar. 'Here is the proof that the Lord Dezraed is innocent of any crime.'

'If we stay here, we'll end up as dead as this one. We have to move.'

The soldier ignored Callis and slowly reached out a hand towards the dead man's head. The wind whistling through the chamber grew louder. Something clattered behind Callis making him spin around, raising his sword. He saw nothing but the sea of smiling skeletons. He turned back, shaking his head.

The figure on the throne snapped its head up to look straight into Callis' eyes.

He cried out and staggered backwards. The figure rose, drifting up from its throne and into the air, throwing its silk-wrapped head backwards to reveal a gaunt and terrible face, a half-necrotised, feminine visage with eyes the colour of deep water. A crown of thorns rested upon the creature's brow.

'*Il thua ca na men,*' it hissed, in a voice like splintering glass. '*Worach mach bar!*'

And then the spirit opened its mouth and screamed.

The sound drove a knife through Callis' heart. He collapsed onto his back, mouth open in horrified agony as his chest tightened and his muscles tensed so hard that he felt the bones of his left hand pop from their sockets. He spat blood, and his vision swam with crimson. That awful sound. It was a keening wail of pure misery and hatred. His heart skipped a beat and he tried to breathe, but found he could not draw in the air. Panic gripped him and he almost blacked out.

Abruptly, the keening stopped. Callis lay there, unable to breathe, unable to move. Slowly, awfully, the spectre drifted above him, staring down at him with malice. The spirit bent down to embrace him, placing its ice-cold fingers upon each side of his head. He gazed into its night-black eyes and saw nothing but a deep and unquenchable hatred. His terror was absolute.

The spirit's mouth yawned open, exposing blackened teeth. It came closer and closer. He tried to scream but could not form the sound.

Suddenly, the wraith's eyes snapped off to the side, widening first in surprise, then in rage. A sword swept through the air. The spectre hissed as the silver metal swept through its incorporeal form. It spiralled away from the strike in a wisp of green-white light. Callis felt a hand grab him by the shirt and lift him upright. It was Toll. The witch hunter raised his pistol, the barrel a mere inch from Callis' temple. As they heard the first awful, discordant notes of the spirit's keening wail, Toll fired. The flash of the muzzle left a scar of light across Callis' vision, and he was thrown backwards.

This close to their ears, in the cramped confines of the low chamber, the effect of the gunshot was akin to a cannon discharging. Callis heard nothing but a painful, piercing ringing. He gasped for breath, blue in the face, and finally sucked in a ragged mouthful of air. He saw Toll, standing before the floating spectre, one hand clasped to the comet symbol around his neck, the other wielding his silver rapier. The spirit rushed forward, its ragged mouth torn open in a silent scream, its dagger seeking the witch hunter's neck. As the ghost swept in, Toll hurled himself to the side, slashing at the insubstantial body of the creature. The banshee screeched, then whirled and came for the witch hunter again. This time, Toll reached to his belt and hurled a handful of white powder. The spirit recoiled, mouth twisted in agony. It slashed its dagger across and Toll fell back, a spurt of blood erupting from his left shoulder. The witch hunter's sword spun away into the field of bones. The banshee swooped towards the prone man, hands reaching for Toll's throat.

Callis scrambled to his feet, almost tripping over the corpse of Captain Celtegar. The man lay staring sightlessly up at the ceiling, blood pouring from his eyes and mouth. Callis dived for Toll's fallen rapier and took it up in two hands. It was light and perfectly balanced – even holding it seemed to still his thudding heart. The banshee wrapped its bony fingers around Toll's throat. The witch hunter kicked, struggling and gasping for breath.

Callis leapt forwards and drove the tip of the rapier into the spirit's side. The banshee arched its back and began to jerk, sickly green light pouring from its mouth as it spasmed. It turned to look at Callis, and the pure, cold hatred on its withered face almost stole the strength from his sword arm. He drove the blade into that awful visage and right down the creature's throat.

The spirit rose into the air and, even through the ringing in his ears, Callis could hear its awful, high-pitched screech, this time a sound of pain. Then, in a blinding flash that hurled him from his feet, the banshee came apart, erupting into a thousand motes of baleful light. Around them, the bones of the kneeling dead crumbled into dust.

Callis collapsed to the ground, panting, exhausted.

It took several minutes for the ringing in their ears to subside. Even then, it did not completely disappear, nor did the pain fade away.

They lay there for a long while, neither speaking. Eventually, Toll hauled himself upright and extended a hand to Callis, dragging him to his feet. The ringing in his ears was agonising still, a piercing pain that jolted through his mind like a lance of fire.

'We should return the body,' said Toll at last, his voice muffled as if it were echoing over a great distance. 'That should spell the end of the Junica and Dezraed feud, at least until they find another reason to come after one another.'

'Doesn't feel like much of a victory,' sighed Callis.

'They rarely do,' said Toll. 'Leave the glorious victories to the soldiers, Callis. We deal in solutions.'

They took hold of the body of the lost Junica boy, and began to drag him towards the tunnel at the rear of the grotto. Callis glanced towards the fallen Captain Celtegar as they left.

'We'll send someone to claim his remains and those of his soldiers,' said Toll. 'And a priest to see these folk get a proper burial.'

It was a long, awkward struggle to haul the dead body up the sloping channel, but eventually they clawed their way out of a bank of close-packed soil and back into the gloom of the Ulwhyr. Callis sucked in a mouthful of air and slumped to his knees.

'I never thought I'd be glad to see this place,' he said.

'You slew the White Witch,' came a voice from behind them. They spun to see Ghedren leaning against the thick trunk of an age-old hardwood tree. He had his bow drawn and raised, aimed straight at Callis. Yet there was only defeat in his eyes, and slowly he lowered the weapon. 'You are not the first. Just because she is gone for now, it does not mean she will not return. Nor that our children are safe. Killing you now will change nothing.'

Callis charged at the man, grabbed him by the neck and hurled him to the floor. Ghedren did not struggle, even when he drew his sword and pressed it to the man's neck.

'You led me there to die,' Callis snarled.

It was a familiar sensation to Callis. The bitter sting of betrayal, and the sick surge of shame and rage as he realised how easily he had been manipulated. Was this how it always ended, he wondered? Trusting someone, only for them to drive their rapier into your unguarded spine.

'Do it,' said Ghedren. 'Kill me, if you must. I do not begrudge your fury. I am sorry that it came to this, but I had no choice. She always returns, Armand. She always takes her due. The curse cannot be broken.'

'The children?' said Toll.

Ghedren nodded, a single tear trickling down his face.

'When it began, I do not know,' he said. 'Before my father's time, and before his father's. A tithe borne of her hatred for the living and her sorrow for a life that was taken from her, some say. The firstborn child of the tribal elder must be delivered unto the White Witch, lest her wrath fall upon all others. Every generation, another sacrifice. By giving one life to sate her fury, the people may survive.'

'Lord Junica's son,' said Callis. 'You led him to that beast as well?'

'There are no longer any tribes, but the White Witch still demands her due. The Azyrites rule over us, and so they must pay the blood price. We tried to explain. We tried to tell them what lay within these woods, and the danger they courted by straying into the depths of the Ulwhyr in search of profit. The silksteel plantations, they strayed into her domain. We tried to warn them that her wrath would be terrible unless an offering was made, but they would not listen. They would not believe. And so, for the good of all, I acted.'

'The Dezraed soldiers,' said Toll. 'How did you dispose of them?'

'Their feud with Aldrec Junica was real enough,' said Ghedren. 'It was simple fortune that I was there that night, accompanying my lord's son to the house of his mistress. We passed the Dezraed soldiers on the road. They were drunk and eager for a fight. Aldrec was never one to back down. Insults were exchanged and swords drawn. He slew one of their number and the rest pursued him. I saw a chance and took advantage of it. I led him deep into the Ulwhyr. The Dezraed followed, and one by one they were claimed by the forest.'

Callis slammed the man's head against the ground. 'And what? Murdering us was an attempt to cover up your crimes?'

Ghedren closed his eyes.

'I did not wish to kill you,' he said, his voice soft and sad. 'But I knew you would never understand what is at stake. You would not stop until you found out the truth.'

'The witch is dead,' said Toll. 'If you had trusted us enough to tell us the truth, lives could have been saved. Including, perhaps, your own.'

'You ended nothing,' snapped Ghedren, shaking his head frantically. 'You think brave warriors have not fought the White Witch before? She is tied to this place, to the very spirit of this forest. No blade can lay her low. She has haunted these trails for centuries. Perhaps even longer. She will return, and her vengeance will be more terrible than ever. It is the children that will pay the price for your actions.' He sighed. 'I am ready to face my death. I know, in my heart, I did the only thing that I could have done. Do as you must.'

'My boy,' whispered Lord Junica. There were no tears in the old man's eyes, but his voice broke. Callis looked away. He'd hardly taken to the man, but he knew all too well how it felt to bury a loved one.

Aldrec Junica lay in repose upon the bed of a carriage, his eyes closed and his arms folded across his chest. They had taken him to the local mission – a humble yet sturdy chapel of Sigmar, attended to by an elderly, grey-bearded priest who had performed the rites and consecrated the body with blessed oils. Candles fluttered in the chill breeze. Callis gazed at the benevolent, stained-glass figures that looked down from the chapel's spire. Saints of old. Warriors and heroes, witnesses to this sad little ceremony.

'He was slain by a wraith,' said Toll. 'A banshee of the forest. The Dezraeds played no part in it. In fact, it was one of your own who led your son to his death.'

Two guards dragged Ghedren forward. Lord Junica stared at him, his mouth trembling.

'Ghedren?' he whispered. *'You?'*

The prisoner raised his head and met his master's gaze.

'I am sorry for your loss,' he said. 'But it was the only way. I tried to tell you. The White Witch required your son's life.'

Junica staggered over to the kneeling man and struck him across the face.

'Everything I have done for you,' his voice shook with rage. 'Everything you have been given, and you betray me? You murder my boy? My firstborn son?'

He struck Ghedren over and over, his blows growing weaker every time. Toll caught his arm as it fell again, and ushered the man away.

'Enough,' said the witch hunter. 'Come.'

He led Junica out through the doors of the chapel and into the central plaza of Marshpoint. The guards led the bound Ghedren after them. He met Callis' eyes as they passed, but looked quickly away. There was much that Callis wanted to ask the man, but the time for questions was long gone now. Ranks of Junica soldiers stood in an honour guard outside the Sigmarite chapel, banners fluttering from their raised spears. There were a few-score locals too, crowded around the edge of the square, no doubt wondering what all the fuss was about. Nearby, a small force of Dezraed soldiers mounted on horseback watched the ceremony with bored expressions on their faces.

'Well, a sad business. But over now, at least,' said Lord Dezraed, who sat upon the open step of his carriage, wrapped in thick furs to fend off the blustery wind. 'Only the matter of a formal apology remains.'

'What?' hissed Lord Junica, eyes widening in outrage.

'For your baseless insinuations,' Dezraed said, as if the answer was perfectly reasonable. 'Accusing me of this horrible crime, when it was your own man all along.'

'You'll get no apology from me,' snarled Junica. His hands curled into fists. 'Now leave. I have an execution to prepare.'

He turned to Ghedren.

'You'll suffer for what you've done,' he hissed. 'You'll beg for death, but I will not be so merciful as to grant it. I will break you down, inch by inch, and I will take pleasure in every moment.'

'These natives must be kept in line. I agree we must let them know we will not tolerate such betrayal,' said Dezraed, nodding his great slab of a head.

'I will ensure you live a long time before I am finished with you,' snarled Junica. Ghedren looked up and met his gaze.

'I believe,' Toll began, 'that it is the task of the Order of Azyr to administer justice here.'

He drew his pistol and fired a single shot. There was a burst of pink mist and Ghedren toppled like a sack of grain. He struck the cobbles hard, and a pool of blood flowed out from his broken body.

'No,' screamed Lord Junica. 'He was mine. *Mine!*'

'You will bury your dead son and return to your duties. The plantations shall reopen, and you will restart the patrols. Both of you.'

At this, he turned and jabbed a finger at Dezraed.

'I should have you both dragged back to Excelsis in chains,' spat Toll. 'You have displayed incompetence, foolishness and borderline treason. Your petty feud has not only endangered this town, but it has risked the lives of loyal soldiers by denying them the supplies they require. Now my patience with this farce is at an end. The fighting stops, or I swear I will make you both regret your actions for the rest of your miserable lives. Do you understand?'

'I am a son of a great house,' Lord Junica snarled. 'I have powerful friends in Azyrheim–'

'You are a minor scion of a great house,' said Toll. 'You are here only because the other lords of the Junica House have more pressing matters to attend to. You are replaceable, and you will be replaced if you cannot perform your duties. Do you understand? Both of you?'

There was a long silence.

'Say the words,' said Toll. 'Say that you understand.'

'I... understand,' said Lord Dezraed.

'I understand,' growled Lord Junica through gritted teeth, as if each word was a knife in his gut.

'You have a month to get your affairs in order,' said Toll.

With that, the witch hunter strode off, Callis rushing after him. They made their way to the southern gate, and the guards waved them through. Callis' heart sank a little as he saw the marsh striders looming above the jetty, chewing on clumps of moss. Their wizened guide was back, already stowing their saddlebags upon the beasts' flanks. Another few days of back-aching discomfort awaited. The joy of it.

'I can't deny that was satisfying,' said Callis.

'I'm glad you found it amusing,' said Toll. 'Perhaps we should discuss your own failures.'

Callis blinked. 'What?'

'Why do you think I brought you here?'

'Because it serves you well to have someone who can handle a sword guarding your back?'

'I can throw glimmerings into any tavern in Excelsis to strike someone who knows how to fight. I brought you because you're sharp, and you know when to draw steel and when not to. But that's only part of this trade, Armand. What allows us to survive is the ability to read people, to see beyond the obvious to the deeper truth. I brought you here to see if you were ready to do that. You failed.'

'You knew Ghedren was the traitor?'

'As you would have, had you not been blinded by your dislike of the Dezraed and the Junica. You let your own personal opinions cloud your judgement, and you gave your trust to a man who had not earned it.'

Callis had never truly felt at home in the Freeguilds, but at that moment, he recalled the simple clarity of his former life with a wistful fondness. Recently, it seemed that even when he was sure he was doing the right thing, it turned out otherwise.

Toll hooked one foot into the stirrups on the side of one of the marsh striders, and hauled himself onto its back. He squinted down at Callis, pulling his hat down low to block the hazy light that filtered through the grey clouds.

'This is a lesson, not an admonishment. We all make mistakes, but in this line of work they have a habit of getting you killed. God-King knows I've put my trust in the wrong person before – you know that better than anyone. Learn from this. Next time, I may not be there to haul you out of the flames. Now, come. We must be back in Excelsis within the next two days. We have new business to attend to.'

YOUR NEXT READ

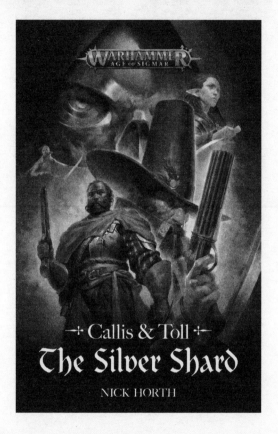

CALLIS AND TOLL: THE SILVER SHARD
by Nick Horth

Witch Hunter Hanniver Toll and his companion, former Freeguild soldier Armand Callis, brave the deadly seas and jungles of the Taloncoast as they try to prevent their nemesis, Ortam Vermyre, from seizing an artefact that can reshape reality.

HUNTING SHADOWS

Andy Clark

Introducing

NEAVE BLACKTALON

KNIGHT-ZEPHYROS

Neave Blacktalon prowled in the shadow of a towering throne, through the cool shade of the ancient monolith and back out into searing heat, then back through shadow again. The Knight-Zephyros' whirlwind axes were lashed firmly to her armoured back. They were ready to be drawn forth at a heartbeat's notice, and her hands itched to swing them.

'The sooner something gives me the excuse...' she murmured to herself, keen to be moving, hunting again.

She had her helm off, the better to stretch her superhuman senses out and taste her surroundings. Her hawk-like vision, her acute senses of taste, smell and hearing, her incredible sensitivity to vibrations in the air and soil – all were bent to absorbing every detail of this region of Aqshy. Known as the Brazen Plains, this region was as rugged as any she had seen in the Realm of Fire. Neave could tell that the cracked earth upon which she paced had been fertile until about three decades ago, when some catastrophe had scoured away the topsoil and salted what remained. She could sense the tectonic rumbling of a range of volcanoes two hundred miles due east, and tracked the passage of an arid dust-storm perhaps half that distance to her south.

Neave hunted alone. She had done so for four years and two Reforgings, through a dozen hunts for the most dangerous quarry Sigmar could assign her, and she had never once failed to bring down her mark. Of course, it was different when her Vanguard chamber, the Shadowhammers, marched out as one. Neave could strategise and lead as well as the next Stormcast officer, and she knew the value of the warriors she fought alongside. They were Hammers of Sigmar, first forged and still the mightiest of all Sigmar's Stormhosts. Yet even at such times, she was the one to hunt her mark amidst the mayhem of the battlefield. She was the one to launch herself upon them at the crucial moment, whirlwind axes singing a terrible dirge as they clove the air again and again.

Her comrades fought to give her the opening she required, but it was Neave who ended the hunt.

Alone.

'But not this time, apparently,' she said aloud, stopping for a moment in the throne's shadow and staring up at it. A remnant of some old and magnificent wonder from the Age of Myth, the marble throne jutted drunkenly from the bedrock, pitted and riven. 'This time I am to have aid in my hunt. Why?'

Neave resumed her pacing, flicking irritated glances westwards. She sensed her comrades drawing closer from that direction, travelling at speed. The missive had been brought to her by an aetherwing, one of the highly intelligent birds of prey that aided the Stormcast Vanguard. The creature had found her as she loped across the Brazen Plains, tracking her mark.

The bird had swept overhead and cried at her to halt in its eerie, singsong voice. Neave had done so, waiting while the aetherwing banked and settled in the skeletal branches of a nearby emberwood. She had listened with surprise, then annoyance, as the bird relayed Lord-Aquilor Danastus' orders to her.

She was to proceed ten miles east, whereupon she would find

the ancient throne. There she was to await rendezvous with Tarion Arlor, a Knight-Venator, and a band of Palladors who would aid her in her hunt. The aetherwing had no answers for her as to why. Blacktalon had merely been bid obey, and so, though she burned to be about the hunt, she had done so.

'They come, at last,' she breathed as she picked out a thin dust trail rising to the west. The unforgiving light of Hysh shone from on high, glinting off burnished sigmarite as her comrades approached. The Knight-Venator was aloft, soaring on crystalline wings with his bright-burning star-eagle wheeling around him impatiently. Below, a crackling surge of energy and whirling dust showed where the Palladors rode their wyndshifting steeds.

Neave jogged out from the throne's shadow, making sure she was clearly visible. The last thing she needed, she thought, was to catch an arrow in the throat from a surprised Knight-Venator. The star-eagle spotted her first and gave a piercing cry, swooping down towards her. The Stormcasts followed and, as the eagle shot overhead and alighted atop the throne's back, Tarion Arlor spread his crystalline pinions and dropped from the sky. He thumped down twenty feet from Neave, raising a cloud of dry dust, then stood tall and favoured her with an honest smile.

Arlor went helmless, like her, noted Neave. He was built big, even for a Stormcast, and she saw from the way he carried himself that his was a solid and resolute sort of strength. She noted the relaxed grip that he maintained upon his bow, the tribal tattoos worn proudly upon his face and the way his quick gaze assessed her as frankly as she assessed him.

The Palladors appeared a moment later, lightning crackling and winds howling as they transmuted from their ephemeral form to solid flesh and bone. There were four of them, Neave saw, armoured warriors wielding stormstrike javelins. They sat astride rangy gryph-chargers that clacked their beaks and clawed the ground with their fore-talons. She recognised the Palladors' leader, and a smile quirked one corner of her mouth.

'Kalparius Foerunner, well met,' said Neave. Typical protocol would be for her to greet the Knight-Venator first, as a warrior of equal rank to her own. Neave had little interest in such niceties, preferring to acknowledge those rare warriors that had fought alongside her and earned her respect.

'Lady Blacktalon,' said Kalparius and inclined his head in greeting. 'It has been some time.'

'Two years since we hunted the daemon Horticulous on the Thassenine Peninsula,' said Neave. 'Have you fared well?'

'Well enough, despite our enemies' efforts,' said Kalparius. From his body language Neave saw the Pallador was pleased she had remembered him by name, though too taciturn to let it show.

'Neave Blacktalon, it is good to meet you at last,' said Arlor.

'We have fought upon the same field more than once,' she said. 'Was that not sufficient?'

'We have fought against the same foes, at the same time, but we have never fought as comrades,' said Tarion. 'You are the most famed of the Shadowhammers, Lady Blacktalon. I look forward to hunting at your side.'

'The mark is away eastwards,' said Neave, masking her irritation at the talismanic way in which the rest of her Vanguard chamber regarded her. 'In waiting for your arrival I've allowed it to extend its lead. If it reaches the volcano fields, it will become far harder to track.'

Arlor's smile vanished. 'The township of Sigenvale lies in that direction. Our orders from the Lord-Aquilor are to call upon that settlement on our march and garner what information we can from the locals.'

'If they lie in the mark's path, there may not be any locals left to question,' said Neave. 'We can waste no more time. Come.'

Neave turned and set off eastwards. As a Knight-Zephyros, Neave's inhuman abilities extended into unnatural swiftness, agility and reactions. Now she put them to good use, accelerating away in a blur of motion that quickly left the shattered throne far behind.

Moments later, Tarion appeared low overhead, keeping pace with her upon his outspread wings. His star-eagle spiralled alongside him, and to Neave's right streaking shimmers of lightning and air marked where the Palladors, too, had matched her speed.

'You can keep up, at least,' called Neave. 'I can infer from this that your orders weren't to actively hamper my hunt?'

'There's more to our orders, Lady Blacktalon,' said Arlor, raising his voice to be heard over the swift whip of the wind. 'Did Sigmar tell you of your prey before you set out?'

'When Sigmar gives me a mark, it is like an epiphany,' Neave replied. 'I feel his power flow through me and I sense the prey, a notion of the direction in which it lies. At the same moment I may learn a little of my prey, of its transgressions against Sigmar and why it must be slain. I know of this thing that it is a horror hidden behind a pall of shifting darkness, and that it is ruinously power-ful. A trail of devastated settlements and slaughtered heroes lies in its wake. I know also that there must be more to this fiend than that, for Sigmar does not set me a mark unless they have earned his personal ire.'

'I don't know what this thing has done to anger Sigmar,' said Arlor. 'But I know that, since you began your hunt, word has reached us of the quarry wreaking further havoc. They say it tore down Fort Dunhaven and slaughtered the entire garrison, then ripped its way along the Wounded Road and left three trade caravans and all their guards in bloody tatters. Chaos warbands are stirring in the wilds at word of this thing's deeds. We have not long driven the enemy back from this region and, if this murderous shadow continues its rampage, it risks becoming a rallying point behind which a fresh Chaos onslaught may gather.'

'I saw the ruins of Dunhaven,' said Blacktalon. 'The carnage was hideous. I was not aware of the cult stirrings, but I can well believe it.'

Now the presence of these reinforcements began to make sense to her. There was grand strategy in play, and Lord-Aquilor

Danastus prized expediency above all else. Even the sanctity of Sigmar's hunt.

'The Lord-Aquilor feels that this matter must be concluded swiftly, and with no chance of the quarry's escape,' said Tarion. 'That is why we are not your only reinforcements.'

'Who else?' asked Neave.

'Beyond Sigenvale, upon the headland above Brimstone Lake, we are to rendezvous with the cogfort *Iron Despot*,' said Tarion. 'The mobile fortress and all of its garrison will be at our disposal.'

Neave almost missed a step as she shot an incredulous glance up at Tarion.

'A cogfort?' she asked. Sent marching out from several of the cities of Order since the end of the Realmgate Wars, the cogforts were the crowning achievement of the Ironweld engineers. Land battleships propelled on huge clockwork-and-girder spider's legs, each cogfort was a mobile armoured fortress with a garrison of well over a hundred human and duardin souls and bearing enough artillery and sorcerous ordnance to level a Dreadhold, or to break an enemy army in two. These vast war engines had not existed for long, but they had already garnered great favour amongst the forces of Order.

Lord-Aquilor Danastus was not given to grand gestures or strategic wastefulness. That he believed Neave's hunt required this level of support was sobering. She glanced again at Tarion and saw her own thoughts mirrored upon his face. Neave set her jaw and ran on, west across the plains towards Sigenvale.

Her ominous sense of the mark grew surer with every footfall.

Neave knew something was wrong even before Tarion's star-eagle, Krien, gave a piercing shriek.

They had travelled for a day and a night, and on into the next morning, relying upon the supreme fortitude that was Sigmar's gift to his Stormcast Eternals. The hunting party had spoken little. They were Hammers of Sigmar, grimly determined to see their duty done, and all their thought was bent towards its prosecution.

Now, though, as they wended their way along the tail end of the Wounded Road through a nameless gorge, they slowed.

'I smell smoke, and blood,' said Neave as they drew to a halt in the lee of a mound of boulders. The part of Neave's mind that was always alive to her surroundings noted that several of the boulders were actually graven chunks of statuary, piled in a tumble and eroded over long years.

'Krien sees something beyond the mouth of the gorge,' said Tarion, landing beside her. 'He's going to circle high and scout. If there are foes, they're less likely to notice him than they are me.'

Neave bristled at Tarion's presumption. 'Spread out and take positions here,' she said, continuing as though he hadn't spoken. 'Stay concealed and ready for trouble.'

Foerunner's Palladors obeyed, splitting two-and-two to either side of the gorge, dismounting their steeds and melting back into the hard shadows. Tarion went right without offering further comment, dropping in behind the remains of a stone pillar and nocking a crackling arrow to his bowstring. Neave remained behind the boulders, sinking into a crouch and watching where the road sloped steeply up to the mouth of the gorge.

The storm she had expected the day before had changed direction, moving ahead of them on capricious Aqshyan winds. Its trailing clouds streaked the sky, softening the hot glare of daylight to merely intense. Still, heat already baked off the rocks in waves. Dawn had come barely an hour before. Neave assumed that by midday this region would be viciously hot, and wondered how the peoples of Sigenvale coped.

If the peoples of Sigenvale remained at all, that was.

Nothing moved save a few skittering lizards, and minutes later Neave caught the speck in the sky that was Tarion's returning eagle. Krien flew on, over their heads as though nothing more than a wild bird of prey, then circled casually down before streaking back along the gorge to alight on Tarion's gauntlet.

Neave waited as Tarion leant his head close to his eagle's, locking eyes with the fierce bird. Its plumage glowed with celestial light, and it bobbed its head. Tarion murmured to Krien and the star-eagle made low, guttural sounds in return.

Tarion jogged across to join Neave.

'Krien sees no foes, just the destruction they have left,' he said. 'Our conversations are never what you would call precise, but from what I can garner Sigenvale lies in ruin. That said, just because Krien doesn't see enemies, doesn't mean they're not concealed and waiting in ambush.'

'The mark could be lurking here,' said Neave. 'But it's doubtful. It is as though my sense of it is dulled by something, some obfuscatory magic or charm. I felt the same at Dunhaven, a warding that interferes with my gifts. I think we should bypass the town and press on. I will know if we overtake the mark, allowing us to double back and surround it here. Otherwise, haste is our ally.'

She caught the subtle frown that Tarion suppressed before it could spread across his face, the slight tensing of his shoulders.

'You disagree?' asked Neave.

'Not that we should make haste,' said Tarion. 'But there may be survivors.'

'You believe they might tell us more of our quarry?' she asked.

This time, Tarion didn't try to hide his displeasure. 'I was more of a mind that if anyone lives in Sigenvale then it is our duty to aid them.'

Neave snorted. 'Danastus has sent me a bleeding heart, has he?'

'We are the protectors of all Sigmar's subjects,' said Tarion, surprised. 'We have a duty to these people. We were like them, once, and we would not have wished to be left in the dirt.'

Neave took a breath. Could the mark be here behind some warding veil, ready to spring its trap? She didn't think so, but the interference with her gifts was maddening. She felt Tarion awaiting her decision. Though they were technically of equal rank, *he* had joined *her* hunt, and so by the customs of the Shadowhammers she had primacy. She contemplated ordering that they press on.

'What if we stop to help a handful of wounded survivors, only for the mark to slaughter another town because we didn't catch it in time?' she asked him.

'What if we aid any survivors here, *and* then catch up to the quarry in time to stop it hurting anyone else?' he countered. 'We are Hammers of Sigmar. Anything short of excellence is failure.'

'Ah, not a bleeding heart then,' she said, concealing her irritation at Arlor's challenge behind a wry smile. 'An optimist. That's infinitely more dangerous. Very well, we perform a quick sweep through Sigenvale. Strictly reconnaissance and information gathering. If we locate any survivors, we do what we can for them, but we don't get bogged down. We move on before Hyshian apogee.'

'Understood,' said Tarion, shooting a quick hand-gesture to the Palladors, who remounted their steeds.

'Kalparius, you take the left flank, Arlor you're on the right,' said Neave. 'We're hardly inconspicuous, so move fast and keep your eyes open. We'll meet in the town square, or whatever they have that passes for one. If the mark *is* here, don't try to engage alone.' *That's my job*, she thought wryly, knowing she wouldn't follow her own advice.

'Krien will circle high and give warning if he sights any threat,' said Tarion.

So saying, he sent his star-eagle winging up into the shimmering blue. Neave, Tarion and the Palladors climbed the slope to the mouth of the gorge and then split, each following their allotted paths.

As Neave crested the rise, she saw the ruin of Sigenvale. The town lay in a bowl-shaped depression perhaps a mile across and followed a rough grid of streets that cross-hatched the dry bedrock. Neave estimated Sigenvale had consisted of around sixty structures, predominately long, low builds wrought from quarried stone blocks. Their outsides had been painted white to reflect the intense heat, and diaphanous silken awnings had been raised on wooden poles to shelter the streets and rooftops. Gardens had grown on each flat roof, irrigated via capacious moisture traps and sheltered by the silk screens fluttering above. A high wall of dressed and cut stone surrounded the entire settlement, guard-towers dotted along its length with the barrels of Freeguild cannons jutting from their embrasures.

Neave could picture the place as it had been, bustling with weathered frontier-folk and hard-eyed militia.

Now it was a gutted carcass.

An entire section of the wall had been torn down and its sundered stones scattered for dozens of yards. Flyblown corpses were strewn around the breach in such a state of dismemberment that Neave couldn't tell from this distance how many had actually been slain. The bodies continued inside the walls, as did the destruction. Buildings had been toppled as though by the strike of some huge weapon or the swipe of immense claws. Corpses lay in heaps, the blood slicks around them dry, brown and cracked by the heat.

'Sigmar's Hammer,' breathed Neave. She accelerated into a swift lope that brought her down the slope to the breach in the walls in under a minute. There she slid into the lee of the wall and paused. The ground was blackened, as though fire had washed across it. The edges of the breach were scorched and cracked by heat-damage, and the ghastly corpses of Sigenvale's defenders were little more than charred meat.

'Like Dunhaven,' muttered Neave. She crouched, slipping off both gauntlets and pressing her bare palms to the stone of the wall, and the bedrock of the ground.

Neave regulated her breathing, and allowed her heartbeat to settle into a slow, distant thump. She closed her eyes and focused her superhuman senses.

The stink of blood, gallons of it splattered on every surface and baked dry by the sun. Stone and soil mixed with spilt viscera and faeces. The stench of putrefaction setting in, hastened by the heat.

The sound of the wind through shattered stone and broken glass. A slow creak, something metal shifting in the hot plains' breeze. The flap of torn silk. The drone of insects.

Vibrations through the bedrock, her allies closing in around the settlement, skittering lizards, the distant tectonic stirring of restive volcanoes.

And something else, a shifting deeper within the ruins of Sigenvale. Something large and heavy, she thought, moving as softly as it could.

Neave replaced her gauntlets and unhitched her helm from her belt, lowering it into place. She unshipped her whirlwind axes and stalked through the rent in Sigenvale's walls. A street circled the town directly behind the wall, with other roadways radiating in from it like the spokes of a cart wheel, then winding crooked through the low buildings as they made for the town's heart.

Neave found more bodies scattered here. Many were torn to shreds. Others, she saw, were crushed into pulp, their bones shattered and their flesh burst like split gourds. Most had had their heads torn from their bodies, and Neave was disturbed to note that she couldn't see most of the missing crania.

The mark didn't discriminate. It had butchered soldiers and townsfolk alike with equal savagery.

The buildings had suffered as badly as the people. Neave saw walls staved in, doorways ripped from hinges and lying dozens of yards away, great gouges torn from them. A glance inside the nearest structure made her wish she hadn't. A larger humanoid figure huddled protectively over several smaller beings. That was all the identification she could make, as they had all been burned black, their remains melting to fuse with the wall and floor of the gutted structure.

Neave shuddered, then was still as she felt again the heavy shifting from deeper within the town. As the mournful wind moaned through the ruins, Neave felt her hackles rise. She turned away from what had once been a home and prowled deeper into the town.

A movement on high caught Neave's attention and her grip tensed on her axes, but it was nothing more than the hot winds stirring a tattered awning overhead. She felt the pressure wave that rolled ahead of Kalparius' Palladors, sweeping in through the town from her left. It was like a localised storm front, and Neave picked up her pace. Whatever she felt lurking here, it couldn't fail to note the Palladors' arrival.

Sure enough, she felt that heavy shifting again, more urgent now. Flies rose in buzzing clouds as Neave jogged down the street and rounded a corner past an overturned wagon. She groped for the sense of her mark, but the sensation was maddeningly vague.

'Could be here, could be miles away,' she muttered. 'Wherever it is, I'd dearly like to know how it's interfering with my gifts from Sigmar.'

Metal screeched against metal beyond the next row of buildings, and Neave envisioned wreckage being thrust aside. She sensed the Palladors closing in from the left and Tarion, an ozone tinge and crackle of power, moving in from the right. If the mark was here, she thought, it was just around the next corner and they were about to converge upon it as one.

Then Krien swooped low overhead and gave a piercing cry. That was enough to propel Neave into a full sprint, dust-devils whirling up in her wake as she accelerated down the body-strewn street. She wove around the tumbled wreckage of awning poles, flipped neatly over the flapping tangle of silk that clung to them, then slid to a halt behind the corner of the last building before the town square. She leaned around the shattered stonework, perceiving something huge moving at increasing speed across the open space. There came a snarl and – taking in a dark, scaly hide and long, hooked claws – Neave accelerated into a charge.

The beast must have weighed several tons and was all muscle and belligerence. Emerging from a ruined storehouse on the south side of the square, it hulked like a Stardrake at the shoulders, while its lantern-jawed head was set low between a quartet of powerful fore-limbs. Its cluster of reptilian eyes swivelled in Neave's direction and a hook-clawed arm swept out.

Neave was faster. Sliding under the blow at the speed of a

galloping gryph-charger, she scissored her axe-blades through the monster's wrist and neatly severed its hand. Neave rose from the slide and ducked under the huge creature's jaw, spinning as she went and hacking both blades up through its throat.

Black gore spurted, and Neave slid free on her back, using the last of her momentum to perform a neat backward roll and coming back to her feet facing the beast.

It staggered, gore spilling from the ragged wound in its neck. The beast let out a gurgling roar, more blood spraying from its crocodilian maw, and doggedly tried to pursue her. Krien streaked in front of the monster's eyes, causing it to rear back and, as it did, a trio of Tarion's crackling arrows whistled down to thump into its chest.

The monster gave a snarl as lightning tore through its body, then stumbled as it tried to wheel again. At that moment the Palladors swept into the square from the opposite end and, not even slowing, bore down upon the creature with their javelins lowered like lances.

Foerunner and his cavalrymen hit the beast like a hammer blow. It swung two of its taloned limbs to ward them off, but Neave watched, impressed, as one rider leaned back in his saddle to evade the blow while the other leapt his steed clear over the hurtling limb.

The monster staggered, bewildered, bleeding in rivers, then sagged. Neave hefted one of her axes and hurled it. The weapon spun end over end and crunched home between the monster's eyes. It gave a last burbling groan, then toppled onto its face.

Neave stood for a moment, head cocked to one side, waiting.

'It was not the mark,' she said, unsurprised as she felt her dim sense of her prey remain unchanged.

'That much was obvious,' said Tarion, landing nearby. 'This thing didn't cause all that death and devastation.'

'It didn't unleash any sort of fire, either,' said Neave. 'Whatever we're hunting, he, she or it has burned half this town black.'

'Corpsejaw,' said Foerunner, cantering back around on his gryph-charger. The half-avian steed clacked its beak in disgust. 'They're a local scavenger species. Saw them during the purge of the Chamrian Hills. Our friend here didn't do this, he just moved in and started scavenging once the dust settled.'

'I think he's the only thing that was left alive here,' said Neave. 'We move on.'

Arlor nodded grimly. 'This was wasted time,' he said. 'My apologies, Lady Blacktalon.'

'Not necessary,' replied Neave. 'For one thing, the devastation here is more extreme than in Dunhaven. That was bad, but there's more fury now, more ferocity.'

'As though the mark is gathering pace,' mused Tarion.

'As though the more carnage it wreaks, the more dangerous it becomes,' said Neave.

'Do you believe that we seek an it, not a he or she?' asked Foerunner. His Palladors had gathered behind him and watched the approaches to the square intently.

'If the mark is a being like you or I, then either they are employing some manner of weapons I cannot fathom, or ride upon some dire beast,' said Neave. 'No warrior's blade caused the massive wounds and destruction we've seen here. The ground is hard, but rock and stone both bear the imprint of tracks, something with long talons and the weight to drive them deep.'

'The entire town looks as though a feral gryph-hound got loose in a pyklin enclosure,' said Tarion. 'This was a rampage, a slaughter wrought by something that attacked everything that moved as though on instinct.'

'Murderously thorough, though,' said Neave. 'And it must have happened shockingly fast. I haven't seen a single body beyond the walls, have you?'

'No one had time to flee,' said Foerunner.

'The mark can obfuscate my sense of its presence, is possessed of murderous strength and unholy weapons, and we must assume that it can move every bit as fast as we can. I believe that even as we hunt this thing, we risk being hunted in turn.'

A moment of silence settled across the Stormcast Eternals as they considered this. The wind sighed miserably through the baking-hot streets. Flies danced. Silk flapped from broken poles like grave markers.

Then, far to the west, something rose into the cloud-scattered sky and detonated in a crimson starburst. Another projectile sailed up after it, spreading another slowly fading bloom of red light and smoke against the tattered storm clouds. As the sky-fires burst, Neave felt dread settle like a lead weight on her heart. She knew what they meant even before Tarion spoke.

'Flares, from *Iron Despot*,' said Tarion.

'Signalling for aid.'

'No. Combat,' said Tarion. 'They've engaged.'

Dunhaven and Sigenvale lay butchered already. Neave wondered if the same was about to happen again.

'Move,' said Neave, determined to ensure that it did not, and broke into a run. Her comrades followed. The Hammers of Sigmar left the corpse of Sigenvale behind them to rot in the fierce heat.

The Stormcasts had been on the move for almost four hours, maintaining a swift pace as the baked earth and tough grass of the plains transformed into cracked stone, basalt outcroppings and sheer-sided chasms. Now, with the storm clouds thickening above and a misty, blood-warm rain falling, they were nearing Brimstone Lake. Neave could see the land rising like a clenched fist before them, forming a rocky headland that jutted out over the churning waters. Fumes rose from the vast lake, and an acrid stench hung on the air.

Beyond, the rising mass of the nearest volcano was now clearly visible, only a few miles distant, black fumes boiling up from its caldera to mingle with the storm clouds. The rest of the chain marched away westwards at its back, and Neave sincerely hoped that they caught up to their quarry before it could vanish into that savage region.

'More flares,' called Tarion from above.

'I see them,' replied Neave. 'White smoke.'

Tarion's face hardened. 'They have ceased combat. According to Danastus' briefing, white smoke is their appeal for aid. This is their last resort.'

'What manner of thing could threaten a cogfort single-handed?' wondered Neave aloud.

'The flares rose from the southern bank of the lake, near the foot of the volcano,' called Tarion. 'The hunt moves ahead.'

'And we must yet again dash to catch up,' snarled Neave, frustrated. 'We halted at Sigenvale to offer mercy to ghosts while the living go to their graves ahead of us. If *Iron Despot* falls, Arlor, it will be because you slowed my hunt.'

'Lady Blacktalon, I–'

'Save your words, only actions matter now,' snapped Neave, increasing her pace and leaving Tarion to flounder in her wake.

They passed the headland, and Neave saw the deep tread-marks of the cogfort sunk into the bedrock. She could see its trail where it had stomped down from the north, the deeper indentations where it had settled its weight and awaited their arrival, and the more ragged gouges in the stone that suggested acceleration as it had moved away south and west along the bank of the lake. It would hardly take skill like Neave's to follow such a track. She saw, as well, a few telltale talon marks like those she had spotted at Dunhaven and in Sigenvale.

'It looks as though they gave chase,' called Neave. She caught the sound of distant booms, rolling through the misty veil.

'Cannon fire,' said Foerunner.

The sounds of combat grew closer as they dashed along the edge of the lake. Neave's frustration redoubled as whatever was occurring remained veiled from her sight. Down here by the lake, a mixture of reeking mist, sheets of rain and the sulphurous fumes rolling from the volcano conspired to drop visibility to a few dozen feet. The Stormcasts were forced to slow lest they run headlong into sudden danger.

Tarion dropped low so that he flew just above his comrades'

heads, Krien tucking in close on his wing. The Palladors spread out to either flank, remaining wholly corporeal.

Neave motioned for silence. The mark must surely be close, and she could feel heavy vibrations rolling through the bedrock. A mighty flash lit the haze ahead. The sound of an explosion rolled over them, muffled by the mists and rain, and the ground convulsed.

Neave and her comrades pressed on, towards whatever catastrophe had occurred. Neave thought she knew, but she wanted to confirm it with her own eyes.

The mists proved deceptive, warping distances. Tension built in Neave's chest as she and her companions pressed forward. Her nerves sang with a sense of peril. Lightning crackled through the clouds above and reached down to form phantom trees of light that stretched between the lake and the skies. Thunder rumbled, and Neave cursed the sound as its echoes rolled over her. Between the increasing wrath of the storm, the throaty rumble of the volcano looming above them and the muffling veils of vapour, even her senses were of little more use than those of a mortal hunter.

It was like being smothered. Was this how mortals lived all the time, so unsure of what lay around the next corner, behind the next scad of cloud or veil of smoke? Was this how *she* had once lived?

Then, quite suddenly, the mist and fumes parted.

'By Sigendil's light,' gasped one of the Palladors.

Neave's reprimand to him for breaking the silence died on her lips as she absorbed the sight that lay before her. She had seen a cogfort once before, stalking towards an unknown horizon. She knew how this one should look: an ironclad fortress with thick, armoured towers rising from within a central wall. Cannons and fire-throwers jutting from hatches all over its superstructure. Firesteps thronging with Freeguild soldiery, dark glass filling the portholes of the command bridge high above, proud banners and thaumatransferric veins rising above its conical slate roof. And the legs – the eight huge, articulated cogwork legs with their steam conduits and hydraulic supports and complex webs of cables that kept them rising and falling with the same fastidious gait as some immense spider.

Iron Despot barely resembled that proud memory. The machine lay on its side at the rocky base of the volcano, three legs torn away entirely. The rest tangled around it, so much oil-slicked wreckage. The fall had sundered the fortress, splitting its flanks like overripe fruit and allowing segments of pipework, decking and mechanical innards to spill out. The incongruous details were the most horrifying: half a wooden stairway jutting proud here, a bent and buckled mess-table protruding there with scraps of food still smeared across its surface. Neave saw talon-marks in the metal of the cogfort's shattered walls, and here and there a gouge in the hard stone upon which it lay.

Corpses lay around the cogfort where the fall had hurled them. Others sprawled amidst the ruins, just as bloodied, just as dead.

Neave cast a glance around, straining her senses to their limits to detect any threat.

Tarion landed beside her and placed a gauntlet upon her shoulder. Neave shrugged his hand away angrily and gestured at the carnage that surrounded them. She stared hard into his eyes and saw that he caught her meaning.

This is your fault, her stare said. Your insistence on delay left us too late to intervene. She saw pain in his eyes and realised that Arlor already knew and owned that guilt. He bowed his head slightly in acknowledgement, then gestured here and there amidst the ruin. Neave realised he was drawing her attention to the flames that crawled across the wreckage. They were white-hot, sizzling with an unnatural intensity and chewing away at metal and rock as happily as flesh and wood.

The fires still burned, she realised. The mark could not long have lit them.

She held up a clenched fist, ordering her comrades to halt and maintain their position in the shadow of the fort. They obeyed, drawing into a tight armoured circle and keeping watch into the mists.

Neave surveyed the fallen fort a second time, forcing herself to start again, dispassionate, taking in every detail. The shores of the lake lay just yards away, and she realised from the angle at which the cogfort lay, and the tracks still visible around its shattered bulk, that it had been backing towards the water when it fell. The lake's muddy banks were churned into an oil-streaked stew where one of the cogfort's legs must have taken a swiping step and slipped over the mud. It looked as though they were trying to back into the lake itself.

A desperate plan.

Neave spotted one of the missing cogwork legs, lying some distance away. She took note of the deep gouges in the leg, the snapped cables and twisted stubs of metal. It had been ripped clean off.

The fort's upper towers had broken across the rocky slopes of the volcano itself, several landing perilously close to rents that split its dark skin, glowing with hellish light and belching thick clouds of smoke. The heat from the rents had melted the wrecked superstructure and burned several human corpses that had been flung from the highest spires.

Tarion leaned close to Neave and murmured in her ear. 'We should give chase, before the mark gets away again. I could not bear the weight of further deaths upon my conscience. Have you a sense of its location?'

Neave closed her eyes and reached out. She ignored the crackle of flames and the groan of stressed metal, the stench of sulphur and brimstone that billowed from the bubbling lake and from the slopes above. Lightning exploded above them with a volley of dry cracks. Thunder bellowed. Neave barely heard them, focusing her attention upon the mark.

'Not everyone on that cogfort can have died in the crash,' she whispered to Tarion. 'The mark has been thorough, again. It left no man nor duardin alive. Even if it is large and powerful enough to massacre settlements and drag down a cogfort, that must have taken it some time. It can't have gone... far...'

Neave's eyes snapped open. Every fibre of her being burned with an adrenal surge of warning. She looked again at the muddy shore of the lake, where the cogfort's rear limb had taken a single, swiping step. Where it had reduced the ground to a mangled mess in which no tracks would show.

Where the shallows boiled like a cauldron.

'It's still here,' she hissed.

The surface of the lake exploded as something vast erupted from its depths.

The thing was as much forged brass and black iron as it was wet muscle, taut sinew and exposed bone spars. It was massive, taller at the shoulder than a Dreadfort wall and built so heavily that it was as though a fortress had mutated and come to predatory life. Neave caught sight of blazing furnace eyes and razor-sharp brass teeth in its hound-like head, a massive collar of spiked brass that encircled its neck, talons the size of battering rams and an armoured body into whose flanks were cut deep rents. Furious fiery light shone from those rib-like gaps, and as the abomination burst from the sizzling waters, black fumes belched out of them as though from the stacks of an Ironweld factory.

Despite its immense size and heavy metallic body, the beast moved blisteringly fast. It covered the ground to the Stormcasts before they had so much as drawn breath and swept a massive foreclaw through their ranks.

Neave leapt straight up, backflipping over the brass claw as it swept below her like some baroque siege engine. Tarion shot past her, taking to the air like a streak of lightning. The Palladors were less fortunate, two of their number failing to wyndshift away in time. Blood sprayed. Torn flesh rained down as the monster's talon obliterated its victims, sending the sundered corpses of two gryph-chargers bouncing and rolling to a stop amidst the wreckage of the fort.

Two bolts of lightning arced skyward, Stormcast souls rushing back to the heavens to be Reforged.

Neave landed with catlike grace and found herself immediately on the defensive. No time to mourn the fallen, but time enough to let their deaths stoke her anger, adrenaline and speed. She leapt back from another hurtling claw swipe, then rolled aside as the monster's jaws clanged shut where she had lain a split second before. Neave managed to lash out with her whirlwind axes as she rolled back to her feet; sparks rained down as they clanged from the abomination's metal skull to no appreciable effect.

'It's some form of accursed daemon engine,' barked Tarion.

'It's immense,' cried Neave, weaving aside again as the monster slammed a claw into the ground with enough force to crack the bedrock. 'Like a Khornate Flesh Hound grew to the size of a living castle! How did such a thing come to be?' Sulphurous waters were still boiling away from its slick muscle-and-metal body, creating a choking cloud of steam that mingled with the black smoke churning from the thing's insides.

A volley of crackling bolts whipped in from the side, peppering the armour around one of the daemon hound's eyes and causing it to recoil with a growl like a furnace door being thrown open. Neave didn't waste time thanking Kalparius and his remaining Pallador – she just took the momentary opening and accelerated away from the beast.

Crackling arrows streaked down as Tarion drew and loosed, drew and loosed far faster than any mortal warrior could have. The lightning-wreathed shafts impacted along the beast's spine in blasts of white light. Neave cursed as she realised that, again, the attacks had done as good as nothing. Her eyes danced across its mountainous form as it moved, seeking weaknesses and vulnerabilities. Its armour plates looked utterly impervious to anything short of sustained cannon fire, and clearly even that hadn't availed the cogfort. Perhaps the wet muscle and sinew that entwined its limbs, she thought.

Then the engine opened its jaws wide with a terrible shriek of hinging metal. Phosphorous flame leapt within its gullet.

'Arlor, get clear,' yelled Neave, in the instant before a spear of white-hot flame roared up from the daemon hound's throat. Tarion had seen the threat coming, yet the engine moved with the speed of an onrushing avalanche. He barely managed to weave aside, crying out in pain as searing flames licked up the right side of his body. Neave saw the Knight-Venator's armour catch light, and his crystal wing-veins crack in the intense heat. What kind of hellish fires could catch in forged sigmarite? thought Neave with growing horror. Surely this gigantic abomination must have been loosed from Khorne's own daemonic forges, to possess such hideous gifts.

Tarion spiralled away, smoke boiling from his scorched form, and Krien gave a desolate cry.

'Foerunner, attract the abomination's attention,' shouted Neave. 'I'm going to try for its living flesh.'

Kalparius shot Neave a salute and spurred his gryph-charger, gesturing for his remaining warrior to follow his lead. The two Palladors rode hard, straight at the daemon hound, and lightning cracked overhead as they unleashed another salvo of boltstorm shots. Crackling blasts burst across the monster's face and it gave a howl of fury before loosing another pyrotechnic blast from its maw. The Palladors wyndshifted out of the path of the searing beam, and it bored a blazing rent in the flank of the fallen cogfort.

Blacktalon seized upon the hound's moment of distraction. She ran up a sloping armour plate that had broken away from the cog-fort's superstructure and leapt, axes raised high, sailing through the air and slamming down on the monster's back. Neave buried both axes into a huge clump of flensed muscle that bunched and corded along the hound's brass spine. Molten ichor sprayed, spattering her armour and faceplate and hissing as it warped the sigmarite.

Neave had an instant to be grateful she was wearing her helm, before the daemon hound bucked underneath her. She had half hoped its fury might make it insensible to her presence. Instead, the beast twisted and snarled, shaking its massive body left and right and almost dislodging her. Worse, Neave could feel furnace heat rapidly building, radiating up from the monster's metal skin and through the soles of her armoured feet.

She couldn't run with burned feet, she thought, and she couldn't fight if she couldn't run. This close, she could hear the daemon engine's mechanical innards thundering away like some pandemoniac factory. She was surrounded by black smoke that choked her lungs and fouled her vision. She realised that, for all her speed and huntress' instincts, she didn't even know where to begin to try to bring down a monster so vast and strange.

Knowing she couldn't remain still any longer, Neave ripped her axes free and began to run along the creature's back towards the nape of its neck. She recalled seeing a great mass of muscle and sinew bunched between its shoulder blades. Perhaps, if she broke enough of those connections, she could behead the beast? For a second, she questioned what would happen if she couldn't, but then crushed the notion down. Panic lay that way, and the realisation that if this thing slew them all, it would have free rein to continue its slaughter.

How many more lives would be lost if they failed here? How much more death would be laid upon their shoulders?

Neave made it ten paces before the daemon hound bucked again, footfalls pounding the bedrock as it turned a maddened half-circle trying to dislodge her. Neave's balance and agility were superb, and she rode out the violent motion, hacking her axes into every visible fleshy substructure as she passed. Boiling ichor spurted in her wake, but the wounds seemed only to increase her mark's fury.

The hillock of wet muscle rose ahead of Neave and she saw a webwork of capillary-strung tendons stretched like hawser cables between it and the brazen collar that encircled the beast's neck. Pivoting on the balls of her feet to avoid being thrown loose again, Neave spun and swung her axes in a vicious arc. Their blades met the nearest tendon and rebounded as though they had struck a castle wall. Neave felt a moment's horror. She had never seen anything resist her blades so completely.

The daemon hound chose that moment to wrench itself sideways, slamming bodily against the crumpled cogfort. Already off balance from the unexpected deflection of her axes, Neave was thrown from her feet and felt a sickening lurch in the pit of her stomach as she plunged over the hound's shoulder and down to hit the ground at its feet.

Neave managed to control her fall, but only barely. She landed on one shoulder and rolled, hissing at the jarring pain that shot through her arm and down her back. She turned the roll into a rising start and began to run, but the hound slammed a claw down and managed to clip Neave's leg. There came a tearing of metal, a crunch of bone and a vicious stab of agony, and Neave crashed down on her face. Fury and despair warred within her at the thought that she was about to be slain, that this abomination was about to best her and be freed to continue its slaughter. She was about to fail Sigmar for the first time, and the thought appalled her.

Neave rolled onto her back in time to see Kalparius and his surviving Pallador riding hard at the hound, shooting as they went.

They were trying to buy her time, Neave knew. But the blow to the head had stunned her momentarily, and with her shattered leg, she simply couldn't move fast enough.

Tons of metal and roaring fire rushed overhead as the beast lunged, bounding right over Neave to swat the remaining Pallador through the air. His body hit the waters of the lake and sank like a stone, before his soul flashed up from the surface in a geyser of steam.

Kalparius was, if anything, less fortunate still. He hauled his gryph-charger into a hard turn, trying to weave between the hound's legs to reach Neave. Impossibly fast, the hound's muzzle darted down and its jaws clanged shut, taking Foerunner's head from his shoulders with shocking precision. A second bite a moment later sliced the Pallador's steed clean in half, the gryph-charger shrieking its last even as Kalparius' soul shot heavenwards.

'We've failed,' breathed Neave through a haze of pain. 'We've failed. Damn this monster.'

The thought was utterly unacceptable and, spurred by a fresh burst of rage and determination, Neave hauled herself into a crouch. She looked up at the underbelly of the beast, seeing more ironwork, bone, muscle and brass. Circular metal hatches were built into the creature's torso, all but obscured by black smoke and bound shut with brass chains. They had unholy runic sigils etched into them, Chaos designs that stung Neave's eyes worse than the smoke.

Were the hatches there to allow access? They couldn't be. Not if they were chained from the outside. They must be hatches behind which something was bound, then.

She had no more time for thought, as the daemon hound circled with pounding footfalls and prepared to attack her again. Neave forced herself to stand, pain screaming through the broken bones in her right leg, and held her axes down and out to either side, blades glinting. The monster's face drew level with her own, furnace eyes burning, hot breath gusting around her. Neave stared back, unflinching. She felt disgust and defiance as she locked eyes with the immense beast, and sudden scorn. It was so powerful, so unbelievably mighty, yet it did naught but destroy like a mindless beast. If this was all that the Dark Gods had to offer, they might well wreak a trail of destruction across the realms, but no amount of unholy strength would prevent Sigmar's armies from winning this war in the end.

'You can kill me now,' she said. 'But I will come for you again and again, and in the end it is you who will fall.'

She'd died before.

She knew its wrench.

She prepared herself for the wash of pain.

A storm of arrows whistled down and peppered the monster's muzzle. Explosions of lightning drove its head aside, before a shrieking crimson comet shot down and raked glowing talons across the beast's left eye.

The daemon hound reared back with a roar so loud that Neave

could feel her ears bleeding. Beyond the beast, perched upon a wrecked spar of cogfort battlement, she saw Tarion beckoning her. He pointed at the shadowy rent in the fort's flank below his position.

Neave summoned as much speed as she could on her mangled leg. Every footfall was blinding pain, but she kept moving, and as the hound came after her Tarion drove it back with another volley of shots to the face. Krien spiralled past, causing the maddened daemon hound to lash out with a massive claw. The star-eagle spiralled up and away, giving a mocking shriek as he shot towards the storm clouds above.

Neave lunged up a metal slope, footfalls clanging, and threw herself into the darkened interior of the fort. She heard a rush of metal and a thunderous impact behind her and was spilled from her feet as the fortress shook. Looking back, Neave saw one blazing eye staring at her through the rent in the fort's flank, then it was replaced by the hound's yawning jaws.

'Oh no, no, no, no...' gasped Neave as she dragged herself along the wall of the tilted corridor and fell desperately through a buckled doorway that yawned surreally in the 'floor'. Neave slid out of control down a ruptured deck and crunched into the heap of wreckage that had piled up against the chamber's far wall. She cried out in pain as the bones in her leg ground together.

Then came fire, filling the doorway with white-hot light. Neave felt the heat from the blast, even thirty feet down, and saw the metal of the door frame glow and begin to drip molten gobbets.

Then the fire was gone.

There came another thunderous clang, then another. A metallic snarl carried through the fort's hull, and the structure shook around Neave as it suffered another thunderous blow.

'For once, I am the cornered prey,' she murmured. Neave heard the tortured shriek of metal, then another blow shook the chamber. Junked furniture and discarded weapons shifted beneath her.

'Neave!' She heard Tarion's voice, distant, echoing through the cogfort. His cry was answered by a muffled howl from outside and another ripping sound.

Concentrating on the echoes of Tarion's voice, Neave hauled herself across the drift of wreckage and through another door that had burst open in the chamber's sloping wall. She found herself in a shrine to Sigmar, with a high ceiling and an altar that had fallen and smashed against a pane of stained glass. Spars of rock jutted up through the shattered window, and bits of broken glass twinkled, their representation of Sigmar fractured into a hundred pieces.

'Neave, where are you?' She heard Tarion again, closer, his voice tight with controlled panic. She began to scale the pews that had been bolted to the metal floor. Neave found bodies amongst the pews, broken and dangling where they had knelt in prayer before the end. A couple of soldiers, what looked like an alchemist of some sort, and a figure she was relatively sure was the fort's cook.

Neave climbed on and, grabbing both sides of the doorframe in what was now the ceiling, she hauled herself up into another skewed corridor. There were more bodies here, Freeguild soldiers lying with their necks broken and bodies mangled by the fall. Fire had swept along it, and Neave saw that it had issued from the fort's secondary engine room – a metal plate was bolted to the wall, its blackened lettering still just visible in the half-light that fell through small rents in the hull. A duardin lay beneath it, his Ironweld garb a blackened and bloody mess.

The fort shook again, and a howl of rage echoed from outside. Something heavy thumped down at the other end of the corridor, and Neave spun, axes raised.

'Tarion,' she said quietly, her voice tinged with relief. The Knight-Venator hastened to meet her, his cracked wings tucked close. She could see from the way he moved that he was in significant pain. His armour was fused and melted down one side.

'Your leg,' he said.

'Broken,' she replied. 'Nothing I cannot ignore until the job's done. You look worse.'

'I am not dead yet,' said Tarion, and to Neave's surprise he shot her a lopsided grin. She felt herself respond in kind.

'We soon will be if we cannot come up with a way to defeat this beast,' said Neave, keeping her voice pitched low. There came another rending clang from somewhere close, shaking the corridor and causing oil to spatter down through rents in the wall.

'Its hide seems proof against our weapons,' said Tarion. 'Direct assault isn't going to work, not with two of us. It'd take an army to bring that thing down.'

'I could distract it and allow you to make a break for freedom, but it wouldn't do us any good,' said Neave. 'That damned collar around its neck, it's thick with Khornate runes. Wards against magic of every sort. I would bet my blades that's what's been interfering with my gifts, obscuring the beast from my sight. If we lost it here, by the time we tracked it down again it could have an army rallied behind it.'

'I was not for a moment suggesting that one of us flee for aid,' said Tarion, and Neave realised he was affronted. 'I meant only that we need to come up with another way to defeat the beast.'

The cogfort shook violently, and there came a tearing of metal. Daylight spilled into the corridor as the section housing the secondary boiler room tore backwards and away. The duardin corpse slithered bonelessly out of the hole, and the daemon hound's furious visage filled the ragged gap in the corridor's end.

'Move,' urged Neave, and both she and Tarion dashed along the corridor as fast as they could go. Neave felt pain ripping up through her mangled leg. She gritted her teeth and ignored the trail of blood she left behind her as she limped along. Again, the fort shook, and another chunk of superstructure tore away behind them as massive claws ripped through it.

'We can't hurt it with our weapons, we don't have the numbers to overwhelm it,' said Tarion as they ducked through a hatchway into what looked like a destroyed map room. 'What else do we have to work with? Did you see any weaknesses, any hints at how to bring it down?'

'The tendons around its neck looked promising, but they're tougher than forged steel,' said Neave as they lurched across the shaking chamber and scrambled up a heap of wreckage and corpses to reach the hatch above. 'Its underbelly. There are hatches in its underbelly, chained shut,' she exclaimed.

'What if, even after we break the chains, whatever is in there does not care to vacate?' asked Tarion. 'That's a powerful second skin it's wearing. Would you give up armour that destructive?'

They reached the top of the stairwell only to find their passage blocked by an iron hatch. It had crumpled in its frame, something huge and heavy buckling the wall beside it. Tarion and Neave gripped it and tried between them to wrench it open. The hatch started to give with a groan, but wouldn't shift any further.

'Damnation,' spat Neave, thumping one fist against the wall. Behind them, they heard the shriek and groan of metal tearing. Smoke billowed up through the stairwell.

'It's going to flush us, then burn us,' said Tarion.

Neave snapped her head around to stare at him. 'Tarion, that's brilliant,' she said.

'It... what?' he replied.

'I'll lead the mark,' she said. 'You get airborne, shadow us, and when I signal–'

The wall of the corridor tore inwards, huge metal talons raking through it as easily as though it were paper. Neave ducked, snarling in pain as a talon-tip raked a furrow through the back-plate of her armour. Tarion gave a yell of alarm as he was caught up in the mangled mass of metal and wood and ripped out of the cogfort's corridor.

'Tarion!' yelled Neave, scrambling up through the rent, grabbing buckled pipes and severed girders as she dragged herself onto the cogfort's outer skin. She saw the hound had clambered halfway up onto the wreck. It had Tarion trapped within its curled talons and was raising him towards its enormous maw.

Neave hobbled as fast as she could towards the beast, mind racing as she tried to figure out a way to get Tarion free. She saw a sudden crackle of light, and then the monster's talons were blown open in a thunderous flash. Tarion was flung away, plunging off the side of the cogfort and vanishing from sight.

Neave had no time to work out what had happened, and no choice but to hope that her comrade was alive, and that he had understood and was capable of following her plan.

She would have to trust Tarion. The thought made her uncomfortable, but at this point it was their best chance.

Neave's darting eyes quickly picked out the best route off the side of the cogfort. She moved as fast as she could, ignoring the jarring pain that shot up her leg, clambering and slithering between the buckled plates and jutting spars before lurching along the inside of the fort's lower rampart and dropping ten feet to the bedrock. A gasp of pain escaped her, but Neave kept moving.

'Come on, you mindless abomination,' she muttered as she set off up the volcano's slope. 'You've hunted down every living thing that's crossed your path since I've been on your trail. Don't tell me you're getting lazy now.'

Neave was rewarded by a tectonic thump behind her, the impact so hard it made dirt jump from the bedrock and almost spilled her from her feet. She didn't need to look back to know that the beast was chasing her; the ominous sound of rumbling furnaces, screeching metal and iron clangour told her everything she needed to know.

Neave ran as fast as she could, accelerating as swiftly as she dared on her shattered leg. She controlled the tight fear that tried to constrict her chest and force its way up her throat, the tinge of dread between her shoulder blades where she expected the monster's claws to smash down any second. She determinedly shut out the agony that shot up through her thigh, into her hip, then up into her spine, growing worse with every footfall. She knew by the end of this mission the limb was going to be so badly ruined that they'd be forced to reforge her anyway, even if she survived.

Neave kept running, right through pain that would have rendered a mortal warrior unconscious. She climbed the slope, up through veils of smoke and fume, and as she went a fiery glow spread before her. She was closing in on the rents she had seen in the volcano's flanks. She just had to hope that her mark didn't catch her before–

A shriek of warning sounded from above, and Neave threw herself sideways with a silent surge of gratitude to Krien. She rolled behind a basalt outcrop just as white-hot fire billowed around her. It blazed furiously, and Neave swore as she felt her armour heating up.

The fiery blast swept away the vapours. Just upslope from her position, Neave saw the vents yawning wide and molten hot.

'One last effort,' she snarled through gritted teeth, but doubts clamoured in her mind. What if Tarion was already dead, and she just hadn't seen his soul escape? What if he hadn't fully understood the plan? What if he simply let her down?

Neave shut the clamour down, cutting off the voices of panic as though she had dropped a portcullis before them.

'He's out there and he'll do his duty,' she told herself. 'He's a damned Hammer of Sigmar. Besides, if I stay here any longer my armour's going to melt and scald me to death anyway.'

With that, Neave bunched her muscles and launched herself into a desperate charge. She pounded upslope, staying in the lee of the boulder as long as she could. The beast's fiery breath still washed around her, but it was jolting as the hound charged up the slope to run her to ground. Expending every iota of her focus and skill, Neave wove through the firestorm, still accelerating, knowing she had to be moving fast enough or it would all be for naught.

Metal pounded on stone behind her.

Fire washed around her in a furious tide.

Pain rolled through her in a nauseating storm.

The chasm yawned suddenly at her feet and, with a scream of effort and a last burst of speed, Neave leapt. As she pushed off on her left foot she spun so that she revolved over the hellish glare of the lava below and passed through the unbearable heatwash in a pirouette. Sure enough, the hound was almost on top of her, bounding closer in vast strides.

Neave had one chance. She drew back her arm and, sighting through the blistering heat haze, she hurled an axe with all her might.

She hit bedrock beyond the chasm shoulders first, and the breath was driven from her body. At the same moment, her axe spun end over end through the air and struck the chained hatch in the hound's underbelly. Crimson sparks exploded as the chain was severed and Neave's axe ricocheted away. The daemon hound, still ploughing forwards with all the momentum of an ironclad avalanche, reared to step over the rent. As it did so, the unchained hatch buckled as though struck from within, and then exploded open.

Light burst outwards, tinged in the impossible hues of insanity, and Neave gritted her teeth as a deranged howl erupted from the open hatch. Through a haze of pain and heat she saw *something* writhing, an ephemeral presence formed from swirling energy that seemed torn between bursting free, or drawing back into the hound's shell like a startled sea creature.

The daemon hound's foreclaws slammed down on Neave's side of the rent, hard enough to send cracks radiating through the bedrock. The huge engine hesitated, its smouldering muzzle just feet from Neave, its fiery eyes flickering with the indecision of the entity bound within.

She took a deep breath and closed her eyes as the shimmering colours sucked back into the torn remains of the hatch, and fire billowed anew in the creature's maw. It had been a desperate plan to begin with...

Tarion swept out of the smoke above the rent, his star-forged arrow crackling upon his bowstring. The Knights-Venator could summon these mighty projectiles only rarely, but they struck with the unleashed fury of a thousand thunderbolts.

Now, Tarion loosed his straight down into the exposed heart of the volcano. Neave grinned wolfishly up at the looming monster, and an instant later a thunderblast ripped through the depths of the rent. Primordial wrath and celestial fury raced outwards, mingling with the natural ferocity of the Realm of Fire. In any other realm, such a plan might have come to naught, but the volcanoes of Aqshy were proud and passionate entities, and their wrath was easily triggered. Tarion's arrow was more than enough.

The ground convulsed, and an almighty blast of molten rock and searing flame jetted up from the rent. It struck the hound's underbelly, and Neave heard an ululating shriek of outrage as gallons of molten magma funnelled up through the hatch to spew into the engine's heart.

The daemon hound convulsed. Neave squirmed backwards on her elbows and heels, leaving a blood trail across the rock. The monster's eyes blazed orange-white, and for an instant it looked almost shocked, before the brass plates of its muzzle deformed and exploded outwards like an obscene flower blooming. Fire and spinning chunks of metal rained around Neave, who rolled onto her front and scrambled as best she could away from the explosion.

She heard furious blasts rippling behind her, the snap of tensed cables letting go, the scream and moan of melting metal and something unnatural and monstrous being hurled out of the mortal plains and into realms beyond the sight of living things.

She threw herself forwards as the ground shook again, and rolled over in time to see the hound's huge claws dragging deep furrows through the rock as its gutted carcass slid backwards into the rent. There came a final blast of volcanic fury, a crashing and rending of mechanical destruction and a billowing cloud of black smoke, then the hound was gone.

Neave's sense of her mark vanished at the same moment.

Utterly exhausted, mind swimming with pain, she slumped back on the hot, hard rock of the volcano's flank and allowed herself to pass out.

* * *

Some hours later, Neave and Tarion stood upon the bank of Brimstone Lake, their armour battered and blackened, their flesh burned and raw. Neave's leg was splinted with metal and bandages salvaged from within the cogfort, and they had dressed Tarion's burns as best they could. Krien sat nearby, ripping busily into something small, furry and unfortunate that he had caught amongst the rocks of the upper slopes.

'That could have been us,' said Neave, nodding at the bird's bloody meal.

'Your plan worked, though, Lady Blacktalon,' said Tarion approvingly.

'Neave,' she said. 'I think we're past titles, don't you?'

'Neave,' repeated Tarion with a smile.

'I've never faced something that was a deadlier predator than myself,' said Neave, shaking her head. The next words left her mouth only grudgingly, but she forced them out regardless. 'Alone, I would have stood no chance of besting it. Thank you, Tarion. We don't make the most terrible team.'

'High praise indeed,' chuckled Tarion, but she could hear in his voice that he was pleased with the grudging compliment. 'We'll have to thank our selfless Palladors once they're Reforged, if they all make it through,' he said, sobering.

Neave grunted an acknowledgement, staring out over the lake. 'We will see them beyond the anvils,' she said. 'Meantime, I'm sure there will be another hunt for us.'

'Us?' asked Tarion, smiling again.

'You pulled a fistful of arrows out of your quiver, didn't you?' she asked. 'When it had you in its talon.'

'It was the only thing I could think of,' he confessed. 'When they exploded, it hurt like Reforging itself, I'll tell you that.'

Neave shook her head. 'It worked. Anyone crazed enough to try something like that, and sharp enough to still finish that hunt alive? Yes, Tarion, I think I'll hunt alongside you again,' she said. 'But in the meantime, we should return to the heavens. All joking aside, it's going to take time to heal this battle-damage, and the war is never done. Beat me back to the Realmgate and I might even deign to have you accompany me in the hunt for my next mark.'

'I can fly, and you are running on a broken leg,' Tarion said flatly.

'Well, then that just makes it a fair race, doesn't it, Arlor?' grinned Neave, and set off along the lakeside. Behind her, Tarion barked a laugh and took to the air. Krien shrieked in irritation as he was forced to cast aside the last of his meal to give chase.

At their backs the volcano rumbled on, the last molten remnants of Neave's quarry dissolving deep within its fiery heart.

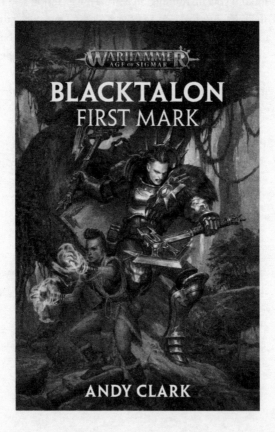

SHIPRATS

C L Werner

Introducing

BROKRIN ULLISSONN

DUARDIN, KHARADRON OVERLORDS

Carefully, the heavy-set duardin warrior raised his weapon. His eyes narrowed, fixating on his victim. He appeared unfazed by the gloom of the darkened hold, his vision sharp enough to pick out a marrow-hawk soaring through a thunderstorm. The duardin judged the distance, allowed for the air currents that buffeted the moored aether-ship and estimated how much strength to bring to bear against his foe.

The shovel came cracking down, striking the deck with such force that a metallic ping was sent echoing through the hold. Drumark cursed as the target of the descending spade leapt upwards and squeaked in fright. The brown rat landed on his foot, squeaked again, then scampered off deeper into the hold.

Furious, Drumark turned and glowered at the other spade-carrying duardin gathered in the *Iron Dragon*'s hold. Arkanauts, endrin-riggers, aether-tenders and even a few of the ship's officers gave the angry sergeant anxious stares.

'Right! Now they are just begging to be shot! I am getting my decksweeper!' Drumark swore, not for the first time.

Brokrin, the *Iron Dragon*'s captain, stepped towards Drumark. 'You are not shooting holes in the bottom of my ship,' he snapped at him. 'We have enough problems with the rats. If you go shooting holes in the hull we won't be able to take on any aether-gold even if we do find a rich cloud-vein.'

Drumark jabbed a thumb down at his boot. 'It peed on my foot. Only respect for you, cap'n, keeps me from getting a good fire going and smoking the vermin out.'

'That is some sound thinking,' Horgarr, the *Iron Dragon*'s endrin-master scoffed. He pressed his shovel against the deck and leaned against it as he turned towards Drumark. 'Start a fire in the ship's belly. Nothing bad could happen from that. Except the fifty-odd things that immediately come to mind.'

Brokrin shook his head as Drumark told Horgarr exactly what he thought of the endrinmaster's mind. No duardin had any affection for rats, but Drumark's hatred of them was almost a mania. His father had died fighting the pestiferous skaven and every time he looked at a rat he was reminded of their larger kin. It made him surly and quick to anger. This would be the third fight between the two he would have to break up since coming down into the *Iron Dragon*'s holds. Unable to find any aether-gold, the ironclad had put in at Greypeak, a walled human city with which Barak-Zilfin had a trading compact. The grain the city's farmers cultivated was well regarded by the Kharadron and would fetch a good price in the skyhold. Not as much as a good vein, but at least there would be something for the aether-ship's backers.

At least there would be if the rats that had embarked along with the grain left anything in good enough condition to sell. There were more than a few Kharadron who claimed that the *Iron Dragon* was jinxed and that her captain was under a curse. Sometimes he found himself wondering if his detractors were right. This was not the first time Brokrin's ship had suffered an infestation of vermin, but he could not recall any that had been so tenacious as these. Whatever they did to try to protect their cargo, the rats found some way around it. They were too clever for the traps old Mortrimm set for them, too cunning to accept the poisoned biscuits Lodri made for them. Even the cat Gotramm had brought aboard had been use-less – after its first tussle with one of the rats it had found itself a spot up in the main endrin's cuppola and would claw anyone who tried to send it below deck again.

'These swine must have iron teeth.' The bitter observation was given voice by Skaggi, the expedition's logisticator. Tasked with balancing profit against expense and safeguarding the investment of the expedition's backers, every ounce of grain despoiled by the rodents stung Skaggi to the quick. He held a heavy net of copper wire in his hands, extending it towards Brokrin so he could see the holes the rats had gnawed. 'So much for keeping them out of the grain. We will be lucky if they do not start in for the beer next.'

Skaggi's dour prediction made Drumark completely forget about his argument with Horgarr. He looked in horror at Skaggi. An instant later, he raised the shovel overhead and flung it to the floor.

'That is it!' Drumark declared. 'I am bringing my lads down here and we will settle these parasites here and now!' He turned to Brokrin, determination etched across his face. 'You tell Grundstok thunderers to hunt rats, then that is just what we will do. But we will do it the way we know best.'

Skaggi's eyes went wide with alarm, his mind turning over the expense of patching over the holes the thunderers would leave if they started blasting away at the rats. He swung around to Brokrin, his tone almost frantic. 'We will be ruined,' he groaned. 'No profit, barely enough to pay off the backers.'

Drumark reached out and took hold of the copper net Skaggi was holding. 'If they can chew through this, they can chew their way into the beer barrels. Me and my thunderers are not going dry while these rats get drunk!'

The sound of shovels slapping against the floor died down as the rest of the duardin in the hold paused in their efforts to hear what Drumark was shouting about. Many of them were from his

Grundstok company and looked more than ready to side with their sergeant and trade spades for guns.

'The rats will not bother the beer while they still have grain to eat,' Brokrin stated, making sure his words were loud enough to carry to every crewman in the hold. How much truth there was in the statement, he did not know. He did know it was what Drumark and the others needed to hear right now.

'All due respect, cap'n,' Drumark said, 'but how long will that be? Swatting them with shovels just isn't enough and we have tried everything else except shooting them.'

Brokrin gave Drumark a stern look. 'I've said it before, and now I'm saying it again – you are not shooting holes in *my* ship.' The chastened sergeant held Brokrin's gaze for a moment, then averted his eyes. The point had been made.

'What are we going to do?' Gotramm asked. The youthful leader of the *Iron Dragon*'s arkanauts, he had watched with pointed interest the exchange between Brokrin and Drumark.

'I know one thing,' Horgarr said, pulling back his sleeve and showing the many scratches on his arm. 'That cat is staying right where it is.' The remark brought laughs from all who heard it, even cracking Drumark's sullen mood.

Brokrin was more pensive. Something Drumark had said earlier had spurred a memory. It was only now that his recollection fell into place. 'The toads,' he finally said. The newer members of the crew glanced in confusion at their captain, but those who had served on the *Iron Dragon* before her escape from the monster Ghazul knew his meaning.

'Some years ago,' Brokrin explained to them, 'we sailed through a Grimesturm and a rain of toads fell on our decks. They were everywhere, even worse than these rats. You could not sit without squashing one or take a sip of ale without having one hop into your mug.

'To rid the ship of her infestation,' Brokrin continued, 'we put in at the lamasery of Kheitar. The lamas prepared a mixture of herbs, which we burned in smudge pots. The smoke vexed the toads so much that they jumped overboard of their own accord.'

'You think the lamas could whip up something to scare off rats?' Gotramm asked.

Brokrin nodded. 'Kheitar is not far out of our way. There would be little to lose by diverting our course and paying the lamasery a visit.'

'Kheitar is built into the side of a mountain,' Horgarr said. 'Certainly it will offer as good an anchorage as the peak we're moored to now.'

Skaggi's eyes lit up, an avaricious smile pulling at his beard. 'The lamas are renowned for their artistic tapestries as well as their herbalism. If we could bargain with them and get them to part with even one tapestry we could recover the loss of what the rats have already ruined.'

'Then it is decided,' Brokrin said. 'Our next port of call is Kheitar.'

The lamasery's reception hall was a stark contrast to the confined cabins and holds of the *Iron Dragon*. Great pillars of lacquered wood richly carved with elaborate glyphs soared up from the teak floor to clasp the vaulted roof with timber claws. Lavish hangings hung from the walls, each beautifully woven with scenes from legend and lore. Great urns flanked each doorway, their basins filled with a wondrously translucent sand in which tangles of incense sticks slowly smouldered. Perfumed smoke wafted sluggishly through the room, visible as a slight haze where it condensed around the great platform at the rear of the chamber. Upon that platform stood a gigantic joss, a golden statue beaten into the semblance of an immensely fat man, his mouth distorted by great tusks and his head adorned by a nest of horns. In one clawed hand the joss held forward a flower, his other resting across his lap with the remains of a broken sword in his palm.

Brokrin could never help feeling a tinge of revulsion when he looked at Kheitar's idol. Whoever had crafted it, their attention to detail had been morbid. The legend at the root of the lamas' faith spoke of a heinous daemon from the Age of Chaos that had set aside its evil ways to find enlightenment in the ways of purity and asceticism. Looking at the joss, Brokrin felt less a sense of evil redeemed than he did that of evil biding its time. The duardin with him looked similarly perturbed, all except Skaggi, who was already casting a greedy look at the tapestries on the walls.

The young initiate who guided the duardin into the hall stepped aside as Brokrin and his companions entered. He bowed his shaved head towards a bronze gong hanging just to the left of the entrance. He took the striker tethered to the gong's wooden stand and gave the instrument three solid hits, each blow sending a dull reverberation echoing through the chamber.

'Take it easy,' Brokrin whispered when he saw Gotramm from the corner of his eye. The young arkanaut had reached for his pistol the moment the gong's notes were sounded. 'If we aggravate the lamas they might not help get rid of the rats.'

Gotramm let his hand drop away from the gun holstered on his belt. He nodded towards the joss at the other end of the hall. 'That gargoyle is not the sort of thing to make me feel at ease,' he said.

'The cap'n is not saying to close your eyes,' old Mortrimm the navigator told Gotramm. 'He is just saying do not be hasty drawing a weapon. Abide by the Code – be sure who you set your axe against, and why.'

Brokrin frowned. 'Let us hope it does not come to axes. Barak-Zilfin has a long history trading with the lamas.' Even as he said the words, they felt strangely hollow to him. Something had changed about Kheitar. What it was, he could not say. It was not something he could see or hear, but rather a faintly familiar smell. He turned his eyes again to the daemon-faced joss, wondering what secrets it was hiding inside that golden head.

Movement drew Brokrin's attention away from the joss. From behind one of the hangings at the far end of the hall, a tall and sparingly built human emerged. He wore the saffron robes of Kheitar's lamas, but to this was added a wide sash of green that swept down across his left shoulder before circling his waist. It was the symbol that denoted the high lama himself. The uneasy feeling Brokrin had intensified, given something solid upon which to focus. The man who came out from behind the tapestry was middle-aged, his features long and drawn. He certainly was not the fat, elderly Piu who had been high lama the last time the *Iron Dragon* visited Kheitar.

The lama walked towards the duardin, but did not acknowledge their presence until after he had reached the middle of the hall and turned towards the joss. Bowing and clapping his hands four times, he made obeisance to the idol. When he turned back towards the duardin, his expression was that of sincerity itself.

'Peace and wisdom upon your path,' the lama declared, clapping his hands together once more. A regretful smile drew at the corners of his mouth. 'Is it too much to hope that the Kharadron overlords have descended from the heavens to seek enlightenment?' He shook his head. 'But such, I sense, is not the path that has led you here. If it is not the comfort of wisdom you would take away from here, then what comfort is it that we can extend to you?'

Although Brokrin was the *Iron Dragon*'s captain, it was Skaggi who stepped forwards to address the lama. Of all the ship's crew, the logisticator had the glibbest tongue. 'Please forgive any intrusion, your eminence,' he said. 'It is only dire need which causes us to intrude upon your solitude. Our ship has been beset by an infestation of noxious pests. Terrible rats that seek...'

The lama's serenity faltered when Skaggi began to describe the situation. A regretful look crept into his eyes. 'We of Kheitar are a peaceful order. Neither meat nor milk may pass our lips. Our hands are not raised in violence, for like Zomoth-tulku, we have forsaken the sword. To smite any living thing is to stumble on the path to ascension.'

Brokrin came forwards to stand beside Skaggi. 'Your order helped us once before, when hail-toads plagued my ship. The high lama, Piu, understood the necessity of removing them.'

The lama closed his eyes. 'Piu-tulku was a wise and holy man.

Cho cannot claim even a measure of his enlightenment.' Cho opened his eyes again and nodded to Brokrin. 'There are herbs which could be prepared. Rendered down they can be burned in smudge pots and used to fumigate your ship.' A deep sigh ran through him. 'The smoke will drive the rats to flee. Would it be too great an imposition to ask that you leave them a way to escape? Perhaps keep your vessel moored here so they can flee down the ropes and reach solid ground.'

Skaggi's eyes went wide in shock. 'That would cause the lamasery to become infested.' He pointed at the lavish hangings on the walls. 'Those filthy devils would ruin this place in a fortnight! Think of all that potential profit being lost!'

Cho placed a hand against his shoulder. 'It would remove a stain from my conscience if you would indulge my hopes. The death of even so small a creature would impair my own aspirations of transcendence.'

'My conscience would not permit me to cause such misery to my benefactors,' Brokrin stated. 'But upon my honour and my beard, I vow that I will not use whatever herbs you provide us without ensuring the rats can make landfall without undue hazard.'

'It pleases me to hear those words,' Cho said. 'I know the word of your people is etched in stone. I am content. It will take us a day to prepare the herbs. Your ship will be safe where it is moored?'

'We are tied to the tower above your western gate,' Mortrimm stated. He gestured with his thumb at Brokrin. 'The cap'n insisted we keep far enough away that the rats wouldn't smell food and come slinking down the guide ropes.'

'Such consideration and concern does you credit, captain,' Cho declared. He suddenly turned towards Skaggi. 'If it is not an imposition, would it be acceptable to inquire if the tapestries we weave here still find favour among your people?'

The question took Skaggi by such surprise that the logisticator allowed excitement to shine in his eyes before gaining control of himself and resuming an air of indifference. Brokrin could tell that he was about to undervalue the worth of Kheitar's artistry. It was a prudent tactic when considering profit but an abominable one when thinking in terms of honour.

'Your work is applauded in Barak-Zilfin,' Brokrin said before Skaggi could find his voice. The logisticator gave him an imploring look, but he continued just the same. 'There are many guildhalls that have used your tapestries to adorn their assemblies, and poor is the noble house that has not at least one hanging from Kheitar on its walls.'

With each word he spoke, Brokrin saw Skaggi grow more perturbed. Cho remained implacable, exhibiting no alteration in his demeanour. Then the high lama turned towards the wall from which he had emerged. Clapping his hands together in rapid succession, he looked aside at the duardin.

'I thank you for your forthrightness,' Cho said. 'Your honesty makes you someone we can trust.' There was more, but even Brokrin lost the flow of Cho's speech when the hangings on the walls were pushed aside and a group of ten lamas entered the hall. Each pair carried an immense tapestry rolled into a bundle across their shoulders. To bring only a few tapestries out of Kheitar was considered a rewarding voyage. Was Cho truly offering the duardin five of them?

Cho noted the disbelief that shone on the faces of his guests. He swung around to Skaggi. 'I have noticed that you admire our work. I will leave it to you to judge the value of the wares I would offer you.' At a gesture from the high lama, the foremost of his followers came near and unrolled their burden. Skaggi didn't quite stifle the gasp that bubbled up from his throat.

The background of the tapestry was a rich burgundy in colour and across its thirty-foot length vibrant images were woven from threads of sapphire blue, emerald green and amber yellow. Geometric patterns that transfixed the eye formed a border around visions of opulent splendour and natural wonder. Soaring mountains with snowy peaks rose above wooded hills. Holy kings held court from gilded thrones, their crowns picked out with tiny slivers of jade wound between the threads. Through the centre of the tapestry a stream formed from crushed pearl flowed into a silver sea.

'Magnificent,' the logisticator sputtered before recovering his composure.

'It gladdens me that you are content with our poor offerings,' Cho told Skaggi. He looked back towards Brokrin. 'It is my hope that you would agree to take this cargo back to your city. Whatever price you gain from their sale, I only ask that you return half of that amount to the lamasery.'

'Well… there are our expenses to be taken into account…' Skaggi started. However good a deal seemed, the logisticator was quick to find a way to make it better.

'Of course you should be compensated for your labours,' Cho said, conceding the point without argument. 'Captain, are you agreeable to my offer?'

'It is very generous and I would be a fool to look askance at your offer,' Brokrin replied. 'It may be some months before we can return here with your share.'

'That is understood,' Cho said. He gestured again to the lamas carrying the tapestries. 'Pack the hangings for their journey. Then take them to the Kharadron ship.'

The unaccountable uneasiness that had been nagging at Brokrin asserted itself once more. 'I will send one of my crew to guide your people and show them the best place to put your wares.' He turned to Mortrimm. 'Go with them and keep your wits about you,' he whispered.

'You expect trouble?' Mortrimm asked.

Brokrin scratched his beard. 'No, but what is it the Chuitsek nomads say? "A gift horse sometimes bites." Just make sure all they do is put the tapestries aboard.'

Nodding his understanding, Mortrimm took his position at the head of the procession of lamas. Because of their heavy burdens, the navigator was easily able to match their pace despite one of his legs being in an aethyric brace. Brokrin and the other duardin watched as the tapestries were conducted out of the hall.

'Should I go with them, cap'n?' Skaggi asked. 'Make certain they do not mar the merchandise when they bring it aboard?'

'I think these lamas know their business,' Gotramm retorted. 'They are the ones who sweated to make the things and they have just as much to lose as we do if they get damaged.'

Unlike the banter between Drumark and Horgarr, there was a bitter edge to what passed between Gotramm and Skaggi. There was no respect between them, only a kind of tolerant contempt. Brokrin started to intercede when something Cho had said suddenly rose to mind. He turned towards the high lama. 'You called your predecessor Piu-tulku? Is not tulku your word for the revered dead?'

'The holy ascended,' Cho corrected him. 'Among the vulgar it is translated as "living god". You have yourself seen the ancient tulkus who have followed Zomoth-tulku's transcendence.'

Brokrin shuddered at the recollection. Deep within the lamasery there were halls filled with niches, each containing the mummified husk of a human. They were holy men who had gradually poisoned themselves, embalming their own bodies while they were still alive in a desperate search for immortality. The lamas considered each of the corpses to still be alive, tending their clothes and setting bowls of food and drink before them each morning. He thought of Piu and the last time he had seen the man. There had been no hint that he had been undergoing this ghastly process of self-mummification.

'I was unaware Piu had chosen such a path,' Brokrin apologised.

Cho smiled and shook his head. 'Piu-tulku did not choose the path. The path chose him. A wondrous miracle, for he has transcended the toils of mortality yet still permits his wisdom to be shared with those who have yet to ascend to a higher enlightenment.' His smile broadened. 'Perhaps if you were to see him, speak with him, you would understand the wisdom of our order.'

That warning feeling was even more persistent now, but Brokrin resisted the urge to play things safe. Something had changed at Kheitar and whatever it was, he would bet it had to do with Piu's unexpected ascension. Glancing over at Gotramm and then at Skaggi, he made his decision. 'We would like very much to meet with Piu-tulku.'

Cho motioned for the initiate by the door to come over to them. 'I am certain Piu-tulku will impart much wisdom to you, but to enter his august presence you must set aside your tools of death.' He pointed at the axes and swords the duardin carried. 'Leave those behind if you would see the tulku. I can allow no blades in his chambers.'

Brokrin nodded. 'You have nothing to fear, your grace. Our Code prohibits us from doing harm to any who are engaged in fair trade with us.' He slowly unbuckled his sword and proffered it to the initiate. 'We will follow your custom.'

Slowly the three duardin removed their blades, setting them on the floor. Gotramm started to do the same with his pistol, but Cho had already turned away. Brokrin set a restraining hand on Gotramm's.

'He said blades,' Brokrin whispered. 'Unless asked, keep your pistol.' He brushed his hand across the repeater holstered on his own belt. 'We will respect their custom, as far as they ask it of us.'

Brokrin gave a hard look at Cho's back as the high lama preceded them out of the hall. 'If he is being honest with us, it will make no difference. If he is not, it might make all the difference in the realms.'

Drumark escorted the lamas down into the *Iron Dragon*'s hold. He had tried to choose the cleanest compartment in which to put the precious cargo, but even here there was the fug of rat in the air. 'This is the best one,' he said. 'You can put them down here.'

'You think they will be safe?' asked Mortrimm. Like the sergeant, he could smell the stink of rat. He looked uneasily at the bamboo crates the lamas carried, wondering how long it would take a rat to gnaw its way through the boxes.

'As long as there is grain, the little devils will keep eating that,' Drumark spat, glowering at a fat brown body that went scooting behind a crate when the light from his lantern shone upon it. 'It will be a while before they start nibbling on this stuff.' He turned his light on the sallow-faced lamas as they carefully set down the crates and started to leave the hold. 'Tell your friends to get that poison ready on the quick. If we do not smoke out these vermin, your tapestries will be gnawed so badly we will have to sell them as thread.'

The warning put a certain haste in the lamas' step as they withdrew from the hold. Mortrimm started to follow them as the men made their way back onto the deck. He had only taken a few steps when he noticed that Drumark was still standing down near the tapestries.

'Are you coming?' Mortrimm asked.

'In a bit,' Drumark answered, waving him away. Mortrimm shook his head and left the hold.

Alone in the rat-infested hold, Drumark glowered at the shadows. The stink of vermin surrounded him, making his skin crawl. Instead of withdrawing from the stench, he let his revulsion swell, feeding into the hate that boiled deep inside him. Rats! Pestiferous, murderous fiends! Whatever size they came in, they had to be stamped out wherever they were found. He would happily do his part. He owed that much to his father, burned down by the foul magics of the loathsome skaven.

Drumark looked at the crates and then back at the noisy shadows. Despite his talk with Mortrimm and the lamas, he was anything but certain the rats would spare the tapestries. The vermin were perverse creatures and might gnaw on the precious hangings out of sheer spite. Well, if they did, they would find a very irritable duardin waiting for them.

Checking one last time to be certain Mortrimm was gone, Drumark walked over to a dark corner near the door and retrieved the object he had secreted there without Brokrin's knowledge. He patted the heavy stock of his decksweeper. 'Some work for you before too long,' he told it. Returning to his original position, he doused the lantern. Instantly the hold was plunged into darkness. Drumark could hear the creaking of the guide ropes as the ship swayed in its mooring, the groan of the engines that powered the ironclad's huge endrin, the scratch of little claws as they came creeping across the planks.

Gradually his eyes adjusted to the gloom and Drumark could see little shapes scurrying around the hold. Soon the shapes became more distinct as his eyes became accustomed to the dark. Rats, as fat and evil as he had ever seen. There must be a dozen of them, all scurrying about, crawling over barrels, peeping into boxes, even gnawing at the planks. He kept his eyes on the crates with the tapestries, all laid out in a nice little row. The moment one of the rats started to nibble at them he would start shooting.

But the rats did not nibble the crates. Indeed, Drumark began to appreciate that the animals were conspicuously avoiding them. At first he thought it was simply because they were new, a change in their environment that the vermin would have to become comfortable with first. Then one of the rats did stray towards the row, fleeing the ire of one of its larger kin. The wayward rodent paused in mid-retreat, rearing up and sniffing at the crates.

Drumark could not know what the rat smelled, but he did know whatever it was had given the rodent a fright. It went scampering off, squeaking like a thing possessed. The rest of the vermin were soon following it, scrambling to their bolt holes and scurrying away to other parts of the ship. Soon Drumark could not hear their scratching claws any more.

Keeping his decksweeper at the ready, Drumark sat down beside the door. He stayed silent as he watched the crated tapestries, his body as rigid as that of a statue. In the darkness, he waited.

The wait was not a long one. A flutter of motion spread through the rolled tapestry at the end of the row. Faint at first, it increased in its agitation, becoming a wild thrashing after a few moments, the cloth slapping against the bamboo that enclosed it. Someone – or something – was inside the rolled tapestry and trying to work its way out. Eyes riveted on the movement, Drumark rose and walked forwards. He aimed his decksweeper at the tapestry. Whatever had hidden itself inside, it would find a warm reception when it emerged.

The thrashing persisted, growing more wild but making no headway against the framework that surrounded the tapestry. Whatever was inside was unable to free itself. Or unwilling. A horrible suspicion gripped Drumark. There were four more tapestries and while his attention was focused on this one, he was unable to watch the others.

Drumark swung around just as a dark shape came leaping at him from the shadows.

The decksweeper bellowed as he fired into his attacker. Drumark saw a furry body go spinning across the hold, slamming into the wall with a bone-crunching impact. He had only a vague impression of the thing he had shot. He got a better look at the creature that came lunging at him from one of the other crates.

Thin hands with clawed fingers scrabbled at Drumark as the creature leapt on him. Its filthy nails raked at his face, pulling hair from his beard. A rat-like face with hideous red eyes glared at him before snapping at his throat with chisel-like fangs. He could feel a long tail slapping at his legs, trying to hit his knees and knock him to the floor.

Drumark brought the hot barrel of his decksweeper cracking up into the monster's jaw, breaking its teeth. The creature whimpered and tried to wrest free from his grip, but he caught hold of its arm and gave it a brutal twist, popping it out of joint. The crippled creature twisted away, plunging back down on top of the crates.

Any sense of victory Drumark might have felt vanished when he raised his eyes from the enormous rat he had overcome. Six more of its kind had crawled out from their hiding places in the tapestries, and unlike the one he had already fought, these each had knives in their paw-like hands. They stood upright on their hind legs, chittering malignantly as they started towards the lone duardin.

'Skaven!'

The cry came from the doorway behind Drumark. The discharge of his decksweeper had brought Horgarr and several others of the crew rushing into the hold, concerned that the sergeant had finally lost all restraint with the rats infesting the ship. Instead they found a far more infernal pestilence aboard.

The arrival of the other duardin dulled the confidence that shone in the eyes of the skaven infiltrators. The mocking squeaks took on an uncertain quality. Ready to pounce en masse on Drumark a moment before, now the creatures hesitated.

'What are you waiting for, lads!' Drumark shouted to Horgarr and the others. 'The bigger the rat, the more of our beer it will drink! Get the scum!'

The sergeant's shouts overcame the surprise that held the other duardin. Armed with shovels and axes, Horgarr led the crew charging across the hold. Their backs against the wall, the skaven had no choice but to make a fight of it.

As he rearmed his decksweeper and made ready to return to the fray, a terrible thought occurred to Drumark. The tapestries and their devious passengers had come from the lamasery. A place from which Captain Brokrin had not yet returned.

'Hold them here!' Drumark told Horgarr. 'I have to alert the rest of the ship and see if we can help the cap'n!'

The young initiate held the ornate door open for Cho and the duardin as they entered the shrine wherein Piu-tulku had been entombed after his ascension. The room was smaller than the grand reception hall, but even more opulently appointed. The hangings that covered its walls were adorned with glittering jewels, the pillars that supported its roof were carved from blackest ebony and highlighted with designs painted in gold. The varnished floor creaked with a musical cadence as the visitors crossed it, sending lyrical echoes wafting up into the vaulted heights of its arched ceiling.

Ensconced upon a great dais flanked by hangings that depicted the wingless dragon and the fiery phoenix, the living god of Kheitar reposed. Piu was still a fat man, but his flesh had lost its rich colour, fading to a parchment-like hue. He wore black robes with a sash of vivid blue – the same raiment that had been given to the mummies Brokrin had seen in the lamasery's vaults. Yet Piu was not content to remain in motionless silence. Just as the duardin had decided that the lamas were delusional and that their late leader was simply dead, the body seated atop the dais opened its eyes and spoke.

'Enter and welcome,' the thing on the dais said. The voice was dull and dry with a strange reverberation running through it. 'Duardin-friends always-ever welcome in Kheitar.' It moved its head, fixing its empty gaze in Cho's general direction. 'Have you given help-aid to our guests?'

'Yes, holy tulku!' Cho said, bowing before the dais. 'The tapestries have been sent to their ship, as you commanded.'

The thing swung its head back around, facing towards the duardin. It extended its hands in a supplicating gesture. The effect was marred by the jerky way in which the arms moved. Brokrin could hear a faint, unnatural sound as Piu moved its head and hands, something between a pop and a whir. He had seen such artificial motion before, heard similar mechanical sounds. The tulku was similar to an aethyric musician he'd seen in the great manor of Grand Admiral Thorgraad, a wondrous machine crafted in the semblance of a duardin bard. The only blight on the incredible automaton's music had been the sound of the pumps inside it sending fuel through its pipes and hoses.

Whatever the esoteric beliefs of Kheitar, what sat upon the dais was not an ascended holy man. It was only a machine.

Piu began to speak again. 'It is to be hope-prayed that we shall all profit-gain from...'

Brokrin stepped past Cho and glared at the thing on the dais. 'I do not know who you are, but I will not waste words with a puppet.' The outburst brought a gasp of horror from the initiate at the door. Cho raced forwards, prostrating himself before the dais and pleading with Piu to forgive him for such insult.

Brokrin gave the offended lamas small notice. His attention was fixed to the hangings behind Piu's dais. There was a ripple of motion from behind one of them. Pushing aside the snake-like dragon, a loathsome figure stalked into view. He was taller than the duardin but more leanly built, his wiry body covered in grey fur peppered with black. A rough sort of metal hauberk clung to his chest while a strange helm of copper encased most of his rodent-like head. Only the fanged muzzle and the angry red eyes were left uncovered. A crazed array of pouches and tools swung from belts and bandoliers, but across one shoulder the humanoid rat wore a brilliant blue sash – the same as that which adorned Piu.

'Now you may speak-beg,' the ratman growled as he stood beside Piu. His hairless tail lashed about in malicious amusement as he smelled the shock rising off the duardin.

'Mighty Kilvolt-tulku,' Cho cried out. 'Forgive me. I did not know they were such barbarians.'

Kilvolt waved aside the high lama's apology. He fixed his gruesome attention on Brokrin. 'No defiance, beard-thing,' he snarled, pointing a claw at either side of the room. From behind the hangings a pack of armoured skaven crept into view, each carrying a vicious halberd in his claws. 'Listen-hear. I know-learn about your port-nest. Your clan-kin make-build ships that fly-climb higher than any others. I want-demand that secret.'

'Even if I knew it,' Brokrin snapped at Kilvolt, 'I would not give it to you.'

The skaven bared his fangs, his tail lashing angrily from side to side. 'Then I take-tear what I want-need! Already you let-bring my warriors into your ship.' He waved his paw at Cho. 'The tapestries this fool-meat gave you.' He gestured again with his paws, waving at the skaven guards that now surrounded the duardin. 'If they fail-fall, then I have hostages to buy the secret of your ship. Torture or ransom will give-bring what I...'

Kilvolt's fur suddenly stood on end, a sour odour rising from his glands. His eyes were fixed on the pistols hanging from the belts Brokrin and Gotramm wore. He swung around on Cho, wrenching a monstrous gun of his own from one of the bandoliers. 'I order-say take-fetch all-all weapons!' The skaven punctuated his words by pulling the trigger and exploding Cho's head in a burst of blood and bone.

The violent destruction of the lama spurred the duardin into action. With the skaven distracted by the murder on the dais, Brokrin and Gotramm drew their pistols. Before the ratmen could react, the arkanaut captain burned one down with a shot to its chest, the aethyric charge searing a hole through its armour. Brokrin turned towards Kilvolt, but the skaven took one glance at the multi-barrelled volley pistol and darted behind the seated Piu-tulku.

Instead Brokrin swung around and discharged his weapon into the skaven guards to his right. The volley dropped two of the rushing ratmen and sent another pair squeaking back to the doorways hidden behind the hangings, their fur dripping with blood. Gotramm was firing again, but the skaven were more wary of their foes now, ducking around the pillars and trying to use them as cover while they advanced.

'We are done for,' Skaggi groaned, keeping close to the other duardin. Alone among them, the logisticator really had come into the room unarmed. 'We have to negotiate!' he pleaded with Brokrin.

'The only things I have to say to skaven come out of here,' Brokrin told Skaggi, aiming his volley pistol at the guards trying to circle around him. The ratmen were unaware the weapon had no charge and seeing it aimed in their direction had them falling over themselves to gain cover.

A crackle from the dais presaged the grisly impact that sent an electric shock rushing through Brokrin. The armour on his back had been struck by a blast from Kilvolt himself. Feeling secure that the duardin were distracted by his henchrats, he had returned to the attack. The oversized rings that adorned one of his paws pulsated with a sickly green glow, a light that throbbed down to them via a series of hoses that wrapped around his arm before dipping down to a cannister on his belt.

The heavy armour Brokrin wore guarded him against the worst of the synthetic lightning. He turned his volley pistol towards the dais. Kilvolt flinched, ducking back behind the phony tulku. As he did, the ratman's eyes fixated on something behind the duardin captain.

'The boy-thing!' Kilvolt snarled from behind Piu. 'Stop-kill boy-thing, you fool-meat!'

Brokrin risked a glance towards the door. It had been flung open and the initiate was racing into the hall outside, screaming at the top of his lungs. Immediately half a dozen of the skaven were charging after him, determined to stop him from alerting the other lamas about what was happening in Piu's shrine.

The ratmen made it as far as the door before a duardin fusillade smashed into them. Skaven bodies were flung back into the shrine, battered and bloodied by a concentrated salvo of gunfire. Just behind them came their executioners, Drumark leading his Grundstok thunderers.

The surviving guards squeaked in fright at the unexpected appearance of so many duardin and the vicious despatch of their comrades. The creatures turned and fled, scurrying back into their holes behind the wall hangings. A few shots from the thunderers encouraged them to keep running.

'The leader is up there!' Brokrin told his crew, waving his pistol at the dais. 'There are tunnels behind the tapestries. Keep him from reaching them.'

Even as Brokrin gave the command, Kilvolt came darting out from behind the dais. His retreat would have ended in disaster, but the skaven had one last trick to play. To cover his flight, he had sent a final pawn into the fray. Piu-tulku rose from its seat and came lurching towards the duardin. There was no doubting the mechanical nature of the thing now. Every jerky motion of its limbs was accompanied by a buzzing whirr and the sour smell of leaking lubricants. Its hands were curled into claws as it stumbled towards Brokrin, but the face of Piu still wore the same expression of contemplative serenity.

'Right! That is far enough!' Drumark cried out, levelling his decksweeper at the automaton. When the Piu-thing continued its mindless approach, he emptied every barrel into it. The shot ripped through the thing's shell of flesh and cloth. In crafting his 'tulku' Kilvolt had stitched the flayed skin of Piu over a metal armature. The armature was now exposed by Drumark's blast as well as the nest of hoses and wires that swirled through its body.

Despite the damage inflicted on it, the automaton staggered onwards. Drumark glared at it in silent fury, as though it were a personal affront that it remained on its feet. While the sergeant fumed, Brokrin took command. 'Thunderers!' he called out. 'Aim for its spine! Concentrate your shots there!'

The thunderers obeyed Brokrin's order, fixing their aim at the core of the Piu-thing. Shots echoed through the shrine as round after round struck the automaton. Under the vicious barrage, the thing was cut in half, its torso severed and sent crashing to the floor. The legs stumbled on for several steps before slopping over onto their side and kicking futilely at the floor.

'And stay down!' Drumark bellowed, spitting on the fallen automaton.

Gotramm seized hold of the sergeant's arm. 'We have to get back to the ship! There are more of them in the hold with those tapestries!'

'Already sorted out,' Drumark declared. 'By now Horgarr should be done tossing their carcasses overboard. I figured you might be having trouble over here so me and the lads grabbed one of the lamas and found out where you were.'

Brokrin felt a surge of relief sweep through him. The *Iron Dragon* was safe. At least for now. He turned his eyes to the dragon tapestry and the tunnel Kilvolt had escaped into. Even now the skaven were probably regrouping to make another attack.

'Everybody back to the ship,' Brokrin said. 'The sooner we are away from here the better.' He gave Skaggi an almost sympathetic look. 'When we get back we will have to dump the tapestries over the side as well. We can't take the chance the skaven put some kind of poison or pestilence on them.'

Skaggi clenched his fist and rushed to the wall. With a savage tug he brought one of the hangings crashing down to the floor. 'If we have to throw out the others then we had better grab some replacements on our way out!' Catching his intention, Gotramm and some of the thunderers helped Skaggi pull down the other tapestries. The hangings were quickly gathered up and slung across the shoulders of the duardin.

'What about the rat poison, cap'n?' Drumark asked as they hurried through halls that were empty of either lamas or skaven.

'We cannot trust that either,' Brokrin told him. 'We must do without it.' He gave the sergeant a grim smile. 'I hope you remember where you put your spade.'

Drumark sighed and shook his head. 'I remember, but overall I would rather stay here and shoot skaven than play whack-a-rat with a shovel.'

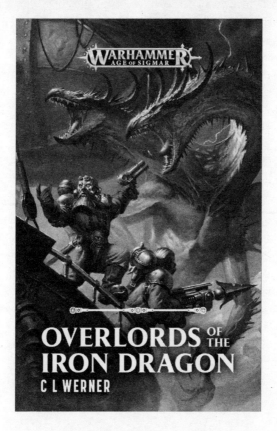

ABOUT THE AUTHORS

Dan Abnett has written over fifty novels, including *Anarch*, the latest instalment in the acclaimed Gaunt's Ghosts series. He has also written the Ravenor and Eisenhorn books, the most recent of which is *The Magos*. For the Horus Heresy, he is the author of *Horus Rising*, *Legion*, *The Unremembered Empire*, *Know No Fear* and *Prospero Burns*, the last two of which were both *New York Times* bestsellers. He also scripted *Macragge's Honour*, the first Horus Heresy graphic novel, as well as numerous Black Library audio dramas. Many of his short stories have been collected into the volume *Lord of the Dark Millennium*. He lives and works in Maidstone, Kent.

David Annandale is the author of the Warhammer Horror novel *The House of Night and Chain* and the novella *The Faith and the Flesh*, which features in the portmanteau *The Wicked and the Damned*. His work for the Horus Heresy range includes the novels *Ruinstorm* and *The Damnation of Pythos*, and the Primarchs novels *Roboute Guilliman: Lord of Ultramar* and *Vulkan: Lord of Drakes*. For Warhammer 40,000 he has written *Warlord: Fury of the God-Machine*, the Yarrick series, and several stories involving the Grey Knights, as well as titles for The Beast Arises and the Space Marine Battles series. For Warhammer Age of Sigmar he has written *Neferata: Mortarch of Blood* and *Neferata: The Dominion of Bones*. David lectures at a Canadian university, on subjects ranging from English literature to horror films and video games.

Andy Clark has written the Warhammer 40,000 novels *Fist of the Imperium*, *Kingsblade*, *Knightsblade* and *Shroud of Night*, as well as the novella *Crusade* and the short story 'Whiteout'. He has also written the novels *Gloomspite* and *Blacktalon: First Mark* for Warhammer Age of Sigmar, and the Warhammer Quest Silver Tower novella *Labyrinth of the Lost*. He lives in Nottingham, UK.

Aaron Dembski-Bowden is the *New York Times* bestselling author of the Horus Heresy novels *The Master of Mankind*, *Betrayer* and *The First Heretic*, as well as the novella *Aurelian* and the audio drama *Butcher's Nails*, for the same series. He has also written the Warhammer 40,000 novels *Spear of the Emperor* and *Ragnar Blackmane*, the popular Night Lords series, the Space Marine Battles book *Armageddon*, the novels *The Talon of Horus* and *Black Legion*, the Grey Knights novel *The Emperor's Gift* and numerous short stories. He lives and works in Northern Ireland.

John French is the author of several Horus Heresy stories including the novels *The Solar War*, *Praetorian of Dorn*, *Tallarn* and *Slaves to Darkness*, the novella *The Crimson Fist*, and the audio dramas *Dark Compliance*, *Templar* and *Warmaster*. For Warhammer 40,000 he has written *Resurrection*, *Incarnation* and *Divination* for The Horusian Wars and three tie-in audio dramas – the Scribe award-winning *Agent of the Throne: Blood and Lies*, as well as *Agent of the Throne: Truth and Dreams* and *Agent of the Throne: Ashes and Oaths*. John has also written the Ahriman series and many short stories.

David Guymer's work for Warhammer Age of Sigmar includes the novels *Hamilcar: Champion of the Gods* and *The Court of the Blind King*, the audio dramas *The Beasts of Cartha*, *Fist of Mork*, *Fist of Gork*, *Great Red* and *Only the Faithful*. He is also the author of the *Gotrek & Felix* novels *Slayer*, *Kinslayer* and *City of the Damned* and the Gotrek audio dramas *Realmslayer* and *Realmslayer: Blood of the Old World*. For The Horus Heresy he has written the novella *Dreadwing*, the Primarchs novel *Ferrus Manus: Gorgon of Medusa*, and for Warhammer 40,000 *The Eye of Medusa*, *The Voice of Mars* and the two Beast Arises novels *Echoes of the Long War* and *The Last Son of Dorn*. He is a freelance writer and occasional scientist based in the East Riding, and was a finalist in the 2014 David Gemmell Awards for his novel *Headtaker*.

Guy Haley is the author of the Siege of Terra novel *The Lost and the Damned*, as well as the Horus Heresy novels *Titandeath*, *Wolfsbane* and *Pharos*, and the Primarchs novels *Konrad Curze: The Night Haunter*, *Corax: Lord of Shadows* and *Perturabo: The Hammer of Olympia*. He has also written many Warhammer 40,000 novels, including *Belisarius Cawl: The Great Work*, *Dark Imperium*, *Dark Imperium: Plague War*, *The Devastation of Baal*, *Dante*, *Darkness in the Blood*, *Baneblade* and *Shadowsword*. His enthusiasm for all things greenskin has also led him to pen the eponymous Warhammer novel *Skarsnik*, as well as the End Times novel *The Rise of the Horned Rat*. He has also written stories set in the Age of Sigmar, included in *War Storm*, *Ghal Maraz* and *Call of Archaon*. He lives in Yorkshire with his wife and son.

Rachel Harrison is the author of the Warhammer 40,000 novel *Honourbound*, featuring the character Commissar Severina Raine, as well the accompanying short stories 'Execution', 'Trials', 'Fire and Thunder', 'A Company of Shadows', and 'The Darkling Hours', which won a 2019 Scribe Award in the Best Short Story category. Also for Warhammer 40,000 she has written the novel *Mark of Faith*, the novella *Blood Rite*, numerous short stories including 'The Third War' and 'Dishonoured', the short story 'Dirty Dealings' for Necromunda, and the Warhammer Horror audio drama *The Way Out*.

Justin D Hill is the author of the Necromunda novel *Terminal Overkill*, the Warhammer 40,000 novels *Cadia Stands* and *Cadian Honour*, the Space Marine Battles novel *Storm of Damocles* and the short stories 'Last Step Backwards', 'Lost Hope' and 'The Battle of Tyrok Fields', following the adventures of Lord Castellan Ursarkar E. Creed. He has also written 'Truth Is My Weapon', and the Warhammer tales 'Golgfag's Revenge' and 'The Battle of Whitestone'. His novels have won a number of prizes, as well as being *Washington Post* and *Sunday Times* Books of the Year. He lives ten miles uphill from York, where he is indoctrinating his four children in the 40K lore.

Nick Horth is the author of the novels *City of Secrets* and *Callis and Toll: The Silver Shard*, the novellas *Heart of Winter* and *Thieves' Paradise*, and several short stories for Age of Sigmar. Nick works as a background writer for Games Workshop, crafting the worlds of Warhammer Age of Sigmar and Warhammer 40,000. He lives in Nottingham, UK.

Nick Kyme is the author of the Horus Heresy novels *Old Earth*, *Deathfire*, *Vulkan Lives* and *Sons of the Forge*, the novellas *Promethean Sun* and *Scorched Earth*, and the audio dramas *Red-Marked*, *Censure* and *Nightfane*. His novella *Feat of Iron* was a *New York Times* bestseller in the Horus Heresy collection, *The Primarchs*. Nick is well known for his popular Salamanders novels, including *Rebirth*, as well as the Cato Sicarius novels *Damnos* and *Knights of Macragge*. His work for Age of Sigmar includes the short story 'Borne by the Storm', included in the novel *War Storm*, and the audio drama *The Imprecations of Daemons*. His most recent title is the Warhammer Horror novel *Sepulturum*. He lives and works in Nottingham.

Graham McNeill has written many Horus Heresy novels, including *The Crimson King*, *Vengeful Spirit* and his *New York Times* bestsellers *A Thousand Sons* and the novella *The Reflection Crack'd*, which featured in *The Primarchs* anthology. Graham's Ultramarines series, featuring Captain Uriel Ventris, is now six novels long, and has close links to his Iron Warriors stories, the novel *Storm of Iron* being a perennial favourite with Black Library fans. He has also written the Forges of Mars trilogy, featuring the Adeptus Mechanicus, and the Warhammer Horror novella *The Colonel's Monograph*. For Warhammer, he has written the Warhammer Chronicles trilogy *The Legend of Sigmar*, the second volume of which won the 2010 David Gemmell Legend Award.

Sandy Mitchell is the author of a long-running series of Warhammer 40,000 novels about the Hero of the Imperium, Commissar Ciaphas Cain, as well as the audio drama *Dead In The Water*. He has also written a plethora of short stories, including 'The Last Man' in the *Sabbat Worlds* anthology, along with several novels set in the Warhammer World. He lives and works in Cambridge.

Josh Reynolds' extensive Black Library back catalogue includes the Horus Heresy Primarchs novel *Fulgrim: The Palatine Phoenix*, and three Horus Heresy audio dramas featuring the Blackshields. His Warhammer 40,000 work includes the Space Marine Conquests novel *Apocalypse, Lukas the Trickster* and the Fabius Bile novels. He has written many stories set in the Age of Sigmar, including the novels *Shadespire: The Mirrored City, Soul Wars, Eight Lamentations: Spear of Shadows*, the Hallowed Knights novels *Plague Garden* and *Black Pyramid*, and *Nagash: The Undying King*. He has written the Warhammer Horror novel *Dark Harvest*, and novella *The Beast in the Trenches*, featured in the portmanteau novel *The Wicked and the Damned*. He has recently penned the Necromunda novel *Kal Jerico: Sinner's Bounty*. He lives and works in Sheffield.

Gav Thorpe is the author of the Horus Heresy novels *The First Wall, Deliverance Lost, Angels of Caliban* and *Corax*, as well as the novella *The Lion*, which formed part of the *New York Times* bestselling collection *The Primarchs*, and several audio dramas. He has written many novels for Warhammer 40,000, including *Ashes of Prospero, Imperator: Wrath of the Omnissiah* and the Rise of the Ynnari novels *Ghost Warrior* and *Wild Rider*. He also wrote the *Path of the Eldar* and *Legacy of Caliban* trilogies, and two volumes in The Beast Arises series. For Warhammer, Gav has penned the End Times novel *The Curse of Khaine*, the Warhammer Chronicles omnibus *The Sundering*, and recently wrote the Age of Sigmar novel *The Red Feast*. In 2017, Gav won the David Gemmell Legend Award for his Age of Sigmar novel *Warbeast*. He lives and works in Nottingham.

Chris **Wraight** is the author of the Horus Heresy novels *Scars* and *The Path of Heaven*, the Primarchs novels *Leman Russ: The Great Wolf* and *Jaghatai Khan: Warhawk of Chogoris*, the novellas *Brotherhood of the Storm*, *Wolf King* and *Valdor: Birth of the Imperium*, and the audio drama *The Sigillite*. For Warhammer 40,000 he has written *The Lords of Silence*, *Vaults of Terra: The Carrion Throne*, *Vaults of Terra: The Hollow Mountain*, *Watchers of the Throne: The Emperor's Legion*, the Space Wolves novels *Blood of Asaheim* and *Stormcaller*, and many more. Additionally, he has many Warhammer novels to his name, including the Warhammer Chronicles novel *Master of Dragons*, which forms part of the *War of Vengeance* series. Chris lives and works in Bradford-on-Avon, in south-west England.

Danie Ware is the author of the novellas *The Bloodied Rose*, *Wreck and Ruin* and the short story 'Mercy', all featuring the Sisters of Battle. She lives in Carshalton, South London, with her son and two cats and has long-held interests in role-playing, re-enactment, vinyl art toys and personal fitness.

C L Werner's Black Library credits include the Age of Sigmar novels *Overlords of the Iron Dragon, Profit's Ruin, The Tainted Heart* and *Beastgrave,* the novella 'Scion of the Storm' in *Hammers of Sigmar,* and the Warhammer Horror novel *Castle of Blood.* For Warhammer he has written the novels *Deathblade, Mathias Thulmann: Witch Hunter, Runefang* and *Brunner the Bounty Hunter,* the Thanquol and Boneripper series and Warhammer Chronicles: The Black Plague series. For Warhammer 40,000 he has written the Space Marine Battles novel *The Siege of Castellax.* Currently living in the American south-west, he continues to write stories of mayhem and madness set in the Warhammer worlds.